HOLLYWOOD STATION

and

HOLLYWOOD CROWS

Also by Joseph Wambaugh

Fiction

Hollywood Moon
Floaters
Finnegan's Week
Fugitive Nights
The Golden Orange
The Secrets of Harry Bright
The Delta Star
The Glitter Dome
The Black Marble
The Choirboys
The Blue Knight
The New Centurions

Non-Fiction

Fire Lover
The Blooding
Echoes in the Darkness
Lines and Shadows
The Onion Field

HOLLYWOOD STATION

and

HOLLYWOOD CROWS

Joseph Wambaugh

Quercus

This omnibus edition published in 2009 by Quercus
Hollywood Station first published in Great Britain in 2007 by Quercus
Hollywood Crows first published in Great Britain in 2008 by Quercus

21 Bloomsbury Square
London
WC1A 2NS

Hollywood Station copyright © 2006 by Joseph Wambaugh
Hollywood Crows copyright © 2008 by Joseph Wambaugh

A CIP catalogue record for this book is available
from the British Library

ISBN 978 1 84916 098 8

Printed and bound in Great Britain by CPI Bookmarque, Croydon

10 9 8 7 6 5 4 3 2 1

HOLLYWOOD STATION

ACKNOWLEDGEMENTS

Special thanks for the terrific anecdotes and wonderful cop talk goes to officers of the Los Angeles Police Department: Chate Asvanonda, Matt Bennyworth, Michael Berchem, Wendi Berndt, Vicki Bynum, Laura Evens, Heather Gahry, Brett Goodkin, Chuck Henry, Craig Herron, Jack Herron (ret.), Brian Hospodar, Andy Hudlett, Jeff Injalls, Rick Jackson, Dennis Kilcoyne, Al Lopez, Tim Marcia, Kathy McAnany, Roger Murphy, Bill Pack, Mike Porter, Rosie Redshaw, Tom Redshaw, Dave Sigler, Bill Sollie, Olivia Spindola, Joe Witty.

And to officers of the San Diego Police Department: Mark Amancio, Pete Amancio, Andra Brown, Brett Burkett, Laurie Cairncross, Blaine Ferguson, Pete Griffin (ret.), Mike Gutierrez, Gerry Kramer, Vanessa Holland, Charles Lara, Vic Morel, Tony Puente (ret.), Andy Rios, Steve Robinson, Steve Sloan, Elliott Stiasny, Alex Sviridov, Don Watkins, Joe Winney.

And to officers of the Palm Springs Police Department: Dave Costello, Don Dougherty, Steve Douglas, Mitch Spike.

And to special agents of the Federal Bureau of Investigation: Matt Desarno, Jack Kelly (ret.).

And to author James Ellroy for urging this return to LAPD roots.

ONE

'Wanna play pit bull polo, dude?'

'What's that?'

'It's something I learned when I worked Metro Mounted Platoon.'

'It's weird thinking of you as a cowboy cop.'

'All I know about horses is they're assholes, man. But we got the overtime there. You know my little Beemer? I wouldn't have that if I hadn't worked Metro. My last year in Metro I made a hundred grand plus. I don't miss those crazy horses but I miss that OT money. And I miss wearing a Stetson. When we worked the mini-riot at the Democrats convention, a hot little lobbyist with nipples big enough to pack up and leave home said I looked like a young Clint Eastwood in that Stetson. And I didn't carry a Beretta nine then. I carried a six-inch Colt revolver. It looked more appropriate when I was sitting on a horse.'

'A wheel gun? In this day and age?'

'The Oracle still carries a wheel gun.'

'The Oracle's been on the job nearly fifty years. He can wear a codpiece if he wants to. And you don't look like Clint Eastwood, bro. You look like the guy in *King Kong*, except you got even more of a beak and your hair is bleached.'

'My hair is sun-streaked from surfing, dude. And I'm even two inches taller in the saddle than Clint was.'

'Whatever, bro. I'm a whole foot taller on the ground than Tom Cruise. He's about four foot ten.'

'Anyways, those pacifist demonstrators at the convention

center were throwing golf balls and ball bearings at our horses, when twenty of us charged. And dude, when you get stepped on by a fifteen-hundred-pound animal, it sucks *bad*. Only one horse went down. He was twenty-eight years old, name of Rufus. That fried him. Had to retire him after that. One of those Jamba Juicers threw a lit trash bag at the one I was riding, name of Big Sam. I beat that bitch with my koa.'

'Your what?'

'It's like a samurai sword made of koa wood. The baton's about as useless as a stalk of celery when you're up there on a horse seventeen hands high. Supposed to strike them in the clavicle, but guess what, she juked and I got her upside the head. Accidentally, wink wink. She did a loop de loop and ended up under a parked car. I saw a horse get stuck with a knitting needle by one of those tree fuckers. The horse was fried after that. Too much stress. They retired him to Horse Rescue. They all get fried sooner or later. Just like us.'

'That sucks. Sticking a horse.'

'That one got a TV interview at least. When cops get hurt, nothing. Who gives a fuck? When a horse gets hurt, you get on TV, maybe with that Debbie D-cup news bunny on channel five.'

'Where'd you learn to ride?'

'Griffith Park. A five-week course at the Ahmanson Training Center. Only horse I ever rode before that was on a merry-go-round, and I don't care if I ever ride another one. Got the job 'cause my sister-in-law went to high school with the platoon lieutenant. Horses're assholes, man. An RTD bus can pass you three inches away at sixty miles an hour and the horse doesn't blink. A little piece of paper blows in his face all of a sudden and he bucks you clear over a pile of tweakers and base heads sleeping on a skid-row sidewalk at Sixth and San Pedro. And you end up in Momma Lucy's shopping cart with her aluminum cans and refundable bottles. That's how I got a hip replacement at the age of thirty. Only thing I wanna ride now is a surfboard and my Beemer.'

'I'm thirty-one. You look a lot older than me.'

'Well I ain't. I just had a lot to worry about. They gave me a doctor that was so old he still believed in bleeding and leeches.'

'Whatever, bro. You might have progeria. Gives you those eyelid and neck wrinkles, like a Galapagos turtle.'

'So you wanna play pit bull polo or not?'

'What the fuck is pit bull polo?'

'Way I learned, they trailered ten of us down to Seventy-seventh Street on a night when they decided to sweep a three-block row of crack houses and gangsta cribs. Whole fucking area is a crime scene. Living next to that is what razor wire was made for. Anyways, all those Bloods and Crips have pit bulls and rotties and they let them run loose half the time, terrorizing the hood and eating any normal dogs they see. And the whole fucking pack of gangsta dogs flew into a blood lust the second they saw us coming in and they attacked like we were riding T-bones and ribeyes.'

'How many did you shoot?'

'Shoot? I need this job. You gotta be richer than Donald Trump and Manny the plumber to fire your piece in today's LAPD, especially at a dog. You shoot a human person and you get maybe two detectives and a team from Force Investigation Division to second-guess you. You shoot a dog and you get three supervisors and four detectives plus FID, all ready to string yellow tape. Especially in the 'hood. We didn't shoot them, we played pit bull polo with the long sticks.'

'Oh, I get it. Pit bull polo.'

'Man, I rode through them, whacking those killer bulls, yelling, "One chukker for my team! Two chukkers for my team!" I only wish I coulda whacked their owners.'

'Bro, a chukker is a period of play. I know 'cause I watched a special on the Royal Family. Horny old Charles was playing a chukker or two for Camilla with big wood in his jodhpurs. That old babe? I don't see it.'

'Whatever. You down with that or not?'

'Yeah, I'm down. But first I wanna know, did anyone beef you for playing polo with the gangsta bulls?'

'Oh yeah, there's always an ABM who'll call IA, his councilman, and maybe long distance to Al Sharpton, who never saw a camera he didn't hug.'

'ABM?'

'You ain't a 'hood rat, are ya? ABM. Angry black male.'

'Spent my nine years in Devonshire, West Valley, and West L.A. before I transferred here last month. ABMs ain't never been filed on my desk top, bro.'

'Then don't go to a police commission or council meeting. ABMs are in charge. But we don't have hardly any living in Hollywood. In fact, nowadays most of south L.A. is Latino, even Watts.'

'I been reading that the entire inner city is mostly Latino.'

'Where the fuck have the brothers gone to? I wonder. And why is everybody worrying about the black vote if they're all moving to the suburbs? They better worry about the Latino vote, because they got the mayor's office now and they're about one generation away from reclaiming California and making us do the gardening.'

'You married? And which number is it?'

'Just escaped from number two. She was Druid-like but not as cuddly. One daughter three years old. Lives with Momma, whose lawyer won't be satisfied till I'm homeless on the beach eating seaweed.'

'Is number one still at large?'

'Yeah, but I don't have to pay her nothing. She took my car, though. You?'

'Divorced also. Once. No kids. Met my ex in a cop bar in

4

North Hollywood called The Director's Chair. She wore a felonious amount of pancake. Looked too slutty for the Mustang Ranch and still I married her. Musta been her J Lo booty.'

'Starter marriages never work for cops. You don't have to count the first one, bro. So how do we play pit bull polo without horses? And where do we play?'

'I know just the place. Get the expandable baton outta my war bag.'

The Salvadoran gang *Mara Salvatrucha*, aka MS-13, began at Los Angeles High School less than twenty years earlier but was now said to have ten thousand members throughout the United States and seven hundred thousand in Central American countries. Many residents of state prison displayed tattoos saying 'MS' or 'MS-13.' It was an MS-13 crew member who was stopped on a street in North Hollywood in 1991 by Officer Tina Kerbrat, a rookie just months out of the LAPD academy, who was in the process of writing him a citation for drinking in public, nothing more than that, when the MS-13 'cruiser' shot her dead. The first LAPD woman officer to be murdered in the line of duty.

Later that evening a besieged Mexican resident living east of Gower Street called Hollywood Station to say that she saw an LAPD black-and-white with lights out driving loops around a dirty pink apartment building that she had reported to the police on several occasions as being full of *Mara Salvatrucha* gang members.

On the other occasions, the officers at the desk kept trying to explain to the Mexican woman about gang injunctions and probable cause, things she did not understand and that did not exist in her country. Things that apparently denied protection to people like her and her children from the criminals in that ugly pink building. She told the officer about how their vicious dogs had mauled and killed a collie belonging to her neighbor Irene, and how all the children were unable to walk safely in the streets. She also said that two of the dogs had been removed by people from the city pound but there were still enough left. More than enough.

The officers told her they were very sorry and that she should contact the Department of Animal Services.

The Mexican woman had been watching a Spanish-language channel and was almost ready for bed when she first heard the howling that drew her to the window. There she saw the police car with lights out, speeding down the alley next to the apartment building, being pursued by four or five barking dogs. On its second pass down the alley, she saw the driver lean out the window and swing something that looked like a snooker stick at one of the brutes, sending it yelping and running back into the pink building. Then the car made another loop and did it to another big dog, and the driver yelled something that her daughter heard from the porch.

Her daughter stumbled sleepily into the tiny living room and said in English, 'Mamá, does chukker mean something very bad, like the F word?'

The Mexican woman called Hollywood Station and spoke to a very senior sergeant whom all the cops called the Oracle. She wanted to say thank you for sending the officers with the snooker stick. She was hopeful that things might improve around the neighborhood. The Oracle was puzzled but thought it best not to question her further. He simply said that he was glad to be of service.

When 6-X-32's lights were back on and they were cruising Hollywood Boulevard, the driver said, 'Dude, right there's where my career with the Mounted Platoon ended. That's where I decided that overtime pay or not, I was going back to normal patrol.'

His partner looked to his right and said, 'At Grauman's Chinese Theater?'

'Right there in the courtyard. That's where I learned that you never ride a horse on the Hollywood Walk of Fame.'

'Bad juju?'

'Bad footing.'

Sid Grauman's famous theater seemed somehow forlorn these days, dwarfed and sandwiched by the Hollywood & Highland Center, better known as the Kodak Center, containing two blocks of shopping and entertainment. It was home to the Kodak Theatre and the Academy Awards and was overrun by tourists day and night. But the Chinese Theater still held its own when it came to Hollywood weirdness. Even this late, there were a number of costumed creatures posing for photos with tourists who were mainly photographing the shoe and handprints in the famous forecourt. Among the creatures were Mr. Incredible, Elmo, two Darth Vaders, Batman, and two Goofys, one short, one tall.

'They pose with tourists. Pix for bucks,' the driver said to his partner. 'The tourists think the creatures work for Grauman's, but they don't. Most of them're crackheads and tweakers. Watch little Goofy.'

He braked, making the nighttime traffic go around their black-and-white. They watched the shorter of the two Goofys hassling four Asians tourists who no doubt had refused to pay him for taking his photo or hadn't paid enough. When Goofy grabbed one of the two Asian men by the arm, the cop tooted his horn. When Goofy looked up and saw the black-and-white, he gave up panhandling for the moment and tried to disappear into the throng, even though his huge Goofy head loomed over all but the tallest tourist.

The driver said, 'The subway back there is a good escape route to the 'hood. Dealers hang out by the trains, and the hooks hang around the boulevard.'

'What's a hook?'

'A guy that approaches you and says, "I can hook you up with what you need." These days it's almost always crystal.

Everybody's tweaking. Meth is the drug of choice on the Hollywood streets, absolutely.'

And that made him think of his last night at Metro, which was followed by the replacement surgery and a right hip more accurate than a barometer when it came to predicting sudden temperature drops and wind-chill factor.

On that last night in the Mounted Platoon, he and another mounted cop were there for crowd suppression, walking their horses along Hollywood Boulevard all calm and okey-dokey, along the curb past the Friday-night mobs by the subway station, moseying west, when he spotted a hook looking very nervously in their direction.

He'd said to his partner, who was riding a mare named Millie, 'Let's jam this guy.'

He dismounted and dropped his get-down rope. His partner held both horses and he approached the hook on foot. The hook was a sweaty, scrawny white guy, very tall, maybe even taller than he was, though his LAPD Stetson and cowboy boots made him tower. That's when it all went bad.

'I was talking to a hook right about there,' he said to his partner now, pointing to the sidewalk in front of the Kodak Center. 'And the dude just turned and rabbitted. Zip. Like that. And I started after him, but Major freaked.'

'Your partner?'

'My horse. He was fearless, Major was. Dude, I'd seen him chill in training when we were throwing firecrackers and flares at him. I'd seen other horses rear up on their hind legs and do a one-eighty while Major stood his ground. But not that night. That's the thing about horses, they're assholes, man.'

'What'd he do?'

'First, Major reared clear up tall and crazy. Then he bit my partner on the arm. It was like somebody cranked up his voltage. Maybe a tweaker shot him with a BB gun, I don't

8

know. Anyways, I stopped chasing the hook, fuck him, and ran back to help my partner. But Major wouldn't calm down until I made like I was going to climb in the saddle. Then I did something very stupid.'

'What's that?'

'I climbed in the saddle, intending to ride him back to the trailer and call it a night. I did that instead of leading him back, which anybody without brain bubbles woulda done under the circumstances.'

'So?'

'He freaked again. He took off. Up onto the sidewalk.'

The moment would be with him forever. Galloping along the Walk of Fame, kicking up sparks and scattering tourists and panhandlers and purse snatchers and tweakers and pregnant women and costumed nuns and SpongeBob and three Elvises. Clomping over top of Marilyn Monroe's star or James Cagney's or Elizabeth Taylor's or fucking Liberace's or whoever was there on this block of the Walk of Fame because he didn't know who was there and never checked later to find out.

Cursing the big horse and hanging on with one hand and waving the creepy multitudes out of his way with the other. Even though he knew that Major could, and had, run up a flight of concrete steps in his long career, he also knew that neither Major nor any horse belonging to the Mounted Platoon could run on marble, let alone on brass inserts on that marble sidewalk where people spilled their Starbucks and Slurpees with impunity. No horse could trample Hollywood legends like that, so maybe it *was* the bad juju. And very suddenly Major hydroplaned in the Slurpees and just… went… *down*.

His partner interrupted the sweat-popping flashback. 'So what happened, bro? After he took off with you?'

'First of all, nobody got hurt. Except Major and me.'

'Bad?'

'They say I ended up in John Wayne's boot prints right there in Grauman's forecourt. They say the Duke's fist print is there too. I don't remember boots or fists or nothing. I woke up on a gurney in an RA with a paramedic telling me yes I was alive, while we were screaming code three to Hollywood Pres. I had a concussion and three cracked ribs and my bad hip, which was later replaced, and everybody said I was real lucky.'

'How about the nag?'

'They told me Major seemed okay at first. He was limping, of course. But after they trailered him back to Griffith Park and called the vet, he could hardly stand. He was in bad shape and got worse. They had to put him down that night.' And then he added, 'Horses are *such* assholes, man.'

When his partner looked at the driver, he thought he saw his eyes glisten in the mix of light from the boulevard—fluorescence and neon, headlights and taillights, even reflected glow from a floodlight shooting skyward—announcing to all: This is Hollywood! But all that light spilling onto them changed the crispness of their black-and-white to a wash of bruised purple and sickly yellow. His partner wasn't sure, but he thought the driver's chin quivered, so he pretended to be seriously studying the costumed freaks in front of Grauman's Chinese Theater.

After a moment the driver said, 'So anyways, I said fuck it. When I healed up I put in for Hollywood Division because from what I'd seen of it from the saddle it seemed like a pretty good place to work, long as you got a few hundred horses under you instead of one. And here I am.'

His partner didn't say anything for a while. Then he said, 'I used to surf a lot when I worked West L.A. Lived with my leash attached to a squealy. I had surf bumps all over my knees, bro. Getting too old for that. Thinking about getting me a log and just going out and catching the evening glass.'

'Awesome, dude. Evening glass is way cool. Me, after I transferred to Hollywood I sorta became a rev-head, cruising in my Beemer up to Santa Barbara, down to San Diego, revving that ultimate driving machine. But I got to missing being in the green room, you know? In that tube with the foam breaking over you? Now I go out most every morning I'm off duty. Malibu attracts bunnies. Come along sometime and I'll lend you a log. Maybe you'll have a vision.'

'Maybe I'll get a brain wave out there on evening glass. I need one to figure out how to keep my second ex-wife from making me live under a tree eating eucalyptus like a fucking koala.'

'Of course you're gonna get a surf jacket soon as these hodads around Hollywood Station find out. Everybody calls me Flotsam. So if you surf with me, you *know* they're gonna call you...'

'Jetsam,' his partner said with a sigh of resignation.

'Dude, this could be the beginning of a choiceamundo friendship.'

'Jetsam? Bro, that is wack, way wack.'

'What's in a name?'

'Whatever. So what happened to the Stetson after you played lawn dart in Grauman's courtyard?'

'No lawn in that courtyard. All concrete. I figure a tweaker picked it up. Probably sold it for a few teeners of crystal. I keep hoping to someday find that crankster. Just to see how fast I can make his body heat drop from ninety-eight point six to room temperature.'

As they were talking, 6-X-32 got a beep on the MDT computer. Jetsam opened and acknowledged the message, then hit the en route key and they were on their way to an address on Cherokee Avenue that appeared on the dashboard screen along with 'See the woman, 415 music.'

'Four-fifteen music,' Flotsam muttered. 'Why the hell can't the woman just go to her neighbor and tell them to turn down the goddamn CD? Probably some juice-head fell asleep to Destiny's Child.'

'Maybe Black Eyed Peas,' Jetsam said. 'Or maybe Fifty Cent. Crank up the decibels on that dude and you provoke homicidal urges. Heard his album called *The Massacre*?'

It wasn't easy to find a parking place near the half block of apartment buildings, causing 6-X-32 to make several moves before the patrol car was able to squeeze in parallel between a late-model Lexus and a twelve-year-old Nova that was parked far enough from the curb to be ticketed.

Jetsam hit the at-scene button on the keyboard, and they grabbed their flashlights and got out, with Flotsam grumbling, 'In all of Hollywood tonight there's probably about thirteen and a half fucking parking places.'

'Thirteen now,' Jetsam said. 'We got the half.' He paused on the sidewalk in front and said, 'Jesus, I can hear it from here and it ain't hip-hop.'

It was the *Schreckensfanfare*, the 'Fanfare of Terror,' from Beethoven's Ninth.

A dissonant shriek of strings and a discordant blast from brass and woodwinds directed them up the outside staircase of a modest but respectable two-story apartment building. Many of the tenants seemed to be out this Friday evening. Porch lights and security lights were on inside some of the units, but it was altogether very quiet except for that music attacking their ears, assaulting their hearing. Those harrowing passages that Beethoven intended as an introduction to induce foreboding did the job on 6-X-32.

They didn't bother to seek out the complainant. They knocked at the apartment from which that music emanated like a scream, like a warning.

'Somebody might be drunk in there,' Jetsam said.

'Or dead,' Flotsam said, half joking.

No answer. They tried again, banging louder. No answer. Flotsam turned the knob, and the door popped open as the hammering timpani served the master composer by intensifying those fearful sounds. It was dark except for light coming from a room off the hallway.

'Anybody home?' Flotsam called.

No answer. Just the timpani and that sound of brass shrieking at them.

Jetsam stepped inside first. 'Anybody home?'

No answer. Flotsam reflexively drew his nine, held it down beside his right leg and flashed his light around the room.

'The music's coming from back there.' Jetsam pointed down the dark hallway.

'Maybe somebody had a heart attack. Or a stroke,' Flotsam said.

They started walking slowly down the long, narrow hallway toward the light, toward the sound, the timpani beating a tattoo. 'Hey!' Flotsam yelled. 'Anybody here?'

'This is bad juju,' Jetsam said.

'Anybody home?' Flotsam listened for a response, but there was only that crazy fucking music!

The first room off the hall was the bedroom. Jetsam switched on the light. The bed was made. A woman's pink bathrobe and pajamas were lying across the bed. Pink slippers sat on the floor below. The sound system was not elaborate, but it wasn't cheap either. Several classical CDs were scattered on a bookcase shelf beside the speakers. This person lived in her bedroom, it seemed.

Jetsam touched the power button and shut off that raging sound. Both he and his partner drew a breath of relief as though bobbing to the surface from deep water. There was another room at the far end of the hallway, but it was dark. The only other light came from a bathroom that served this two-bedroom unit.

Flotsam stepped to the bathroom doorway first and found her. She was naked, half in half out of the bathtub, long pale legs hanging over the side of the tub. She had no doubt been a pretty girl in life, but now she was staring, eyes open in slits, lips drawn back in that familiar snarl of violent death he'd seen on others: Don't take me away! I'll fight to stay here! Alive! I want to stay alive!

Jetsam drew his rover, keyed it, and prepared to make the call. His partner stayed and stared at the corpse of the young woman. For a few seconds Flotsam had the panicky idea that she might still be alive, that maybe a rescue ambulance would have a chance. Then he moved one step closer to the tub and peeked behind the shower curtain.

There were arterial spurts all over the blue tile of the wall even to the ceiling. The floor of the tub was a blackening vat of viscosity and from here he could see at least three chest wounds and a gaping gash across her throat. At that second but not before, the acrid smell of blood and urine almost overwhelmed him, and he stepped out into the hallway to await the detectives from Hollywood Station and from Scientific Investigation Division.

The second bedroom, apparently belonging to a male roommate, was tidy and unoccupied at the moment, or so they thought. Jetsam had shined his light in there in a cursory check while talking on the rover, and Flotsam had glanced in, but neither had bothered to enter the bedroom and look inside the small closet, its door ajar.

While the two cops were back in the living room making a few notes, careful not to disturb anything, even turning on the wall switch with a pencil, a young man entered from the darkened hallway behind them.

His voice was a piercing rasp. He said, 'I love her.'

Flotsam dropped his notebook, Jetsam the rover. Both cops wheeled and drew their nines.

'Freeze, motherfucker!' Flotsam screamed.

'Freeze!' Jetsam added redundantly.

He was frozen already. As pale and naked as the young

woman he'd murdered, the young man stood motionless, palms up, freshly slashed wrists extended like an offering. Of what? Contrition? The gaping wrists were spurting, splashing fountains onto the carpet and onto his bare feet.

'Jesus Christ!' Flotsam screamed.

'Jesus!' Jetsam screamed redundantly.

Then both cops holstered their pistols, but when they lunged toward him the young man turned and ran to the bathroom, leaping into the tub with the woman he loved. And the cops gaped in horror as he curled himself fetally and moaned into her unhearing ear.

Flotsam got one latex glove onto his hand but dropped the other glove. Jetsam yelled into the rover for paramedics and dropped both latex gloves. Then they jumped onto him and tried to drag him up, but all the blood made his thin arms slip through their hands, and both cops cursed and swore while the young man moaned. Twice, three times he pulled free and plopped onto the bloody corpse with a splat.

Jetsam got his handcuff around one wrist, but when he cinched it tight the bracelet sunk into the gaping flesh and he saw a tendon flail around the ratchet and he yelled, 'Son of a bitch! Son of a bitch!' And he felt ice from his tailbone to his brain stem and for a second he felt like bolting.

Flotsam was bigger and stronger than Jetsam, and he muscled the rigid left arm out from under the chest of the moaning young man and forced it up behind his back and got the dangling bracelet around the wrist. And then he got to see it sink into the red maw of tendon and tissue and he almost puked.

They each got him by a handcuffed arm and they lifted him but now all three were dripping and slimy from his spurting blood and her thickening blood and they dropped him, his head hitting the side of the tub. But he was past pain and only moaned more softly. They lifted again and got him out of the tub and dragged him out into the hallway, where Flotsam slipped and fell down, the bleeding man on top of him still moaning.

A neighbor on her balcony screamed when the two panting cops dragged the young man down the outside stairway, his naked bloodslimed body bumping against the plastered steps in a muted plop that made the woman scream louder. The three young men fell in a pile onto the sidewalk under a street lamp, and Flotsam got up and began ransacking the car trunk for the first-aid kit, not knowing for sure what the hell was in it but pretty sure there was no tourniquet. Jetsam knelt by the bleeding man, jerked his Sam Browne free, and was trying to tie off one arm with an improvised tourniquet made from his trouser belt when the rescue ambulance came squealing around the corner onto Cherokee, lights flashing and siren yelping.

The first patrol unit to arrive belonged to the sergeant known as the Oracle, who double-parked half a block away, leaving the immediate area to RA paramedics, Hollywood detectives, evidence collectors from Scientific Investigation Division, and the coroner's team. There was no mistaking the very old patrol sergeant, even in the darkness. As his burly figure approached, they could see those pale service stripes on his left sleeve, rising almost to his elbow. Forty-six years on the Job rated nine hash marks and made him one of the longest-serving cops on the entire police department.

'The Oracle has more hash marks than a football field,' everybody said.

But the Oracle always said, 'I'm only staying because the divorce settlement gives my ex half my pension. I'll be on the Job till that bitch dies or I do, whichever comes first.'

The bleeding man was unmoving and going gray when he was blanketed and belted to the gurney and lifted into the rescue ambulance, both paramedics working to stem the now oozing blood but shaking their heads at the Oracle, indicating that the young man had probably bled out and was beyond saving.

Even though a Santa Ana wind had blown into Los Angeles from the desert on this May evening, both Flotsam and Jetsam were shivering and wearily gathering their equipment which was scattered on the sidewalk next to a concrete planter containing some hopeful pansies and forget-me-nots.

The Oracle looked at the blood-drenched cops and said, 'Are you hurt? Any injuries at all?'

Flotsam shook his head and said, 'Boss, I think we just had a tactical situation they never covered in any class I've taken at the academy. Or if they did, I fucking missed it.'

'Get yourselves to Cedars for medical treatment whether you need it or not,' the Oracle said. 'Then clean up real good. Might as well burn those uniforms from the looks of them.'

'If that guy has hepatitis, we're in trouble, Sarge,' Jetsam said.

'If that guy has AIDS, we're dead,' Flotsam said.

'This doesn't look like that kind of situation,' the Oracle said, his retro gray crewcut seeming to sparkle under the streetlight. Then he noticed Jetsam's handcuffs lying on the sidewalk. He flashed his beam on the cuffs and said to the exhausted cop, 'Drop those cuffs in some bleach, son. I can see chunks of meat jammed in the ratchets.'

'I need to go surfing,' Jetsam said.

'Me too,' Flotsam said.

The Oracle had acquired his sobriquet by virtue of seniority and his penchant for dispensing words of wisdom, but not on this night. He just looked at his bloody, hollow-eyed, shivering young cops and said, 'Now, you boys get right to Cedars ER and let a doc have a look at you.'

It was then that D2 Charlie Gilford arrived on the scene, a gumchewing, lazy night-watch detective with a penchant for bad neckties who was not a case-carrying investigator, his job being only to assist. But with more than twenty years at Hollywood Station, he didn't like to miss anything sensational that was going down and loved to offer pithy commentary on whatever had transpired. For his assessments they called him Compassionate Charlie.

During that evening's events on Cherokee Avenue, after he'd received a quick summary from the Oracle and called a homicide team from home, he took a look at the gruesome scene of murder and suicide, and at the bloody trail marking the grisly struggle that failed to save the killer's life.

Then Compassionate Charlie sucked his teeth for a second or two and said to the Oracle, 'I can't understand young coppers anymore. Why would they put themselves through something like that for a selfsolver? Shoulda just let the guy jump in the tub with her and bleed out the way he wanted to. They coulda sat there listening to music till it was over. All we got here is just another Hollywood love story that went a little bit sideways.'

TWO

It had always seemed to Farley Ramsdale that the blue mailboxes, even the ones on some of the seedier corners of Hollywood, were much more treasure-laden and easier to work than the resident boxes by most of the upmarket condos and apartments. And he especially liked the ones outside the post office because they got really full between closing time and 10 p.m., the hour he found most propitious. People felt so confident about a post office location that they dropped a bonanza in them, sometimes even cash.

The hour of 10 p.m. was midday for Farley, who'd been named by a mother who just loved actor Farley Granger, the old Hitchcock thriller *Strangers on a Train* being one of her favorites. In that movie Farley Granger is a professional tennis player, and even though Farley Ramsdale's mother had signed him up for private lessons when he was in middle school, tennis had bored him silly. It was a drag. School was a drag. Work was a drag. Crystal meth was definitely not a drag.

At the age of seventeen years and two months, Farley Ramsdale had gone from being a beads 'n' seeds pot head to a tweaker. The first time he smoked crystal he fell in love, everlasting love. But even though it was far cheaper than cocaine, it still cost enough to keep Farley hopping well into the night, visiting blue mailboxes on the streets of Hollywood.

The first thing Farley had to do that afternoon was pay a visit to a hardware store and buy some more mousetraps.

Not that Farley worried about mice—they were scampering around his rooming house most of the time. Well, it wasn't a rooming house exactly, he'd be the first to admit. It was an old white-stucco bungalow just off Gower Street, the family home deeded to him by his mother before her death fifteen years ago, when Farley was an eighteen-year-old at Hollywood High School discovering the joys of meth.

He'd managed to forge and cash her pension checks for ten months after her death before a county social worker caught up with him, the meddling bitch. Because he was still a teenager and an orphan, he easily plea-bargained down to a probationary sentence with a promise to pay restitution, which he never paid, and he began calling the two-bedroom, one-bath bungalow a rooming house when he started renting space to other tweakers who came and went, usually within a few weeks.

No, he didn't give a shit about mice. Farley needed ice. Nice clear, icy-looking crystal from Hawaii, not the dirty white crap they sold around town. Ice, not mice, that's what he worried about during every waking hour.

While browsing through the hardware store, Farley saw a red-vested employee watching him when he passed the counter where the drill bits, knives, and smaller items were on display. As if he was going to shoplift the shitty merchandise in this place. When he passed a bathroom display and saw his reflection in the mirror, now in the merciless light of afternoon, it startled him. The speed bumps on his face were swollen and angry, a telltale sign of a speed freak, as his kind used to be known. Like all tweakers he craved candy and sweets. His teeth were getting dark and two molars were hurting. And his hair! He had forgotten to comb his fucking hair and it was a whirling tangle with that burnt-straw look, hinting at incipient malnutrition, marking him even more as a longtime crystal-smoking tweaker.

He turned toward the employee, an East Asian guy

younger than Farley and fit-looking. Probably a fucking martial arts expert, he thought. The way Korea Town was growing, and with a Thai restaurant on every goddamn street and Filipinos emptying bedpans in the free clinics, pretty soon all those canine-eating, dog-breath motherfuckers would be running City Hall too.

But come to think of it, that might be an improvement over the chili-dipping Mexican asshole who was now the mayor, convincing Farley that L.A. would soon be ninety percent Mexican instead of nearly half. So why not give the slopes and greasers knives and guns and let them waste each other? That's what Farley thought should happen. And if the south end niggers ever started moving to Hollywood, he was selling the house and relocating to the high desert, where there were so many meth labs he didn't think the cops could possibly hassle him very much.

Since he couldn't shake that slit-eyed asshole watching him, Farley decided to stop browsing and headed for the shelf containing the mousetraps and rat poison, whereupon the Asian employee walked up to him and said, 'Can I help you, sir?'

Farley said, 'Do I look like I need help?'

The Asian looked him over, at his Eminem T-shirt and oily jeans, and said in slightly accented English, 'If you have rats, the springloaded rat traps are what you want. Those glue traps are excellent for mice, but some larger rodents can pull free of the glue pads.'

'Yeah, well, I don't have rats in my house,' Farley said. 'Do you? Or does somebody eat them along with any stray terriers that wander in the yard?'

The unsmiling Asian employee took a deliberate step toward Farley, who yelped, 'Touch me and I'll sue you and this whole fucking hardware chain!' before turning and scuttling away to the shelf display of cleaning solutions, where he grabbed five cans of Easy-Off.

When he got to the checkout counter, he grumbled to a frightened teenage cashier that there weren't enough English-speaking Americans left in all of L.A. to gang-fuck Courtney Love so that she'd even notice it.

Farley left the store and had to walk back to the house, since his piece-of-shit white Corolla had a flat tire and he needed some quick cash to replace it. When he got to the house, he unlocked the dead bolt on the front door and entered, hoping that his one nonpaying tenant was not at home. She was a shockingly thin woman several years older than Farley, although it was hard to tell, with oily black hair plastered to her scalp and tied in a knot at the nape of her neck. She was a penniless, homeless tweaker whom Farley had christened Olive Oyl after the character in *Popeye*.

He dumped his purchases on the rusty chrome kitchen table, wanting to catch an hour of shut-eye, knowing that an hour was about all he could hope for before his eyes snapped open. Like all tweakers, he was sometimes awake for days, and he'd tinker with that banged-up Jap car or maybe play video games until he crashed right there in the living room, his hand still on the controls that allowed him to shoot down a dozen video cops who were trying to stop his video surrogate from stealing a video Mercedes.

No such luck. Just as he fell across the unmade bed, he heard Olive Oyl clumping into the house from the back door. Jesus, she walked heavy for a stick of a woman. *River Dance* was quieter. He wondered if she had Hep C by now. Or Christ! Maybe AIDS? He'd never shared a needle on the rare occasions when he'd skin-popped ice, but she'd probably done it. He vowed to quit boning her and only let her blow him when he was totally desperate.

Then he heard that tremulous little voice. 'Farley, you home?'

'I'm home,' he said. 'And I need to catch some z's, Olive. Take a walk for a while, okay?'

'We working tonight, Farley?' She entered the bedroom.

'Yeah,' he said.

'Want a knobber?' she asked. 'Help you to sleep.'

Jesus, her speed bumps were worse than his. They looked like she scratched them with a garden tool. And her grille showed three gaps in front. When the hell had she lost the third tooth? How come he hadn't noticed before? Now she was skinnier than Mick Jagger and sort of looked like him except older.

'No, I don't want a knobber,' he said. 'Just go play video games or something.'

'I think I got a shot at some extra work, Farley,' she said. 'I met this guy at Pablo's Tacos. He does casting for extras. He said he was looking for someone my type. He gave me his card and said to call next Monday. Isn't that cool?'

'That's so chill, Olive,' he said. 'What is it, *Night of the Living Dead, Part Two*?'

Unfazed, Olive said, 'Awesome, ain't it? Me, in a movie? Of course it might just be a TV show or something.'

'Totally awesome,' he said, closing his eyes, trying to unwire his circuits.

'Of course he might just be some Hollywood Casanova wanting in my pants,' Olive said with a gap-toothed grin.

'You're perfectly safe with Hollywood Casanovas,' Farley mumbled. 'You got nothing to spank. Now get the fuck outta here.'

When she was gone he actually succeeded in falling asleep, and he dreamed of basketball games in the gym at Hollywood High School and boning that cheerleader who had always dissed and avoided him.

Trombone Teddy had a decent day panhandling on Hollywood Boulevard that afternoon. Nothing like the old days, when he still had a horn, when he'd stand out there on the boulevard and play cool licks like Kai Winding and J.J.

23

Johnson, jamming as good as any of the black jazzmen he'd played with in the nightclub down on Washington and La Brea forty years ago, when cool jazz was king.

In those days the black audiences were always the best and treated him like he was one of them. And in fact he had gotten his share of chocolate cooz in those days, before pot and bennies and alcohol beat him down, before he hocked his trombone a hundred times and finally had to sell it. The horn had gotten him enough money to keep in scotch for oh, maybe a week or so if he remembered right. And no trash booze for Teddy. He drank Jack then, all that liquid gold sliding down his throat and warming his belly.

He remembered those old days like it was this afternoon. It was yesterday he couldn't recall sometimes. Nowadays he drank anything he could get, but oh, how he remembered the Jack and the jazz, and those sweet mommas whispering in his ear and taking him home to feed him gumbo. That's when life was sweet. Forty years and a million drinks ago.

While Trombone Teddy yawned and scratched and knew it was time to leave the sleeping bag that was home in the portico of a derelict office building east of the old Hollywood Cemetery, time to hit the streets for some nighttime panhandling, Farley Ramsdale woke from his fitful hour of sleep after a nightmare he couldn't remember.

Farley yelled, 'Olive!' No response. Was that dumb bitch sleeping again? It burned his ass how she could be such a strung-out crystal fiend and still sleep as much as she did. Maybe she was shooting smack in her twat or someplace else he'd never look and the heroin was smoothing out all the ice she smoked? Could that be it? He'd have to watch her better.

'Olive!' he yelled again. 'Where the fuck are you?'

Then he heard her sleepy voice coming from the living room. 'Farley, I'm right here.' She'd been asleep, all right.

'Well, move your skinny ass and rig some mail traps. We got work to do tonight.'

'Okay, Farley,' she yelled, sounding more alert then.

By the time Farley had taken a leak and splashed water on his face and brushed most of the tangles out of his hair and cursed Olive for not washing the towels in the bathroom, she had finished with the traps.

When he entered the kitchen, she was frying some cheese sandwiches in the skillet and had poured two glasses of orange juice. The mousetraps were now rigged to lengths of string four feet long. He picked up each trap and tested it.

'They okay, Farley?'

'Yeah, they're okay.'

He sat at the table knowing he had to drink the juice and eat the sandwich, though he didn't want either. That was one good thing about letting Olive Oyl stay in his house. When he looked at her, he knew he had to take better care of himself. She looked sixty years old but swore she was forty-one, and he believed her. She had the IQ of a schnauzer or a U.S. congressman and was too scared to lie, even though he hadn't laid a hand on her in anger. Not yet, anyway.

'Did you borrow Sam's Pinto like I told you?' he asked when she put the cheese sandwich in front of him.

'Yes, Farley. It's out front.'

'Gas in it?'

'I don't have no money, Farley.'

He shook his head and forced himself to bite into the sandwich, chew and swallow. Chew and swallow. Dying for a candy bar.

'Did you make a couple auxiliary traps just in case?'

'A couple what?'

'Additional different fucking traps. With duct tape?'

'Oh yes.'

Olive went to the little back porch leading to the yard and got the traps from the top of the washer, where she'd put them. She brought them in and placed them on the drain board. Twelve-inch strips of duct tape, sticky side out with strings threaded through holes cut in the tape.

'Olive, don't put the sticky side down on the fucking wet drain board,' he said, thinking that choking down the rest of the sandwich would take great willpower. 'You'll lose some of the stickiness. Ain't that fucking obvious?'

'Okay, Farley,' she said, looping the strings around knobs on the cupboard doors and hanging them there.

Jesus, he had to dump this broad. She was dumber than any white woman he'd ever met with the exception of his Aunt Agnes, who was a certifiable retard. Too much crystal had turned Olive's brain to coleslaw.

'Eat your sandwich and let's go to work,' he said.

Trombone Teddy had to go to work too. After sundown he was heading west from his sleeping bag, thinking if he could panhandle enough on the boulevard tonight he was definitely going to buy some new socks. He was getting a blister on his left foot.

He was still eight blocks from tall cotton, that part of the boulevard where all those tourists as well as locals flock on balmy nights when the Santa Anas blow in, making people's allergies act up but making some people antsy and hungry for action, when he spotted a man and woman standing by a blue mailbox half a block ahead of him at the corner of Gower Street. The corner was south of the boulevard on a street that was a mix of businesses, apartments, and houses.

It was dark tonight and extra smoggy, so there wasn't any starlight, and the smog-shrouded moon was low, but Teddy could make them out, leaning over the mailbox, the man doing something and the woman acting like a lookout or something. Teddy walked closer, huddling in the shadows of a two-story office building where he could see them better. He may have lost part of his hearing and maybe his chops on the trombone, and he'd lost his sex drive for sure, but he'd always had good vision. He could see what they were doing. Tweakers, he thought. Stealing mail.

Teddy was right, of course. Farley had dropped the mousetrap into the mailbox and was fishing it around by the string, trying to catch some letters on the glue pad. He had something that felt like a thick envelope. He fished it up slowly, very slowly, but it was heavy and he didn't have enough of it stuck to the pad, so it fell free.

'Goddamnit, Olive!'

'What'd I do, Farley?' she asked, running a few steps toward him from her lookout position on the corner.

He couldn't think of what to say she'd done wrong, but he always yelled at her for something when life fucked him over, which was most of the time, so he said, 'You ain't watching the streets. You're standing here talking is what.'

'That's because you said "Goddamnit, Olive,"' she explained. 'So that's why I—'

'Get back to the fucking corner!' he said, dropping the mousetrap into the blue mailbox.

Try as he might, he couldn't hook the glue trap onto the thick envelope, but after giving up on it, he did manage to sweep up several letters and even a fairly heavy ten-by-twelve-inch envelope that was nearly as thick as the one he couldn't catch. He tried the duct tape, but it didn't work any better than the mousetrap.

He squeezed the large envelope and said, 'Looks like a movie script. Like we need a goddamn movie script.'

'What, Farley?' Olive said, running over to him again.

'You can have this one, Olive,' Farley said, handing her the envelope. 'You're the future movie star around here.'

Farley tucked the mail under Olive's baggy shirt and inside her jeans in case the cops stopped them. He knew the cops would bust him right along with her but he figured he'd have a better shot at a plea bargain if they didn't actually find any evidence on his person. He was pretty sure that Olive wouldn't snitch him off and would go ahead and take the rap. Especially if he promised that her bed in the house would be there when she got out. Where else did she have to go?

They walked right past one of the old homeless Hollywood street people when they rounded the corner by the car. He scared the shit out of Farley when he stepped out of the shadows and said, 'Got any spare change, Mister?'

Farley reached into his pocket, took out an empty hand and said to Teddy, 'April Fool, shitbag. Now get the fuck outta my face.'

Teddy watched them walk to an old blue Pinto, open the doors, and get in. He watched the guy turn on the lights and start the engine. He stared at the license plate for a minute and said the number aloud. Then he repeated it. He knew he could remember it long enough to borrow a pencil from somebody and write it down. The next time a cop rousted him for being drunk in public or panhandling or pissing in somebody's storefront, maybe he could use it as a get-out-of-jail-free card.

THREE

There were happier partners than the pair in 6-X-76 on Sunday of that May weekend. Fausto Gamboa, one of the most senior patrol officers at Hollywood Station, had long since surrendered his P3 status, needing a break from being a training officer to rookies still on probation. He had been happily working as a P2 with another Hollywood old-timer named Ron LeCroix, who was at home healing up from painful hemorrhoid surgery that he'd avoided too long and was probably just going to retire.

Fausto was always being mistaken for a Hawaiian or Samoan. Though the Vietnam veteran wasn't tall, only five foot nine, he was very big. The bridge of his nose had been flattened in teenage street fights, and his wrists, hands, and shoulders belonged on a guy tall enough to easily dunk a basketball. His legs were so massive he probably could have dunked one if he'd uncoiled those calf and thigh muscles in a vertical leap. His wavy hair was steel-gray and his face was lined and saddle leather-brown, as though he'd spent years picking cotton and grapes in the Central Valley as his father had done after arriving in California with a truckload of other illegal Mexican immigrants. Fausto had never set eyes on a cotton crop but somehow had inherited his father's weathered face.

Fausto was in a particularly foul mood lately, sick and tired of telling every cop at Hollywood Station how he'd lost in court to Darth Vader. The story of that loss had traveled fast on the concrete jungle wireless.

*

It wasn't every day that you get to write Darth Vader a ticket, even in Hollywood, and everyone agreed it could only happen there. Fausto Gamboa and his partner Ron LeCroix had been on patrol on an uneventful early evening when they got a call on their MDT computer that Dark Vader was exposing himself near the corner of Hollywood and Highland. They drove to that location and spotted the man in black cycling down Hollywood Boulevard on an old Schwinn three-speed bike. But there was often more than one Darth Vader hanging around Grauman's, Darths of different ethnicity. This one was a diminutive black Darth Vader.

They weren't sure they had the right Darth until they saw what had obviously prompted the call. Darth wasn't wearing his black tights under his black shorts that evening, and his manhood was dangling off the front of the bike saddle. A motorist had spotted the exposed trekkie meat and had called the cops.

Fausto was driving and he pulled the car behind Darth Vader and tooted the horn, which had no effect in slowing down the cyclist. He tooted again. Same result. Then he turned on the siren and blasted him. Twice. No response.

'Fuck this,' Ron LeCroix said. 'Pull beside him.'

When Fausto drew up next to the cyclist, his partner leaned out the window and got Darth's attention by waving him to the curb. Once there, Darth put down the kickstand, got off the bike, and took off his mask and helmet. Then they saw why their attempts to stop him had been ineffective. He was wearing a headset and listening to music.

It was Fausto's turn to write a ticket, so he got out the book and took the trekker's ID.

Darth Vader, aka Henry Louis Mossman, said, 'Wait a minute here. Why you writing me?'

'It's a vehicle code violation to operate a bike on the streets wearing a headset,' Fausto said. 'And in the future, I'd advise you to wear underwear or tights under those short shorts.'

'Ain't this some shit?' Darth Vader said.

'You couldn't even hear our siren,' Fausto said to the littlest Darth.

'Bullshit!' Darth said. 'I'll see you in court, gud-damnit! This is a humbug!'

'Up to you.' Fausto finished writing the ticket.

When the two cops got back in their car that evening and resumed patrol, Fausto said to Ron LeCroix, 'That little panhandler will never take me to court. He'll tear up the ticket, and when it goes to warrant, we'll be throwing his ass in the slam.'

Fausto Gamboa didn't know Darth Vader.

After several weeks had passed, Fausto found himself in traffic court on Hill Street in downtown L.A. with about a hundred other cops and as many miscreants awaiting their turn before the judge.

Before his case was called, Fausto turned to a cop in uniform next to him and said, 'My guy's a loony-tune panhandler. He'll never show up.'

Fausto Gamboa didn't know Darth Vader.

Not only did he show up, but he showed up in costume, this time wearing black tights under the short shorts. All courtroom business came to a standstill when he entered after his name was called. And the sleepy-eyed judge perked up a bit. In fact, everyone in the courtroom—cops, scofflaws, court clerk, even the bailiff—was watching with interest.

Officer Fausto Gamboa, standing before the bench as is the custom in traffic court, told his story of how he'd gotten the call, spotted Darth Vader, and realized that Darth didn't know his unit was waving in the breeze. And that he couldn't be made to pull over because he was wearing a headset and listening to music, which the cops discovered after they finally stopped the spaceman.

When it was Darth's turn, he removed the helmet and mask, displaying the headset that he said he wore on the day in question. He did a recitation of the vehicle code section that prohibits the wearing of a headset while operating a bike on city streets.

Then he said, 'Your Honor, I would like the court to observe that this headset contains only one earpiece. The vehicle code section clearly refers to both ears being blocked. This officer did not know the vehicle code section then and he don't know it now. The fact is, I did hear the officer's horn and siren but I did not think that it was for me. I wasn't doing nothing illegal, so why should I get all goosey and pull over jist because I hear a siren?'

When he was finished, the judge said to Fausto, 'Officer, did you examine the headset that Mr. Mossman was wearing that day?'

'I saw it, Your Honor,' Fausto said.

'Does this look like the headset?' the judge asked.

'Well... it looks... similar.'

'Officer, can you say for sure that the headset you saw that day had two earpieces, or did it have only one, like the headset you are looking at now?'

'Your Honor, I hit the siren twice and he failed to yield to a police vehicle. It was obvious he couldn't hear me.'

'I see,' the judge said. 'In this case I think we should give the benefit of the doubt to Mr. Mossman. We find him not guilty of the offense cited.'

There was applause and chortling in the courtroom until the bailiff silenced it, and when business was concluded, Darth Vader put on his helmet and with every eye still on him said to all, 'May the force be with you.'

Now Ron LeCroix and his hemorrhoids were gone, and Fausto Gamboa, still smarting from having his ass kicked by Darth Vader, gave the Oracle a big argument the moment he learned that he was being teamed with Officer Budgie Polk. When Fausto was a young cop, women didn't work regular patrol assignments at the LAPD, and he sneered when he said to the Oracle, 'Is she one of them who maybe trades badges with a boyfriend copper like they used to do class rings in my day?'

'She's a good officer,' the Oracle said. 'Give her a chance.'

'Or is she the kind who gets to partner with her boyfriend and hooks her pinkie through his belt loop when they walk the boulevard beat?'

'Come on, Fausto,' the Oracle said. 'It's only for the May deployment period.'

Like the Oracle, Fausto still carried an old six-inch Smith & Wesson revolver, and the first night he was paired with this new partner, he'd pissed her off after she asked him why he carried a wheel gun when the magazine of her Beretta 9-millimeter held fifteen rounds, with one in the pipe.

'If you need more than six rounds to win a gunfight, you deserve to lose,' he'd said to her that night, without a hint of a smile.

Fausto never wore body armor, and when she asked him about that too, he had said, 'Fifty-four cops were shot and killed in the United States last year. Thirty-one were wearing a vest. What good did it do them?'

He'd caught her looking at his bulging chest that first night and said, 'It's all me. No vest. I measure more around the chest than you do.' Then he'd looked at her chest and said, 'Way more.'

That really pissed her off because the fact was, Budgie Polk's ordinarily small breasts were swollen at the moment. Very swollen. She had a four-month-old daughter at home being watched by Budgie's mother, and having just returned to duty from maternity leave, Budgie was actually a few pounds lighter than she had been before the pregnancy. She didn't need thinly veiled cracks about her breast size from this old geezer, not when her tits were killing her.

Her former husband, a detective working out of West L.A. Division, had left home two months before his daughter was born, explaining that their two-year marriage had been a 'regrettable mistake.' And that they were 'two mature people.' She felt like whacking him across the teeth with her baton, as well as half of his cop friends whom she'd run into since she came back to work. How could they still be pals with that dirtbag? She had handed him the keys to her heart, and he had entered and kicked over the furniture and ransacked the drawers like a goddamn crack-smoking burglar.

And why do women officers marry other cops in the first place? She'd asked herself the question a hundred times since that asshole dumped her and his only child, with his shit-eating promise to be prompt with child-support payments and to visit his daughter often 'when she was old enough.' Of course, with five years on the Job, Budgie knew in her heart the answer to the why-do-women-officers-marry-other-cops question.

When she got home at night and needed to talk to somebody about all the crap she'd had to cope with on the streets, who else would understand but another cop? What if she'd married an insurance adjuster? What would he say when she came home as she had one night last September after answering a call in the Hollywood Hills, where the owner of a three-million-dollar hillside home had freaked on ecstasy and crack and strangled his ten-year-old step-daughter, maybe because she'd refused his sexual advances, or so the detectives had deduced. Nobody would ever know for sure, because the son of a bitch blew half his head away with a four-inch Colt magnum while Budgie and her partner were standing on the porch of the home next door with a neighbor who said she was sure she'd heard a child screaming.

After hearing the gunshot, Budgie and her partner had

run next door, pistols drawn, she calling for help into the keyed mike at her shoulder. And while help was arriving and cops were leaping out of their black-and-whites with shotguns, Budgie was in the house gaping at the body of the pajama-clad child on the master bedroom floor, ligature marks already darkening, eyes hemorrhaging, pajamas urine-soaked and feces-stained. The step-father was sprawled across the living room sofa, the back cushion soaked with blood and brains and slivers of bone.

And a woman there, the child's crack-smoking mother, was screaming at Budgie, 'Help her! Resuscitate her! Do something!'

Over and over she yelled, until Budgie grabbed her by the shoulder and yelled back, 'Shut the fuck up! She's dead!'

And that's why women officers seemed to always marry other cops. As poor as the marital success rate was, they figured it would be worse married to a civilian. Who would they talk to after seeing a murdered child in the Hollywood Hills? Maybe male cops didn't have to talk about such things when they got home, but women cops did.

Budgie had hoped that when she returned to duty, she might get teamed with a woman, at least until she stopped lactating. But the Oracle had said everything was screwed during this deployment period, with people off IOD from an unexpected rash of on-duty injuries, vacations, and so forth. He had said, she could work with Fausto until the next deployment period, couldn't she? All of LAPD life revolved around deployment periods, and Fausto was a reliable old pro who would never let a partner down, the Oracle said. But shit, twenty-eight days of this?

Fausto longed for the old days at Hollywood Station when, after working the night watch, they used to gather in the upper parking lot of the John Anson Ford Theater, across from the Hollywood Bowl, at a spot they called the Tree and have a few brews and commiserate. Sometimes badge bunnies would show up, and if one of them was sitting in a car, sucking face with some cop, you always could be sure that another copper would sneak up, look in the window, and yell, 'Crime in progress!'

On one of those balmy summer nights under what the Oracle always called a Hollywood moon, Fausto and the Oracle had sat alone at the Tree on the hood of Fausto's VW bug, Fausto, a young cop back from Vietnam, and the Oracle, a seasoned sergeant but less than forty years old.

He'd surprised Fausto by saying, 'Kid, look up there,' referring to the lighted cross on top of the hill behind them. 'That'd be a great place to have your ashes spread when it's your turn. Up there, looking out over the Bowl. But there's even a better place than that.' And then the Oracle told young Fausto Gamboa about the better place, and Fausto never forgot.

Those were the grand old days at Hollywood Station. But after the last chief's 'Reign of Terror,' nobody dared to drive within a mile of the Tree. Nobody gathered to drink good Mexican brew. And in fact, this young generation of granola-crunching coppers probably worried about *E. coli* in their Evian. Fausto had actually seen them drinking organic milk. Through a freaking straw!

So here she was, Budgie thought, riding shotgun on Sunset Boulevard with this cranky geezer, easily older than her father, who would have been fifty-two years old had he lived. By the number of hash marks on Fausto's sleeve, he'd been a cop for more than thirty years, almost all of it in Hollywood.

To break the ice on that first night, she'd said, 'How long you been on the Job, Fausto?'

'Thirty-four years,' he said. 'Came on when cops wore hats and you had to by god wear it when you were outta the car. And sap pockets were for saps, not cell phones.' Then he paused and said, 'Before you were on this planet.'

'I've been on this planet twenty-seven years,' she said. 'I've been on the Job just over five.'

The way he cocked his right eyebrow at her for a second and then looked away, he appeared to be saying, So who gives a shit about your history?

Well, fuck him, she thought, but just as night fell and she was hoping that somehow the pain in her breasts would subside, he decided to make a little small talk. He said, 'Budgie, huh? That's a weird name.'

Trying not to sound defensive, she said, 'My mother was Australian. A budgie is an Australian parakeet. It's a nickname that stuck. She thought it was cute, I guess.'

Fausto, who was driving, stopped at a red light, looked Budgie up and down, from her blond French-braided ponytail, pinned up per LAPD regulations, to her brightly shined shoes, and said, 'You're what? Five eleven, maybe six feet tall in your socks? And weigh what? About as much as my left leg? She shoulda called you "Storkie."'

Budgie felt it right then. Worse breast pain. These days a dog barks, a cat meows, a baby cries, she lactates. This bastard's gruff voice was doing it!

Take me to the substation on Cherokee,' she said.

'What for?' Fausto said.

'I'm hurting like hell. I got a breast pump in my war bag. I can do it in there and store the milk.'

'Oh, shit!' Fausto said. 'I don't believe it! Twenty-eight days of this?'

When they were halfway to the storefront, Fausto said, 'Why don't we just go back to the station? You can do it in the women's locker room, for chrissake.'

'I don't want anyone to know I'm doing this, Fausto,' she said. 'Not even any of the women. Somebody'll say something, and then I'll have to hear all the wise-ass remarks from the men. I'm trusting you on this.'

'I gotta pull the pin,' Fausto said rhetorically. 'Over a

thousand females on the Job? Pretty soon the freaking chief'll have double-X chromosomes. Thirty-four years is long enough. I gotta pull the pin.'

After Fausto parked the black-and-white at the darkened storefront substation by Musso & Frank's restaurant, Budgie grabbed the carryall and breast pump from her war bag in the trunk, unlocked the door with her 999 key, and ran inside. It was a rather empty space with a few tables and chairs where parents could get information about the Police Activity League or sign up the kids for the Police Explorer Program. Sometimes there was LAPD literature lying around, in English, Spanish, Thai, Korean, Farsi, and other languages for the polyglot citizenry of the Los Angeles melting pot.

Budgie opened the fridge, intending to put her blue ice packs in the freezer, and left her little thermal bag beside the fridge, where she could pick it up after going off duty. She turned on the light in the john, deciding to pump in there sitting on the toilet lid instead of in the main room, in case Fausto got tired of waiting in the car and decided to stroll inside. But the smell of mildew was nauseating.

She removed the rover from her Sam Browne, then took off the gun belt itself and her uniform shirt, vest, and T-shirt. She draped everything on a little table in the bathroom and put the key on the sink. The table teetered under the weight, so she removed her pistol from the gun belt and laid it on the floor beside her rover and flashlight. After she'd been pumping for a minute, the pain started subsiding. The pump was noisy, and she hoped that Fausto wouldn't enter the storefront. Without a doubt he'd make some wisecrack when he heard the sucking noise coming from the bathroom.

Fausto had clicked onto the car's keyboard that they were code 6 at the storefront, out for investigation, so that they wouldn't get any calls until this freaking ordeal was over.

And he was almost dozing when the hotshot call went out to 6-A-77 of Watch 3.

The PSR's urgent voice said, 'All units in the vicinity and Six-Adam-Seventy-seven, shots fired in the parking lot, Western and Romaine. Possibly an officer involved. Six-A-Seventy seven, handle code three.'

Budgie was buttoning her shirt, just having stored the milk in the freezer beside her blue ice packs. She had slid the rover inside its sheath when Fausto threw open the front door and yelled, 'OIS, Western and Romaine! Are you through?'

'Coming!' she yelled, grabbing the Sam Browne and flashlight while still buttoning her shirt, placing the milk and the freezer bags in the insulated carryall, and running for the door, almost tripping on a chair in the darkened office as she was fastening the Sam Browne around her waspish waist.

There were few things more urgent than an officer-involved shooting, and Fausto was revving the engine when she got to the car and she just had time to close the door before he was ripping out from the curb. She was rattled and sweating and when he slid the patrol car around a corner, she almost toppled and grabbed her seat belt and... oh, god!

Since the current chief had arrived, he'd decided to curtail traffic collisions involving officers busting through red lights and stop signs minus lights and siren while racing to urgent calls that didn't rate a code 3 status. So henceforth, the calls that in the old days would have rated only a code 2 status were upgraded to code 3. That meant that in Los Angeles today the citizens were always hearing sirens. The street cops figured it reminded the chief of his days as New York's police commissioner, all those sirens howling. The cops didn't mind a bit. It was a blast getting to drive code 3 all the time.

Because the call wasn't assigned to them, Fausto couldn't drive code 3, but neither the transplanted easterner who headed the Department nor the risen Christ could keep LAPD street cops from racing to an OIS call. Fausto would slow at an intersection and then roar through, green light or not, making cars brake and yield for the black-and-white. But by the time they got to Western and Romaine, five units were there ahead of them and all officers were out of their cars, aiming shotguns or nines at the lone car in the parking lot, where they could see someone ducking down on the front seat.

Fausto grabbed the shotgun and advanced to the car closest to the action, seeing it belonged to the surfers, Flotsam and Jetsam. When he looked over at Budgie trailing beside him, he wondered why she wasn't aiming hers.

'Where's your gun?' he said, then added, 'Please don't tell me it's with the milk!'

'No, I have the milk,' Budgie said.

'Just point your finger,' he said and was stunned to see that, with a sick look on her face, she did it! After a pause, he said, 'I have a two-inch Smith in my war bag, wanna borrow it?'

Still pointing her long, slender index finger, Budgie said, 'Two-inch wheel guns can't hit shit. I'm better off this way.'

Fausto came as close to a guffaw as he had in a long time. She had balls. And she was quick, he had to give her that. Then he saw the car door open, and two teenage Latino boys got out with their hands up and were quickly proned-out and cuffed.

The code 4 was broadcast by the PSR, meaning there was sufficient help at the scene. And to keep other eager cops from coming anyway, she added, 'No officer involved.'

Fausto saw one of those surfers, Flotsam, heading their way. Fausto thought about how back when he was a young copper, there was no way in hell bleached hair would be allowed. And what about his partner, Jetsam, swaggering along beside him with his dark blond hair all gelled in little spikes two inches long? What kind of shit was that? It was time to retire, Fausto thought again. Time to pull the pin.

Flotsam approached Fausto and said, 'Security guard at the big building there got hassled by some homies when he caught them jacking up a car to steal the rims. Dumb ass capped one off in the air to scare them away. They jumped in the car and hid, afraid to come out.'

'Sky shooting,' Fausto snorted. 'Guy's seen too many cowboy movies. Shouldn't allow those door shakers to carry anything more than a bag of stones and a slingshot.'

'You should see the ride they were working on,' Jetsam said, joining his partner. 'Nineteen thirty-nine Chevy. Completely restored. Cherry. Bro, it is sweet!'

'Yeah?' Fausto was interested now. 'I used to own an old 'thirty-nine when I was in high school.' Turning to Budgie, he said, 'Let's take a look for a minute.' Then he remembered her empty holster and thought they'd better get away before somebody spotted it.

He said to Flotsam and Jetsam, 'Just remembered something. Gotta go.'

Budgie was thrown back in her seat as they sped away. When she shot him a guilty look, he said, 'Please tell me that you didn't forget your key too.'

'Oh shit,' she said. 'Don't you have your nine-nine-nine key?'

'Where's your freaking keys?'

'On the table in the john.'

'And where is your freaking gun, may I ask?'

'On the floor in the john. By the keys.'

'And what if my nine-nine-nine key's in my locker with the rest of my keys?' he said. 'Figuring I didn't have to bother, since I have an eager young partner.'

'You wouldn't leave your keys in your locker,' Budgie said without looking at him. 'Not you. You wouldn't trust a young partner, an old partner, or your family dog.'

He looked at her then and seeing a tiny upturn at the corner of her lips thought, She really has some balls, this one. And some smart mouth. And of course she was right about him—he would never forget his keys.

Fausto just kept shaking his head as he drove back to the storefront substation. Then he grumbled more to himself than to her, 'Freaking surfers. You see that gelled hair? Not in my day.'

'That isn't gel,' Budgie said. 'Their hair is stiff and sticky from all the mai tai mix getting dumped on their heads in the beach bars they frequent. They're always sniffing around like a pair of poodles and getting rejected. And please don't tell me it wouldn't be like that if there weren't so many women officers around. Like in your day.'

Fausto just grunted and they rode without speaking for a while, pretending to be scanning the streets as the moon was rising over Hollywood.

Budgie broke the silence when she said, 'You won't snitch me off to the Oracle, will you? Or for a big laugh to the other guys?'

With his eyes focused on the streets, he said, 'Yeah, I go around ratting out partners all the time. For laughs.'

'Is there a bathroom window in that place?' she asked. 'I didn't notice.'

'I don't think there's any windows,' he said. 'I hardly ever been in there. Why?'

'Well, if I'm wrong about you and you don't have a key, and if there's a window, you could boost me up and I could pry it open and climb in.'

His words laden with sarcasm, Fausto said, 'Oh, well, why not just ask me if I'd climb in the window because you're a new mommy and can't risk hurting yourself?'

'No,' she said, 'you could never get your big ass through any window, but I could if you'd boost me up. Sometimes it pays to look like a stork.'

'I got my keys,' he said.

'I figured,' she said.

For the first time, Budgie saw Fausto nearly smile, and he said, 'It hasn't been a total loss. At least we got the milk.'

At about the same time that Fausto Gamboa and Budgie Polk were gathering her equipment at the substation on Cherokee, Farley Ramsdale and Olive Oyl were home at Farley's bungalow, sitting on the floor, having smoked some of the small amount of crystal they had left. Scattered all around them on the floor were letters they had fished out of seven blue mailboxes on that very busy evening of work.

Olive was wearing the glasses Farley had stolen for her at the drugstore and was laboriously reading through business mail, job applications, notices of unpaid bills, detached portions of paid bills, and various other correspondence. Whenever she came across something they could use, she would pass it to Farley, who was in a better mood now, sorting some checks they could possibly trade and nibbling on a saltine because it was time to put something in his stomach.

The crystal was getting to him, Olive thought. He was blinking more often than usual and getting flushed. Sometimes it worried her when his pulse rate would shoot up to 150 and higher, but if she mentioned it, he just yelled at her, so she didn't say anything.

'This is a lot of work, Farley,' she said when her eyes were getting tired. 'Sometimes I wonder why we don't just make our own meth. Ten years ago I used to go with a guy who had his own meth lab and we always had enough without working so hard. Till the chemicals blew up one day and burned him real bad.'

'Ten years ago you could walk in a drugstore and buy all the goddamn ephedrine you wanted,' Farley said. 'Nowadays a checkout clerk'll send you to a counter where they ask for ID if you try to buy a couple boxes of Sudafed. Life ain't easy anymore. But you're lucky, Olive. You get to live in my house. If you were living in a ratty hotel room, it'd be real dangerous to do the work we do. Like, if you used a hot credit card or a phony name to get your room like you always did before, you'd lose your protection against search and seizure. The law says you have no expectation of privacy when you do that. So the cops could kick your door down without a search warrant. But you're lucky. You live in my house. They need a search warrant to come in here.'

'I'm real lucky,' Olive agreed. 'You know so much about the law and everything.' She grinned at him and he thought, *Kee-rist*, those fucking teeth!

Olive thought it was nice when she and Farley were at home like this, working in front of the TV. Really nice when Farley wasn't all paranoid from the tweak, thinking the FBI and the CIA were coming down the chimney. A couple times when he'd hallucinated, Olive really got scared. They'd had a long talk then about how much to smoke and when they should do it. But lately she thought that Farley was breaking his own rules when she wasn't looking. She thought he was into that ice a whole lot more than she was.

'We got quite a few credit-card numbers,' he said. 'Lots of SS numbers and driver's license info and plenty of checks. We can trade for some serious glass when we take this stuff to Sam.'

'Any cash, Farley?'

'Ten bucks in a card addressed to "my darling grand-child." What kinda cheap asshole only gives ten bucks to a grandchild? Where's the fucking family values?'

'That's all?'

'One other birthday card, "to Linda from Uncle Pete." Twenty bucks.' He looked up at Olive and added, 'Uncle Pete's probably a pedophile, and Linda's probably his neighbor's ten-year-old. Hollywood's full of freaks. Someday I'm getting outta here.'

'I better check on the money,' Olive said.

'Yeah, don't cook it to death,' Farley said, thinking that the saltine was making him sick. Maybe he should try some vegetable soup if there was a can left.

The money was in the tub that Farley had placed on the screened back porch. Eighteen five-dollar bills were soaking in Easy-Off, almost bleached clean. Olive used a wooden spoon to poke a few of them or flip them over to look at the other side. She hoped this would work better than the last time they tried passing bogus money.

That time Olive almost got arrested, and it scared her to even think about that day two months ago when Farley told her to buy a certain light green bonded paper at Office Depot. And then they took it to Sam, the guy who rented them his car from time to time, and Sam worked for two days cutting the paper and printing twenty-dollar bills on his very expensive laser printer. After Sam was satisfied, he told Olive to spray the stack of bogus twenties with laundry starch and let them dry thoroughly. Olive did it, and when she and Farley checked the bills, he thought they were perfect.

They stayed away from the stores like the mini-market chains that have the pen they run over large bills. Farley wasn't sure if they'd bother with twenties, but he was afraid to take a chance. A mini-market clerk had told Farley that if the clerk sees brown under the pen, it's good; black or no color is bad. Or something like that. So they'd gone to a Target store on that day two months ago to try out the bogus money.

In front of the store was a buff young guy with a mullet passing out gay pride leaflets for a parade that was being organized the following weekend. The guy wore a tight yellow T-shirt with purple letters across the front that said 'Queer Pervert.'

He'd offered a handbill to Farley, who pointed at the words on the T-shirt and said to Olive, 'That's redundant.'

The guy flexed his deltoids and pecs, saying to Farley, 'And it could say "Kick Boxer" too. Want a demonstration?'

'Don't come near me!' Farley cried. 'Olive, you're a witness!'

'What's redundant, Farley?' Olive asked, but he said, 'Just get the fuck inside the store.'

Olive could see that Farley was in a bad mood then, and when they were entering, they were partially blocked by six women and girls completely covered in chadors and burkas, two of them talking on cells and two others raising their veils to drink from large Starbucks cups.

Farley brushed past them, saying, 'Why don't you take those Halloween rags back to Western Costume.' Then to Olive, 'Wannabe sand niggers. Or maybe Gypsies boosting merchandise under those fucking mumus.'

One of the women said something angrily in Arabic, and Farley muttered, '*Hasta lasagna* to you too. Bitch.'

There were lots of things that Olive had wanted to buy, but Farley said they were going to maintain control until they tested the money once or twice with small purchases. Farley kept looking at a CD player for $69.50 that he said he could sell in five minutes at Ruby's Donuts on Santa Monica Boulevard, where a lot of tranny streetwalkers hung out.

Olive had always been tenderhearted and she felt sorry for all those transsexuals trapped between two genders. Some of those she'd talked to had had partial gender-changing operations, and a couple of them had endured the complete change, Adam's apple surgery and all. But Olive could still tell they hadn't been born as women. They seemed sad to Olive and they were always nice to her long before she'd met Farley, when she was panhandling and selling ecstacy for a guy named Willard, who was way mean. Many times a tranny who'd just turned a good trick would give Olive five or ten dollars and tell her to go get something to eat.

'You look nervous,' Farley said to Olive as they wandered around the Target store.

'I'm only a little nervous,' Olive said.

'Well, stop it. You gotta look like a normal person, if that's possible.' Farley eyed a very nice twenty-one-inch TV set but shook his head, saying, 'We gotta start small.'

'Can we just do it now, Farley?' Olive said. 'I just wanna get it over with.'

Farley left the store and Olive took the CD player to the checkout counter, the most crowded one so that she'd encounter a clerk who was too busy to be looking for bogus money. Except that just as the shopper ahead of her was paying for a purchase of blankets and sheets, a manager stepped over and offered to relieve the harried young check-out clerk. He glanced at Olive when he was taking care of the other customer, and Olive had a bad feeling.

She had a real bad feeling when it was her turn and he said suspiciously, 'Will you be paying by check?'

'No, cash,' Olive said innocently, just as a roving store employee walked up to the manager and nodded toward Olive. The roving guy said, 'Where's your friend?'

'Friend?' Olive said.

'Yes, the man who insulted the Muslim ladies,' he said. 'They complained and wanted me to throw him out of the store.'

Olive was so shaken, she didn't notice that she'd dropped the three twenties on the counter until the manager picked them up and held them up to the light and ran them through his fingers. And Olive panicked. She bolted and ran past shoppers with loaded carts, through the doors to the parking lot, and didn't stop until she was on the sidewalk in front.

When Farley found her walking on the sidewalk and picked her up, she didn't tell him about the guy and the complaint from the Muslim women. She knew it would just make him madder and get him in a terrible mood, so she said that the checkout clerk felt the money and said, 'This paper is wrong.' And that's why Farley went back to Sam, who told him to try to get good paper by bleaching real money with Easy-Off.

So today they were trying it again but with real money. She wore her cleanest cotton sweater and some low-rise jeans that were too big, even though Farley had shoplifted them from the junior's section at Nordstroms. And she wore tennis shoes for running, in case things went bad again.

'This time it won't go bad,' Farley promised Olive while he parked in front of RadioShack, seemingly determined to buy a CD player.

When they were out and standing beside the car, he said, 'This time you got real paper from real money, so don't sweat it. And it wasn't easy to get hold of all those five-dollar bills, so don't blow this.'

'I don't know if they look quite right,' Olive said doubtfully.

'Stop worrying,' Farley said. 'You remember what Sam told you about the strip and the watermark?'

'Sort of,' Olive said.

'The strip on the left side of a five says five, right? But it's small, very hard to see. The president's image on the right-side watermark is bigger but also hard to see. So if they hold the bill up to the light and their eyes start looking left to right or right to left, whadda you do?'

'I run to you.'

'No, you don't run to me, goddamnit!' He yelled it, then looked around, but none of the passing shoppers were paying any attention to them. He continued with as much patience as he could muster. 'These dumb shits won't even notice that the strip ain't for a twenty-dollar bill and that the watermark has a picture of Lincoln instead of Jackson. They just go through the motions and look, but they don't see. So don't panic.'

'Until I'm sure he's onto me. Then I run out to you.'

Farley looked at the low, smog-laden sky and thought; Maintain. Just fucking maintain. This woman is dumb as a clump of dog hair. Slowly he said, 'You do not run to me. You never run to me. You do not know me. I am a fucking stranger. You just walk fast out of the store and head for the street. I'll pick you up there after I make sure nobody's coming after you.'

'Can we do it now, Farley?' Olive said. 'Pretty soon I'll have to go to the bathroom.'

The store was bustling when they entered. As usual, there were a few street people lurking around the parking lot begging for change.

One of the street people recognized Farley and Olive. In fact, he had their license number written down on a card, saving it for a rainy day, so to speak. Farley and Olive never noticed the old homeless guy who was eyeballing them as they entered. Nor did they see him enter the store and approach a man with a 'Manager' tag on his shirt.

The homeless guy whispered something to the manager, who kept his eye on Farley and Olive for the whole ten minutes that they browsed. When Farley walked out of the store, the manager still watched him, until he was sure that Farley wasn't coming back in. Then the manager reentered the store and watched Olive at the checkout counter.

Slick, Olive thought. It's working real slick. The kid at the checkout took the four bogus twenties from Olive's hand and began ringing up the purchase. But then it happened.

'Let me see those bills.'

The manager was talking to the kid, not to Olive. She hadn't seen him standing behind her, and she was too startled by his arrival to do anything but freeze.

He held the bills up to the late-afternoon light pouring through the plate glass, and she saw his eyes moving left to right and right to left, and she didn't care if Farley said they're too dumb to match up strips and watermarks and all that Farley Ramsdale goddamn bullshit! Olive knew exactly what to do and did it right at that instant.

Three minutes later Farley picked her up sprinting across the street against a red light, and he was amazed that Olive Oyl could move that fast, given her emaciated condition. A few minutes after that, Trombone Teddy walked into RadioShack and the manager told him that yes, they were crooks and had tried to pass bogus twenties. He handed Teddy several dollars from his pocket and thanked him for the tip. All in all, Teddy thought that his day was beginning quite fortuitously. He wished he could run into those two tweakers more often.

FOUR

Wondering why in the hell she'd volunteered to read her paper when none of them knew what she did for a living, Andi McCrea decided to sit on the corner of the professor's desk just as though she wasn't nervous about criticism and wasn't scared of Professor Anglund, who'd squawked all during the college term about the putative abuse of civil liberties by law enforcement.

With her forty-fifth birthday right around the corner and her oral exam for lieutenant coming up, it had seemed important to be able to tell a promotion board that she had completed her bachelor's degree at last, even making the Dean's List unless Anglund torpedoed her. She hoped to convince the board that this academic achievement at her time of life—combined with twenty-four years of patrol and detective experience—proved that she was an outstanding candidate for lieutenant's bars. Or something like that.

So why hadn't she just gracefully declined when Anglund asked her to read her paper? And why now, nearly at the end of the term, at the end of her college life, had she decided to write a paper that she knew would provoke this professor and reveal to the others that she, a middle-aged classmate old enough to be their momma, was a cop with the LAPD? Unavoidable and honest answer: Andi was sick and tired of kissing ass in this institution of higher learning.

She hadn't agreed with much of what this professor and others like him had said during all the years she'd struggled here, working for the degree she should have gotten two decades ago, balancing police work with the life of a single mom. Now that it was almost over, she was ashamed that she'd sat silently, relishing those A's and A-pluses, pretending to agree with all the crap in this citadel of political correctness that often made her want to gag. She was looking for self-respect at the end of the academic trail.

For this effort, Andi wore the two-hundred-dollar blue blazer she'd bought at Banana instead of the sixty-dollar one she'd bought at The Gap. Under that blazer was a button-down Oxford in eye-matching blue, also from Banana, and no bling except for tiny diamond studs. Black flats completed the ensemble, and since she had had her collar-length bob highlighted on Thursday, she'd figured to look pretty good for this final performance. Until she got the call-out last night: the bloodbath on Cherokee that kept her from her bed and allowed her just enough time to run home, shower and change, and be here in time for what she now feared would be a debacle. She was bushed and a bit nauseated from a caffeine overload, and she'd had to ladle on the pancake under her eyes to even approach a look of perkiness that her classmates naturally exuded.

'The title of my paper is, "What's Wrong with the Los Angeles Police Department,"' Andi began, looking out at twenty-three faces too young to know Gumby, fourteen of whom shared her gender, only four of whom shared her race. It was to be expected in a university that prided itself on diversity, with only ten percent of the student population being non-Latino white. She had often wanted to say, 'Where's the goddamn diversity for me? I'm the one in the minority.' But never had.

She was surprised that Professor Anglund had remained in his chair directly behind her instead of moving to a position where he could see her face. She'd figured he was getting too old to be interested in her ass. Or are they ever?

She began reading aloud: 'In December of nineteen

ninety-seven, Officer David Mack of the LAPD committed a $722,000 bank robbery just two months before eight pounds of cocaine went missing from an LAPD evidence room, stolen by Officer Rafael Perez of Rampart Division, a friend of David Mack's.

'The arrest of Rafael Perez triggered the Rampart Division police scandal, wherein Perez, after one trial, cut a deal with the district attorney's office to avoid another, and implicated several cops through accusations of false arrests, bad shootings, suspect beatings, and perjury, some of which he had apparently invented to improve his plea bargain status.

'The most egregious incident, which he certainly did not invent, involved Perez himself and his partner, Officer Nino Durden, both of whom in nineteen ninety-six mistakenly shot a young Latino man named Javier Ovando, putting him into a wheelchair for life, then falsely testified that he'd threatened them with a rifle that they themselves had planted beside his critically wounded body in order to cover their actions. Ovando served two years in prison before he was released after Perez confessed.'

Andi looked up boldly, then said, 'Mack, Perez, and Durden are black. But to understand what came of all this we must first examine the Rodney King incident five years earlier. That was a bizarre event wherein a white sergeant, having shot Mr. King with a Taser gun after a long auto pursuit, then directed the beating of this drunken, drug-addled African American ex-convict. That peculiar sergeant seemed determined to make King cry uncle, when the ring of a dozen cops should have swarmed and handcuffed the drunken thug and been done with it.'

She gave another pointed look at her audience and then went on: 'That led to the subsequent riot where, according to arrest interviews, most of the rioters had never even heard of Rodney King but thought this was a good chance to act out and do some looting. The riot brought to Los Angeles a commission headed by Warren Christopher, later to become U.S. secretary of state under President Bill Clinton, a commission that determined very quickly and with very little evidence, that the LAPD had a significant number of overly aggressive, if not downright brutal, officers who needed reining in. The LAPD's white chief, who, like several others before him, had civil service protection, was soon to retire.

'So the LAPD was placed under the leadership of one, then later a second African American chief. The first, an outsider from the Philadelphia Police Department, became the first LAPD chief in decades to serve without civil service protection at the pleasure of the mayor and city council, a throwback to the days when crooked politicians ran the police force. His contract was soon bought back by city fathers dissatisfied with his performance and his widely publicized junkets to Las Vegas.

'The next black chief, an insider whose entire adult life had been spent with the LAPD, was in charge when the Rampart Division scandal exploded, making the race card difficult for anyone to play. This chief, a micromanager, seemingly obsessive about control and cavalier about officer morale, quickly became the enemy of the police union. He came to be known as Lord Voldemort by street cops who'd read *Harry Potter*.

'David Mack, Rafael Perez, and Nino Durden went to prison, where Mack claimed to belong to the Piru Bloods street gang. So, we might ask: Were these cops who became gangsters, or gangsters who became cops?'

Scanning their faces, she saw nothing. She dropped her eyes again and read, 'By two thousand two, that second black chief, serving at the pleasure of City Hall, hadn't pleased the politicians, the cops, or the local media. He retired but later was elected to the city council. His replacement was another cross-country outsider, a white chief this time, who had been

New York City's police commissioner. Along with all the changes in leadership, the police department ended up operating under a "civil rights consent decree," an agreement between the City of Los Angeles and the United States Department of Justice wherein the LAPD was forced to accept major oversight by DOJ-approved monitors for a period of five years but which has just been extended for three years by a Federal judge based on technicalities.

'And thus, the beleaguered rank and file of the formerly proud LAPD, lamenting the unjustified loss of reputation as the most competent and corruption-free, and certainly most famous, big-city police department in the country, finds itself faced with the humiliation of performing under outside overseers. Mandated auditors can simply walk into a police station and, figuratively speaking, ransack desks, turn pockets inside out, threaten careers, and generally make cops afraid to do proactive police work that had always been the coin of the realm with the LAPD during the glory days before Rodney King and the Rampart Division scandal.

'And of course, there is the new police commission, led by the former head of the L.A. Urban League, who uttered the following for the *L.A. Times* before he took office. Quote: "The LAPD has a longstanding institutionalized culture in which some police officers feel that they have the tacit approval of their leadership… to brutalize and even kill African American boys and men." End quote. This baseless and crudely racist slander is apparently okay with our new Latino mayor, who appointed him claiming to want harmony in the racial cauldron where the police must do their job.'

Andi looked again at the blank stares as she prepared for her parting shot and said, 'Finally, all of the layers of oversight, based on the crimes of a few cops—costing millions annually, encouraged by cynical politicians and biased reporting and fueled by political correctness gone mad—

have at last answered the ancient question posed by the Roman poet Juvenal in the first century A.D. He too was worried about law enforcement abuse, for he asked, "But who would guard the guards themselves?" At the Los Angeles Police Department, more than nine thousand officers have learned the answer: Everybody.'

With that, Andi turned to glance at Anglund, who was looking at papers in his lap as though he hadn't heard a word. She said to the class, 'Any questions?'

Nobody answered for a long moment, and then one of the East Asians, a petite young woman about the age of Andi's son, said, 'Are you a cop or something?'

'I am a cop, yes,' Andi said. 'With the LAPD, and have been since I was your age. Any other questions?'

Students were looking from the wall clock to the professor and back to Andi. Finally, Anglund said, 'Thank you, Ms. McCrea. Thank you, ladies and gentlemen, for your diligence and attention. And now that the spring quarter is so close to officially concluding, why don't you all just get the hell out of here.'

That brought smiles and chuckles and some applause for the professor. Andi was about to leave, when Anglund said, 'A moment, Ms. McCrea?'

He waited until the other students were gone, then stood, hands in the pockets of his cords, linen shirt so wrinkled that Andi thought he should either send it out or get his wife an ironing board. His gray hair was wispy, and his pink scalp showed through, flaked with dandruff. He was a man of seventy if he was a day.

Anglund said, 'Why did you keep your other life from us until the end?'

'I don't know,' she said. 'Maybe I only like to don the bat suit when night falls on Gotham City.'

'How long have you been attending classes here?'

'Off and on, eight years,' she said.

'Have you kept your occupation a secret from everybody in all that time?'

'Yep,' she said. 'I'm just a little secret keeper.'

'First of all, Ms. McCrea... is it Officer McCrea?'

'Detective,' she said.

'First of all, your paper contained opinions and assertions that you may or may not be able to back up and not a few biases of your own, but I don't think you're a racist cop.'

'Well, thank you for that. That's mighty white of you, if that's an acceptable phrase.' Thinking, *There goes the Dean's List. She'd be lucky to get a C-plus out of him now.*

Anglund smiled and said, 'Sorry. That was very condescending of me.'

'I bored them to death,' Andi said.

'The fact is, they don't really give a damn about civil liberties or police malfeasance or law enforcement in general,' Anglund said. 'More than half of today's university students cannot even understand the positions put forth in newspaper editorials. They care about iPods and cell phones and celluloid fantasy. The majority of this generation of students don't read anything outside of class but magazines and an occasional graphic novel, and barely contemplate anything more serious than video downloading. So, yes, I think you failed to provoke them as you'd obviously intended to do.'

'I guess my son isn't so different after all, then,' she said, seeing her first C-plus morphing into a C-minus.

'Is he a college student?'

'A soldier,' she said. 'Insisted on joining because two of his friends did.'

Anglund studied her for a few seconds and said, 'Iraq?'

'Afghanistan.'

Anglund said, 'Despite the flaws in your thesis, I was impressed by the passion in it. You're part of something larger than yourself, and you feel real pain that uninformed outsiders are harming the thing you love. I don't see much of that passion in classrooms anymore. I wish you'd revealed your other life to us earlier.'

Now she was confused, fatigued and confused, and her nausea was increasing. 'I wouldn't have done it today, Professor,' Andi said, 'except my forty-fifth birthday is coming up in two weeks and I'm into a midlife crisis so real it's like living with a big sister who just wants to dress up in thigh-highs and a miniskirt and dance the funky chicken. No telling what kind of zany thing I'll do these days. And last night I got called out on a murder-suicide that looked like O.J. Simpson was back in town, and I'm exhausted. But I'm not half as tired or stressed as two young cops who had to wallow in a bloodbath doing a job that nobody should ever have to do. And when it was all over, one of them asked me back at Hollywood Station if I had some moisturizing cream. Because he surfed so much he thought his neck and eyelids looked like they belonged on a Galapagos turtle. I felt like just hugging him.'

Then the catch in her voice made her pause again, and she said, 'I'm sorry. I'm babbling. I've gotta get some sleep. Good-bye, Professor.'

As she gathered her purse and books, he held up his class folder, opened it, and pointed to her name, along with the grade he'd given her presentation when he'd sat there behind her, when she'd thought he wasn't listening. It was an A-plus.

'Good-bye, Detective McCrea,' he said. 'Take care in Gotham City.'

Andi McCrea was driving back to Hollywood Division (she'd never get used to calling it Hollywood Area, as it was supposed to be called these days but which most of the street cops ignored) to assure herself that all the reports from last night's murder-suicide were complete. She was a D2 in one of the three homicide teams, but they were so shorthanded at Hollywood Station that she had nobody else around today who could help with the reports from her current cases, not even the one that had solved itself like the murder-suicide of the night before.

She decided to send an FTD bouquet to Professor Anglund for the A-plus that guaranteed her the Dean's List. That old socialist was okay after all, she thought, scribbling a note saying 'flowers' after she wheeled into the Hollywood Station south parking lot in her Volvo sedan.

The station parking lots were more or less adequate for the time being, considering how many patrol units, plain-wrap detectives units, and private cars had to park there. If they were ever brought up to strength, they'd have to build a parking structure, but she knew that it wasn't likely that the LAPD would ever be brought up to strength. And when would the city pop for money to build a parking structure when street cops citywide were complaining about the short-age of equipment like digital cameras and batteries for rifle lights, shotgun lights, and even flashlights. They never seemed to have pry bars or hooks or rams when it was time to take down a door. They never seemed to have anything when it was needed.

Andi McCrea was bone-weary and not just because she had not slept since yesterday morning. Hollywood Division's workload called for fifty detectives, but half that many were doing the job, or trying to do it, and these days she was always mentally tired. As she trudged toward the back door of Hollywood Station, she couldn't find her ring of keys buried in the clutter of her purse, gave up, and walked to the front door, on Wilcox Avenue.

The building itself was a typical municipal shoe box with a brick facade the sole enhancement, obsolete by the time it was finished. Four hundred souls were crammed inside a rabbit warren of tiny spaces. Even one of the detectives' interview rooms had to be used for storage.

By habit, she walked around the stars on the pavement in front of the station without stepping on them. There was nothing like them at other LAPD stations, and they were exactly like the stars on the Hollywood Walk of Fame except that the names imbedded in the marble were not the names of movie stars. There were seven names, all belonging to officers from Hollywood Station who had been killed on duty. Among them were Robert J. Coté, shot and killed by a robber, Russell L. Kuster, gunned down in a Hungarian restaurant by a deranged customer, Charles D. Heim, shot to death during a drug arrest, and Ian J. Campbell, kidnapped by robbers and murdered in an onion field.

The wall plaque said 'To Those Who Stood Their Ground When in Harm's Way.'

Hollywood Station was also different from any other in the LAPD by virtue of the interior wall hangings. There were one-sheet movie posters hanging in various places in the station, some but not all from cop movies based in Los Angeles. A police station decorated with movie posters let people know exactly where they were.

Andi was passed in the corridor leading to the detective squad room by two young patrol officers on their way out. Although there were several older cops working patrol, Hollywood Division officers tended to be young, as though the brass downtown considered Hollywood a training area, and perhaps they did.

The short Japanese American female officer she knew as Mag something said hi to Andi.

The tall black male officer whose name she didn't know said more formally, 'Afternoon, Detective.'

Six-X-Sixty-six had been asked by the vice sergeant to pop into a few of the adult bookstores to make sure there weren't lewd-conduct violations taking place in the makeshift video rooms. A pair of Hollywood Station blue suits making unscheduled visits went a long way toward convincing the termites to clean up their act, the vice sergeant had told them. Mag Takara, an athletic twenty-six-year-old, and the shortest officer at Hollywood Station, was partnered in 6-X-66 with Benny Brewster, age twenty-five, from southeast L.A., who was one of Hollywood's tallest officers.

One morning last month, the Oracle had spotted a clutch of male cops in the parking lot after roll call convulsing in giggles at Mag Takara, who, after putting her overloaded war bag into the trunk, couldn't close the lid because it was sprung and yawned open out of reach.

Mag's war bag was on wheels, jammed with helmet and gear. She had also been carrying a Taser, an extra canister of pepper spray, a beanbag shotgun, a pod (handheld MDT computer), her jacket, a bag of reports, a flashlight, a side-handle baton as well as a retractable steel baton, and the real we-mean-business shotgun loaded with double-aught buck that would be locked in the rack inside the car. She was so short she had to go around to the rear window of the patrol car and close the trunk by walking her hands along the length of the deck lid until it clicked shut.

The Oracle watched her for a moment and heard the loudest of the cops tossing out lines to the others like, 'It's a little nippy, wouldn't you say? A teeny little nippy.'

The Oracle said to the jokester, 'Bonelli, her great-grand-parents ran a hotel on First Street in little Tokyo when yours were still eating garlic in Palermo. So spare us the ethnic wisecracks, okay?'

Bonelli said, 'Sorry, Sarge.'

While the cops were all walking to their patrol cars, the Oracle said, 'I gotta balance that kid out.' And he'd assigned Benny Brewster to partner with Mag for the deployment period to see how they got along. And so far, so good, except that Benny Brewster had a cultural hangup about adult bookstores when it came to gay porn.

'Those sissies creep me out,' he said to Mag. 'Some of the gangstas in Compton would cap their ass, they saw the stuff we see all over Hollywood' is how he explained it.

But Mag told him she didn't give a shit if the fuck flicks were gay or straight, it was all revolting. One of her former cop boyfriends had tried to light her fire a couple of times by showing her porn videos in his apartment after dinner, but it seemed to her that act two of all those stories consisted of jizz shots in a girl's face, and how that could excite anybody was way beyond her.

Despite his hangup about gay men, Benny seemed to her like a dedicated officer, never badge-heavy, never manhandling anybody who didn't need it, whether gay or straight, so she had no complaints. And it was very comforting for Mag when Benny was standing behind her, eye-fucking some of those maggots who liked to challenge little cops, especially little female cops.

They met Mr. Potato Head in the first porn shop they checked out. It was on Western Avenue, a dingier place than most, with a few peep rooms where guys could look at video and jerk off with the door locked, but this one had a makeshift theater, a larger room with three rows of plastic chairs posing as theater seats, and a large screen along with a quality projector hanging from the ceiling.

The theater was curtained off by heavy black drapes and there was no lighting inside, except for what came from the screen. The occasional visit from uniformed cops was supposed to discourage the viewers from masturbating in public, whether alone or in tandem, while they watched two or three or five guys porking whatever got in front of them. To background hip-hop lyrics about rape and sodomy.

Benny walked down one aisle, looking like he wanted to get it over with, and Mag started down the other, when she heard him say, 'Do your pants up and come with me!'

The viewer had been so involved in what he was doing

that he hadn't seen that very tall black cop in a dark blue uniform until he was standing three feet away. He lost the erection he'd been stroking, as did just about all of the other guys in the room, but Mag figured some of these dudes were so bent that the presence of the law, the danger of it all, probably enhanced the thrill.

She shined her light across the chair to see what was going on but he had already pulled up and belted his pants. He was being led by the elbow toward the black curtain and Benny kept saying, 'Damn!'

When they got him out of the video room, Mag said, 'What? Six-forty-seven-A?' referring to the penal code section for lewd conduct in public.

Benny looked at the guy, at the black elastic straps wound around his wrists, and said, 'What were you doing in there, man? Besides displayin' your willie. What're them straps on your wrists all about?'

He was a fiftyish plump, bespectacled white guy with a pouty mouth and a fringe of brown hair. He said, 'I'd prefer not to explain at this time.'

But when they took him to a glass-windowed holding tank at Hollywood Station, they found out. He gave a short demonstration that caused Benny to exit the scene shortly after the prisoner dropped his pants and unhooked the intricately connected elastic straps that encircled his waist, wound under his crotch from each wrist, and finally threaded through holes in the end of a potato. Which he reached behind and removed from his anal cavity with a magician's flourish and not a little pride of invention.

Performing before five gaping cops who happened by the glass window, the prisoner then demonstrated that if he sat on one buttock and manipulated the straps attached to his wrists, he could adeptly pull the potato halfway out simply by raising his arms, then force it back into its 'magic cave' by sitting on it. He looked like he was conducting an orchestra.

Arms raised, potato out, then sit. Arms raised, potato out, then sit. And so forth.

'Probably keeping time with the background music on the video,' Mag suggested. The guy was ingenious, she had to give him that.

'I ain't handling the evidence,' Benny said to Mag. 'No way. In fact, I wanna transfer outta this lunatic asylum. I'll work anywhere but Holly-weird!'

It disappointed her. *Holly-weird.* Why did they all have to say it?

By end-of-watch, Benny would find a gift box tied with a ribbon in front of his locker and a card bearing the name 'Officer Brewster.' Inside the box was a nice fresh Idaho potato to which someone had attached plastic eyes and lips, along with a handwritten note that said, 'Fry me, bake me, mash me. Or bite me, Benny. Love ya.—Mr. Potato Head.'

FIVE

There was always a male cop at LAPD with 'Hollywood' attached to his name, whether or not he worked Hollywood Division. It was usually earned by the cop's outside interest in things cinematic. If he did an occasional job with a TV or movie company as a technical advisor, you could be sure everyone would start calling him 'Hollywood Lou' or 'Hollywood Bill.' Or in the case of aspiring thespian Nate Weiss— who so far had only done some work as an extra on a few TV shows—'Hollywood Nate.' After he got bitten by the show business bug, he enrolled at a gym and worked out obsessively. With those brown bedroom eyes and dark, wavy hair just starting to gray at the temples, along with his newly buffed physique, Nate figured he had leading-man potential.

Nathan Weiss was thirty-five years old, a late bloomer as far as show business was concerned. He, along with lots of other patrol officers in the division, had done traffic control and provided security when film companies were shooting around town. The pay was excellent for off-duty cops and the work was easy enough but not as exciting as any of them had hoped. Not when all those hot actresses only popped their heads out of their trailers for a few minutes to block out a scene if the director wasn't satisfied with a stand-in doing it. Then they'd disappear again until it was time to shoot it.

Most of the time, the cops weren't up close for the shooting itself, and even when they were, it quickly became boring. After the master shot, they'd do two-shots of the principals, with close-ups and reverse angles, and the actors had to do it over and over. So most of the cops would quickly get bored and hang around the craft services people, who supplied all the great food for the cast and crew.

Hollywood Nate never got bored with any of it. Besides, there were a lot of hot chicks doing below-the-line work and ordinary grunt work on every shoot. Some of them were interns who dreamed of someday being above-the-line talent: directors, actors, writers, and producers. When Nate had a lot of overtime opportunities, he actually made more money than just about all of those cinematic grunts. And unlike them, Nate did not have to suffer the biggest fear in show business: My Next Job.

Nate loved to display his knowledge of the Business when talking to some little hottie, maybe a gofer running errands for the first assistant director. Nate would say things like 'My usual beat is around Beachwood Canyon. That's old Hollywood. A lot of below-the-line people live there.'

And it was one of those gofers who had cost Nate Weiss his less than happy home two years back, when his then-wife, Rosie, got suspicious because every time the phone rang one time and stopped, Nate would disappear for a while. Rosie started making date and time notations whenever one ring occurred, and she compared it with his cell phone bills. Sure enough, Nate would call the same two numbers moments after the one-ring calls she noted. Probably the slut had two cell phones or two home numbers, and it would be just like Nate to think two separate numbers would fool Rosie if she got suspicious.

Rosie Weiss bided her time, and one cold winter morning Nate came home from work at dawn telling her he was just all tuckered out from an overtime hunt for a cat burglar in Laurel Canyon. Rosie thought, Sure, an alley cat, no doubt. And she did a little experiment in Nate's car while he slept, and then managed to just go about her business for the rest of the day and that evening.

The next day, when Nate went to work, he sat in the roll-call room listening to the lieutenant droning on about the U.S. Department of Justice consent decree that the LAPD was under and hinting that the cars that were working the Hispanic neighborhoods on the east side should be turning in Field Data Reports on non-Hispanics, even though there were none around.

Cops did what cops were doing from Highland Park to Watts, those who worked African American 'hoods and Latino barrios. LAPD officers were inventing white male suspects and entering them on FDRs that contained no names or birth dates and were untraceable. Therefore, an abundance of white male field interviews could convince outside monitors that the cops were not racial profiling. In one inner-city division, there was a 290 percent increase in non-Hispanic white male nighttime pedestrian stops, even though nobody had ever seen a white guy walking around the 'hood at night. Even with a flat tire, a white guy would keep riding on the rims rather than risk a stop. Cops said that even a black-and-white had to have a sign in the window saying 'Driver carries no cash.'

This was the federal consent decree's version of 'don't ask, don't tell': We won't ask where you got all those white male names on the FDRs if you don't tell us.

Before the watch commander had arrived at roll call, a cop said aloud, 'This FDR crap is so labor-intensive it makes embryonic cloning look like paint matching.'

Another said; 'We should all just become lawyers. They get paid a lot to lie, even if they have to dress up to do it.'

So it seemed that the Department of Justice, instead of promoting police integrity, had done just the opposite, by making liars out of LAPD street cops who had to live under the consent decree for five years and then had to swallow the demoralizing three-year extension.

During that ponderous roll call, Hollywood Nate was

dozing through the consent decree sermon and got surprised when the Oracle popped his head in the door, saying, 'Sorry, Lieutenant, can I borrow Weiss for a minute?'

The Oracle didn't say anything until they were alone on the stairway landing, when he turned to Nate and said, 'Your wife is downstairs demanding to speak to the lieutenant. She wants a one-twenty-eight made on you.'

Nate was mystified. 'A personnel complaint? Rosie?'

'Do you have any kids?'

'Not yet. We've decided to wait.'

'Do you want to save your marriage?'

'Sure. It's my first, so I still give a shit. And her old man's got bucks. What's happened?'

'Then cop out and beg for mercy. Don't try weasel words, it won't work.'

'What's going on, Sarge?'

Hollywood Nate got to see for himself what was going on when he, Rosie, and the Oracle stood in the south parking lot beside Nate's SUV on that damp and gloomy winter night. Still baffled, Nate handed his keys to the Oracle, who handed them to Rosie, who jumped into the SUV, started it up, and turned on the defroster. As the windows were fogging prior to clearing, she stepped out and pointed triumphantly at what her sleuthing had uncovered. There they were, in the mist on the windshield in front of the passenger seat: oily imprints made by bare toes.

'Wears about a size five,' Rosie said. Then she turned to the Oracle and said, 'Nate always did like little spinners. I'm way too zoftig for him.'

When Nate started to speak, the Oracle said, 'Shut up, Nate.' Then he turned to Rosie and said, 'Mrs. Weiss...'

'Rosie. You can call me Rosie, Sergeant.'

'Rosie. There's no need to drag the lieutenant into this. I'm sure that you and Nate—'

Interrupting, she said, 'I called my dad's lawyer today

while this son of a bitch was sleeping it off. It's over. Way over. I'm moving everything out of the apartment on Saturday.'

'Rosie,' the Oracle said. 'I'm positive that Nate will be very fair when he talks with your lawyer. Your idea of making an official complaint for conduct unbecoming an officer would not be helpful to you. I imagine you want him working and earning money rather than suspended from duty, where he and you would lose money, don't you?'

She looked at the Oracle and at her husband, who was pale and silent, and she smiled when she saw beads of sweat on Nate's upper lip. The asshole was sweating on a damp winter night. Rosie Weiss liked that.

'Okay, Sergeant,' she said. 'But I don't want this asshole to set foot in the apartment until I'm all moved out.'

'He'll sleep in the cot room here at the station,' the Oracle said. 'And I'll detail an officer to make an appointment with you to pick up whatever Nate needs to tide him over until you're out of the apartment.'

When Rosie Weiss left them in the parking lot that evening, she had one more piece of information to impart to the Oracle. She said, 'Anyway, since he got all those muscles in the gym, the only time he can ever get an erection is when he's looking in the mirror.'

After she got in her car and drove away, Nate finally spoke. He said, 'A cop should never marry a Jewish woman, Sarge. Take it from me, she's a terrorist. It's code red from the minute the alarm goes off in the morning.'

'She's got good detective instincts,' the Oracle said. 'We could use her on the Job.'

Now, his wife was married to a pediatrician, no longer entitled to alimony, and Nate Weiss was a contented member of the midwatch, taking TV extra work as much as he could, hoping to catch a break that could get him into the Screen Actors Guild. He was sick of saying, 'Well, no, I don't have a SAG card but...'

Hollywood Nate had hoped that 2006 would be his breakthrough year, but with summer almost here, he wasn't so sure. His reverie ended when he got a painfully vigorous handshake from his new partner, twenty-two-year-old Wesley Drubb, youngest son of a partner in Lawford and Drubb real estate developers, who had enormous holdings in West Hollywood and Century City. Nate got assigned with the former frat boy who'd dropped out of USC in his senior year 'to find himself' and impulsively joined the LAPD, much to the despair of his parents. Wesley had just finished his eighteen months of probation and transferred to Hollywood from West Valley Division.

Nate thought he'd better make the best of this opportunity. It wasn't often he got to partner with someone rich. Maybe he could cement a friendship and become the kid's big brother on the Job, maybe persuade him to chat up his old man, Franklin Drubb, about investing in a little Indie film that Nate had been trying to put together with another failed actor named Harley Wilkes.

The cops often called their patrol car their 'shop' because of the shop number painted on the front doors and roof. This so that each car could be easily identified by an LAPD helicopter, always called an 'airship.' When they were settled in their shop and out cruising the streets that Nate like to cruise no matter which beat he was assigned, the eager kid riding shotgun swiveled his head to the right and said, 'That looks like a fifty-one-fifty,' referring to the Welfare and Institutions Code section that defines a mental case.

The guy was a mental case, all right, one of the boulevard's homeless, the kind that shuffle along Hollywood Boulevard and wander into the many souvenir shops and adult bookstores and tattoo parlors, bothering the vendors at the sidewalk newsstands, refusing to leave until somebody gives them some change or throws them out or calls the cops.

He was known to the police as 'Untouchable Al' because he roamed freely and often got warned by cops but was never arrested. Al had a get-out-of-jail-free card that was better than Trombone Teddy's any old day. This evening he was in a cranky mood, yelling and scaring tourists, causing them to step into the street rather than pass close to him there on the Walk of Fame.

Nate said, 'That's Al. He's untouchable. Just tell him to get off the street. He will unless he's feeling extra grumpy.'

Hollywood Nate pulled the black-and-white around the corner onto Las Palmas Avenue, and Wesley Drubb, wanting to show his older partner that he had moxie, jumped out, confronted Al, and said, 'Get off the street. Go on, now, you're disturbing the peace.'

Untouchable Al, who was drunk and feeling very grumpy indeed, said, 'Fuck you, you young twerp.'

Wesley Drubb was stunned and turned to look at Nate, who was out of the car, leaning on the roof with his elbows, shaking his head, knowing what was coming.

'He's having a bad hair day,' Nate said. 'A dozen or so are hanging out his nose.'

'We don't have to take that,' Wesley said to Nate. Then he turned to Al and said, 'We don't have to take that from you.'

Yes, they did. And Al was about to demonstrate why. As soon as Wesley Drubb pulled on his latex gloves and stepped forward, putting his hand on Al's bony shoulder, the geezer shut his eyes tight and grimaced and groaned and squatted a bit and let it go.

The explosion was so loud and wet that the young cop leaped back three feet. The sulfurous stench struck him at once.

'He's shitting!' Wesley cried in disbelief. 'He's shitting his pants!'

'I don't know how he craps on cue like that,' Nate said.

'It's a rare talent, actually. Kind of the ultimate defense against the forces of truth and justice.'

'Gross!' the young cop cried. 'He's shitting! Gross!'

'Come on, Wesley,' Hollywood Nate said. 'Let's go about our business and let Al finish his.'

'Fucking young twerp,' Untouchable Al said as the black-and-white drove swiftly away.

While Untouchable Al was finishing his business, an extraordinary robbery was taking place at a jewelry store on Normandie Avenue owned by a Thai entrepreneur who also owned two restaurants. The little jewelry store that sold mostly watches was this week offering a very special display of diamonds that the proprietor's twenty-nine-year-old nephew, Somchai 'Sammy' Tanampai, planned to take home when he closed that evening.

The robbers, an Armenian named Cosmo Betrossian and his girlfriend, a Russian masseuse and occasional prostitute named Ilya Roskova, had entered the store just before closing, wearing stocking masks. Now Sammy Tanampai sat on the floor in the back room, his wrists duct-taped behind his back, weeping because he believed they would kill him whether or not they got what they wanted.

Sammy forced his eyes from roaming to his son's cartoon-plastered lunch box on a table by the back door. He'd placed the diamonds in little display trays and velvet bags and stacked them inside the lunch box next to a partially consumed container of rice, eggs, and crab meat.

Sammy Tanampai thought they might be after the watches, but they didn't touch any of them. The male robber, who had very thick black eyebrows grown together, raised up the stocking mask to light a cigarette. Sammy could see small broken teeth, a gold incisor, and pale gums.

He walked to where Sammy was sitting on the floor, pulled Sammy's face up by jerking back a handful of hair, and said in heavily accented English, 'Where do you hide diamonds?'

Sammy was so stunned he didn't respond until the large blond woman with the sulky mouth, garishly red under the stocking mask, walked over, bent down, and said in less accented English, 'Tell us and we will not kill you.'

He started to weep then and felt urine soak his crotch, and the man pointed the muzzle of a .25 caliber Raven pistol at his face. Sammy thought, What a cheap-looking gun they are about to shoot me with.

Then his gaze involuntarily moved toward his child's lunch box and the man followed Sammy's gaze and said, 'The box!'

Sammy wept openly when the big blond woman opened the lunch box containing more than a hundred and eighty thousand wholesale dollars' worth of loose diamonds, rings, and ear studs and said, 'Got it!'

The man then ripped off a strip of duct tape and wrapped it around Sammy's mouth.

How did they know? Sammy thought, preparing to die. Who knew about the diamonds?

The woman waited by the front door and the man removed a heavy object from the pocket of his coat. When Sammy saw it he cried more, but the duct tape kept him quiet. It was a hand grenade.

The woman came back in, and for the first time Sammy noticed their latex gloves. Sammy wondered why he hadn't noticed before, and then he was confused and terrified because the man, holding the spoon handle of the grenade, placed it between Sammy's knees while the woman wrapped tape around his ankles. The grenade spoon dug into the flesh of his thighs above the knees and he stared at it.

When the robbers were finished, the woman said, 'You better got strong legs. If you relax too much your legs, you shall lose the handle. And then you die.'

And with that, the man, holding Sammy's knees in place, pulledthe pin and dropped it on the floor beside him.

Now Sammy did wail, the muffled sound very audible even with his mouth taped shut.

'Shut up!' the man commanded. 'Keep the knees tight or you be dead man. If the handle flies away, you be dead man.'

The woman said, 'We shall call police in ten minutes and they come to help you. Keep the knees together, honey. My mother always tell me that but I do not listen.'

They left then but didn't call the police. A Mexican dishwasher named Pepe Ramirez did. He was on his way to his job in Thai Town, driving past the boss's jewelry store, and was surprised to see light coming from the main part of the store. It should have been closed. The boss always closed before now so he could get to both his restaurants while they were preparing for the dinner crowd. Why was the boss's store still open? he wondered.

The dishwasher parked his car and entered the jewelry store through the unlocked front door. He spoke very little English and no Thai at all, so all he could think to call out was 'Meester? Meester?'

When he got no answer, he walked cautiously toward the back room and stopped when he heard what sounded like a dog's whimper. He listened and thought, No, it's a cat. He didn't like this, not at all. Then he heard banging, a loud muffled series of thumps. He ran from the store and called 911 on his brand-new cell phone, the first he'd ever owned.

Because of his almost unintelligible English and because he hung up while the operator was trying to transfer the call to a Spanish speaker, his message had been misunderstood. Other undocumented migrants had told him that the city police were not *la migra* and would not call Immigration unless he committed a major crime, but he was uncomfortable around anyone with a uniform and badge and thought he should not be there when they came.

It came out over the air as an 'unknown trouble' call, the kind that makes cops nervous. There was enough known trouble in police work. Usually such a call would draw more than one patrol unit as backup. Mag Takara and Benny Brewster got the call, and Fausto Gamboa and Budgie Polk were the first backup to arrive, followed by Nate Weiss and Wesley Drubb.

When Mag entered the store, she drew her pistol and following her flashlight beam walked cautiously into the back room with Benny Brewster right behind her. What she saw made her let out a gasp.

Sammy Tanampai had hopelessly banged his head against the plasterboard wall, trying to get the attention of the dishwasher. His legs were going numb and the tears were streaming down his face as he tried to think about his children, tried to stay strong. Tried to keep his knees together!

When Mag took two steps toward the jeweler, Benny Brewster shined his light on the grenade and yelled, 'WAIT!'

Mag froze and Fausto and Budgie, who had just entered by the front door, also froze.

Then Mag saw it clearly and yelled, 'GRENADE! CLEAR!' And nobody knew what was going on or what the hell to do except instinctively to draw their guns and crouch.

Fausto did not clear out. Nor did the others. He shouldered past Benny, plunged into the back room, and saw Mag standing two feet from the taped and hysterical Sammy Tanampai. And Fausto saw the grenade.

Sammy's face was bloody where he'd snagged the tape free on a nail head, and he tried to say something with a crumpled wad of tape stuck to the corner of his mouth. He gagged and said, 'I can't... I can't...'

Fausto said to Mag, 'GET OUT!'

But the littlest cop ignored him and tiptoed across the room as though motion would set it off. And she reached carefully for it.

Fausto leaped forward after Sammy unleashed the most despairing terrifying wail that Mag had ever heard in her life when his thigh muscles just surrendered. Mag's fingers were inches from the grenade when it dropped to the floor beneath her and the spoon flew across the room.

'CLEAR CLEAR CLEAR!' Fausto yelled to all the cops in the store, but Mag picked up the grenade first and lobbed it into the far corner behind a file cabinet.

Instantly, Fausto grabbed Mag Takara by the back of her Sam Browne and Sammy Tanampai by his shirt collar and lifted them both off the floor, lunging backward until they were out of the little room and into the main store, where all six cops and one shopkeeper pressed to the floor and waited in terror for the explosion.

Which didn't come. The hand grenade was a dummy.

No fewer than thirty-five LAPD employees were to converge on that store and the streets around it that night: detectives, criminalists, explosives experts, patrol supervisors, even the patrol captain. Witnesses were interviewed, lights were set up, and the area for two blocks in all directions was searched by cops with flashlights.

They found nothing of evidentiary value, and a detective from the robbery team who had been called in from home interviewed Sammy Tanampai in the ER at Hollywood Presbyterian Hospital. The victim told the detective that the male robber had briefly smoked a cigarette but none had been found by detectives at the scene.

Sammy grew lethargic because the injection they had given him was making him sleepy, but he said to the detective, 'I don't know how they knew about the diamonds. The diamonds arrived at ten o'clock this morning and we were going to show them tomorrow to a client from Hong Kong who requested certain kinds of pieces.'

'What kind of client is he?' the detective asked.

'My uncle has dealt with him for years. He is very wealthy. He is not a thief.'

'About the blond woman who you think was Russian, tell me more.'

'I think they were both Russians,' Sammy said. 'There are lots of Russians around Hollywood.'

'Yes, but the woman. Was she attractive?'

'Perhaps so. I don't know.'

'Anything out of the ordinary?'

'Big breasts,' Sammy said, opening and closing his aching jaw and touching the wounded flesh around his mouth, his eyelids drooping.

'Have you ever gone to any of the nightclubs around here?' the detective asked. 'Several of them are Russian owned and operated.'

'No. I am married. I have two children.'

'Anything else that you remember about either of them?'

'She made a joke about keeping my knees together. She said that she never did. I was thinking of my children then and how I would never see them again. And she made that joke. I hope you get to shoot them both,' Sammy said, tears welling.

After all the cops who'd been in the jewelry store were interviewed back at the station, Hollywood Nate said to his young partner, 'Some gag, huh, Wesley? Next time I work on a show, I'm gonna tell the prop man about this. A dummy grenade. Only in Hollywood.'

Wesley Drubb had been very quiet for hours since their trauma in the jewelry store. He had answered questions from detectives as well as he could, but there really wasn't anything important to say. He answered Nate with, 'Yeah, the joke was on us.'

What young Wesley Drubb wanted to say was, 'I could

have died tonight. I could have… been… *killed* tonight! If the grenade had been real.'

It was very strange, very eerie, to contemplate his own violent death. Wesley Drubb had never done that before. He wanted to talk to somebody about it but there was no one. He couldn't talk about it to his older partner, Nate Weiss. Couldn't explain to a veteran officer like Nate that he'd left USC for this, where he'd been on the sailing team and was dating one of the hottest of the famed USC song girls. He'd left it because of those inexplicable emotions he felt after he'd reached his twenty-first birthday.

Wesley had grown sick of college life, sick of being the son of Franklin Drubb, sick of living on Fraternity Row, sick of living in his parents' big house in Pacific Palisades during school holidays. He'd felt like a man in prison and he'd wanted to break out. LAPD was a break-out without question. And he'd completed his eighteen months of probation and was here, a brand-new Hollywood Division officer.

Wesley's parents had been shocked, his fraternity brothers, sailing teammates, and especially his girlfriend, who was now dating a varsity wide receiver—everyone who knew him was shocked. But he hadn't been sorry so far. He'd thought he'd probably do it for a couple of years, not for a career, for the kind of experience that would set him apart from his father and his older brother and every other goddamn broker in the real-estate firm owned by Lawford and Drubb.

He thought it would be like going into the military for a couple of years, but he wouldn't have to leave L.A. Like a form of combat that he could talk about to his family and friends years later, when he inevitably became a broker at Lawford and Drubb. He'd be a sort of combat veteran in their eyes, that was it.

Yes, and it had all been going so well. Until tonight. Until that grenade hit the floor and he stared at it and that little officer Mag Takara picked it up with Fausto Gamboa roaring in his ears. That wasn't police work, was it? They never talked about things like that in the academy. A man with a hand grenade between his knees?

He remembered a Bomb Squad expert lecturing them at the police academy about the horrific event of 1986 in North Hollywood when two LAPD officers were called in to defuse an explosive device in a residential garage, rigged by a murder suspect involved in a movie studio/labor union dispute. They defused it but were unaware of a secondary device lying there by a copy of *The Anarchist's Cookbook*. The device went off.

What Wesley remembered most vividly was not the description of the gruesome and terrible carnage and the overwhelming smell of blood, but that one of the surviving officers who had just gotten inside the house before the explosion was having recurring nightmares two decades later. He would waken with his pillow soaked with tears and his wife shaking him and saying, 'This has *got* to stop!'

For a while this evening, after he'd completed his brief statement, after he was sitting in the station quietly drinking coffee, Wesley Drubb could only think about how he'd felt trying to dig with his fingernails into the old wooden floor of that jewelry store. It had been an instinctive reaction. He had been reduced to his elemental animal core.

And Wesley Drubb asked himself the most maddeningly complex, dizzying, profound, and unanswerable question he'd ever asked himself in his young life: How the fuck did I get here?

When Fausto Gamboa got changed into civvies, he met Budgie on the way to the parking lot. They walked quietly to their cars, where they saw Mag Takara already getting into her personal car and driving away.

Fausto said, 'It used to drive me crazy seeing that kid doing her nails during roll call. Like she was getting ready to go on a date.'

'I'll bet it won't annoy you anymore, will it?' Budgie said.

'Not as much,' Fausto Gamboa conceded.

SIX

This was supposed to be a routine interview of a missing juvenile, nothing more. Andi McCrea had been sitting in her little cubicle in the detective squad room staring at a computer screen, putting together reports to take to the DA's office in a case where a wife smacked her husband on the head with the side of a roofing hammer when, after drinking a six-pack of Scotch ale, he curled his lip and told her that the meatloaf she'd worked over 'smelled like Gretchen's snatch.'

There were two things wrong with that: First, Gretchen was her twice-divorced, flirtatious younger sister, and second, he had a panicstricken look on his face that denuded the feeble explanation when he quickly said, 'Of course, I wouldn't know what Gretchen's...' Then he began again and said, 'I was just trying for a Chris Rock kind of line but didn't make it, huh? The meatloaf is fine. It's fine, honey.'

She didn't say a word but walked to the back porch, where the roofer kept his tool belt, and returned with the hammer just as he was taking the first bite of meatloaf that smelled like Gretchen's snatch.

Even though the wife had been booked for attempted murder, the guy only ended up with twenty-three stitches and a concussion. Andi figured that whichever deputy DA the case was taken to would reject it as a felony and refer it to the city attorney's office for a misdemeanor filing, which was fine with her. The hammer victim reminded her of her ex-husband, Jason, now retired from LAPD and living in

Idaho near lots of other coppers who had fled to the wilderness locales. Places where local cops only write on their arrest reports under race of suspects either 'white' or 'landscaper.'

Jason had been one of those whom several other women officers had sampled, the kind they called 'Twinkies,' guys who aren't good for you but you have to have one. Andi had been young then, and she paid the price during a five-year marriage that brought her nothing good except Max.

Her only child, Sergeant Max Edward McCrea, was serving with the U.S. Army in Afghanistan, his second deployment, the first having been in Iraq at a time when Andi was hardly ever able to sleep more than a few hours before waking with night sweats. It was better now that he was in Afghanistan. A little better. Eighteen years old, just out of high school, he had gotten the itch, and there was nothing she could do to keep him from signing that enlistment contract. Nothing that her ex-husband could do either, when for once Jason had stepped up and acted like a father. Max had said he was going into the army with two other teammates from his varsity football team, and that was it. Iraq for him, tension headaches for her, lying awake in her two-story house in Van Nuys.

After getting her case file in order, Andi was about to get a cup of coffee, when one of the Watch 2 patrol officers approached her cubicle and said, 'Detective, could you talk to a fourteen-year-old runaway for us? We got a call to the Lucky Strike Lanes, where he was bowling with a forty-year-old guy who started slapping him around. He tells us he was molested by the guy, but the guy won't talk at all. We got him in a holding tank.'

'You need the sex crimes detail,' Andi said.

'I know, but they're not here and I think the kid wants to talk but only to a woman. Says the things he's got to say are too embarrassing to tell a man. I think he needs a mommy.'

'Who doesn't?' Andi sighed. 'Okay, put him in the interview room and I'll be right there.'

Five minutes later, after drinking her coffee, and after getting the boy a soft drink and advising him for the second time of his rights, she nodded to the uniformed officer that he could leave.

Aaron Billings was delicate, almost pretty, with dark ringlets, wide-set expressive eyes, and a mature, lingering gaze that she wouldn't have expected. He looked of mixed race, maybe a quarter African American, but she couldn't be sure. He had a brilliant smile.

'Do you understand why the officers arrested you and your companion?' she asked.

'Oh, sure,' he said. 'Mel was hitting me. Everyone saw him. We were right there in the bowling alley. I'm sick of it, so when they asked for our ID I told them I was a runaway. I'm sure my mom's made a report. Well, I think she would.'

'Where're you from?'

'Reno, Nevada.'

'How long have you been gone?'

'Three weeks.'

'Did you run away with Mel?' Andi asked.

'No, but I met him the next day when I was hitchhiking. I was sick of my mother. She was always bringing men home, and my sister and me would see them having sex. My sister is ten.'

'You told the officer that Mel molested you, is that right?'

'Yes, lots of times.'

'Tell me what happened from when you first met.'

'Okay,' the kid said, and he took a long drink from the soda can. 'First, he took me to a motel and we had sex. I didn't want to but he made me. Then he gave me ten dollars. Then we went to the movies. Then we had Chinese food at a restaurant. Then we decided to drive to Hollywood and maybe see movie stars. Then Mel bought

83

vodka and orange juice and we got drunk. Then we drove to Fresno and parked at a rest stop and slept. Then we woke up early. Then we killed two people and took their money. Then we went to the movies again. Then we drove to Bakersfield. Then—'

'Wait a minute!' Andi said. 'Let's go back to the rest stop!'

Twenty minutes later Andi was on the phone to the police in Fresno, and after a conversation with a detective, she learned that yes, a middle-aged couple had been shot and killed where they'd obviously been catching a few hours' sleep en route from Kansas to a California vacation. And yes, the case was open with no suspects and no evidence other than the .32 caliber slugs taken from the skulls of both victims at the postmortem.

The detective said, 'We just don't have any leads.'

Andi said, 'You do now.'

When Andi's supervisor, D3 Rhonda Jenkins, came in late that afternoon after a long day in court testifying in a three-year-old murder case, she said, 'My day sucked. How was yours?'

'Tried to keep busy on a typical May afternoon in Hollywood, USA.'

'Yeah? What'd you do?' Rhonda asked, just making conversation as she slipped off her low-heeled pumps and massaged her aching feet.

Deadpan, Andi said, 'First I made calls on two reports from last night. Then I reread the case file on the pizza man shooting. Then I interviewed a banger down at Parker Center. Then I had some coffee. Then I cleared a double homicide in Fresno. Then I wrote a letter to Max. Then—'

'Whoa!' Rhonda said. 'Go back to the double homicide in Fresno!'

'That bitch! You couldn't find her heart with a darkfield microscope,' Jetsam complained to his partner.

Flotsam, who was attending community college during the day, said, 'Dude, you are simply another victim of the incestuous and intertwined and atavistic relationships of the law-enforcement community.'

Jetsam gaped at Flotsam, who was driving up into the Hollywood Hills, and said, 'Just shove those college-boy words, why don't you.'

'Okay, to be honest,' said Flotsam, 'from that photo you showed me, she was spherical, dude. The woman looked to me like a fucking Teletubby. You were blinded by the humongous mammary glands is all. There was no real melding of the hearts and minds.'

'Melding of the…' Jetsam looked at his partner in disbelief and said, 'Bro, the bitch's lawyer wants everything, including my fucking fish tank! With the only two turtles I got left! And guess what else? The federal consent decree ain't gonna end on schedule because that asshole of a federal judge says we're not ready. It's all political bull-shit.'

'Don't tell me that,' Flotsam said. 'I was all ready to yell out at roll call, "Free at last, free at last, Lord God Awmighty, free at last!"'

'I'm outrageously pissed off at our new mayor,' Jetsam said, 'turning the police commission into an ACLU substation. And I'm pissed off at my ex-wife's lawyer, who only wants me to have what I can make recycling aluminum cans. And I'm pissed off living in an apartment with lunging fungus so aggressive it wants to tackle you like a linebacker. And I'm pissed off at my former back-stabbing girlfriend. And I'm pissed off at the Northeast detective who's boning her now. So all in all, I feel like shooting somebody.'

And, as it happened, he would.

The PSR radio voice alerted all units on the frequency to a code 37, meaning a stolen vehicle, as well as a police pursuit in progress of said vehicle.

Ever the pessimist, Jetsam said, 'Devonshire Division. He'll never come this far south.'

The more optimistic Flotsam said, 'You never know. We can dream.'

Jetsam said, 'Since our politician chief won't let us pursue unless the driver's considered reckless, do you suppose this fucking maniac has crossed the reckless-driving threshold yet? Or does he have to run a cop off the road first?'

They listened to the pursuit on simulcast as it crossed freeways and surface streets in the San Fernando Valley, heading in the general direction of North Hollywood. And within a few minutes it was in North Hollywood and heading for the Hollywood Freeway.

'Watch them turn north again,' Jetsam said.

But the pursuit did not. The stolen car, a new Toyota 4Runner, turned south on the Hollywood Freeway, and Jetsam said, 'That one has a pretty hot six under the hood from what I hear. Bet he'll double-back now. Probably some homie. He'll double-back, get near his 'hood, dump the car, and run for it.'

But the pursuit left the Hollywood Freeway and turned east on the Ventura Freeway and then south on Lankershim Boulevard. And now the surfer team looked at each other and Jetsam said, 'Holy shit. Let's go!'

And they did. Flotsam stepped on it and headed north on the Hollywood Freeway past Universal City and turned off in the vicinity of the Lakeside Country Club, where by now a dozen LAPD and CHP units were involved, as well as a television news helicopter, but no LAPD airship.

And it was here that the driver dumped the car on a residential street near the country club, and he was into a yard, over a fence into another yard, onto the golf course, running across fairways, and then back into a North Hollywood residential street where nearly twenty cops were out on foot, half of them armed with shotguns.

Even though a North Hollywood Division sergeant was at the abandoned stolen car, trying to inform the communications operator that there was sufficient help at the scene, cars kept coming, as happens during a long pursuit like this. Soon there were L.A. Sheriff's Department units as well as more CHP and LAPD cars, with the TV helicopter hovering and lighting up the running cops below.

Flotsam drove two blocks west of the pandemonium and said, 'Wanna get out and go hunting for a while? You never know.'

'Fucking A,' Jetsam said, and they got out of their car with flashlights extinguished and walked through a residential alley behind family homes and apartment buildings.

They could hear voices on the street to their right, where other cops were searching, and Flotsam said, 'Maybe we better turn our flashlights on before somebody caps one off at us.'

Then a voice yelled, 'There he is! Hey, there he is!'

They ran toward the voice and saw a young cop with ginger hair and pink complexion sitting astride an eight-foot block wall dividing an apartment complex from the alley.

He saw them, or rather, he saw two shadow figures in blue uniforms, and said, 'Up there! He's in that tree!'

Flotsam shined his light high into an old olive tree, and sure enough, there was a young Latino up there in an oversize white T-shirt, baggy khakis, and a head bandana.

The young cop yelled, 'Climb down now!' And he pointed his nine at the guy with one hand while with his other hand he shined his light on the treetop.

Flotsam and Jetsam got closer, and the guy in the tree looked down at the young cop straddling the wall and said, 'Fuck you. Come up and get me.'

Flotsam turned to Jetsam and said, 'Tweaked. He's fried on crystal.'

'Ain't everybody?' Jetsam said.

The young cop, who had 'probationer' written all over him, pulled out his rover but before keying it said, 'What's our location? Do you guys know the address here?'

'Naw,' Jetsam said. 'We work Van Nuys Division.'

Now, that was weird, Flotsam thought. Why would his partner tell the boot that they worked Van Nuys instead of telling the truth?

Then the young cop said, 'Watch him, will you? I gotta run out to the street and get the address.'

'Just go out front and start yelling,' Jetsam said. 'There's coppers all over the block.'

Flotsam also found it strange that Jetsam had turned his flashlight off and was standing in deep shadow under a second tree. Almost as though he didn't want the kid to be able to see him clearly. But why? That they had driven a short distance out of their division wasn't a big deal.

After the rookie ran out onto the street in front, Jetsam said, 'Fucking boot doesn't know what to do about a thief in a tree.'

They stood looking up at the guy who squinted down at their light beams, and Flotsam said, 'What would you do besides wait for backup?'

Jetsam looked up and yelled, 'Hey asshole, climb down here.'

The car thief said, 'I'm staying here.'

'How would you like me to blow you outta that tree?' Jetsam shouted, aiming his .40 caliber Glock at him. 'I feel like shooting somebody tonight.'

'You won't shoot,' the kid said. 'I'm a minor. And all I did was joyride.'

Now Jetsam was really torqued. And not for the first time he noticed that the young cop had left his Remington bean-bag shotgun with the bright green fore and aft stocks propped against the wall.

'Check this out, partner,' he said to Flotsam. 'That

probey grabbed a beanbag gun instead of the real thing. Now he's probably looking for a chain saw to cut the fucking tree down.'

Touching his pepper spray canister, Flotsam said, 'Wish he was closer, dude. A little act-right spray would do wonders for him.' Then Flotsam looked at Jetsam and Jetsam looked at Flotsam and Flotsam said, 'No. I know what you're thinking, but no. Stay real, man!'

But Jetsam said in a quiet voice, 'That boot never saw our faces, bro. There's coppers all over the neighborhood.'

'No,' Flotsam said. 'A beanbag gun is not to be used for compliance purposes. This ain't pit bull polo, dude.'

'I wonder if it would induce some compliance here.'

Flotsam said. 'I don't wanna know.'

But Jetsam, who had never shot anyone with a beanbag or anything else, reached into his pocket, put on a pair of latex gloves so as to not leave latent prints, picked up the shotgun, pointed it up into the tree, and said, 'Hey *vato*, get your ass down here right now or I'll let one go and blow you outta that tree.'

The muzzle of the gun looked big enough to hold a popsicle, but it didn't scare the car thief, who said, 'You and your *puto* partner can just kiss my—'

And the muzzle flash and explosion shocked Flotsam more than the kid, who let out a shriek when the beanbag struck him in the belly.

'Ow ow ow, you pussy!' the kid yelled. 'You shot me, you pussy! Owwwwwwww!'

So Jetsam let go with another round, and this time Flotsam ran to the street in front of the apartment complex and saw no less than five shadow figures yelling and running their way while the kid howled even louder and started climbing down.

'Let's get the fuck outta here!' Flotsam said, after running back to Jetsam and grabbing him by the arm.

'He's coming down, bro,' Jetsam said with a dazed expression.

'Toss that tube!' Flotsam said, and Jetsam dropped the shotgun on the grass and scurried after his partner.

Both cops ran back down the alley through the darkness toward their car, and neither spoke until Flotsam said, 'Man, there'll be IA investigators all over this one, you crazy fucker! You ain't even allowed to shoot white guys like that!'

Still running, and gradually realizing that he'd just violated a whole lot of Department regulations, if not the penal code itself, Jetsam said, 'The homie never saw us, bro. The lights were always in his eyes. The little boot copper didn't see our faces neither. Shit, he was so excited he couldn't ID his own dick. Anyways, this is North Hollywood Division. We don't work here.'

'The best-laid plans of mice and rats,' Flotsam said. Then he had a panicky thought. 'Did you go code six?' he said, referring to the safety rule of informing communications of their location when leaving the car. 'I can't remember.'

Jetsam also panicked for a moment, then said, 'No, I'm sure I didn't. Nobody knows we're here in North Hollywood.'

'Let's get the fuck back to our beat!' Flotsam said when they reached their car, unlocked it, and got inside.

He drove with lights out until they were blocks from the scene and heard the PSR voice say 'All units, code four. Suspect in custody. Code four.'

They didn't talk at all until they were safely back cruising Hollywood Boulevard. Then Jetsam said, 'Let's get code seven. Our adventure's made me real hungry all of a sudden. And bro, your shit's kinda weak lately. We gotta jack you up somehow. Why don'tcha get one of those healthy reduced-fat burritos swimming in sour cream and and guacamole.' Then he added, 'It musta been those two shots I gave that homie, but I feel mega-happy now.'

And Flotsam could only gape when Jetsam suddenly began to sing the U2 hit: 'Two shots of happy, one shot of saaaaad. You think I'm no good, well I know I've been baaaaad.'

'You're scary, dude,' Flotsam said. 'You're as scary as a doctor putting on one rubber glove.'

Jetsam kept on singing: 'Took you to a place, now you can't get back. Two shots of happy, one shot of saaaaaad.'

Flotsam kept driving toward Sunset Boulevard and finally said, 'I wanna take you up to the Director's Chair first night we're off together. Have a few beers. Shoot some pool or darts.'

'Okay, I got nothing better to do, but I never been fond of the joint. Don't you wanna go someplace where there ain't so many cops?'

Flotsam said, 'I love a bar with a sign that says "No shirt, no shoes, no badge, no service." Besides, there's always a few badge bunnies around that'll pork any copper, even you.'

Jetsam said, 'Thank you, Dr. Ruth. Why're you so concerned with my sex life all of a sudden?'

Flotsam said, 'It's me I'm thinking about, dude. You gotta take your mind off your ex and her lawyer and that hose monster that dumped you. Either that or in order to protect my career and pension I gotta go find that Northeast detective she's snogging.'

'What for?'

'To cap him. We can't go on like this. You hearing me, dude?'

Cosmo Betrossian had always denied that he was even loosely associated with the so-called Russian Mafia. The federal and local authorities called everybody from the former USSR and eastern Europe 'Russian Mafia.' That is, everyone Cosmo knew, because everyone Cosmo knew was involved in illegal activity of one sort or another. The designations didn't make any sense to Cosmo, who, even though he had grown up in Soviet Armenia and spoke some bastardized Russian, was no more a Russian than George Bush was. He figured that American cops were just full of shit as far as eastern European immigrants were concerned.

But because of their obsession with Russian Mafia, he had to be careful when he had any business dealing with Dmitri, the owner of the Gulag, a nightclub on Western Avenue that wasn't in the best part of town but had a well-lit, well-guarded parking lot. Young people from all over the west side, even Beverly Hills and Brentwood, were not afraid to drive east to Little Siberia, as some called it.

The Gulag's food was good and they poured generous drinks and Dmitri gave them the recorded familiar rock sounds they wanted, which kept the dance floor jammed until closing time. And on the occasional 'Russian Night' Dmitri advertised live entertainment: Russian dancers, balalaikas, violins, and a beautiful singer from Moscow. It brought Dmitri a very wealthy clientele who had emigrated to Los Angeles from all over the former USSR, whether or not they were into legitimate business or smuggling or money laundering. But this night was not going to be one of the Russian nights.

A week had passed since the robbery, and Cosmo felt confident going to Dmitri. The police were even less of a worry. Nobody he knew had even been questioned. Early in the evening, he drove to the Gulag, entered, and went to the bar. He knew the bartender whom the Americans called 'Georgie' because he was from the Republic of Georgia, and asked to see Dmitri. The bartender poured him a shot of ouzo and Cosmo waited for the bartender to deal with two cocktail waitresses at the service bar who were giving the bartender more happy hour drink orders than he could handle.

The nightclub was typical for Hollywood in that there was an area set aside for private parties. In the Gulag the private area was upstairs, with plush green sofas lining walls papered in garish streaks of color—somebody's idea of 'edgy,' that favorite cliché of Hollywood scenesters, the other being 'vibe.' The Gulag was edgy. The Gulag vibed mysterious.

On this evening, the jock was just setting up and he spun some soft-rock standards for the end of the extended happy hour. There were two guys repairing some strobes and spots before the crowd arrived and bodies got writhing in the dance-floor pit. Busboys and waiters were wiping off tables and chairs and dusting the seats in the cuddle-puddle booths on the raised level for those customers who tipped the manager Andrei.

After ten minutes, Cosmo was directed upstairs into Dmitri's surprisingly spartan office where he found the club owner at his desk, slippered feet up, smoking a cigarette in a silver holder, and watching S&M porn on his computer screen. Everybody said that Dmitri indulged in all kinds of exotic sex. He was forty-one years old, not tall, had a slight build, soft hands, and bloodshot blue eyes, and was wearing a chestnut hair weave. He looked unexceptional and harmless in a white linen shirt and chinos, but Cosmo was very scared of him. He had heard things about Dmitri and his friends.

The club owner knew that Cosmo's Russian was extremely poor and Dmitri adored current American slang, so he had always spoken English to Cosmo. Without getting up he said, 'Here comes a happenink guy! A guy who always has it go-ink on! Hello, Cosmo!'

He reached out with one of those soft hands and slapped palms with Cosmo, who said, 'Dmitri, thank you for this talk. Thank you, brother.'

'You got some-think I need?'

'Yes, my brother,' Cosmo said, sitting in the client chair in front of the desk.

'Not credit-card information, I hope. In gen-yural I am not into credit cards no more, Cosmo. I am moving into other directions.'

'No, brother,' Cosmo said. 'I have brought for you something to show.' And with that he produced a single diamond, one of the larger stones from the jewelry store robbery, and put it gingerly on the desk.

Dmitri lowered his feet onto the floor and looked at the stone. He smiled at Cosmo and said, 'I do not know diamonds. But I have a friend who knows. Do you have more?'

'Yes,' Cosmo said. 'Much more. Many rings and earrings too. All very beautiful stones.'

Dmitri looked impressed. 'You are grow-ink in America!' he said. 'No more business with addicts?'

'Addicts do not have diamonds,' Cosmo said. 'I think you shall buy all my diamonds and sell for big profit, my brother.'

'It is possible that I should be een-wolved with you again, Cosmo,' Dmitri said, smiling. 'You are perhaps now a big man in America.'

'I wish to bring every diamond soon. I wish to sell for only thirty-five thousands. The news lady on TV say the diamonds worth maybe two, three hundred thousands.'

'The hand grenade!' Dmitri said with a grin. 'So it was you! But thirty-five thousand? You must bring me high-quality stones for thirty-five thousand.'

'Okay, brother,' Cosmo said. 'I shall bring.'

'I need perhaps one month to make my deal and to get so much cash for you,' Dmitri said. 'And to make sure that police do not arrest you in meantime.'

'I am very sad to hear that,' Cosmo said, sweat popping on his forehead. 'I must get money now.'

Dmitri shrugged and said, 'You may take your treasure to somebody else, Cosmo. No problem.'

Cosmo had nobody else for something like this, and he knew that Dmitri was aware of it.

'Okay,' Cosmo said. 'I wait. Please call me when you have money.'

'Now that you are grow-ink into a businessman,' Dmitri said as Cosmo bowed slightly and prepared to leave, 'you should shave between the eyebrows. Americans like two eyebrows, not one.'

On the night that Jetsam fired two shots of happy with no shot of sad, another shooting would take place, this one in Hollywood Division, that would provoke several shots of sad for two of the officers involved.

The code 3 call was given to 6-A-65 of Watch 3, directing them to a residential street on the west side of Hollywood, an area that seldom was the source of such calls. Half the cars on the midwatch rolled on it when the PSR said the words 'Man with a gun.'

The assigned car, thanks to lights and siren, got there seconds before the others, but two of the midwatch units roared in before the officers of 6-A-65 were out of the car. One of the midwatch units was driven by Mag Takara. Her partner, Benny Brewster, jumped out with a shotgun, and then another car from Watch 3 arrived. Eight cops, four with shotguns, approached the house from which the call had emanated. The porch lights were out, and the street was quite dark. The decision whether to approach the porch did not have to be made. The front door to the house swung open, and the cops at the scene could scarcely believe what they were seeing.

A thirty-eight-year-old man, later identified as Roland Tarkington, owner of the house, stepped out onto the porch.

It would be learned that his father had once owned large chunks of commercial property in Hollywood but had lost it all in bad investments, leaving his only child, Roland, the house and sufficient money to exist. Roland was waving a document in one hand and had the other hand behind his back.

In the glare of half a dozen flashlight beams plus a spotlight trained on him by the closest black-and-white, Roland spoke not a word but held up the paper as though it were a white flag of surrender. He struggled down the concrete steps from his porch and advanced toward the cops.

The thing that had the cops amazed was Roland Tarkington's size. He would be measured the next day during a postmortem at five feet six inches. His weight would be listed on the death report as just over 540 pounds. The shadow of Roland Tarkington thrown onto the walk behind him was vast.

After Benny Brewster shouted, 'Let's see the other hand!' there was a cacophony of voices:

'Show us your other hand!'

'Both hands in the air, goddamnit!'

'Get down on the sidewalk!'

'Watch that fucking hand! Watch his hand!'

A probationary cop from Watch 3 left his training officer and crept along the driveway forty feet from the standoff as the obese man stopped, still silently waving the white paper. The probationer was in a position to see behind Roland Tarkington's back and yelled, 'He's got a gun!'

As though on cue, another Hollywood performance ended when Roland Tarkington showed them what he was hiding, suddenly aiming what looked like a .9-millimeter semiautomatic pistol at the closest cop.

And he was hit by two shotgun blasts fired by separate officers from Watch 3 and five rounds from pistols fired by two other Watch 3 officers. Roland Tarkington, despite his great bulk, was lit up by bright orange muzzle blasts, lifted off his feet, and thrown down on his back, where he bled out, dying within seconds, his heart literally shredded. Another five police pistol rounds that missed had riddled the front of the house as Roland Tarkington fell.

Neighbors then poured out of their homes, and voices were yelling, and at least two women across the street were wailing and crying. The Oracle, who arrived just as the rounds exploded in the night, picked up the blood-spattered paper lying on the grass beside the dead man. Roland Tarkington's gun turned out to be a realistically designed water pistol.

The second cop to have fired his shotgun said, 'What's it say, Sarge?'

The Oracle read aloud: '"I offer my humble apologies to the fine officers of the LAPD. This was the only way I could summon the courage to end my life of misery. I ask that my remains be cremated. I would not want anyone to have to carry my body to our family plot at Forest Lawn Cemetery. Thank you. Roland G. Tarkington."'

None of the midwatch units had been in a position to fire, and Mag said to Benny, 'Let's get outta here, partner. This is bad shit.'

When they were back at their car putting the shotgun into the locked rack, Mag heard two cops talking to the Oracle.

One said, 'Goddamnit! Goddamn this bastard! Why didn't he take poison? Goddamn him!'

The Oracle said to the cop, 'Get in your car and get back to the station, son. FID will be arriving soon.'

Another voice said to the Oracle, 'I'm not a fucking executioner! Why did he do this to me? Why?'

The final comment was made by the night-watch detective, Compassionate Charlie Gilford, who showed up as the black-and-whites were driving away. The RA was double-parked, a paramedic standing over the huge mound of bloody flesh that had been Roland Tarkington, glad that the crew from the coroner's would be handling this one.

Compassionate Charlie picked up the water pistol, squeezed the trigger, and when no water squirted out said, 'Shit, it ain't even loaded.' Then he shined his light on the blasted gaping chest of Roland Tarkington and said, 'You would have to call this a heartrending conclusion to another Hollywood melodrama.'

SEVEN

The following Friday evening saw throngs on Hollywood Boulevard at another of the endless red carpet ceremonies, this one at the Kodak Theatre, where show business back-slaps and hugs itself before returning to everyday backbiting and seething in never-ending bouts of jealousy over a colleague's getting a job that should have been given to Me! Show business's unmentioned prayer: Please, God, let me succeed and let them... fail.

The midwatch was in terrible shape as far as deployment was concerned. Fausto was on days off and so was Benny Brewster. Budgie Polk saw the Oracle working at his desk and found it reassuring to see all those hash marks on his left sleeve, all the way up to his elbow. He wore not his heart on his sleeve, but his life. Forty-six years. Nine service stripes. Who could push him around? The Oracle had said he was going to break the record of the detective from Robbery-Homicide Division who'd retired in February with fifty years of service. But sometimes, like now, he looked tired. And old.

The Oracle would be sixty-nine years old in August, and it was all there around his eyes and furrowed brow, all the years with the LAPD. He'd served seven chiefs. He'd seen chiefs and mayors come and go and die. But in those old glory days of LAPD, he couldn't have imagined he'd be serving under a federal consent decree that was choking the life out of the police department he loved. Proactive police work had given way to police paranoia, and he seemed to internalize it more than anyone else. Budgie watched him unscrew a bottle of antacid liquid and swallow a large dose.

Budgie had been hoping to team up with Mag Takara, but after Budgie walked into the watch commander's office and had a look at the lineup, she took the Oracle aside in the corridor, where she said privately, 'Did the lieutenant decide on the assignments tonight, Sarge?'

'No, I did,' he told her, but he stopped talking when Hollywood Nate interrupted by bounding in the back door with three rolls of paper, carrying them like they were treasure maps.

'Wait'll you see these, Sarge,' he said to the Oracle.

He handed two to Budgie while he carefully unrolled the third, revealing a movie one-sheet for Billy Wilder's *Sunset Boulevard*, starring William Holden and Gloria Swanson.

'Don't we have enough movie posters around the station?' the Oracle said.

'But this one's in great shape! It's a copy, but it's a pretty old copy. And in beautiful condition. I'm getting the frames donated tomorrow.'

'All right, put them up in the roll-call room with the others,' the Oracle said, running his hand over his gray crewcut. 'I guess anything's better than looking at all these inmate green walls. Whoever designed our stations must've got his training in Albania during the cold war.'

'Way cool, Sarge,' Nate said. 'We'll decide where to put the others later. One's for *Double Indemnity*, and the other's for *Rebel Without a Cause*, with James Dean's face right under the title. Lots of great shots of Hollywood in those movies.'

'Okay, but pick places where citizens can't see them from the lobby,' the Oracle said. 'Don't turn this station into a casting office.'

After Hollywood Nate had sprinted up the stairs, the Oracle said to Budgie, 'I'm a sucker for young cops who respect old things. And speaking of old things, with Fausto off I thought you wouldn't mind working with Hank Driscoll for a few days.'

Budgie rolled her eyes then. Hank aka 'B.M.' Driscoll was someone nobody liked working with, especially young officers. It wasn't that he was old like Fausto—he had nineteen years on the Job and was only a little over forty—but it was like working with your whiny aunt Martha. The B.M. sobriquet that the other cops hung on him was for Baron Münchhausen, whose invented illnesses resulted in medical treatment and hospitalization, a disorder that came to be known in the psychiatric community as Munchausen syndrome.

B.M. Driscoll probably had more sick days than the rest of the midwatch combined. If they had to arrest a junkie with hepatitis, B.M. Driscoll would go to his doctor with symptoms within forty-eight hours and would listen doubtfully when assured that his claims were medically impossible.

The ten-hour shift of Watch 5 crawled by when you had to work with him. Older cops said that if you felt that life was flying by too quickly, you could bring time almost to a standstill just by working a whole twenty-eight-day deployment period with B.M. Driscoll.

He was tall and wiry, the grandson of Wisconsin farmers who came to California during the Great Depression, which he claimed kept his parents from eating properly, so they passed unhealthy genes down to him. He kept his sparse brown hair clipped almost as close as the Oracle's because he believed it was more hygienic. And he was twice divorced, the mystery being how he found anyone but a psychiatrist to marry him in the first place.

However, there was one event in his career that made him a bit of a police legend. Several years earlier, when he was working patrol in the barrio of Hollenbeck Division, he became involved in a standoff with a drug-crazed, facially tattooed homeboy who was threatening to cut his girl-friend's throat with a Buck knife.

Several cops were there in the middle of the street, point-ing shotguns and handguns and cajoling and threatening to no avail. Officer Driscoll was holding a Taser gun, and at one point during the standoff when the homie lowered the blade long enough to wave it during his incoherent rant, B.M. Driscoll fired. The dart struck the homeboy in the left chest area, penetrating the pack of cigarettes in his shirt pocket as well as his butane lighter. Which was ignited by a lit cigarette. Which caused the guy to burst into flames. Which ended the standoff.

They got the shirt off the homeboy before he was seri-ously burned and threw him into a rescue ambulance, and B.M. Driscoll became something of a celebrity, especially among the Latino cruisers where he was known as 'the dude with the flame thrower.'

But whether he was a legend or not, Budgie Polk was very unhappy about her assignment. She said to the Oracle, 'Just tell me one thing, Sarge. Tell me that you're not keeping me and Mag apart because I'm just back from maternity leave and she's a little munchkin. I can't explain to you how degrading it is when that happens to us women. When male supervisors say stuff like "We're splitting you up for your own safety." After all the shit we women have gone through to get where we are on this Job.'

The Oracle said, 'Budgie, I promise you that's not why I put you with Driscoll instead of Mag. I don't think of you in those terms. You're a cop. Period.'

'And that's not why you put me with Fausto? So the old war horse could look after me?'

'Haven't you caught on by now, Budgie?' the Oracle said. 'Fausto Gamboa has been a bitter and depressed man since he lost his wife to colon cancer two years ago. And both their sons are losers, so they don't help him any. When Ron LeCroix had to get his hemorrhoids zapped, it looked like a perfect time to team up Fausto with somebody young and alive. Preferably a woman, to soften him up a little bit. So I didn't assign him to you for your benefit. I did it for him.'

They didn't call him the Oracle for nothing, Budgie thought. She was painted into a corner now with nowhere to go. 'Hoisted by my own ponytail' was all she could mutter.

The Oracle said, 'Put some cotton in your ears for a few days. Driscoll's actually a decent copper and he's generous. He'll buy your cappuccino and biscotti every chance he gets. And not because you're a woman. That's the way he is.'

'I hope I don't catch bird flu or mad cow just listening to him,' Budgie said.

When they got to their patrol unit, Budgie driving, B.M. Driscoll threw his war bag into the trunk and said, 'Try not to get in my breathing zone if you can help it, Budgie. I know you've got a baby, and I wouldn't want to infect you. I think I could be coming down with something. I'm not sure, but I've got muscle pain and sort of feel chills down my back. I had the flu in October and again in January. This has been a bad year for my health.'

The rest was lost in radio chatter. Budgie tried to concentrate on the PSR's voice and tune his out. She was reminded of an event she'd first heard about when she transferred to Hollywood Division and met Detective Andi McCrea. Other women officers particularly enjoyed the story.

It seemed that several years ago an LAPD officer from a neighboring division was shot by a motorist he'd pulled over for a ticket. Andi McCrea was a uniformed cop in Hollywood Division at that time, and several night-watch units were assigned to patrol their eastern border, where the suspect was last seen abandoning his car after a short pursuit.

It was past end of watch, and cars were working overtime, in communication with one another and checking alleys, storage yards, and vacant buildings, with no sign of the shooter. Then Andi got the word who the officer was: an academy classmate of hers, and he was badly wounded. She'd been relentless that night, shining her spotlight beam onto rooftops, even into trees, and her older male partner, like B.M. Driscoll, was a complainer. Not about imaginary illnesses, but about his need for rest and sleep. He was an unreliable shiftless cop.

Andi McCrea, according to all accounts, endured it for two hours, but after listening to him say, 'We ain't gonna find nobody, let's get the hell outta here and go end of watch—this is bullshit,' she grimly turned north to the Hollywood Freeway, pulled onto the ramp, and stopped.

When her partner said, 'What're we stopping here for?' Andi said, 'Something's wrong. Get out and look at the right front tire.'

He griped about that too, but complied, and when he was out of the car shining his beam onto the tire, he said, 'There's nothing wrong here.'

'There sure as hell is something wrong here, you worthless asshole,' Andi said and drove off, leaving him on the freeway ramp, his rover still on the seat and his cell phone in his locker at the station.

Andi continued searching for another hour and only stopped when the search was called off, after which she drove to the station, still hacked off and ready to take her medicine.

The Oracle was waiting for her, and as she was unloading her war bag from the trunk, he said, 'Your partner arrived about a half hour ago. Flagged down a car. He's torqued. Stay away from him.'

'Sarge, we were hunting a maggot who shot a police officer!' Andi said.

'I understand that,' the Oracle said. 'And knowing him, I can imagine what you had to put up with. But you don't dump a body on the freeway unless it's dead and you're a serial killer.'

'Is he making his complaint official?'

'He wanted to but I talked him out of it. Told him it would be more embarrassing for him than for you. Anyway, he's getting his long-awaited transfer to West L.A., so he'll be gone at the end of the deployment period.'

That's how it had ended, except that it was a favorite story of cops at Hollywood Station who knew Andi McCrea. And B.M. Driscoll's whining about his flu symptoms reminded Budgie Polk of the story. It put a little smile on her face, and she thought, How far does he have to push me? Could I get away with it like Andi did? After all, there is precedent here.

And though Budgie was starting to enjoy certain things about working with Fausto now that he'd mellowed a little, wouldn't it be great to be teamed with Mag Takara? Just for girl talk if nothing else. During code 7, when they were eating salads at Soup Plantation, they could kid around about eye candy on the midwatch, saying things like, 'Would you consider doing Hollywood Nate if you thought he could ever keep his big mouth shut about it?' Or, 'How much would it take for you to do either of those two log heads, Flotsam or Jetsam, if you could shoot him afterward?' Girl talk cop-style.

Mag was a cool and gutsy little chick with a quiet sense of humor that Budgie liked. And being of Japanese ethnicity, Mag would no doubt be down for code 7 at the sushi bar on Melrose that Budgie couldn't persuade any of the male officers to set foot in. Of course, two women as short and tall as Mag and Budgie would be butts of stupid male remarks, along with the usual sexist ones that all women officers have to live with unless they want to get a rat jacket by complaining about it. The lamest: What do you call a black-and-white with two females in it? Answer: a tuna boat.

And while Budgie was thinking of ways to trade B.M. Driscoll for Mag Takara without pissing off the Oracle, Mag was thinking of ways to trade Flotsam for anybody at all. With Jetsam on days off, they were teamed for the first time, short and tall, quiet and mouthy. And oh god! He kept sliding his sight line over onto her every time she was looking out at the streets, and if this kept up, he'd be rear-ending a bus or something.

'Where shall we go for code seven?' he asked when they hadn't been on patrol for twenty minutes. 'And don't say the sushi bar on Melrose, where I've seen your shop parked on numerous occasions.'

'I won't, then,' she said, punching in a license plate on a low rider in the number two lane, figuring this surfer probably takes his dates to places with paper napkins and tap water.

Hoping for a smile, he said, 'For me an order of sushi is a dish containing unretouched, recently dead mollusks. Stuff like that lays all over the beach in low tide. You like to surf?'

'No,' Mag said, unamused.

'I bet you'd look great shooting a barrel. All that gorgeous dark hair flowing in the wind.'

'A barrel?'

'Yeah, a tube? A pipe? Riding through as the wave breaks over you?'

'Yeah, a barrel.' This loghead's had too many wipeouts, she thought. He's gone surfboard-simple, that's what.

'In one of those bikinis that's just a piece of Lycra the size of a Toll House cookie.'

Just get me through the night and away from this hormone monster, Mag thought. Then she did some serious eye rolling when Flotsam said, 'A surfer might predict that this could be the beginning of a choiceamundo friendship.'

Wesley Drubb got to drive, and he liked that. Hollywood Nate was sitting back doing what he did best, talking show business to his young partner, who didn't give a shit about the movie theater that Nate pointed out there at Fairfax and Melrose, one that showed silent films.

'There was a famous murder there in the nineties,' Nate informed him, 'involving former owners. One got set up by a business partner who hired a hit on him. The hit man is now doing life without. "The Silent Movie Murder," the press called it.'

'Really,' Wesley said, without enthusiasm.

'I can give you a show-business education,' Nate said. 'Never know when it could come in handy working this division. I know you're rich and all, but would you ever consider doing extra work in the movies? I could introduce you to an agent.'

Wesley Drubb hated it when other officers talked about his family wealth and said, 'I'm not rich. My father's rich.'

'I'd like to meet your dad sometime,' Nate said. 'Does he have any interest in movies?'

Wesley shrugged and said, 'He and my mom go to movies sometimes.'

'I mean in filmmaking.'

'His hobby is skeet shooting,' Wesley said. 'And he's done a little pistol shooting with me since I came on the Department.'

'Guns don't have it going on, far as I'm concerned,' Nate said. 'When I talk millimeters, it's not about guns and ammo, it's about celluloid. Thirty-five millimeters. Twenty-four frames per second. I have a thousand-dollar digital video camera. Panavision model. Sweet.'

'Uh-huh,' Wesley said.

'I know a guy, him and me, we're into filmmaking. One of these days when we find the right kind of investor, we're gonna make a little Indie film and show it at the festivals. We have a script and we're very close. All we need is the right investor. We can't accept just anybody.'

They were stopped at a residential intersection in east Hollywood, a street that Wesley remembered hearing about. He looked at a two-story house, home of some Eighteenth Street crew members.

Hollywood Nate was just about to pop the question to Wesley about whether he thought that Franklin Drubb would ever consider including a start-up production company in his investment portfolio, when a head-shaven white guy in faux-leather pants, studded boots, and a leather jacket over a swelling bare chest completely covered by body art walked up to the passenger side of the patrol car and tapped loudly on Nate's window.

It startled both of them, and Nate rolled down the window and said, 'What can I do for you?' keeping it polite but wary.

The man said in a voice soft and low, 'Take me to Santa Monica and La Brea.'

Hollywood Nate glanced quickly at Wesley, then back to the guy, shining his flashlight up under the chin, seeing those dilated cavernous eyes, and said to him, 'Step back away from the car.' Nate got out and Wesley quickly informed communications that 6-X-72 was code 6 at that location. Then he put the car in park, turned off the engine, tucked the keys in the buckle of his Sam Browne and got out on the driver's side, walking quickly around the front of the car, flashlight in one hand, the other on the butt of his Beretta.

The man was a lot older than he looked at first when Nate walked him to the sidewalk and had a good look, but he was wide shouldered, with thick veins on his well-muscled arms, and full-sleeve tatts. It was very dark and the street lamp on the corner was out. An occasional car passed and nobody was walking on the residential street.

Then the guy said, 'I'm a Vietnam vet. You're a public servant. Take me to Santa Monica and La Brea.'

Hollywood Nate looked from the guy to his partner in disbelief and said, 'Yeah, you're a Vietnam vet and you got napalm eyes to prove it, but we're not a taxi. What're you fried on, man? X, maybe?'

The man smiled then, a sly and secretive smile locked in place just this side of madness. He opened his vest, showing his bare torso, and ran his hands over his own waist and buttocks and groin under the tight imitation-leather pants and said, 'See, no weapons. No nothing. Just beautiful tattoos. Let's go to Santa Monica and La Brea.'

Hollywood Nate glanced again at his partner, who looked springloaded, and Nate said, 'Yeah, I see. You got more tatts than Angelina Jolie, but you ain't her. So we're not driving you anywhere.' Then he uttered the Hollywood Station mantra, 'Stay real, dude.'

Those eyes. Nate looked again with his flashlight beam under the guy's chin. Where did he find those eyes? They didn't fit his face somehow. They looked like they belonged to somebody else. Or something else.

Nate looked at Wesley, who didn't know what the hell to do. The man hadn't broken any laws. Wesley didn't know if he should ask the guy for ID or what. He waited for a cue from Nate. This was getting very spooky. An unhinged 5150 mental case for sure. Still, all he'd done was ask for a ride. Wesley remembered his academy instructor saying as long as they weren't a danger to themselves or others, they couldn't be taken to the USC Medical Center, formerly the old county hospital, for a seventy-two-hour hold.

Nate said to the man, 'The only place this car goes is jail. Why don't you walk home and sleep it off, whatever it is gave you those eyes.'

The man said, 'War gave me these eyes. War.'

Cautiously, Nate said, 'I think we're gonna say good night to you, soldier. Go home. Right now.'

Nate nodded to his partner and backed toward the police

car, but when he got in and closed the door and Wesley got in on the driver's side and started the engine, the transmission still in park, the man ran to the car and kicked the right rear door with those studded boots, howling like a wolf.

'Goddamn!' Nate yelled, keying the mike and yelling, 'Six-X-Seventy-two, officers need help!' He gave the location, then threw open his door and jumped out with his baton, which he lost during the first thirty seconds of the fight.

Wesley jumped from the driver's side, not removing the keys, not even turning off the engine, ran around the car, and leaped onto the back of the madman who had Nate's baton with one hand and Nate in a headlock.

All those muscles that Hollywood Nate had found in his gym, that had impressed badge bunnies in the Director's Chair saloon, weren't impressing this lunatic one bit. And even when Wesley hurled his 210-pound body onto the guy, he still kept fighting and kicking and trying to bite like a rabid dog.

Wesley tried the Liquid Jesus on him but the OC can was clogged and it created a pepper-spray mist in front of his own face that almost blinded him. Then he tried again but got more on Hollywood Nate than on the suspect, so he gave up and dropped the canister.

And pretty soon they had tussled, tumbled, and rolled across the lawn of a sagging two-story residence belonging to Honduran immigrants, into the side yard, and then clear into the backyard, where Hollywood Nate was starting to panic as he felt his strength waning. And he thought he might have to shoot this fucking lunatic after he felt the guy trying to grab his sidearm.

And while the battle was raging, some of the Eighteenth Street cruisers from another two-story house looked out the window, and a few of them came out to get a better look and root for the guy to kick some LAPD ass. When their pit bulls tried to follow, they leashed them, knowing that lots of other cops would be coming soon.

The dogs seemed to enjoy the fight even more than the crew did and began snarling and barking, and whenever the leather-clad madman growled and kicked at Wesley Drubb, who was administering LAPD-approved baton strikes, the dogs would bark louder. And then Loco Lennie happened on the scene.

Loco Lennie was not a member of Eighteenth Street but he was oh, such a wannabe. He was too young, too stupid, and too impulsive even for the cruisers to use him as a low-level drug delivery boy. Loco Lennie wasn't watching the fight with the five members of the crew and their crazed dogs. Loco Lennie couldn't take his eyes off the black-and-white that Wesley Drubb had left in gear, engine running, key in the ignition, in his haste to help Hollywood Nate. And Loco Lennie saw a chance to make a name for himself that would live forever in the minds and hearts of these cruisers who had so far rejected him.

Loco Lennie ran to the police car, jumped in, and took off, yelling, 'Viva, Eighteenth Street!'

Hollywood Nate and Wesley Drubb didn't even know that their shop had been stolen. By now they had the guy pinned against the single-car garage of the ramshackle house, and young Wesley was learning that all of the leg and arm strikes he'd been taught at the academy weren't worth a shit when battling a powerful guy who was maybe cooked on PCP or just plain psychotic.

And before the first help came screeching around the corner, siren yelping louder than the homie dogs and even louder than this howling mental case who was trying desperately to bite Hollywood Nate, the cop locked his forearm and biceps in a V around the man's throat. Nate applied all the pressure he could manage to the carotid arteries while Wesley exhausted himself, whacking the guy everywhere from the guy's wingspan on down to his lower legs with little effect.

Flotsam and Mag, Budgie and B.M. Driscoll, and four officers from Watch 3 all came running to the rescue just as the guy was almost choked out, his brain oxygen starved from the infamous choke hold, the carotid restraint that had killed several people over the decades but had saved the lives of more cops than all the Tasers and beanbag guns and side-handle batons and Liquid Jesus and the rest of the nonlethal weapons in their arsenal put together. A form of nonlethal force that, in this era of DOJ oversight and racial politics and political correctness, was treated exactly the same as an officer-involved shooting. And that would require almost as much investigation and as many reports as if Hollywood Nate had shot the guy in defense of his life with a load of double-aught buckshot.

When it looked as though the situation was in hand, one of the dogs belonging to the cruisers did what guard dogs do, after he saw the cops piling out of their black-and-whites and running in the direction of his homeboys. He sprang forward, breaking free of the leash, and raced directly at B.M. Driscoll, who had barely set foot on the sidewalk. When B.M. Driscoll saw those slobbering jaws and those bared fangs and malevolent eyes coming at him, he bellowed, drew his nine, and fired twice, missing once but then killing the dog instantly with a head shot.

The gunfire seemed to stop all action. Hollywood Nate realized that the maniac was choked out, and he let the guy fall to the ground, unconscious. Wesley Drubb looked toward the street for the first time and said, 'Where's our shop?'

Now that the entertainment had ended, the homies and their still-living dogs turned and retreated to their house without complaint about the unlicensed animal they'd lost. And there was lots of talk among them about how Loco

Lennie had *pelotas* made of stainless steel. Maybe they should reconsider Loco Lennie as a cruiser, they agreed, if he didn't get himself dusted by some cop who spotted him in the stolen police car.

When Flotsam saw the leather-clad lunatic lying on the ground, he said to Mag, 'Let's do rock-paper-scissors to see who gets the mouth on CPR.'

But as Mag was running to the car to look for her personal CPR mask, the unconscious man started breathing again on his own. He moaned and tried to get up but was quickly handcuffed by Hollywood Nate, who then collapsed beside him, his face bruised and swollen.

It was then that Flotsam noticed something clinging to the guy's bald head. He shined his light on it and saw 'Weiss.' Hollywood Nate's name tag had been pulled off and was sticking to the guy's bare scalp.

'Get me a Polaroid!' Flotsam yelled.

By the time the Oracle had arrived and instructed Flotsam and Mag to ride with him and to give their car to Hollywood Nate and Wesley Drubb, the handcuffed man was alert, and he said to Hollywood Nate, 'You can only hurt me in a physical state.'

And Nate, who was still trying to get his own breathing back to normal, rolled his aching shoulders and answered, 'That's the only state we live in, you psycho motherfucker.'

The Oracle warned that now they might have two FID teams out there: one on the dog shooting and another because Hollywood Nate had applied the dreaded choke hold. Force Investigation Division would have to be convinced that B.M. Driscoll had acted in fear of great bodily injury and that Hollywood Nate had choked out the madman as a last resort in the immediate defense of a life, namely his own.

'Not one but two FID roll-outs on the same freaking incident,' the Oracle moaned.

Flotsam said sympathetically, 'LAPD can't get enough layers of oversight, Boss. Somebody flipped the pyramid and we're under the pointy tip. We got more layers than a mafia wedding cake.'

When a plain-wrapper detective unit pulled up in front and parked, the Oracle wondered how FID could have gotten there so fast but then saw that it was only the night-watch detective Compassionate Charlie, as usual experiencing morbid curiosity. He was wearing one of his Taiwanese checked sport coats that made people ask if it was flame retardant. Charlie got out, picked some food from his teeth, and surveyed the scene for one of his sage pronouncements.

Flotsam talked for a few minutes to one of the Eighteenth Street crew who had lingered to be sure the dog was dead, and after the short conversation, the surfer jogged up to the Oracle and said, 'Boss, I think we have some extenuating circumstances in this shooting that might help you with those rat bastards from FID.'

'Yeah, what's that?'

Pointing to the deceased pit bull, Flotsam said, 'A homie told me the dog was just ghetto elk when they found him.'

'What?'

'You know, one of those stray dogs that roam around the 'hood? One of the cruisers found the dog down in Watts, brought him here and let him in their pack. But last month the dog came down with terminal cancer and they were just going to put him down any day now.'

'So?'

Compassionate Charlie butted into the conversation, saying to the Oracle, 'Don't you get it? Haven't you read about dogs that can smell malignant tumors?'

'Now, what in hell is your point, Charlie?' the Oracle wanted to know. He didn't have time for this goofy surfer or for one of Charlie's on-scene analyses.

Compassionate Charlie shook his head sadly, sucked his

teeth, and said, 'You can call this just another touching drama among the many that occur nightly on the streets of Hollywood. The fucking mutt knew he had cancer, so he decided to do honor to his crew and commit suicide-by-cop.'

Young Wesley Drubb felt sort of dazed for the remainder of the watch. His mind kept wandering away from the issues at hand. For instance, when they drove their prisoner to Central Jail at Parker Center, where medical treatment was available for him, all Wesley could think about when they drove past the parking lot was, Why is the entrance gate blocked with a steel barrier, and the exit gate is wide open with no metal spikes? A terrorist could just drive in the exit. Are we stupid, or what? His mind was wandering like that.

After the prisoner was treated prior to being booked for battery on a police officer, Hollywood Nate and Wesley Drubb decided to go to Cedars for treatment of contusions and abrasions, and in Nate's case muscle spasms. As to the prisoner, Nate told Wesley it would be up to the DA's office to decide if the arrestee was permanently nuts or only temporarily nuts from PCP or whatever a blood test might reveal. Drug-induced craziness would not be a defense in a criminal case, but life-induced craziness like his war experiences might keep him from a jail sentence and put him in a mental ward for a short vacation.

Wesley Drubb's mind remained unfocused for more than an hour. He got alarmed by remarks made by a jail employee who had taken his sweet time returning from the long lunch break that their union had recently won for them.

When their prisoner was strip-searched, the black detention officer studied the darkening welts all over the guy's body and said, 'He looks like a zebra.'

Wesley Drubb had never dreamed a man fifty-seven years old could fight like that and was still trying to sort his feelings about the first act of violence he'd ever committed on another human being in his entire life. And sick from the worry and stress of having lost his police car, he tried to explain the prisoner's bruises by saying, 'We had no choice.'

The jailor chuckled at the shaken young cop and said, 'Boy, lucky for you he's a peckerwood. If this cat was black, you would be facing the wrath of the city council, the United States Department of Justice, and the motherfuckin' ghost of Johnnie Cochran.'

Loco Lennie may or may not have heard the PSR's voice informing all units that 6-X-72's car had been stolen, and he may or may not have opened the text messages sent by other units to 6-X-72 after they'd learned of the incident.

One message said, 'When we see you, you are dead meat.'

Another said, 'We will shoot you and burn your body.'

Another, apparently from a K-9 unit, said, 'Trooper will eat on your sorry ass for as long as he wants. Before you die.'

In any case, Loco Lennie figured he had made his point to the crew, so he abandoned the police car only ten blocks from his house. He found a rock lying beside a chain-link fence, picked it up, and threw it at the windshield, just as a parting shot. Then Loco Lennie sprinted home in glory.

When, at the end of their long and awful duty tour, they were painfully walking to their personal cars, Wesley Drubb, who had been silent most of the night, said to Hollywood Nate, 'I don't care what they taught me in my years at USC. I don't care how unscientific it is. All I know is that since coming on this Job, I no longer believe in evolution. I believe in Creationism.'

'And why is that?' Nate asked.

'For instance, that guy tonight? An evolved form of life could not resemble something like that.'

EIGHT

After stopping at the Gulag for a happy hour drink, Cosmo Betrossian was driving his eighteen-year-old Cadillac east on Sunset to Korea Town, where he was living temporarily, and thinking of how impressed Dmitri had been with him during their meeting last week. This was where he belonged, with people like Dmitri. Cosmo was forty-three years old, too old to be dealing with people addicted to crystal meth. Too old to be buying the paper they'd stolen from mailboxes or from purses left in cars and then shopping the credit-card information to the other freaks at the public libraries and cyber cafés, where they sold stolen information and dealt drugs on the Internet.

Cosmo and Ilya had never committed an armed robbery prior to the jewelry store job. The hand grenade idea came from something he had heard from one of the addicts who had read about it in a San Diego newspaper. The reason the addict had mentioned it to Cosmo at all was that the robbers who did it were Armenians who were supposed to be connected with Russian Mafia. Cosmo had to laugh. He had stolen their idea and their modus operandi, and it had been easy. And it had all come to him because he was an Armenian émigré.

The knowledge about the diamonds' arriving on the premises had come to him by way of another of the addicts he had been dealing with for several months. It was information from an invoice receipt acknowledging delivery, sent by the jewelry store to a Hong Kong supplier. Along with that stolen letter had been another one, also bearing the jewelry store's return address, sent to a customer in San Francisco, telling the customer that an 'exciting delivery' of stones had arrived and were just what the customer had in mind when last he'd visited the Los Angeles store. The letters had been stolen from a mailbox by an addict who traded a bag full of credit-card and check information along with the letters in question for four teeners of crystal meth that Cosmo had bought for two hundred fifty dollars and used as trade bait.

He'd been doing business with tweakers for over a year and only on one occasion did he and Ilya smoke some crystal with them, but neither had liked the high, although it did sexually arouse them. They preferred cocaine and vodka. Cosmo had told the addicts that he and Ilya were more normal, old-fashioned people.

The thing that really had him excited now was that the robbery had been easy. It gave him a great thrill to make that jeweler weep and piss all over himself. Cosmo had fucked Ilya all night after they had done the robbery. And she too admitted that it had been sexually stimulating. Though she said that she would not participate in any more armed robberies, he thought that he could persuade her.

Ilya was waiting for him when he got back to their apartment. As soon as they sold the diamonds, they would be moving, maybe to a nicer apartment in Little Armenia. Their two-room hovel over a residential garage had been rented to them by a Korean who never asked questions about the men, both white and Asian, who visited Ilya in that apartment for a 'massage' and left within an hour or so. Ilya had formerly done a lot of out-call work, until she got arrested in a hotel room on a sting by a handsome vice cop who had flash money and nice clothes and rings on his fingers. Ilya wept when he showed his badge that night. She had been naive enough then to think that the handsome stranger had possibilities beyond a quick blow job.

Ilya was thirty-six years old and without a lot of years left for this kind of life, which is how she got teamed up with Cosmo. He'd promised to take care of her, promising that she'd never get arrested again and that he'd make enough money that she'd seldom have to sell her ass. But so far, she was making more money with her ass than he was making with the addicts who brought him things to trade for drugs.

Cosmo saw the outside light on after he'd parked half a block away and walked through the alley to the garage apartment with its termite-eaten stairway leading up. He was puzzled because she did not have a massage scheduled. He had specifically asked her about that. He felt a rush of fear through his bowels because it could mean a warning from her. But no, he could see her moving past the window. If cops were there, she'd be sitting, probably handcuffed. He took the stairs two at a time stealthily and opened the door without announcing his presence.

'Hi, Cosmo!' Olive Oyl said, with a gap-toothed smile, sitting on the small settee.

'Evening, Cosmo,' Farley said with his usual smirk, sitting next to Olive.

'Hello to you, Olive. Hello to you, Farley,' Cosmo said. 'You did not call me. I am not expecting you to come here tonight.'

'They called me,' Ilya said, 'after you went to Dmitri's.'

Cosmo shot her a look. Stupid woman. She mentioned Dmitri in front of these addicts. He turned to Farley and said, 'What is it you bring for me?'

'A business proposition,' Farley said, still smirking.

Puzzled, Cosmo looked at Ilya. Her blond hair was pulled straight back in a tight bun, which she would never do if she was expecting guests, even addict customers like these. And her makeup was haphazardly applied, and there were dark lines under her eyes. He guessed that she had been taking one of her long afternoon naps when the freaks called, and hadn't really pulled herself together before their arrival. Ilya showed Cosmo a very worried face.

'What business?' Cosmo asked.

'Sort of a partnership,' Farley said.

'I do not understand.'

'We figure that the last stuff we brought you was worth more than the few teeners you gave us. A whole lot more.'

'It is very hard thing to sell credit-card information and the banking paper today. Everyone who do crystal can make many deals today. Everybody know about—how they call it?'

'Identity theft,' Farley said.

'Yes,' Cosmos said. 'So I do not make enough money to pay me back for crystal I give to you, Farley.'

'Four lousy teeners,' Farley reminded him. 'That's one-quarter of an ounce. In your country maybe seven grams, right? What'd you pay, sixty bucks a teener?'

Cosmo was getting angry and said, 'We do a deal. It is done. Too late for to complain, Farley. It is done. You go someplace else next time, you don't like us.'

Cosmo's tone disturbed Olive, who said, 'Oh, we like you, Cosmo, and we like Ilya too! Don't we, Farley?'

'Shut up, Olive,' Farley said. 'I'm a smart man, Cosmo. A very smart man.'

Olive was about to verbally agree, but Farley elbowed her into silence. 'Cosmo, I read every fucking thing that I bring to people I deal with. I read those letters from a certain jewelry store. I thought maybe you could do something with it. Like maybe sell the information to some experienced burglar who might tunnel in through the roof when the store was closed and steal the stones. It never occurred to me that somebody might go in with guns and take over the place like Bonnie and Clyde. See, I'm not a violent man and I didn't think you were.'

Now Ilya looked like she was about ready to cry, and Cosmo glowered at her. 'You talk shit, Farley,' he said.

'I watch lots of TV, Cosmo. Smoking glass does that to you. Maybe I don't read the papers much anymore but I watch lots of TV. That hand grenade trick made all the local news shows the night you did it. Shortly after I'd brought the jewelry store's letters to you.'

All Cosmo could say was 'You talk shit, Farley.'

'The description they gave on the news was you.' Then he looked at Ilya, saying, 'And you, Ilya. I been thinking this over. I can hardly think of anything else.'

Cosmo was now glancing wildly from Farley to Ilya and back again. 'I do not like this talk,' he said.

'There's one more letter you should have,' Farley said. 'But I didn't bring it with me. I left it with a friend.' Farley felt a pang of fear shoot through him when he added, 'If I don't get home safe and sound tonight, he's going to deliver the letter to the Hollywood police station.'

Olive looked quizzically at Farley and said, 'Me too, Farley. Safe and sound, right?'

'Shut up, Olive,' Farley said, smelling his own perspiration now, thinking how the TV news bunny said the guy was waving around a pistol on the night of the robbery.

After a long silence, Cosmo said, 'You want from me what?'

'Oh, about fifteen thousand,' Farley said.

Cosmo jumped to his feet and yelled, 'You crazy! You crazy man!'

'Don't touch me!' Farley cried. 'Don't touch me! I gotta arrive home safe and sound or you're toast!'

Olive put her arms around Farley to calm him down and stop his shaking. Cosmo sat back down, sighed, ran his fingers through his heavy black hair, and said, 'I give you ten. I give you ten thousands sometime next month. Money will come in the month of June. I have nothing today. Nothing.'

Farley figured he'd better settle for the ten, and he was trembling when he and Olive stood. He took her hand.

Violence was not his gig. A man like this looking at him with murder in his face? All this was new to Farley Ramsdale.

Farley said, 'Okay, but don't try to sneak outta town. I got somebody watching the house twenty-four-seven.'

Then, before Cosmo could reply and frighten him again, Farley and Olive scuttled down the staircase, Farley yelping out loud when he almost stepped on a half-eaten rat by the bottom step. A black feral cat hissed at him.

By the time they reached the doughnut shop on Santa Monica where the tweakers hung out, Farley had recovered somewhat. In fact, he was feeling downright macho thinking about the ten large that would be theirs next month.

'I hope you don't think that goat eater had me scared,' he said to Olive, even though he'd been so shaky he'd had to pull over and let her take the wheel.

'Of course not, Farley,' Olive said. 'You were very brave.'

'There's nothing to be scared of,' he said. 'Shit, they used a phony hand grenade, didn't they? I'll bet their gun was phony, too. What'd that news reader with the tits call it? A "semiautomatic pistol"? I'll bet it was a fucking toy gun dressed up to look bad.'

'It's hard to believe Cosmo and Ilya would shoot anybody,' Olive agreed.

'Trouble is,' Farley reminded her, 'we ain't got enough glass to last till next month. We gotta get to the cyber café and do some business. Like, right away.'

'Right away, Farley.' She wished they had some money for a good meal. Farley was looking more like a ghost than he ever had.

The cyber café they chose was in a strip mall. It was a large two-story commercial building with at least a hundred computers going day and night. There was lots of business that could be done on the Internet. A tweaker could buy drugs from an on-line bulletin board or maybe do a little whoring on the Internet—male or female, take your choice. Money could be wired from one account to another. Or a tweaker could just sit there phishing for pin numbers and credit-card information. The computers were cheap and could be rented by the hour. Just like the dragons working the corner by the cyber café.

One of the dragons, a six-foot-tall black queen in full drag with a blond wig, short red sheath, three-inch yellow spikes, red plastic bracelets, and yellow ear loops, spotted Farley and Olive and approached them, saying, 'You holding any crystal tonight?' The dragon had scored from Farley on a few occasions when he was dealing crack.

'No, I need some,' Farley said.

The dragon was about to return to the corner to hustle tricks in passing cars, when a very tall teenage crackhead, also African American, with his baseball cap on sideways, wearing a numbered jersey and baggy knee-length jams and high-top black sneakers, looking goofy enough to be shooting hoops for a living in the NBA, approached the dragon and said, 'Hey, Momma, where can I get me some? I needs it bad, know what I'm sayin'?'

'Uh-huh,' the dragon said. 'I know what you're sayin', doodlebug.'

'Well, whatchoo gonna do about it, Momma? I got somethin' to trade, know what I'm sayin'?'

'And what is that?'

He took several rocks wrapped in plastic from his pocket and said, 'This'll take you on a trip to paradise, know what I'm sayin'?'

Pointing to the computer center, the dragon said, 'Go in there and sell it, then. Get some United States legal tender and come back and we'll talk.'

'I come back and show you tender, I make you do more than talk. I make you scream, know what I'm sayin'?'

'Uh-huh,' said the dragon, and when the kid went strutting into the cyber café, the dragon said to Farley and Olive, 'Don't see too many black folk around Hollywood these days 'cept for jive-ass cracked-out niggers like that, come up here from south L.A. to hustle and steal. Jist havin' them around is bad for my bidness. Fuck things up for everyone.' Then the dragon grinned and added, 'Know what I'm sayin'?'

'If we get any crystal tonight, we'll share with you,' Olive said to the drag queen. 'I remember when you shared with us.'

Farley shot Olive his shut-the-fuck-up look, and the dragon caught it. 'That's okay, honey, your old man needs tweak a lot more than I do, from the looks of him.'

Before Olive, which Farley referred to as B.O., he used to do lots of business here. He'd steal a car stereo and sell it at the cyber café on a rented computer. The money was wired on eBay to the Western Union office, where Farley would pick it up and cash it. Then he was back to the cyber café to buy his glass. It was hard for him to imagine life away from this place.

They entered and Farley began looking for someone he could work. He saw a dude he'd been arrested with in a drug sweep a few years back, sitting at one of the computers by the door. Farley stood behind the guy for a minute to see if the guy had it going.

The e-mail message said, 'Need tickets to Tina Turner concert. And want to sit in 8th row. Have teenager with me.'

'That's a fucking cop,' Farley said to the tweaker, who jumped and spun around on his chair. 'Dude, you are doing e-mail with a cop.' He couldn't remember the tweaker's name.

'Yo, Farley,' the tweaker said. 'What makes you think?'

'Every fucking cop on the planet knows Tina Turner is

code for tweak. And eighth row? Dude, think about it. What else could it be but an eight ball, right? And teenager means teener, very fucking obviously. So you're either dealing with the stupidest tweaker in cyberspace or a fucking narc. He's using dopey code that nobody uses anymore 'cause anybody can figure it out.'

'Maybe you're right,' the tweaker said. 'Thanks, man.'

'So if I just did you a favor, how about doing me one?'

'I got no ice to share and no cash to loan, Farley. Catch you later.'

'Ungrateful, simpleminded motherfucker,' Farley said to Olive when he rejoined her. 'When we got busted down at Pablo's Tacos two years ago and taken to Hollywood Station in handcuffs, we had to drop our pants and bend over and spread. And crystal went flying out his ass. He told the cop it didn't belong to him. Said he was just holding it for some parolee who pulled a knife and made him put the ice in his ass when the cops surrounded the taco joint.'

'Did you see it happen?' Olive asked.

'What?'

'The parolee with the knife, making him put the crystal up there! God, I'll bet your friend was scared!'

Farley Ramsdale was speechless at times like this and thought that she'd be better off dead. Except that she was so stupendously stupid she actually seemed to enjoy living. Maybe that's the way to cope with life, Farley thought. Get as brain-cooked as Olive and just enjoy the ride as long as it lasts.

When he looked at her, she smiled at him, showing her gums, and a tiny bubble popped out from the left gap in her grille when she said, 'I think there's a little bit of pot left at home. And we could boost you some candy and a bottle of vodka from the liquor store on Melrose. The old Persian man that works nights is almost blind, they say.'

'Persian is a fucking cat, Olive,' Farley said. 'He's an Iranian. They're everywhere, like cockroaches. This is Iran-geles, California, for chrissake!'

'We'll get by, Farley. You should eat something. And you should not get discouraged, and try to always remember that tomorrow's another day.'

'Jesus Christ,' Farley said, staring at her. '*Gone with the Fucking Wind*!'

'What, Farley?'

Farley, who, like most tweakers, stayed up for days watching movie after movie on the tube, said, 'You're what woulda happened to Scarlett O'Hara in later life if she'd smoked a chuck wagon load of Maui ice. She'd have turned into you! "Tomorrow is another fucking day"!'

Olive didn't know what in the world he was raving about. He needed to go to bed whether he could sleep or not. It had been a terrible day for him. 'Come on, Farley,' she said. 'Let's go home and I'll make you a delicious toasted cheese sand-wich. With mayonnaise on it!'

Nobody on the beach or in the whole state of California was madder than Jetsam that early morning of June 1. That's what he said to Flotsam when he met him at Malibu and unloaded his log from the Bronco and stopped to stare at the ocean. Both were wearing black wet suits.

The sky was a glare of gold rising up, and smudges of gray scudded low over the horizon. Looking away, Jetsam stared at the smog lying low in wispy veils, and at the bruised, glowering clouds that were curdling down onto all the fucking places where people lived in despair. Jetsam turned and looked out to sea, to the hopeful horizon glis-tening like an endless ribbon of silver, and for a long moment he didn't speak.

'What's wrong, dude?' Flotsam asked.

'I got stung Thursday night, bro!' Jetsam said.

'Stung?'

'A fucking IA sting! If you'da been on duty, you'da got stung with me. I was working with B.M. Driscoll. Poor fucker might as well set fire to homies and shoot dogs. He's always in trouble.'

'What happened?'

'You know that IA sting they did down in Southeast—when was it, last year? Year before? The one where they put the gun in the fucking phone booth?'

'I sorta remember the gist of it,' Flotsam said while Jetsam waxed the old ten-foot board as he talked.

'On that one, the fucking incompetents working the sting detail at IA leave a gun by a phone booth with one of their undercover guys standing nearby. They put out some kinda phony call to get a patrol unit there. Deal is, a patrol unit they're interested in is gonna come by, see the dude, do an FI, and see the gun there in plain view. The patrol unit's gonna ask what he knows about the gun and the dude's gonna say, "Who, me?" like the brothers always say down there. Then IA, who's watching from ambush, hope the coppers are gonna arrest the brother and claim he was carrying the gun. And if they're real lucky, maybe slap the brother around after he mouths off to them. And if they hit the jackpot, call him a nigger, which of course will get them a death row sentence and a lethal injection. And then maybe they can have a party for a job well done. But not that time. It goes sideways.'

'What happened? A shooting, right?'

'Some homies happen to be cruising by before the black-and-white shows up. These cruisers see a strange brother there who ain't one of their crew and they pop a cap at him. And then the IA cover team comes to the rescue and they fire back but don't really engage. I thought cops're supposed to engage hostile fire, but this is the rat squad. They see life different from regular coppers. So the homies get away, and what does IA do? They grab their sting gun and they get the hell out, and they don't hang around for an FID investigation. So they break every fucking rule the rest of us have to play by during these times. Their excuse was they had to protect the identity of their undercover officer.'

'That is bullshit, dude,' Flotsam said. 'When you apply seven-pound pull on a six-pound trigger, you stay and talk to the Man and make the reports. Undercover is over when the muzzle flashes.'

'Except for those rat bastards.'

'So how did they sting you Thursday night?'

'That's what makes me so mad. They used the same fucking gag, the unimaginative assholes! I thought at first they must be after B.M. Driscoll. He told me he was involved in a shaky shooting before he transferred to Hollywood and was worried about it. One of those deals where he capped a Mexican illegal who drove his car straight at him when the guy was trying to escape after a long car pursuit. The next day, he gets a phone call at the station from an irate citizen who says, 'You gotta come mow my lawn now. You shot my gardener.'

Flotsam said, 'Yeah, our chief says we're supposed to just jump out of the way of cars coming at us, maybe wave a cape like a matador. Then start chasing again, long as we don't endanger anybody but ourselves. Anything but shooting a thief who might be a minor. Or an ethnic. I wish somebody'd make a chart about which ethnics are unshootable nowadays and have Governor Arnold give them a sticker for their license plates. So we'd know.'

Jetsam said, 'Retreat goes against a copper's personality traits. Maybe they want us to just go back to the drive-and-wave policy, like we did under Lord Voldemort.'

'Maybe they should just put trigger locks on all our guns.'

'Anyways, B.M. Driscoll's convinced himself he's targeted by IA,' Jetsam said. 'Checks his house for listening devices every couple weeks. But you know him, he gets a hay fever cough and thinks it's cancer.'

'So how about Thursday night's sting? Are you saying they dropped a gun by a phone booth?'

'Purse,' Jetsam said.

Jetsam said it was a phone booth on Hollywood Boulevard of course, where lots of tourists might do something dumb like that. A phone booth by the subway station. He remembered how it had annoyed him when it popped on their computer screen. No big deal. An unnamed person had called in to say that there was a purse left in the phone booth. And the call was assigned to 6-X-32, on a night when B.M. Driscoll was Flotsam's stand-in.

B.M. Driscoll, who was riding shotgun, said, 'Shit. Found property to book. What a drag. Oh well, it'll give me a chance to get my inhaler outta my locker. I'm getting wheezy.'

'You ain't wheezy,' Jetsam said. The guy's imagined health issues were wearing Jetsam down to the ground. 'My ex was wheezy. Got an asthma attack every time I put a move on her in bed. That was about once every deployment period. Little did I know that her and the plumber down the street were laying pipe twice a week.'

Jetsam parked in a red zone by the intersection of Hollywood and Highland while B.M. Driscoll said, 'I don't like steroid inhalers but there's nothing more fundamental than breathing.'

When Jetsam was getting out of the car, B.M. Driscoll said, 'Be sure to lock it.'

He wasn't worried about their shotgun rack getting pried open or their car getting hot-wired. He was worried about his two uniforms they'd just picked up from the cleaners, which were hanging over the backseat.

After locking the car, Jetsam took his baton and ambled toward the phone booth, letting B.M. Driscoll lag behind and finish his medical monologue on the treatment of asthma with steroid inhalers at a distance where Jetsam could hardly hear him.

It was the kind of early summer evening when the layer of smog burnished the glow from the setting sun and threw a golden light over the Los Angeles basin, and somehow over Hollywood in particular. That light said to people: There are wondrous possibilities here.

Feeling the dry heat on his face, looking at the colorful creatures surrounding him, Jetsam saw tweakers and hooks, panhandlers and ordinary Hollywood crazies, all mingling with tourists. He saw Mickey Mouse and Barney the dinosaur and Darth Vader (only one tonight) and a couple of King Kongs.

But the guys inside the gorilla costumes weren't tall enough to successfully play the great ape, and he saw a guy he recognized as Untouchable Al walk up to one of them and say, 'King Kong, my ass. You look more like Cheetah.'

Jetsam turned away quickly because if there was a disturbance, he wanted no part of Untouchable Al, especially not here on Hollywood Boulevard where the multitudes would witness the dreadful inevitable outcome.

A team of bike cops, one man and one woman whom Jetsam knew from Watch 3, pedaled by slowly on the sidewalk, over those very famous three-hundred-pound slabs of marble and brass dedicated to Hollywood magic and the glamour of the past.

The bike cops nodded to him but continued on their way when he shook his head, indicating that nothing important had brought him here. He thought they looked very uncool in their bike helmets and those funny blue outfits that the other cops called pajamas.

When B.M. Driscoll caught up with him, he said, 'Don't this look a little bit strange? I mean, a purse is left here by an unknown person-reporting?'

Jetsam said, 'Whaddaya mean?'

B.M. Driscoll said, 'They're out to get me.'

'Who?'

'Internal Affairs Group. In fact, the whole goddamn Professional Standards Bureau. I got grilled like an Al-Qaeda terrorist by a Force Investigation Team when I popped the cap at the goddamn crackhead that tried to run over me. I tell you, IA's out to get me.'

'Man, you gotta go visit the Department shrink,' Jetsam said. 'You're soaring way out there, bro. You're sounding unhinged.'

But B.M. Driscoll said, 'I'll tell you something, if that purse is still there in the midst of this goddamn boulevard carnival, it means one thing. An undercover team has chased away every tweaker that's tried to pick it up during the last ten minutes.'

And now Jetsam started getting paranoid. He began looking hard at every tourist nearby. Could that one be a cop? That one over there looks like he could be. And that babe pretending to be reading the name on one of the marble stars down on the sidewalk. Shit, her purse is bulging like maybe there's a Glock nine and handcuffs in there.

When they were standing at the phone booth and saw a woman's brown leather handbag on the phone booth tray, B.M. Driscoll said, 'The purse is still there. Nobody's picked it up. No tweaker. No dogooder. It's still there. If there's money in it, you can bet your ass this is a sting.'

'If there's money in it, I gotta admit you might have a point here,' Jetsam said, looking behind him for the babe with the bulge in her handbag. And goddamnit, she was looking right at him! Then she gave him a little flirtatious wave and walked away. Shit, just a badge bunny.

B.M. Driscoll picked up the purse and opened it as though he was expecting a trick snake to jump out, removed the thick leather wallet, and handed it to Jetsam, saying, 'Tell me I'm wrong.'

Jetsam opened it and found a driver's license, credit cards, and other ID belonging to a Mary R. Rollins of Seattle, Washington. Along with $367 in currency.

'Bro, I think you ain't paranoid,' Jetsam said. 'Forget what I said about the shrink.'

'Let's take this straight to the station and make a ten-ten,' B.M. Driscoll said, referring to a property report.

'Let's take this to the Oracle,' Jetsam said. 'Let's call information for a phone number on Mary Rollins. Let's check and see if this ID is legit. I don't like to be set up like I'm a fucking thief.'

'It's not you,' B.M. Driscoll said, and now he was twitching and blinking. 'It's me. I'm a marked man!'

When they got to the station, they found the Oracle in the john, reading a paper. Jetsam stood outside the toilet stall and said, 'You in there, Boss?'

Recognizing the voice, the Oracle replied, 'This better be more important than your overwhelming excitement that surf's up tomorrow. At my age, taking a dump is serious business.'

'Can you meet Driscoll and me in the roll-call room?'

'In due time,' the Oracle said. 'There's a time for everything.'

They chose the roll-call room for privacy. The Oracle examined the purse and contents, and as he looked at this angry suntanned surfer cop with his short hair gelled up like a bed of spikes, and at his older partner twitching his nose like a rabbit, he said to them, 'You're right. This has to be a sting. This is unadulterated bullshit!'

Flotsam and Jetsam were lying in the sand next to their boards, by their towels and water, when Jetsam, reaching this part of the story, stopped to take a long pull from his water bottle.

Flotsam said, 'Don't stop, dude. Get to the final reel. What the fuck happened?'

Jetsam said, 'What happened was the Oracle came on like El Niño, and everybody stayed outta his way. The Oracle was hacked off, bro. And I got to see what all those hash marks give you.'

'What besides death before your time?'

'Humongous prunes and no fear, bro. The Oracle jumped their shit till the story came out. It was a sting, but as usual, Ethics Enforcement Section fucked up. It wasn't meant for B.M. Driscoll. He's so straight he won't even remove mattress tags, but they wouldn't say who it was meant for. Maybe somebody on Watch three. We think communications just gave the call to the wrong unit.'

Flotsam said, 'EES should stick to catching cops who work off-duty jobs when they're supposed to be home with bad backs. That's all they're good for.'

'Being an LAPD cop today is like playing a game of dodgeball, but the balls are coming at us from every-fucking-where,' Jetsam said.

Flotsam looked at his partner's thousand-yard stare, saying, 'Your display is on screen saver, dude. Get the hard drive buzzing and stay real.'

'Okay, but I don't like being treated like a thief,' Jetsam said.

Flotsam said, 'They gotta play their little games so they can say, "Look, Mr. Attorney General, we're enforcing the consent decree against the formerly cocky LAPD." Just forget about it.'

'But we got sideswiped, bro.'

'Whaddaya mean?'

'They burned us.'

'For what?'

'The undercover team saw B.M. Driscoll's uniforms hanging in the car. They had to nail us for something after we didn't fall for their stupid sting, so we're getting an official reprimand for doing personal business on duty.'

'Stopping at the cleaners?'

'You got it, bro.'

'What'd the Oracle say about that?'

'He wasn't there at the time. He'd already headed out for Alfonso's Tex Mex when a rat from PSB showed up. One of those that can't stop scratching all the insect bites on his candy ass. And the watch commander informed us we were getting burned.'

'That is way fucked, dude. You know how many man hours were wasted on that chickenshit sting? And here we are, with half the bodies we need to patrol the streets.'

'That is life in today's LAPD, bro.'

'How's your morale?'

'It sucks.'

'How would it be if I got you laid Thursday night?'

'Improved.'

'There's this badge bunny I heard about at the Director's Chair. Likes midnight swims at the beach, I hear.'

'I thought you said you'd fallen in love with Mag Takara?'

'I am in love, but it ain't working too good.'

'You said it was hopeful.'

'Let's hit it, dude,' Flotsam said to change the subject, grabbing his board and sprinting for the surf. He plunged into a cold morning breaker and came up grinning in the boiling ocean foam.

After Jetsam paddled out to his partner, he looked at Flotsam and said, 'So what happened between you and Mag? Too painful to talk about?'

'She's got it all, dude. The most perfect chick I ever met,' Flotsam said. 'Do you know what the Oracle told me? When he walked a beat in Little Tokyo a hundred years ago, he got to know the Takara family. They own a couple of small hotels, three restaurants, and I don't know how much rental property. That little honey might have some serious assets of her own someday.'

'No wonder you're in love.'

'And she is such a robo-babe. You ever see more beautiful lips? And the way she walks like a little panther? And her skin like ivory and the way her silky hair falls against her gracefully curving neck?'

Sitting astride his surfboard, Jetsam said, '"Gracefully curving"... bro, you are way goony! Stay real! This could just be false enchantment because she grabbed that dummy hand grenade and tossed it that time.'

Flotsam said, 'Then I got way pumped the last night we worked together. I knew after my days off, you and me would be teamed for the rest of the deployment period, so I took the bit in my teeth and I went for it. I said something like, "Mag, I hope I can persuade you to grab a bikini and surf with me on the twilight ocean with the molten sun setting into the darkling sea."'

'No, bro!' Jetsam said. 'No darkling sea! That is sooo non-bitchin'!' He paused. 'What'd she say to that?'

'Nothing at first. She's a very reserved girl, you know. Finally, she said, "I think I would rather stuff pork chops in my bikini and swim in a tank full of piranhas than go surfing with you at sunset, sunrise, or anytime in between."'

'That is like, way discouraging, bro,' Jetsam said somberly. 'Can't you see that?'

Flotsam and Jetsam weren't the only ones complaining about the LAPD watchers that day. One of the watchers, D2 Brant Hinkle, had been biding his time at Internal Affairs Group. He was on the lieutenant's list but was afraid that the list was going to run out of time before an opening came for him. He was optimistic now that all of the black males and females of any race who'd finished lower on the written and oral exam than he had but got preference had already been selected. Even though he wasn't a D3 supervisor, he'd had enough prior supervisory experience in his package to qualify for the lieutenant's exam, and he'd done pretty well on it. He didn't think anyone else could leapfrog over him before the list expired.

It had been an interesting two-year assignment at IAG, good for his personnel package but not so good for the stomach. He was experiencing acid reflux lately and was staring down the barrel at his fifty-third birthday. With twenty-nine years on the Job this was his last realistic chance to make lieutenant before pulling the pin and retiring to... well, he wasn't sure where. Somewhere out of L.A. before the city imploded.

Brantley Hinkle was long divorced, with two married daughters but no grandchildren yet, and he tried for a date maybe twice a month after he heard a colleague his age say, 'Shit, Charles Manson gets a dozen marriage proposals a year, and I can't get a date.'

It made him realize how seldom he had a real date, let alone a sleepover so he'd been making more of an effort lately. There was a forty-year-old divorced PSR whose honeyed tones over the police radio could trigger an incipient erection. There was an assistant district attorney he'd met at a retirement party for one of the detectives at Robbery-Homicide Division. There was even a court reporter, a Pilates instructor in her spare time, who was forty-six years old but looked ten years younger and had never been married. She'd whipped him into better shape with a diet and as much Pilates as he could stand. His waistband got so loose he couldn't feel his cell phone vibrating.

So he was in decent condition and still had most of his hair, though it was as gray as pewter now, and he didn't need glasses, except for reading. He could usually connect with one of the three women when he was lonely and the need arose, but he hadn't been trying lately. He was more focused on leaving Professional Standards Bureau and getting back to a detective job somewhere to await the promotion to lieutenant. If it came.

At IAG Brant Hinkle had seen complaints obsessively investigated for allegations that would have been subjects of fun and needling at retirement parties back in the days before the Rodney King beating and the Rampart scandal. Back before the federal consent decree.

And they weren't just coming from citizens; they were coming from other cops. He'd had to oversee one where a patrol sergeant his age looked at a woman officer in a halter bra and low-ride shorts who had just come from working out. Staring at her sweaty belly, the sergeant had sighed. That was it, he'd sighed. The woman officer beefed the sergeant, and that very expensive sigh got him a five-day suspension for workplace harassment.

Then there was the wrestling match at arrest-and-control school, where a male officer was assigned to wrestle with a woman officer in order to learn certain holds. The male cop said aloud to his classmates, 'I can't believe I get paid for this.'

She'd beefed him, and he'd gotten five days also.

Yet another involved a brand-new sergeant who, on his way to his first duty assignment as a sergeant, happened to spot one of the patrol units blow a stop sign on their way to a hot call that the unit had not been assigned. The sergeant arrived at his new post, and immediately he wrote a 1.28 personnel complaint.

Within his first month, that sergeant, a man who wore his new stripes with gusto, called one of the officers on his watch a 'dumbbell.' The officer made an official complaint against him. The sergeant got a five-day suspension. The troops cheered.

Under the federal consent decree with the legions of LAPD overseers, the cops were turning on each other and eating their own. It was a different life from the one he'd lived when he'd joined the world-famous LAPD, uncontested leader in big-city law enforcement. In Brant Hinkle's present world, even IAG investigators were subjected to random urine tests conducted by Scientific Investigation Division.

The IAG investigators who had preceded him said that during Lord Voldemort's Reign of Terror, they sometimes had six Boards of Rights—the LAPD equivalent of a military court martial—going on at one time, even though there were only five boardrooms. People had to wait in the corridors for a room to clear. It was an assembly line of fear, and it brought about the phenomenon of cops lawyering up with attorneys hired for them by their union, the Los Angeles Police Protective League.

The more senior investigators told him that at that time, everyone had joked grimly that they expected a cop to walk out of his Board of Rights after losing his career and pension and leap over the wrought-iron railing of the Bradbury Building into the courtyard five stories down.

The Bradbury Building, at 304 South Broadway, was an incongruous place in which to house the dreaded Professional Standards Bureau, with its three hundred sergeants and detectives, including the Internal Affairs Group, all of whom had to handle seven thousand complaints a year, both internally and externally generated against a police force of nine thousand officers. The restored 1893 masterpiece, with its open-cage elevators, marble staircases, and five-story glass roof, was probably the most photographed interior in all of Los Angeles.

Many a film noir classic had been shot inside that Mexican-tile courtyard flooded with natural light. He could easily imagine the ghosts of Robert Mitchum and Bogart exiting any one of the balcony offices in trench coats and fedoras as ferns in planter pots cast ominous shadows across their faces when they lit their inevitable smokes. Brant knew that nobody dared light a cigarette in the Bradbury Building today, this being twenty-first-century Los Angeles, where smoking cigarettes is a PC misdemeanor, if not an actual one.

Brant Hinkle was currently investigating a complaint against a female training officer in a patrol division whose job it had been to bring a checklist every day for a sergeant to sign off. After a year of this bureaucratic widget counting, where half the time she couldn't find a sergeant, she'd just decided to create one with a fictitious name and fictitious serial number.

But then the 'fraud' was discovered, and no check forger had ever been so actively pursued. IAG sent handwriting exemplars downtown to cement the case against the hapless woman whom the brass was determined to fire. But as it turned out, there was a one-year statute on such offenses, and they couldn't fire her. In fact, they couldn't do anything except transfer her to a division that might cause her a long drive and make her miserable, this veteran cop who had had an unblemished record but had finally succumbed to the deluge of audits and paperwork.

Brant Hinkle and his team were secretly happy that she'd kept her job. Like Brant, just about all of them were using IA experience as a stepping stone to promotion and weren't the rats that street cops imagined them to be.

As Brant Hinkle put it, 'We're just scared little mice stuck in a glue trap.'

Once when they were all bemoaning the avalanche of worthless and demoralizing complaints that the oppressive oversight armies had invited, Brant said to his colleagues, 'When I was a kid and *Dragnet* was one of the biggest hits on TV, Jack Webb's opening voice-over used to say, "This is the city. Los Angeles, California. I work here… I'm a cop." Today all we can say is, "This is the city. Los Angeles, California. I work here… I'm an auditor."'

Probably the most talked-about investigation handled by

Brant Hinkle during these we-investigate-every-complaint years was the one involving a woman who had become obsessed with a certain cop and made an official complaint against him, signed and dated, maintaining, 'He stole my ovaries.'

It had to be investigated in full, including with lengthy interviews. There had to be an on-the-record denial by the police officer in question, who said to Brant, 'Well, I'm glad IA is taking her complaint seriously. There could be something to this ovary theft. After all, you guys are trying real hard to steal my balls, and you've just about done it.'

It was probably at that moment that Brant Hinkle spoke to his boss about a transfer back to a divisional detective squad.

NINE

Watch 5, the ten-hour midwatch, from 5:15 p.m. to 4:00 a.m. with an unpaid lunch break (code 7), had about fifty officers assigned to it. Five of them were women, but three of those women were on light duty for various reasons, and there were only two in the field, Budgie and Mag. And what with days off, sick days, and light duty, on a typical weekend night it was difficult for the Oracle to find enough bodies to field more than six or eight cars. So when one of the vice unit's sergeants asked to borrow both of the midwatch women for a Saturday night mini-version of the Trick Task Force, he got an argument.

'You've got the biggest vice unit in the city,' the Oracle said. 'You've got half a dozen women. Why don't you use them?'

'Only two work as undercover operators and they're both off sick,' the vice sergeant said. 'This isn't going to be a real task force. No motor cops as chase units. No big deal. We only wanna run a couple operators and cover units for a few hours.'

'Why can't you put your uniformed women on it?'

'We have three. One's on vacation, one's on light duty, one's pregnant.'

'Why not use her?' the Oracle said. 'It's a known fact that there's a whole lotta tricks out there who prefer pregnant hookers. Something about a mommy fixation. I guess they want spanked.'

'She's not pregnant enough to notice, but she's throwing

up like our office is a trawler in a perfect storm. I ask her to walk the boulevard, she'll start blowing chunks on my shoes.'

'Aw shit,' the Oracle said. 'How're we supposed to police a city when we spend half the time policing ourselves and proving in writing that we did it?'

'I don't answer trick questions,' the vice sergeant said. 'How about it? Just for one night.'

When the Oracle asked Budgie Polk and Mag Takara if they'd like to be boulevard street whores on Saturday night, they said okay. He only got an argument from Budgie's partner, Fausto Gamboa.

Fausto walked into the office, where three supervisors were doing paperwork, and being one of the few patrol officers at Hollywood Station old enough to call the sixty-eight-year-old sergeant by his given name, he said to the Oracle, 'I don't like it, Merv.'

'What don't you like, Fausto?' the Oracle asked, knowing the answer.

'Budgie's got a baby at home.'

'So what's that got to do with it?'

'Sometimes she lactates. And it's painful.'

'She'll deal with it, Fausto. She's a cop,' the Oracle said, while the other sergeants pretended to not be listening.

'What if she gets herself hurt? Who's gonna feed her baby?'

'The cover teams won't let her get hurt. And babies don't have to have mother's milk.'

'Aw shit,' Fausto said, echoing the Oracle's sentiments about the whole deal.

After he'd gone the Oracle said to the other two sergeants, 'Sometimes my ideas work too well. Fausto's not only gotten out of his funk, I think he's about to adopt Budgie Polk. Her kid'll probably be calling him Grandpa Fausto in a couple years.'

*

Cosmo Betrossian was a whole lot unhappier than Fausto Gamboa. He had diamonds to deliver to Dmitri at the Gulag soon and he had to kill that miserable addict Farley Ramsdale and his stupid girlfriend, Olive, sometime before then. Farley's claim that he had someone watching Cosmo and Ilya's apartment was so ridiculous Cosmo hadn't given it a thought. And as to Farley's other claim, that he had a letter that would be delivered to the police if something happened to him, well, the addict had seen too many movies. Even if there was a letter, let the police try to prove the truth of it without the writer and his girlfriend alive to attest to its veracity.

Cosmo was going to make them disappear, and he would have liked to talk to Dmitri about that. Dmitri would have some good ideas about how to make someone vanish, but if Dmitri learned about the tweakers, he might see them as potential trouble and back out of the arrangement. No, Cosmo would have to deal with them with only Ilya to help. And it would not be easy. Other than a gang rival back in Armenia whom he had shot to death when he was a kid of eighteen, Cosmo had never killed anyone. Here in America he had never even committed violent crime until the jewelry store robbery. His criminal life had been relegated to the smuggling of drugs, which he did not use himself, fencing stolen property, and in recent years, identity theft, which he'd learned from a Gypsy.

He'd met the Gypsy in a Hollywood nightclub on the Sunset Strip. Cosmo had been frequenting the Strip then, doing low-level cocaine sales. But the Gypsy introduced him to a new world. He showed Cosmo how easy it was to walk into the Department of Motor Vehicles, armed with a bit of personal data stolen by common mail thieves like Farley Ramsdale, and tell a DMV employee that he needed a new driver's license because he'd changed his address and misplaced his license. At first the DMV employees would ask for a Social Security Number but seldom if ever bothered to pull up the photo of the legitimate license holder to compare it with the face before them. They'd just take a new photo and change the address to the location where the license would be sent, and business would be concluded.

Cosmo and the Gypsy normally used an address of a house or apartment in their neighborhood where the occupant worked during the day. And either Cosmo or the Gypsy would check their neighbor's mailbox every day until the driver's license arrived. Later, when the DMV started asking for a birth certificate, Cosmo learned that with the information from the stolen mail, it was a simple matter for the Gypsy to make a credible birth certificate that would satisfy most DMV employees.

Cosmo and the Gypsy got so lazy that instead of going to the DMV, they started using a CD template that was making the rounds among all the identity thieves. It showed how to make driver's licenses, Social Security cards, auto insurance certificates, and other documents.

Stealing credit-card numbers became a bonanza. They could buy just about anything. They could even buy automobiles, and since car dealers were all covered by insurance, they were the easiest. By the time the legitimate card owners got their statements, Cosmo and the Gypsy would be off that card and on to another. Sometimes the credit-card statements went to bogus addresses supplied by Cosmo and the Gypsy, so legitimate card owners wouldn't discover the account was delinquent until they tried to buy something of value.

The Gypsy had an interior decorator working with them at that time. She said it was amazing how many people on the affluent west side of town kept their old cards, even ATM cards, thrown into a drawer somewhere. Nobody seemed to care much. The credit-card company only took a hit if the card was presented in person by the thief. If the business was done on the Internet or by phone, the credit-card company was not liable. Banks and credit-card companies had long delays in catching up, and identity thefts were so paper intensive the police were overwhelmed.

For a while Cosmo and the Gypsy had gotten so successful they were hoping to deal with the Russians whose eastern European contacts hacked into U.S. banks and lending institutions for card numbers, then ordered high-quality embossing and encoding strips from China. As it was, they just did their business online in the cyber cafés or by phone and ordered merchandise to be sent to addresses they'd cased. FedEx would drop the parcels on the porch while the resident was at work, and they would be picked up by Cosmo while the Gypsy waited in their car. The resident would be shocked when, after a few months of this, the police showed up at the home with a search warrant for all that stolen property.

Then one day without warning the Gypsy and the interior moved to New York without notifying Cosmo until they were there. And that was that. Cosmo continued limping through the world that the Gypsy had sailed through, and now Cosmo was dealing with tweaker mail thieves and doing cyber café networking as best he could. He had almost been arrested twice and was losing confidence now that everybody was doing identity theft.

The big break had come in the batch of mail stolen by Farley Ramsdale, when he had found the letter about the diamonds, and Cosmo had committed his first violent crime in America. He was stunned to learn that he liked it. It had thrilled him, that feeling of power over the jewelry store proprietor. Seeing the fear in his eyes. Hearing him weep. Cosmo had had complete control over everything, including that man's life. The feeling was something he could never put into words, but he believed that Ilya felt some of it too. If another chance at a safe and profitable armed robbery came up, he knew he would take it.

But of immediate concern to him was Farley Ramsdale and Olive. And Cosmo was very worried about Ilya as a partner in homicide. Could she do what it took, he wondered. He hadn't spoken with her about the two addicts, not since they had come to the apartment with their blackmail threat. Cosmo sensed that Ilya knew what had to be done but wanted him to deal with it alone. Well, it was not going to work that way. He couldn't do it alone. They wouldn't trust him. Ilya was a very smart Russian, and he needed a plan with her involved.

Hollywood Nate Weiss and Wesley Drubb were having another one of those Hollywood nights, that is, a night of very strange calls. It always happened when there was a full moon over the boulevard and environs.

Actually, the Oracle, who'd read a book or two in his long life, forewarned them all at roll call, saying, 'Full moon. A Hollywood moon. This is a night when our citizens act out their lives of quiet desperation. Share your stories tomorrow night at roll call and we'll give the Quiet Desperation Award to the team with the most memorable story.' Then he added, 'Beware, beware! Their flashing eyes, their floating hair!'

Nate's facial bruises from the fight with the veteran who wanted a ride were healing up well, and though he would never admit it to anyone, he was secretly wishing they'd given the psycho the goddamn ride he'd wanted. His black eye had actually cost him a job as an extra on a low-budget movie being shot in Westwood.

Wesley was driving again, and with the Oracle going to bat for him, he hoped that there wouldn't be disciplinary action for letting their shop get stolen and trashed by the little homie who hadn't been arrested yet but whom detectives had identified. The Oracle had written in his report that Wesley's failure to shut off the engine and take the keys when he'd jumped out of the car was understandable given the extreme urgency of helping his partner subdue the very violent suspect.

Hollywood Nate said that since Wesley had just finished his probation it wouldn't cost him his job, but Nate figured he'd be getting a few unpaid days off. 'Forgiveness is given in church, in temple, and by the Oracle, but it ain't written into the federal consent decree or the philosophy of Internal Affairs,' Nate warned young Wesley Drubb.

Their first very strange call occurred early in the evening on Sycamore several blocks from the traffic on Melrose. It came from a ninety-five-year-old woman in a faded cotton dress, sitting in a rocker on her front porch, stroking a calico cat. She pointed out that the man who lived across the street in a white stucco cottage 'hadn't been around for a few weeks.'

She was so old and shriveled that her parchment skin was nearly transparent and her colorless hair was thinned to wisps. Her frail legs were wrapped in elastic bandages, and though she was obviously a bit addled she could still stand erect, and she walked out onto the sidewalk unaided.

She said, 'He used to have a cup of tea and cookies with me. And now he doesn't come, but his cat does and I feed her every day.'

Hollywood Nate winked at Wesley and patted the old woman on the shoulder and said, 'Well, don't you worry. We'll check it out and make sure he's okay and tell him to drop by and have some tea with you and give you his thanks for feeding his cat the past few weeks.'

'Thank you, Officer,' she said and returned to her rocker.

Hollywood Nate and Wesley strolled across the street and up onto the porch. The few feet of dirt between the house and sidewalk hadn't been tended in a long time but was too patchy and water-starved to have done more than spread a web of crabgrass across its length. There seemed to be several seedy and untended small houses along this block, so there was nothing unusual about this one.

Hollywood Nate tapped on the door and when they received no answer said, 'The guy might have gone out of town for the weekend. The old lady doesn't know a few weeks from a few days.'

Or a few years, as it turned out.

When Wesley Drubb opened the letter slot to take a look, he said, 'Better have a look at this, partner.'

Nate looked inside and saw mail piled up nearly to the mail slot itself. It looked to be mostly junk mail, and it completely covered the small hallway inside.

'Let's try the back door,' Nate said.

It was unlocked. Nate figured to find the guy dead, but there was no telltale stench, none at all. They walked through a tiny kitchen and into the living room, and there he was, sitting in his recliner in an Aloha shirt and khaki pants.

He was twice as shriveled as his former friend across the street. His eyes, or what was left of them, were open. He'd obviously been a bearded man, but the beard had fallen out onto his chest along with most of the hair on his head, and the rest clung in dried patches. Beside his chair was a folding TV tray, and on it was his remote control, a *TV Guide*, and two vials of heart medication.

Wesley checked the jets on the kitchen range and tried light switches and the kitchen faucet, but all utilities had been turned off. On the kitchen table was an unused ticket to Hawaii, explaining the Aloha shirt. He'd been practicing.

Nate bent over the *TV Guide* and checked the date. It was two years and three months old.

Wesley asked Hollywood Nate if this could possibly be a crime scene because the dead man's left leg wasn't there.

Nate looked in the corner behind the small sofa and there it was, lying right near the pet door where his cat could come and go at will. There was almost no dried flesh left on the foot, just tatters from his red sock hanging on bone. The leg had apparently fallen off.

'Good thing he didn't have a dog,' Nate said. 'If grandma across the street had found this on her front porch, she might've had a heart attack of her own.'

'Should we call paramedics?' Wesley said.

'No, just the coroner's crew. I'm pretty sure this man's dead,' said Hollywood Nate.

When they got back to the station at end-of-watch and everyone was comparing full-moon stories, they had to agree that the Quiet Desperation Award went to Mag Takara and Benny Brewster, hands down.

It began when a home owner living just west of Los Feliz Boulevard picked up the phone, dialed 911, gave her address, and said, 'The woman next door is yelling for help! Her door is locked! Hurry!'

Mag and Benny acknowledged the code 3 call, turned on the light bar and siren, and were on their way. When they got to the spooky old two-story house, they could hear her from the street yelling, 'Help me! Help me! Please help me!'

They ran to the front door and found it locked. Mag stepped out of the way and Benny Brewster kicked the door in, splintering the frame and sending the door crashing against the wall.

Once inside the house they heard the cries for help increase in intensity: 'For God's sake, help me! Help me! Help me!'

Mag and Benny ascended the stairs quickly, hearing car doors slam outside as Fausto and Budgie and two other teams arrived. The bedroom door was slightly ajar and Mag stood on one side of it, Benny on the other, and being cops, they instinctively put their hands on their pistol grips.

Mag nudged the door open with her toe. There was

silence for a long moment and they could hear the loud tick of a grandfather clock as the pendulum swept back and forth, back and forth.

Then, in the far corner of the large bedroom suite, the voice: 'Help me! Help me! Help me!'

Mag and Benny automatically entered in a combat crouch and found her. She was a fifty-five-year-old invalid, terribly crippled by arthritis, left alone that night by her bachelor son. She was sitting in a wheelchair by a small round table near the window, where she no doubt spent long hours gazing at the street below.

She was holding a .32 semiautomatic in one twisted claw and an empty magazine in the other. The .32 caliber rounds were scattered on the floor where she'd dropped them.

Her surprisingly youthful cheeks were tear-stained, and she cried out to them, 'Help me! Oh, please help me load this thing! And then get out!'

There were two detectives working overtime at Hollywood Station that night. One was Andi McCrea, who had been given the job of finishing what she'd started innocently a few weeks ago as a stand-in for the absent sex crimes detail. But she didn't mind a bit because that was the first time in her career that she had solved a double homicide without knowing a damn thing about it.

The kid from Reno was in Juvenile Hall awaiting his hearing. But more important, his forty-year-old fellow killer, Melvin Simpson, a third-strike ex-con from the San Francisco Bay Area who had been in Reno on a gambling junket, was going to be charged with capital murder.

Now detectives in Las Vegas were also interested in Simpson, since it was discovered through his credit-card receipts that he'd also been in their city for a week. With no means of employment he'd had enough money to gamble in both places, and it turned out that a high-tech engineer from

Chicago who was attending a convention had been robbed and murdered at a rest stop outside Las Vegas on the day that Simpson had checked out of his hotel.

The ballistics report hadn't been completed yet, but Andi had high hopes. Wouldn't this be something to talk about to the oral board at the next lieutenant's exam. It might even rate a story in the *L.A. Times*, except that nobody read the *Times* anymore or any newspaper, so there was no point getting excited about that part of it.

The other detective working late that night was Viktor Chernenko, a forty-three-year-old immigrant from Ukraine, one of two naturalized citizens currently working at Hollywood Station, the other being from Guadalajara, Mexico. Viktor had a mass of wiry, dark hair that he called 'disobedient,' a broad Slavic face, a barrel of a body, and a neck so thick he was always popping buttons.

Once when his robbery team was called to a clinic in east Hollywood to interview the victim of a violent purse snatching, the receptionist saw Viktor enter and said to a woman waiting in the lobby, 'Your cab is here.'

And he was just about the most dedicated, hardworking, and eager-to-please cop that Andi McCrea had ever encountered.

Viktor had emigrated to America in September 1991, a month after the coup that led to the collapse of the Soviet Union, at a time when he was a twenty-eight-year-old captain in the Red Army. His exit from the USSR was unclear and mysterious, leading to gossip that he'd defected with valuable intelligence and was brought to Los Angeles by the CIA. Or maybe not. No one knew for sure, and Viktor seemed to like it that way.

He was the one that LAPD came to when they needed a Russian translator or a Russian-speaking interrogator, and consequently he had become well known to most of the local gangsters from former Iron Curtain countries. And that was why he was working late. He had been assigned to assist the robbery team handling the 'hand grenade heist,' as the jewelry store robbery came to be called. Viktor had been contacting every émigré that he knew personally who was even remotely involved with the so-called Russian Mafia. And that meant any Los Angeles criminal from the Eastern bloc, including the YACS: Yugoslavians, Albanians, Croatians, and Serbs.

Viktor was educated well in Ukraine and later in Russia. His study of English had helped get him promoted to captain in the army before most of his same age colleagues, but the English he'd studied in the USSR had not included idioms, which would probably confound him forever. That evening, when Andi twice offered to get him some coffee, he had politely declined until she asked if she could bring him a cup of tea instead.

Using her proper name as always, he said, 'Thank you, Andrea. That would strike the spot.'

During his years in Los Angeles, Viktor Chernenko had learned that one similarity between life in the old USSR and life in Los Angeles—life under a command economy and a market economy— was that a tremendous amount of business was transacted by people in subcultures, people whom no one ever sees except the police. Viktor was fascinated by the tidal wave of identity theft sweeping over Los Angeles and the nation, and even though Hollywood detectives did not deal directly with these cases—referring them downtown to specialized divisions like Bunco Forgery—almost everybody Viktor contacted in the Hollywood criminal community had something or other to do with forged or stolen identity.

After several conversations with the jewelry store victim, Sammy Tanampai, as well as with Sammy's father, Viktor was convinced that neither of them had had any dealings, legitimate or not, with Russian gangsters or Russian prostitutes. Sammy Tanampai was positive that he had heard a Russian accent from the woman, or something similar to the accents he'd heard from Russian émigrés who'd temporarily settled in cheap lodgings that his father often rented to them in Thai Town.

It was during a follow-up interview that Sammy said to Viktor Chernenko, 'The man didn't say many words, so I can't be exactly sure, but the woman's accent sounded like yours.'

The more that Viktor thought about how these Russians, if they were Russians, had gotten the information about the diamonds, the more he concluded that it could have come from an ordinary mail theft. Sipping the tea that Andi had brought him, he decided to make another phone call to Sammy Tanampai.

'Did you mail letters to anyone about the diamonds?' he asked Sammy after the jeweler's wife called him to the phone.

'I did not. No.'

'Do you know if your father did so?'

'Why would he do that?'

'Maybe to a client who wanted the kind of diamonds in your shipment? Something like that?'

And that stopped the conversation for a long moment. When Sammy spoke again he said, 'Yes. My father wrote to a client in San Francisco about the diamonds. He mentioned that to me.'

'Do you know where he mailed the letter?' Viktor asked.

'I mailed it,' Sammy said. 'In a mailbox on Gower, several blocks south of Hollywood Boulevard. I was on my way to pick up my kids at the day-care center. Is that important?'

'People steal letters from mailboxes,' Viktor explained.

After he hung up, Andi said, curious, 'Are you getting somewhere on the jewelry store case?'

With a smile, Viktor said, 'Tomorrow I shall be looking

through the transient book to see if many homeless people are hanging around Hollywood and Gower.'

'Why?' Andi asked. 'Surely you don't think a homeless person pulled a robbery that sophisticated?'

With a bigger smile, he said, 'No, Andrea, but homeless people can steal from mailboxes. And homeless people see all that happens but nobody sees homeless people, who live even below subculture. My Russian robbers think they are very clever, but I think they may soon find that they have not pulled the fuzz over our eyes.'

One of the reasons given for putting Budgie Polk and Mag Takara out on the boulevard on Saturday night was that Compstat had indicated there were too many tricks getting mugged by opportunist robbers and by the whores themselves. And everyone knew that many of the robberies went unreported because tricks were married men who didn't want mom to know where they went after work.

Compstat was the program of the current chief of police that he'd used when he was police commissioner of the NYPD and that he claimed brought down crime in that city, even though it was during a time when crime was dropping all over America for reasons demographic that had nothing to do with his program. Still, nobody ever expressed doubts aloud and everybody jumped onboard, at least feigning exuberance for the big chief's imported baby, pinching its cheeks and patting its behind when anyone was watching.

Brant Hinkle of Internal Affairs Group thought that Compstat might possibly have helped in New York, with its thirty thousand officers, maybe even in Boston, where the chief had served as a street cop. Perhaps it might be a worthwhile tool in many vertical cities where thousands live and work directly on top of others in structures that rise several stories. But that wasn't the way people lived in the transient, nomadic sprawl of the L.A. basin. Where nobody knew their neighbors' names. Where people worked and lived close to the ground with access to their cars. Where everyone owned a car, and freeways crisscrossed residential areas as well as business districts. Where only nine thousand cops had to police 467 square miles.

When crime occurred in L.A., the perpetrator could be blocks or miles away before the PSR could even assign a car to take a report. If she could find one. And as far as flooding an area with cops to deal with a crime trend, the LAPD didn't have half enough cops to flood anything. They could only leak.

There were a few occasions when Brant Hinkle got to see Compstat in action, during the first couple of years after the new chief arrived. That was when the chief, perhaps a bit insecure on the Left Coast, brought in a journalist crony from New York who had never been a police officer and made a special badge for him saying 'Bureau Chief.' And gave him a gun permit so he'd have a badge and gun like a real cop. That guy seemed to do no harm, and he was gone now and the chief of police was more acclimated and more secure, but Compstat remained.

Back then the chief had also brought several retired cops from New York, as though trying to re-create New York in L.A. They would put on a little slide show with two or three patrol captains sitting in the hot seat. On a slide would be a picture of an apartment building, and one of the retired NYPD cops with a loud voice and a Bronx accent would confront the LAPD captains and say, 'Tell us about the crime problems there.'

And of course, none of the captains had the faintest idea about the crime problems there or even where 'there' was. A two-story apartment building? There were hundreds in each division, thousands in some.

And the second-loudest guy, maybe with a Brooklyn accent, would yell in their faces, 'Is the burglary that occurred there on Friday afternoon a single burglary or part of a trend?'

And a captain would stammer and sweat and wonder if he should take a guess or pray for an earthquake.

However, Brant Hinkle learned that there were some LAPD officers who loved the Compstat sessions. They were the street cops who happened to hate their captains. They got a glow just hearing about their bosses melting in puddles while these abrasive New Yorkers sprayed saliva. At least that's how it was described to the cops who wished they could have been there to watch the brass get a taste of the shit they shoveled onto the troops. The street cops would've paid for tickets.

As far as the troops at Hollywood Station were concerned, the East Coast chief was not Lord Voldemort, and that alone was an answered prayer. And he did care about reducing crime and response time to calls. And he did more than talk about troop morale; he allowed detectives to take their city cars home when they were on call instead of using their private cars. And of great importance, he instituted the compressed work schedule that Lord Voldemort hated, which allowed LAPD cops to join other local police departments in working four ten-hour shifts a week or three twelve-hour shifts instead of the old eight-to-five. This allowed LAPD cops, most of whom could not afford to live in L.A. and had to drive long distances, the luxury of three or four days at home.

As far as Compstat was concerned, the street cops were philosophical and fatalistic, as they always were about the uncontrollable nature of a cop's life. One afternoon at roll call, the Oracle, who was old enough and had enough time on the Job to speak the truth when no one else dared, asked the lieutenant rhetorically, 'Why doesn't the brass quit sweating Compstat? It's just a series of computer-generated pin maps is all it is. Give the chief a little more time to settle down in his new Hollywood digs and go to a few of those Beverly Hills cocktail parties catered by Wolfgang Puck. Wait'll he gets a good look at all those pumped-up weapons of mass seduction. He'll get over his East Coast bullshit and go Hollywood like all the clowns at city hall.'

When his transfer came through, Brant Hinkle was overjoyed. He had hoped he would get Hollywood Detectives and had had an informal interview months earlier with their lieutenant in charge. He had also had an informal interview with the boss of Van Nuys Detectives, the division in which he lived, and did the same at West L.A. Detectives, pretty sure that he could get one of them.

When he reported, he was told he'd be working with the robbery teams, at least for now, and was introduced around the squad room. He found that he was acquainted with half a dozen of the detectives and wondered where the rest were. He counted twenty-two people working in their little cubicles on computers or phones, sitting at small metal desks divided only by three-foot barriers of wallboard.

Andi McCrea said to him, 'A few of our people are on days off, but this is about it. We're supposed to have fifty bodies, we have half that many. At one time ten detectives worked auto theft, now there're two.'

'It's the same everywhere,' Brant said. 'Nobody wants to be a cop these days.'

'Especially LAPD,' Andi said. 'You should know why. You just left IA.'

'Not so loud,' he said, finger to lips. 'I'd like to keep it from the troops that I did two years on the Burn Squad.'

'Our secret,' Andi said, thinking he had a pretty nice smile and very nice green eyes.

'So where's my team?' he asked Andi, wondering how old she was, noticing there was no wedding ring.

'Right behind you,' she said. He turned and suffered an

enthusiastic Ukrainian handshake from Viktor Chernenko.

'I am not usually a detective of the robbery teams,' Viktor said, 'but I am Ukrainian, so now I am a detective of robbery teams because of the hand grenade heist. Please sit and we shall talk about Russian robbers.'

'You'll enjoy this case,' Andi said, liking Brant's smile more and more. 'Viktor has been very thorough in his investigation.'

'Thank you, Andrea,' Viktor said shyly. 'I have tried with all my effort to leave no stone upright.'

The Oracle decided maybe he himself should win honorable mention for the Quiet Desperation Award on that full-moon evening. He had just returned from code 7 and had severe heartburn from two greasy burgers and fries, when the desk officer entered the office and said, 'Sarge, I think you need to take this one. A guy's on the phone and wants to speak to a sergeant.'

'Can't you find out what it's about?' the Oracle said, looking in the desk drawer for his antacid tablets.

'He won't tell me. Says he's a priest.'

'Oh, crap!' the Oracle said. 'Did he say his name is Father William, by any chance?'

'How'd you know?'

'There's a Hollywood moon. He'll keep me on the phone for an hour. Okay, I'll talk to him.'

When the Oracle picked up the phone, he said, 'What's troubling you this time, Father William?'

The caller said, 'Sergeant, please send me two strong young officers right away! I need to be arrested, handcuffed, and utterly humiliated! It's urgent!'

TEN

On Saturday, June 3, Officer Kristine Ripatti of Southwest Division was shot by an ex-con who had just robbed a gas station. Her partner killed the robber but got harassed by homies while he was trying to help the wounded officer, whose spinal wound paralyzed her from the waist down. When Fausto learned that Officer Ripatti, age thirty-three, also had a baby girl, he began to agonize over his partner's upcoming assignment.

When Saturday night arrived, Budgie and Mag got whistles from one end of the station to the other. Budgie grinned and flipped them off and tried not to look too self-conscious. She was wearing a push-up bra that wasn't comfortable given her condition, a lime-green jersey with a plunging neck under a short vest to hide the wire and mike, and the tightest skirt she'd ever worn, which the teenager next door had let her borrow.

The neighbor kid had gotten into the spirit of the masquerade by insisting that Budgie try on a pair of her mother's three-inch stilettos, and they fit, for despite being so tall, Budgie had small feet. A green purse with a shoulder strap completed the ensemble. And she wore plenty of pancake and the brightest creamiest gloss she owned, and she didn't spare the eyeliner. Her braided blond ponytail was combed out and sprinkled with glitter.

Flotsam checked her out and said to Jetsam, 'Man, talk about bling!'

Fausto looked at her with disapproval, then took a five-shot, two-inch Smith & Wesson revolver from his pocket and said, 'Put this in your purse.'

'I don't need it, Fausto,' Budgie said. 'My security team'll be watching me at all times.'

'Do like I say, please,' Fausto said.

Because it was the first time he'd ever said please to her, she took the gun and noticed him looking at her throat and chest. She reached up and unfastened the delicate gold chain and handed the chain and medal to him, saying, 'What kind of whore wears one of these? Hold it for me.'

Fausto took the medal in his hand and said, 'Who is this, anyways?'

'Saint Michael, patron saint of police officers.'

Handing it back to her, he said, 'Keep him in your purse right alongside the hideout gun.'

Mag, who wasn't thin like Budgie and was nearly a foot shorter, had all the curves she needed without enhancement, and came off as more of a bondage bitch. She wore a black jersey turtleneck, black shorts, black plastic knee boots that she had bought for this occasion, and dangling plastic earrings. She'd tied back her glossy blunt cut in a severe bun.

Her look said, 'I will hurt you but not too much.'

When the rest of the midwatch gave Mag the same cat calls and whistles, she just struck a pose and slapped her right hip and shot them a steaming look, saying, 'How would you like me to whip you with a licorice rope?'

During the regular roll call, the vice cops escorted their borrowed undercover operators to their office to get them wired and briefed about the elements of 647b of the penal code, which criminalized an offer of sex for money. The decoys had to remain passive without engaging in an entrapment offer, while the cagier of the tricks would try to make them do it, knowing that entrapment would vitiate an arrest if it turned out that the hookers were cops.

After roll call, the Oracle took Fausto Gamboa aside and said privately, 'Stay away from Budgie tonight, Fausto. I mean it. You start hovering around the boulevard in a black-and-white, you'll screw it up for everybody.'

'Nobody should be giving that job to a new mother is all I got to say,' Fausto grumbled and then turned and went to partner with Benny Brewster for the night.

When Budgie and Mag were sitting in the backseat of a vice car being driven out onto east Sunset Boulevard, Mag, who had been loaned to the Trick Task Force on one other occasion, and Budgie, who had never worked as an undercover operator, kept their energy up with a lot of nervous chatter. After all, they were about to step out onto the stage, find their marks, and wait for the vice cop director to say 'Action!' All the time knowing that the part they were playing brought with it an element of danger that higher-paid Hollywood performers never had to face. But both women were eager and wanted to do well. They were smart, ambitious young cops.

Budgie noticed that her hands were trembling, and she hid them under the green plastic purse. She wondered if Mag was as nervous and said to her, 'I wanted to wear a little halter top but I figured if I did, they wouldn't be able to hide the wire.'

'I wanted my belly ring showing,' Mag said. 'But I thought the same thing about concealing the mike. I still like my ring but I'm glad I resisted the impulse to get the little butterfly above the tailbone when it was so popular.'

'Me too,' Budgie said, finding that just doing girl talk calmed her. 'Tramp stamps are out. And I'm even thinking of losing my belly ring. My gun belt rubs on it. Took almost a year to heal.'

'Mine used to rub,' Mag said, 'but now I put a layer of cotton over it and some tape before I go on duty.'

'I got mine right after work one day,' Budgie said. 'I wore my uniform to work in those days to save time for a biology class I was taking at City College. You should've seen the guy when I walked in and took off my Sam Browne. He gawked at me like, I'm putting a belly ring on a cop? His hands were shaking the whole time.'

Both women chuckled, and Simmons, the older vice cop, who was driving, turned to his partner Lane in the passenger seat and said, 'Popular culture has definitely caught up with the LAPD.'

Before they were dropped off at separate busy blocks on Sunset Boulevard, the older vice cop said to Mag, 'The order of desirability is Asian hookers first, followed by white.'

'Sorry, Budgie,' Mag said with a tense grin.

'Bet I'll catch more,' Budgie said also with a tense grin. 'I'll get all the midgets with a tall blonde fantasy.'

'For now I want you just one block apart,' Simmons said. 'There's two chase teams of blue suits to pull over the tricks after you get the offer, and two security teams including us who'll be covering you. One is already there watching both corners. 'You might have some competition who'll walk up to you and ask questions, suspecting you're cops. You're both too healthy looking.'

'I can look very bad very easily,' Budgie said.

'Won't that mess up our play?' Mag asked. 'If we get made by some hooker?'

'No,' he said. 'They'll just catch a ride ten blocks farther east and stay away from you. They know if you're cop decoys, we're close by watching out for you.'

Lane said, 'Most tricks're sick scum, but this early in the evening you might catch some ordinary businessmen driving west from the office buildings downtown. They know that better-class whores work the Sunset track and once in a while they look for a quickie.'

Budgie said, 'I haven't been in Hollywood all that long,

but I've been in on some drug busts as transporting officer for trannies and dragons. One of them might recognize me.'

'The trannies mostly work Santa Monica Boulevard,' Simmons explained. 'They do good business with all those parolees-at-large who like that track because they got a taste for dick and ass when they were in the joint. They're disease-ridden. They avoid needles for fear of AIDS, then smoke ice and take it up the toboggan run. Does that make sense? Meth is an erotic drug. Don't even shake hands with trannies or dragons without wearing gloves.'

Knowing it was Budgie's first show, Lane said to her, 'If you should see an Asian hooker on the Sunset track you can figure she might be a transsexual. Sometimes Asian trannies make good money up here because they can fool the straight tricks. Goose bumps from shaving don't show as much on them. They might arrive just before the bars close, when the tricks're too drunk to see straight. But all trannies and dragons should be considered violent felons in dresses. They like to steal a trick's car when they can, and most tricks don't like to admit how the car got stolen, so the tranny or dragon never ends up on the stolen report as a suspect.'

Simmons said, 'Just avoid all the other hookers if possible—straights, dragons, and trannies.'

'*Other* hookers?' said Budgie.

He said, 'Sorry, you're starting to look so convincing I got confused.'

When the women were dropped off half a block from the boulevard, Simmons said, 'If a black trick hits on you, go ahead and talk but look for a too-cool manner and a cool ride. He may be one of the pimps from a Wilshire track checking out the competition, or trying to muscle in. He may talk shit and try to pimp you out and we would love that to happen, but keep both feet on the sidewalk. You never load up. Never get in a car. And remember, sometimes there's interference on the wire and we can't always make out exactly what the tricks're saying to you, so we take our cues from what you say. The wires have been known to fail completely. If you ever get in trouble, the code word is "slick." Use it in a sentence and we'll all come running. If necessary yell it out. Remember: "slick."'

After all that, they were both back to being nervous when they got out. Each spoke in a normal voice into their bras and then heard the cover unit say to Simmons and Lane on their radio band, 'Got them loud and clear.'

The older vice cop seemed clearly more safety conscious, and he said, 'Don't take this wrong. I hope I'm not being sexist, but I always tell new operators, don't take foolish chances for a misdemeanor violation like this. You're competent cops but you're still women.'

'Hear me roar,' Budgie said without conviction.

The younger vice cop said, 'Showtime!'

Both women had some twilight action within the first ten minutes. Budgie traded looks with a blue-collar white guy in a GMC pickup. He circled the block only once, then pulled off Sunset and parked. She walked over to his car, mentally rehearsing the lines she might use to avoid an accusation of entrapment. She needn't have worried.

When she bent down and looked at him through the passenger window, he said, 'I don't have time for anything but a very sweet head job. I don't want to go to a motel. If you're willing to get in and do it in the alley behind the next corner, I'll pay forty bucks. If you're not, see you later.'

It was so fast and so easy that Budgie was stunned. There was no parrying back and forth, no wordplay to see if she might be a cop. Nothing. She didn't quite know how to respond other than to say, 'Okay, stop a block down Sunset by the parking lot and I'll come to you.'

And that was all she had to do, other than signal to her

security team by scratching her knee that the deal was done. Within a minute a black-and-white chase unit from Watch 3 squealed in behind the guy, lit him up with their light bar and a horn toot, and in ten minutes it was over. The trick was taken back to the mobile command post, a big RV parked two blocks from the action taking place on Sunset Boulevard.

At the CP were benches for the tricks, some folding party tables for the arrest reports, and a computerized gadget to digitally fingerprint and photograph the shell-shocked trick, after which he might be released. If he failed the attitude test or if there were other factors such as serious priors or drug possession, he would be taken to Hollywood Station for booking.

If it turned out to be a field release, the trick would find his car outside the command post, having been driven there by one of the uniformed cops, but the trick wouldn't be driving it home. The cars were usually impounded, the city attorney's office believing that impound is a big deterrent to prostitution.

Budgie was taken in a vice car to the command post, where she completed a short arrest report after telling the guy who wired her that she didn't need to hear the tape of her conversation with the trick. He was sitting there glaring at her.

He said, 'Thanks a lot.' And mouthed the word 'cunt.'

Budgie said to a vice cop, 'Maybe it's just a hormonal funk I'm in, but I'm starting to hate his guts.'

The vice cop said to Budgie, 'He's the kind of shit kicker that spent his happiest days line dancing and blowing up mailboxes.' Then to the glowering trick he said, 'This is Hollywood, dude. Let's do this cinema vérité.'

The trick scowled and said, 'What the fuck's that?'

The vice cop said, 'You just keep mouthing off, and pretend we're not in your face with a hidden video camera

165

for a scene maybe you can later interpret for momma and the kiddies.'

Mag's first came a few minutes after Budgie's. He was a white guy driving a Lexus, and from the looks of him, one of those downtown businessmen on his way home to the west side. He was more cautious than Budgie's trick and circled the block twice. But Mag was a trick magnet. He pulled around the corner after his second pass and parked.

The vice cops had said that they expected long tall Budgie to get some suspicious questions about being a police decoy, but Mag was so small, so exotic, and so sexy that she should reassure anybody. And indeed, the businessman was not interested in her bona fides.

He said, 'You look like a very clean girl. Are you?'

'Yes, I am,' she said, tempted to try a Japanese accent but changed her mind. 'Very clean.'

'I think you're quite beautiful,' he said. Then he looked around warily and said, 'But I have to know you're clean and safe.'

'I'm a very clean girl,' Mag said.

'I have a family,' he said. 'Three children. I don't want to bring any diseases into my home.'

To calm him down, Mag said, 'No, of course not. Where do you live?'

'Bel Air,' he said. Then he added, 'I've never done anything like this before.'

'No, of course not,' she said. Then came the games.

'How much do you charge?'

'What're you looking for?'

'That depends on how much you charge.'

'That depends on what you're looking for.'

'You're truly lovely,' he said. 'Your legs are so shapely yet strong.'

'Thank you, sir,' she said, figuring that matching his good manners was the way to go.

'You should always wear shorts.'

'I often do.'

'You seem intelligent. So obliging. I'll bet you know how to cater to a man.'

'Yes, sir,' she said, thinking, Jesus, does he want a Geisha or what?

'I'm old enough to be your father,' he said. 'Does that trouble you?'

'Not at all.'

'Excite you?'

'Well… maybe.'

And with that, he unzipped his fly and withdrew his erect penis and began masturbating as he cried out, 'You're so young and lovely!'

For the benefit of the cover team and because of her genuine surprise, Mag yelled into her bra, 'Holy shit! You're spanking the monkey! Get outta here!'

For a minute she forgot to scratch her knee.

Within two minutes the uniformed chase team lit up and stopped the Lexus, and when her vice cop security team pulled up, Mag said, 'Damn, he just jizzed all over his seventy-five-thousand-dollar car!'

After arriving back at the mobile CP, where the guy was booked for 647a of the penal code, lewd conduct in a public place, Mag was feeling a little bit sorry for the sick bastard.

Until after his digital photographing and fingerprinting, when he turned to Mag and said, 'The truth is, you have fat thighs. And I'll just bet you have father issues.'

'Oh, so you're a psychologist,' Mag said. 'From looking at my thighs you have me all figured out. So long, Daddy dearest.'

Then she turned to leave and noticed a handsome young

vice cop named Turner looking at her. She blushed and involuntarily glanced at her thighs.

'They're gorgeous like the rest of you,' Turner said. 'Father issues or not.'

Mag Takara hooked three tricks in two hours, and Budgie Polk got two. When Budgie's third trick, a lowlife in a battered Pontiac, offered her crystal for pussy, Budgie popped him for drug possession.

'How's that? Felony prostitution,' she said, grinning at Simmons when she arrived back at the CP.

'You're doing great, Budgie,' Simmons said. 'Have fun, but stay alert. There's lotsa real weird people out here.'

Mag met one of them ten minutes later. He was a jug-eared guy in his early forties. He drove a late-model Audi and wore clothes that Mag recognized as coming from Banana. He was the kind of guy she'd probably have danced with if he'd asked her at one of the nightclubs on the Strip that she and her girlfriends sometimes visited.

He'd been hanging back when other tricks flitted around her, making nervous small talk for a moment but then driving away in fear. Fear of cops, or fear of robbery, or fear of disease—there was plenty of fear out there mingling with the lust and sometimes enhancing it. There were plenty of neuroses.

When the guy in the Audi took his turn and talked to Mag, broaching the subject of sex for money very tentatively, he became the second guy of the evening to get so excited so fast that he unzipped his pants and exposed himself.

Mag said into her bra, 'Oh my! You're masturbating! How exciting!'

'It's you!' he said. 'It's you! I'd pay you for a blow job, but I'm tapped out. And I can't get old Jonesy stiff, goddamnit!'

And while the chase team was speeding toward the corner, the headlights from a large van lit up the interior of the Audi. Mag looked more closely, and it was true: Jonesy was not stiff. But it was bright crimson!

'Good god!' Mag said. 'Are you bleeding down there?'

He stopped and looked at her. Then he released his flaccid member and said, 'Oh, that. It's just lipstick from the other three whores that sucked it tonight. That's where all my money went.'

A bit later, Budgie violated an order from Simmons by not keeping her feet on the pavement. She couldn't believe it when a big three-axle box truck hauling calves pulled around the corner and parked in the only place he could, in the first alley north.

She couldn't resist this one, approaching the cab of the truck, even though it was very dark in the alley. She climbed up on the step and listened nervously when the scar-faced trucker in a wife beater and cowboy hat said, 'Fifty bucks. Here. Now. Climb on up and suck me off, honey.'

This one was so bizarre that when the second cover team showed up, one of the vice cops said to the guy, 'Wonder what your boss would say if we booked you into jail and impounded your vehicle.'

Budgie said to the cowboy, 'Are they going to be slaughtered?'

The cowboy was so pissed off he didn't answer at first but then said, 'I suppose you don't eat veal? I suppose you shoot your goddamn lobsters before you put them in boiling water? Gimme a break, lady.'

This one presented so many logistical problems that after a field release the cowboy was allowed to continue on his way with his cargo.

When Budgie was finished at the CP and taken back to her corner on Sunset Boulevard, she tried not to remember the doomed calves bawling. It was the first time that evening that she was truly sad.

Budgie wasn't standing on Sunset Boulevard for three minutes when a Hyundai with Arkansas plates pulled up with two teenagers inside. She was still feeling depressed about the calves and about the pathetically reckless husbands and fathers she and Mag had hooked tonight, and she wondered what diseases all these losers would bring home to their wives. Maybe the fatal one. Maybe the Big A.

She could see right away what she was dealing with here: a pair of Marines. Both had tan lines from the middle of their foreheads down, and skinned whitewalls with an inch or two of hair on top. Both were wearing cheap T-shirts with glittery names of rock groups across the front, shirts that they'd probably just bought from a souvenir shop on Hollywood Boulevard. Both had dopey nervous smiles on their dopey young faces, and after being inexplicably sad, Budgie was now inexplicably mad.

The passenger said to her, 'Hey, good-lookin'!'

Budgie walked to the car and said, 'If you say, "Whatchya got cookin'?" I might have to shoot you.'

The word "shoot" changed the dynamic at once. The kid said, 'I hope you're not carrying a gun or something?'

'Why?' Budgie said. 'Can't a girl protect herself out here?'

The kid tried to recover some of his bravado and said, 'Know where we could get some action?'

'Action,' Budgie said. 'And what do you mean by that?'

The passenger glanced at the driver, who was even more nervous, and said, 'Well, we'd like to party. Know what I mean?'

'Yeah,' Budgie said. 'I know what you mean.'

'If it's not too expensive,' he said.

'And what do you mean by that?' Budgie said.

'We can pay seventy bucks,' the kid said. 'But you have to do both of us, okay?'

'Where're you stationed?' Budgie asked, figuring a chase or cover team was getting ready.

'Whadda you mean?' the passenger said.

'I was born at night, but not last night.' They're no more than eighteen, she thought.

'Camp Pendleton,' the kid said, losing his grin.

'When're you leaving for Iraq?'

The kid was really confused now, and he looked at the driver and back to Budgie and trying to retrieve some of the machismo said, 'In three weeks. Why, are you going to give us a free one out of patriotism?'

'No, you dumb little jarhead asshole,' Budgie said. 'I'm gonna give you a pass so you can go to Iraq and get your dumb little ass blown up. I'm a police officer and there's a team of vice cops one minute away, and if you're still here when they arrive you'll have some explaining to do to your CO. Now, get the fuck outta Hollywood and don't ever come back!'

'Yes, ma'am!' the kid said. 'Thank you, ma'am!'

And they were gone before her cover team drove slowly past the corner, and Budgie saw that cute vice cop named Turner shake his head at her, then shrug his shoulders as if to say, It's okay to throw one back, but don't make a habit of it.

The vice cops knew that their operators would need a break about now, so they suggested code 7 at a nearby Burger King, but Mag and Budgie asked to be dropped at a Japanese restaurant farther west on Sunset. They figured that the male officers wouldn't eat raw fish, and they'd had enough of that gender for a while. Thirty minutes to rest their feet and talk about their night's work would be a blessing. The vice cops dropped them and said they'd pick them up for one more hour and then call it a night.

Turner said, all the time looking at Mag, 'Another hour and it's a wrap.'

When Budgie and Mag got inside the restaurant, Budgie said, 'Jesus, in this division *all* the coppers use movie expressions.'

Mag ordered a plate of mixed sashimi, and Budgie a less courageous sushi plate, trying to observe protocol and not blatantly scrape the wooden chopsticks together, as so many round-eyes did at sushi joints. She lowered them to her lap and did it, dislodging a few splinters from the cheap disposable utensils.

Budgie said, 'Do I ever regret borrowing these stilettos.'

'My canines are barking too,' Mag said, looking down.

'How many you hooked so far?'

'Three,' she said.

'Hey, I pulled ahead by one,' Budgie said. 'And I threw a pair back. Jarheads from Camp Pendleton. I was the righteous bitch from hell they'll always remember.'

'I haven't found any worth throwing back,' Mag said. 'Lowest kind of scum is what I've met. Maybe I shouldn't have worn the S&M wardrobe.'

'You still into competitive shooting?' Budgie asked. 'I read about you in the *Blue Line* when I worked Central.'

'Kinda losing interest,' Mag said. 'Guys don't like to shoot with me. Afraid I'll beat them. I even stopped wearing the distinguished expert badge on my uniform.'

'Know what you mean,' Budgie said. 'If we girls even talk about guns, we're gay, right?'

'U.S. Customs had a recent shoot that I was asked to compete in. Until I saw it was called "Ladies Pistol Shoot." Can you believe that? When I got asked, I said, "Oh, goodie. With high tea and cotillion?" The guy from Customs didn't get it.'

Budgie said, 'I had three guys tonight ask me if I was a cop. I was tempted to say, 'Would you like to ask that again with your dick in my mouth?'

Both laughed, and Mag said, 'I got a feeling Simmons

would call that entrapment. Did you get a good look at Turner? Mr. eye candy?'

'I got a good look at him getting a good look at you,' Budgie said.

'Maybe he's into bondage bitches,' Mag said.

'I got a feeling he'd be interested if you wore overalls and combat boots.'

'Wonder if he's married.'

'God, why do we inbreed with other cops?' Budgie said. 'Why not cross-pollinate with firemen or something?'

'Yeah, there must be other ways to fuck up our lives,' Mag said. 'But he sure is cute.'

'Probably lousy in bed,' Budgie said. 'The cute ones often are.'

Mag said, 'Couldn't be as bad as a twisted detective from Seventy-seventh Street I used to date. The kind that buys you two drinks and expects to mate in his rape room within the hour. He actually stole one of my thongs, the creep.'

Budgie said, 'I hooked a drunk tonight who could hardly drive the car. When the cover team called a shop to take him to jail, he asked me if I was seeing someone. Then he asked me if I could get him out of jail. He asked me a dozen questions. When they took him away I had to tell him, "Yes, I'm seeing someone. No, I can't get you out of jail. No, I can't help it that you have strong feelings for me. And no, this encounter was not caused by fate, it was caused by Compstat." Christ, I just turn on my dumb-blonde switch and they can't let go. The guy tried to hug me when they were writing the citation! He said he forgave me.'

Mag said, 'One trick wanted to really hurt me when they badged him, I could tell. He was eye-fucking me the whole time they were writing him up, and he said, "Maybe I'll see you out on the street sometime, Officer."'

'What'd you say?'

'I said, "Yeah, I know you're bigger than me. I know you can kick my ass. But if I ever run into you and you ever try it, I will shoot you until you are dead. I will shoot you in the face, and you'll have a closed-casket funeral."'

Budgie said, 'When I was a boot I used to say to creepy vermin like that, "You don't get any status points for hitting a girl. But if you try it, my partners will pepper-spray you and kick *your* ass big time."'

'Whadda you tell them these days?'

'I don't. If nobody's looking, I just take out the OC spray and give them a shot of Liquid Jesus. For a while my partners were calling me "OC Polk."'

Mag said, 'The only really scary moment I had tonight was when one trick pulled a little too far off Sunset, and I had to walk past the parking lot. And a big rat ran right across my foot!'

'Oh, my god!' Budgie said. 'What'd you do, girl?'

'I screamed. And then I had to quick tell the cover team that everything was okay. I didn't want to admit it was only a rat.'

Budgie said, 'I'm terrified of rats. Spiders too. I would've cried.'

'I almost did,' Mag said. 'I just had to hang on.'

'How's your sashimi?'

'Not as fresh as I like it. How's your sushi?'

'Healthy,' Budgie said. 'With Fausto I eat burritos and get more fat grams than the whole female population of Laurel Canyon consumes in a week.'

'But they burn calories shopping for plastic surgeons and prepping their meals,' Mag said. 'Imagine laying out a weekly diet of celery stalks and carrot strips according to feng shui.'

Budgie thought about how pleasant and restful it was just to sit there and drink tea and talk to another girl.

*

During the last hour, Budgie hooked one more trick, and Mag wanted to soar past her with two, but business was slowing. They had only thirty minutes to go when Mag saw a cherry-red Mercedes SUV with chrome wheels drive slowly past. The driver was a young black man in a three-hundred-dollar warm-up suit and pricey Adidas. He made one pass, then another.

Mag didn't return his smile the way she had been doing to other tricks that night, including two who were black. This guy made her think one word: 'pimp.' Then she realized that if she was right, this could be the topper of the evening. A felony bust for pimping. So on his next pass, she returned the smile and he pointed just around the corner and parked the SUV. A hip-hop album was blasting out, and he turned it down to talk.

When she approached cautiously, he said, 'What's a matter, Momma, ain't you into chocolate delight?'

Yeah, he's a pimp, she thought, saying, 'I like all kind of delights.'

'I bet you do,' he said. 'Jump on in here and le's talk bidness.'

'I'm okay out here.'

'What's wrong?' he said. 'You a cop or somethin'?'

He smiled big when he said it, and she knew he didn't believe it. She said, 'I can talk out here.'

'Come on in, baby,' he said, and his pupils looked dilated. 'I might got somethin' for you.'

'What?' she said.

'Somethin'.'

'What something?'

'Get in,' he said, and she didn't like the way he said it this time. He was amped, all right. Maybe crack, maybe crystal.

'I don't think so,' she said and started to walk away. This wasn't going right.

He opened the door of the SUV and jumped out, striding

around the back and standing between her and Sunset Boulevard. She was about to use the code word 'slick' but thought about what it would mean if she brought down a pimp. She said, 'You better talk fast because I don't have time for bullshit.'

And he said, 'You think you gonna come and work this corner? You ain't, not without somebody lookin' out for you. And that ain't no bullshit. That is righteous.'

'Whadda do you mean?' Mag said.

'I'm gonna be your protector,' he said.

'Like my old man?' she said. 'I don't need one.'

'Yes, you do, bitch,' he said. 'And the protection has started. So how much you made tonight so far? Working on my corner. On my boulevard.'

'I think you better get outta the way, Slick,' Mag said. And now she was definitely scared and could see one of the vice cops running across Sunset Boulevard in her direction.

She was still looking for her mobile cover team when he said, 'I'm gonna show you what is slick.'

And she was shocked when his fist struck. She hadn't seen coming it at all. Her face had been turned toward the boulevard while she waited for her security, thinking, Hurry up. Her head hit the pavement when she fell. Mag felt dizzy and sick to her stomach and tried to get up, but he was sitting on top of her, big hands all over her, looking for her money stash.

'In yo pussy?' he said, and she felt his hands down there. Felt his fingers exploring inside her.

Then she heard car doors slam and voices shouting and the pimp screaming, and she got so sick she vomited all over her bondage bitch costume. And the curtain descended on the last performance of the evening.

Fausto Gamboa was driving when he heard the gut-churning 'Officer down' and that an ambulance was racing code 3 to the Sunset Boulevard whore track. He almost gave Benny Brewster whiplash cranking the steering wheel hard left and blowing a stop sign like it wasn't there. Speeding toward Sunset Boulevard.

'Oh, god!' he said. 'It's one of the girls. I knew it. I knew it.'

Benny Brewster, who had worked with Mag Takara for most of the deployment period, said, 'I hope it's not Mag.'

Fausto glanced sharply at him and felt a rush of anger but then thought, I can't blame Benny for hoping it's Budgie. I'm hoping it's Mag. That was an awful feeling, but there was no time to sort it out. When he made the next left he felt two wheels almost lifting.

The Oracle had been taking code 7 at his favorite taco joint on Hollywood Boulevard when the call came out. He was standing beside his car, working on his second *carne asada* taco and sucking down an enormous cup of *horchata*, Mexican rice water and cinnamon, when he heard 'Officer down.'

He was the first one at the scene other than all the security teams and the paramedics loading Mag into the ambulance. Budgie was sitting in the backseat of a vice car, weeping, and the pimp was handcuffed and lying on the sidewalk near the alley, crying out in pain.

Simmons, the oldest of the vice cops, said to the Oracle, 'We got another ambulance coming.'

'How's Mag?'

'Pretty bad, Sarge,' Simmons said. 'Her left eye was lying out on her cheek. The bones around the eye socket were just about crushed, from what I could see.'

'Oh no,' the Oracle said.

'He hit her once and she fell back and her head bounced off the sidewalk. I think she was awake sort of when we first rolled up, but not now.'

The Oracle pointed to the pimp and said, 'How about

him?' And then he saw it in the vice cop's face when Simmons hesitated and said, 'He resisted.'

'Do you know if FID has been notified?'

'Yeah, we called our boss,' Simmons said. 'They'll all be here soon.'

The vice cop's eyes didn't meet the Oracle's when he finally said, 'There's a guy in the liquor store might want to make a complaint about... how we handled the arrest. He was yammering about it. I told him to wait until Force Investigation Division arrives. I'm hoping he'll change his mind before then.'

'I'll talk to him,' the Oracle said. 'Maybe I can calm him down.'

When the Oracle was walking toward the liquor store, he saw a young vice cop pacing nervously and being spoken to very earnestly by one of the other vice cops. The second ambulance arrived, and the Oracle heard the pimp moan when they put him on the litter.

In the liquor store, the elderly Pakistani proprietor completed a transaction for a customer, then turned to the Oracle and said, 'Are you here for my report?'

'What did you see?' the Oracle asked.

'I hear car doors slam. I hear a man scream. Loud. I hear shouts. Curses. A man screams more. I run out. I see a young white man kicking a black man on the ground. Kick kick kick. Curses and kicks. I see other white men grab the young man and pull him away. The black man continues the screams. Plenty of screams. I see handcuffs. I know these are policemen. I know they come to this block to arrest the women of the street. That is my report.'

'There will be some investigators coming to talk to you,' the Oracle said, leaving the liquor store.

Budgie and one vice car were gone. Four vice cops and two cars were still there. The young cop who had been pacing when the Oracle arrived walked up to him and said,

'I know I'm in trouble here, Sarge. I know there's a civilian witness.'

'Maybe you want to call the Protective League's hotline and get lawyered up before making any statements,' the Oracle said.

'I will,' the vice cop said.

'What's your name, son?' the Oracle asked. 'I can't remember anybody's name anymore.'

'Turner,' he said. 'Rob Turner. I never worked your watch when I was in patrol.'

'Rob,' the Oracle said, 'I don't want you making any statements to me. Call the League. You have rights, so don't be afraid to exercise them.'

It was obvious that Turner trusted the Oracle by reputation, and he said, 'I only want you to know… everybody to know… that when I arrived, that fucking pimp was sitting on her with his hands down inside her pants. That beautiful girl, her face was a horrible sight. I want all the coppers to know what I saw when I arrived. And that I'm not sorry for anything except losing my badge. I'm real sorry about that.'

'That's enough talking, son,' the Oracle said. 'Go sit in your car and get your thoughts together. Get lawyered up. You've got a long night ahead of you.'

When the Oracle returned to his car to make his notifications, he saw Fausto and Benny Brewster parked across the street, talking to a vice cop. They looked grim. Fausto crossed the street, coming toward him, and the Oracle hoped this wasn't going to be an I-told-you-so, because he wasn't in the mood, not a bit.

But all Fausto said to him before he and Benny Brewster left the scene was 'This is a crummy job, Merv.'

The Oracle opened a packet of antacid tablets, and said, 'Old dogs like you and me, Fausto? It's all we got. Semper cop.'

ELEVEN

Early that morning Mag Takara underwent surgery at Cedars Sinai to reconstruct facial bones, with more surgeries to follow, the immediate concern being to save the vision in her left eye. After being booked into the prison ward at USCMC, the pimp, Reginald Clinton Walker, also went under the knife, to have his ruptured spleen removed. Walker would be charged with felony assault because of the great bodily injury suffered by Officer Takara, but of course the serious charge of felony assault on a police officer could not be alleged in this case.

There wasn't a cop on the midwatch who didn't think that the felony assault and the pimping allegation wouldn't be the subject of plea bargain negotiations, but both the area captain and the patrol captain vowed that they'd do all they could to keep the DA onboard for a vigorous felony prosecution. However, a caveat was added, because as soon as Walker filed a multimillion-dollar lawsuit against the LAPD and the city for having his spleen destroyed, who could say what the outcome would be?

That afternoon, an hour before midwatch roll call, the floor nurse at Cedars saw a tall man in T-shirt and jeans with a dark suntan and bleached streaky hair enter the ward, carrying an enormous bouquet of red and yellow roses. Sitting outside the room of Officer Mag Takara were her mother, father, and two younger sisters, who were crying.

The nurse said, 'Are those for Officer Takara, by chance?'

'Yeah.'

'I thought so,' she said. 'You're the fourth. But she can't see anybody today except immediate family. They're waiting outside her room for her to have her dressing changed. You can talk to them if you like.'

'I don't wanna bother them,' he said.

'The flowers are beautiful. Do you want me to take them?'

'Sure,' he said. 'Just put them in her room when you get a chance.'

'Is there a card?'

'I forgot,' he said. 'No, no card.'

'Shall I tell her who brought them?'

'Just tell her... tell her that when she's feeling better, she should have her family take her to the beach.'

'The beach?'

'Yeah. The ocean is a great healer. You can tell her that if you want.'

At midwatch roll call the lieutenant was present, along with three sergeants, including the Oracle. He got the job of explaining what had happened and having it make sense, as though that were possible. The cops were demoralized by the events on Sunset Boulevard the night before, and they were angry, and all the supervisors knew it.

When he was asked to be the one to talk about it, the Oracle said to the lieutenant, 'In his memoir, T. E. Lawrence of Arabia said old and wise means tired and disappointed. He didn't live long enough to know how right he was.'

At 5:30 p.m. the Oracle, sitting next to the lieutenant, popped a couple of antacid tablets and said to the assembly of cops in the roll call room, 'The latest report is that Mag is resting and alert. There doesn't appear to be any brain damage, and the surgeon in charge says that they're optimistic about restoring vision in her eye. At least most of the vision.'

The room was as quiet as the Oracle had ever heard it, until Budgie Polk, her voice quavering, said, 'Will she look... the same, do they think?'

'She has great surgeons taking care of her. I'm sure she'll look fine. Eventually.'

Fausto, who was sitting next to Budgie, said, 'Is she coming back to work after she's well?'

'It's too soon to say,' the Oracle said. 'That will depend on her. On how she feels after everything.'

'She'll come back,' Fausto said. 'She picked up a grenade, didn't she?'

Budgie started to say something else but couldn't. Fausto patted her hand for a second.

The Oracle said, 'The detectives and our captains have promised that the pimp will go to the joint for this, if they can help it.'

B.M. Driscoll said, 'Maybe they can't help it. I'm sure he's got half a dozen shysters emptying his bedpan right this minute. He'll make more money from a lawsuit than he could make from every whore on Sunset.'

'Yeah, our activist mayor and his handpicked, cop-hating police commissioner will be all over this one,' Jetsam said. 'And we'll hear from the keepers of the consent decree. No doubt.'

Before the Oracle could answer, Flotsam said, 'I suppose the race card will be played here. Dealt from the bottom of the deck, as usual.'

That's what the lieutenant hadn't wanted, the issue of race entering what he knew would be a heated exchange today. But race affected everything in Los Angeles from top to bottom, including the LAPD, and he knew that too.

Looking very uncomfortable, the lieutenant said, 'It's true that the media and the activists and others might have a field day with this. A white cop kicking the guts out of a black arrestee. They'll want Officer Turner not just fired but prosecuted, and maybe he will be. And you'll hear accusations that this proves we're all racists.'

'I got somethin' to say about it, Lieutenant.'

Conversation stopped then. Benny Brewster, the former partner of Mag Takara, the only black cop on the midwatch and in the room except for a night-watch sergeant sitting on the lieutenant's right, had something to say about what? The race card? White on black? The lieutenant was very uncomfortable. He didn't need this snarky shit.

Every eye was on Benny Brewster, who said, 'If it was me that got there first instead of Turner and seen what he seen, I'd be in jail. 'Cause I'da pulled my nine and emptied the magazine into that pimp. So I'd be in jail now. That's all I got to say.'

There was a murmur of approval, and a few cops even clapped. The lieutenant wanted to give them a time-out, wanted to restore order, and was trying to figure out how to do it, when the Oracle took over again.

The Oracle looked at all those faces, wondering how it was possible that they could be so young. And he said to them, 'The shield you're wearing is the most beautiful·and most famous badge in the world. Many police departments have copied it and everyone envies it, but you wear the original. And all these critics and politicians and media assholes come and go, but your badge remains unchanged. You can get as mad and outraged as you want over what's going to go down, but don't get cynical. Being cynical will make you old. Doing good police work is the greatest fun there is. The greatest fun you'll ever have in your lives. So go on out tonight and have some fun. And Fausto, try to get by with only two burritos. Speedo weather's coming up.'

After they had handled two calls and written one traffic ticket, Budgie Polk turned to Fausto Gamboa and said, 'I'm okay, Fausto. Honest.'

Fausto, who was riding shotgun, said, 'Whaddaya mean?'

'I mean you gotta quit asking me if I want you to roll up the window or where do I wanna have code seven or do I need my jacket. Last night is over. I'm okay.'

'I don't mean to be a—'

'Nanny. So you can stop now.'

Fausto got quiet then, a bit embarrassed, and she added, 'The Li'l Rascals didn't want Darla in their clubhouse either. But we're in. So you can all just live with it, especially you, you cranky old sexist.'

Budgie glanced sideways at him and he quickly looked out at the boulevard, but she saw a little bit of a smile that he couldn't hide.

Things got back to normal when Budgie went after a silver Saab that pulled out of Paramount Studios heading west a good three seconds late at the first traffic signal. The driver had a cell to his ear.

'Jesus,' she said, 'what's he doing, talking to his agent?'

When they had the Saab pulled over, the driver tried charming Budgie, whose turn it was to write one. He said with an attempt at a flirtatious grin, 'I couldn't have busted the light, Officer. It didn't even turn yellow until I was in the intersection.'

'You were very late on the red signal, sir,' Budgie said, looking at his license, then at the guy, whose grin came off as smarmy and annoying.

'I would never argue with a police officer as attractive as you,' he said, 'but couldn't you be a little mistaken on the light? I'm a very careful driver.'

Budgie started walking back to her car, putting her citation book on the hood to write while Fausto kept his eyes on the driver, who quickly got out and came back to her. Budgie nodded at Fausto that she could handle this schmuck, and Fausto stayed put.

'Before you start writing,' he said, all the charm gone

now, 'I'd like to ask for a break here. One more ticket and I'll lose my insurance. I'm in the film business, and I need a driver's license.'

Without looking up, Budgie said, 'Oh, you've had other citations, have you? I thought you said you were a careful driver.'

When she began writing he stormed back to his car, got behind the wheel, and made a call on his cell.

Budgie finished the citation and took it to him, but Fausto stayed glued to the right side of the guy's car, watching his hands like the guy was a gangbanger. She knew that Fausto was still playing guardian angel, but what the hell—it was kind of comforting in a way.

After finishing, she presented the ticket and said, 'This is not an admission of guilt, only a promise to appear.'

The driver snatched the ticket book from her hand, scrawled his signature, and gave it back to her, saying in a low voice that Fausto couldn't hear, 'I'll just bet you get off on fucking over men, don't you? I'll bet you don't even know what a cock looks like that doesn't have batteries included. I'll see you in court.'

Budgie removed his copy, handed it to him, and said, 'I know what a cassette player looks like with batteries included. This.' And she patted the rover on her belt that was the size of a cassette player. 'Let's have a jury trial. I'd love for them to hear what you think of women police officers.'

Without a word he drove away, and Budgie said to the disappearing car, 'Bye-bye, cockroach.'

When Fausto got in the car he said, 'That is an unhappy citizen.'

'But he won't take me to court.'

'How do you know.' She patted the rover.

'He said naughty things and I recorded them on my little tape machine.'

Fausto said, 'Did he fall for that dumb gag?'

'Right on his ass,' she said.

'Sometimes you're not quite as boring as other young coppers,' Fausto said to her, then added, 'How you feeling?'

'Don't start that again.'

'No, I mean the mommy stuff.'

'I may have to stop at the milking station later.'

'I'm gonna keep your gun in the car with me next time,' Fausto said.

Farley Ramsdale was in an awful mood that afternoon. The so-called ice he bought from some thieving lowlife greaser asshole at Pablo's Tacos, where tweakers did business 24/7, had turned out to be shitty. The worst part was having to sit there for an hour waiting for the guy and listening to hip-hop blasting from the car of a pair of basehead smokes who were also waiting for the greaseball. What were they doing in Hollywood?

It turned out to be the worst crystal he'd ever scored. Even Olive complained that they'd been screwed. But it got them tweaked, the proof being that they were both awake all night, pulse rates zooming, trying to fix a VCR that had stopped rewinding. They had parts all over the floor, and they both fell asleep for an hour or so just before noon.

When Farley woke up, he was so disgusted he just kicked the VCR parts under the couch among all the dust balls and yelled, 'Olive! Wake up and get your skinny ass in motion. We got to go to work, for chrissake.'

She was off the couch before he stopped grumbling, and said, 'Okay, Farley. Whatcha want for breakfast?'

Farley pulled himself painfully to his feet. He just had to stop passing out on the couch. He wasn't a kid anymore and his back was killing him. Farley looked at Olive, who was staring at him with that eager, gap-toothed grille, and he stepped closer and looked into her mouth.

'Goddamnit, Olive,' he said. 'Have you lost another tooth lately?'

'I don't think so, Farley,' she said.

He couldn't remember right now either. He had a headache that felt like Nelly or some other nigger was rapping inside his skull. 'You lose another tooth and that's it. I'm kicking your ass outta here,' he said.

'I can get false teeth, Farley!' Olive whined.

'You look enough like George Washington already,' he said. 'Just get the goddamn oatmeal going.'

'Can I first run over to see Mabel for a couple minutes? She's very old, and I'm worried about her.'

'Oh, by all means, take care of the local witch,' he said. 'Maybe next time she makes a stew outta rats and frogs, she'll save a bowl for us.'

Olive ran out of the house, across the street and down three houses to the only home on the block that had weeds taller than those in Farley's yard. Mabel's house was a wood-frame cottage built decades after Farley's stucco bungalow, during the 1950s era of cheap construction. The paint was blistered, chipped, and peeling in many places, and the screen door was so rusted a strong touch would make chunks crumble away.

The inside door was open, so Olive peered through the screen and yelled, 'Mabel, you there?'

'Yes, Olive, come in!' a surprisingly strong voice called back to her.

Olive entered and found Mabel sitting at the kitchen table drinking a cup of tea with lemon slices. She had a few vanilla cookies on a saucer next to a ball of yarn and knitting needles.

Mabel was eighty-eight years old and had owned that cottage for forty-seven years. She wore a bathrobe over a T-shirt and cotton sweatpants. Her face was lined but still held its shape. She weighed less than one hundred pounds but had lots more teeth than Olive. She lived alone and was independent.

'Hello, Olive, dear,' Mabel said. 'Pour yourself a nice cup of tea and have a cookie.'

'I can't stay, Mabel. Farley wants his breakfast.'

'Breakfast? At this time of day?'

'He slept late,' Olive said. 'I just wanted to make sure you're okay and see if you need anything from the market.'

'That's sweet of you, dear,' Mabel said. 'I don't need anything today.'

Olive felt a stab of guilt then because every time she shopped for Mabel, Farley kept at least five dollars from Mabel's change, even though the old woman was surviving on Social Security and her late husband's small pension. Once Farley had kept thirteen dollars, and Olive knew that Mabel knew, but the old woman never said a word.

Mabel had no children or other relatives, and she'd told Olive many times that she dreaded the day when she might have to sell her cottage and move into a county home, where the money from her cottage sale would be used by county bureaucrats to pay for her keep the rest of her life. She hated the thought of it. All Mabel's old friends had died or moved away, and now Olive was the only friend she had in the neighborhood. And Mabel was grateful.

'Take some cookies with you, dear,' Mabel said. 'You're getting so thin I'm worried about you.'

Olive took two of the cookies and said, 'Thanks, Mabel. I'll look in on you later tonight. To make sure you're okay.'

'I wish you could watch TV with me some evening. I don't sleep much at all anymore, and I know you don't sleep much. I see your lights on at all hours.'

'Farley has trouble sleeping,' Olive said.

'I wish he treated you better,' Mabel said. 'I'm sorry to say that, but I really do.'

'He ain't so bad,' Olive said. 'When you get to know him.'

'I'll save some food for you in case you stop in tonight,' Mabel said. 'I can never eat all the stew I cook. That's what happens to old widows like me. We're always cooking the way we did when our husbands were alive.'

'I'll sneak over later,' Olive said. 'I love your stew.'

Pointing at her orange tabby cat, Mabel said, 'And Olive, if Tillie here comes around your house again, please bring her when you come.'

'Oh, I love having her,' Olive said. 'She chases away all the rats.'

Late that afternoon, they were finally on the street, the first day that they'd gotten Farley's car running and Sam's Pinto returned to him.

'Goddamn transmission's slipping on this fucking Jap junker,' Farley said. 'When we collect from the Armenian, I'm thinking of looking around for another ride.'

'We also need a new washing machine, Farley,' Olive said.

'No, I like my T-shirts stiff enough to bust a knife blade,' he said. 'Makes me feel safe around all those greaseballs at Pablo's Tacos.' He was thinking, When Cosmo pays me, bye-bye, Olive. Barnacles are less clingy than this goofy bitch.

He lit a smoke while he drove and, as so often happened since his thirtieth birthday three years ago, he started feeling nostalgic about Hollywood. Remembering how it was when he was a kid, back in those glorious days at Hollywood High School.

He blew smoke rings at the windshield and said, 'Look out the window, Olive, whadda you see?'

Olive hated it when he asked questions like that. She knew if she said the wrong thing, he'd yell at her. But she was obedient and looked at the commercial properties on the boulevard, here on the east side of Hollywood. 'I see… well… I see… stores.'

Farley shook his head and blew more smoke from his nose, but he did it like a snort of disgust that made Olive nervous. He said, 'Do you see one fucking sign in your mother tongue?'

'In my...'

'In English, goddamnit.'

'Well, a couple.'

'My point is, you might as well live in fucking Bangkok as live near Hollywood Boulevard between Bronson and Normandie. Except here, dope and pussy ain't a bargain like over there. My point is that gooks and spics are everywhere. Not to mention Russkies and Armos, like those fucking thieves Ilya and Cosmo, who wanna take over Hollywood. And I must not forget the fucking Filipinos. The Flips are crawling all over the streets near Santa Monica Boulevard, taking other people's jobs emptying bedpans and jacking up their cars on concrete blocks because no gook in history ever learned to drive like a white man. Do you see what's happening to us Americans?'

'Yes, Farley,' she said.

'What, Olive?' he demanded. 'What's happening to us Americans?'

Olive felt her palms, and they were moist and not just from the crystal. She was on the spot again, having to respond to a question when she had no idea what the answer was. It was like when she was a foster child, a ward of San Bernardino County, living with a family in Cucamonga, going to a new school and never knowing the answer when the teacher called on her.

And then she remembered what to say! 'We'll be the ones needing green cards, Farley,' she said.

'Fucking A,' he said, blowing another cloud through his nose. 'You got that right.'

When they reached the junkyard and he drove through the open gate, which was usually kept chained, he parked near the little office. He was about to get out but suddenly learned why the gate was open. They had other security now.

'Goddamn!' Farley yelled when a Doberman ran at the car, barking and snarling.

The junkyard proprietor, known to Farley as Gregori, came out of his office and shouted 'Odar!' to the dog, who retreated and got locked inside.

When Gregori returned, his face stained with axle grease, he wiped his hands and said, 'Better than chaining my gate. And Odar don't get impressed by police badges.'

He was a lean and wiry man with inky thinning hair, wearing a sweat shirt and grease-caked work pants. Inside the garage a late-model Cadillac Escalade, or most of it, was up on a hydraulic lift. The car lacked two wheels and a front bumper, and two Latino employees were working on the undercarriage.

Olive remained in the car, and when Gregori and Farley were alone, Farley presented a stack of twenty-three key cards to Gregori, who looked them over and said, 'What hotel do these come from?'

'Olive gets them by hanging around certain hotels on the boulevards,' Farley said. 'People leave them at the front desk and in the lobby by the phones. And in the hotel bars.'

Then Farley realized he was making it sound too easy, so he said, 'It's risky and time-consuming, and you need a woman to do it. If you or me tried hanging around a hotel, their security would be all over us in no time. Plus, you gotta know which hotel has the right key cards. Olive has that special knowledge but she ain't sharing it.'

'Five bucks apiece I give you.'

'Come on, Gregori,' Farley said. 'These key cards are in primo condition. The perfect size and color. With a good-looking mag strip. You can buy those bogus driver's licenses from Cosmo and they'll glue to the front of the card just perfect. They'll pass inspection with any cop on the street.'

'I don't talk to Cosmo in a long time,' Gregori said. 'You see him lately?'

'Naw, I ain't seen him in a year,' Farley lied. Then, 'Look, Gregori, for very little money every fucking wetback that works in all your businesses can be a licensed driver tomorrow. Not to mention your friends and relatives from the old country.'

'Friends and relatives from Armenia can get real driver's license,' Gregori said imperiously.

'Of course they can,' Farley said, apologetically. 'I just meant like when they first get here. I been in a couple of Armenian homes in east Hollywood. Look like crap on the outside, but once you get inside, there's a fifty-two-inch TV and a sound system that'd blow out the walls if you cranked it. And maybe a white Bentley in the garage. I know you people are real smart businessmen.'

'You know that, Farley, then you know I ain't paying more than five dollars for cards,' Gregori said, taking out his wallet.

When Farley accepted the deal and was driving back to the boulevard to score some crystal, he said to Olive, 'That cheap communist cocksucker. You see what was up on that lift?'

'A new car?' Olive said.

'A new Escalade. That Armo gets one of his greasers to steal one. Then they strip it right down to the frame and dump the hot frame with its hot numbers. They search every junkyard in the county till they find a wrecked Escalade. They buy the frame, bring it here, and reassemble all the stolen parts right onto their cold frame, then register it at DMV. It's a real Armo trick. They're like fucking Gypsy tribes. Cosmo's one of them. We shoulda nuked all the Soviet puppet states when we had the chance.'

'I'm scared of Cosmo, Farley,' Olive said, but he ignored her, still pissed off at the price he got for the key cards.

'Hear what he called his dog? Odar. That's what Armenians call us non-Armos. Fucking goat eater. If I wasn't a man of property, I'd get outta Hollywood and away from all these immigrant assholes.'

'Farley,' Olive said. 'When your mom left you the house, it was paid for, right?'

'Of course it was paid for. Shit, when my parents bought the house, it only cost about thirty-nine grand.'

'You could sell it for a lot now, Farley,' Olive said. 'We could go somewhere else and not do this thing with Cosmo and Ilya.'

'Pull yourself together,' he said. 'This is the biggest score of my life. I ain't walking away. So just deal with it.'

'We could stop using crystal,' Olive said. 'You could go into rehab, and I really think I could kick if you was in rehab.'

'Oh, I see,' he said. 'I've led you into a life of drugs and crime, is that it? You were a virgin cheerleader before you met me?'

'That ain't what I mean, Farley,' she said. 'I just think I could kick if you did.'

'Be sure to tell that to the casting director when he asks you to tell him all about yourself. You were a good girl seduced into the life by a wicked, wicked man. Who, by the way, provides you with a house and car and food and clothes and every fucking thing that makes life worthwhile!'

Farley parked four blocks from Hollywood Boulevard to keep from getting a ticket, and they walked to one of the boulevard's tattoo parlors, one owned by a member of an outlaw bikers gang. A nervous young man was in a chair being worked on by a bearded tattoo artist with a dirty blond ponytail wearing a red tank top, jeans, and sandals. He was drawing what looked like a unicorn on the guy's left shoulder.

The artist nodded to Farley, dabbed some blood from his customer's arm, and said to him, 'Be right back.' Then he walked to a back room, followed by Farley.

When Farley and the tattoo artist were in the back, Farley said, 'A pair of teens.'

The artist left him, entered a second room and returned in a few minutes with the teeners of crystal in plastic bindles.

Farley gave the guy six twenty-dollar bills and returned to the front, where Olive stood admiring the design on the young man's shoulder, but the guy just looked sick and full of regret.

Olive smiled and said to him, 'That's going to be a beautiful tattoo. Is it a horse or a zebra?'

'Olive, let's go,' Farley said.

Walking to the car, Farley said, 'Fucking bikers're lousy artists. People get bubbles under the skin. All scarred up. Hackers is what they are.'

They were halfway home and stopped at a traffic signal when Olive blurted, 'Know what, Farley? Do you think it might be a little bit big for us? I mean, trying to make Cosmo give us ten thousand dollars? Don't it scare you a little bit?'

'Scare me?' he said. 'I'll tell you what I been thinking. I been thinking about pulling the same gag on that cheap fucking Gregori, that's what I been thinking. Fuck him. I ain't doing business with the cheap bastard no more, so I wonder how he'd like it if I phoned him up and said I was gonna call the cops and tell them what I know about his salvage business. I wonder how he'd like reaching in that fat wallet and pulling out some real green to shut me up.'

Olive's hands were sweating more now. She didn't like the way things were changing so fast. The way Farley was changing. She was very scared of Cosmo and even scared of Ilya.

She said, 'I think it will be just awful to meet with Cosmo and collect the money from him. I'm very worried about you, Farley.'

Farley looked surprised and said, 'I'm not stupid, Olive. The fucker robbed the jewelry store with a gun. You think I'm gonna meet him in some lonely place or something? No way. It's gonna happen in a nice safe place with people around.'

'That's good,' Olive said.

'And you're gonna do it, of course. Not me.'

'Me?'

'It's way safe for you,' Farley said. 'It's me he hates. You'll be just fine.'

At 7 p.m. that evening, Gregori phoned his business acquaintance Cosmo Betrossian and had a conversation with him in their language. Gregori told Cosmo that he had had a visitor and had bought some hotel key cards from Farley, the dope fiend that Cosmo had introduced to him last year when identification was needed for employees working in Gregori's salvage yard.

'Farley? I have not seen the little freak in a very long time,' Cosmo lied.

'Well, my friend,' Gregori said, 'I just need to know if the thief can still be trusted.'

'In what way?'

'People like him, they sometimes become police informants. The police trade little fishes for big whales. They might consider me to be a whale.'

Cosmo said, 'You can trust him in that way. He is such a worthless addict that the police would not even want to deal with him. But you cannot lend him money. I was stupid enough to do that.'

'Thank you,' Gregori said. 'Perhaps I could buy you and your lovely Ilya a dinner at the Gulag some evening?'

'I would like that, thank you,' Cosmo said. 'But I have an idea. Perhaps you can do something for me?'

'Of course.'

'I would be very grateful next month on a night I shall designate if you would call Farley and tell him you need more key cards because several new employees have arrived from Mexico with family members. Offer him more than you paid today. Then tell him to deliver the cards to your salvage yard. After dark.'

'My business is closed before dark. Even on Saturday.'

'I know,' Cosmo said, 'but I would like you to give me a duplicate gate key. I will be at the salvage yard when Farley arrives.'

'Wait a moment,' Gregori said. 'What does this mean?'

'It is only about the money he owes me,' Cosmo said reassuringly. 'I want to scare the little dope fiend. Maybe make him give me what money he has in his pocket. I have a right.'

'Cosmo, I do not do violence, you know that.'

'Of course,' Cosmo said. 'The most I will do is to keep his car until he pays me. I will take his keys and drive his car to my place and make him walk home. That is all.'

'That is not a theft? Could he call the police?'

Cosmo laughed and said, 'It is a business dispute. And Farley is the last man in Hollywood to ever call the police. He has never worked an honest day in his life.'

'I am not sure about this,' Gregori said.

'Listen, cousin,' Cosmo said. 'Drop the key at my apartment after work this evening. I cannot be there because of other business, but Ilya will be there. She will make you her special tea. In a glass, Russian-style. What do you say?'

Gregori was silent for a moment, but then he thought of Ilya. That great blond Russian Ilya with her nice plump, long legs and huge tits.

He was silent too long, so Cosmo said, 'Also, I will give you one hundred dollars for your trouble. Gladly.'

'All right, Cosmo,' Gregori said. 'But there must not be violence on my property.'

After Cosmo hung up, he said to Ilya in English, 'You shall not believe our good fortune. In a few hours Gregori of the junkyard shall come here with a key. I promise to him one hundred for the key. Behave nice. Give to him your glass of tea.'

Two hours later when Gregori arrived, he discovered that, true to his word, Cosmo was not there. Ilya invited him in and after he put the salvage yard gate key on the table, he was asked to sit while she put on the tea kettle.

Ilya wore a red cotton dress that hiked up every time she bent over even slightly, and he could see those white plump thighs. And her breasts were spilling from her bra, which Gregori could see was black and lacey.

After putting two glasses and saucers and cookies on the table, Ilya said in English, 'Cosmo is gone all evening. Business.'

'Do you get the lonesomeness?' Gregori asked.

'I do,' she said. 'Gregori, Cosmo promises to pay you one hundred?'

'Yes,' Gregori said, unable to take his eyes from those white ballooning breasts.

'I have it for you, but...'

'Yes, Ilya?'

'But I must buy shoes and Cosmo is not a generous man, and perhaps I may tell him that I paid money, but...'

'Yes, Ilya?'

'But perhaps we do like Americans say...'

'Yes, Ilya?'

'And fuck the brains from outside of our heads?'

The tea was postponed, and within two minutes Gregori was wearing only socks, but he suddenly began to fret about Cosmo and said, 'Ilya, you must promise. Cosmo must never learn we do this.'

Unhooking her bra and removing her black thong, Ilya said, 'Gregori, you have nothing to fear about. Cosmo says that in America someone fuck someone in every business deal. One way or other.'

TWELVE

Hollywood Nate always said that there were two kinds of cops in Hollywood Division: Starbucks and 7-Eleven types. Nate was definitely a Starbucks guy, and lucky for him his protégé Wesley Drubb came from a family that had never set foot in a 7-Eleven store. Nate couldn't work very long without heading for either the Starbucks at Sunset and La Brea or the one at Sunset and Gower. On the other hand, there were Hollywood Division coppers (7-Eleven types) who chose to take code 7 at IHOP. Nate said that eating at IHOP would produce enough bad cholesterol to clog the Red Line subway. He seldom even patronized the ever-popular Hamburger Hamlet, preferring instead one of the eateries in Thai Town around Hollywood Boulevard and Kingsley. Or one of the more health-conscious joints on west Sunset that served great lattés.

The hawkish handsome face of Nate Weiss had now recovered from his battle with the war veteran who insisted on a ride to Santa Monica and La Brea. The last Nate heard about the guy was that he'd plea-bargained down to simple battery and would no doubt soon be returning to drugs and flashbacks and a hankering for another ride to Santa Monica and La Brea.

Nate was back to pumping iron at the gym and jogging three times a week and had an appointment to meet a real agent who might advance his career immeasurably. Being one of the few officers at Hollywood Station who loved to work all the red carpet events at Grauman's or the Kodak

Theatre, where sometimes hundreds of officers were needed, he'd met the agent there.

'You know, Wesley,' Nate said, 'about that little Indie film I've been trying to put together? Had a chance to talk to your old man about it yet?'

'Not yet, Nate,' Wesley said. 'Dad's in Tokyo. But I wouldn't get my hopes up. He's a very conservative man when it comes to business.'

'So am I, Wesley, so am I,' Nate said. 'But this is as close to a no-brainer as it gets in the film business. Did I tell you I'm getting my SAG card?'

'I'm not sure if you told me or not,' Wesley said, thinking, Does he ever stop? The guy's thirty-five years old. He'll be a star about the time USC trades its football program for lacrosse.

'Every time I do a union job as a nonunion extra, I get a voucher. One more job and I'll have enough vouchers and pay stubs. Then I'm eligible to join the Screen Actors Guild.'

'Awesome, Nate,' Wesley said.

When Hollywood Nate lay in bed after getting off duty, he had latté dreams and mocha fantasies of life in a high canvas chair, wearing a makeup bib, never dating below-the-line persons, using the word 'energy' at least once in every three sentences, and living in a house so big you'd need a Sherpa to find the guest rooms. Such was the dream of Hollywood Nate Weiss.

As for young Wesley Drubb, his dream was muddled. Lately he'd been spending a lot of time trying to convince himself that he had not made a horrible mistake dropping out of USC, not graduating and going on for an MBA. He often questioned the wisdom of moving away from the Pacific Palisades family home into a so-so apartment in West Hollywood that he couldn't have easily afforded without a roommate. And not without the personal checks he was secretly receiving from his mother's account, checks that he had nobly refused to cash for several months until he'd finally succumbed. What was he proving? And to whom?

After the hand grenade incident and the fight in which Nate got hurt worse than he pretended, Wesley had confided in his brother, Timothy, hoping his older sibling would give him some advice.

Timothy, who had been working for Lawford and Drubb only three years, knocking down more than $175,000 last year (their father's idea of starting at the bottom), said to him, 'What do you get out of it, Wesley? And please don't give me any undergraduate existential bullshit.'

Wesley had said, 'I just... I don't know. I like what I do most of the time.'

'You are such an asshole,' his brother said, ending the discussion. 'Just try to only get crippled and not killed. It would be the end of Mom if she lost her baby boy.'

Wesley Drubb didn't think that he was terribly afraid of getting crippled or killed. He was young enough to think that those things happened to other guys, or other girls, like Mag Takara. No, the thing that he couldn't explain to his brother or his dad or mom, or any of his fraternity brothers who were now going to grad school, was that the Oracle was right. This work was the most fun he would ever have on any job.

Oh, there were boring nights when not much happened, but not too boring. On the downside, there was the unbelievable oversight that LAPD was presently going through, which created loads of paperwork and media criticism and a level of political correctness that a civilian would never understand or tolerate. But at the end of the day, young Wesley Drubb was having fun. And that's why he was still a cop. And that's why he just might remain one for the foreseeable future. But his thought process went off the rails at that point. At his age, he couldn't begin to fathom what the words 'foreseeable future' truly meant.

After Hollywood Nate had his Starbucks latté and was in a good mood, they got a call to Hollywood and Cahuenga, where a pair of Hollywood's homeless were having a twilight punch-out. Neither geezer was capable of inflicting much damage on the other unless weapons were pulled, but the fight was taking place on Hollywood Boulevard, and that would not be tolerated by the local merchants. Project Restore Hollywood was in full bloom, with everyone dreaming of more and more tourists and of someday making seedy old Hollywood glam up like Westwood or Beverly Hills or Santa Barbara minus the nearby ocean.

The combatants had taken their fight to the alley behind an adult bookstore and had exhausted themselves by throwing half a dozen flailing punches at each other. They were now at the stage of standing ten feet apart and exchanging curses and shaking fists. Wesley parked the shop on Cahuenga north of Hollywood Boulevard, and they approached the two ragbag old street fighters.

Nate said, 'The skinny one is Trombone Teddy. Used to be a hotlicks jazzman a truck load of whiskey ago. The *real* skinny one I've seen around for years, but I don't think I've ever talked to him.'

The *real* skinny one, a stick of a man of indeterminate age but probably younger than Trombone Teddy, wore a filthy black fedora and a filthier green necktie over an even filthier gray shirt and colorless pants. He wore what used to be leather shoes but were now mostly wraps of duct tape, and he spent most evenings shuffling along the boulevard raving at whoever didn't cross his palm with a buck or two.

It was hardly worth worrying about who would be contact and who would be cover with these two derelicts, and Hollywood Nate just wanted to get it over with, so he waded in and said, 'Jesus, Teddy, what the hell're you doing fighting on Hollywood Boulevard?'

'It's him, Officer,' Teddy said, still panting from exertion. 'He started it.'

'Fuck you!' his antagonist said with the addled look these guys get from sucking on those short dogs of cheap port.

'Stay real,' Nate said, looking at the guy and at his shopping cart crammed with odds and ends, bits and bobs. There was no way he wanted to bust this guy and deal with booking all that junk.

Wesley said to the skinniest geezer, 'What's your name?'

'What's it to ya?'

'Don't make us arrest you,' Nate said. 'Just answer the officer.'

'Filmore U. Bracken.'

Trying a positive approach, Wesley smiled and said, 'What's the U for?'

'I'll spell it for you,' Filmore replied. 'U-p-y-u-r-s.'

'Upyurs?' Wesley said. 'That's an unusual name.'

'Up yours,' Nate explained. Then he said, 'That's it, Filmore, you're going to the slam.'

When Nate took latex gloves from his pocket, Filmore said, 'Upton.'

Before putting the gloves on, Nate said, 'Okay, last chance. Will you just agree to move along and leave Teddy here in peace and let bygones be bygones?'

'Sure,' Filmore U. Bracken said, shuffling up to Teddy and putting out his hand.

Teddy hesitated, then looked at Nate and extended his own hand. And Filmore U. Bracken took it in his right hand and suckered Teddy with a left hook that, pathetic as it was, knocked Trombone Teddy on the seat of his pants.

'Hah!' said Filmore, admiring his own clenched fist.

Then the latex gloves went on both cops, and Filmore's bony wrists were handcuffed, but when he was about to be walked to their car, he said, 'How about my goods?'

'That's worthless trash,' Hollywood Nate said.

'My anvil's in there!' Filmore cried.

Wesley Drubb walked over to the junk, gingerly poked around, and underneath the aluminum cans and socks and clean undershorts probably stolen from a Laundromat found an anvil.

'Looks pretty heavy,' Wesley said.

'That anvil's my life!' their prisoner cried.

Nate said, 'You don't need an anvil in Hollywood. How many horses you see around here?'

'That's my property!' their prisoner yelled, and now an asthmatic fat man waddled out the back door of an adult bookstore and said, 'Officer, this guy's been raising hell on the boulevard all day. Hassling my customers and spitting on them when they refuse to give him money.'

'Fuck you too, you fat degenerate!' the prisoner said.

Nate said to the proprietor, 'I gotta ask you a favor. Can he keep his shopping cart inside your storage area here until he gets outta jail?'

'How long will he be in?'

'Depends on whether we just book him for plain drunk or add on the battery we just witnessed.'

'I don't wanna make a complaint,' Trombone Teddy said.

'Shut up, Teddy,' Hollywood Nate said.

'Yes, sir,' said Teddy.

'I ain't as drunk as he is!' the prisoner said, pointing at Teddy.

He was right and everyone knew it. Teddy was reeling, and not from the other geezer's punch.

'Okay, tell you what,' Nate said, deciding to dispense boulevard justice. 'Filmore here is going to detox for a couple hours and then he can come back and pick up his property. How's that?'

Everyone seemed okay with the plan, and the store owner

pushed the shopping cart to the storage area at the rear of his business.

While Nate was escorting their prisoner to the car, Trombone Teddy walked over to Wesley Drubb and said, 'Thanks, Officer. He's a bad actor, that bum. A real mean drunk.'

'Okay, anytime,' Wesley said.

But Teddy had a card in his hand and extended it to Wesley, saying, 'This is something you might be able to use.'

It was a business card to a local Chinese restaurant, the House of Chang. 'Thanks, I'll try it sometime,' Wesley said.

'Turn it over,' Teddy said. 'There's a license number.'

Wesley flipped the card and saw what looked like a California license plate number and said, 'So?'

Teddy said, 'It's a blue Pinto. Two tweakers were in it, a man and a woman. She called him Freddy, I think. Or maybe Morley. I can't quite remember. I seen them fishing in a mailbox over on Gower south of the boulevard. They stole mail. That's a federal offense, ain't it?'

Wesley said, 'Just a minute, Teddy.'

When he got back to his partner, who had put Filmore U. Bracken in the backseat of the car, Wesley showed him the card and said, 'Teddy gave me this license number. Belongs to tweakers stealing from mailboxes. The guy's name is Freddy or Morley.'

'All tweakers steal from mailboxes,' Hollywood Nate said, 'or anything else they can steal.'

It seemed to Wesley that he shouldn't just ignore the tip and throw the license number away. But he didn't want to act like he was still a boot, so he went back to Teddy, handed him the card, and said, 'Why don't you take it to a post office. They have people who investigate this sort of thing.'

'I think I'll hang on to it,' Teddy said, clearly disappointed.

Driving to the station, Nate got to thinking about the secretary who worked for the extras casting office he'd visited last Tuesday. She had given him big eyes as well as her phone number. He thought that he and Wesley could pick up some takeout, and he could sit in the station alone somewhere and chat her up on his cell.

'Partner, you up for burgers tonight?' he asked Wesley.

'Sure,' Wesley said. 'You're the health nut who won't eat burgers.'

And then, thinking of the little secretary and what they might do together on his next night off, and how she might even help him with her boss the casting agent, Nate felt a real glow come over him. What he called 'Hollywood happy.'

He said, 'How about you, Filmore, you up for a burger?'

'Hot damn!' the derelict said. 'You bet!'

They stopped at a drive-through, picked up four burgers, two for Wesley, and fries all around, and headed for the station.

When they got there, Nate said to their prisoner, 'Here's the deal. I'm giving you not only a burger and fries, but a get-out-of-jail-free pass. You're gonna sit in the little holding tank for thirty minutes and eat your burger, and I'll even buy you a Coke. Then, after my partner writes an FI card on you for future reference, I'm gonna let you out and you're gonna walk back up to the boulevard and get your shopping cart and go home to your nest, wherever that is.'

'You mean I ain't going to jail or detox?'

'That's right. I got an important phone call to make, so I can't waste time dicking around with you. Deal?'

'Hot damn!' Filmore said.

When their passenger got out of the car in the station parking lot, Wesley looked at the car seat and said to Filmore, 'What's that all over the seat? Beach sand?'

'No, that's psoriasis,' said Filmore U. Bracken.

'Oh, gross!' Wesley cried.

*

B.M. Driscoll and Benny Brewster caught the call to the apartment building on Stanley north of Fountain. They were half a block from the L.A. Sheriff's Department jurisdiction of West Hollywood, and later Benny Brewster thought about that and wished it could've occurred just half a block south.

The apartment manager answered their ring and asked them inside. It was by no means a down-market property. In fact, B.M. Driscoll was thinking he wouldn't mind living there if he could afford the rent. The woman wore a blazer and skirt and looked as though she had just come home from work. Her silver-streaked hair was cut like a man's, and she was what is called handsome in women her age.

She said, 'I'm Cora Sheldon, and I called about the new tenant in number fourteen. Her name is Eileen Leffer. She moved in last month from Oxnard and has two young children.' She paused and read from the rental agreement, 'A six-year-old son, Terry, and a seven-year-old daughter, Sylvia. She said she's a model and seemed very respectable and promised to get us references but hasn't done it yet. I think there might be a problem.'

'What kinda problem?' Benny asked.

'I work during the day, but we never see or hear a peep from the kids. The owner of the building used to rent our furnished units to adults only, so this is new to me. I've never been married, but I think normal kids should be heard from sometimes, and these two are not. I don't think they're enrolled in any school. Even on weekends when I'm home, I never hear or see the kids.'

'Have you investigated?' B.M. Driscoll asked. 'You know, knocked on the door with maybe an offer of a friendly cup of coffee?'

'Twice. Neither time was there a response. I'm worried. I have a key, but I'm afraid to just open the door and look.'

'We got no probable cause to enter,' Benny said. 'When was the last time you knocked on the door?'

'Last night at eight o'clock.'

'Gimme the key,' B.M. Driscoll said. 'And you come with us. If there's nobody home, we all just tiptoe away and nobody's the wiser. We wouldn't do this except for the presence of little kids.'

When they got to number fourteen, Benny knocked. No answer. He tapped sharply with the butt of his flashlight. Still no answer.

Benny called out, 'Police officers. Anybody home?' and knocked again.

Cora Sheldon was doing a lot of lip biting then, and B.M. Driscoll put the pass key in the lock and opened the door, turning on the living room light. The room was messy, with magazines strewn around and a couple of vodka bottles lying on the floor. The kitchen smelled of garbage, and when they looked in, they saw the sink stacked with dirty dishes. The gas range was a mess with something white that had boiled over.

B.M. Driscoll switched on a hallway light and looked into the bathroom, which was more of a mess than the kitchen. Benny checked the master bedroom, saw an unmade bed and a bra and panties on the floor, and returned with a shrug.

The other bedroom door was closed. Cora Sheldon said, 'The second bedroom has twin beds. That would be the children's room.'

B.M. Driscoll walked to the door and opened it, turning on the light. It was worse by far than the master bedroom. There were dishes with peanut butter and crackers on the floor and on the dresser top. In front of the TV were empty soda cans, and boxes of breakfast cereal were lying on the floor.

'Well, she's not much of a housekeeper,' he said, 'but other than that?'

'Partner,' Benny said, pointing at the bed, then walking to

it and shining his light at wine-dark stains. 'Looks like blood.'

'Oh my god!' Cora Sheldon said as B.M. Driscoll looked under the bed and Benny went to the closet, whose door was partially open.

And there they were. Both children were sitting under hanging garments belonging to their mother. The six-year-old boy began sobbing, and his seven-year-old sister put her arm around him. Both children were blue-eyed, and the boy was a blond and his sister a brunette. Neither had had a decent wash for a few days, and both were terrified. The boy wore shorts and a food-stained T-shirt and no shoes. The girl wore a cotton dress trimmed with lace, also food-stained. On her feet she wore white socks and pink sneakers.

'We won't hurt you, come on out,' Benny said, and Cora Sheldon repeated, 'Oh my god!'

'Where's your mommy?' B.M. Driscoll asked.

'She went with Steve,' the girl said.

'Does Steve live here?' Benny asked, and when Cora Sheldon said, 'I didn't rent to anyone named—' he shushed her by putting up his hand.

The little girl said, 'Sometimes.'

B.M. Driscoll said, 'Have they been gone for a long time?'

The little girl said, 'I think so.'

'For two days? Three days? Longer?'

'I don't know,' she said.

'Okay, come on out and let's get a look at you,' he said.

Benny was inspecting the stain on the bed, and he said to the girl, 'Has somebody hurt you?'

She nodded then and started crying, walking painfully from the closet.

'Who?' Benny asked. 'Who hurt you?'

'Steve,' she said.

'How?' Benny asked. 'How did he hurt you?'

'Here,' she said, and when she lifted her cotton dress

slightly, they saw dried blood crusted on both legs from her thighs down, and what looked like dark bloodstains on her lace-trimmed white cotton socks.

'Out, please!' Benny said to Cora Sheldon, taking both children by the hands and walking them into the living room, first closing the bedroom door to protect it as a crime scene.

B.M. Driscoll grabbed his rover to inform detectives that they had some work to do and that they needed transportation to the hospital for the children.

'Wait in your apartment, Ms. Sheldon,' Benny said.

Looking at the children, she said, 'Oh,' and then started to weep and walked out the door.

When she had gone, the girl turned to her younger brother and said, 'Don't cry, Terry. Mommy's coming home soon.'

It was nearly midnight when Flotsam and Jetsam were in the station to get a sergeant's signature on a robbery report. A drag queen claimed to have been walking down the boulevard on a legitimate errand when a car carrying two guys stopped and one of them jumped out and stole the drag queen's purse, which contained fifty dollars as well as a 'gorgeous' new wig that cost three hundred and fifty. Then he'd punched the drag queen before driving away.

Jetsam was in the process of calling to see what kind of record the dragon had, like maybe multiple prostitution arrests, when the desk officer asked Flotsam to watch the desk while he ran upstairs and had a nice hot b.m.

Flotsam said okay and was there when a very angry and outraged Filmore U. Bracken came shuffling into the lobby.

Flotsam took a look at the old derelict and said, 'Dude, you are too hammered to be entering a police station of your own volition.'

'I wanna make a complaint,' the codger said.

'What kinda complaint?'

'Against a policeman.'

'What'd he do?'

'I gotta admit he bought me a hamburger.'

'Yeah, well, I can see why you're mad,' Flotsam said. 'Shoulda been filet mignon, right?'

'He brought me here for the hamburger and left my property with a big fat degenerate at a dirty bookstore on Hollywood Boulevard.'

'Which dirty bookstore?'

'I can point it out to you. Anyways, the degenerate didn't watch my property like he said he would and now it's gone. Everything in my shopping cart.'

'And what, pray tell, was in your cart?'

'My anvil.'

'An anvil?'

'Yeah, it's my life.'

'Damn,' Flotsam said. 'You're a blacksmith? The Mounted Platoon might have a job for you.'

'I wanna see the boss and make a complaint.'

'What's your name?'

'Filmore Upton Bracken.'

'Wait here a minute, Mr. Bracken,' Flotsam said. 'I'm going to talk this over with the sergeant.'

While Jetsam waited for the Oracle to approve and sign the crime report, Flotsam went to the phone books and quickly looked up the law offices of Harold G. Lowenstein, a notorious and hated lawyer in LAPD circles who had made a living suing cops and the city that hired them. Somebody was always saying what they would do to Harold G. Lowenstein if they ever popped him for drunk driving.

Flotsam then dialed the number to the lobby phone. After the eighth ring, as he started to think his idea wasn't going to work, the phone was picked up.

Filmore Upton Bracken said, 'Hello?'

'Mr. Bracken?' Flotsam said, doing his best impression of Anthony Hopkins playing a butler. 'Am I speaking to Mr. Filmore Upton Bracken?'

'Yeah, who's this?'

'This is the emergency hotline for the law offices of Harold G. Lowenstein, Esquire, Mr. Bracken. A Los Angeles police officer just phoned us from Hollywood Station saying that you may need our services.'

'Yeah? You're a lawyer?'

'I'm just a paralegal, Mr. Bracken,' Flotsam said. 'But Mr. Lowenstein is very interested in any case involving malfeasance on the part of LAPD officers. Could you please come to our offices tomorrow at eleven a.m. and discuss the matter?'

'You bet I can. Lemme get a pencil from the desk here.'

He was gone for a moment, and Flotsam could hear him yelling, 'Hey, I need a goddamn pencil!'

When Filmore returned, he said, 'Shoot, brother.'

Flotsam gave him the address of Harold G. Lowenstein's Sunset Strip law office, including the suite number, and then said, 'Mr. Bracken, the officer who just phoned on your behalf said that you are probably without means at present, so do not be intimidated if our somewhat sheltered employees try to discourage you. Mr. Lowenstein will want to see you personally, so don't take no for an answer from some snippy receptionist.'

'I'll kick ass if anybody tries to stop me,' Filmore said.

'That's the spirit, Mr. Bracken,' Flotsam said, his accent shifting closer to the burr of Sean Connery and away from Anthony Hopkins.

'I'll be there at eleven.'

Filmore was waiting in the lobby when Flotsam returned, saying, 'Mr. Bracken? The sergeant will see you now.'

Filmore drew himself up on his tiptoes to lock eyeballs

with the tall cop and said, 'Fuck the sergeant. He can talk to my lawyer. I'm suing all you bastards. When I'm through, I'll own this goddamn place, and maybe if you're lucky I'll buy you a hamburger sometime. Asshole.'

And with that, Filmore Upton Bracken shuffled out the door with a grin as wide as Hollywood Boulevard.

When B.M. Driscoll and Benny Brewster went end-of-watch in the early morning hours, they found Flotsam and Jetsam in the locker room, sharing Filmore Upton Bracken adventures with Hollywood Nate and Wesley Drubb.

After the chuckles subsided, Nate said to Flotsam and Jetsam, 'By the way, you guys're invited to a birthday party. My newest little friend is throwing it at her place in Westwood. Might be one or two chicks from the entertainment industry for you to meet.'

'Any of the tribe coming?' Flotsam asked. 'No offense, but I got a two-Jew limit. Three or more Hollywood hebes gather and they start sticking political lapel pins on every animate and inanimate object in sight, which might include my dead ass.'

'Why, you filthy anti-Semitic surfer swine,' Nate said.

'You inviting Budgie?' Flotsam asked.

'Probably,' Nate said.

'Okay, we'll come. My partner admires her from afar.'

They stopped the banter when B.M. Driscoll and Benny Brewster came in looking very grim. Both began quickly and quietly undressing.

'What's wrong with you guys?' Jetsam asked. 'They taking Wrestlemania off the air?'

'You don't wanna know,' B.M. Driscoll said, almost tearing the buttons from his uniform shirt as though he just wanted *out* of it. 'Bad shit. Little kids.'

'So lighten up,' Flotsam said. 'Don't you guys listen to the Oracle? This Job can be fun. Get happy.'

Suddenly, Jetsam did his Bono impersonation, singing, 'Two shots of happy, one shot of saaaaaad.'

Benny Brewster peeled off his body armor and furiously crammed the vest into the locker, saying, 'No shots of happy tonight, man. Just one shot of sad. *Real* sad.'

THIRTEEN

Excuse me, please, Andrea,' Viktor Chernenko said late in the morning. There were only six detectives in the squad room, the rest being out in the field or in court or, in the case of Hollywood detectives, nonexistent due to the manpower shortage and budget constraints.

'Yes, Viktor?' Andi said, smiling over her coffee cup, fingers still on the computer keyboard.

'I think you are looking very lovely today, Andrea,' Viktor said with his usual diffident smile. 'I believe I recognize your most beautiful yellow sweater from the Bananas Republic, where my wife, Maria, shops.'

'Yeah, I bought it there.'

Then he walked back to his cubicle. This was the way with Viktor. He wanted something, but it might take him half a day to get around to asking. On the other hand, nobody ever paid her the compliments that Viktor did when he needed a woman detective for something or other.

Andi was glad to see that Brant Hinkle was still teamed with Viktor, and because of that she'd probably agree to do whatever Viktor got around to requesting. Ever since Brant had arrived, her belief in his possibilities kept increasing. She'd checked him out by now and found that he'd just turned fifty-three, had only been married and divorced once —a rarity among cops these days—had two adult married daughters, and based on his serial number, had about five more years on the Job than she had. In other words, he was a likely prospect. And she knew he was interested by the way he looked at her, but as yet he hadn't made a move.

Another twenty minutes passed and she was about to go out in the field and call on a couple of witnesses to a so-called attempted murder where a pimp/boyfriend slapped around a whore and fired two shots in her direction when she ran away. Without a doubt, the whore would have changed her mind by now or had it changed for her and all would be forgiven. But Andi needed to go through the motions just in case tomorrow night he murdered her.

'Andrea,' Viktor said when he approached her desk the second time.

'Yes, Viktor.'

'Will you be so kind to help Brant and me? We have a mission for a woman, and as you see, today you are the only woman here.'

'How long will it take?'

'A few hours, and I would be honored to buy your lunch.'

Andi glanced over at Brant Hinkle, who was talking on the phone, wearing little half-glasses as he wrote on a legal pad, and she said, 'Okay, Viktor. My damaged hooker can wait.'

Viktor drove east to Glendale with Andi beside him and Brant in the backseat. Viktor was very solicitous, apologizing because the air conditioner didn't work in their car.

'So okay,' Andi said, 'all I have to do is tail this Russian guy from his job at the auto parts store to wherever he eats lunch?'

Viktor said, 'We have been told that he always walks to a fast-food place, but there are several that are close by.'

Brant said, 'Viktor's informant says this guy Lidorov is very tail conscious, but he probably won't be looking for a woman to be on him.'

'And all we do is get a DNA sample?'

'That is all,' Viktor said. 'My informant is sometimes reliable, sometimes not.'

'Your evidence for a DNA comparison isn't all that reliable either,' she said, turning in her seat to look at Brant, who raised his eyebrows as if to say, Viktor is obsessive.

Viktor said, 'Andrea, when I did my follow-up investigation and found the cigarette butt in that jewelry store far behind the cabinet, I know in my heart it was left there by the suspect.'

'Even though the victim was too terrified to remember for sure if the guy left the butt or took it with him,' Brant said doubtfully.

'It is an intestines feeling,' Viktor said. 'And this Russian in Glendale has two convictions for armed robbery of jewelry stores.'

'I've heard you say you're not sure the man from the jewelry store two-eleven is even a Russian,' Andi said.

Viktor said, 'The accent that the store owner heard from the man was different from the woman's. But everybody is Russian Mafia to people in Hollywood. Actually, Glendale has a very big Armenian population. Many go to the Gulag, where my tip has come from. Criminals from all over former USSR go to the Gulag to drink and dine, including criminals from former Soviet Armenia. But for now, we have this Russian who was a jewel robber in his past life.'

'This isn't much to go on,' Andi said.

'We have nothing else,' Viktor said. 'Except I believe that a theft of mail from a certain mailbox on Gower is where the information about the diamonds was learned about. If only I could get a clue to the mail thief.'

'We can't stake out every mailbox in the area, Viktor,' Brant said.

'No, Brant, we cannot,' Viktor said. 'So that is why I would like to try this thing today. I know it is a far shot.'

They parked on the next block, and Viktor diligently watched the front door of the auto parts store through binoculars while Andi turned in her seat to chat with Brant about how he liked Hollywood so far and where was he on the lieutenant's list.

Brant was surprised to learn that Andi had a son in the army serving in Afghanistan, and said, 'Don't think I say this to all the ladies, but really, you don't look old enough.'

'I'm plenty old enough,' she said, hoping she hadn't blushed. Next thing, she'd be batting her lashes if she didn't get hold of herself.

'I think Afghanistan's fairly quiet these days,' he said.

'Last year he was in Iraq,' she said. 'I don't like to think about how I felt during those months.'

Brant was quiet then, feeling very lucky to have daughters living safe lives. He couldn't imagine how it must feel to have your only child over there in hell. Especially for coppers, whose assertive, in-your-face personality is of absolutely no use in such a situation. To just feel helpless and frightened all the time? He believed it must be extra hard for the parents who are police officers.

Viktor lowered the binoculars, picked up a mug shot from his lap, and said, 'It is Lidorov. He is wearing a black shirt and jeans. He has what looks like hair made of patent leather and has a gray mustache and is of medium size. He is walking toward the big mall half a block from the auto parts store.'

Andi was dropped on the east side of the mall and walked inside a minute after Lidorov entered. At first she thought she'd lost him, but heading toward the food court she spotted him.

Lidorov paused before the Greek deli, where two Latino men were making gyros, then moved on to an Italian takeout, where another young Latino was expertly tossing a pizza. Then he settled on Chinese fast food and ordered something in a carton along with a soft drink in a takeout cup. From another Latino.

Andi watched from the Italian side and wondered if

chopsticks would be better or worse than forks for the collecting of DNA evidence. But Lidorov shook his head when offered chopsticks and took a plastic fork instead. He sat down at one of three small tables in front of the counter and ate from the carton and sipped his drink and ogled any young women who happened to pass by.

When he got up, she was ready to bus his table for him and scoop up the fork and the drinking straw. But she never got the chance. He took the unfinished carton of food with him along with the cup and strolled back toward the entrance, drinking from the straw. She assumed the fork was in the carton, so now what?

Lidorov went out the door into the sunlight, stretched a little, and strolled right past two perfectly good trash receptacles where he could have dropped the carton and the cup.

Litter, you bastard! Andi thought, following as far as she dared. But since there were few pedestrians on the sidewalk, she crossed over to the other side of the street and waited to be picked up.

When Viktor drove alongside, she got in and said, 'Sorry, Viktor. He's taking his lunch back to the store.'

'Is okay, Andrea,' Viktor said.

'Whoops!' Brant said, looking through the binoculars. 'He's not a litterbug.'

Two minutes later they were parked just east of the little strip mall that housed the auto parts store. Next to the wall in the parking lot was a very tall trash dumpster sitting on a thick concrete slab. All three detectives were standing in front of it with the lid raised.

Viktor and Brant, who were both more than six feet tall, pulled themselves up, their feet off the asphalt, and peered down inside the dumpster.

After getting back down, Viktor said to Andi, 'Do you want the news that is good or the news that is not so good?'

'Good,' Andi said.

Brant said, 'Looks like they dumped the trash this morning. There's hardly anything in there. We can see the Chinese takeout carton and the drinking cup and straw.'

'Bad news?'

'We can't reach it without somebody climbing inside,' Brant said.

'Well, I guess one of you fashion plates is going to get your suit dirty,' Andi said.

'Andrea,' said Viktor, 'I am so outside of good shape that I truly do not think I can do it. I am thinking that if I spread my coat over the top here so that you do not mess up the beautiful sweater from Bananas, you could lie down over the top here and reach down and get the fork and the straw?'

'And how do I keep from falling in right on my head?'

'We would each hold you by a leg,' Brant said.

'Oh, you think it's a good idea too?'

'I swear to you, Andi,' Brant said. 'I don't think I could do it without a ladder. And if we mess around here much longer, somebody's gonna see us and the element of surprise will be lost. Even if we do get a match, he'll be long gone, maybe clear back to Russia.'

'My heroes,' Andi said, slipping off her pumps. 'Good thing I'm wearing long pants.'

With each man holding a bare foot, Andi was boosted up to the edge of the dumpster, lying across Viktor's suit coat, and very reluctantly she allowed herself to be lowered upside down until she got hold of the carton and the cup.

'Get me outta here. It stinks,' she said.

When they were back in the car, the fork and drinking straw in a large evidence envelope, Viktor said, 'My coat must go to the cleaners. How is your sweater, Andrea?'

'Other than busting a bra strap and bruising my belly and thighs, I'm okay. This lunch better be good, Viktor.'

It was. Viktor took them to a whimsically designed Russian restaurant on Melrose, where they had borscht and black bread and blinis and hot tea in a glass. And even got to hear dreamy Russian violins coming from the sound system, with Viktor acting every inch the host.

'Sometimes they make Ukrainian dishes here,' he told them, as they drank their tea.

'I don't think I'll do Pilates tonight,' Andi said. 'You guys stretched every muscle in my body.'

'Speaking of muscles, yours are way better developed than mine,' Brant said. 'Your legs are buff. I mean, they felt strong when I was holding them.'

That look again. Andi was sure he'd make a move after today's little exercise. Maybe after they got back to the station and Viktor was otherwise occupied.

'I try to stay in shape in case I'm called on for dumpster diving,' she said. 'They should make it an event in the police Olympics.'

When Viktor went to the restroom, Brant said, 'Andi, I was wondering if maybe sometime you might like to join me for dinner at a new trendier-than-trendy-ever-gets restaurant called Jade that I've been reading about.'

Thinking, At last! she said, 'I'd like to have dinner with you, but that's pretty pricey. I read a review.'

He said, 'My daughters're long past child support and my ex remarried ten years ago, so I'm independently comfortable. But on second thought, maybe I'm too old for a place like Jade.'

'You look younger than I do,' she said.

'Bless you, my child,' Brant said. 'So is it a date?'

'Yeah, let's try it on Thursday to avoid the weekend rush. Wonder how I should dress.'

'Anything you wear would look great,' he said, and dropped his eyes in a shy way after he said it.

Andi thought, Those green eyes! This one's going to take me to heaven or bust me down to the ground. Her heart was pounding when Viktor returned to the table.

'There is one thing for sure,' Viktor said to them when he gave his credit card to the waiter, 'even if Lidorov is not our robber, it will be good to have his DNA profile. He is a violent thief. And a leopard cannot change its freckles.'

It was a different thief, newly seduced by the heady excitement of power and control, who that very afternoon was in the process of committing the second armed robbery of his life. But his chain-smoking companion was not the least bit seduced as they sat in a stolen car in a crowded parking lot, waiting. She wished that his Russian wasn't hopeless, and that she didn't have to convey her fears in English.

'I warn you, Cosmo,' Ilya said, looking like a clown to Cosmo in her red wig, wearing big sunglasses. 'This is a foolish thing that we do.'

'Dmitri told me is okay.'

'Fuck, Dmitri!' Ilya snapped, and Cosmo impulsively backhanded her across the face, regretting it at once.

He said, 'Dmitri say that this is what he plan for long time. He say he is looking for someone like me and you to do it. We are lucky, Ilya. Lucky!'

'We get killed!' she said, wiping her eyes with tissue and touching up her mascara.

'We get rich,' he said. 'You seen how the man in the jewelry store do when he seen my gun? He piss on his pants. You seen him cry, no? The guards with money do not wish to die. Dmitri say the money is paid back by insurance company. The guards shall see the gun and they shall give the money to me. You going to see.'

Cosmo, now wearing a Dodgers cap and sunglasses, had received the call from Dmitri the afternoon prior. Cosmo had thought it was about the diamonds, and when he showed up at the Gulag just before happy hour, he was sent upstairs to the private office.

Cosmo had not been surprised to see Dmitri sitting feet

up, much as he'd seen him last time, again watching porn on his computer screen. But this time it was kiddie porn. When Cosmo entered, Dmitri turned down the sound on the speakers but left the screen on, glancing at it from time to time.

'Did you wish to talk about diamonds?' Cosmo said in English, as always.

'No,' Dmitri said. 'But I been giving much thinking about the happen-ink guy Cosmo, who is my friend. I think about how you get the diamonds and how we going to do the deal for the diamonds very soon. I think maybe you ready for bigger job.'

'Yes?' Cosmo said, and Dmitri knew the look. He had him.

'It feels how? Strong? Sexy? Like fuck-ink when you point the gun in the face of a man. Am I correct, Cosmo?'

'Feels okay,' Cosmo said. 'Yes, I don't mind.'

'So, I have a job where you can get big money. Cash. At least one hundred thousand, maybe lot more.'

'Yes?'

'You know the kiosk in the big mall parking lots? The ATM machine kiosk? I know about one. I know exactly when money will come. Exactly.'

'Big armor car?' Cosmo said. 'I cannot rob the armor car, Dmitri.'

'No, Cosmo,' Dmitri said. 'Only a van. Two guys. They bring money inside a big, how you say, canister? Like soldier in Russia use for ammunition? One man must go behind kiosk, open door with key. Lock self in. Reload machine with nice green bullets from ammunition can.'

'Please, Dmitri, how you know about this?'

'Everyone drink at the Gulag sometime,' Dmitri said, chuckling in that way of his that scared Cosmo. He could imagine Dmitri chuckling like that if he was slitting your eyes.

'These men have guns, Dmitri.'

'Yes, but they be only regular security guard. They are contract out for these deliveries. I know about the two men. They will not die to save money. Insurance will pay anyways. Everybody know that. Nobody lose noth-ink except insurance company. No problem.'

'Two guys, two guns, two keys?'

'Yes, two keys for, how you say, internal security. You must take money before first guy get to kiosk. That is why I think of you. You prove at jewelry store you got lot of guts. And you got woman with big tits.'

'Ilya?'

'Yes. I give you exact day and time. Ilya is there to do business at ATM machine. Ilya know how to distract man who walks from van with money can. Other guy have a habit. Always the same. He wait until partner get to kiosk. Then he get out and come with his key.' Dmitri grinned and said, 'One minute all you need, you happen-ink guy. You rock, Cosmo!'

And now here they were, sitting in a busy Hollywood parking lot, waiting in the fifteen-year-old red Mazda that Dmitri's Georgian bartender had stolen for them with instructions to wipe it clean and abandon it somewhere east of Hollywood.

Ilya had gathered herself now, but every time she turned toward him he saw a hateful glare. He had slapped her around before, but this time it was different. He could smell his stale sweat and the fear on her. He thought she might leave him after this. But if Dmitri was right about how much would be in the can, he would just pay her off and let her go.

He had a passing thought about trying to reduce Dmitri's fifty percent by saying that the amount of money in the can was far less than advertised. It gave him a thrill to think about that, but it was tempered when he thought of Dmitri's sinister chuckle. And for all he knew, one of the security guards might be Dmitri's informer. And might know exactly how much money he was delivering.

Cosmo looked at his Rolex knock-off and said, 'Ilya, go to kiosk now.'

The blue Chevy van looked like anything but an armored car, much to Cosmo's relief. And it sat there a few minutes, just as Dmitri said it would, while the guards looked around but saw nothing out of the ordinary. Just shoppers coming and going to the mall stores. Only one woman, a bosomy redhead was at the ATM machine, looking very frustrated.

Her black purse was beside her on the tray and she took out her cell phone and appeared to be making a call. Then she threw her cell phone into the purse disgustedly and looked around as though she needed... what? She appeared to be trying her ATM card again but failed to make it work and just walked a short distance away, looking toward the electronics store across the parking lot. Maybe for her husband?

One of the guards glanced at the other. This was their last stop of the day and they couldn't sit there all evening because of one goofy woman. The passenger got out, slid open the door of the van, grabbed the only canister remaining, and slid the door closed. Then he walked from the van to the kiosk, and when he got to the front of it he saw that the red-haired woman was crying.

The six o'clock news would give the security guard's age as twenty-five. He was an 'actor' who had been in Hollywood from Illinois for three years, looking for work and trying to get a SAG card. He had been with the security service for eighteen months. His name was Ethan Munger.

'Are you okay?' Ethan Munger said to Ilya, only pausing for a moment.

She was wiping her cheeks with the tissue and said, 'I cannot make the card work.' And when she put the tissue back inside her purse, she pulled out the Raven .25 caliber pistol, one of the cheap street guns that Cosmo had been given by the bartender. Ilya pointed it at the astonished young guard.

The driver of the van keyed his mike, announced the robbery, and jumped out of the van, his pistol drawn. He ran around the back of the van, where Cosmo Betrossian, crouched below a parked car, said, 'Drop the gun or die!'

The driver dropped the gun and put his hands in the air, lying facedown when ordered to do so. It was just as Dmitri had promised, no problem.

But Ethan Munger was a problem. The young guard began backing toward the van, unaware that his partner had been disarmed. Ethan Munger had his free hand in the air, the other holding the metal container. And he said, 'Lady, you don't want to do this. Please put that little gun away. It will probably blow up in your face. Just put it away.'

'Drop the can!' Ilya screamed it. And it was all she could do not to burst into tears, she was so scared.

'Just don't get excited, lady,' the young guard said, still backing up with Ilya coming toward him.

It seemed to Ilya like minutes had passed, but it was only seconds, and she expected to hear sirens because several passing shoppers were looking and a woman was yelling, 'Help! Somebody call the police!' Another woman was shouting into her cell phone.

Then Cosmo came running up behind the young security guard with a pistol in each hand. Ethan Munger turned, saw Cosmo, and perhaps from having seen too many Hollywood films or played too many action videos tried to draw his pistol. Cosmo shot the young guard with the other guard's pistol. Three times in the chest.

Ilya didn't grab the can. She just put her pistol in her purse and ran screaming back toward the stolen car, the gunfire ringing in her ears. Within a minute, which seemed like ten, Cosmo jerked open the back door of the car and threw the can and two guns inside. And for one terrible moment couldn't get the old Mazda to start. Cosmo turned the key off, then on again three times, and it started and they sped from the parking lot.

Watch 5 was just loading up their war bags and other equipment when the code 3 hotshot call was given to 6-A-65 of Watch 2. And of course all the midwatch officers started throwing gear into their shops, jumping in, and squealing out of the station parking lot. They headed in the general direction of the robbery but really hoped they'd spot the red Mazda containing a dark-haired man wearing a baseball cap and a red-haired woman on the way. It wasn't often that there was a robbery and shooting of a security guard to start off their evening.

Benny Brewster and B.M. Driscoll of 6-X-66 were the last midwatch car out of the parking lot, which didn't surprise Benny. B.M. Driscoll had to run into the station at the last minute to get a bottle of antihistamine tablets from his locker because the early summer Santa Anas were killing him. Benny Brewster just sat and drummed his fingers on the steering wheel and thought about how miserably unlucky he had been in losing a heroic cop like Mag Takara and inheriting a hypochondriac whom nobody wanted.

Benny had visited Mag three times in the hospital and called her every day since she'd been home with her parents. He wasn't sure if her misshapen left cheekbone would ever be rebuilt to look exactly the way it was supposed to look. Mag said that the vision in her left eye was only about sixty percent of what it had been but that it was expected to improve. Mag promised Benny that she was coming back on duty, and he told her sincerely that he longed for the day.

There was still no court date set for the pimp who had assaulted her. Mag had suggested to Benny that with the huge lawsuit filed against the city for internal injuries suffered from the kicks by Officer Turner, maybe some sort of deal was coming down. A deal where the pimp would plea-bargain to county jail time instead of prison hard time, and a settlement would be made with the financially strapped city. Mag said she was very sorry for Turner, who had resigned in lieu of being fired and was awaiting word about whether he would be prosecuted.

'I jist wish I coulda been there, Mag,' Benny said when last they'd talked about it.

Mag had looked at her tall black partner and said, 'I'm glad you weren't, Benny. You've got a good career ahead of you. I predicted that to the Oracle first time you worked with me.'

Benny Brewster was still thinking about all of that when B.M. Driscoll finally got in the car and said, 'Let's not roll down the windows unless we have to.' Then he sniffed and blew his nose, taking another tissue from the box that he put on the floor beside the shotgun rack.

Benny started the car and drove slowly from the parking lot, saying disgustedly, 'Fucking two-eleven suspects that shot the guard're probably outta the county by now.'

B.M. Driscoll didn't respond, only taking off his glasses and cleaning them with a tissue so that he could better read the dosage on the antihistamine bottle.

All that Cosmo Betrossian could think about as he drove away from the scene of the robbery while the young security guard lay dying was the bartender at the Gulag. Cosmo was going to ask Dmitri to torture and kill that Georgian if he and Ilya were not killed themselves in the next few minutes. The stolen Mazda that the bartender assured him was in good working order had stalled at the first traffic light. And as Cosmo sat there grinding and grinding the starter, a police car sped past, light bar flashing and siren screaming, going to the very place from which they had just escaped.

228

'Let us get out of the car!' Ilya said.

'The money!' Cosmo cried. 'We have money!'

'Fuck money,' Ilya said.

The engine almost started, but he flooded it. He waited and tried again and it kicked over, and the Mazda began lurching south on Gower.

Cosmo decided that she was right, that they must get out and flee on foot. 'Son of bastard!' he screamed. 'I kill fucking Georgian that give me this car!'

'We leave it now?' Ilya said. 'Stop, Cosmo.'

Then the idea came to him. 'Ilya,' he said, 'you know where we be now?'

'Yes, Gower Street,' she said. 'Stop the car!'

'No, Ilya. We be almost at the house of the miserable addict Farley.' Ilya had never been to Farley's house and could not see the significance of this. 'So who gives damn about fucking tweaker? Stop the car! I get out!'

Cosmo realized that he was a block and a half away, that was all. A block and a half. 'Ilya, please do not jump out. Farley has little garage! Farley always park his shit car on the street so is easy to push it.'

'Cosmo!' she screamed again. 'I am going to kill you or me! Stop this car! Let me out!'

'Two minutes,' he said. 'We be at house of Farley. We put this car in garage of Farley. Our money shall be safe. We shall be safe!'

The Mazda bucked and shuddered its way down Gower to the residential street of Farley Ramsdale. Cosmo Betrossian was afraid that the car wouldn't make the final turn, but it did. And as though the Mazda had a mind and a will, it seemed to throw itself in a last lurching effort up the slightly sloping driveway, where it sputtered and died beside the old bungalow.

Cosmo and Ilya got out quickly, and Cosmo opened the garage door and threw some boxes of junk and an old, rusty bike from the garage into the backyard, making room for the Mazda. Cosmo and Ilya both had to push the car into the garage. Cosmo tucked both pistols inside his belt, grabbed the container of money, and closed the termite-riddled door.

They went to the front door of the bungalow and knocked but got no answer. Cosmo tried the door and found it locked. They went to the back door, where Cosmo slipped the wafer lock with a credit card, and they entered to await the return of their new 'partners.'

Cosmo thought that now he had more reason than ever to kill the two tweakers, and that he must do it right after they entered the house. But not with the gun. The neighboring homes were too close. But how? And would Ilya help him?

The canister contained $93,260, all of it in twenty-dollar bills. By the time they had finished counting it, Ilya had smoked half a dozen cigarettes and seemed calm enough, except for her shaking hands. Cosmo began giggling and couldn't stop.

'Is not so much as Dmitri promised, but I am happy!' Cosmo said. 'I am not greedy pig.' That tickled him so much he giggled more. 'I must call Dmitri soon.'

'You kill the guard,' Ilya said soberly. 'They catch us, we go to the house of death.'

'How can you know he is dead?'

'I saw bullets hit him. Three. Right here.' She touched her chest. 'He is dead man.'

'Fucking guy,' Cosmo said, testy now. 'He did not give up money. Dmitri say no problem. The guard shall give up money. Not my fault, Ilya.'

Ilya shook her head and lit yet another cigarette, and Cosmo lit a smoke of his own while he stuffed stacks of money back into the can, leaving out eight hundred, which he divided with Ilya, saying, 'This make you not so much worried about the house of death, no?'

He took the container back out to the car, wanting to

lock it in the trunk, but the ignition key did not work the trunk lock. He cursed the Georgian again and put the container in the backseat of the Mazda and locked the door.

When he returned to the house, Ilya was lying on the battered sofa as though she had a terrible headache. He went over to her and knelt, feeling very aroused.

He said to her, 'Ilya, remember how much sex we feel when we rob the diamonds? I feel that much sex now. And you? How would you like to fuck the brains outside my head?'

'If you touch me now, Cosmo,' she said, 'I swear I shall shoot the brains outside your head. I swear this by the Holy Virgin.'

Less than a mile away, Farley and Olive sat in Sam's Pinto, having borrowed it once again, parked by the cyber café. They saw several tweakers entering and then leaving after having done their Internet business, but they saw no one who they thought might have some decent crystal for purchase.

'Let's try the taco stand,' Farley said. 'We gotta get Sam's car back to him before it gets dark and pick up our piece of shit. He musta fixed the carburetor by now. One good thing about tweakers, Sam can sit around his kitchen table with my carburetor in a million pieces and he actually enjoys himself. Like a fucking jigsaw puzzle or something. There's fringe benefits from crystal if you stop and think about it.'

'I'm glad the police cars and ambulances stopped their sirens,' Olive said. 'They were giving me a headache.'

She was like a goddamn dog, Farley thought. Supersensitive hearing even when not tweaked. She could sit in a restaurant and hear conversations on the other side of a crowded room. He thought he should figure out a way to use that, the only talent she possessed.

'Something musta happened at one of the stores in

the mall,' Farley said. 'Maybe some fucking Jew actually charged a fair price. That would cause a bunch of greasers to drop dead of shock and tie up some ambulances.'

He was driving out of the parking lot and turning east when a southbound car at the intersection also turned east and drove in front of him, making Farley slam on his brakes.

'Fuck you!' Farley yelled out the window at the elderly woman driver after he flipped her the bird.

He hadn't gone half a block when he heard the horn toot behind him. He looked in the mirror and said, 'Cops! My fucking luck!'

Benny Brewster said to B.M. Driscoll, 'You're up.'

The older cop wiped his runny nose with Kleenex, pushed his drooping glasses back up, sighed, and said, 'I'm really not well enough to be working tonight. I shoulda called in sick.'

Then he got out, approached the car on the driver's side and saw Farley Ramsdale fumbling in his wallet for his driver's license. Olive looked toward the policeman on her right and saw Benny Brewster looking in at her and at the inside of the car.

'Hi, Officer,' Olive said.

'Evening,' Benny said.

As B.M. Driscoll was examining his driver's license, Farley said, 'What's the problem?'

B.M. Driscoll said, 'You pulled out of the lot into the traffic lane, causing a car to brake hard and yield. That's a traffic violation.'

Benny said to Farley, 'Sir, how about showing the officer your registration too.'

Farley said, 'Aw shit, this ain't my car. Belongs to a friend, Sam Culhane. My car's at his house getting fixed by him.'

When he quickly reached over to the glove compartment, Benny's hand went to his sidearm. There was nothing in the glove box except a flashlight and Sam's garage opener.

'Tell the officer, Olive,' he said. 'This is Sam's car.'

'That's right, Officer,' Olive said. 'Our car is getting its carburetor redone. Sam has it all over the table like a jigsaw.'

'That'll do,' Farley said to her. Then turning to B.M. Driscoll, he said, 'I got a cell here. You can use it and call Sam. I'll dial him for you. This ain't a hot car, Officer. Hell, I just live ten blocks from here by the Hollywood Cemetery.'

Benny Brewster looked over the top of the car to his partner and mouthed the word 'tweakers.'

Then, while B.M. Driscoll was returning to their car to run a make on Farley Ramsdale and the car's license number and to write up the traffic citation, Benny decided to screw with the tweakers, saying to Farley, 'And if we followed you to your house just to verify you're who your license says you are, would you invite us inside?'

'Why not?' Farley said.

'Would there be anything in your house that you wouldn't want us to find?'

'Wait a minute,' Farley said. 'Are you talking about searching my house?'

'How many times have you been in jail for drug possession?' Benny asked.

'I been in jail three times,' Olive said. 'Once when this guy I used to know made me shoplift some stuff from Sears.'

'Shut the fuck up, Olive,' Farley said. Then to Benny he said, 'If you don't write me the ticket, you can search me and search this car and you can search Olive here and you can come to my house and I'll prove whatever you want proved, but I ain't letting you do a fishing expedition by looking in my underwear drawer.'

'Underwear floor, you mean,' Olive said. 'Farley always throws his underwear on the floor and I gotta pick them up,' she explained.

'Olive, I'm begging you to shut up,' Farley said.

Benny looked up and saw B.M. Driscoll returning with the citation book and said, 'Too late. Looks like the citation's already written.'

B.M. Driscoll looked over the roof at his tall partner and said, 'Mr. Ramsdale has a number of arrests for drug possession and petty theft, don't you, Mr. Ramsdale?'

'Kid stuff,' Farley mumbled, signing the traffic ticket.

'I didn't write you for not having a registration,' B.M. Driscoll said. 'But tell your friend, Samuel Culhane... where does he live, by the way?'

'On Kingsley,' Olive said. 'I don't know the number.'

B.M. Driscoll nodded at Benny and said, 'That checks.' Then to Farley he said, 'Have a good evening, Mr. Ramsdale.'

When they were once again on their way to the taco stand to score some ice that Farley now needed desperately, he said to Olive, 'You see what happens when you pin a badge on a nigger? That fucking Watusi wanted to go on a fishing expedition in my house.'

'Maybe we shoulda just invited them home to see that you're a property owner and the stuff on your driver's license is correct,' Olive said. 'And it wouldn'ta mattered if they searched. We got nothing but a glass pipe at home, Farley. That's why we're out here. We got no crystal, no nothing at home.'

Farley turned and stared at her until he almost rear-ended a pickup in front of him, then said, 'Invite cops home to search? I suppose you'da made coffee for them?'

'If we had any,' she said, nodding. 'And if they didn't write the traffic ticket. It's always best to be friendly with the police. Being mean will just bring you more trouble.'

'Jesus Christ!' Farley cried. 'And then what? Maybe you woulda told them you were going to fuck them both to be friendly? Well, I hope not, Olive. Because making terroristic threats is a felony!'

FOURTEEN

Budgie and Fausto were the first of the midwatch teams to break away from the hunt for the red Mazda. Virtually every car had driven east toward gang territory and the less affluent neighborhoods where most of Hollywood's street criminals resided, but the suspects' descriptions could have put them anywhere. By now the cars were looking for a male, white or possibly Hispanic, in his midforties, of medium height and weight, with dark hair. He was wearing a Dodgers cap and sunglasses, a blue tee, and jeans. His companion was a female, white, also about forty, tall and full-figured, with red hair that two Latino women said looked like a cheap wig. The woman with the gun wore sunglasses also, a tight, multicolored cotton dress, and white espadrilles. Both witnesses commented on her large 'bosoms.'

A supplemental description was given to the communications operator by Viktor Chernenko during an on-scene interview thirty minutes after the shooting, when the area around the ATM machine was taped off and controlled by uniformed officers. Even though Viktor knew that the Bank Squad from Robbery-Homicide Division would be handling this one, he was confident that these were the suspects from the jewelry store.

When the report call came in on their MDT, Fausto said to Budgie, 'Well, by now they're in their hole. Best we could hope for is to spot the abandoned Mazda. They probably dumped it somewhere.'

The report they were assigned was for attempted murder, which in Hollywood could mean anything. This was, after all, the land of dreams and fantasy. They were sent to a quite expensive, artsy-craftsy, split-level house in Laurel Canyon, certainly not an area where attempted murders occurred frequently. The fact that there was no code assigned to the call made them think that whoever took the call at Communications didn't think it was worthy of urgent response.

The caller was waiting on his redwood balcony under a vaulted roof. He waved after they parked, and they began climbing the outside wooden staircase. It was still nearly an hour before sunset so they didn't need to light their way, but it was dark from shadows cast by all of the ferns and palms and bird of paradise plants on both sides of the staircase.

Fausto, who was getting winded from the steep climb, figured that the gardeners must make a bundle.

The caller held open the door and said, 'Right this way, officers.'

He was seventy-nine years old and dressed in an ivory-white bathrobe with satin lapels, and leather monogrammed slippers. He had dyed-auburn transplants and a gray mustache that used to be called a toothbrush. He introduced himself as James R. Houston but added that his friends called him Jim.

The inside of the house said 1965: shag carpets, lime-green-flowered sofa, Danish modern dining room furniture, and even an elaborate painted clown in a gilded frame resembling the ones that the late actor-comedian Red Skelton had painted.

When Fausto said, 'By any chance is that a Red Skelton?' and got a negative reply, Budgie said, 'Who's Red Skelton?'

'A famous comic actor of yesteryear,' the man said. 'And a fine painter.'

Only after their host insisted did they agree to have a glass of lemonade from a pitcher on the dining room table.

Then he said to Fausto, 'Even though I don't have the honor of owning a Red Skelton clown painting, I did work with him in a movie. It was in nineteen fifty-five, I think. But don't hold me to that.'

Of course, he was implying that he was an actor. Budgie Polk had learned by now that in Hollywood Division, when a suspect or victim says he's an actor, a cop's automatic response is 'And what do you do when you're not acting?'

When she said this to him, he said, 'I've dabbled in real estate for years. My wife owns some rental property that I manage. Jackie Lee's my second wife.' Then he corrected himself and said, 'Actually, my third. My first wife died, and my second, well...' With that he made a dismissive gesture and then said, 'It's about my present wife that I've called you here.'

Budgie opened her report binder and said, 'Is someone trying to murder her?'

'No,' he said, 'she's trying to murder me.'

Suddenly his hand holding the glass of lemonade began to tremble, and the ice cubes tinkled.

With his long experience in Hollywood crime, Fausto took over. 'And where is your wife now?'

'She's gone to San Francisco with her sister-in-law. They'll be back Monday morning, which is why I felt safe to call you here. I thought you might like to look for clues like on...'

'CSI,' Fausto said. These days it was always the CSI TV show. Real cops just couldn't measure up.

'Yes,' he said. 'CSI.'

'How is she trying to kill you?' Fausto asked.

'She's trying to poison me.'

'How do you know that?' Budgie asked.

'I get a stomachache every time she cooks a meal. I've started going out to dinner a lot because I'm so frightened.'

'And you wouldn't have any physical evidence, would

you?' Budgie asked. 'Something that you've saved? Like they do on *CSI*?'

'No,' he said. 'But it happens every time. It's a gradual attempt to murder me. She's a very sophisticated and clever woman.'

'Is there any other evidence of her homicidal intent that you can offer?' Fausto asked.

'Yes,' he said. 'She's putting a toxic substance in my shoes.'

'Go on,' Budgie said. 'How do you know?'

'My feet are always tired. And the soles sometime hurt for no reason.'

Fausto glanced at his watch and said, 'Anything else?'

'Yes, I believe she's putting a toxic substance in my hats.'

'Let me guess,' Fausto said. 'You have headaches?'

'How did you know?'

'Here's the problem as I see it, Mr. Houston,' Fausto said. 'If we arrest her, a high-priced shyster like the ones Michael Jackson hires would look at all this evidence and say, your wife's a lousy cook, your shoes're too tight, and so's your hat. You see where I'm coming from?'

'Yes, I take your point, Officer,' he said.

'So I think what you should do is put this aside for now and call us back when you have more evidence. A lot more evidence.'

'Do you think I should risk my life eating her food to collect the evidence?'

'Bland food,' Fausto said. 'It's not easy to disguise poison in bland dishes. Go ahead and enjoy your mashed potatoes and vegetables and a steak or some chicken, but not fried chicken. Just don't go for the spicy stuff and avoid heavy sauces. That's where it could be risky. And buy some shoes that are a half size bigger. Do you drink alcohol with dinner?'

'Three martinis. My wife makes them.'

'Cut back to one martini. It's very hard to put a toxic dose in only one martini. Have it after dinner but not just before bedtime. And only wear hats when you go out in the sun. I think all of this will disrupt a murder plot or flush out the perpetrator.'

'And you'll come back when we have more to go on?'

'Absolutely,' Fausto said. 'It will be a pleasure.'

There was no pleasure to be had in the house of Farley Ramsdale. Three hours had passed since Cosmo and Ilya had pushed the car into the little garage, and still Farley and Olive had not come home. At one point Cosmo thought Ilya was asleep, lying there on the couch with her eyes closed.

But when he got up to look out the window at the darkened street, she said, 'Stay back from the window. Every police in Hollywood looks for a man in a blue shirt and a woman with the hair that they shall know is a wig. We cannot call a taxi here. A driver shall think of us when he hears about the robbery. Then police may come here and talk to Farley and he is going to know it was us and he shall tell them.'

'Shut up, Ilya. I must think!'

'We cannot go to a bus. We may be seen by police. We cannot call any of your friends to come for us unless you wish to share money with them because they shall find out. We are in a trap.'

'Shut up!' Cosmo said. 'We are not in the trap. We have the money. It is dark now.'

'How do we go home, Cosmo? How?'

'Maybe the car will start now.'

'I shall not put myself in that car!' Ilya said. 'Every cop looks for that car. Every cop in Hollywood! Every cop in all Los Angeles!'

'The car must stay here,' he agreed. 'We put the money in shopping bags. There are paper bags in the kitchen.'

'I understand,' Ilya said. 'We walk away from this house because we do not dare to call the taxi to come here? And then we call from my cell phone and taxi is going to meet us out on the street someplace where we hide in shadows? And we get taxi to leave us a few streets from our apartment?'

'Yes. That is exactly correct.'

'And then Farley and Olive come home to find a car in garage and pretty soon when they turn on TV they see about robbery and the death of the guard and how the killer looks like and you don't think they know who done it? And you think they do not call police and say, Is there reward for the name of killers? The car is here. You do not think this shall happen, Cosmo?'

Cosmo sat down then and put his head in his hands. He had been thinking for three hours, and there was no alternative. He had planned to kill Farley and Olive at the junkyard just before getting the money for the diamonds, but now? He had to kill them when they walked in this house. Yet he could not risk gunfire.

He went over to Ilya and knelt on the floor beside her and said, 'Ilya, the two addicts must die when they come home. We got no choice. We got to kill them. Maybe with knife from the kitchen. You must help me, Ilya.'

She sat up and said, 'I will not kill nobody else with you, Cosmo. Nobody.'

'But what must we do?' he pleaded.

'Tell them what we done. Make them partner. Give them half of money. Make them help us to push that goddamn car away from here and leave it or set fire on it. Then they drive us home. And while all this happens, we just got to hope the cops do not see us. That is what we do, Cosmo. We do not kill nobody else.'

'Please, Ilya! Think!'

'If you try to kill Farley and Olive, you shall have to kill me. You cannot stab us all, Cosmo. I shall shoot you if I can.'

And with that, she drew the pistol from her purse, got up, and walked across the room to the sagging TV viewing chair, where she sat down with the gun in her lap.

'Please do not make fool talk,' Cosmo said. I must call Dmitri. But not now. Not today. I do not talk to Dmitri yet. We must see what is what before I call him.'

'We shall get caught,' she said. 'Or killed.'

'Ilya,' he said, looking at her. 'Let us make love, Ilya. You shall feel much better if we make love.'

'Do not come close to me or it shall end here with guns, and you cannot let guns shoot on this quiet street, Cosmo. Or maybe you also wish to stab every neighbor too?'

Budgie and Fausto were back on patrol looking for something to do, when Budgie said, 'Let's go by Pablo's Tacos and jam up a tweaker or two. Maybe we'll shake loose some crystal. We could use an observation arrest on our recap.'

'Okay,' Fausto said, turning east on the boulevard. 'But whatever you do, don't order a taco in that joint. 'You heard about the tweaker at Pablo's that shoved bindles of crystal up his bung and tried to say his partner made him do it? Well, sometimes he cooks there.'

Farley was absolutely livid by now, and Olive was getting an upset stomach from the stress. For the tenth time, he cried out, 'Ain't there a goddamn teener or two left in this fucking town?'

'Please, Farley,' Olive said. 'You'll make yourself sick.'

'I need some ice!' he said. 'Goddamnit, Olive, we been fucking around for hours!'

'Maybe we should try the doughnut shop again.'

'We tried it twice!' Farley said. 'We tried every goddamn place I can think of. Can you think of a place we ain't tried?'

'No, Farley,' she said. 'I can't.'

Farley raised himself up and looked to his right and saw

6-X-76 parking in the lot. A tall blond female cop got out, along with an old rhino who Farley figured must be a Mexican, or these days a Salvadoran, and that was even worse.

Farley turned his face away and said, 'Olive, tell me these two cops ain't gonna jack us up. Not twice in one night, for chrissake!'

'They're looking at us,' Olive said. Then Farley heard her say cheerfully, 'Good evening, officers.'

Farley put both hands on the steering wheel so they wouldn't get goosey and blow his fucking head off, and the female cop said, 'Evening. Waiting for someone?'

Farley pointed to Olive and said, 'Yeah, she's an actress. Waiting to get discovered.'

That did it. Fausto said, 'Step outta the car.'

Since this had happened to Farley dozens of times in his life, he kept his hands in plain view when Fausto pulled open the driver's door. Farley got out, shaking his head and wondering why oh why did everything happen to him?

Fausto patted him down and said, 'Let's see some ID.'

When Olive got out, Budgie looked at Olive's scrawny torso covered only by a short T-shirt, revealing a sunken belly and bony hips. Her jeans were child size, and Budgie perfunctorily patted the pockets to see if she felt any bindles of crystal. Then Budgie shined her flashlight beam on Olive's inner forearms, but since Olive had seldom skin-popped, there weren't any tracks.

Farley said, 'Gimme a break, *amigo*. Some of your *compadres* already rousted us tonight. They ran a make on us and on the car and then gave me a fucking ticket. Can I reach in my glove box and prove it to you?'

'No, stay here, *amigo*,' Fausto said, painting it with sarcasm. To Budgie he said, 'Partner, take a look in the glove compartment. See if there's a citation in there.'

She opened the glove compartment and retrieved the

traffic ticket, saying, 'B.M. Driscoll wrote it right after roll call. Near the cyber café.'

'I'll bet it never occurred to you, *amigo*,' Fausto said, 'that maybe the reason you get stopped by so many cops is because you hang out where tweakers score their crystal. Did that ever flash on your computer screen?'

Farley thought he better lose the Spanish words because they didn't work with this fucking greaseball, so he tried a different tack. 'Officer, please help yourself. You don't even have to ask. Search my car.'

And Budgie said, 'Okay,' and she did.

While she was searching, Farley said, 'Yes, I got a minor record for petty theft and possession of crystal meth. No, I don't have drugs on me. If you want, I'll take off my shoes. If we weren't standing out here, I'd take off my fucking pants. I'm too tired to reason with you guys anymore. Just do what you gotta do and let me go home.'

Olive said, 'We even told the other officers they could come home with us,' Olive said helpfully. 'We don't care if you search our house. You can do a fishing exposition, we don't care.'

'Olive,' Farley said, 'I'm begging you. Shut the fuck up.'

'Is that right?' Budgie said. 'You're so clean you'd take us home right now and let us search your house, no problem?' To Fausto, 'Whadda you think of that, partner?'

'Is that what you'd do?' Fausto asked Farley, as he wrote a quick FI card. 'Take us to your crib? You're that clean?'

'Man, at this point I'm just tempted to say yes. If you'd let me go lay in bed, you could turn the fucking place upside down, inside and out. And if you find any dope in that house, it would mean that Olive here must have a secret boyfriend who's supplying her. And if Olive could find a boyfriend, then there really are miracles and maybe I'll win the California lottery. And if I do, I'll move clear outta this fucking town and away from you people, because you're killing me, man, you're killing me!'

Fausto looked at the anguished clammy face of Farley Ramsdale, handed him his driver's license, and said, 'Dude, you better get into rehab ASAP. The trolley you're riding is at the last stop. Nothing left ahead but the end of the line.'

When Fausto and Budgie were back in their car, she said to Fausto, 'I'm tempted to drive by the address on that FI a little later.'

'What for?'

'That guy's gotta score some crystal. They'll be smoking ice and getting all spun out tonight or he'll be in a strait-jacket. He's that close to losing it completely.'

Ilya was on her feet, pacing and smoking. Cosmo was the one on the couch now, exhausted from arguing with her.

'How long we sit at this place?' he asked lethargically.

'Almost six hours,' she said. 'We can't wait no more. We got to go.'

'Without our money, Ilya?'

'Did you wipe all evidence from the car, Cosmo?'

'I tell you yes, okay? Now please shut up.'

'Did you empty the cigarette tray in the car? That is evidence.'

'Yes.'

'Get can of money out from the car.'

'You got idea, Ilya? Wonderful. You don't like my ideas. Like we must kill the addicts.'

'Shut up, Cosmo. You will put can of money under this house. Find a little door that go under this house. Put can in there.'

She began emptying ashtrays into a paper bag from the kitchen, and he said, 'Ilya, the car? It cannot travel! What are you thinking about?'

'We are leaving it.'

'Here? Ilya, you are crazy person! Farley and Olive—'

In charge now, she interrupted, 'Did you take things out from garage?'

'Yes, a bike and few boxes. Goddamn garage, full of junk. Almost no room for a goddamn car.'

'As I thought,' she said. 'Put all junk back in.'

'What are you thinking about, Ilya?'

'They are addicts, Cosmo. Look at this house. Trash all around. Junk all around. They do not park car in garage. They do not go in garage almost never. The car must stay for few days. They shall not even know it.'

'And us?'

'Take a shirt from Farley. Look inside bedroom. I am going to remove my wig and we shall walk few blocks from here to phone taxi. It is a little bit safe now. Then we go home.'

'All right, Ilya,' he said. 'But you sleep on top of this idea tonight: The addicts must die. We got no other road to travel. You must soon see that.'

'I must think,' she said. 'Now we go. Hurry.'

When Cosmo came back into the living room from the bedroom, he was wearing a dirty long-sleeved patterned shirt over his T-shirt. 'Hope you happy now, Ilya,' he said. 'Before we get home I shall be bit a hundred times by tiny creatures that crawl inside Farley's clothes.'

After the cops left them in the Pablo's Tacos parking lot, Farley said, 'Olive, I think we gotta go home and white-knuckle it. We ain't gonna score tonight.'

'There's almost a quart of vodka there,' Olive said. 'I'll mix it with some packets of punch and you can just drink as much as you can.'

'Okay,' he said. 'That'll get me through the night. It'll have to.'

'I just hope it won't make you throw up,' Olive said. 'You're so thin and tired-looking.'

'It won't,' he said.

'And I'll make you something delicious to eat.'

'That'll make me throw up,' he said.

When they arrived at Farley's house, he was almost too tired to climb the porch steps, and when he did and they were inside, Olive said, 'Farley, it smells like smoke in here.'

He threw himself on the couch and grabbed the TV remote, saying 'Olive, it should. We smoke crystal in here in case you forgot. Every chance we get, which ain't often enough these days.'

'Yes, but it smells like old cigarette smoke. Don't you notice it?'

'I'm so fucking tired, Olive,' he said, 'I wouldn't smell smoke if you set fire to yourself. Which wouldn't be a bad idea.'

'You'll feel better after a meal,' said Olive. 'How does a toasted cheese sandwich sound?'

The PSR putting out the broadcast decided to have a bit of fun with 6-X-32's call to Grauman's Chinese Theater. She put it out as a hotshot.

Flotsam and Jetsam listened incredulously when, after the electronic beep, she said, 'All units in the vicinity and Six-X-ray-Thirty-two, see the woman on Hollywood Boulevard west of Highland. A battery in progress. Batman versus Spiderman. Batman last seen running into Kodak Center. Person reporting is Marilyn Monroe. Six-X-Thirty-two, handle code three.'

When they got to the scene, Marilyn Monroe was waving at them from the courtyard of Grauman's Chinese Theater and tourists were snapping photos like crazy. B.M. Driscoll and Benny Brewster rolled in right behind them.

Jetsam, who was driving, said, 'Which Marilyn is it, do you think? One of them is hot, bro. Know which one I mean?'

'It ain't the hot one,' Flotsam said.

Their Marilyn was striking the famous over-the-air-vent pose, but there was no air blowing up her dress. She had the Monroe dress and her pricey wig was excellent. Even her coy but sensuous Monroe smile was right on the money. The problem was, she was six feet three inches tall and wasn't a woman.

Flotsam got out first and saw Spiderman sitting on the curb holding his head and rubbing his jaw. Jetsam went over to him and got the details, which of course involved a turf fight between two tourist hustlers.

While Flotsam was talking to Marilyn Monroe, a tourist begged them to move stage left so he could get Grauman's in the background. Marilyn did it gladly. After a moment's hesitation during which several tourists needled him for being a poor sport, Flotsam moved with her and put up with about a hundred photo flashes from every direction.

Finally Marilyn said, 'It was terrible, Officer! Batman struck Spiderman with a flashlight for no reason at all. He's a pig, Batman is. I have always found Spiderman to be a love. I hope you find that cape-wearing rat and toss his fat ass in jail!'

There was quite a bit of applause then, and Marilyn Monroe flashed a smile that could only be called blinding in its whiteness.

As Flotsam was trying to get information from Marilyn Monroe, he was surrounded by all three Elvises. They worked in tandem only on big Friday nights like this one, and seeing the commotion went for the chance at real publicity. And they weren't disappointed. The first TV news van to have heard the police broadcast was dropping a cameraman and reporter at the corner of Hollywood and Highland just as the Elvises gathered.

The Presleys were all talking at once to Flotsam: Skinny Elvis, Fat Elvis, and even Smellvis, he of the yellow sweat stains under the arms of his ice-cream suit, which made tourists hold their breath during his cuddly photo shoots.

'Batman will never eat lunch in this town again!' Skinny Elvis cried.

'Spiderman rules!' Fat Elvis cried.

'I am an eye witness to the caped crusader's vicious attack!' Smellvis announced to the crowd, and he was so rank that Flotsam had to backpedal a few steps.

Flotsam asked B.M. Driscoll to check out the Kodak Center, and when he asked, 'What's the guy look like?' Flotsam said, 'Just hook up any guy you see wearing a cape and hanging upside down somewheres. If it turns out to be Count Dracula, just apologize.'

The midwatch cops didn't know that there was an undercover team at work in the midst of the crowd, posing as tourists with backpacks and cameras. The UC team had Tickle Me Elmo under arrest for manhandling a female tourist after she'd snapped his picture and refused to pay his three-dollar tariff.

Elmo had grabbed her by the arm and said, 'Well you can kiss my ass, bitch!' and next thing he knew, the UC cops had him up against the wall of the Kodak Center and removed his head, inside of which they found more than two hundred dollar bills and a gram of cocaine.

Now the tourists turned on Elmo for photos, but the TV camera crew was still concentrating on Marilyn Monroe, until Benny Brewster said to Flotsam, 'Hey man, Elmo had dope in his head!'

Upon hearing this, the news team swung their cameras toward Elmo, who was yelling that his head was dope-free when he'd put the costume on, implying a police frame-up.

Jetsam decided to help search the Kodak Center, where after a few minutes Batman was spotted. It was a brief chase, since Batman's ample gut was hanging over his utility belt, and he was just slogging along in front of the Kodak

Theatre when Jetsam jumped him from behind. For a minute or two Jetsam feared that the exhausted Batman was going into cardiac arrest after he was proned out and cuffed.

Jetsam said to B.M. Driscoll, 'How do you do CPR through a bat mask and breast-plate?'

When Jetsam finally got outside Grauman's forecourt with his handcuffed and forlorn prisoner, crowds gathered, camera bulbs flashed, and the news bunny ran up to him, saying, 'Officer, did you have trouble catching up with Batman? Was it an exciting chase?'

The surfer cop struck a semi-heroic pose for the camera and said, 'Weak sauce.' Then he quickly walked Batman to the black-and-white, where he was put into the backseat.

This particular news bunny was a relentless journalist and proud of it. She hurried after Jetsam and stood next to the police car, making a point of handing her mike to one of the guys in her crew so she could appear to confront the cop empty-handed.

'"Weak… sauce"?' said the news bunny to Jetsam, with arching, perfectly penciled eyebrows, and a lip-licking smile that stopped the surfer cop in his tracks. 'Can you translate that term for us? Off the record?'

Jetsam gaped at her cleavage. And goddamn, she licked her lips again! He looked at her camera crew, who were back on the sidewalk and couldn't even see his face, and he leaned down with his mouth close to her ear and whispered, 'It just means, without his Batmobile he ain't shit.'

Then with a devil-may-care wink, he whirled and hopped into the car behind the wheel. He was tickled to see the news bunny direct the crew to shoot coverage of 6-X-32 as he was driving off.

What Jetsam didn't see, however, was the news bunny fingering the little mike she had wired inside the collar of her jacket. And the triumphant smile she gave to her sound man was even twice as sexy as the one she'd given Jetsam.

On the late news, the producer bleeped out *shit*, but from the context the audience knew what had been said. Then the news bunny appeared on camera, this time directly in front of Grauman's Chinese Theater.

With her Hollywood insider's saucy grin, she said to her audience, 'This is your intrepid reporter coming to you from Hollywood Boulevard, where even superheroes must bow to the forces of LAPD justice—who are anything but... weak sauce.'

The watch commander told Jetsam that he'd probably get another official reprimand or even a little suspension for the manner of his 'interview.'

Cosmo did not waken until 1 p.m. the next afternoon. The smell of Ilya's tea brought him around, and at first he felt a stab of panic. What if she'd gone back to get the money? But then he heard her and the sound of dishes being washed, so he entered the bathroom and showered.

When he came into the kitchen, she was at the table smoking and drinking a glass of hot tea. Another glass was poured and awaited him. Neither spoke until he drank some and lit a cigarette of his own, and then he said, 'How long you are awake?'

'Three hours,' she said. 'I am thinking many thoughts.'

'And what is the new idea?'

'How much Dmitri is going to give for the diamonds?'

'Twenty thousands,' he lied.

'Okay,' she said. 'Give to him the diamonds. No charge. We keep the money.'

'All the money?'

'No, we share with Farley and Olive. We make the best bargain we can. Then we get out of Los Angeles. Go to San Francisco. Start over. No more guns. No more death.'

'Ilya, Dmitri know how much money we got. Do you not turn on TV and hear about it?'

'No,' she said. 'I have no wish to hear more.'

'The news tell how much we got. Dmitri shall want half.'

'We may leave Los Angeles with almost fifty thousand, even Farley if take away half. We cannot give Dmitri no money. We give him diamonds.'

'Is not enough. He shall kill us, Ilya. I know he is mad now because I did not make a call to him. I know he is very mad.'

'We are leaving Los Angeles.'

'He shall find us and kill us in San Francisco.'

'We take a chance.'

'You think Farley and Olive do not tell police about us after we give them money?'

'No. They must have drugs. They must have money for drugs. After they take half of money, they are, how you say it, partners in the crime. They cannot tell police nothing. We shall wait two, maybe three days. I tell you the addicts will not know the Mazda is in garage. And under the house they never go in all their life. We are okay for two, three days. We hide here.'

'Ilya, we may keep half money and give other half to Dmitri.' Then he almost told the truth about the diamond deal, saying, 'I think I may bargain with Dmitri. I think I say to him I must have thirty-five thousands for diamonds. So, we shall have almost eighty-five thousands and we stay in Los Angeles. All of this if you permit me to kill the addicts. I know how. You shall not need to do nothing.' He was finished now, but he decided to add a postscript. He said, 'Please, Ilya. You love the life here. You very much love the life in Hollywood. Am I correct?'

Ilya's mascara was running when she got up and went to the tea kettle on the stove. She stood there for a long moment before speaking. With her back to him she said, 'All right, Cosmo. Kill them. And do not never talk of it. Never!'

FIFTEEN

The southeastern part of Hollywood Division, near Santa Monica Boulevard and Western Avenue, was the turf of Latino gangs, including Eighteenth Street cruisers and some Salvadorans from the huge MS-13 gang. White Fence, one of the oldest Mexican American gangs was active around Hollywood Boulevard and Western, and Mexican Mafia, aka MM or El Eme, was only here and there but in some ways was the most powerful gang of all and could even operate lethally from inside state prisons. There were no black gangs in the Hollywood area, like the Crips or Bloods of south central and southeast L.A., because there were very few blacks living in the Hollywood area.

Wesley Drubb was steeped in this what was to him exciting information, having been permitted to gain new experience by working on loan for two nights with 6-G-1, a Hollywood Division gang unit. But now while driving on Rossmore Avenue, which bordered the Wilshire Country Club, his gang chatter seemed ludicrously inappropriate and especially annoying to Hollywood Nate Weiss.

Wesley said, 'The California Department of Corrections estimates that El Eme has nearly two hundred members in the prison system.'

'You don't say.' Nate was gazing up at the luxurious apartment buildings and condos on both sides of his favorite Los Angeles street.

'They're usually identified by a tattoo of a black hand with an *M* on the palm of it. In the Pelican Bay Maximum

Security Prison, an MM gang member had sixty thousand dollars in a trust account before it was frozen by authorities. He was doing deals from inside the strictest prison!'

'Do tell.' Nate imagined Clark Gable in black tie and Carole Lombard in sable, both smiling at the doorman as they went off for a night on the town. At the Coconut Grove, maybe.

Then he tailored the fantasy to fit Tracy and Hepburn, even though he knew that neither of them had ever lived on the street. But what the hell, it was his fantasy.

Wesley said, 'Big homies have been known to order hits from their prison cells. If you're "in the hat" or "green-lighted," it means you're targeted.'

'Weird,' Nate said. 'Green-lighted in the movie business means you got the okay to do the picture. In Hollywood it means you're alive. In prison it means you're dead. Weird.'

Wesley said, 'They told me that sometimes in Hollywood we might encounter southeast Asian gangsters from the Tiny Oriental Crips and the Oriental Boy Soldiers. Ever run into them?'

'I don't think so,' Nate said. 'I've only encountered more law-abiding and sensitive Asians who would bury a cleaver in your neck if you ever referred to them as Orientals.'

Wesley said, 'And the Asian gang whose name I love is the Tiny Magicians Club, aka the TMC.'

'Jesus Christ!' Nate said. 'TMC is The Movie Channel! Isn't anything fucking sacred anymore?'

Wesley said, 'I already knew about the civil injunctions to keep gang members in check, but did you know the homies have to be personally served with humongous legal documents that set forth all terms of the injunction? Two or three gang members congregating can violate the injunction, and even possession and use of cell phones can be a violation. Did you know that?'

Nate said, 'Possession of a cell phone by any person of

253

the female gender who is attempting to operate a motor vehicle should be a felony, you ask me.'

Wesley said, 'I might get to examine the tattoos and talk to some crew members and hear about their gang wars next time.'

'Do I detect a 'hood rat in the making?' Nate said, yawning. 'Are you gonna be putting in a transfer, Wesley? Maybe to Seventy-seventh Street or Southeast, where people keep rocket launchers at home for personal protection?'

'When I got sent to Hollywood I heard it was a good misdemeanor division. I guess I wanna go to a good felony division. I've heard that in the days before the consent decree, Rampart Division CRASH unit used to have a sign that said "We intimidate those who intimidate others." Imagine how it was to work that Gang Squad.'

Nate looked at Wesley the way he'd look at a cuppa joe from Dunkin' Donuts or a Hostess Ding Dong and said, 'Wesley, the days of LAPD rock 'n' rule are over. It's never coming back.'

Wesley said, 'I just thought that someplace like Southeast Division would offer more... challenges.'

'Go ahead, then,' Nate said. 'You can amuse yourself on long nights down there by going to drug houses and yelling "Police!" then listening to toilets flushing all over the block. Cop entertainment in the 'hood. Watching cruisers throw gang signs beats the hell outta redcarpet events, where the tits extend from Hollywood Boulevard to infinity, right?'

Wesley Drubb was eager indeed to do police work in gang territory, or anyplace where he might encounter real action. He was growing more and more tense and nervous with Nate boring him to death by directing him far from the semi-mean streets of Hollywood for his endless sorties into Hollywood's past. The gang turf was there and he was here. Touring!

Quiet now, Wesley chewed a fingernail as he drove. Nate

finally noticed and said, 'Hey pard, you look especially stressed. Got girlfriend troubles maybe? I'm an expert on that subject.'

Wesley wasn't far enough from his probationary period to say, 'I am fucking bored to death, Nate! You are killing me with these trips through movie history!'

Instead, he said, 'Nate, do you think we should be cruising around the country club? This is Wilshire Area. We work in Hollywood Area.'

'Stop saying area,' Nate said. 'Division sounds more coplike. I can't stand these new terms for everything.'

'Okay, Hollywood Division, then. We're out of it right now. This is Wilshire Division.'

'A few blocks, big deal,' Nate said. 'Look around you. This is gorgeous.'

Hollywood Nate was referring to Rossmore Avenue, where the elegant apartment buildings and pricey converted condos had names like the Rossmore, El Royale, the Marlowe, and Country Club Manor, all of them a short walk from the very private golf course. They were built in the French, Spanish, and Beaux Arts styles of Hollywood's Golden Age.

Seeing that Wesley lacked enthusiasm for the architecture, Nate said, 'Maybe you'd like to cruise by the Church of Scientology Celebrity Center? We might spot John Travolta. But we can't hassle any of their so-called parishioners or we'll get beefed by their fascist security force. Do you know they even beefed our airship one time? Said they wanted to make their headquarters an LAPD no-fly zone.'

Wesley said, 'No, I don't have much interest in Scientology or John Travolta, to tell you the truth.'

'This looks like we're in Europe,' Nate said, as the setting sun lit the entry of the El Royale. 'Can't you see Mae West sashaying out that door with a hunky actor on her arm to a limo waiting on the street?'

'Mae West' was how Wesley Drubb's father referred to the life jackets he kept aboard a seventy-five-foot power yacht that he used to own and kept docked at the marina. Wesley didn't know that they were named after a person, but he said, 'Yeah, Mae West.'

'Someday I'll be living in one of those buildings,' Nate said. 'The local country clubs used to restrict Jews. And actors. I've heard it was Randolph Scott who told them, "I'm not an actor and I've got a hundred movies to prove it." But then I heard it was Victor Mature. Even John Wayne, and he didn't hardly play golf. It's a good Hollywood story no matter who said it.'

Wesley had never heard of the first two actor-golfers and was getting a tightness in his neck and jaw muscles. He was even grinding his teeth and only relaxed when Nate sighed and said, 'Okay, let's go find you a bad guy to put in jail.'

And at last, with an enormous sense of relief, Wesley Drubb was permitted to drive away from reel Hollywood and head for the real one.

Darkness fell as they were passing the Gay and Lesbian Center, and Nate said, 'That's where they can go to let their hair down. Or their hair extensions. There's a place for everyone to dream in Hollywood. I don't know why you can't be satisfied.'

A few minutes later, on Santa Monica Boulevard, Wesley said, 'Look how that guy's walking. Let's shake him.'

Nate looked across the street at a pale and gaunt forty-something guy in a crew neck, long-sleeved sweater and jeans, walking along the boulevard with his hands in his pockets.

'Whadda you see that I don't see?'

'He's a parolee-at-large, I bet. He walks like they do in the prison yard.'

'You learned a lot with the gang unit,' Nate said. 'Maybe even something worthwhile, but I haven't noticed it yet.'

Wesley said, 'The parole officers are a few months behind in getting warrants into their computer, but we could check him anyway, okay? Even if there's no warrant, maybe he's holding some dope.'

'Maybe he's cruising for a date,' Nate said. 'This is Santa Monica Boulevard, home of boy love and homo-thugs. He might be looking for somebody like the one he left in prison. A guy with a tattoo of a naked babe on his back and an asshole like the Hollywood subway.'

'Can we check him?'

'Yeah, go ahead, get it outta your system,' Nate said.

Wesley pulled up several yards behind the guy, and both cops got out and lit him with their flashlight beams.

He was used to it. He stopped and took his hands out of his pockets. With a guy like this preliminaries were few, and when Wesley said, 'Got some ID?' the guy shot them a grudging look of surrender and without being asked pulled up the sweater sleeves, showing his forearms, which were covered with jailhouse tatts over old scar tissue.

'I don't use no more,' he said.

Nate moved the beam of his light near the man's face and said, 'Your eyes are down right now, bro.'

'I drink like a Skid Row alky,' the ex-con said, 'but I don't shoot up. I got tired of getting busted for eleven five-fifty. I was always under the influence and I just kept getting busted. Like, I was serving life in prison a few weeks at a time.'

Wesley wrote an FI card on the guy, whose ID said his name was Brian Allen Wilkie, and ran the information on the MDT, coming back with an extensive drug record but no wants or warrants.

Before they let him go, Nate said, 'Where you headed?'

'Pablo's to get a taco.'

'That's tweakerville,' Nate said. 'Don't tell me you're smoking glass now instead of shooting smack?'

'One day at a time, man,' Brian Wilkie said. 'I wouldn't want my PO to know, but I'm down to booze and a little meth now and then. That's an improvement, ain't it?'

'I don't think that's what AA means by one day at a time, man,' Nate said. 'Stay real.'

A few minutes later, when Wesley drove past Pablo's Tacos, they saw an old car parked in front and a pair of skinny tweakers in a dispute with another guy who also had tweaker written all over him. The argument was so animated that the tweakers didn't see the black-and-white when Wesley parked half a block away and turned out the lights to watch.

'Maybe one of them'll stab the other,' Nate said. 'And you can pop him for a felony. Or better yet, maybe one of them'll pull a piece and we can get in a gunfight. Would that relieve your boredom?'

Farley Ramsdale was waving his arms like one of those people with that terrible disease whose name she couldn't remember, and Olive was getting scared. Spit was running down Farley's chin and he was screaming his head off because the tiny tweaker that they knew as Little Bart wouldn't sell one of the two teeners he was holding. Farley refused to meet his excessive price and had tried to bargain him down.

Olive thought it was mean and wrong of Little Bart, because Farley had often sold to him at a decent price. But all this screaming was just going to get them in trouble.

'You are an ungrateful chunk of vomit!' Farley yelled. 'Do you remember how I saved your sorry ass when you needed ice so bad you were ready to blow a nigger for it?'

Little Bart, who was about Farley's age and whose neck bore a tattoo of a dog collar all the way around, said, 'Man, things're bad, real bad these days. This is all I got and all I'm gonna have for a while. I gotta pay the rent.'

'You little cocksucker!' Farley yelled, doubling his fist.

'Hey, dude!' Little Bart said, backing up. 'Take a chill pill! You're freaking!'

Olive stepped forward then and said, 'Farley, please stop. Let's go. Please!'

Suddenly, Farley did something he had never done in all the time they'd been together. He smacked her across the face, and she was so stunned she stared at him for a moment and then burst into tears.

'That's enough,' Wesley said, and got out of the car, followed by Hollywood Nate.

Farley never saw them coming but Little Bart did. The tiny tweaker said, 'Uh-oh, time to go.'

And he started to do just that, until Wesley said, 'Hold it right there.'

A few minutes later, Little Bart and Farley were being patted down by Wesley and Hollywood Nate while Olive wiped her tears on the tail of her jersey.

'What's this all about?' Farley said. 'I ain't done nothing.'

'You committed a battery,' Wesley said. 'I saw it.'

'It was an accident,' Farley said. 'Wasn't it, Olive? I didn't mean to hit her. I was just making a point with this guy.'

'What point is that?' Nate said.

'About whether George W. Bush is really as dumb as he looks. It was a political debate.'

Little Bart wasn't really worried, because the ice was under the rear floor mat of his car, which was half a block down the street. So he just had to chill and not piss off the cops, and then he figured he could skate.

When Nate pulled Farley ten yards away from the other two, Farley yelled back, 'Olive, tell these guys it was an accident!'

'Shut the fuck up,' Nate said. 'Where's your car?'

'I ain't got a car,' Farley lied, and after he did it, he wondered why he had lied. There was no crystal in his car. He hadn't smoked any glass for two and a half days. That's why his nerves were shot. That's why he was on the verge of strangling Little Bart. He was just so sick of being hassled by cops that he lied. Lying was a form of rebellion against all of them. All of the assholes who were fucking with him.

For the next twenty minutes, the shakes were written, and each name was run through CII, with a rap sheet showing for Farley Ramsdale but none for Olive O. Ramsdale. Farley finally stopped bitching and Olive stopped crying.

Little Bart actually began trying to talk politics to Farley to go along with the George Bush crack, but the cops obviously weren't buying it. They knew that some kind of drug deal was going down, and Little Bart just didn't want to give them a good reason to try his car keys in the doors of the eight cars that were parked within half a block of Pablo's. And he especially didn't want them to look under the floor mat.

Farley thought the cops were going to prolong this for as long as possible, but the younger cop ran up to the other one and said, 'Kidnapping in progress, Omar's Lounge on Ivar! Let's go, Nate!'

When Farley and Olive and Little Bart were left standing there outside Pablo's Tacos, Farley said to Little Bart, 'Those cops saved your fucking life.'

Bart said, 'Dude, you need some help. You're way out there. Way, way out there.' And he ran to his car and drove off.

Olive said, 'Farley let's go home now and—'

'Olive,' he said, 'if you say you'll make me a delicious cheese sandwich, I swear I'll knock your fucking tooth out.'

Hollywood detectives had been forced to investigate a number of date rapes, called acquaintance rapes by the police. It was usually 'I woke up naked with somebody I didn't know. I was drugged.'

The cases were never prosecuted. Evidentiary requirements necessitated an immediate urine test, but the date rape drugs metabolized in four to six hours. It was always too late for the special analysis that had to be done outside the LAPD crime lab, which did only basic drug screening of controlled substances. In fact, as defense lawyers argued, too much booze produced much the same effect as a date rape drug.

The date rape cases were reported to Hollywood Station by persons of both genders, but only once was there a criminal filing by the District Attorney's Office. The victim had vomited shortly after the encounter, and the drug was able to be recovered and identified.

Six-X-Seventy-six was the unit to receive the code 3 call to Omar's Lounge but Budgie and Fausto were beaten to the call by Wesley Drubb and Hollywood Nate, followed closely by Benny Brewster and B.M. Driscoll, complaining of motion sickness caused by Benny's fast driving.

The first units to arrive gave way to Budgie and Fausto, since they were assigned the call, and Budgie entered the nightclub to interview the victim. Even though Fausto was the report writer on this night and Budgie was driver, she took over with the report because the victim was a woman.

When they were being escorted to a private office inside the nightclub, Fausto whispered to her, 'This joint gets sold to somebody new just about every time they change the tablecloths. It's impossible to keep track of who the owner is, but you can bet your ass it's a Russian.'

Sara Butler was sitting in the office being tended to by a cocktail waitress who wore a starched white shirt, black bow tie and black pants. The waitress was a natural blonde and pretty, but the kidnap victim, who was about Budgie's age, was both prettier and unnaturally more blond. The straps on her black dress were held together with safety pins, and her pantyhose was in shreds around her ankles. Her knees were scraped and bleeding, as were both her palms. Mascara and eye liner were smeared all over her cheeks, and she was wearing most of her lipstick on her chin. She was angry and she was drunk.

The cocktail waitress was applying ice in a napkin to the victim's right knee when the cops walked in. A faux fur coat was draped across the chair behind the young woman.

Budgie sat down and said, 'Tell us what happened.'

'I was kidnapped by four Iranians,' Sara Butler said.

'When?' Budgie asked.

'About an hour ago,' Sara Butler said.

Budgie looked at Fausto, who nodded and went out to broadcast a code 4, meaning sufficient help at the scene, since the suspects were long gone.

'What did you say when you called it in?' Budgie asked. 'We were under the impression that it had just occurred.'

'I don't know what I said, I was so upset.'

'Okay,' Budgie said. 'From the beginning, please.'

After she'd given all of the contact information for the report, and after listing her occupation as actress, Sara Butler said, 'I was supposed to meet my girlfriend here but she called me on my cell and said her husband came home from a trip unexpectedly. And I thought I might as well have a drink since I was here.'

'You had more than one?'

'I don't know how many I had.'

'Go on.'

'I got talking to some guy at the bar and he started buying me martinis. I didn't have that many.'

Worrying about the liquor license, the cocktail waitress looked at Budgie and said, 'We wouldn't serve anyone who's drunk.'

'Continue, please,' Budgie said to Sara Butler.

'So pretty soon I started feeling weird. Dizzy in a weird way. I think the guy slipped me a date rape drug but I didn't drink enough of it to knock me cold.'

'How many martinis did you drink?'

'No more than four. Or possibly five.'

'That could knock a hippo cold,' Budgie said. 'Go on.'

'The guy who bought me the martinis offered to drive me home. Said he had a black Mercedes sedan and a driver parked right in front. Said he'd be in the car. I said okay and went to the ladies room to freshen up.'

'Weren't you worried about the date rape drug?' Budgie asked.

'Not then. I only thought about it after the kidnapping.'

'Okay, continue.'

'Then I left the club, and there was a long black car at the curb and I went to the back door which was open and got in. And goddamn! There were four drunken Iranians in the car and one of them closed the door and they took off with me, just laughing their asses off. And I realized that it was a limo and I was in the wrong car and I yelled at them to stop and let me out.'

'How did you know they were Iranians?'

'I go to acting class with two Iranians and they're always jabbering in Farsi. I know Iranians, believe me. Or Persians, as they prefer to call themselves when they live in a free country, the bastards.'

'Okay, and then?'

'They were groping me and kissing me and I scratched one on the face and he told the driver to stop and they pushed me out of the car right onto the street and I ran back here. I want them arrested and prosecuted for kidnapping.'

'Kidnapping might be very hard to allege in this case,' Budgie said, 'but let's get the report finished and see what the detectives think.'

'I don't care what the detectives think,' Sara Butler said. 'I've done half their job for them already.'

And with that she produced a tissue that was carefully

folded, and said, 'These are fingernail scrapings from the Iranian's face. And my coat there can be examined for latent fingerprints.'

'We can't get fingerprints from fur,' Budgie said.

'Officer, don't tell me what you can't do,' Sara Butler said. 'My father's a lawyer and I won't have my report swept under the rug by your detectives. The dirt from my dress will identify where I was lying in the gutter in case someone says I wasn't pushed from the car. And those fingernail scrapings will positively identify one of my assailants after a DNA analysis.' She paused and said, 'And channel seven is on the way.'

'Here?'

'Yes, I called them. So I suggest you take this case very seriously.'

'Tell me, Ms. Butler,' Budgie said. 'Do you watch *CSI*?'

'All the time,' Sara Butler said. 'And I know that some cheap lawyer for the Iranians might say I got into the car by design and not by accident, but I have that covered as well.'

'I'm sure you do,' Budgie said.

'The man who bought me the martinis can testify that he had a car waiting for me, and that will prove I just made a mistake and got into the wrong car.'

'And I suppose you have the man's name and how we can contact him?'

'His name is Andrei. He's a Russian gentleman who said he worked as manager at the Gulag in east Hollywood. And he gave me a business card from there. I think you should check on him and see if he's ever been accused of doctoring a girl's drink either at his nightclub or elsewhere. I still think I was affected too suddenly by the martinis.'

'Anything else you'd like to add?' Budgie said, intending to get the hell out before a news team arrived.

'Only that I intend to have my father call the Gulag or go to the nightclub in person if necessary to make sure someone from the police department properly investigates my crime report. Now, if you'll excuse me, I've got to pull myself together for channel seven.'

When Budgie got back outside, Fausto, who had stepped into the office during part of the interview, said, 'Would you call that a righteous felony or an example of first-stage alcoholism and a slight PMS issue?'

'For once, you sexist old bastard,' Budgie said, 'I think you got it right.'

Dmitri would have been even angrier, if that were possible, had he known that Andrei, his night manager, had been out on his night off trying to pick up a woman who subsequently got herself involved with the police. Dmitri did not want the police at his place of business ever, not for any reason. But this night he had cops all over the place, including Andi McCrea, who'd been called in from home by the night-watch detective Compassionate Charlie Gilford.

When Charlie told Andi that he was having trouble reaching other members of the homicide unit, two of whom were sick with the flu that was going around, she suggested he try one of the detectives from Robbery, and gave him Brant Hinkles's cell number.

Charlie rang up Brant Hinkle and told him there was a murder at the Gulag and asked if he'd be willing to help out Andi. Brant said he thought he could manage and that he'd be there ASAP.

Then Brant closed his cell and looked over at Andi, naked in bed beside him, and said, 'That is a very dirty trick.'

She kissed him, jumped out of bed, and said, 'You'd rather investigate a homicide with me than lie here alone all night, wouldn't you?'

'I guess I would at that,' Brant said. 'Is that what you would call a commitment?'

Andi said, 'When two cops are committed, the definition

is similar to the one meaning residents of an asylum. Let's go to work.'

There had been a large private party in the VIP section on the upper level of the Gulag, an area roped off and guarded by a bouncer. Dmitri had assigned two waitresses for the party and wished he'd scheduled three when the party grew much larger than had been expected. Soon the sofas along the walls and every chair was occupied in layers, young women sitting on the laps of any guy who would permit it. Everyone else was standing three deep by a railing, watching the mass of dancers writhing in the pit down below on ground level.

They were foreign students from a technical college attending this gathering put together by a party promoter who dealt with various Hollywood nightclubs. Most at the soirée were Arabs, some were Indians, a few were Pakistanis. And there were two uninvited guests from south L.A. who were members of the Crips gang, out for a night in Hollywood, one of whom claimed to be a cousin of the promoter.

Dmitri had installed a video camera on the patio outside, where customers could go for a smoke, and it was there on the patio that the crime occurred. One of the young Arabs, a twenty-two-year-old student, didn't like something that the taller of the two Crips said to his girlfriend, and a fight started. The taller Crip, who wore a raspberry-colored fedora over a head rag, got knocked down by the Arab with some help from his friends. While several people were separating the combatants, the shorter of the two Crips, the quiet one, walked behind the Arab, reached around, and stabbed him in the belly.

Then both Crips ran from the patio and out through the nightclub's front door as people screamed and an ambulance was called. The young Arab lay thrashing and bled out, displaying no signs of life even before the RA and the first black-and-whites arrived. Still, he was taken straight to Hollywood Presbyterian Hospital while a paramedic worked on him futilely.

It was B.M. Driscoll and Benny Brewster who sealed off the area and kept as many actual eyewitnesses in place as they could, but the nightclub had started emptying fast after word got out about the stabbing. When Andi McCrea and Brant Hinkle arrived (in separate cars so as to stay discreet), Benny Brewster and B.M. Driscoll were writing down information from half a dozen of the Arabs and two of their American girlfriends, who were crying.

Benny Brewster briefed Andi by pointing out the party promoter, Maurice Wooley, a very worried black man who was sitting at the far end of the now-empty bar drinking a tall glass of Jack. He was plump, in his midfifties and wearing a conservative, double-breasted gray suit. He was also bleary-eyed from the booze.

Benny said to him, 'Mr. Wooley, this is Detective McCrea. Tell her about the homie that did the stabbing.'

'I really don't know much about him,' the promoter said to Andi. 'He's jist somebody from Jordan Downs, where I grew up, is all. I don't live down there no more.'

'I understand he's your cousin,' Andi said.

'A much younger cousin to my play cousin,' the promoter said quickly. 'I don't know his real name.'

Benny Brewster abruptly changed tack, glared at him, and said, 'So what's your cousin to your play cousin's street name? Whadda you call him?'

The promoter's jowls waddled slightly and he said, 'Doobie D. That's all I ever did call him, Doobie D. I swear on my momma's grave.'

Benny scowled and said, 'Maybe your momma has room for one more in there.'

Andi said, 'What's his phone number?'

'I dunno,' the promoter said, twisting his zircon ring nervously, glancing every few seconds at the tall black cop, who looked about ready to grab him by the throat.

Andi said, 'This officer tells me you invited him here as your guest tonight.'

'That's 'cause I run into him on the street when I went to visit my momma. He said he wanna go to one of them Hollywood parties I promote. And me, I'm a fool. I say, okay, when I get one, I'm gonna let you know. So I get this job and I let him know and I comp him in here as my guest. With one of his crew. And look at the grief I get.'

'If you don't have his number, how did you reach him?'

'I jist have his e-mail address,' the promoter said, handing Andi his cell phone. 'His cell company is one of them that you can e-mail or phone.'

When they were finished at the Gulag and ready to go, Andi was approached by a man with an obvious hairpiece and a peculiar smile. He extended his hand to both detectives and said, 'I am Dmitri Sikhonov, proprietor of the Gulag. I am sick to my heart from the terrible think that has een-wolved my club tonight. I shall be of service if you need any-think. Any-think at all.'

He gave them his card and bowed slightly.

'We may have some questions for you tomorrow,' Andi said.

'On the back of the card is my cell number,' he said. 'Anytime you wish to call Dmitri. Please, I shall be at your service.'

After getting back to the station, Andi Googled Doobie D's Internet provider from the text message. Then she left a phone message with the provider, requesting that the customer's name and phone number be pulled up, with the assurance that a search warrant would be faxed to them in the morning before the provider faxed the account information to her.

Andi said to Brant, 'We'll write a three-page search warrant and run it over to the Hollywood court tomorrow. Have you ever done it?'

'I'm real rusty,' he said.

'The provider will triangulate from the cell site towers. If we're real lucky and Doobie D uses his phone, the provider will call us every hour or so to tell us where he is. It's like a GPS on the cell phone. If he disposes of the cell, we're outta luck.'

'Are we gonna finally get home to get the rest of our night's sleep, do you think?'

Looking at those green eyes of his, she said, 'Is that all you're thinking about, sleep?'

'It's *one* of the things I'm thinking about,' he said.

SIXTEEN

The Oracle showed up at roll call that Thursday evening with a detective whom most of them had seen around the station and a few of the older cops knew by name.

The Oracle said, 'Okay, listen up. This is Detective Chernenko. He has a few things to say to you, and it's important.'

Viktor stood before them in his usual rumpled suit with food stains on the lapels and said, 'Good evening to you. I am investigating the jewelry store two-eleven where your Officer Takara was so very brave. And I also have very much interest in the two-eleven of three days ago at the ATM where the guard was killed. I am thinking that the same two people did both of them and now everybody agrees with me.

'What I wish is that you watch out for anybody who might be stealing from a mailbox. It is a crime very typical of addicts, so you might watch for tweakers who are hanging around the blue mailboxes on the corners of the streets. Especially in the area of Gower south of Hollywood Boulevard. If you find a suspect, look for a device like string and tape that they use to fish in a mailbox. If you find nothing, please write a good FI on the suspect and leave it for me at end-of-watch. Any question?'

Wesley Drubb turned and glanced at Hollywood Nate who looked sheepish, obviously thinking what Wesley was thinking.

Fausto Gamboa, the old man of the midwatch, said, 'Why Gower south of the boulevard, Viktor? Can you share it with us?'

'Yes, it is no big secret, Fausto,' Viktor said. 'It is a very small clue. I believe that information about the jewels was learned from a letter stolen from a mailbox there on Gower.'

Wesley Drubb looked at Hollywood Nate again but couldn't wait to see if Nate was going to admit that they might have lost a lead several days ago. Wesley raised his hand.

The Oracle said, 'Yeah, Drubb. Got a question?'

Wesley said, 'Last week we got a call about two homeless guys fighting on Hollywood Boulevard. One of them said that a couple weeks before, he saw a guy and a woman stealing mail from a blue mailbox a few blocks south of Hollywood Boulevard on Gower.'

That didn't elicit too much excitement in itself but Viktor was mildly interested and said, 'Did he provide more details than that?'

Looking at Nate again. 'Yes, he did. He said the guy was driving an old blue Pinto. And his partner was a woman. And he heard the woman call him Freddy or Morley.'

'Thank you, Officer,' Viktor said. 'I will check recent FIs for the name of Freddy and the name of Morley, but of course that will not be easy.'

The Oracle saw Wesley glance at Hollywood Nate again, and he said to Wesley, 'I think you're not through, Drubb. Was there something more?'

'Yes, Sarge,' Wesley said. 'The homeless guy had a card with the mail thief's license number written on it.'

Now Viktor's mouth dropped open. 'Fantastic!' he said. 'Please present me with this card, Officer!'

Wesley looked sheepish, and being loyal to his partner said, 'I'm afraid I gave the card back to him.'

Hollywood Nate spoke up then, saying, 'I told him to give

it back. I figured, what the hell, just some tweakers stealing mail, happens all the time. It was my fault, not Drubb's.'

'We're not talking fault here,' said the Oracle. 'What was the name of the homeless guy with the card? Where can Detective Chernenko find him?'

'They call him Trombone Teddy,' Nate said. 'We wrote an FI on him and the other homeless geezer who knocked him on his ass. But neither one of them has a real address. They don't live anywhere, guys like that.'

The Oracle said to Hollywood Nate, 'Weiss, you and Drubb are on a special detail tonight. Don't clear for calls. Just stay off the air and go out there and find Trombone Teddy. Get that license number for Detective Chernenko.'

'I'm sorry, Sarge,' a chastened Hollywood Nate said.

'Do not feel too badly, Officer,' Viktor said. 'These suspects are no doubt lying down low for a few days but soon must act. Our balls are in their court.'

On very busy nights the midwatch units sometimes compared notes for who would get the BHI prize for Bizarre Hollywood Incident of the evening. Six-X-Thirty-two got an honorable mention for a call to east Hollywood, where an Eighteenth Street gang member was loitering by a liquor store with two other homies. A Lebanese store clerk got scared because the guy obviously was hiding something large under his sweatshirt. In the age of terrorism the clerk was afraid that the Eighteenth Street cruisers might be getting ready to bomb his store because he'd once called the cops on one of their crew who had shoplifted a bottle of gin.

Flotsam and Jetsam were the responders, and they had the three cruisers against the wall of the liquor store, assisted by Hollywood Nate and Wesley Drubb, who were tired of looking for Trombone Teddy. Wesley was thrilled that they'd been close enough to provide cover when gang members were involved.

With flashlights and neon from the store lighting him up, the shortest homie, a head-shaved, tattoo-covered, twenty-one-year-old in baggy walking shorts and an enormous cut-off sweatshirt, was looking over his shoulder at them. The cops liked the homie low-slung baggies because they often fell down and tripped them when they ran from cops. But this cruiser had something huge bulging from his chest.

Flotsam drew his nine and holding it down by his leg, said, 'Okay, homes, turn around and raise up your sweat-shirt real slow. Let's see what you're hiding.'

When he did, they saw the yellow pages of the Los Angeles telephone directory taped to his chest with elastic wrap.

'What in the hell is that?' Flotsam said.

'It's a phone book,' the cruiser said.

'I know it's a phone book. But why do you have it taped to your chest?'

The gangster looked around and said, 'An old *veterano* from White Fence is after me, man. You think I'm gonna just stand around a take a bullet without some protection?'

'Bro, do you know what you've done here?' Jetsam said to him. 'I think you can take this nationwide. You've just designed an affordable bulletproof vest for the inner city!'

On Saturday, two days after Cosmo and Ilya had hidden the stolen car and the money at the house of Farley Ramsdale, Cosmo decided that they had hidden out as long as they dared. He had phoned Gregori at the junkyard that morning and arranged for one of Gregori's Mexicans to drive the tow truck to Farley's address. Cosmo insisted that timing was important and that the truck should arrive at 7 p.m.

'Why do you buy an old car that will not operate?' Gregori asked him in Armenian.

'For Ilya. We need two cars,' Cosmo said. 'I will give you the repair job and pay three hundred dollars for the tow because it is on Saturday evening. Also, I shall tip your driver another fifty if he arrives at precisely seven p.m.'

'You are generous,' Gregori said. 'And when do you return to me the spare key for my yard that I left with Ilya?'

'On Monday morning,' Cosmo said. 'When I come to see how much repairs the Mazda needs.'

'All right, Cosmo,' Gregori said. 'My driver is named Luís. He speaks pretty good English. He will tow the car to our yard.'

'Thank you, my brother,' Cosmo said. 'I shall see you on Monday.'

When he finished his call to Gregori, Ilya, who was lying on the bed smoking and staring at an old MGM musical on TV, said, 'So today you do what you do?'

'You wish to hear my plan, Ilya?'

'I know I say do not tell me. I have a change of mind about some things. Now I wish you to tell how you get rid of the car and get our money. Do not tell me more than that.'

'Okay, Ilya,' he said. 'I shall be at the house of Farley at seven o'clock to help truck driver to take away the car. I shall give to truck driver fifty dollars to call me when he get the car to junkyard of Gregori. If he do not call me, I shall know that police have him and stolen car he is towing. Then we take our money and our diamonds and fly to San Francisco and never come back.'

She said, 'But maybe yesterday or today Farley has found the car or found our money and made call to police and they are there to wait for you.'

'If I do not phone you at seven-thirty that all is okay, you take taxi to airport and fly to San Francisco with diamonds. And God bless you. Please have good life. I shall never tell the police nothing about you. Never.'

'You take big risk, Cosmo.'

'Yes, but I think is okay. I think Farley and Olive do not

look in garage or under house. All they look for is drugs. Nothing else.'

'How you can be sure that Farley and Olive will not be there at the house when you go there at seven o'clock, Cosmo?'

'Now you ask question you say you not wish to know.'

'You are correct. Do not tell me.'

The unanswered question had a simple answer. Cosmo was going to phone Farley to arrange a business meeting and then arrive at Farley's at six p.m., carrying a canvas bag. In the bag he would have his gun, a roll of duct tape and a kitchen knife that he had sharpened when Ilya had gone to the liquor store for cigarettes. If Farley and Olive were at home, he would knock, be admitted on the pretext of paying the blackmail money, take them prisoner at gunpoint and tape their wrists and their mouths. Then cut their throats. Just another addict murder, the police would think. Probably a drug deal gone bad.

If for some reason Farley and Olive could not be home at the appointed hour, there was an alternate plan that involved the spare key to the junkyard. They would be lured there tomorrow by a call from Gregori about buying more key cards. Cosmo would ambush them there and dispose of their bodies somewhere in east Los Angeles. Just another addict murder.

As for the car, if the tow driver phoned his cell, telling him that the towing had been accomplished, Cosmo would go to Gregori's junkyard on Monday morning and tell Gregori he'd changed his mind about repairing the car and ask him to crush the Mazda for scrap. For one thousand dollars cash Cosmo was sure that Gregori would ask no questions and do it.

He could not see a flaw in his plan. It was foolproof. He wished that Ilya would permit him to tell her about all of it. She would be impressed by how much thought he had put into it. The only thing that worried him was that Dmitri might be so angry Cosmo hadn't called him that he would think he was being betrayed and maybe send Russian thugs looking for him.

His hands were shaking at 5:15 p.m. while driving to Farley's house. He decided to make the two crucial calls that would possibly decide his fate. The first was to the cell number that Dmitri said was the only one he should use after the job was done.

It rang five times, and then, 'Yes.'

'Dmitri, it is me.'

'I know who,' Dmitri said. 'I am think-ink that you had run away from me. That will be a stupid think to do.'

'No, no, Dmitri. We are being quiet for two, three days.'

'Do not tell me more. When do I see you for all of our business? You have thinks for me.'

'There is more I must complete, Dmitri. Maybe I come to you tonight.'

'I like that,' Dmitri said.

'Maybe I must wait for Monday morning.'

'I do not like that.'

'There are two peoples—'

'Enough!' Dmitri said, interrupting him. 'I do not want to hear about your business. If you do not call me tonight, I shall be here on Monday. If I do not see you on Monday, you are very stupid person.'

'Thank you, Dmitri,' Cosmo said. 'I shall be correct in my business with you.'

After hanging up, Cosmo made the second crucial call, to Farley Ramsdale's cell number, but got only his voice mail. It was the first time this had ever happened. The addict never slept and was always open for business deals. It staggered him. He would try again in thirty minutes. He still had the alternate plan for Farley and Olive, but this did not bode well. He had all of the killing tools with him and he was ready.

Where in the hell was Olive? She knew they were almost down to their last dollar and had to work the mailboxes or maybe try again to pass some of the bogus money they still had. Or just go to a RadioShack or Best Buy and try to boost a DVD player to sell at the cyber café. Things were that desperate!

But where was the stupid bitch? All Farley knew was she went out searching the goddamn neighborhood for that crazy Mabel's fucking cat! He was about to go out looking for her, when he got a cell call from Little Bart.

When he recognized the voice he said, 'Whadda you want?'

'I felt bad the way things were left between us,' Little Bart said.

'So you're calling to say you wanna send me flowers?'

'I wanna do a deal with you.'

'What kinda deal?'

'I want you to deliver a couple of brand-new computers to a real nice house on the west side of Laurel Canyon.'

'Deliver them how?'

'In your car.'

'Why don't you deliver them?'

'I lost my driver's license on a DUI.'

'That's the only reason?'

'And I hurt my back and can't carry them.'

'They ain't very heavy. Tell you what, how about I deliver in your car?'

'They impounded my car when they popped me.'

'Uh-huh. So how much do I get for this delivery?'

'Fifty bucks.'

'Good-bye, Bart,' Farley said.

'No, wait! A hundred bucks. It'll take you a half hour, tops.'

'One fifty.'

'Farley, I'm not making much on this. They aren't the very best top-of-the-line computers.'

'I don't risk my ass delivering hot computers that you're too chickenshit to deliver for less than one twenty-five.'

'Okay, deal.'

'When?'

'Can you meet me at Hollywood and Fairfax in twenty minutes? I'll be standing on the corner and I'll walk and you follow me to where you pick up and deliver. The merchandise is in a garage there. Then when you got it, I'll ride with you to the drop-off address.'

'Why will you walk to the pickup location instead of riding with me?'

'I can't be anywhere near this pickup. I can't explain.'

'And you'll have the money?'

'Half. I'll give you the other half when the job's done.'

'Can you make it later? I can't find that goddamn bitch of mine.'

'You don't need her.'

'Who the hell you think does the heavy lifting?' Farley said. 'And she goes in first in case there's anything chancy going on.'

'We can't wait for her. Twenty minutes, Farley,' Bart said.

Farley looked all over the street but still no Olive. He made a quick stop at Mabel's and found the old witch reading Tarot cards in which Olive believed with all her heart.

Farley peered through the rusted screen. 'Hey, Mabel, you seen Olive?'

'Yes, she's out looking for Tillie. I think Tillie might be pregnant. She's acting peculiar and roaming around as though she's looking for a nest. She was once a feral cat, you know. I took her in and tamed her.'

Farley said, 'Yeah, I'm sure you got a Humane Society award. If you see Olive, tell her I had to do a quick job and she should wait for me at home.'

'All right, Farley,' Mabel said. 'It might interest you to know that the cards don't look good for you,' she added. 'Maybe you should stay home too.'

She heard him mumble 'Crazy old bitch' when he left her porch.

Olive was in the backyard of a neighbor six houses away, looking for Tillie and chatting with the neighbor about the beautiful white camellias that bordered her property. And Olive just loved the pink and white azaleas that climbed the fence. Olive told her that someday she hoped to have a garden. The woman offered to teach Olive the basics and to get her started with the proper seeds and a few young plants.

Olive thought she heard Farley's Corolla, excused herself, and running to the street saw his taillights at the stop sign. She yelled but he didn't hear her and was gone. Olive then went home, hoping he wasn't mad at her.

There he was on the northeast corner of Hollywood and Fairfax, jumping around like he had to take a leak. Or had to score some tweak, more likely, Farley figured. He didn't like any part of this. Little Bart couldn't drive because he had no license? When did that ever stop a tweaker from driving? He couldn't carry a computer because his back hurt? He couldn't ride in Farley's car to the garage where the computers were? What was this shit all about?

Little Bart walked over to his car and said, 'Just follow me real slow for half a block. When I get to the house, I'll point with my finger behind my back. Then you drive into the driveway and go to the garage. The door will open manually. Get the computers and pick me up two blocks north.'

While he was driving slowly behind Bart, he missed Olive more than he had in the eighteen months they'd been together. This was a very bad deal. Bart was scared to pick up the merchandise, which meant that Bart didn't trust the thief who'd stolen the computers, or the fence who'd hired Bart to deliver them.

If Olive were here, there'd be no problem. He'd drop her off at the pickup address and let her go into the garage and check it out. If the cops were there and grabbed her, he'd just keep on moving down the road. If there was one thing he was sure of, Olive would never rat him out. She'd take the hit and do the time if she had to and come to him when she got out of jail, just as though nothing had happened.

But Olive wasn't here. And that fucking Little Bart was pointing at a house, a modest one for this neighborhood. Then Bart kept walking north. Farley parked across from the house and looked at the garage.

The house wasn't unlike his own. It was in that ubiquitous California style that everyone calls Spanish, which means nothing other than tile roof and stucco walls. The longer he looked at it, the worse he felt about the whole arrangement.

Farley got out of the car and walked across the street to the house. He went to the front door and rang the bell. When he got no answer, he went to the side door, which was only forty feet from the garage, banged on the door, and yelled, 'Olive, you there? Hellooooo? Olive?'

It was then that two Hollywood Division detectives came out of the garage, badged him, put him against the wall, patted him down and then dragged him back into the garage. There was nothing in the garage except a workbench, some tools and tires, and two boxes containing new computers.

'What is this?' he said.

'You tell us,' the older detective said.

'My girlfriend, Olive, went to lunch with a pal of hers and gave me the pal's address. This is it.'

'Right,' the younger detective said. 'What've you been in jail for?'

'Petty kid stuff is all,' Farley said. 'What's this all about?'

'You been busted for burglary?'

'No.'

'Receiving?'

'Receiving what?'

'Don't fuck with us. Receiving stolen property.'

'No, just kid stuff. Drug possession. Petty theft a couple times.'

'Are you going to use the S-O-D-D-I defense?'

'What's that?'

'Some other dude did it.'

'I'm innocent!' Farley cried.

'Well, partner,' the younger detective said to the other. 'Let's take kid stuff here to the station. Looks like our surprise party is blown.'

'Hey, man,' Farley said, 'I musta wrote down the wrong address is all. My girlfriend Olive's gonna be looking for me. If you'll let me call her, she'll tell you.'

'Turn around, kid stuff,' the older detective said. 'Put your hands behind your back.'

After they handcuffed Farley, they led him out to the street, where a detective car drove up from wherever it had been hidden. Then they searched his Corolla, but of course it was clean. There wasn't even a roach in the ashtray.

When they got to the station, Farley saw some movie posters on a wall. What the fuck kind of police station has movie posters on the wall? Farley thought. And how did he get in this horror flick? All he knew was, if he'd had Olive with him, he wouldn't be here. That dumb bitch just got his ass busted!

It was after five o'clock and Farley hadn't come home and hadn't called. Olive was tired and she was very hungry. She remembered what Mabel had said about saving some food for her. She wondered if Mabel might let her help cook the meal. She'd like that, and getting to eat and chat with Mabel.

When she got to Mabel's the old woman was delighted to see her.

'I'm sorry, Mabel,' she said. 'I can't find Tillie.'

'Don't worry, dear,' Mabel said. 'She'll turn up. She always does. She's still a bit of a wild thing. Tillie's got a touch of Gypsy in her soul.'

'Would you like me to help you cook?'

'Oh, yes,' Mabel said. 'If you'll promise to stay and have supper with me.'

'Thank you, Mabel,' Olive said. 'I'll be real happy to join you for supper.'

'Then we'll play gin. If you don't know how, never mind, I'll teach you. I know all about cards. Did I ever tell you I used to make good money telling fortunes with cards? That was sixty-five years ago.'

'Really?'

'Really. There are certain legal technicalities about foretelling the future that I didn't follow. I was arrested twice and taken to Hollywood Station for ignoring those silly technicalities.'

'You, arrested?' Olive couldn't imagine it.

'Oh, yes,' Mabel said. 'I was a bit of a naughty girl in my time. The old police station was a lovely building constructed in nineteen thirteen, the year my parents got married. When I was born, they named me for the silent-screen star Mabel Normand. I never had any siblings. You know, I used to date a policeman from Hollywood Station. He was the one who arrested me the second time and persuaded me to stop telling fortunes for money. He was killed in the war. One week after D-day.'

Loving Mabel's stories and gossip about the old days in Hollywood, Olive hated to interrupt her, but she thought about Farley and said, 'Mabel, let me run home and leave a note for Farley so he'll know where I'm at. Be right back!'

'Hurry, dear,' Mabel said. 'I'll tell you lots of tales about life in the golden age of Hollywood. And we'll play cards. This is going to be such fun!'

SEVENTEEN

Cosmo Betrossian cursed the traffic. He cursed Los Angeles for being the most car-dependent, traffic-choked city in the world. He cursed the Georgian bartender who gave him the stolen car that almost got him captured. But most of all he cursed Farley Ramsdale and his stupid woman. He sat in traffic on East Sunset Boulevard looking at all of the signs around him in the languages of the Far East, and he cursed them too.

Then he heard the siren and for a few seconds it terrified him until he saw an ambulance weaving through traffic on the wrong side of Sunset, obviously trying to get to the traffic accident that had him gridlocked. Glancing repeatedly at his Rolex knockoff, he cursed.

First, they left him in an interrogation room for what seemed like an hour, only letting him go to the bathroom once and then watching him piss, just like the goddamn probation officer who used to make him piss in a bottle twice a month. With no sympathy for the fact that it was hard to piss with someone watching to make sure you piss from your own dick and not from a bottle of clean piss stashed in your underwear.

Then one of the two detectives came in and gave him a bad-cop interrogation about a goddamn warehouse burglary of electronic equipment that he knew nothing about. Then the other detective played good cop and came in and gave him a cup of coffee. Then the bad cop took over and played the game all over again until Farley's hands were shaking and his pulse was vibrating.

Farley knew they didn't buy the wrong-address story, but he stuck with it. And he was pretty sure they were starting to think he hadn't been involved in the warehouse burglary but was just some tweaker with exactly $3.65 in his pocket, hired only to pick up and deliver.

He would have given up Little Bart instantly if he thought it would help him, but something in good cop's tone last time around told him he was going to be released. Except that bad cop came in and walked him to a holding tank with a wooden bench, where they locked him in. And every cop walking by could look through the big glass window and gawk at him like he was a fucking spider monkey at the Griffith Park zoo.

When Watch 5 left roll call at 6 p.m., several of them passed by the holding tank and did gawk at him.

'Hey, Benny,' B.M. Driscoll said to his partner. 'Is that the tweaker we wrote the ticket to?'

'Yeah,' Benny Brewster said. Then he tapped on the glass and said to Farley, 'What happened, man? They catch you selling ice?'

'Fuck you,' Farley mumbled, and when Benny laughed and walked away, Farley growled, 'You're the one oughtta be in a zoo with the rest of the silverbacks, you fucking ape.'

Budgie and Fausto saw Benny talking to someone in the holding tank, and Budgie looked in and said, 'Fausto, that's the guy we FI'd at the taco stand.'

Fausto looked at Farley and said, 'Oh yeah, the tweaker with the skinny girlfriend. Bet they got him doing a deal at Pablo's. They never learn, they never change.'

When Hollywood Nate and Wesley walked past the holding tank, Nate heard Fausto's remark, took a look inside, and said, 'Shit, everyone knows that dude. Hey, Wesley, check this out.'

Wesley looked in and said, 'Oh yeah. That's what's-his-name— Rimsdale? No, Ramsdale.'

'Farley,' Nate said. 'Like the old movie star Farley Granger.'

'Who?' Wesley said.

'Never mind,' Nate said. 'Let's go look for Trombone Teddy. We gotta find him or I'll have stress dreams tonight about chasing an old geezer who keeps holding me off with the slide of his gold trombone.'

'Do you really have dreams like that?'

'No,' Nate said, 'but it would make a good dream sequence in a screenplay, don't you think?'

One of the sergeants on Watch 2 was a forty-year-old black woman, Wilma Collins. She had a good reputation with the troops but had a persistent weight problem that the coppers at Hollywood Station joked about. She wasn't actually obese but they called her a 'leather stretcher.' Her Sam Browne had a lot to hold in place.

Everyone knew that a few hours before end-of-watch, Sergeant Collins liked to sneak into IHOP and load up on buttermilk pancakes swimming in butter, with sausages and fried eggs and butter-drenched biscuits. They made lots of cholesterol and clogged-arteries jokes about Sergeant Collins.

When the surfer team were loading their war bags and getting ready to hit the streets, the entire parking lot and the watch commander's office suddenly erupted. Some of those who heard it had to sit for a moment until they could gain control. It became a Hollywood Station moment.

It seems that Sergeant Collins had left her rover behind on the counter at IHOP, because a message was sent on the Hollywood frequency by a Mexican busboy who had keyed the mike and talked into the rover.

The busboy said, 'Hello, hello! Chubby black police lady?

Hello, hello! You leave radio here! Hello! Chubby black lady? You there, please? Hello, hello!'

Hollywood Nate and Wesley Drubb didn't say much to each other when they left roll call. Nate was driving and Wesley had never seen him so intent on watching the street.

At last Wesley said, 'I had to mention Trombone Teddy at roll call.'

'I know you did,' Nate said. 'The real mistake I made was I shoulda told you to take Teddy's license number and at least write the info on the FI card.'

'I shoulda done that on my own,' Wesley said.

'You're barely off probation,' Nate said. 'You're still in the yessir boot-mode. It was my fault.'

'We'll find Teddy,' Wesley said.

'I hope he still has the card,' Nate said. Then, 'Hey, it was a business card, right? What was the business?'

'A Chinese restaurant. Ching or Chan, something like that.'

'House of Chang?'

'Yeah, that was it!'

'Okay, let's pay them a visit.'

The tow truck was parked in front of Farley Ramsdale's house and the Mexican driver was knocking on the door when Cosmo Betrossian came squealing down the street in his old Cadillac. The traffic had disrupted everything.

He got out and ran toward the porch, saying to the driver, 'I am friend of Gregori. I am the one.'

'Nobody home here,' the Mexican said.

'Is not important,' Cosmo said. 'Come. Let us get the car.'

He ran to the garage, opened the termite-eaten door, and was relieved to see that the garage was just as he'd left it.

'Let us push it out to the street,' Cosmo said. 'We must work fast. I have important business.'

The Mexican and Cosmo easily pushed the car back down the driveway, Cosmo jumping in to steer after they got it going. The driver knew his job and in a few minutes had the Mazda hooked up and winched. It was all that Cosmo could do to keep from running back up the driveway and snatching the big can full of money from under the house.

Before he got in the truck to drive away, the driver said to Cosmo, 'I call you in thirty minute?'

'No, I need more time. Call me in one hour. Traffic very bad tonight. I give you time to get to the yard of Gregori. Then you call, okay?'

'Okay,' the Mexican said, waiting for the promised bonus.

Cosmo opened his wallet and gave the driver fifty dollars and said, 'Put it back where junk cars go. Okay?'

As soon as the truck was halfway down the block, Cosmo went to the trunk of the Cadillac and removed the bag of killing tools. He was going to wait at least an hour for them to show up.

He walked quickly back up the driveway to the rear yard of the house and was shocked to see the little access panel hanging open. He dropped the bag and threw himself onto the dirt, crawling under the house. The can of money was gone!

Cosmo screamed an Armenian curse, got up, took the gun from the bag, and ran to the back porch. He didn't even bother slipping the lock with his credit card like last time. He kicked the flimsy door open and ran inside, prepared to kill anybody in the house after he tortured the truth out of them.

There was no one. He saw a note on the kitchen table in a scrawl. It said, 'Gone to eat with Mabel. Will bring delishus supper for you.'

His alternate plan to lure them to Gregori's junkyard, where they could easily be killed, was finished. They had his money. They would never go near him now except to collect the blackmail money from the diamond robbery. They would ask for even more now that they knew about the ATM robbery and the murder of the guard. They must have discovered the Mazda too. Farley had stolen their money, and he would want more money to keep his mouth shut about everything.

Maybe all he could do was give the diamonds to Farley. Give him everything and tell him to do the deal with Dmitri himself. Then beg Dmitri to kill both addicts after they were forced to tell where the money was, and beg Dmitri to be fair with the money split even though so many things had gone wrong. After all, if Dmitri's Georgian bartender hadn't given him a stolen car that could barely run, this would not have happened.

Or maybe he should just go home and get Ilya and the diamonds and head for the airport. It was too much for him to work out. He needed Ilya. She was a very smart Russian and he was far out of his depth. He would do whatever she wanted him to do.

Cosmo took his killing bag and went out to his car. He had never been so demoralized in his life. If the Cadillac failed to start, he would just take the pistol from the bag and shoot himself. But it started and he drove home to Ilya. When he was only two blocks from their apartment his cell rang.

He answered and the driver's voice said, 'Mister, I am at Gregori's with the car. No problem. Everything okay.'

The stolen car was okay, but of course everything else was far from okay.

At 7:15 p.m. Farley was released from the holding tank and told that he was free to go.

Bad cop said to him, 'We know you're connected to those computers, but right now we're gonna let you walk. I suspect you'll see us again.'

'Speaking of walk,' Farley said. 'My car's there where you grabbed me. How about a ride back up there?'

'You got a lotta 'tude, dude,' bad cop said. 'We're not running a taxi service.'

'Man, you hassle me, you keep me here for hours when I ain't done nothing wrong. The least you can do is take me back to my car.'

The Oracle heard the bitching and came out of the sergeant's office, saying to Farley, 'Where do you need to go?'

Farley looked at the old sergeant and said, 'Fairfax, just north of Hollywood Boulevard.'

The Oracle said, 'I'm going out now. I'll give you a lift.'

Fifteen minutes later, when the Oracle dropped him at his car, Farley said, 'Thanks a lot, Sergeant. You're okay.'

The Oracle offered the Hollywood mantra: 'Stay real, Farley. Stay real.' But he knew that this tweaker would not. Who in Hollywood ever did?

'Teddy?' Mrs. Chang said when Hollywood Nate had a Latino busboy call her from the kitchen. 'He eat here?'

'He's a bum,' Nate said.

'Bum?' she said, grappling with the English meaning.

'Homeless,' Wesley said. 'Street person.'

'Oh, street person,' she said. 'Him I know. Teddy. Yes.'

'Does he come here?'

'Sometime he come to back door,' Mrs. Chang said. 'Come at maybe seven o'clock, sometime later. And we give him food we got to throw away. Teddy. Yes. He sit in kitchen and eat. Nice man. Quiet. We feel sorry.'

'When did you last see him?' Wesley asked.

'Tuesday night maybe. Hard to remember.'

Nate began writing in his notebook and said, 'When he comes again, I want you to call this number. Ask that Six-X-Seventy-two come right away. I've written it down for you.

We don't want to arrest him. We just have to talk to him. Understand?'

'Yes, I call.'

The house was dark when Farley got home, and the garage door was open. Why would Olive go in the garage? There was nothing in there but junk.

He unlocked the front door and entered, yelling, 'Olive! You here?'

She was not, and he went into the kitchen to see if there was any orange juice left and found the back door kicked open!

'Son of a bitch!' he said.

This was the first time that burglars had struck his house, although several houses on the block had been hit by daytime thieves in the past two years. But the TV was still there. He went into the bedroom and saw that the radio-CD player was still there. Nobody had ransacked the bedroom drawers. This wasn't like house breakers. It wasn't the way he worked when he himself was a daytime burglar fifteen years ago.

Then he saw the note on the kitchen table. Mabel. He should have known. The fucking old ghost probably was reading tarot cards for Olive and time had gotten away from the skinny moron. He went into the bedroom to strip down and take a shower and then he saw that something was different. The closet was half empty. All of Olive's clothes were missing, including the jacket he'd shoplifted for her Christmas present. He opened the drawer and saw that her underwear and socks were gone too. She'd bailed on him!

The note. He ran out the front door and across the street to Mabel's. It was such a warm evening that her door was open, and he could see that the TV was on. He put his hands up to the screen door to peer inside and said, 'Mabel!'

The old woman shuffled in from the back bedroom of the cottage, wearing pajamas, a bathrobe, and fuzzy slippers, and said, 'Farley? What're you doing here?'

'Do you know where Olive is?'

'Why, no.'

'She left a note saying she was having supper with you.'

'Yes, she did. And Olive found Tillie under your house where she'd made a nice little den for herself. Tillie's in my bedroom now, the little brat. I never have completely domesticated her.'

'Did Olive say where she was going when she left?'

'Yes, home.'

Farley had to sit down and ponder that when he got back to the house. Everything was going wrong lately. His entire world was upside down. Without a dollar to her name, that toothless fucking scarecrow had abandoned his ass! This was impossible! That imbecile Olive Oyl had actually dumped Farley Ramsdale, who'd given her everything!

This time it was Cosmo who was lying on the bed trying to quell a throbbing headache. He had quickly briefed Ilya on what had happened and then fell on his knees beside her chair and kissed her hands.

He is beaten, Ilya thought. Cosmo is crying for Mommy. He would never strike her again.

Ilya prepared her third glass of hot tea and lit a cigarette with the butt of the last and finally said, 'Cosmo, all is a fuckup.'

'Yes, Ilya,' he murmured painfully.

'I think we must pack the suitcase and make ready to fly away.'

'Yes, Ilya,' Cosmo said. 'What you say, I do.'

'On other hand,' she said, looking from one palm to the other for emphasis, 'we do not know for absolute truth that Farley has our money.'

'Ilya, please!' Cosmo said. 'The money is gone. Farley is gone. I cannot get to Farley with cell. Farley always have cell with him. He is addict. Addict must have cell.'

'One way we find out,' she said. 'Sit up, Cosmo!'

He obeyed instantly.

'Call Farley. Go with plan. Tell him Gregori need key cards. Many more. Will pay top money. Let us hear what he shall say.'

Cosmo's head was aching too much for this but it was impossible not to obey her. He felt as though he was back in Soviet Armenia and the Comrade Chairman himself had spoken. He was afraid of her now. He dialed.

'Hello!' Farley yelled into his cell.

Cosmo was stunned. He couldn't speak for a moment and Farley said, 'Olive? Is that you?'

Looking at Ilya, Cosmo said, 'Is me, Farley.'

'Cosmo?' Farley said. 'I thought it was Olive. That fucking tweaker has up and disappeared!'

'Olive?' Cosmo said. 'Gone?'

He saw the wry smile turn up the corners of Ilya's mouth, and he said, 'You know where she go to?'

'No,' Farley said. 'The cunt. I ain't got a clue.'

Ilya was mouthing the words 'Ask him,' and Cosmo said, 'I very sorry, Farley. You know Gregori? He need more cards right away.'

'Key cards? Cosmo, you forgot that you and me got a little business deal coming up? You think I'm gonna keep waiting? You think I'm gonna fuck around with key cards?'

'Please, Farley,' Cosmo said. 'Do this for me. I owe big favor to Gregori. Just drop off cards at his junkyard tonight. He work to midnight. He will give you fast hundred fifty. You buy crystal.'

The word 'crystal' struck a chord with Farley. He wanted to smoke ice more than he'd ever wanted anything in his life. This was the kind of deal where he desperately needed

Olive. If she were here, he'd drive her over there to the junk-yard and send her in. If Cosmo had a plan to waste them, he'd have to settle for Olive. Goddamn her!

'I only got about ten of the primo cards left,' Farley said.

'Is enough,' Cosmo said. 'Gregori got a bunch new worker who must have driving license. Gregori so cheap his old worker not stay long. Always new worker.'

'Is that dog in the yard?'

'I tell Gregori to tie up dog. No problem.'

'You tell Gregori to call me. If he says come, I come. He ain't a violent type. He's a businessman. You I ain't so sure about.'

'Okay, I call Gregori now,' Cosmo said. 'And if he say come?'

'Then I'll be there at nine o'clock. Tell Gregori to put the money in a bag and stick the bag between the links of the gate. If the money's there, I'll drive in and give him the cards.'

'Okay, Farley,' Cosmo said. Then he added, 'Call me if Olive come home.'

'Why?'

'I think I got good job for her.'

'You better have my big bucks this weekend, Cosmo,' Farley said. 'Let me worry about Olive if she comes home.'

When Cosmo closed the cell, Ilya took a great puff from her cigarette, sucked it into her lungs, and with her words enveloped in smoke clouds said, 'If he go to junkyard tonight, he don't know nothing about ATM robbery.'

'But I shall kill him anyways. The diamond blackmail shall end.'

'Blackmail still there, Cosmo. Olive has our money and Olive know all about both our jobs. Olive is full of danger for us. Not Farley so much.'

'But I shall kill him anyways?'

'Yes, he must die. Olive may give up the blackmail. She got lot of money now. She buy lot of drugs and die happy in two, three years.'

'Our money,' he said.

'Yes, Cosmo. She got our money, I think so. Call Gregori now. Say again and make him to believe you only scare Farley to pay a debt he owe you. Tell Gregori you will pay money for the Mazda on Monday.'

Before phoning Gregori, Cosmo said, 'Ilya, you tell me. When Gregori come to bring key to junkyard, you fuck him. No?'

'Of course, Cosmo,' she said. 'Why?'

'If he getting scared about Farley, scared about Mazda that I want to crush to scrap, is okay if I tell him you wish to make him glass of tea one more time? To make him calm?'

'Of course, Cosmo,' she said. 'My tea is best in all of Hollywood. Ask Gregori. Ask anybody who taste my tea.'

Six-X-Seventy-two got the call twenty minutes after they'd left the House of Chang. Hollywood Nate spun a U-ee and floored it. He craved redemption.

When they got back to the restaurant, Mrs. Chang tossed her head in the direction of the kitchen. And there they found Trombone Teddy sitting at the chopping block by the back door, happily scarfing down a huge bowl of pan-fried noodles.

'Teddy,' Nate said. 'Remember us?'

'I ain't causing no trouble,' he said. 'They invited me in here.'

'Nobody says you're causing trouble,' Nate said. 'A couple questions and you can sit and enjoy your noodles.'

Wesley said, 'Remember the fight you had on the boulevard? We're the officers that got the call. You gave me a card with a license number on it. Remember?'

'Oh yeah!' Teddy said, a noodle plastered to his beard. 'That son of a bitch sucker-punched me.'

'That's the night,' Nate said. 'Do you still have the card? With the license number?'

'Sure,' Teddy said. 'But nobody wants it.'

'We want it now,' Wesley said. Trombone Teddy put down his fork and searched inside his third layer of shirts, dug into a pocket with grimy fingers, and pulled out the House of Chang business card.

Wesley took it, looked at the license number, and nodded to Nate, who said, 'Teddy, what kind of car was it that the mail thief was driving?'

'An old blue Pinto,' Teddy said. 'Like I wrote down on the card.'

'And what did the guy look like?'

'I can't remember no more,' Teddy said. 'A white guy. Maybe thirty. Maybe forty. Nasty mouth. Insulted me. That's why I wrote down the license number.'

'And his companion?' Wesley said.

'A woman. That's all I can remember.'

'Would you recognize either of them if you saw them again?' Nate said.

'No, they was just dark shadows. He was just a dark shadow with a nasty mouth.'

'Tell us again what she called him,' Wesley said.

'I don't remember,' Teddy said.

'You told me Freddy,' Wesley said.

'Did I?'

'Or Morley?'

'If you say so. But it don't ring a bell now.'

'Have you seen them either before or after that?'

'Yeah, I saw them try to hustle a clerk in a store.'

'When?'

'A few days after he insulted me.'

'What store?'

'Coulda been like a Target store. Or maybe it was Radio-Shack. Or like a Best Buy store. I can't remember. I get around.'

'At least,' Nate said, 'you got another good look at them, right?'

'Yeah, but I still can't remember what they look like. They're white people. Maybe thirty years old. Or forty. But they could be fifty. I can't tell ages no more. You can check with the guy at the store. He gave me a ten-buck reward for telling him they were crooks. They had a bogus credit card. Or bogus money. Something like that.'

'Jesus,' Nate said, looking at Wesley in frustration.

Wesley said, 'If we can find the store and find the guy who saw them, at least you can say that they're the same two people who stole from the mailbox, isn't that right?'

'He stole from the mailbox,' Teddy said. 'She didn't. I got a feeling she's okay. He's a total asshole.'

Wesley said, 'If the detectives need to talk to you, where can they find you?'

'There's an old empty office building on that street on the east side of Hollywood Cemetery. I'm living there for now. But I come here a few nights a week for supper.'

'Can you remember anything else?' Hollywood Nate said, taking a ten-dollar bill from his wallet and putting it on the chopping block.

'Hell, half the time I can't remember what day it is,' Teddy said. Then he looked at them and said, 'What day is it, anyways?'

Viktor Chernenko was known for working late, especially with his obsession to solve the jewelry store robbery and the ATM robbery-murder, and most of the veteran cops from Hollywood Station were aware of it. Nate knew it and was busting stop signs and speeding to the station faster than he'd driven to the House of Chang.

They ran into the detective squad room and were over-joyed to see Viktor still there, typing on his computer key-board.

'Viktor,' Nate said. 'Here it is!'

Viktor looked at the business card, at the license number and the words 'blue Pinto' written on it, and he said, 'My mail thief?'

Since he had been on the initial callout, Brant worked all day in southeast L.A. with Andi on the Gulag homicide. Doobie D, whom they had identified through data received from his cell provider, was Latelle Granville, a twenty-four-year-old member of the Crips with an extensive record for drug sales and weapons violations. He had begun using his cell in the afternoon.

With a team of detectives from Southeast Division assist-ing, the cell towers eventually triangulated him to the vicin-ity of a residence on 103rd Street known to be the family home of a Crips cruiser named Delbert Minton. He had a far more extensive record than Latelle Granville and turned out to be the Crip who had been fighting with the slain student. Both were arrested at Minton's without incident and taken back to Hollywood Station for interview and booking. Both Crips refused to speak and demanded to call their lawyers.

It had been a very long day, and the detectives were hungry and tired from working well into an overtime evening. Then Andi returned a phone call from a cocktail waitress, one of the people she'd interviewed at the Gulag on the night of the murder. At that time, the waitress, Angela Hawthorn, had told Andi she was at the service bar fetching drinks when the fight broke out and had seen nothing. So why was she calling now? Andi wondered.

'This is Detective McCrea,' Andi said when the woman answered her cell.

'Hello,' Angela Hawthorn said. 'I'm at home. I don't work at the Gulag anymore. Dmitri fired me because I wouldn't put out for one of his rich Russian customers. I have some information that might help you.'

'I'm listening,' Andi said.

'Up in the corner of the building by the window to Dmitri's office there's a video camera that sees everything on the smoking patio. During the party I'm pretty sure it was there like it always is. But when you showed up it wasn't there. Dmitri probably took it down so you wouldn't see it.'

'Why would he do that?'

'He's paranoid about bad publicity and cops and court-rooms. And he doesn't want trouble with black hoodlums. In fact, he doesn't want black customers. He just wouldn't want to be involved in your murder case. Anyways, if you get that camera from him I'll bet you'll see that black guy sticking the knife in that kid. Just keep my name out of it, okay?'

When Andi hung up, she said to Brant, 'Do you need money?'

'Why?'

'You're going to be getting even more overtime. There might be video at the Gulag with our murder shown right there on it!'

Brant looked around, but all the other detectives had gone home. Only the night-watch detective Compassionate Charlie was there, with his feet up on the desk, sucking his teeth as usual, reading the *LA Times* sports page.

'I'm all you got?' he said.

'Don't be a wuss. This is more fun than being an IA weasel, isn't it?'

'I don't know,' he said. 'I'm starting to miss the Burn Squad. At least I got fed every once in a while.'

'When we're all through tonight, I'm making you a very late supper with a bottle of good Pinot I've been saving. How's that sound?'

'Suddenly I'm renewed,' he said.

'One thing, though,' Andi said. 'I think I should call Viktor. We might find a Russian translator very useful if this nightclub owner starts lyin' and denyin' like he probably will. Viktor is a master at handling those people, a kick-ass skill he learned in the bad old days with the Red Army.'

'He's just getting home by now,' Brant said. 'He won't be pleased.'

'He owes me,' Andi said. 'Didn't I do a dumpster dive for him? Didn't it cost me a busted bra strap?'

Eavesdropping as usual, Compassionate Charlie said, 'Hey, you guys looking for Viktor? He left in a hell of a hurry with Hollywood Nate and that big kid Nate works with. I love to watch Viktor run. Like a bear on roller skates.'

EIGHTEEN

The blue Pinto was registered to a Samuel R. Culhane who lived on Winona Boulevard. Viktor Chernenko was sitting in the backseat of the black-and-white, concerned about whiplash with Hollywood Nate still driving in his high-speed redemption mode.

Wesley said to Viktor, 'You know, Detective, the only problem here is that the first time we talked to Trombone Teddy he said the guy's name sounded like Freddy or Morley.'

'Maybe Samuel sold the car to a Freddy,' Nate said. 'Stay positive.'

'Or lent the car to Morley,' Viktor added.

The house was almost a duplicate of Farley Ramsdale's old Hollywood bungalow except it was in good repair and had a small lawn in front with geraniums along the side of the house and a bed of petunias by the front porch.

Wesley ran to the rear of the house to prevent escape. It was dusk, and he didn't need a flashlight yet. He took cover behind the garage and waited.

Viktor took the lead and knocked, with Nate standing to his left.

Samuel R. Culhane wasn't as thin as Farley but he was in a late stage of methamphetamine addiction. He had pustules on his face and a permanent twitch at the corner of his right eye. He was several years older than Farley and balding, with a bad comb-over. And though he couldn't see Hollywood Nate standing beside the guy at the door, he knew instantly that Viktor was a cop.

'Yeah?' he said cautiously.

Viktor showed his badge and said, 'We need to talk to you.'

'Come back with a warrant,' Samuel Culhane said and started to close the door, but Viktor stopped it with his foot and Nate pushed past and into the room, touching the badge pinned to his shirt, saying, 'This is a brass pass, dude.'

When the back door opened and Nate whistled to him, Wesley entered and saw the tweaker sitting on the couch in the living room looking glum. Viktor was formally reading the guy his rights from a card that every cop, including Viktor, had memorized.

Nate handed Samuel Culhane's driver's license to his partner and said, 'Run him, Wesley.'

After Viktor had finished with the rights advisement, he said to the unhappy homeowner, 'You are not pleased to see us?'

'Look,' Samuel Culhane said, 'you ain't searching my house without a warrant, but I'll talk to you long enough to find out what the hell this is all about.'

'We must find out where you were on a certain night.'

'What night?'

'Three weeks ago. You were driving your Pinto with a lady friend, no?'

'Hah!' Samuel Culhane said. 'Driving with a lady friend? No! I'm gay, dude. Gayer than springtime. You got the wrong guy.'

Persisting, Viktor said, 'You were driving on Gower south of Hollywood Boulevard that evening.'

'And who says so?'

'You were seen.'

'Bullshit. I got no reason to drive down Gower in the evening. In fact, I don't even go out till around midnight. I'm a night person, man.'

'There was a woman in your car,' Viktor said.

'I told you I'm gay! Do I gotta blow you to prove it? Wait a minute, what crime was I supposed to've done?'

'You were seen at a mailbox.'

'A mailbox?' he said. 'Oh, man, now I get it. You're gonna try to fuck me with a mail theft.'

Wesley came in then and handed an FI card to Viktor on which he'd scribbled some of Samuel R. Culhane's rap sheet entries.

Reading, Viktor said, 'You have been arrested for fraud... one, two times. Once for counterfeiting. This is, as they say, consistent with the theft of U.S. mail from a public mailbox.'

'Okay, fuck this,' Samuel Culhane said. 'I ain't spending a night in jail till you guys get your shit together and figure out you got the wrong guy. I'll come right out and tell you what's what if you'll go away and leave me be.'

'Proceed,' Viktor said.

'I rented my Pinto for a week to a guy I know. I got another car. He lives down there off Gower with an idiot tweaker who calls herself his wife but they ain't married. I warned them both, don't fuck around and do any deals in my Pinto. They didn't listen to me, did they? I'll show you where he lives. His name's Farley Ramsdale.'

Hollywood Nate and Wesley Drubb looked at each other and said it simultaneously and with such gusto that it startled not only Samuel Culhane but Viktor Chernenko as well.

'Farley!'

That goddamn Olive, she never puts anything in its proper place. Farley was still thinking of Olive in the present tense although he knew in his heart that she was in the past. He had to admit there were things he was going to miss. She was like those Bedouin women who walk through minefields while the old man stays fifty yards behind on the donkey and follows in her footsteps. Never less than obedient. Until now.

Finally he found the key cards in the bottom drawer of the kitchen together with the egg timer she'd never used and a badly burned skillet that she did use. They were the best key cards they'd ever stolen, and they had always fetched a good price. Just the right size and color, with just the right mag code to look exactly like a righteous California driver's license once they slapped the bogus facsimile on the front. He was going to have to find another woman partner to hang around that particular hotel and get more of them. Maybe a halfway classy woman who would never arouse suspicion. He tried to think of a halfway classy woman he might know but gave up trying immediately.

Of course he knew that the junkyard rendezvous was very dangerous and might be a trick of Cosmo's to kill them, but after he'd told Cosmo that Olive had boogied and Cosmo still wanted him to make delivery, he figured it was probably okay. That fucking Armo wouldn't dare try to kill him with Olive out there able to dime him to the cops if Farley went missing. Would he?

He might. Farley had never dealt with anyone as violent as Cosmo, so that's why he'd devised a little plan of his own. Sure, he was going to drive to that lonely junkyard on that lonely fucking road in east L.A., where no white man in his right mind would roam around at night. But he wasn't stepping one toe out of his car, no way. He was going to drive up, wrong side of the road to that fence, reach out, and grab the paper bag. And if the money was in there, he'd pull into the yard, spin a sweeping U-turn, blow his horn until Gregori came out, toss him the paper bag with the key cards in it, and zip on out of that yard and back to white man's country—if Hollywood could be called white man's country these days.

And if there wasn't a trap at all and Gregori got insulted by his method of delivery and threatened not to do business with him anymore, too fucking bad. Gregori shouldn't hang with gun-packing Armos like Cosmo. He should stick with thieving, chiseling, bloodsucking Armos like himself. Yeah, Farley thought with waxing confidence as he fantasized about the glass he'd be smoking tonight, where's the glitch in *that* plan?

Suddenly he was hungry from all that thinking, but he couldn't bear the thought of a cheese sandwich. He had a yearning for Ruby's doughnuts, especially for a couple of those big fat cream-filled, chocolate-covered specials. He found the emergency twenty-dollar bill he had stashed in his underwear drawer, where Olive would never look, then propped up the broken back door as best he could and left for Ruby's. Like Pablo's Tacos and the cyber café, Ruby's Donuts was one of the last stops on the Tweakerville Line.

He saw a couple of tweakers he knew in the parking lot, looking hungry but not for doughnuts. Come to think of it, this was the first time he'd ever gone to Ruby's looking for something to put in his stomach. The Hollywood nights were growing more and more strange and weird and scary for Farley Ramsdale, and he couldn't seem to stop it from happening.

They didn't really need Samuel R. Culhane to lead them to Farley's house. A call took care of that. The FI file was full of shakes involving Farley Ramsdale and Olive O. Ramsdale, and it also had their correct address as shown on his driver's license. Like other tweakers, they were always getting stopped and FI'd. But Viktor pretended that Culhane's presence was needed just to be sure that if left alone, he wouldn't make a warning call to Farley.

Driving his Pinto, Samuel L. Culhane did as he was told and led 6-X-72 and Viktor Chernenko to Farley's house, where he slowed and indicated the house with his left-turn signal. Then he took off for home while the cops parked and piled out of the black-and-white, approaching the house with their flashlights off.

As before, Wesley went to cover the back door. He found it partially ajar, one hinge hanging loose, and propped in place by a kitchen chair. Nate and Viktor got no response and there were no lights on in the house. Wesley checked the empty garage.

'He's a typical tweaker,' Nate said to Viktor. 'Out hunting for crystal. When he finds it he'll come home.'

'I must arrange for a stakeout,' Viktor said. 'I feel very strong that this Farley Ramsdale stole the letter from the mailbox that led to the jewel robbery. Yet it is only a feeling. But I am positive that the jewel robbers are the ATM killers. This shall be the biggest case of my career if I can prove that I am correct.'

'This could be one for the TV news and the *L.A. Times*,' Hollywood Nate said.

'It is more than possible,' Viktor said.

Hollywood Nate paused for a moment and only one word came to him: 'publicity.' He thought about walking into a casting office with a *Times* under his arm. Maybe with his picture in it.

'Viktor,' he said, 'since we've been in on this with you so far, how about calling us if the guy shows up? We'd be glad to transport for you or help you search for evidence—whatever. We were there during the grenade trick and we sorta feel like this is our case too.'

'Detective,' Wesley added. 'This could be the biggest thing I've ever accomplished in my whole life. Please call us.'

'You may be sure,' Viktor said, 'that I shall personally call you. I am not going home tonight until I have a talk with Mr. Farley Ramsdale and his friend who calls herself Olive O. Ramsdale. And if you wish, you can go now and look for them at tweaker hangouts. Perhaps we do not have enough to tie them into crimes but we do not have to just sit back and cool our toes.'

*

Now Ilya was lecturing Cosmo as she would a child, and he sat there with a cigarette in his nicotine-stained fingers, taking it gladly, a man bereft of ideas.

'Understand me, Cosmo, and trust,' she said. 'Olive is gone and Farley will not get out of his car in the junkyard of Gregori. He will not, because of you. Do not think all people are as stupid as…' She stopped there and said, 'You must kill him in his car. Outside the yard.'

'Ilya, I cannot find no place to hide myself outside. It is open road and no cars parked on the road at night. Where can I hide myself?'

'Think on it,' Ilya said. 'Use the brain. After you kill him you take him away in his car. You park one mile away. You leave. You go back to the yard and get our car.'

Interrupting, 'How must I get back to the yard? Call taxi?'

'No!' she said. 'You do not! You want police to find out that taxi takes somebody from a scene of dead body to the junkyard of Gregori? Goddamn, Cosmo!'

'Okay, Ilya. Sorry. I walk back.'

'Then you and me, we drive to Dmitri. You have some diamonds in your pocket. Not too many. You give diamonds to Dmitri. His man inspect diamonds. You say, please bring money downstairs to the nightclub. Give to Ilya. I shall be sitting at the bar. He give me money, I go to ladies room and get the remaining diamonds from where I hide them in a safe place. Lots of people around in the nightclub. We shall be safe.'

'But Ilya,' Dmitri said. 'You forget about ATM money.'

'No, I do not forget. You must tell Dmitri mostly truth.'

'Ilya! He shall kill me!'

'No, he wants ATM money. You tell him we know where to find Olive. You tell him we shall find her tomorrow. We shall get money and kill her. We shall bring half of money to Dmitri like our deal say we do.'

'He shall be very angry,' a despairing Cosmo said. 'He shall kill me.'

'Dmitri wish to kill someone? Tell him to kill his goddamn Georgian who give us a goddamn car that don't run!'

'Then, what we do tomorrow? We cannot find Olive. We cannot get money to Dmitri.'

'The Americans have saying, Cosmo. I am not for sure what each word mean but I understand the idea. Tomorrow we get the fuck out of Dodge.'

The Oracle was having a bad night. The lieutenant was off and he was watch commander, so he had to deal with the angry phone call from the lawyer, Anthony Butler.

'Mr. Butler,' he said, 'the detectives have gone home, so if you'll just call back tomorrow.'

'I have been waiting all day for your detectives!' the lawyer said. 'Or rather my daughter has. Do you know she was given a date rape drug at a place called Omar's Lounge?'

'Yes, I've pulled the report and looked it over as you requested, but I'm not a detective.'

'I talked to your nighttime detective twenty minutes ago. The man's an idiot.'

The Oracle didn't argue with that one but said, 'I will personally make sure that the detective commander knows about your call, and he will send someone to your office tomorrow.'

'The man Andrei who tried to drug my daughter knows she got in the wrong car. He probably knows the police were called. And how do we know that he's not a friend of the Iranians? Maybe he can identify them. What if this was a filthy little plot involving Andrei and the Iranian pigs? I'm shocked that nobody has been to the Gulag to at least identify this Andrei.'

The Oracle said, 'If he's really the manager of the Gulag,

he's got a good job and he's not going anywhere. He'll be there tomorrow. And being an attorney, you must understand how impossible it would be to prove that she'd been given a drug last night.'

The lawyer said, 'I want to know if the man has a history of this sort of thing. Sara is my only child, Sergeant. A security officer from our corporation is going to accompany me and my daughter to the Gulag this evening, and she's going to point him out if he's there, and we're going to get his name and address. I intend to make the bastard's life a misery with or without the help of detectives from Hollywood Station.'

'No, no, Mr. Butler,' the Oracle said. 'Don't go to the Gulag and stir things up. That'll just end up a real mess for everyone. Tell you what, I'll go there myself tonight and talk to the guy and get all the necessary information that the detectives can act on. How's that?'

'You give me your personal guarantee, Sergeant?'

'You have it,' the Oracle said.

After he hung up, the Oracle called 6-X-76 to the station while he read through the report in its entirety. This was the kind of petty crap that wore him down more than anything, that made him feel old.

Whenever anybody asked him how old he was, the Oracle always answered, 'I'm the same age as Robert Redford, Jack Nicholson, Jane Fonda, Warren Beatty, and Dustin Hoffman.'

He'd always figured that ageless images of Hollywood stars would somehow mitigate what the mirror was showing him: jagged furrows running down his cheeks and encircling his neck, a sagging jawline, deepening creases between his hazel eyes.

But the trick didn't work anymore. Many of the young coppers would say, 'Who's Warren Beatty?' Or ask what movie Jane Fonda ever played in. Or say, 'Jack Nicholson's the dumpy old guy that goes to the Laker games, right?' He opened the desk drawer and swallowed a dose of antacid liquid from the bottle.

When 6-X-76 entered the watch commander's office, the Oracle said, 'This so-called kidnapping at Omar's Lounge is a piece of shit, right?'

'A smelly one, Sarge,' Budgie said. 'The woman insisted on a kidnapping report. She threatened lawsuits. She called a TV news crew, but I didn't hear anything more, so I guess they also figured it was a piece of shit. Her old man's some kind of politically connected lawyer, according to her.'

'He just called.'

'She's an actress,' Fausto said, and at Hollywood Station that explained a lot.

The Oracle nodded and said, 'Just to keep the peace I'll run up to the Gulag later tonight and get Andrei's name and address so that when her daddy calls, the detectives can pacify him. We don't need any more personnel complaints around here.'

'What time you going?' Fausto asked.

'In a couple hours.'

'We'll meet you there and take you to Marina's.'

'What's that?'

'New Mexican restaurant on Melrose.'

'I'm not rich enough for Melrose.'

'No, this is a little family joint. I'll buy.'

'Is there a rehab for Tex-Mex addiction? I've got permanent heartburn.'

'Whatever you say.'

The Oracle hesitated and said, 'Home-made tortillas? And *salsa fresca*?'

'I been hearing good things,' Fausto said.

'Okay, I'll call and let you know when I'm at the Gulag,' the Oracle said.

'Catch you in five, Fausto,' Budgie said, obviously going to the bathroom.

When she was gone, the Oracle said, 'I'm doing car assignments for the next deployment period. How do you feel about Budgie?'

'Whaddaya mean?'

'You didn't want to work with a woman, but you did me a favor. I don't wanna ask for a favor two months in a row if you still feel the same way.'

Fausto didn't speak for a moment. He looked up at the ceiling and sighed as though it were a tough decision and then said, 'Well, Merv, if you're on the spot again and need me to help out...'

'We're so shorthanded that figuring out deployment is awful hard these days,' the Oracle said. 'It would make things easier for me.'

'She's a good enough young copper,' Fausto said, 'but I think she could benefit from having an old dog like as a shepherd for a while longer.'

'I'm glad you feel that way, Fausto,' the Oracle said. 'Thanks for helping me out.'

'Well, I better go collect her,' Fausto said. 'These split tails take a long time to get unrigged just to take a pee. We oughtta come up with some kind of loincloth uniform for them.'

The Oracle saw Fausto go out the back door to the parking lot to wait, and he caught Budgie coming out of the bathroom.

'Budgie,' he said, 'you got any objections to working another deployment period with the old walrus?'

'No, Sarge,' she said, smiling. 'We have an understanding, Fausto and me. We're actually a pretty good team.'

'Thanks,' he said. 'Working with you has done wonders for him. He looks and acts ten years younger. Sometimes I think I'm a genius.'

'We all know that, Sarge,' Budgie said.

*

Farley arrived at the junkyard at the appointed time and parked fifty yards away with his lights out. If any shadow figure that even slightly resembled Cosmo Betrossian walked up to that fence, he was going to drive away, money or no money. But in ten minutes nothing moved. He had to get close to see if the gate was open and a paper bag was stuffed through the chain link, so he drove slowly toward the yard, lights still out. He heard dogs barking at another yard closer to his car. It reminded him of Odar, the oversized Doberman guard dog that was named for non-Armenians.

He was on the wrong side of the road now, but there was so little nighttime traffic on the junkyard road that it didn't matter. Behind the fences were stripped and wrecked cars on both sides of the road as well as huge cranes. He saw small office buildings, or RVs serving as office buildings, and larger buildings where cars could be dismantled or reassembled. And all was dark except for security lights on some of the buildings and along some of the roadside fences.

When he was drifting close to Gregori's car gate, lights out, he could see by moonlight that it was open. And he could see something white in the chain-link mesh. Apparently the bag containing the money was there.

He lowered his window, snatched the bag from the wire, and drove back up the road a safe distance, where he parked. He opened the bag and turned on the overhead light, and there it was—$150 in tens and twenties. He counted it twice. Then excitement began to replace his fear. He thought about the ice he'd be smoking tonight. That was all he could think about for a moment, but then he realized he had to deliver.

Farley drove back boldly now and wheeled into the junkyard with his lights on and his windows rolled up and the doors locked. Odar, tied to a long wire line that allowed him to run from the gate to the office, was barking and snarling, but there was nobody around the gate at all, nothing except an oil drum up against the fence. Farley felt so safe that he made a leisurely U-turn in the yard, blew his horn three times, lowered the window, and tossed the bag of key cards onto the asphalt and headed back to the gate.

His headlight beams caught just enough of Cosmo Betrossian climbing out of the empty drum! Farley had time to step on the accelerator hard, but by the time he got to the gate, Cosmo had swung it closed!

The Corolla slammed into the gate and stopped, its left headlight broken and its front fender driven into the tire. The engine died, and in utter panic Farley turned the key off and on as Cosmo ran up to the car, a pistol in his hand.

'Stop, Farley!' Cosmo yelled. 'I shall not hurt you!'

Farley was sobbing when the engine finally kicked over, and he slammed the shift into reverse and backed all the way across the yard, bashing into the door of the office, breaking both taillights and jerking his head back.

Odar was going mad! The dog was snapping and snarling and barking hoarsely, his muzzle white with froth. He was lunging at the car that was crashing and smashing things. Lunging at the running man who had showed up two hours after his master leashed him to the wire and left him. Odar wanted to attack! Anybody! Anything!

Farley dropped the shift into low and gunned it, aiming at Cosmo, who leaped aside and fired a shot through the passenger window behind Farley's head. Farley drove for the gate and rammed it a second time. The car shuddered and recoiled again but the gate still stood. He looked in his side-view mirror and saw Cosmo running toward the car, gun in one hand, flashlight in the other.

Farley reversed it again and floored the accelerator. The tires spun and burned and smoked and the car jetted in reverse and Cosmo leaped out of the way again and fired a second shot and a third, the recoil taking both rounds over the top of the Corolla's roof.

The car was hurtling backward with its driver not

knowing which way to turn, but turn he did, this time avoiding a rear-end crash into the office building. Then Farley slammed on the brakes and spun to a stop, his head still reeling.

He could see the blur in his headlights and knew it was Cosmo Betrossian coming to kill him, so he dropped it in low and gunned it and jerked the wheel left, uncertain if Cosmo was still there, even though he could hear the gunfire and see muzzle flashes coming at him. Farley's damaged left front fender just clipped Cosmo on the hip and he flew twenty feet across the asphalt, landing on that same hip, losing his pistol in a jumble of scrap metal and grease rags.

Farley knew he'd hit Cosmo and he floored it again, driving right at the gate, but at the last second he mashed on the brakes, got out, and ran to the gate, expecting to be struck in the back of the head by a bullet. Farley threw back the steel bolt and swung the gate almost open but when he turned he saw Cosmo staggering toward him, without a pistol now but carrying a metal bar that he'd picked up from the scrap heap. Cosmo was limping and cursing in his language. And coming at him.

Farley got the gate all the way open and headed for the driver's seat but he was too late. Cosmo was on him and the bar smashed the driver's side window after Farley ducked. Then Farley was running with Cosmo after him, running into the darkness, running toward the rows of stacked cars waiting to be crushed, then toward another row waiting to be stripped and sold for parts.

Odar had had all he could handle. These two intruders running through his yard were too much for him. His canine adrenaline was overflowing and he took a run, a long run at both men, and the leash drew as tight as piano wire and the overhead line that held the leash snapped. And Odar, eyes aflame, fangs bared, his entire face covered in foam, narrowed those demon eyes and came at them.

Farley saw Odar first and scrambled on top of a wrecked Plymouth pulling himself onto the roof. Cosmo saw Odar too but had no time to swing at him with the bar, and taking a cue from Farley, he leaped onto the deck lid of a wrecked Audi, scuttling up onto the roof with Odar behind him, his black coat glistening in the moonlight.

The dog vaulted up, slipped, fell from the car onto the ground, then tried again and in a few seconds was standing on the Audi roof dragging his leash. But Cosmo had jumped from the roof of the Audi to the hood of a Pontiac and from the Pontiac across to the roof of a nearly stripped Suburban. Suddenly, Odar abandoned the chase of Cosmo and switched his attention to Farley, who was also leapfrogging cars and partially stripped car bodies, until he turned around, horrified to see the goddamn dog doing the same and coming after *him*!

Cosmo's injured hip began to freeze up on him now, and Farley caught his breath on the roof of an old Cadillac while the confused dog crouched on the hood of a Mustang between them, looking from one man to the other, uncertain which he should attack.

Cosmo began speaking to the dog in Armenian then, trying to win him over with the language the animal was used to hearing. He began issuing gentle commands in his mother tongue.

Farley, who was not as badly injured as Cosmo but every bit as exhausted, also tried persuading the dog, but when Farley tried to speak, he was blubbering and hysterical and tears ran down into his mouth as he cried, 'Don't listen to him, Odar! You're like me! I'm an odar, too! Kill him! Kill the fucking Armo!'

Odar started for Farley then and Farley screamed like a woman. The scream of terror triggered something in the attack animal. The dog whirled, hurtled from deck lid to hood to roof, flying at Cosmo like a missile, driving Cosmo off the car onto the ground. The dog's momentum took him with Cosmo and he landed on the ground at a twisting angle, yelped in pain, and came up limping badly. Within seconds he was unable to walk at all on his left rear leg, and hardly at all on his right.

By then Farley was running for his car, and he made it and jumped in but was unable to start it. Weeping, he flooded the engine, then turned off the ignition and locked the door as Cosmo limped to the scrap heap where he'd lost the pistol. But Cosmo's flashlight was gone too, and he could only dig his hands into the twisted metal until he found the gun, cutting a finger to the bone in the process.

Farley tried the ignition again and the car started! He dropped it into low and stomped the accelerator at the same instant that Cosmo appeared at the passenger window and fired five rounds through the glass, missing with the first four. The fifth and last round entered through Farley's right armpit as his hand was cranking the wheel left and the car was digging out and burning rubber.

Out of the fight, the dog sat on his right hip, snarling and howling at Cosmo, who limped to his Cadillac which had been concealed behind the office building, started it up, and tried to drive after Farley. But Cosmo hadn't driven a quarter of a mile before he had to pull off the road, rip off his T-shirt, and use it to stem the blood that was flowing from a nasty head gash and running into his eyes and blinding him.

Farley is a quarter of a mile down that junkyard road before he knows he's been shot. He reaches down with his left hand, feels the warm wetness, and begins bawling. Still, he keeps driving, one headlight lighting the road in front, smashed fenders scraping both front tires.

Farley loses track of time but just follows his instincts onto east Sunset Boulevard, where it begins near downtown Los Angeles. Sometimes Farley stops for traffic lights, sometimes not, and he never sees the police car that spots him cruising through a red light at Alvarado as several motorists slam on brakes and blow horns and yell at him.

He is driving leisurely now through all those ethnic neighborhoods where people speak the languages of Latin America, Southeast Asia, and the Far East as well as Russian and Armenian and Arabic and a dozen other languages he hates. Heading west, heading toward Hollywood, heading home.

Farley Ramsdale does not hear the police siren either and of course has no knowledge that a Rampart Division unit has broadcast a pursuit of a white Corolla along with his license number and his location and direction, causing Hollywood Division cars to start heading for Sunset Boulevard, everyone convinced that this incredibly reckless drunk will blow at least a .25 on the Breathalyser because he's weaving along Sunset at only thirty miles an hour, causing oncoming traffic to veer right and stop, and is apparently oblivious to the sirens and the queue of black-and-whites that have joined in behind the pursuit car.

At Normandie Avenue Farley crosses into Hollywood Division, still heading west. But he's not in a car any longer. Farley Ramsdale is fifteen years younger and is in the gymnasium at Hollywood High School shooting hoops in an intramural game, and they are all threepointers that find only net. *Swoosh!* And that cheerleader who always disses him is now giving him the big eye. He'll be boning her tonight, that's for sure.

At the corner of Gower Street his foot slips from the accelerator and the car drifts slowly into the rear of a parked Land Rover and the engine dies. Farley never sees the officers of Hollywood Division midwatch who know him— Hollywood Nate and Wesley Drubb and B.M. Driscoll and Benny Brewster, and Budgie Polk and Fausto Gamboa—and those who don't.

All out of their cars, guns drawn, the cops run very warily toward the Corolla now that Nate's broadcast has alerted all units that the pursued car is wanted in connection with a robbery investigation. They are yelling things, but Farley doesn't hear that either.

Hollywood Nate was the first to reach the car, and he smashed the rear driver's side window open and unlocked the driver's door. When Nate jerked open the door and saw all the blood, he holstered his nine and yelled for someone to call an RA.

Farley Ramsdale's eyes were rolled back showing white, his eyelids fluttering like wings as he went into shock and died long before the rescue ambulance reached Sunset Boulevard.

NINETEEN

Cosmo could not stop cursing as he drove west toward Hollywood. He kept looking at his watch without knowing why. He kept thinking of Ilya, of what she would say, of what they would do. He kept wondering how long it would take that miserable addict Farley to phone the police and tell them about the jewelry store robbery. At least Farley couldn't tell them about the ATM robbery and the killing of the guard. Ilya was correct. Farley did not know about that or he would not have come to Gregori's tonight. But that was very little consolation now.

His finger was throbbing and so was his head. He had a laceration just inside the hairline and it was still oozing blood. His finger would need suturing and maybe his head would as well. Almost every bone and muscle ached. He wondered if his hip was broken. Should he go home? Would the police be waiting for him there?

Tonight he had used the Beretta 9-millimeter pistol that he'd taken from the guard. He thought it would be much more accurate than the cheap street gun he had used in the robberies. And what good did it do him? But at least he still had rounds left in the magazine. He had no intention of living his life in prison like an animal. Not Cosmo Betrossian.

He opened his cell and phoned Ilya. If she did not answer, it meant that the police were already there.

'Yes?' Ilya said.

'Ilya! You are okay?'

'Yes, I am okay. Are you okay, Cosmo?'

'Not okay, Ilya. Nothing is correct.'

'Shit.'

'I am bleeding on my hand and head. I need bandage on my wounds and I need a new shirt and I need a cap to hide blood. Not the cap from that day.'

'I threw the baseball cap away, Cosmo. I am not so stupid.'

'I shall be home soon. I must be putting gas in my car. I think there is more safety if we drive to San Francisco.'

'Shit.'

'Yes, Farley may be calling police now. Make all things ready to travel. I shall see you soon.'

Before she began packing their clothes Ilya went to the closet shelf and removed the bag of rings and earrings and loose diamonds. She left a sufficient sampling of each for Cosmo to show to Dmitri. Then she put the rest in a very safe place.

The intersection of Sunset Boulevard and Gower Street was a very busy place, completely blocked off by police. Viktor Chernenko was there, having left the stakeout at Farley Ramsdale's house. The house would now be the object of a hastily written search warrant as soon as Viktor got back to the office. After Hollywood Nate told him that the homicide victim was definitely his person of interest, Farley Ramsdale, Viktor began to think of Farley as having been much more ambitious than a petty mail thief. Whatever his connection to the Russian robbers it had gotten him killed.

And when word got to the detective squad room that the pursuit suspect had ended up dead, shot at some location east of Hollywood Division but wanted by Viktor Chernenko, it stirred a lot of interest from the usually disinterested night-watch detective Compassionate Charlie Gilford.

Andi McCrea and Brant Hinkle were just getting ready to leave for the Gulag to follow up on their own homicide case and try to get their hands on Dmitri's videotape, when Compassionate Charlie looked their way.

Andi said, 'Don't even think about it, Charlie. The guy was shot somewhere outside Hollywood, and I've got all I can handle anyway.'

Compassionate Charlie shrugged and started making calls. When he was through, he put on his checked sport coat and headed for Sunset and Gower so as not to miss a chance to offer commentary on another Hollywood dream gone terribly wrong.

Wesley Drubb was so excited that Hollywood Nate told him to hang on to his seat belt for fear of levitation. Viktor Chernenko had spoken to Robbery-Homicide Division detectives from the Bank Squad who were on the ATM case and had phoned his lieutenant at home. Things were happening so fast it was hard to decide what to do next other than to write a search warrant for the Ramsdale house and hope that they could locate the woman who called herself Olive Ramsdale. Another Hollywood robbery team had the house under surveillance, waiting for her.

There wasn't anything else for 6-X-72 to do at the moment, so Nate and Wesley reluctantly had to go back to the streets and return to ordinary police work.

Viktor said to them, 'I shall write you a commendation for your good performance whether or not we solve this case. And do not forget Olive. You know her. You might see her at the taco stand or the doughnut shop or the cyber café.'

'We'll be looking,' Nate said.

'Keep the eyes skinned,' Viktor said. 'And thank you.'

Andi and Brant had decided to have a quick bite before going to the Gulag. One thing about Russian nightclubs, they stayed open until the last minute the law allowed, so Andi figured they had plenty of time left.

They were in Thai Town, Andi working on a green papaya salad and Brant devouring a red curry with chicken, his eyes watering from the chilis. They each drank two Thai iced coffees, both to soothe their burning mouths and because they needed the caffeine jolt, having had such little sleep in the past two days.

Brant said, 'Since I'm the new kid on the block and bouncing from robbery team to helping you, I think I'll talk to the lieutenant about working homicide full-time. You're shorthanded.'

'Everybody's shorthanded,' Andi said, sipping the iced coffee through a straw.

'It's not that anybody would fight over me,' Brant said. 'The boss knows I'll only be around here until the promotion list gets down to me and I'm appointed.'

'Lieutenant Hinkle,' Andi said. 'It has a nice sound. You'll be a good watch commander.'

'Not as good as you,' Brant said. 'I expect you to knock 'em dead and be near the top of the next list. The troops will love working for you.'

'Why is that?'

'You have a good heart.'

'How do you know what's inside? You've only seen the outside of me.'

'Cop instinct.'

'Careful, buddy. I'm at the age where I get all giddy when a man flatters me like that. I might do something stupid. Like taking you seriously.'

'I'm several years older than you. I'm ready to be taken seriously.'

'Let's postpone this conversation until end-of-watch,' Andi said, 'when I can focus on it.'

'Whatever you say, partner.'

'I say, let's go get a videotape and clear a homicide.'

'Is Viktor still gonna meet us there for a little Russian fast talk?'

'He's a very busy guy tonight but he said he would.'

'To the Gulag, comrade,' Brant said with a smile that crinkled his heavily lashed green eyes and made Andi's toes curl under.

Cosmo was a shocking sight to Ilya when he limped up the stairs. She helped him clean up the head wound and stanch the ooze of blood. As to his finger, she did her best to hold the laceration together with butterfly Band-Aids, then wrapped and taped the finger until they could get to a doctor tomorrow and have it sutured. Where they would have that done, where they would be tomorrow, was anybody's guess. Ilya just wanted to concentrate on getting the money from Dmitri tonight.

'We may run away now, Ilya,' Cosmo said. 'We have diamonds. We find somebody in San Francisco.'

'We are very much hot,' Ilya said. 'Too much happening. We got no time no more. The police shall be coming when Farley informs to them about us. No time to fish for diamond people in San Francisco. We need money now. You know, Cosmo, I may run clear back to Russia. I do not know.'

He didn't know either. All he knew was that he was very much afraid to face Dmitri tonight without the ATM money. And to try to sell him a lie. Dmitri was very smart. More smart than Ilya, he thought.

He made the phone call to the cell number Dmitri had given to him.

'Yes,' Dmitri answered.

'Is me, brother,' Cosmo said.

'Do not say your name.'

'I shall like to come in thirty minute.'

'Okay.'

'You ready to finish business?'

'Yes, and you?'

Cosmo swallowed and said, 'Ready, brother.'

'See you in thirty,' Dmitri said, and somehow Cosmo could see that smile of his.

Cosmo put on the black beret to hide his head wound. It was something that Ilya wore with her black sweater and boots when she wanted to look very sexy. He wore a pale white sport coat and blue slacks and his best cordovan shoes. He tucked the Beretta inside his waistband in the small of his back. He cinched the leather belt tight to hold the pistol there.

Ilya was wearing the tightest red skirt she owned, and a shell with a deep V neckline, the one that made her breasts swell out, and a short black jacket over that, one trimmed with sequins. And since they were going to a Russian club she wore her black knee boots with three-inch heels. She was not short on bling, she thought. Ilya liked that American word: 'bling.'

Cosmo forced a brave smile and said, 'We go to get our thirty-five thousands, Ilya. We go to the Gulag.'

The Oracle looked at the clock. He was getting hungry and this had been a very busy night what with the pursuit driven by a dead man, and Viktor Chernenko tying up one of his midwatch cars, along with more ordinary Hollywood madness breaking out here and there as though there was a full moon. He felt a stab of heartburn and popped a couple of antacid tablets.

He said to the Watch 3 sergeant, 'I gotta go do a PR job to keep some dirtbag of a lawyer from making a personnel complaint on everybody in Hollywood Division who met or failed to meet his goofy daughter who's made a bogus crime report. I just gotta get the name and address of the manager of a nightclub, if the guy really is the manager. Maybe he just has business cards made up to impress the chicks he meets in bars.'

'Which nightclub you going to?' the sergeant asked.

'A Russian joint called the Gulag. You know it?'

'No, but I imagine it's a Russian Mafia hangout. They change and names more often than they change underwear.'

The Oracle said, 'After that, I'll be taking code seven with Fausto and his partner. They found a hot new mama-and-papa Mexican eatery. Call if you need me.'

When the Oracle drove out of the Hollywood Station parking lot, he sent a message to 6-X-76 telling them he was on his way to the Gulag and shouldn't be there for more than fifteen minutes.

The Gulag parking lot was jammed when Cosmo wheeled his Cadillac in. He had to park in the far corner by the trash containers.

'Dmitri should hire valet boys,' Ilya observed nervously.

'Too cheap,' Cosmo said.

They could hear the place rocking the moment they stepped out of their cars. Cosmo snuffed out his cigarette, touched the pistol under his coat, and limped to the entrance with Ilya.

Ilya went to the bar, joined the rows of drinkers trying to get service, and called to the sweaty bartender, 'Excuse me, please.'

A boozy young guy sitting at the bar turned and looked at her face, then at her tits, got up from the bar stool, and said, 'I'll give you my seat if you'll let me buy you a drink.'

Ilya gave him her best professional smile, took his bar stool, and said, 'That is lovely, darling.'

Smiling at her accent, he said, 'Are you Russian?'

'Yes, darling,' she said.

'How about I order you a Black Russian?'

'I prefer a white American,' she said, and the young guy laughed out loud, drunk enough that anything was funny.

Ilya wished that the world had not stopped smoking. She would have given a diamond for a cigarette at this moment.

As busy as he was, Viktor Chernenko had made a promise to Andi McCrea, and a promise was a promise. He looked at his watch and told Compassionate Charlie that he had to quickly run to a Russian nightclub called the Gulag to do a verbal muscle job for Andi in the proprietor's own language. As for the outside detectives who were on their way to the station to help piece together the puzzle of the Ramsdale murder and Hollywood robberies, Viktor planned to stay tonight as long as there was hope of finding Farley Ramsdale's woman. He had a copy of her minor rap sheet for petty theft and drug possession and saw that the name 'Olive Ramsdale' must be a recent alias. She'd given the name 'Mary Sullivan' when she'd been arrested, but who could say if that was her true name?

Then he put in a quick phone call home and got his wife, Maria, on the phone.

'Hello, my darling,' he said. 'This is your most loving husband.'

Compassionate Charlie said, 'What the hell?' and looked at Viktor like he'd just burped pepper spray. Charlie couldn't bear telephone canoodling.

'I am working on the most important matter of my entire career, my little sweetheart,' Viktor said. 'It is possible that I shall be sleeping here in the cot room tonight. I do not know for sure.'

Then Viktor listened with a dopey smile on his broad Slavic face, said, 'Me too!' and actually did kisses into the receiver before he rang off.

'Is this your first marriage, Viktor?' Charlie asked him.

'My first, my last,' Viktor said.

Charlie shook his head and said, 'Must be a Russian thing.'

'I am not Russian,' Viktor said patiently. 'I am Ukrainian.'

Compassionate Charlie said, 'Bring me back some kielbasa if the Gulag looks like a clean joint.'

'That is Polish, not Russian,' Viktor said, heading for the door.

'Polish, Russian, Ukrainian. Gimme a fucking break, Viktor,' Compassionate Charlie whined.

Cosmo knocked at the door to Dmitri's office and heard 'Come.'

When he limped into the office, he saw Dmitri in his high-back chair behind the desk, but not with his feet up this time and not watching exotic porn on the computer screen. An older man in a dark suit and a striped necktie, bald except for a scraggly fringe of gray, was sitting on the leather sofa against the wall.

Standing by the window that looked down on the smoking patio where the murder had occurred was the Georgian bartender, wearing a starched white shirt, a black bow tie, and black pants. His wavy black hair was even thicker than Cosmo's and he had a square, dark jaw that no razor could ever shave clean. He nodded to Cosmo.

Dmitri smiled that unreadable smile and said, 'The happen-ink guy is here! Please to meet Mr. Grushin, Cosmo. And show to him your goods for sale.'

'I have some sample,' Cosmo said, and Dmitri's smile faded and his face seemed to grow pale around the corners of his mouth. So Cosmo quickly added, 'All other diamonds downstairs with Ilya. Not to worry, brother.'

'I do not worry,' Dmitri said, smiling again. 'Why are you so injured?'

'I shall explain after,' Cosmo said. Then he removed a

plastic sandwich bag from his jacket pocket and poured out two rings, three sets of earrings, and five loose diamonds onto Dmitri's desk.

Mr. Grushin got up and walked to the desk. The Georgian pulled the client chair close so he could sit. Mr. Grushin took a jeweler's loupe from his pocket and examined each item under the light of the desk lamp and when he was through nodded to Dmitri, got up, and left the office.

'I may see money now, brother?' Cosmo said.

Dmitri opened the top desk drawer and withdrew three large stacks of currency, placing them on the desk in front of him. He did not ask Cosmo to sit.

'Okay, my friend,' Dmitri said. 'Tell me of ATM. And when I shall receive my half of money you got from there.'

Cosmo felt the dampness under his arms, and his palms were wet when he pointed his uninjured hand at the Georgian and said, 'He gave us a no-good car. The car die when we leave ATM!'

The Georgian said something quickly in Russian to Dmitri that Cosmo couldn't understand, then turned a scowl toward Cosmo and said, 'You lie! The car is good car. I drove car. You lie.'

Now Cosmo felt his stomach gurgle and his bowels rumble and he said, 'No, Dmitri. This Georgian, he lie! We have to drive the car away from ATM and park at the house of guy I know. We almost get caught by police!'

'You lie!' the Georgian said, taking a menacing step toward Cosmo until Dmitri held up his hand and stopped him.

'Enough,' Dmitri said to both men.

'I tell you truth, brother,' Cosmo said. 'I swear.'

'Now, Cosmo, where is money from ATM?' Dmitri asked.

'The man where we must take no-good car, his woman steal our money and run away from her man. But not to worry. We shall find her. We get money.'

'This man,' Dmitri said calmly, 'he does not know noth-ink of me? Noth-ink of the Gulag?'

'No, brother!' Cosmo said. 'Never!'

'And what of this man? What is his name?'

'Farley Ramsdale,' Cosmo said. 'He is addict.'

Dmitri looked in disbelief at Cosmo, then at the Georgian and back to Cosmo, and said, 'You leave my money with addict?'

'No choice, brother!' Cosmo said. 'This Georgian give us car that don't run. And Farley not at home so we got to hide car in his garage and hide money under his house. But goddamn addict woman, she find it and run away!'

Cosmo's mouth was dry as sand now and it made a popping sound each time his lips opened. The Georgian was glaring at him dangerously but Cosmo could hardly take his eyes from the thirty-five thousand dollars. It was a bigger pile of money than he'd imagined.

'Go get Ilya,' Dmitri said. 'Brink her up and I buy you drinks and we complete diamond deal and you tell me how you catch addict woman and tell me when you goink to get me my money from ATM.'

This was the moment he dreaded. This is what Ilya said he must do regardless of the outcome. Cosmo swallowed twice and said, 'No, brother. I take money now and your Georgian come with me down to the bar and Ilya go to bathroom and get diamonds from safe place and give to this Georgian. Lot of peoples down there. Safe for every-body.'

Dmitri laughed out loud at that and said, 'Cosmo, is information on TV and in newspaper correct? How much you find in the box?'

'Ninety-three thousands,' Cosmo said.

'TV lady say hundred thousand,' Dmitri said, 'but never mind, I believe you. So this mean you owe to me forty-six thousand and five hundred dollars and I owe to you thirty-five thousand dollars. So we do mathematics and we discover eleven thousand, five hundred dollars you owe to me. And the diamonds, too. Is very simple, no?'

Cosmo was dripping sweat now. His shirt was soaked and he kept wiping his palms on his trousers, standing there like a child, looking down at this Russian pervert and up at the Georgian thug standing beside him. And he wanted badly just to touch the Beretta, cold against the sweat on his back.

Cosmo said, 'Please to give me three minute to explain how the car this Georgian steal for us is reason for every problem!'

The Oracle was very surprised to see the detective car parked in the red zone on the east side of the nightclub, where he too was forced to park, the packed parking lot being an impossibility. He wondered which detective was in there and why. As he was walking toward the door, a black-and-white slowed and stopped and Fausto gave a short toot to get his attention. The Oracle walked over to the curb, bent down, and said, 'I won't be long, Fausto.'

'Want some company?' Budgie said. 'I've never been inside one of these Russian glam palaces.'

'Okay, but we'll scare the crap outta them,' the Oracle said. 'There's already a detective team in there.'

'For what?' Fausto said.

'Maybe the murder the other night,' the Oracle said. 'Five cops? They'll think they're back in the USSR.'

When the Oracle entered, followed by Fausto and Budgie, he spotted Andi and Brant standing back by the restrooms talking to a guy in a tuxedo who the Oracle figured might be the manager Andrei.

The decibel level was astounding and multicolored lights and strobes were playing all over the dance floor pit, where couples, mostly young, were 'get-tink down,' as Dmitri called it. From her seat at the end of the bar, Ilya couldn't see the three uniformed cops who entered and headed toward a narrow corridor by the kitchen. The Oracle, Fausto, and Budgie attracted some attention but not much, and they surprised the detectives.

Andi had to shout over the music. 'What're you doing here? Don't tell me there's another murder on the patio I haven't heard about?'

The Oracle said to the unhappy-looking guy in the tuxedo, 'Are you Andrei?'

'Yes,' the manager said.

'We'll give you cuts in line with this one,' Andi said to the Oracle. 'We're waiting to see Dmitri, the proprietor.'

The Oracle said to Andrei, 'I need to have a chat with you and get your name and address. I'll explain when we get to a quiet place, if such a thing exists around here.' Then, with a wink at Andi, he indicated Fausto and Budgie and said to Andrei, 'These two're my bodyguards. I take them with me wherever I go.'

Andrei had a what-else-can-go-wrong look on his face then. Just as something else was about to go very wrong.

Dmitri's eyes were half closed as Cosmo glossed over the aftermath of the ATM robbery, leaving out his confrontation tonight with Farley Ramsdale.

And when Cosmo was through, Dmitri said, 'You had to shoot the guard?'

'Yes, Dmitri,' Cosmo said. 'He did not give up money like you say.'

Dmitri shrugged and said, 'Sometimes information on enemy is not correct. Ask President Bush.'

Cosmo was getting his hopes built until Dmitri turned to the and said, 'Okay, maybe is a little piece of truth about the car. Maybe the car is not so good as you think.'

'Dmitri!' the Georgian said, but he saw the look in Dmitri's eye and stopped his protest.

'So, Cosmo,' Dmitri said, 'you are going to get ATM money tomorrow when you catch addict woman, no?'

'That is exactly correct,' Cosmo said.

'Okay, here is what I do for you, Cosmo,' said Dmitri. 'You owe me eleven thousand, five hundred plus diamonds. I am go-ink to cancel the money what you owe me! You get Ilya up here and give me all diamonds and we are even. Tomorrow when you catch addict woman, you keep all ninety-three thousand dollars. Your share, my share. I could not be more generous with my own brother, Cosmo.'

Then Dmitri looked up at the Georgian for validation and got a nod of agreement that said Dmitri was a very reasonable and very generous man.

It was hopeless. Cosmo was the image of despair. As Cosmo was staring at the money on Dmitri's desk, the Russian opened the top drawer and put the first stack back inside. When he reached for the second stack, Cosmo felt that he was outside his body and watching himself pull his coat back and reach behind him for the Beretta.

'Dmitri!' the Georgian yelled, coming up with a small pistol, from where, Cosmo didn't see.

And Dmitri shouted in Russian and opened a second drawer and reached inside for a gun of his own.

Andi said to the other cops and to Andrei the manager, 'We've waited long enough. I'm going to knock on Dmitri's door.'

She was interrupted by one shot followed by two more followed by five! And the two detectives and three uniformed cops ran upstairs. Andi was getting her pistol out of her purse when Fausto and Budgie passed her and both crouched down on one knee, guns extended in two hands aimed at the door of Dmitri's office. The Oracle ran to the other side of the door, and with his old six-inch revolver extended, he backed up, so that all guns, high and low, were deployed diagonally, pointed at the door.

Inside the office, Cosmo Betrossian had pain in his left arm that far exceeded anything he'd suffered this night either from Farley Ramsdale or the killer dog. Cosmo had a through-and-through wound in the biceps that had chipped the bone before exiting, and it burned like liquid fire.

The Georgian was sprawled across Dmitri's desk, spurting blood from an arterial penetration in the neck. But his chest wounds were even more devastating.

Dmitri was sitting back in his chair with a hole in his forehead that was actually a coup de grâce delivered by Cosmo as Dmitri lay dying, having fired the round that wounded Cosmo.

The thundering sounds from the pit below Dmitri's office had actually muffled the sound from the patron's area, and everyone rocked on. From time to time Ilya gazed across the dance floor, wondering why Cosmo had not returned.

Cosmo hoped he didn't faint before he got down to Ilya with the stacks of money inside his shirt against his skin. The money felt good. He was about to put his gun back into his waistband, but thinking that an employee from the kitchen might have heard the shots, he held the gun in front of him with his one good hand and opened the door.

In such confined space it sounded to Fausto like automatic weapon fire that he'd heard in Nam. Budgie later said that it sounded to her like one huge explosion. She couldn't differentiate the separate weapons firing.

Cosmo Betrossian got off exactly one shot, which hit the wall above their heads. He in turn was shot eighteen times with nine rounds missing him, probably as he was twisting and falling. All five cops shot him at least twice, with Fausto and Budgie scoring the most hits.

This being her first shooting, Andi McCrea later said during the FID investigation that it truly was like a slow-motion sequence. She could see, or thought she could see, hot empty shells ejecting into the air from various pistols and slapping against her face.

The Oracle said that in forty-six years, this was the first time he'd ever fired his weapon outside of the police pistol range.

Budgie had the most interesting commentary. She said that in such close confines, all the muzzle blasts and gun smoke had created a condition that, with her mouth wide open and sucking air, got her chewing gum full of grit.

The pandemonium that followed was worse than occurred on the night of the patio stabbing. The customers did hear the roar of the multiple gun shots from the upstairs hallway. Budgie and Fausto ran down the stairs to grab the manager and anybody else who looked like he might know what the hell had happened upstairs to cause the original gunfire. The Oracle made urgent calls on his rover.

By the time Viktor Chernenko pulled up in front, people were pouring from the front door and running for their cars. The parking lot was in such chaos that the cars in the back of the lot could not move. Headlights were flashing and horns were honking. Viktor bulled his way through emerging hysterical customers and took the stairs two at a time.

When he got to the scene of carnage, he said to the Oracle, 'One of these Russians may be the one I am looking for! Maybe the one who shot Farley Ramsdale!'

The Oracle, who was pale and had the worst heartburn of his life, said, 'A busboy told us the one in the chair is the owner. The one lying across the desk is a bartender. The one we shot…'—and he pointed to the ragged, bloody heap lying in the corner just beyond the door—'I don't know who he is. He killed the other two.'

Viktor said, 'You have latex gloves?' and when the Oracle

shook his head, Viktor said, 'Hell with it!' and pulled Cosmo's wallet from his back pocket and ran back down the stairs, his hands stained by Cosmo's blood.

When he got to the sidewalk in front he could hear sirens wailing as patrol units were arriving from all directions.

'Come with me!' Viktor yelled to Wesley Drubb, who had just leaped from their car as Nate was double-parking it.

Wesley followed Viktor to the parking lot, where Viktor looked inside each and every car with his flashlight as the cars took turns trying to funnel out of the narrow driveway. Most cars had couples in them or single men. Less than ten percent of the cars were driven by single women, but for every one that was, Cosmo's flashlight beamed squarely into the driver's face.

He was starting to think that he'd been wrong when he got to the last row of cars, but then he saw a big blond woman with huge breasts behind the wheel of an older Cadillac. Viktor turned to Wesley, his flashlight on Cosmo's driver's license, showing Wesley the name. Then he shined his light on the Cadillac and said, 'Please get a DMV on this license plate! Very fast!'

Viktor hung his badge on his coat pocket, walked up to the driver's door, and tapped on the window with his flashlight, his pistol in hand concealed just below the window ledge. And he smiled.

The woman rolled down the window, smiled back at him, and said, 'Yes, Officer?'

'Your name, please,' Viktor said.

'Ilya Roskova,' she said. 'There is a problem?' Then she looked to see if the queue of cars was moving, but it was not.

'Maybe,' Viktor said. 'And is this your car?'

'No, I borrow this car from a friend. She is a neighbor. I am so stupid I do not even know her family name.'

'May I see the registration?'

Ilya said, 'Shall I look in glove box?'

'By every means,' Viktor said, shining his light on her right hand as well as the glove compartment. His gun coming up a bit higher.

'No,' she said. 'No papers in there.'

'This car belongs to a woman, then?'

'Yes,' Ilya said. 'But not to this woman who sits before you in traffic.' Her smile broke wider, a bit coquettish.

Hollywood Nate and Wesley came running back, and Wesley whispered, 'Cosmo Betrossian. Same as on that driver's license.'

'So you know the owner of the car, then?' Viktor said to Ilya.

'Yes,' Ilya said cautiously. 'Her name is Nadia.'

'Do you know Cosmo Betrossian?'

'No, I do not think so,' Ilya said.

Viktor raised his pistol to her face and said in Russian, 'You will please step from the car with your hands where we can see them at all times, Madame Roskova.'

As Wesley handcuffed Ilya's hands behind her back, she said, 'I shall be calling my lawyer immediately. I am completely full of outrage!'

When they were transporting her to Hollywood Station, Nate said to his partner, 'Well, Wesley, what do you think of your misdemeanor division now?'

TWENTY

At 3 a.m. Ilya Roskova was sitting in the detective squad room, which was more crowded with people than it ever was during daylight hours. There were Force Investigation Division people, there was the area captain, there was the Detective Division commander—everyone had left their beds for this one. And the Gulag had more LAPD cars and personnel swarming around than they ever had customers during happy hour.

What was known so far was that the diamonds found on the desk at the Gulag under the body of the Georgian bartender matched descriptions given by Sammy Tanampai of his jewelry store inventory. The serial number on the Beretta 9-millimeter pistol used by Cosmo Betrossian to kill Dmitri and the Georgian proved to be the weapon taken from the surviving security guard during the ATM robbery.

Viktor Chernenko, the man who had been instinctively correct from the beginning, was told that, along with the captain, he should be prepared to speak to the media in the late morning after he got some much-needed sleep. Viktor predicted that ballistics would show that the bullet that killed Farley Ramsdale came from the same Beretta, and that Farley Ramsdale must have been an accomplice to the robbery and had a falling out with Cosmo Betrossian.

There was a person in the squad room, being guarded by Budgie Polk, who knew if Viktor was correct in both theories, but she wasn't talking. Ilya's wrist was handcuffed to a chair and she'd said *nyet* to every question asked, including whether she understood her constitutional rights. Everyone was waiting for Viktor to find time to try an interview in her language.

Andi McCrea along with the others who had participated in the officer-involved shooting were being separately interviewed by FID and were scattered among several of the station's offices. Andi was the third one finished, and when she came back into the busy squad room, she played the videotape that had been seized along with the other evidence from the desk of Dmitri.

When she watched the video with Brant Hinkle looking over her shoulder, they nodded, satisfied. The stabbing of the student was caught vividly. The identity of the assailant was unmistakable.

'He'll cop a plea when his lawyer sees this,' Andi said.

After packaging the videotape for booking, she looked at Ilya Roskova, sitting in the chair glaring at her stoic guard, Budgie Polk, who had been interviewed for one hour by FID.

Andi pulled Viktor aside and said, 'Have you gotten any information out of her?'

'Nothing, Andrea,' Viktor said. 'She will not speak at all except to ask for cigarettes. And she keeps wanting to go to the bathroom. I was just going to ask Officer Polk to take her.'

Andi kept eying Ilya, looking particularly at her lower body squeezed into that low-rise red skirt, as tight as Lycra. She said, 'Let me take her. Where's her purse?'

He pointed and said, 'Over there on the desk.'

'Does she have cigarettes in there?'

'Yes.'

Andi went to the desk and picked up the purse, then walked over to Ilya Roskova and said, 'Would you like us to take you to the bathroom?'

'Yes,' Ilya said.

'And after that maybe a cigarette?' Andi said.

'Yes.'

'Take the cuff off her, Budgie,' Andi said.

Budgie unlocked the handcuff and the prisoner stood, massaging her wrist for a second, prepared to accompany the cops.

As they started to walk, Andi opened the purse and said to Ilya, 'Yes, I see you have cigarettes in—' Then the purse dropped from Andi's hand onto the floor.

Ilya looked at Andi, who just smiled and said 'I'm sorry' but made no effort to pick up the purse.

Ilya angrily bent over to pick it up, and Andi stepped forward, put her hand on Ilya's shoulder, and forced her down into a full squat with one hand, reaching down toward the purse with her other, saying, 'Here, let me help you, Ms. Roskova.'

And when Ilya was held in the squatting position for a few seconds, making a fish mouth, a diamond hit the floor. Then another. Then a ring with a four-karat stone plinked against the floor and rolled across the squad room, stopping when it hit Viktor's shoe. Diamonds were shooting from that 'safe place' where she'd promised Cosmo to hide them.

Andi reached under Ilya's arm and raised her up, saying, 'We'll let you pee in a urinal and we'll be watching. And Viktor, I think you better put on gloves before you pick up the evidence.'

'Bitch!' Ilya said, as the two women, one on each arm, led her to the door.

'And you can use our bidet,' Budgie said. 'Like the one I have at home. It's called a sink. You jump up on it, but we'll keep the stopper in.'

Brant Hinkle said to Viktor, 'I think she might talk to you now.'

'How did Andi know?' Viktor marveled.

'She noticed right away and told me. No panty line, no thong line, nothing. She guessed that Roskova might want to get rid of them in a hurry first chance she'd get at privacy.'

'But the trick? To put her down in that position? How did she know that trick?'

'Viktor, there're some things you and I didn't learn at detective school that women just know,' Brant Hinkle said.

When Andi and Budgie returned with the cache of diamonds, Budgie said, 'I'm sure glad I didn't have to remove the evidence. I can't even clean out my rain gutters for fear of spiders and other crawly things.'

Late the next day, after getting five hours' sleep in the cot room along with a wardrobe change driven to the station by his wife, Maria, Viktor Chernenko completed his investigation by supervising a thorough search of the car and apartment of Cosmo Betrossian, as well as the house of Farley Ramsdale.

They found Cosmo's Lorcin .380 pistol and the Raven that Ilya had carried during the ATM robbery. At Farley's house they found some stolen mail, a glass pipe for smoking meth, and the usual litter and detritus that are found in the homes of tweakers. There were a few articles of women's clothing, but it appeared that Farley Ramsdale's companion had disappeared.

Viktor and two other detectives inquired at every house on both sides of the street but learned nothing of value. The next-door neighbor, an elderly Chinese man, said in barely understandable English that he had never spoken to Farley and never noticed a woman. The neighbor on the other side was an eighty-two-year-old Romanian who said that she only saw the man and woman coming in late at night and that her night vision was so bad she'd never recognize them in the daylight.

Interviews of other, mostly elderly, residents on the block were equally fruitless. Even when Olive's old mugshot was shown to them, nobody could say that she looked very familiar. She was the kind of person, it seemed, who would live and die on the streets of Hollywood utterly invisible.

Upon reading the news accounts about Farley Ramsdale and the massacre at the Gulag, a very frightened Gregori Apramian called Hollywood Station early in the afternoon to offer information. And after that call, his junkyard was deemed a crime scene and was sealed and scoured by criminalists and detectives from downtown.

Gregori stood in front of his office next to a leashed Doberman who, despite the cast on his rear leg, was snarling and still ready to fight. And scaring the crap out of every cop who got within ten yards.

What Gregori said for the record and what was transcribed onto a police report was: 'I just promise Cosmo to tow the Mazda that night. I don't know about no robberies. Maybe Cosmo bring this guy Farley to my yard to destroy the Mazda? That is what I think. They are going to burn up the Mazda to do the covering up of robberies. But something happen. They get in fight and hurt my Odar. And Cosmo shoot the man Farley. I do not know Farley. I do not know the Russian woman you arrest. I only know Cosmo because we go to same Armenian church sometimes. I am trying to be a friend to a fellow immigrant and be a, how you say, credit to America.'

At the end of his long day, Viktor Chernenko played a tape of Ilya Roskova's interview for the detective lieutenant and both area and station captains. Ilya had stopped saying *nyet* after the diamonds were excreted onto the squad room floor. She had then voluntarily removed the rest in the Hollywood Station bathroom where they were packaged and booked.

Ilya had been advised of her rights in both English and Russian, and she declared her understanding. The interview about her role in both robberies was long and tedious and self-serving. She kept claiming to have been totally in thrall to Cosmo Betrossian, calling herself a mental captive who lived in fear of him.

When one of the captains looked at his watch, Viktor advanced the tape to the portion dealing with the last pieces of the puzzle that remained missing: Olive and the ATM money.

Ilya's voice said, 'Olive was there when Farley did blackmail on Cosmo. When he gave big threat to tell police about the stolen letter. But Olive is, how you say, imbecile. Her brain is in a destroyed condition from drugs. I am very astounded that she have enough of the brain left to find the money Cosmo steal from ATM. Very astounded that she can take the money and vanish into thin smoke.'

Then Viktor's voice said, 'Do you think it is possible that Cosmo was holding back from you? Is it possible that Cosmo hid the money somewhere because he did not wish to share with you?'

After a long pause on the tape, Ilya's voice said angrily, 'Is not possible!' Then she obviously realized that she was blurring her portrait of enslavement and said, 'But of course I was so much in fear that I may be incorrect about what Cosmo can do. He was very much clever. And had two faces.'

Viktor turned off the machine then and said to his superiors, 'So far as I am concerned, we have hit a stone fence. I believe that Cosmo Betrossian took the ATM money from under the house of Farley Ramsdale on the night that the car was towed to the junkyard. I believe that Cosmo Betrossian has disposed of the ATM money with a friend, probably another woman. The Russian pride of Ilya Roskova does not wish to admit such a possibility—that he could have another secret woman and would be leaving her. I believe that Cosmo then tried to tell to Dmitri Sikhonov a false story of Olive stealing the money, but Dmitri was too smart to buy it. And that's when the shooting started.'

'You've been right on so far,' the area captain said. 'So what do you think happened to this woman Olive?'

'I think she finally got scared enough of Cosmo Betrossian to run away from Farley Ramsdale. She is probably living now with some other tweaker. Or maybe just living out on the street. We shall find her dead sometime from an overdose. Truly, she is of no further use to this investigation.'

'Do you think we'll ever find the ATM money?' the station captain asked.

Viktor said, 'We have learned that Cosmo Betrossian loved Russian woman. There is probably one of them shopping on Rodeo Drive with the ATM money. Right now as we talk.'

'Okay, it's a wrap,' the area captain said. 'When you do press interviews on this, just try to avoid mention of the missing money. The other pieces fit perfectly.'

'Yes, sir,' Viktor Chernenko said. 'That is the only fly in the jelly.'

TWENTY ONE

By the time the June deployment period was in full swing at Hollywood Station, things were back to normal. The surfer cops were hitting the beach at Malibu every chance they got. B.M. Driscoll was sure that he had a sinus infection from what to him was a severe allergy season. Benny Brewster had persuaded the Oracle to stick B.M. Driscoll with one of the recent arrivals who didn't know him, and the Oracle complied. Fausto Gamboa and Budgie Polk were an effective team, particularly after Budgie convinced Fausto that he absolutely had to treat her more like one of the guys. Wesley Drubb got his wish and was assigned to a gang unit with a chance to do more hardcore police work. And in a pinch, caused by summer vacations, Hollywood Nate agreed to be a temporary training officer to a brand-new probationer named Marty Shaw, who made Nate nervous by constantly calling him sir.

But best of all for the midwatch, Mag Takara came back to duty. The Oracle thought she should be assigned to the desk until her vision improved a bit more, and she agreed. Mag wore glasses now and would soon be taking sick days for future plastic surgery, but she wanted very much to put on the uniform again, and it was permitted. She learned that she was going to be awarded the Medal of Valor for her actions in the jewelry store on the night of the grenade incident. She said her parents would be very proud.

Mag even thanked Flotsam for the beautiful roses he had brought to the hospital, telling him he was a 'choiceamundo friend.' Flotsam actually blushed.

When Budgie Polk saw Mag, they hugged, and Budgie looked at the cheekbone that showed a slight darkened crater where tissue had not yet fully recovered and said, 'You're still the most gorgeous slut that ever hustled tricks on Sunset Boulevard.'

The deployment period was ending on a night when the homicide team of Andi McCrea and Brant Hinkle was working late after having arrested an aging actor who walked into his agent's office, cold-cocked the guy with an Oscar replica that the actor used as a paperweight, and then threatened to return with a gun.

When Hollywood Nate heard about it he said no jury made up of SAG members would ever convict the actor, and they might even make the agent buy him another fake Oscar.

They were just finishing up that evening when the Oracle entered the detective squad room looking very grim. He said, 'Andi, can you come to the captain's office, please?'

'What's up?' she said, following the Oracle to the captain's office, where she saw a U.S. Army sergeant major holding his hat in both hands.

'Noooo!' Andi cried out, and Brant Hinkle heard and ran to the sound of her voice.

'He's not dead!' the Oracle said quickly. 'He's alive!'

He put his arm around her and led her into the office and closed the door.

The sergeant major said, 'Detective McCrea, we've been informed that your son, Max, has been wounded. I'm really sorry.'

'Wounded,' she said, as though the word were foreign to her.

'It wasn't a roadside bomb, it was an ambush. Automatic weapons and mortars.'

'Oh, my god,' she said and started weeping.

'It's his leg. I'm afraid he's lost his right leg.' Then he

quickly added, 'But it's below the knee. That's much better.'

'Much better,' Andi murmured, hardly hearing, hardly comprehending.

'He's been flown to Landstuhl Regional Medical Center in Germany, and from there he'll go to Walter Reed Army Medical Center in Washington.'

The sergeant major expressed his and the army's gratitude, offered to assist her in any way he could, and said a lot of other things. And she didn't understand a word of it.

When he was finished, Andi thanked him and walked out into the corridor, where Brant Hinkle took her in his arms and said to the Oracle, 'I'll drive her home.'

There wasn't a more excited homeowner in that part of Hollywood than Mabel was these days. She had so much to do. There just weren't enough hours in the day.

First of all, she got a new screen door. It was a nice aluminum door that the man said would last a lifetime. Then he looked at Mabel and she knew he was thinking, It will surely last your lifetime.

Then came the painting of the exterior, which was still going on. Mabel had to keep the windows open all the time in this hot weather, even though there was the awful smell of paint from outside. But it all just added to the excitement. They were going to start painting the interior of the house very soon and putting wallpaper in the kitchen and bathroom. Mabel thought she'd buy a couple of air conditioners before the interior painting started. It was a thrilling time to be alive.

When they were having breakfast, Mabel said to Olive, 'Do you think you're up to going to an NA meeting this afternoon, dear?'

'Oh, sure,' Olive said, still looking pale from having to whiteknuckle it.

'I started going to AA when I was sixty-two years old,'

Mabel said. 'After my husband died, the booze got the best of me. I've been in recovery ever since. You'll meet some grand people there who will always be just a phone call away. I'm sure that the NA meetings are like AA meetings, just a different drug is all. But I have no doubt you'll prevail. You're a strong girl, Olive. You've never had a chance to prove it.'

'I'll be okay, Mabel,' Olive said, trying to eat some scrambled egg.

Mabel's physician had told Olive that a diet of nutritious food was essential for her, and Mabel hadn't stopped cooking since Olive arrived. Mabel had seen that Olive's attempt at unassisted withdrawal from methamphetamine addiction was very hard on her, so Mabel had taken Olive by bus to a doctor who'd treated Mabel for thirty years.

The doctor had examined Olive and given her medication to ease withdrawal symptoms but said that healthy eating was the best medicine, along with abstaining from all drugs forever.

Mabel was pleased watching Olive eat a forkful of scrambled egg and a bite of toast, washing it all down with orange juice. A week earlier she couldn't have done that.

'Dear,' Mabel said, 'do you feel well enough today to talk about the future?'

'Sure, Mabel,' Olive said, realizing that this was the first time in her life that anyone had ever mentioned her future. Olive never thought that she had a future. Or much of a past. She'd always lived in the present.

'As soon as you're well into recovery I'm going to do a quitclaim deed. Do you know what that is?'

'No.'

'I'm going to deed this house to you with the provision that I can live here for the rest of my life.'

Olive looked at Mabel with a blank expression, then said, 'I don't think I understand what you mean.'

347

'That's the least I can do for you after what you've given me,' Mabel said. 'I was going to leave the house to the Salvation Army so the state doesn't get it. That's what will happen to Farley's house, you know. He had no heirs and no will, so the state of California will take it. I think Governor Schwarzenegger is rich enough. He doesn't need my house.'

Olive clearly couldn't grasp it. 'Me?' she said. 'You're giving me your house?'

'All that I ask is that you take care of me as best you can for as long as you can. We can hire one of those nice Filipino girls to help with the unpleasant nursing when I get to that point. I would like to die at home. I think my doctor will help me achieve that wish. He's a good and decent man.'

Suddenly tears ran down Olive's cheeks, and she said, 'I don't want you to die, Mabel!'

'There there, dear,' Mabel said, patting Olive's hand. 'My parents both lived until they were nearly one hundred. I expect I've got some years left.'

Olive got up and took a tissue from the box beside Mabel's chair, then came and sat down at the table again, wiping her eyes.

Mabel said, 'I never use that silly sewing room anymore, so that will be your bedroom. We'll decorate it up real pretty for you. And it has a good closet. We'll take you shopping and fill up that closet.'

Olive just kept looking at Mabel with eyes as quiet and devoted as a dog's and said, 'My own bedroom?'

'Certainly, dear,' Mabel said. 'But of course we'll always have to share the bathroom. You wouldn't mind not having your own bathroom, would you?'

Olive started to say that in her whole life she'd never had her own bathroom. Or her own bedroom. But she was so overwhelmed she couldn't speak. She just shook her head.

Mabel said, 'I think we'll buy a reliable car right away. You can drive, can't you?'

'Oh, yes,' Olive said. 'I'm a good driver.'

'I think when we get our car, the first thing we'll do is take a drive to Universal Studios and do the tour. Have you ever been to Universal Studios?'

'No,' Olive said.

'Neither have I,' Mabel said. 'But we'll need to buy one of those fold-up wheelchairs. I don't believe I could manage the long walk. You wouldn't mind pushing me in a wheel-chair, would you?'

'I'll do anything for you, Mabel,' Olive said.

'Do you have a driver's license?'

'No,' Olive said. 'When I got arrested for DUI, they took mine away. But I know a real nice guy named Phil who makes them. They're very expensive. Two hundred dollars.'

'All right, dear,' Mabel said. 'We have plenty of money, so we'll buy you one of those for now. But someday you should try to get a proper one.'

Thinking of the driver's license, Mabel said, 'Dear, I know your real name is not Olive Oyl.'

'No, that's the name Farley gave me.'

'Yes, he would,' Mabel said. 'What's your real name?'

'Adeline Scully. But nobody knows it. When I got arrested I used a alias.'

'Adeline!' Mabel said. 'Sweet Adeline. I used to sing that song when I was a girl. That's the name that will go on the driver's license. That's who you are from this day forward. Adeline. What a lovely name.'

Just then Tillie, the striped tabby who was lying on the coffee table—a cat who had never heard a negative word spoken to her since Mabel rescued her—finished a can of tuna and slapped the empty can from the table in disgust.

'Oh, goodness,' Mabel said, 'Tillie's getting cross. We'll have to open another can of tuna. After all, if it wasn't for Tillie, we would never be able to have this new and wonder-ful life, would we?'

'No,' Adeline said, smiling at Tillie.

'And mum's the word, Tillie,' Mabel said to the cat.

'I'm real happy, Mabel,' Adeline said.

Looking at her smile like that, Mabel said, 'Adeline, you have such nice thick hair I'll bet a stylist could give you a beautiful cut. Let's both go get our hair done and a manicure. And I was wondering, would you like to have some teeth?'

'Oh, yes!' Adeline said. 'I'd love to have some teeth.'

'That's going to be something we tend to first thing,' Mabel said. 'We're going to buy you some nice new teeth!'

By the start of the new deployment period things were getting better insofar as car assignments were concerned. The Oracle liked the way Mag Takara was recovering and her vision was improving. He was thinking about putting her back on patrol.

Andi McCrea had been to Washington for a week, where she'd visited her son in Walter Reed every day. When she came back to Hollywood, she said she'd seen courage beyond words and that she'd never underestimate her son's generation, not ever again.

There are no worse gossips in the world than cops, and few can keep a secret, so the word got around Hollywood Station that Andi McCrea and Brant Hinkle were getting married. Compassionate Charlie Gilford quickly offered his usual brand of commentary.

'Another double-handcuff ceremony,' he said to Viktor Chernenko. 'Right now they're calling each other darling babycakes and little buttercup. In another six months they'll blow each other's brains out. That's the way it is in Hollywood.'

Viktor was especially happy, having learned that he'd been named Hollywood Station's Detective of the Quarter, and paid no attention to Compassionate Charlie's unromantic notions. He loved the sound of those terms of endearment.

That evening before going home, he phoned his wife and said, 'I am so joyful my darling babycakes. Would it be pleasing if I picked up some Big Macs and strawberry ice cream for my little buttertub?'

TWENTY -TWO

With the July Fourth holiday approaching, the Oracle thought he had midwatch well sorted. When Fausto and Budgie brought in a report for signature, he said, 'Fausto, it's time we took code seven at that other new Mexican restaurant—what's it called?'

'Hidalgo's,' Fausto said.

'I'm buying.'

'You hit the lottery?'

'Time to celebrate. It's summer in Hollywood,' the Oracle said. 'I feel expansive in the summer.'

Fausto looked at the Oracle's ample belly and said, 'I see what you mean.'

'You should talk,' Budgie said to Fausto. Then turning to the Oracle she added, 'I have him on a six-burrito diet. He's already had five this week so he only gets one tonight.'

'Give us a few minutes,' Fausto said. 'I gotta get a DR for a report.'

The Oracle was alone again when he started to feel pain in his upper stomach. That damn heartburn again. He was sweating for no reason and felt he needed some air. He walked out into the lobby, passing below the hanging photos of those slain officers whose names were outside on the Hollywood Station Walk of Fame.

The Oracle looked up at the full moon, a 'Hollywood moon,' he always called it, and sucked in air through his nose, blowing it out his mouth. But he didn't feel better. There was suddenly a dull ache in his shoulder and his back.

A woman was coming to the station to make a report on the theft of her son's bicycle when a loud motorcycle roared by and she saw the Oracle grab his chest and fall to the pavement.

She ran into the station, screaming, 'An officer's been shot!'

Fausto almost knocked her down as he threw open the glass door and ran out, followed by Budgie and Mag Takara, who'd been working at the front desk.

Fausto turned the Oracle over onto his back and said, 'He hasn't been shot.'

Then he knelt beside him and started chest compression. Budgie lifted the Oracle's chin, pinched off his nostrils and started breathing into his mouth as Mag called the rescue ambulance. Several officers ran out of the station and watched.

'Come on, Merv!' Fausto said, counting compressions silently. 'Come back to us!'

The RA arrived quickly, but it didn't matter. Budgie and Mag were both crying when the paramedics loaded the Oracle into the ambulance. Fausto turned and pushed two night-watch cops out of his way and wandered alone into the darkness of the parking lot.

One week later at roll call, the lieutenant said to the midwatch, 'There will not be the usual police funeral for the Oracle. His will was very specific and stated that he'd made other arrangements.'

'He should get a star on the Walk,' Flotsam said.

The lieutenant said, 'Well, that's for our Hollywood Division officers killed on duty.'

'He was killed on duty,' Hollywood Nate said. 'Forty-six years around here? That's what killed him.'

'How about a special star for the Oracle?' Mag Takara said.

The lieutenant said, 'I'll have to talk to the captain about this.'

'If anybody deserves a star,' Benny Brewster said, 'that man does.'

Jetsam said, 'No funeral? We gotta do something, Lieutenant.'

B.M. Driscoll said, 'The Oracle always said he was staying on the job till his ex-wife died so she couldn't get any of his pension. What about her? Did they have kids who might want a funeral?'

Getting rattled, the lieutenant said, 'It's out of my control. He'd made special arrangements, I've been told. He left everything he owned to the L.A. Police Memorial Foundation for scholarships. That's all I know.'

Fausto Gamboa stood up then, the first time he'd ever done such a thing at roll call in his thirty-four-year career. He said, 'The Oracle didn't want any fuss made over him after he was gone. I know that for a fact. We talked about it one night many years ago when we were having a brew up at the Tree.'

B.M. Driscoll said, 'But what's his ex-wife say about it?'

'There is no ex-wife,' Fausto said. 'That was his excuse for being crazy enough to stay on the Job all this time. And if he'd lived, someday they woulda had to tear the badge off his chest to get rid of him. He wouldn'ta liked that at all. He was nearly sixty-nine years old and enjoyed his life and did some good and now he's gone end-of-watch.'

'Didn't he have... anybody?' Mag asked.

'Sure he did,' Fausto said. 'He had you. He was married to the Job and you were his kids. You and others before you.'

The room was still then until Hollywood Nate said, 'Isn't there... one little thing we can do for him? For his memory?'

After a pause, Fausto said with a quivering voice, 'Yeah, there is. Remember how he said the Job is fun? The Oracle always said that doing good police work is more fun than anything you'll ever do in your entire lives. Well, you just go out there tonight and have yourselves some fun.'

As soon as darkness fell on Hollywood, 6-X-76 went on a very special mission. A secret mission known to nobody else at Hollywood Station. They didn't speak as Budgie drove up into the Hollywood Hills to Mount Lee. When they got to their destination, she pulled up to a locked gate and stopped.

Fausto unlocked the gate, saying, 'I had to practically sign in blood to get this key from the park ranger.'

Budgie drove as far as they could on the fire road and then parked. There was no sound but cicadas whirring and a barely audible hum of traffic far below.

Then Budgie and Fausto got out and she opened the trunk. Fausto reached into his war bag and lifted out the urn.

Budgie led the way with her flashlight, but it was hardly needed under the light from a full moon. They walked along the path until they were at the base of the sign. It was four stories high and brilliantly lit.

Budgie looked up at the giant *H* looming and said, 'Be careful, Fausto. Why don't you let me do it?'

'This is my job,' Fausto said. 'We were friends for more than thirty years.'

The ground by the *H* had fallen away, so they walked to the center, to the *Y*, where the ground was intact.

The ladder was in place beside scaffolding, and when he had climbed halfway up, Budgie yelled, 'That's high enough, Fausto!'

But he kept going, puffing and panting, pausing twice until he was all the way to the top. And when he was there, he carefully opened the lid from the urn and turned it upside down, saying, 'Semper cop, Merv. See you soon.'

And the Oracle's ashes blew away into the warm summer

night, against the backdrop of HOLLYWOOD, four stories high, under magical white light supplied by an obliging Hollywood moon.

*

When they were finished with their mission and Budgie had driven them back down to the streets of Hollywood, she broke the silence by saying, 'I've been thinking about cooking a turkey dinner. How about coming over and meeting Katie? I want a photo op of you burping her. I'll buy a small bird for just you and me and my mom.'

'I'll check my schedule,' Fausto said. 'Maybe I can make time.'

Budgie said, 'My dad's been dead for three years but Mom hasn't started dating yet, so it probably won't do you much good to hit on her.'

'Oh, sure,' Fausto said. 'Like I'd hit on an old lady.'

Budgie looked at him and said, 'The old lady is nearly ten years younger than you are, buddy.'

'Yeah?' said Fausto, cocking that right eyebrow. 'So what's she look like?'

'Well, Marty,' Hollywood Nate said to his rookie partner. 'We're going to do some good police work and have some fun tonight. You ready for that?'

'Yes, sir,' the young cop said.

'Goddamnit, Marty,' Nate said, 'save that "sir" crap for your real training officer, who'll probably turn out to be one of those GI junkies who grew up watching TV war movies. Me, I watched Fred Astaire and Gene Kelly musicals. My name's Nate. Remember?'

'Okay, Nate. Sorry.'

'By the way, you like movies?'

'Yes… Nate,' Marty said.

'Your old man wouldn't be rich by any chance, would he?'

'Lord, no,' Marty said.

'Oh, well,' said Nate. 'My last rich partner didn't help my career anyway.'

There was a good crowd on the boulevard, and the young cop turned to Nate and said, 'Sir—I mean, Nate, there's a fifty-one-fifty raising heck over there in front of Grauman's Chinese Theater.'

Without looking, Nate said, 'What's he doing?'

'Waving his arms around and yelling at people.'

'In Hollywood, that's just called communication,' Nate said. 'Nowadays it's hard to tell ordinary boulevard lunatics from people with headsets talking on cells.' But then he glanced toward the famous theater, saw who it was, and said, 'Uh-oh. That guy's a known troublemaker. Maybe we should talk to him.'

Nate pulled the car into a red zone and said to his partner, 'Marty, on this one, you be contact and I'll be cover. I'm gonna stay by the car here and see how you handle him. Think you can deal with it?'

'For sure, Nate,' Marty said with enthusiasm, getting out of the car, collecting his baton, and putting on latex gloves.

The wild man waving his arms saw the young cop coming his way and stopped yelling. He planted his feet and waited.

Young Marty Shaw remembered from academy training that it's usually better to address mental cases in personal terms, so he turned around for a moment and said to Nate, 'Do you remember his name, by chance?'

'Not his full name,' said Hollywood Nate. 'But they call him Al. Untouchable Al.'

HOLLYWOOD CROWS

ONE

'DUDE, YOU BETTER drop that *long* knife,' the tall, suntanned cop said. At Hollywood Station they called him 'Flotsam' by virtue of his being a surfing enthusiast.

His shorter partner, also with a major tan, hair even more suspiciously blond and sun streaked, dubbed 'Jetsam' for the same reason, said, sotto voce, 'Bro, that ain't a knife. That's a bayonet, in case you can't see too good. And why didn't you check out a Taser and a beanbag gun from the kit room, is what I'd like to know. That's what the DA's office and FID are gonna ask if we have to light him up. Like, "Why didn't you officers use nonlethal force?" Like, "Why'd that Injun have to bite the dust when you coulda captured him alive?" That's what they'll say.'

'I thought you checked them out and put them in the trunk. You walked toward the kit room.'

'No, I went to the john. And you were too busy ogling Ronnie to know where I was at,' Jetsam said. 'Your head was somewheres else. You gotta keep your mind in the game, bro.'

Everyone on the midwatch at Hollywood Station knew that Jetsam had a megacrush on Officer Veronica 'Ronnie'

Sinclair and got torqued when Flotsam or anybody else flirted with her. In any case, both surfer cops considered it sissified to carry a Taser on their belts.

Referring to section 5150 of the Welfare and Institutions Code, which all cops used to describe a mental case, Flotsam whispered, 'Maybe this fifty-one-fifty's trashed on PCP, so we couldn't taze him anyways. He'd swat those darts outta him like King Kong swatted the airplanes. So just chill. He ain't even giving us the stink eye. He just maybe thinks he's a wooden Indian or something.'

'Or maybe we're competing with a bunch of other voices he's hearing and they're scarier,' Jetsam observed. 'Maybe we're just echoes.'

They'd gotten nowhere by yelling the normal commands to the motionless Indian, a stooped man in his early forties, only a decade older than they were but with a haggard face, beaten down by life. And while the cops waited for the backup they'd requested, they'd begun speaking to him in quiet voices, barely audible in the unlit alley over the traffic noise on Melrose Avenue. It was there that 6-X-46 had chased and cornered him, a few blocks from Paramount Studios, from where the code 2 call had come.

The Indian had smashed a window of a boutique to steal a plus-size gold dress with a handkerchief hemline and a red one with an empire waist. He'd squeezed into the red dress and walked to the Paramount main gate, where he'd started chanting gibberish and, perhaps prophetically, singing 'Jailhouse Rock' before demanding admittance from a startled security officer who had dialed 9-1-1.

'These new mini-lights ain't worth a shit,' Jetsam said, referring to the small flashlights that the LAPD bought and issued to all officers ever since a widely viewed videotaped arrest showed an officer striking a combative black suspect with his thirteen-inch aluminum flashlight, which caused panic in the media and in the police commission, and resulted in the firing of the Latino officer.

After this event, new mini-flashlights that couldn't cause harm to combative suspects unless they ate them were ordered and issued to new recruits. Everything was fine with the police commission and the cop critics except that the high-intensity lights set the rubber sleeves on fire and almost incinerated a few rookies before the Department recalled all of those lights and ordered these new ten-ouncers.

Jetsam said, 'Good thing that cop used flashlight therapy instead of smacking the vermin with a gun. We'd all be carrying two-shot derringers by now.'

Flotsam's flashlight seemed to better illuminate the Indian, who stood staring up white-eyed at the starless smog-shrouded sky, his back to the graffiti-painted wall of a two-story commercial building owned by Iranians, leased by Vietnamese. The Indian may have chosen the red dress because it matched his flip-flops. The gold dress lay crumpled on the asphalt by his dirt-encrusted feet, along with the cutoffs he'd been wearing when he'd done the smash-and-grab.

So far, the Indian hadn't threatened them in any way. He just stood like a statue, his breathing shallow, the bayonet held down against his bare left thigh, which was fully exposed. He'd sliced the slit in the red dress clear up to his flank, either for more freedom of movement or to look more provocative.

'Dude,' Flotsam said to the Indian, holding his Glock nine in the flashlight beam so the Indian could observe that it was pointed right at him, 'I can see that you're spun out on something. My guess is you been doing crystal meth, right? And maybe you just wanted an audition at Paramount and didn't have any nice dresses to wear to it. I can sympathize with that too. I'm willing to blame it on Oscar de la Renta or whoever made the fucking things so alluring. But you're gonna have to drop that *long* knife now or pretty soon they're gonna be drawing you in chalk on this alley.'

Jetsam, whose nine was also pointed at the ponytailed Indian, whispered to his partner, 'Why do you keep saying *long* knife to this zombie instead of bayonet?'

'He's an Indian,' Flotsam whispered back. 'They always say *long* knife in the movies.'

'That refers to us white men!' Jetsam said. 'We're the fucking *long* knives!'

'Whatever,' said Flotsam. 'Where's our backup, anyhow? They coulda got here on skateboards by now.'

When Flotsam reached tentatively for the pepper-spray canister on his belt, Jetsam said, 'Uncool, bro. Liquid Jesus ain't gonna work on a meth-monster. It only works on cops. Which you proved the time you hit *me* with act-right spray instead of the 'roided-up primate I was doing a death dance with.'

'You still aggro over that?' Flotsam said, remembering how Jetsam had writhed in pain after getting the blast of OC spray full in the face while they and four other cops swarmed the hallucinating bodybuilder who was paranoid from mixing recreational drugs with steroids. 'Shit happens, dude. You can hold a grudge longer than my ex-wife.'

In utter frustration, Jetsam finally said quietly to the Indian, 'Bro, I'm starting to think you're running a game on us. So you either drop that bayonet right now or the medicine man's gonna be waving chicken claws over your fucking ashes.'

Taking the cue, Flotsam stepped forward, his pistol aimed at the Indian's pustule-covered face, damp with sweat on this warm night, eyes rolled back, features strangely contorted in the flashlight beams. And the tall cop said just as quietly, 'Dude, you're circling the drain. We're dunzo here.'

Jetsam put his flashlight in his sap pocket, nowadays a cell-phone pocket, since saps had become LAPD artifacts, extended his pistol in both hands, and said to the Indian, 'Happy trails, pard. Enjoy your dirt nap.'

That did it. The Indian dropped the bayonet and Flotsam said, 'Turn and face the wall and interlace your fingers behind your head!'

The Indian turned and faced the wall, but he obviously did not understand 'interlace.'

Jetsam said, 'Cross your fingers behind your head!'

The Indian crossed his middle fingers over his index fingers and held them up behind his head.

'No, dude!' Flotsam said. 'I didn't ask you to make a fucking wish, for chrissake!'

'Never mind!' Jetsam said, pulling the Indian's hands down and cuffing them behind his back.

Finally the Indian spoke. He said, 'Do you guys have

a candy bar I could buy from you? I'll give you five dollars for a candy bar.'

When Jetsam was walking the Indian to their car, the prisoner said, 'Ten. I'll give you ten bucks. I'll pay you when I get outta jail.'

After stopping at a liquor store to buy their meth-addled, candy-craving arrestee a Nutter Butter, they drove him to Hollywood Station and put him in an interview room, cuffing one wrist to a chair so he could still eat his candy. The night-watch D2, a lazy sensitivity-challenged detective known as 'Compassionate' Charlie Gilford, was annoyed at being pulled away from shows like *American Idol*, which he watched on a little TV he kept concealed in the warren of work cubicles the size of airline restrooms, where he sat for hours on a rubber donut. He loved to watch the panels brutalize the hapless contestants.

The detective was wearing a short-sleeved, wrinkled white shirt and one of his discount neckties, a dizzying checkerboard of blues and yellows. Everyone said his ties were louder than Mötley Crüe, and even older. Charlie got fatigued listening to the story of the window smash on Melrose, the serenade to the guard at Paramount Studios' main gate, the foot chase by the surfer cops, and the subsequent eerie confrontation, all of which Flotsam described as 'weird.'

He said to them, 'Weird? This ain't weird.' And then he uttered the phrase that one heard every night around the station when things seemed too surreal to be true: 'Man, this is fucking Hollywood!' After that, there was usually no need for further comment.

But Charlie decided to elaborate: 'Last year the

midwatch busted a goony tweaker totally naked except for a pink tutu. He was waving a samurai sword on Sunset Boulevard when they took him down. That was weird. This ain't shit.'

When he spotted the acronym for American Indian Movement tattooed on the prisoner's shoulder, he touched it with a pencil and said, 'What's that mean, chief? Assholes in Moccasins?'

The Indian just sat munching on the Nutter Butter, eyes shut in utter bliss.

Then the cranky detective sucked his teeth and said to the arresting officers, 'And by the way, you just had to feed him chocolate, huh? This tweaker don't have enough speed bumps?'

To the Indian he said, 'Next time you feel like breaking into show business, take a look in the mirror. With that mug, you only got one option. Buy a hockey mask and try singing "Music of the Night."'

'I'll give you twenty bucks for another Nutter Butter,' the Indian finally said to Compassionate Charlie Gilford. 'And I'll confess to any crime you got.'

Nathan Weiss, called Hollywood Nate by the other cops because of his obsession, recently waning, to break into the movie business, had left Watch 5, the midwatch, eight months earlier, shortly after the very senior sergeant known as the Oracle had died of a massive heart attack there on the police Walk of Fame in front of Hollywood Station. Nothing was the same on the midwatch after they lost the Oracle. Hollywood Nate had been pulled out of trouble, usually involving women, and spared from disciplinary action more than once by the grizzled forty-six-year veteran supervisor, who had died just short of his sixty-ninth birthday.

Everyone said it was fitting that the Oracle had died on that Walk, where stars honoring Hollywood Division officers killed on duty were embedded in marble and brass just as they were for movie stars on Hollywood Boulevard. The Oracle had been *their* star, an anachronism from another era of policing, from long before the Rodney King riots and Rampart Division evidence-planting scandal. Long before the LAPD had agreed to a Department of Justice 'consent decree' and gotten invaded by federal judges and lawyers and politicians and auditors and overseers and media critics. Back when the cops could be guided by proactive leaders, not reactive bureaucrats more fearful of the federal overseers and local politicians than of the street criminals. The day after the Oracle died, Nathan Weiss had gone to temple, the first time in fifteen years, to say Kaddish for the old sergeant.

All of them, street cops and supervisors, were now smothered in paperwork designed to prove that they were 'reforming' a police force of more than ninety-five hundred souls who ostensibly needed reforming because of the actions of half a dozen convicted cops from both incidents combined. Hundreds of sworn officers had been taken from street duties to manage the paper hurricane resulting from the massive 'reformation.' The consent decree hanging over the LAPD was to expire in two more years, but they'd heard that before and knew it could be extended. Like the war in Iraq, it seemed that it would never end.

The Oracle had been replaced by a university-educated twenty-eight-year-old with a degree in political science who'd rocketed almost to the top of the promotion list with little more than six years of experience, not to mention overcoming disadvantages of race and gender. Sergeant Jason Treakle was a white male, and that wasn't helpful in the diversity-obsessed city of Los Angeles, where fifty-five languages were spoken by students in the school district.

Hollywood Nate called Sergeant Treakle's roll call speeches a perfect meld of George Bush's garbled syntax and the tin ear of Al Gore. During those sessions Nate could hear cartilage crackling from all the chins bouncing off chests as the troops failed to stay awake and upright. He'd hated the rookie sergeant's guts the first time they'd met, when Sergeant Treakle criticized Nate in front of the entire assembly for referring to Officer Ronnie Sinclair as a 'very cool chick.' Ronnie took it as a compliment, but Sergeant Treakle found it demeaning and sexist.

Then, during an impromptu inspection, he'd frowned upon Hollywood Nate's scuffed shoes. He'd pointed at Nate's feet with an arm that didn't look long enough for his body, saying the shoes made Nate look 'unkempt,' and suggested that Nate try spit-shining them. Sergeant Treakle was big on spit shines, having spent six months in the ROTC at his university. Because of his knife-blade mouth, the cops soon referred to him as 'Chickenlips.'

Hollywood Nate, like his idol, the Oracle, had always worn ordinary black rubber-soled shoes with his uniform. He liked to needle the cops who wore expensive over-the-ankle boots to look more paramilitary but then experienced sweaty feet, foot fungus, and diminished running speed. Nate would ask them if their spit-shined boots made it easier to slog through all the snow and ice storms on Sunset and Hollywood Boulevards.

And Hollywood Nate had given up suggesting that field training officers stop making the new PI probationers call them sir or ma'am, as most did. The more rigid and GI of the FTOs seemed to be those who'd never served in the military and they wouldn't think of letting their probies wear the gung-ho boots before finishing their eighteen-month probation. Nate would privately tell the rookies to forget about boots, that their feet would thank them for it. And Nate never forgot that the Oracle had never spit-shined his shoes.

Before the midwatch hit the streets, every cop would ritually touch the picture of the Oracle for luck, even new officers who'd never known him. It hung on the wall by the door of the roll call room. In the photo their late sergeant was in uniform, his retro gray crew cut freshly trimmed, smiling the way he'd always done, more with his smart blue eyes than with his mouth. The brass plate on the frame simply said:

THE ORACLE
APPOINTED: FEB 1960
END-OF-WATCH: AUG 2006
SEMPER COP

Hollywood Nate, like all the others, had tapped the picture frame before leaving roll call on the first evening he'd met his new sergeant. Then he'd gone straight downstairs to the watch commander's office and asked to be reassigned to the day watch, citing a multitude of personal and even health reasons, all of them lies. It had seemed to Nate that an era had truly ended. The Oracle – the kind of cop Nate told everyone he had wanted to be when he grew up – had been replaced by a politically correct, paper-shuffling little putz with dwarfish arms, no lips, and a shoe fetish.

At first, Hollywood Nate wasn't fond of Watch 2, the early day watch, certainly not the part where he had to get up before 5 A.M. and speed from his one-bedroom apartment in the San Fernando Valley to Hollywood Station, change into his uniform, and be ready for 0630 roll call. He didn't like that at all. But he did like the hours of the 3/12 work shift. On Watch 2, the patrol officers worked three twelve-hour days a week during their twenty-eight-day deployment periods, making up one day at the end. That gave Nate four days a week to attend cattle calls and harangue casting agents, now that he'd earned enough vouchers to get his Screen Actors Guild card, which he carried in his badge wallet right behind his police ID.

So far, he'd gotten only one speaking part, two lines of dialogue, in a TV movie that was co-produced by an over-the-hill writer/director he'd met during one of the red carpet events at the Kodak Center, where Nate was tasked with crowd control. Nate won over that director by body blocking an anti-fur protester in a sweaty tank top before she could shove one of those 'I'd Rather Go Naked' signs at the director's wife, who was wearing a faux-mink stole.

Nate sealed the deal and got the job when he told

the hairy protester he'd hate to see *her* naked and added, 'If wearing fur is a major crime, why don't you scrape those pits?'

The movie was about mate-swapping yuppies, and Nate was typecast as a cop who showed up after one of the husbands beat the crap out of his cheating spouse. The battered wife was scripted to look at the hawkishly handsome, well-muscled cop whose wavy dark hair was just turning silver at the temples, and wink at him with her undamaged eye.

To Nate, there didn't seem to be much of a story and he was given one page of script with lines that read: 'Good evening, ma'am. Did you call the police? What can I do for you that isn't immoral?'

During that one-day gig, the grips and gaffers and especially the craft services babe who provided great sandwiches and salads all told Nate that this was a 'POS' movie that might never reach the small screen at all. After she'd said it, Nate knew that his initial impression had been correct: It was a piece of shit, for sure. Hollywood Nate Weiss was already thirty-six years old, with fifteen years on the LAPD. He needed a break. He needed an agent. He didn't have time left in his acting life to waste on pieces of shit.

On the morning after the midwatch surfer cops busted the wooden Indian, Nate Weiss was assigned to a one-man day-watch report car known as a U-boat, which responded to report-writing calls instead of those that for safety reasons required a pair of officers. At 8:30 A.M. Nate did what he always did when he caught a U-boat assignment: He went to Farmers Market at Third and Fairfax for a coffee break.

The fact that Farmers Market was a couple of blocks out of Hollywood Division didn't bother him much. It was a small peccadillo that the Oracle would always forgive. Nate loved everything about that old landmark: the tall clock tower, the stalls full of produce, the displays of fresh fish and meat, the shops and ethnic eateries. But mostly he loved the open-air patios where people gathered this time of morning for cinnamon rolls, fresh-baked muffins, French toast, and other pastries.

Nate ordered a latte and a bagel, taking a seat at a small empty table close enough to eavesdrop on the 'artistes' table.' He'd started doing it after he'd overheard them talking about pitching scripts to HBO and getting financing for small indie projects and doing lunch with a famous agent from CAA who one of them said was a schmuck – all topics of fascination to Hollywood Nate Weiss.

By now, he was almost able to recognize them from their voices without looking at them directly. There was the features director who, due to Hollywood ageism, complained that he couldn't even get arrested at the studios. Ditto for three former screenwriters who were regulars at the table, as well as for a former TV producer. A dozen or more of these would come and go, all males, the average age being seventy-plus, far too old for the youth-obsessed entertainment business that had nurtured them.

A formerly famous painter and sculptor, wearing a trademark black beret, wasn't selling so well these days either. Nate heard him tell the others that when his wife asks him what he wants for dinner, his usual response is, 'Get off my back, will ya?' Then the painter added, 'But don't feel sorry for us. We're getting used to living in our car.'

A former TV character actor wearing a safari jacket from Banana Republic, whose face was familiar to Nate, stood up and informed the others he had to leave and make an important call to a VP in development at Universal to discuss a script he'd been deciding whether or not to accept.

After he'd gone, the director said, 'The poor schlemiel. I'll bet he gets a "Please leave a message" recording from the VP at Universal. That's who he discusses the project with – a machine. Probably has to call back a hundred and thirty-five times to get his whole pitch into the VP's voicemail.'

'I've suspected he's calling the number for highway information when he pretends to be talking to HBO,' the painter said, clucking sadly.

'He never was any good, even in his prime,' the director said. 'Thought he was a method actor. They'd run out of money doing retakes. Twenty tics a take on average.'

'If he had more of a name, they could paint him like a whore and let him do arthritis and Geico commercials, like the rest of those has-beens,' said the has-been TV producer.

'And women?' one of the screenwriters said. 'He thinks we believe his daffy seduction stories. Instead of another face-lift, the old bastard should have his balls stapled to his thigh to keep them from dropping in the toilet.'

'He could do it without anesthetic,' said the oldest

of the screenwriters. 'At his age it's a dead zone down there.'

All of the geezers, who tended to talk over one another in multiple conversations, went silent for a moment when a stunning young woman paused to look into a nearby shop that sold glassware and candles. She wore a canary cotton jersey accented by hyacinth stitching, and $400 second-skin jeans, and stood nearly six feet tall in her Jimmy Choo lilac suede pumps. She had a full, pouty upper lip, and butterscotch blonde hair so luxurious it fanned across her shoulder when she turned to look at a glass figurine and then fell back perfectly into place when she continued walking. Her amazing hair gleamed when spangled sunlight pierced the covered patio and provided honey-colored highlights.

The codgers sighed and snuffled and did everything but drool before resuming their conversations. Nate watched her walk out toward the parking lot. Her remarkable body said Pilates loud and clear, and he could see she wasn't wearing a bra. There in Hollywood, and even in Beverly Hills, Nate Weiss had not seen many showstoppers like her.

By then, Nate was ready to go back to work. It was getting depressing listening to the old guys railing about ageism, knowing in their hearts they'd never work again. He'd noticed that always around 9:30 A.M., they'd get up one by one and make excuses to leave, for important calls from directors, or for appointments with agents, or to get back to scripts they were polishing. Nate figured they all just went home to sit and stare at phones that never rang. It gave him a chill to think that he might be looking at Nathan Weiss a few decades from now.

Nate strolled to the parking lot thirty yards behind the beauty with the butterscotch hair, wanting to see what she drove. He figured her for a Beverly Hills hottie in an Aston Martin with a vanity license plate, compliments of a bucks-up husband or sugar daddy who drove a stately Rolls Phantom. It was almost disappointing when she got into a red BMW sedan instead of something really expensive and exotic.

Impulsively, he jotted down her license number, and when he got back to his black-and-white, ran a DMV check and saw that she lived in the Hollywood Hills, off Laurel Canyon Boulevard in the development called Mt. Olympus, where realtors claimed there were more Italian cypress trees per acre than anywhere else on earth. Her address surprised him a bit. There were lots of well-to-do foreign nationals on Mt. Olympus: Israelis, Iranians, Arabs, Russians, and Armenians, and others from former Soviet bloc countries, some of whom had been suspects or victims in major crimes. A few of the residents reportedly owned banks in Moscow, and it was not uncommon to see young adults driving Bentleys, and teenagers in BMWs and Porsches.

Around the LAPD it was said that mobbed-up former Soviets were more dangerous and cruel than the Sicilian gangsters ever were back in the day. Just five months earlier, two Russians had been sentenced to death in Los Angeles Superior Court for kidnapping and murder. They'd suffocated or strangled four men and one woman in a $1.2 million ransom scheme.

Mt. Olympus was pricey, all right, but not the crème

de la crème of local real estate, and Nate thought that the area didn't suit her style. Luckily, it was in Hollywood Division and he'd often patrolled the streets up there. He figured it was unlikely that this Hills bunny would ever need a cop, but after finally getting his SAG card, Hollywood Nate Weiss was starting to believe that maybe anything was possible.

At 6 P.M. that day, after the midwatch had cleared with communications and was just hitting the streets, and Nate Weiss was an hour from end-of-watch, the electronic beep sounded on the police radio and the PSR's voice said to a midwatch unit, 'All units in the vicinity and Six-X-Seventy-six, a jumper at the northeast corner, Hollywood and Highland. Six-X-Seventy-six, handle code three.'

Hollywood Nate in his patrol unit – which everyone at LAPD called their 'shop' because of the identifying shop numbers on the front doors and roof – happened to be approaching the traffic light west at that intersection. He'd been gazing at the Kodak Center and dreaming of red carpets and stardom when the call came out. He saw the crowd of tourists gathering, looking up at a building twelve stories high, with an imposing green cupola. Even several of the so-called Street Characters who hustled tourists in the forecourt of Grauman's Chinese Theatre were jaywalking or running along the Walk of Fame to check out the excitement.

Superman was there, of course, and the Hulk, but not Spider-Man, who was in jail. Porky Pig waddled across the street, followed by Barney the dinosaur and three of the Beatles, the fourth staying behind to guard the karaoke equipment. Everyone was jabbering and pointing up at the top of the vacant building, formerly a bank, where a young man in walking shorts, tennis shoes, and a purple T-shirt with 'Just Do It' across the front sat on the roof railing, a dozen stories above the street below.

In the responding unit were Veronica Sinclair and Catherine Song, both women in their early thirties who, as far as Nate was concerned, happened to be among the better cops on midwatch. Cat was a sultry Korean American whose hobby was volleyball and whose feline grace made her name a perfect fit. Nate, who had been trying unsuccessfully to date her for nearly a year, loved Cat's raven hair, cut in a retro bob like the girls in the 1930s movies that he had in his film collection. Cat was a divorced mother of a two-year-old boy.

Ronnie Sinclair had been at Hollywood Station for less than a year, but she'd been a heartthrob from the first moment she'd arrived. She was a high-energy brunette with a very short haircut that worked, given her small, tight ears and well-shaped head. She had pale blue eyes, great cheekbones, and a bustline that made all the male cops pretend they were admiring the shooting medals hanging on her shirt flap. The remarkable thing about her was that her childless marriages had been to two police officers named Sinclair who were distant cousins, so Flotsam and Jetsam called her Sinclair Squared. Most of the midwatch officers over the age of thirty were single but had been divorced at least once, including the surfer cops and Hollywood Nate.

The two women were met at the open door of the vacant building by an alarm company employee who said, 'I don't know yet how he got in. Probably broke a window in the back. The elevator still works.'

Ronnie and Cat hurried inside to the elevators, Nate right behind them. And all three stood waiting for the elevator, trying to be chatty to relieve the gathering tension.

'Why aren't you circling the station about now?' Ronnie said, looking at her watch. 'You're almost end-of-watch and there must be a starlet waiting.'

Nate looked at his own watch and said, 'I still have, let's see, forty-seven minutes to give to the people of Los Angeles. And who needs starlets when I have such talent surrounding me?'

When Nate, whose womanizing was legendary at Hollywood Station, shot her his Groucho leer, Ronnie said, 'Forget it, Nate. Ask me for a date sometime when you're a star and can introduce me to George Clooney.'

That caused Hollywood Nate to whip out his badge wallet and proudly remove the SAG card tucked right underneath his police ID, holding it up for Ronnie and Cat to see.

Ronnie looked at it and said, 'Even O.J. has one of those.'

Cat said, 'Sorry, Nate, but my mom wants me to date and marry a rich Buddhahead lawyer next time, not some oh-so-cute, round-eyed actor like you.'

'Someday you'll both want me to autograph an eight-by-ten head shot for you,' Nate said, pleased that Cat thought he was cute, more pleased that she'd called him an actor. 'Then I'll be the one playing hard to get.'

During the ride up in the elevator they didn't speak anymore, growing tense even though the location of the jumper call, here in the heart of Hollywood tourism, made it likely that it was just a stunt by some publicity junkie. The three cops were trying their best not to take it too seriously. Until they climbed to the observation deck encircling the cupola and saw him, shirtless now, straddling a railing with arms outstretched, tennis shoes pressed together, head slightly bowed in the crucifixion pose. This, as tourists, hustlers, tweakers, pickpockets, cartoon characters, and various Hollywood crazies were standing down below, yelling at him to stop being a chickenshit and jump for Jesus.

'Oh, shit!' Cat said, speaking for all of them.

The three cops walked very slowly toward him and he turned around on the railing to face them, wobbling precariously, making onlookers down below either scream or cheer. His sandy, shoulder-length hair was blowing in his face, and his eyes behind wire-rimmed glasses were even more pale blue than Ronnie's. In fact, she thought he looked a lot like her cousin Bob, a drummer in a rock band. Maybe it was that, but she took the lead and the others let her have it.

She smiled at him and said, 'Hey, whadda you say you come on down here and let's talk.'

'Stay where you are,' he said.

She held up her hands, palms forward, and said, 'Okay, okay, I'm cool with that. But how about coming down now?'

'You're going to kill me, aren't you?' he said.

'Of course not,' Ronnie said. 'I just wanna talk to you. What's your name? They call me Ronnie.'

He did not respond, so she said, 'Ronnie is short for Veronica. A lot of people see my name somewhere and think I'm a guy.'

Still he did not respond, so she said, 'Do you have a nickname?'

'Tell them to go,' he said, pointing at Nate and Cat. 'I know they want to kill me.'

Ronnie turned around, but the others had immediately retreated to the door when they heard his demand, Cat saying, 'Be careful, Ronnie!'

Then Ronnie said to him, 'See, they've gone.'

'Take off your gun belt,' he said. 'Or I'll jump.'

'Okay!' Ronnie said, unfastening her Sam Browne and lowering it to her feet, close enough to grab for it.

'Step away from the gun,' he said. 'I know you want to kill me.'

'Why would I kill you?' Ronnie said, taking a single step toward him. 'You're getting ready to kill yourself. You see, that wouldn't make sense, would it? No, I don't wanna kill you. I wanna help you. I know I can if you'll just get down from that railing and talk to me.'

'Do you have a cigarette?' he said, and for a few seconds he swayed in the wind, and Ronnie sucked in a lungful of air, then let it out slowly.

'I don't smoke,' she said, 'but I can have my partner find you a cigarette. Her name's Cat. She's very nice and I bet you'd like her a lot.'

'Never mind,' he said. 'I don't need a cigarette. I don't need anything.'

'You need a friend,' Ronnie said. 'I'd like to be that friend. I have a cousin who looks just like you. What's your name?'

'My name's Randolph Bronson and I'm not crazy,' he said. 'I know what I'm doing.'

'I don't think you're crazy, Randolph,' Ronnie said, and now she could feel sweat running down her temples, and her hands felt slimy. 'I just think you're feeling sad and need someone to talk to. That's why I'm here. To talk to you.'

'Do you know what it's like to be called crazy? And schizophrenic?' he asked.

'Tell me about it, Randolph,' Ronnie said, walking another step closer until he said, 'Stop!'

'I'm sorry!' she said. 'I'll stay right here if it makes you feel better. Tell me about your family. Who do you live with?'

'I'm a burden to them,' he said. 'A financial burden. An emotional burden. They won't be sorry to see me gone.'

After six long minutes of talking, Ronnie Sinclair was fairly certain that the young man was ready to surrender. She found out that he was nineteen years old and had been treated for mental illness most of his life. Ronnie believed that she had him now, that she could talk him down from the railing. She was addressing him as 'Randy' by the time backup arrived on the street, including a rescue ambulance and the fire department, whose engine only served to clog traffic. Still no crisis negotiator from Metropolitan Division had arrived.

And the first supervisor to show up at the scene was Sergeant Jason Treakle, who'd been on a suck-up mission to buy two hamburgers and an order of fries for the night-watch lieutenant. Sergeant Treakle had gotten a brainstorm the moment he'd heard the call. The idea actually made him say 'Wow!' aloud, though he was alone in the car. Then he looked at the bag of burgers next to him, turned on his light bar, and sped to the location of the jumper call.

The young sergeant had recently read about an attempted suicide where a jumper had been talked down by a crisis negotiator who'd bought him a sandwich that they shared while talking at length about the people, real and imagined, who were tormenting him. The crisis negotiator had gotten her photo in the *L.A. Times* and had done several TV interviews.

When the midwatch supervisor ascended to the tower, carrying the bag of burgers, and brushed past Cat Song and Hollywood Nate, Cat said, 'Sergeant Treakle, wait! Ronnie's talking to the guy. Wait, please.'

Hollywood Nate said, 'Don't go out there, Sergeant.'

The sergeant said, 'Don't tell me my job, Weiss.'

Nate Weiss, who had several years in age and job experience on his former supervisor, said, 'Sergeant, nobody should *ever* bust in on a suicide standoff. This might be Hollywood but this is not a movie, and there's no air bag down there.'

'Thanks for your wise counsel,' Sergeant Treakle said with a chilly glance at Nate. 'I'll keep it in mind if you ever become my boss.'

Ronnie turned and saw him striding confidently along the deck and said, 'Sergeant! Go back, please! Let me handle—'

The anguished moan from Randolph Bronson made her spin around. He was staring at the uniformed sergeant with the condescending smile and the bulging paper bag in his hand, into which he was reaching.

The boy's pale eyes had gotten huge behind the eyeglasses. Then he looked at Ronnie and said, 'He's going to kill me!'

And he was gone. Just like that.

The screams from the crowd, a gust of wind, and Cat's and Nate's shouts all prevented Ronnie from hearing her own cry as she lunged forward and gaped over the railing. She saw him bounce once on the pavement. Several bluesuits immediately began holding back the most morbid of the boulevard onlookers.

A few minutes later, there were a dozen more uniforms in the lobby of the building who observed Ronnie Sinclair, eyes glistening, yelling curses into the face of Sergeant Jason Treakle, who had gone pale and didn't know how to respond to his subordinate.

Ronnie didn't remember what she'd yelled, but Cat later said, 'You started dropping F-bombs and it was beautiful. There's nothing Treakle can do about it, because now he knows he was dead wrong. And now that kid is just plain dead.'

When they got out to the street, they were amazed to see that Randolph Bronson's wire-rimmed glasses were still affixed to his face and only one lens was broken. He had not blown apart, as some of them do, but there was a massive pool of blood.

Cat put an arm around Ronnie's shoulder, squeezed it, and said, 'Gimme the keys to our shop. Let me drive us to the station.'

Ronnie handed Cat the car keys without objection.

*   *   *

Compassionate Charlie Gilford, who never missed a newsworthy incident, especially with carnage involved, arrived in time to observe them picking up the body, and he offered his usual on-scene commentary.

The lanky veteran detective sucked his teeth and said to the body snatcher driving the coroner's van, 'So, one of our patrol sergeants thought he could keep this looney tune from a back flip by feeding him a meal, right? Man, this is fucking Hollywood! Everybody knows you can walk a couple blocks to Musso and Frank's and dine with movie stars on comfort food. And Wolfgang Puck's got a joint right inside the Kodak Center with some of the trendiest eats in town. But what does our ass-wipe sergeant do to cheer up a depressed wack job? He brings the dude a fucking Big Mac! No wonder the fruitloop jumped.'

Later that night, Compassionate Charlie Gilford saw Ronnie Sinclair in the report room massaging her temples, waiting for the interrogation from Force Investigation Division, knowing that this one would be handled just like an officer-involved shooting.

The detective said merrily, 'I hear you really carpet bombed Chickenlips Treakle, Ronnie. Hollywood Nate told me you wouldn't hear *that* many "motherfuckers" at a Chris Rock concert. Way to go, girl!'

TWO

IT WAS A FEW WEEKS after the jumper incident that Ronnie Sinclair decided she'd had enough of the midwatch and Sergeant Treakle, who had only received an official reprimand for barging into her crisis negotiation and, in Ronnie's opinion, causing the demise of young Randolph Bronson. She'd discussed her situation with an old sergeant for whom she'd worked at Newton Street Division, now officially called Newton Street Area, since the current LAPD brass had decided that *division* sounded too militaristic. The working cops said the brass were full of shit, and they kept right on referring to police divisions even in the LAPD union's monthly newspaper.

Ronnie's former sergeant suggested that in these repressive times, supervisors like Treakle were harder to get rid of than Rasputin and jock itch. He thought she ought to have a talk with the boss of the Hollywood Division Community Relations Office, or CRO, pronounced 'Crow' by the cops. 'CRO is a good job, Ronnie,' he told her. 'You've done enough hard-core police work for a while. Being a senior lead officer in CRO will give you a leg up when you take your sergeant's oral.'

*   *   *

It had surprised Hollywood Nate to learn that Ronnie Sinclair was seeking the job that had opened up at the Community Relations Office, a job that Nate coveted. The CRO was composed of eighteen cops and two civilian workers led by a twenty-two-year sergeant. Eleven of the officers, both men and women, were senior lead officers, or SLOs, pronounced 'Slows,' and were given a pay bump and wore two silver chevrons on their sleeves with a star beneath them. The SLOs acted as ombudsmen or community liaisons for the Hollywood Division captain. Five were Hispanics and could translate Spanish as needed, and three others were foreign born and could communicate in half a dozen other tongues, but that was only a fraction of the languages spoken in Hollywood. The coppers called their bailiwick Babelwood Division.

The Community Relations Office was housed in a one-story rambling old structure just a wedge shot across the police parking lot. It was dubbed Hollywood South by the troops in the main station, to which the Crows referred as Hollywood North, and which, like all LAPD police facilities, had the architectural charm of a parking garage in Watts.

Among other duties, Crows handled calls from chronic complainers and Hollywood loons, and they could pretty well set their own ten-hour duty tours in their four-day work week. The major efforts of these cops were directed at quality-of-life issues: chronic-noise complaints, graffiti, homeless encampments, abandoned shopping carts, unauthorized yard sales, and aggressive panhandlers. Crows also had the job of overseeing the Police Reserve Program and the Police Explorer

Program for teenagers and directed the Nightclub Committee, the Homeless Committee, the Graffiti Committee, and even the Street Closure Committee.

In 2007, the city of Los Angeles's love for committees was almost as overpowering as its lust for diversity and its multicultural mania, and it would be hard to imagine anywhere with more social experimentation involving the police than LAPD's Hollywood Division. African Americans were the only ethnic group underrepresented in Hollywood demographics, but young black males arrived on the boulevards in large numbers every night, traveling on the subway or in cars from South L.A., many of whom were gang members.

The Crows also had to organize events such as the Tip-A-Cop fund-raiser, the Torch Run for the Special Olympics, and the Children's Holiday Party, and were tasked to help police the antiwar demonstrations, the Academy Awards, and all of the red carpet events at the Kodak Center. In short, they were doing jobs that caused salty old-timers to shake their heads and refer to the CRO as the sissy beat. Crows were often called teddy bears in blue.

They were also called much worse, but there was some envy involved in all of the pejoratives aimed at the Crows, because these officers of Hollywood South had relative freedom and the choice of wearing uniforms or street clothes depending upon the assignment, and they almost always did safe, clean work. Crows generally chose to stay in the job for a long time.

Ronnie had beaten out Hollywood Nate for the first opening in the Community Relations Office and was sent to senior lead officer training at the recruit training center near LAX. An unexpected retirement occurred a month later, and Nate Weiss ended up following Ronnie to the CRO, thinking he had found the spot where he might remain happily until retirement or until he attained show business success, whichever came first. By early summer, he had worked on two more TV movies, with a line of dialogue in each, the plots being for people who watch daytime TV. He was sure that the last one might make it to Spike TV because at the last minute they'd included lots of gratuitous blood and gore for high-school dropouts.

By July 2007, all of the Crows were future millionaires – in theory. One of them had been born in Iraq and had come to the U.S. as a child. He'd touted the wisdom of buying Iraqi dinars to his Crow partner now that the country was in chaos and its money nearly worthless. Through a currency broker, the partner bought one million dinars for $800 U.S. As the broker explained it to them, when Iraq eventually was able to get back to one dinar for one dollar and started being traded in all of the exchanges, 'You'll be millionaires!'

So two other Crows bought a million dinars. Three bought half a million each. Another bought one and a half million, figuring to buy a yacht when he retired. Ronnie Sinclair was very hesitant, but thinking of her aging parents, she bought half a million dinars.

The week after he'd been assigned to the CRO, Nate had one of his vigorous iron-pumping workouts in the high-tech weight room at Hollywood South. After the workout and a mirror examination of his impressive pecs, lats, and biceps, Nate entered the CRO office, sat down at a desk, and carefully studied an Iraqi dinar that one of the others had given to him. Looking at it under a glass and holding it against a lamp, he examined the horse in the watermark as though he knew what he was doing.

'Check it with a jeweler's loupe, why don't you?' said Tony Silva, one of the Hispanic officers. 'It's not counterfeit, if that's what you're thinking.'

'No, but I read in the paper that counterfeiters are bleeding out the ink on these things,' Nate said, 'and using them to make U.S. currency with laser printers.'

'Aren't you gonna buy while you have the chance?' Samuel Dibble, the CRO's only black cop, asked Nate. 'What if Bush's troop surge works and the dinar stabilizes? We'll all be rich. How about you?'

Nate only smiled, trying not to look too condescending, but later said privately to his sergeant, 'Cops are such suckers. Anyone can sell them a bill of goods. They'll invest in anything.'

His sergeant said to him, 'Yeah, I'm in for one million.'

Later, after the new commanding general in Iraq gave a major TV interview and said that the troop surge had a very good chance of success, Hollywood Nate Weiss secretly made a transfer from his savings account, called the currency broker, and bought *two* million dinars without telling any of the others.

Of course, Hollywood Nate's former colleagues, the midwatch officers of Watch 5, were not dreaming of being millionaires. They were just trying to cope with young Sergeant Treakle, whose administrative spanking for bringing the Big Macs to the rooftop standoff had not dampened his zeal or ambition. They knew that Hollywood Division was as shorthanded as the rest of the beleaguered LAPD, so before a supervisor like Sergeant Treakle could get a suspension without pay, he would have to do something *really* terrible. Such as saying something politically incorrect to a member of what had historically been considered a minority group. At least that was the thinking of the midwatch, according to all of the bitching heard around the station.

On one of those summer nights under what the Oracle used to call a Hollywood moon, meaning a full moon that brought out the crazies, Flotsam mentioned the rooftop incident to Catherine Song and said, 'Why couldn't the jumper have been black or Hispanic? That would've pushed Treakle's off button.'

'What about a Korean female?' Cat said back to him. 'We're not potential PC victims?'

'Negative,' Flotsam said. 'You people have got too rich and successful for victimhood. You and me're in the same boat. We could jump off a roof and who cares?'

Sergeant Treakle had teamed them up arbitrarily for one night, assigning Jetsam to ride with a Hispanic probationer whose field training officer was on a sick day. Jetsam didn't like working with a boot, but Flotsam wasn't complaining, and Cat knew why. She was very aware that he had eyes for her, but so did most of the other male officers on the midwatch.

That was when the PSR's radio voice said, ' Six-X-Thirty-two, a four-fifteen fight, Santa Monica and Western, code two.'

'Why can't we get a call in our own backyard once in a while?' Flotsam grumbled as Cat rogered the call. 'Doomsday Dan's working sixty-six with a probie partner. They should be handling it.'

'Dan probably had to run over to the cyber café to rent a computer and watch his foreign stocks tumble,' Cat said. 'Doesn't matter how good the market's doing. He's a great anticipator of international disasters.'

When they got to the location of the call, which turned out to be a bit east of Western Avenue, Cat said, 'Doomsday Dan sure would break out the gloves for this one.'

Four onlookers, two of them Salvadoran gang members, along with a pair of white parolees out looking for some tranny or dragon ass, were watching the disturbance. Transsexuals were preferred by the ex-cons in that all of their hormone treatments and surgery made them more like women, but in a pinch the parolees would settle for a drag queen. The onlookers were watching what had been a pretty good fight between a black drag queen and a white man in a business suit, which was now down to a screaming contest full of threats and gestures.

When the cops got out of the black-and-white, four observers walked quickly away, but a fifth stepped out of the shadows from a darkened doorway. Trombone Teddy was a transient, known to Flotsam from prior contacts. He was a street person nearly eighty years old who panhandled on the boulevards.

Teddy had stayed at the fight scene to watch the denouement, knowing he was drunk enough to get busted but too drunk to care. He wore a Lakers cap, layers of shirts that were now part of him, and nearly congealed trousers the color and texture of just-picked mushrooms. Looking at Teddy made you think fungus.

'I'm a witness,' Trombone Teddy said to Flotsam.

'Go home, Teddy,' the tall cop said, putting his mini-flashlight under his arm, cursing because the little light wouldn't stay there.

'I am home,' Teddy replied. 'I been living right here in this doorway for the last few days. The cops rousted us outta our camp in the hills. Up there we could hear the concerts at the Hollywood Bowl. I was a real sideman in my time, you know. I could blow better than any I ever heard at the Bowl. Back when I was a real person.'

That made Flotsam feel a little bit sad, Trombone Teddy reminiscing about having been a real person. Back in the day.

With the police there as protection, the black dragon, wearing a mauve shell and a black double-slitted skirt, hauled off for one last shot, swinging a silver purse at the white businessman, until Flotsam stepped in and said, 'Back off! Both of you!'

Reluctantly, the dragon stepped back, blonde wig askew, one heel broken off the silver pumps, makeup smeared, panty hose shredded, and yelled, 'He kidnapped me! I barely escaped with my life! Arrest him!'

Flotsam had already patted down the other combatant. He was portly and middle-aged with a dyed-black comb-over that shone like patent leather. A trickle of blood dripped from his nose and he wiped it with a silk handkerchief from his breast pocket.

He handed Flotsam his driver's license and said, 'My name is Milt Zimmerman, Officer. I've never been arrested for anything. This person stole my car keys and took off running to here, where I caught her. My car is two blocks west in an alley. I want her arrested for attempted car theft.'

'Ask this guddamn kidnapper how we got in the alley! Jist ask him!' the dragon cried.

'Step over here with me,' Cat said to the slender drag queen, who listed to starboard on the broken silver pump.

When the combatants were separated, Trombone Teddy staggered back and forth from one pair to the other so as not to miss any of the good parts, and he heard Cat say to the dragon, 'Okay, now give me some ID and tell me what happened.'

The drag queen produced a driver's license bearing the name of Latrelle Johnson, born in 1975, from the silver purse. Cat shined her light on the photo, taken when Latrelle was without eyebrows and lipstick and wig, and Cat decided that the dragon was far better-looking as a man than as a woman.

Cat said, 'Okay, Latrelle, tell me what happened.'

'Please call me Rhonda,' the dragon said. 'That's my name now. Latrelle don't exist no more. Latrelle is dead, and I'm glad.'

'Okay, Rhonda,' Cat said, thinking that sounded kind of sad. 'So what's the story here?'

'He picked me up from the corner two blocks down Santa Monica and offered to take me to a club for some drinks and a dance or two. Me, I'm stupid. I believed him.'

'Uh-huh,' Cat said. 'You just happened to be on this corner waiting for someone to go dancing with?'

'I ain't hookin',' said Rhonda, then after a few seconds added, 'Well . . . I admit I got busted a couple times for prostitution, but tonight I happened to be jist makin' a call at the public phone here by the liquor store.' Rhonda pointed to the phone box behind them.

'Okay, then what?' Cat said, deciding that there would be no kidnapping report and maybe no reports at all, except for a couple of field interrogation cards.

'I thought maybe he was takin' me out to the Strip, but we only got a couple blocks and he whips into an alley and forces me to commit a sex act. I was scared for my life, Officer!'

Milt Zimmerman heard part of that and yelled, 'She's a liar! She wanted it! Then she grabbed my car keys and ran off with them!'

'Okay, pay attention to me, not to them,' Flotsam said, taking Milt Zimmerman by the arm and walking him several steps farther away, while Trombone Teddy drifted toward Cat and Rhonda because their conversation sounded juicier.

Milt Zimmerman said to Flotsam, 'She's lying! I told her I wanted a blow job and she gave it up willingly. Then when she's done she wants an extra twenty. I said no way, and she grabs my keys from the ignition and starts running back here, where I first picked her up. My Cadillac's still back there in the alley!'

'Thing is,' Flotsam said. 'She's a him. You might call her a "shim."'

'I didn't know!' Milt Zimmerman said. 'She looks like a woman!'

'This is Hollywood,' Flotsam said, 'where men are men and so are the women.'

Back by the liquor store Rhonda was starting to reveal more details, causing Trombone Teddy to shuffle closer, his hearing not what it used to be. When Cat came on the Job, she was trained by old male coppers who scorned latex gloves, which cops didn't have back in the day. But looking at Trombone Teddy made Cat glad she was carrying a pair tonight.

She said to the old eavesdropper, 'Get your butt away from here. Now!'

'But I always liked soap opera,' Trombone Teddy said.

Cat reached in her pocket and said, 'Don't make me glove up. If I do, you're going to jail.'

'Yes, ma'am,' Teddy muttered and walked back toward Flotsam, where he knew it wouldn't be nearly as entertaining.

'So what exactly went on in that alley?' Cat asked Rhonda. 'The details.'

Rhonda said, 'At first he seemed real nice. He stopped the car the second we was in the alley. He turned off the motor and started kissin' me. Hard. I said somethin' like, "Easy, baby, give a girl a minute to breathe." Next thing I know, the pants came off.'

'Yours?'

'His. Then he made me do something that I would never do. He said if I didn't do it, he'd get violent. He had very strong hands and I was afraid. When he said it, he reached under my skirt and pulled my panty hose down and my thong clear off!'

'Was it anal sex? Did he bugger you?'

'No! He made *me* bugger *him!* It was humiliatin'. I was so scared, I done it. I don't know how I managed, but I did. And I didn't have no condom neither.'

'I see,' Cat said. 'Then what?'

'Then, when I was through, he said he wanted more and I said no way and tried to get outta the car. And he started cussin' and said he oughtta run over me with his Cadillac. So I jist grabbed his keys, got out, and ran while he was tryin' to pull his pants back up.'

Rhonda took out a tissue and wiped at her mascara then, and Cat wasn't sure if it was for her benefit or if Rhonda was really getting weepy.

Cat said, 'Rhonda, don't make us do a lot of paperwork for nothing here. Tell me the truth. Was there money involved in this incident?'

Rhonda put the tissue back in the purse and said, 'He offered me thirty-five dollars.' Then Rhonda quickly added, 'I didn't ask him for it. He jist offered to give it to me. Not for sex, but like a gift, sorta.'

'If you went dancing with him?'

' Uh-huh,' Rhonda said, sniffling again.

'Stay right here.'

Seeing Cat walking toward him, Flotsam told Milt Zimmerman to stay put, and he met Cat halfway, where they could talk in whispers. Trombone Teddy tried to sidle closer, but when Cat gave him a look, he scuttled away to his doorway bed, muttering, 'I been scared to death of them ever since Pearl Harbor.'

'She's Korean, Teddy. You're safe,' Flotsam informed him.

'North or South?' Teddy asked anxiously.

When Cat and Flotsam were huddled, Flotsam said,

'He claims he picked up the dragon in front of the liquor store by the phone booth. The dragon offered sex for fifty bucks but said okay to thirty-five. They drove to the alley, where he got his steam released from a head job, then the dragon demanded twenty more. He refused and the dragon up and grabbed his keys and ran back to the liquor store.'

'Did he say why Rhonda wanted twenty more after it was over?' Cat asked.

'No, why?'

'If Rhonda's telling most of the truth, it's because the guy wanted something that the more fem dragons like Rhonda are seldom asked to do.'

'Dragons and trannies do anything you want,' Flotsam said, 'which is why they got every kind of plague and pestilence. So what was it?'

'Anal sex,' Cat said.

'So? The dragon found that peculiar?'

'Milton was the catcher, not the pitcher.'

Flotsam said to Cat, 'Lemme track this. You're telling me that Milton ended up being Rhonda's bitch?' He turned to gawk for a moment at the outraged businessman impeccably clothed by Armani, then said, 'Sometimes it gets way too confusing out here.'

All that was left to do was to mollify both of the complainants. The two cops walked over to the businessman, and Flotsam said, 'Mr Zimmerman, do you really wanna make a crime report? Before you answer, lemme tell you that the person over there in the torn skirt says that you paid to be . . .'

'Buggered,' Cat finished it abruptly. 'That doesn't mean you can't be a victim of an attempted car theft, but it might get embarrassing for you and your family if it went to court. Of course, we could disprove Rhonda's allegations by taking you to Hollywood Presbyterian and having a doctor swab your anus for DNA evidence. Whadda you think?'

After a long hesitation, Milt Zimmerman said, 'Well, I'm okay with just forgetting the whole thing and getting the hell away from that lunatic.'

Flotsam said, 'Just stand by for a minute until we see if the other party is satisfied with this outcome.'

When they walked back to the liquor store, Rhonda was hanging up the receiver on a public phone attached to the wall. Cat said, 'Rhonda, you might wanna think this over before you insist on reports for kidnapping or sexual assault. You see, there *was* money involved here, regardless of whether he decided to give it or you asked him for it. Sex and money usually means prostitution.'

'And after all, he's the one that got boned,' Flotsam said to Rhonda. 'So even if we arrested him for assaulting you, his defense lawyer would say he took it in the chute, not you. That this is just a case of tit for tat.'

'Okay,' Rhonda said with a sigh. 'But I will always know that I was the victim, not that freak. And my tits had nothin' to do with it!'

While Milt Zimmerman walked to the alley with the car keys that Cat had retrieved, Rhonda removed the broken silver pump and hobbled down Santa Monica Boulevard in the other direction, disappearing into the night.

'No such thing as rape in Hollywood,' Cat said to Flotsam. 'Just a lot of business disputes.'

Flotsam had the last word, two words, actually. It was what was always said by officers in that unique police division, there in the very heart of Los Angeles. He shook his head in utter bewilderment and said, 'Fucking Hollywood!'

Just then the public phone rang. Cat was heading for their car but Flotsam said, 'They're all afraid of cell phones from watching *The Wire* on TV.'

Flotsam picked it up and in a voice as close to Rhonda's as he could manage said, 'Heloooo.'

As expected, a male voice said, 'Is this Rhonda?'

'It certainly is,' Flotsam said in falsetto.

'I'm the guy who had a little party with you at my apartment three weeks ago,' the caller said. 'Lance. Remember?'

'Ohhhh, yes,' Flotsam said. 'Remind me of your address, Lance.'

Before he hung up, Cat heard him say, 'Get ready to shed those pants, Lance!'

'What's going on in that water-logged brain?' Cat asked with a sloe-eyed glance.

At eleven-thirty, 6-X-32 pulled up in front of an apartment building on Franklin, an upmarket neighborhood where Flotsam and Cat wouldn't have expected a dragon streetwalker to have an outcall date.

Flotsam said to Cat, 'I thought we'd find the guy somewhere like that building near Fountain and Beachwood. That's where a lotta trannies and dragons do business. My partner and me call it Jurassic Park.'

'Why?' Cat asked.

'Because of the occupants. We don't know *what* the hell they are.'

Flotsam shined his spotlight along the second-floor balcony until he spotted Lance's apartment number, then got on the PA and said, 'Attention, Lance! Miss Rhonda regrets she is indisposed and unable to keep her date with you tonight. It's her recurring prostate infection.'

THREE

RONNIE WASN'T SURE how she felt about working at the CRO. It surely wasn't police work, and yet she couldn't stop thinking about how she'd felt when her mother and father and married sister had ganged up on her. It had happened when she'd mentioned her new job to them during a family dinner at her parents' home in Manhattan Beach, where her father owned and operated a successful plumbing supply business.

'I don't even like what they call us,' Ronnie said to them.

'Crows?' her mother said. 'That's cute.'

'How would you like to be called a crow?' Ronnie said.

'I'm too old to appreciate it,' her mother said. 'But on you it's cute.'

Ronnie had felt exceptionally tired that evening, and while her mother and her sister Stephanie were preparing a dinner of roasted halibut and wild rice, Ronnie was sprawled on the sofa with her niece Sarah sitting on her stomach. She'd tried without much success to enjoy a glass of pinot while Sarah prattled on, bouncing incessantly.

After the meal, Ronnie's mother urged her just to relax and listen to her mom's favorite Sting CDs and her father's Tony Bennett albums while the others tidied up. She should have been suspicious of the extra solicitude. Then they all entered the living room and sat down, her mother and sister with a glass of wine each, her father with a beer. And they started in on her.

'The Community Relations Office is where you belong, Ronnie,' her father began. 'You should stay there until you make sergeant. It's a good stepping-stone and there's no reason for you to leave.'

Her mother said, 'You've done your share of dangerous work, honey.'

Stephanie said, 'Do a year or two as a community relations officer, study, and get promoted. I know you think being a street cop is more fun, but you gotta think of the future.'

Her sister had assured her own future by marrying a computer geek who made three million dollars from selling his start-up company and investing it in another computer business, which was soaring.

'What is this, an intervention?' Ronnie said. 'When did you all decide to do good-cop, bad-cop on me?'

'We've been talking about you, it's true,' her mother said. 'We know you're not thrilled with your new job, but you're smart. You can climb the ladder and end up—'

'In a safe desk job somewhere,' Ronnie said, ruefully. 'Build them a desk and they will sit, right?'

Stephanie, who bore a family resemblance to her older sister, said, 'I'll never understand your fascination with being a cop anyway. What's it got you except two failed marriages to other cops?'

'But they were both Sinclairs, so I didn't even have to change my driver's license,' Ronnie said with a smirk, pissed off as she always was when Sanctimonious Stephanie spouted off about Ronnie's bad choices. Both Sinclair husbands had fooled Ronnie at first, but she felt she hadn't gotten enough credit for dumping each of them quickly, as soon as she discovered that one was a secret drinker and the other a philanderer.

'Give your new job a chance,' her father said.

'You might start liking it,' her sister said. 'Making your own hours to suit your own schedule.'

'And I could quit worrying about you,' her mother said.

After that evening, Ronnie decided to give it all she had at the CRO, especially since the sergeant had teamed her with an experienced senior lead officer, Bix Ramstead, to whom Ronnie had been drawn instantly.

Forty-five-year-old Bix Ramstead was thirteen years her senior, on both the Job and the calendar. At six foot one, he was fit and good-looking, with a warm and kindly smile. He had a head full of curls the color of pewter, and smoky gray eyes, and though Ronnie had never dated a man his age, she would have jumped at a chance with Bix. Except that he was married with two children he adored, a sixteen-year-old girl named Janie, and Patrick, who was twelve. Their photos were on his desk and he talked of them often, worrying about whether he'd have enough for their college tuition when the time came. Because of that, he worked as much overtime as he could, and the citizens in his area liked him.

When Ronnie had mentioned Bix to Cat, she'd said, 'Yeah, I was teamed with him a few times, maybe six years ago, when he was working patrol. A complicated guy who never wanted to make sergeant. Not as much fun as some of the gunfighters when you're working the streets. Back then I was always happier with carnivores than with grazers, but I don't need kick-ass partners anymore. Now he'd probably suit me fine. Plus, he's very cute.'

When Ronnie said it was too bad that Bix was married, Cat said, 'He's a little too old for you, and besides, didn't you learn your lesson marrying two cops? I learned from marrying one. Do like me and look for a rich attorney next time. Hang out in lawyer-infested bars. Shysters are all over the place, like Starbucks cups.'

The first appointment Ronnie took with Bix Ramstead was at 'The Birds,' as the cops referred to the Doheny Estates, in 6-A-31's area. It was late morning as they cruised up the hills, surrounded by seven-figure homes on streets named Warbler Way, Robin Drive, Nightingale Drive, Thrush Way, and Skylark Drive. Many movie and rock stars owned high-dollar houses in the Hollywood Hills, some of them serving as occasional homes when their owners were in L.A. Many had great open views, some were on secluded properties. The showbiz residents were fearful of stalkers, burglars, and paparazzi.

'Occasionally, we do burglary walk-throughs,' Bix Ramstead explained to Ronnie while they drove the streets. 'We just point out all the vulnerable places that need protection.'

'Quality of life,' Ronnie said, repeating the CRO mantra.

'You got it,' Bix said with a grin. 'The quality-of-life calls we get up here in the hills are a bit different from the quality-of-life calls in East Hollywood, you'll notice.'

Ronnie looked at the luxury surrounding her and said, 'Their quality is a lot different from my quality, for sure.' She was silent for a moment, then said, 'We still look like police officers, still think like police officers, but we aren't doing police work.'

Bix Ramstead said to her, 'When I was a cop, I spoke as a cop, I understood as a cop, I thought as a cop. But when I became a Crow, I put aside cop-ish things.'

'Who's line is that?' Ronnie said.

'St. Paul to the Corinthians. More or less.' Then he said, 'This is a good job, Ronnie. You'll see. Don't fight it.'

The call to the Community Relations Office that had come from The Birds was from a drummer in a rock band who was definitely on his way down. At one time he'd been hot and mentioned in the same breath with Tommy Lee, but internal dissension between the singer and the lead guitarist, who wrote their material, had broken up the group. The drummer lived with a singer whose career had taken a similar dive. She was known on the Strip as a very bad drinker whose cocaine addiction had gotten her arrested twice.

When they rang the bell, Bix said to Ronnie, 'Look for *Scarface*. He's an icon.'

'Who?' Ronnie said.

It took the rocker a minute to come to the door, and when he did, he looked pale and puzzled. His ginger ringlets hung in his face. He had a week's growth of whiskers, and the wispy, dark soul patch under his lip was plastered with dried food. He wore a 'Metallica' T-shirt and battered designer jeans that Ronnie figured had cost more than the best dress she owned. His arms were covered with full-sleeve tatts and he appeared malnourished.

'Oh, yeah, thanks for coming,' he said, stepping back in bare feet, obviously just recalling that he'd called the police the day before.

When they entered, Ronnie saw his singer girlfriend sprawled in a huge wicker chair inside a garden room just off the foyer. She was listening trancelike to speakers built into the walls on each side of the chair. Ronnie figured it was her voice on the CD singing unintelligible lyrics. Behind her on the wall was a framed one-sheet movie poster of *Scarface,* starring Al Pacino.

The rocker didn't invite them in any farther than the foyer, and Bix Ramstead said, 'How can we help you?'

'We're scared of getting trapped in a fire,' the rocker said, scratching his ribs and his back, even his crotch for a moment, until he remembered that one of the cops was a woman. 'It's the pap. They come around with scopes and watch us from vacant property on the hilltop. And they smoke up there. We're scared they'll start a brush fire. Can you chase them away?'

'Are there any up there now, or do you not know?' Bix asked.

'I don't know. We see them watching us. Always watching.'

'We'll take a drive up the hill and check it out,' Bix said.

'Stop back and let us know,' the rocker said.

'Sure, we'll be back in a little bit.'

When they got in their car and drove up the hill, Ronnie said, 'He's a poster boy for "Just Say No." He's thirty years old, going on eighty. And speaking of posters, how did you know *Scarface* would be there?'

'Rocker plus cocaine plus Hollywood equals *Scarface*,' Bix said. 'The cocaine set loves that movie, especially that dopey scene where Al Pacino's so buzzed he falls face-first into a snowdrift of coke. You can usually find *Scarface* somewhere in all their cribs.'

Ronnie said, 'The first time I drove up to the Hollywood Hills, I saw these homes and figured these were the kind of people who listen to music I never hear on K-Rock. Now I find out there're people here who download tunes from Headbanger's Heaven.'

'Big bucks don't change human nature,' Bix said.

He didn't waste much time on the paparazzi search. Bix drove to the area where homes had not yet been built on the steeper slopes, looked around perfunctorily, then drove back down to the rocker's address and parked in front, where the man was waiting for them in the doorway.

'Well?' the rocker said.

'You were right,' Bix said. 'There were four of them. They had telephoto cameras on tripods. And there were three more driving up while we were talking to the other four. You're a very popular target, it seems.'

'What'd you tell them?' the rocker asked anxiously.

'I told them that I know they're just doing their jobs but that there could be serious repercussions for stalking famous people.'

'I understand they gotta make a living,' the rocker said.

'I reassured them that you understand. That celebrities like you need them and they need you. A reciprocal arrangement, so to speak.'

'Yeah, exactly,' the rocker said. 'Just so they don't start a fire. That's all we're worried about.'

'They promised me that there'd be no smoking up there in the future unless it was done in their van with cigarettes extinguished in the ashtray.'

'They had a van?' the rocker said with a little smile.

'Yes, sir,' Bix said. 'They come prepared for someone like you.' Then he added, 'And your lady, of course.'

The rocker's smile widened and he said, 'Yeah, because of the pap, she's afraid to get in the Jacuzzi without wearing something.'

'The price of fame,' Bix said, nodding sympathetically.

'Well, thanks, Officers,' the rocker said. 'Anything I can do for you, let me know. We played a gig one time for the Highway Patrol.'

'We'll keep that in mind, sir,' Bix said. 'We'd be thrilled to hear you play.'

When they were driving back down toward Sunset Boulevard, Bix said to Ronnie, 'We get a lot of those. I never tell them the truth. They're miserable enough in their failed lives without finding out that there's no paparazzi. That nobody gives a shit anymore.'

Hollywood Nate was supposed to be doing similar CRO work that day, but he took a drive up into the Hollywood Hills on his own, to a neighborhood farther east. On an impulse, he cruised up to Mt. Olympus, sipping a cup of Starbucks latte as he remembered the young woman with butterscotch hair. He hadn't been able to forget her since the day he wrote down her license-plate number at Farmers Market.

Nate parked a block from her home on her very winding street. It was obvious that on her side of the street, there was a good city view. He told himself that he wasn't going to sit there long, only long enough to finish the latte.

Hollywood Nate couldn't understand why he was there in the first place. That is, until he remembered the way she'd moved. Like an athlete, or a dancer, maybe. And the way her hair itself had danced when she'd turned abruptly. He couldn't forget that either. In fact, he was ashamed of himself for doing this, but as long as nobody would ever know, what the hell. He just wanted to see her one more time, to see if she measured up to the image in his memory.

Then Nate thought, What am I, a high-school kid? And he tossed the empty cup on the floor of the car, started the engine, and was just about to head back down, when the garage door opened and the red Beemer backed out. The car turned and drove down the hill with Hollywood Nate Weiss following behind, but far enough to be out of mirror range.

Nate's heart started pumping faster and he knew it wasn't the caffeine. He'd never done anything like this before, had never had the memory of a beautiful woman affect him in this way. Hollywood Nate Weiss had never had to pursue any woman, not in his entire life. And it made him think, I've turned into a goddamn stalker! Now Nate was experiencing something altogether unique for him. Not just shame, but a trace of self-loathing had entered his consciousness.

He said aloud, 'Fuck this!' and was about to abandon this silliness when they were a few blocks from Hollywood Boulevard. But then he saw her car rolling through a boulevard stop without so much as a tap on the brake pedal.

Suddenly, Nate Weiss was no longer in charge. Something took him over. It was like he was watching himself on a movie screen. Without completely willing it, Nate stepped on the accelerator and got close behind her, turning on the light bar and tooting his horn until she glanced at her rearview mirror, pulled over, and parked.

When he got to her driver's-side window, she looked at him with amber eyes that matched her hair and said, 'Ditzy Margot didn't come to a complete stop back there, did she?'

Her cotton jersey that stretched tight over her cleavage was a raspberry shade. Her skirt was eggshell white and was halfway up her suntanned thighs. Those thighs! She *was* an athlete or a dancer, he just knew it.

Nate's hand trembled when he took her driver's license, and his voice was unsteady when he said, 'Yes, ma'am, you ran the stop sign without even trying to stop. Your brake lights didn't glow at all.'

'Damn!' she said. 'I've got so much on my mind. I'm sorry.'

He read the driver's license: Margot Aziz, date of birth 4-13-77. She was six years younger than Nate, yet he felt like a schoolboy again. Stalling for time in order to pull himself together, he said, 'Could I see your registration, ma'am?'

She reached into the glove box for the leather packet containing the owner's manuals, removed the registration and insurance card, handed them to Nate, and said, 'Please don't call me ma'am, Officer. I recently turned thirty, as you see, and I'm feeling ancient. Call me Margot.'

Her lipstick was a creamy raspberry to match her jersey, and her perfect teeth were probably whiter than nature intended. Nate blurted, 'I won't call you ma'am if you don't call me Officer. My name is Nate Weiss.'

She had him and she knew it. The smile widened and she said, 'Do you patrol this area all the time, Nate?'

'Actually, I'm what the other cops call a Crow. I work the Community Relations Office. I don't do regular patrol.'

'You don't look like a crow,' Margot Aziz said. 'More like an eagle, I would say.'

He couldn't remember the last time he'd blushed, but his face felt hot. He said, 'Yeah, I do have a bit of a beak, don't I?'

'No, my husband has a beak,' she said. 'Your nose is barely aquiline. It's very strong and manly. Actually, quite . . . beautiful.'

He wasn't even aware that he'd handed her back her license and registration. 'Well,' he said, 'drive carefully.'

Before he could turn to leave, she said, 'Nate, what does a Crow do?'

He said, 'We deal with quality-of-life issues so that the officers on patrol don't have to. You know, stuff like chronic-noise complaints, graffiti, homeless encampments up near where you live. Stuff like that.'

'Homeless encampments!' she cried, like calling a winning Bingo. 'This is an amazing coincidence because I was going to call Hollywood Station about that very thing. I can see them from my patio. They make noise up there and they light campfires. It's terrible. How lucky to run into you like this. Sometime I'd like you to come by my house and let me point them out. Maybe you can do something about it.'

'Sure!' Nate said. 'Absolutely. When, today?'

'Not today, Nate,' she said quickly. 'Can I have your phone number?'

'Of course,' Nate said, reaching for his business cards. 'I can come and talk to you – and to your husband – anytime up to eight P.M., when I usually go home.'

'My husband and I are separated, in the middle of a divorce,' Margot Aziz said. 'You'll just be talking to me when you come.'

Nate Weiss couldn't give her the card fast enough. He had ordered a custom-made business card with the Hollywood sign across the front of it, alongside an LAPD badge. And under that was his name, serial number, and the city phone number he'd been assigned by the CRO sergeant.

He hesitated for only a few seconds, then wrote his
private cell number on the back of the card and said
to Margot Aziz, 'It might be better for you to call me
on my cell. Sometimes we don't pick up the calls on
our city line right away, but I always pick up my private
cell.'

'Good,' she said. 'Let's keep it personal, Nate.' And
she showed that gleaming smile again, then turned her
head to look for eastbound traffic. Her amazing hair
caught another sunbeam and danced for Nate Weiss.
And she drove away.

A few minutes after he was back in his car, Nate
thought, That Hills bunny just flirted her way out of
a ticket that I was never going to write in the first place,
and I feel like a chump. Separated from her husband?
She'll show that card to him tonight over dinner and
they'll both have a laugh. On Nate Weiss!

Then he thought about her surname, Aziz. Some kind
of Middle East name. She was married to an Arab,
maybe. It didn't feel good for a Jewish cop to think of
this fantastic woman married to a rich Arab. Nate Weiss
wondered how that might have happened.

After leaving Hollywood Nate, Margot Aziz drove to
a nightclub called the Leopard Lounge on Sunset
Boulevard. It was a strip club but topless only, so liquor
could be sold. Her estranged husband also owned a
totally nude strip club, but in that one, no alcoholic
beverages were allowed by the state. In that nightclub,
Ali Aziz had to make money from hugely overpriced
soft drinks, minimums, and cover charges. He spent
most of his time in the Leopard Lounge but frequently

drove to the other club to pick up the cash from his manager.

Margot had made a phone call to be sure that Ali would not be at the Leopard Lounge at this time of day, and she avoided the Mexican employees preparing for the early-evening business, heading for the dressing room. It was not a typical strip club with dim lights and dark colors. Not like Ali's totally nude nightclub, which had faux-leather banquettes, faux-granite columns, and faux-walnut soffits. That one was claustrophobic, with nude prints in gilded frames that Ali thought would provoke fantasies and erections. Margot had been in that kind of strip club often enough.

She'd designed the Leopard Lounge interior herself, despite her husband's complaints about how much money she was spending. This one featured woven-leather chairs surrounding the stage, with terracotta walls and a sandy tile pattern cutting through chocolate-brown carpeting that Ali had insisted on because he'd gotten it cheap. This club had a more open feeling, more inviting to female patrons. At least that was Margot's intent when she did the interior design.

She opened the dressing-room door without knocking, and a lovely Amerasian, twenty-five years old, wearing a terry robe and sitting at the makeup table applying eyeliner, looked up.

'What time's he coming back, Jasmine?' Margot asked.

She walked up behind the young woman and swept Jasmine's long black hair onto one of her surgically enhanced breasts, whose nipples and areolas were rouged. Then she massaged the dancer's neck and shoulders, kissing the right shoulder lightly.

'About seven, seven-thirty,' Jasmine said, placing her delicate fingers over Margot's. 'Not so hard,' she said. 'I strained my shoulder on that goddamn pole last night.' Then she asked, 'Have any luck with your friend? Will he be visiting again soon?'

'Not as soon as I'd like,' Margot said, stopping the shoulder rub and sitting on a chair next to the makeup table. 'He gets attacks of remorse. I think I can pull him out of it, but how soon, I can't say.'

'Shit!' Jasmine said.

'Don't be discouraged,' Margot said. 'I had a lucky break today.'

'Yeah, what kinda break?' Jasmine said listlessly.

'A cop stopped me for a ticket,' Margot said. 'Of course he didn't write it. A handsome, horny cop with no wedding ring on his finger.'

'So what? It's not too hard for someone like you to talk a cop out of a ticket. I've done it myself.'

'There was something about this one,' Margot said. 'I think it could work with him.'

'A substitute?'

'If a second-stringer is needed,' Margot said. 'But let's not give up on our number-one draft pick. He's perfect.'

'Did today's cop try to make a date?'

'I have his cell number,' Margot said. 'If we need it.'

'Tell me something about your husband that I gotta know,' Jasmine said.

'What's that?'

'Does that fucking Arab asshole *ever* get enough blow jobs?'

FOUR

WATCH 5 HIT THE STREETS with a bang that evening. The bang came from a twelve-year cop with a sporty blonde haircut, rosy dumpling cheeks, and just a hint of makeup, whose Sam Browne belt was rumored to be a size 44. Gert Von Braun had recently transferred to Hollywood from Central Division, where she'd been in an officer involved shooting that cops refer to as a 'good' shooting. Gert had encountered an armed bandit running out of a skid row liquor store, loot and gun in hand, at the same moment that Gert, working alone in a report car, was pulling up in front. Steering with her left hand, Gert had fired one-handed through the open passenger window and hit the parolee-at-large with four out of five rounds, killing him instantly, thus making herself a celebrity gunslinger at Central Station.

But Gert was sick of all the skid row derelicts and the smells associated with them: urine and feces, vomit and blood. And, worst of all, the unbearably sweet, sickly smell of decaying flesh from corpses that had lain dead under bridges and in cardboard shelters. Some had been there for so long that even the flies covering them were dead. At least those corpses didn't smell.

And the living weren't much better off, derelicts with their legs and feet covered with clumps of maggots that were eating them alive while the wretches ate whatever they could beg at the back doors of downtown eateries.

The watch commanders were always calling for acid washes at Central Station. They had an air-deodorizing machine going most of the time and burned incense sticks in the report room. Cops would come on duty, sniff the air, and say, 'Is it a three- or four-stick day?'

Finally, Gert Von Braun had decided that Central Division smelled like one huge tennis shoe and she couldn't get the odor out of her uniforms or her nostrils. Hollywood Station was closer to her home in the Valley and smelled much better, even though she knew it was a lot weirder than Central. She'd asked for a transfer and had gotten it.

Coppers at Hollywood Station noticed that Gert carried everything but a rocket launcher in her war bag, which was not actually a bag but a huge black suitcase on wheels. And the cops at Hollywood Station discovered quickly that Gert had 'ETS,' which was what they called explosive temper syndrome, especially when she'd come puffing out of the station into the parking lot, red-faced in the summer heat, dragging her load while her partner lagged behind with a beanbag shotgun as well as the Remington 870 one-shot-and-you-rot model.

It wasn't a good time to start hacking on her, but nobody ever said the surfer cops were founts of wisdom. They always referred to big war bags on wheels as 'wimpy bags for airline employees.' Jetsam nodded toward her nylon suitcase, winked at Flotsam, and said to Gert, 'Excuse me, miss, but is our flight on time?'

Taking the cue, Flotsam said, 'Can we have a beverage before takeoff? And extra peanuts?'

Gert Von Braun, who was only five foot six but outweighed Jetsam, if not the much larger Flotsam, said, 'Shove your peanuts up your ass, you surfboard squids.'

'Oh, that's scandalous,' Flotsam whispered to Jetsam.

'I'm so appalled,' Jetsam whispered back to Flotsam.

Still giving the surfer cops the stink eye, Gert hefted her equipment into the trunk of her shop, closed the lid, and began testing her Portable Officer Data Device System, which she'd checked out at the kit room.

The PODD, pronounced 'pod' by the cops, was one of the instruments of torture encouraged by the monitors of the federal consent decree. It was a handheld instrument resembling a large BlackBerry. In it were the FDRs, or field data reports, which LAPD officers had to fill out for every contact with a suspect that was not the result of a radio call, that is, any stop of a suspect initiated by an officer. On it they had to list the gender, descent, and age of a suspect, and the reason for the stop, also indicating whether there was a pat-down or a more complete search of the suspect's person or car.

The purpose of the FDR was to monitor whether or not cops were engaging in racial profiling, but like everything else connected with the federal consent decree, it discouraged proactive police work. With the mountains of paperwork they already had to endure in order to please their monitoring masters, this one was cumbersome and insulting, and it encouraged otherwise honest cops to dishonestly 'balance out' their legitimate suspect stops of blacks and Latinos by creating nonexistent Asians or white Anglos. And it just generally pissed off everybody connected with it and resulted in yet more cops being taken off the streets to deal with the PODD information.

And at that moment nobody was more pissed off than Officer Gert Von Braun, who checked her PODD and placed it on the deck lid of her shop, trying to ignore the surfer team who were watching her and chortling. Because she was mad at the surfers, and at the PODD, and at herself for transferring to Hollywood Station, her mind had been elsewhere when she loaded the magazine tube of her shotgun. The loading protocol was designed to make the gun 'patrol ready,' that is, four in the magazine and none in the chamber, with the safety on until the gun is ready to be taken from the car and used. Then a final round was to be taken from the butt cuff to top off the magazine.

Probably because she was so hot and distracted by the smirking surfers, and had such a famously short fuse in the first place, she forgot that she'd just loaded the magazine. And she decided to test the action as she usually did before loading any rounds into the gun. Of course, that racked a live round into the chamber, with the safety off.

Gert realized at once what she'd done, and cursing the surfers under her breath for dissing her, she was about to unchamber the round after placing her cell phone beside the PODD on the deck lid of the car.

'Dude, I think we better get our wheels up,' Flotsam

said to his partner. 'Gert has locked in on us with lips drawn, fangs bared, and a shotgun in her paws.'

'Bro, that swamp donkey can shoot with either hand,' Jetsam agreed, eyeing Gert's Distinguished Expert shooting medal on her left pocket flap over her extra-large bosom. 'And her heart pumps Freon to her veins.'

Still glaring at the surfer cops, and trying to think up some crack she could make about their dumb-looking, bleached-out spiky hair, Gert saw that the PODD had bumped the cell phone and it was sliding clear off the deck lid of the car.

She said, 'Shit!' and tried to catch it with her left hand before it hit the asphalt, but she touched the PODD and it started sliding. Now she was trying to catch both instruments with her left hand. And she accidentally touched the trigger with her right.

The evening began with a bang, all right. A big one. Doomsday Dan Applewhite yelled like he'd been shot. He'd been bent over the open trunk of his shop and leapt back from the explosion, twisting clumsily and falling down on his hip. His P1 partner, young Gil Ponce, who was one month from completing his eighteen-month probation, instinctively crouched and drew his Beretta.

Officer Von Braun's shotgun had been pointed skyward, so the explosion did no damage, except to the psyche of Officer Applewhite. Within a minute, there were three supervisors running into the parking lot, including the lieutenant and Sergeant Treakle. Gert Von Braun was scared, mortified, and greatly relieved when she saw that she'd not blown away a cop, though she knew she'd be facing disciplinary action for the accidental discharge.

'You okay?' the lieutenant asked the senior field training officer, whose face had gone white.

'I think so,' Dan Applewhite said. Then he added, 'I'm not sure. I better run over to Cedars and get MT'd. I went down hard.'

To the supervisors of Dan Applewhite, it went without saying that he'd go for medical treatment, since his retirement date was nearing. A paper cut could send him to Cedars-Sinai or Hollywood Presbyterian, demanding a tetanus shot. He was determined to have recorded on paper any injury he'd suffered while on duty as an active cop in case some disability popped up during his retirement years, as he was sure it would.

Gert Von Braun followed the supervisors into the station to give her statement for the 1.28 personnel complaint while the surfer cops jumped into their shop and cleared for calls, hoping they wouldn't somehow get blamed for harassing, enraging, and distracting a recognized gunfighter who wore a size 44 Sam Browne. They needn't have worried, though. Gert was told she'd probably end up with an official reprimand, and she took it like a man.

After the supervisors and Gert Von Braun were gone, Dan Applewhite's twenty-two-year-old boot turned to his shaken partner and said, 'Want me to drive tonight?'

Wordlessly, the older cop handed Gil the keys to their shop. Phantom pains were already burning Dan's left hip and running down into his femur. He wondered if this would lead to eventual hip replacement. He'd heard horror stories of staph infection that crippled patients after hip surgery, and he got a terrifying mental picture of himself trying to negotiate the steps to his apartment with a walker.

Unhappily for the older cop, but happily for his young P1, the ER was jammed with patients who had real injuries that needed treatment. LAPD officer or not, Dan Applewhite was told that he'd have to wait an hour, maybe more, before a doctor could see him.

'How're you feeling now?' Gil asked his partner, whose lean body was twisted gingerly onto his good hip as he sat contorted.

A six-year-old Latino boy whose mother was experiencing contractions was watching Dan Applewhite. Finally he said to the wiry cop, 'Why do you sit down so funny? You look like a blue grass-hopper.'

Dan Applewhite ignored the kid but said to Gil Ponce, 'Let's get the hell outta here. But if anything happens as a result of this, I want you as witness. I'm in pain from my hip . . .'

'To your lip,' Gil said, then with his FTO glaring at him added, 'Sorry. Just trying to cheer you up. Let's get you a cup of coffee.'

Like Hollywood Nate, Doomsday Dan was one of the Starbucks cops and would rather endure severe caffeine deprivation than ever set foot in a 7-Eleven for a cuppa joe. Gil Ponce couldn't understand that, given the price of Starbucks coffee, but his field training officer was a partner who would often buy coffee for both of them, and sometimes even a meal at Hamburger Hamlet or IHOP. Generosity was one of Dan's saving graces that everyone appreciated, and it made working with him tolerable when he was in a dark mood. Gil figured that maybe it was his FTO's way of compensating.

Dan Applewhite was called Doomsday Dan by the other cops because he lived in constant anticipation of calamity, with permanent frown lines and an inverted smile on his lips. He could be assertive and fearless, but after the fact he'd lapse into a funk and imagine the horrors that might befall him for his actions. He'd reach ungloved into a resisting doper's mouth to pull out a five-gram stash of rock cocaine but later conclude that if he was lucky, he'd only contract staph from the encounter, instead of the AIDS virus. He was forty-nine years old and had one year to go before retirement, but he was morbidly convinced he'd never make it. Or if he did, the stock market would crash and bankrupt him, and there he'd be, a retired cop, begging for quarters on Hollywood Boulevard.

'I heard that Donald Trump carries a sterilizer for when he has to shake hands with lots of people,' Flotsam had said to Gil Ponce. 'If I had to work with Doomsday Dan all the time, I'd buy him one. It gets embarrassing when he's on a real downer and you go for a Fat Burger and he gloves up to spritz the table and scrub it down with paper napkins.'

Gil Ponce had hoped that a supervisor would move him to another training officer, but being a P1 with so little time left on his probation, Gil had resigned himself and felt lucky when deployment considerations put him with other partners. Despite Doomsday Dan's pathological pessimism, the older cop had taught Gil a lot, and the twenty-two-year-old boot never doubted that Doomsday Dan was dependable and instructive.

More than once the older cop had lectured Gil on ways to take advantage of his Hispanic status in the diversity conscious LAPD, especially now that the city of L.A. had a Mexican American mayor with political topspin.

'You're Hispanic,' Dan had reminded him. 'So use it when the time comes.'

'But I'm really not,' Gil Ponce finally said to his partner one evening when they were cruising the side streets in East Hollywood, looking for car prowlers. 'Let me explain.'

Gil Ponce had been named after his paternal grandfather, who had immigrated with his parents to Santa Barbara, California, from Peru. All of their children, including Gil's grandfather, had married Americans.

Gilberto Ponce III told Dan that he wished his mother, whose ancestry was a mix of Irish and Scottish, had named him Sean or Ian, but she said it would have dishonored his grandfather, whom young Gil loved as much as he loved his parents. Yet Gil had always felt like a fraud, especially now, when this FTO kept harping about the diversity promotions that a name like his could facilitate in Los Angeles, California, circa 2007.

'Having a Hispanic name is bogus,' Gil finally said that night to the senior officer.

'Read the nameplate on your uniform,' Dan Applewhite retorted. 'You're Hispanic. That means something today. Look around Hollywood Station.

Except for the midwatch, white Anglos are in the minority. Half of the current academy class is Hispanic. L.A. is on the verge of being reclaimed by Mexico.'

'Okay, look at it this way,' the probie said. 'What if my Peruvian grandpa had come from neighboring Brazil, where they have Portuguese names and don't speak Spanish? Would I still rate diversity points?'

'Don't make this too complicated just because you been to college,' Dan said. 'It's all about color and language.'

Gil said, 'I know about as much Spanish as you do, and my skin is lighter than yours and my eyes are bluer. If you wanna work out the math, I'm exactly one-fourth Peruvian, and I don't think any of that is mestizo in the first place.'

'You overanalyze,' Dan Applewhite said, wishing this college boy wouldn't debate every goddamn thing, thinking it really was time for him to retire.

Gil said, 'And if I had the same Peruvian DNA on my mother's side with no Hispanic surname attached to me, we wouldn't be having this discussion. And should Geraldo Rivera's kids rate diversity points? How about Cameron Diaz when she has kids? Or Andy Garcia? Or Charlie Sheen, for chrissake. He's as much Hispanic as I am!'

The conversation was forever ended when Doomsday Dan pulled their shop to the curb, put it in park, and, turning to face his young partner, said, 'This ain't the city of angels, it's the city of *angles,* where everybody's looking for an edge. There're hundreds of languages spoken right here in Babelwood, right? It's all about diversity and preferences and PC. So if the lottery of life gave you an edge, you're gonna accept it and be grateful. Because even though you're a nice kid with potential, I'm telling you right here and now that if you don't shut the fuck up and act like you *been* somewhere, as your FTO I'm gonna decide that you're too goddamn stupid to be a cop and maybe shouldn't even make your probation! Are you tracking?'

Then Dan Applewhite started to sneeze and had to grab his box of tissues and his nasal spray. 'See what you did,' he said, sniffling. 'You stressed me out and activated my allergies.'

When the older cop got his sneezing under control, his young partner thought things over, looked at his training officer, and said in English-accented high-school Spanish, *'Me llamo Gilberto Ponce. Hola, compañero.'*

Wiping his dripping nose, Doomsday Dan said, 'That's better. But you don't have to overdo it. You Hispanics always tend to gild the lily.'

Leonard Stilwell was a thirty-nine-year-old crackhead with a mass of wiry red hair, a face full of freckles, and large, unfocused blue eyes that would have looked believable on a barnyard bovine. He had served two relatively short terms for burglary in the Los Angeles county-jail system but had never been sentenced to state prison. The last conviction resulted from Leonard's having tossed his latex gloves into a Dumpster after successfully completing his work. The cops later found the gloves, and, after cutting off the fingertips, the crime lab had successfully treated the inside of the fingertips and got good latent prints. After that conviction, Leonard Stilwell began watching *CSI*.

The county jail was so overcrowded that nonviolent prisoners like Leonard Stilwell could usually get an early release to make room for rapists, gangbangers, and spouse killers. So Leonard had benefited from all the crime that everyone else was committing and got squeezed out of the county jail onto the streets like toothpaste from a tube. Whenever he was free, he would hurry to old companions to try talking them into an advance against his cut from the next job, then he'd go on a rock cocaine binge for a few days to smoke the miseries of county jail from his memory bank before going back to work. But that had been when he was teamed with master burglar Whitey Dawson, who'd died from a heroin overdose six months earlier, his last words being 'It don't get any better!'

Leonard Stilwell had proved reasonably adept at breaking into liquor storage rooms, which had been Whitey Dawson's specialty, and also showed some competence in refilling empty bottles of premium brands with the cheap stolen booze, then affixing a believable stamp to seal the cap. Twice he'd sold several of the doctored bottles, mixed with legitimate ones, to Ali Aziz of the Leopard Lounge, who had never caught on.

Now with Whitey Dawson gone, Leonard Stilwell was reduced to taking a job. It was the first time in fifteen years that he'd actually drawn a paycheck and he hated every minute of it. He was the only gringo at a second-rate car wash, and when the owner wasn't yelling at him, the other workers were. One of the Mexicans was an old homeboy named Chuey, who sometimes had some decent rock to sell. Chuey never carried the rock on his person and he lived in a cottage in East Hollywood, where Leonard had to drive to if he wanted the dope.

Leonard drove there just after sunset and found Chuey's door wide open. He yelled and finally entered but couldn't find Chuey anywhere. Then he walked into the backyard and found him. Horrified, Leonard ran back inside, picked up Chuey's phone, and called 9-1-1, reporting what he'd found in what he considered to be Spanish-accented English but which was almost indecipherable.

Before he left the cottage, he sublimated his horror long enough to ransack the bedroom until he found Chuey's wallet. He stole $23 from the wallet and got the hell out of there.

Their 'unknown trouble' call came a couple of hours after Dan Applewhite's allergy attack had quieted. Unknown trouble usually meant that somebody had phoned while drunk or hysterical, or sometimes in a language that was unintelligible. But it could mean anything and made cops a bit nervous and more alert.

That part of Hollywood was gang territory, but not the turf of the Salvadorans. This was where older cruisers lived, Mexican American *veteranos* of White Fence. Recent reports identified 463 street gangs in Los Angeles with 38,974 members. But how the LAPD had managed to count heads so precisely was anybody's guess.

'Bring the shotgun,' Dan said to Gil Ponce, who removed the Remington from its barrel-up bed between the seats and racked one into the chamber, topping off the magazine with an extra round.

It was a wood-frame cottage, white paint faded and peeling, the tiny yard full of weeds. A smell of salsa and frying lard was coming through the open door.

'Police!' Dan Applewhite said at the doorway. 'Did somebody call?'

No answer. He took the shotgun from Gil and used the muzzle to push the door farther open. The house was dark but there was light coming from the kitchen. Somebody had eaten at the table recently. The single bedroom was vacant and the bed was made carelessly, a worn bedspread pulled up over a single pillow. A man's clothes were draped over a chair and hanging in the closet, the meager wardrobe consisting of two pairs of khaki trousers, several white tees, and a gray sweatshirt with cutoff sleeves.

The back door was open and Gil shined his light outside into a small rear yard, where he saw a child's tricycle and a plastic wading pool, although the house interior bore no signs of a child living there. On a cheap dresser in the bedroom, he noted four pictures of a smiling Latino boy, and said, 'He's got a son living somewhere, if not here.'

The young cop walked to the back porch of the cottage and noticed that the rear gate was hanging open, facing onto an alley. Across the alley was a firetrap of an apartment building, defaced by gang graffiti, known to house Latino illegal immigrants. The proof of their occupancy was all of the bean and tomato plants in the common areas, where there was an erstwhile flower planter or a patch of earth. It wasn't very late and only a few windows showed light in that three-story building, whose westside owner had been cited for fire code violations.

Gil Ponce walked through the yard and out to the alley, and there he found the object of their call. He was hanging by what appeared to be nylon rope from a climbing spike on a telephone pole between the cottage and the house next to it. He was wearing white cotton briefs and that was all. He was shoeless and there were drizzles of feces running down his legs and over his feet. His neck was stretched a third more than normal and his face had gone from its usual olive tone to purple and black. His torso, arms, neck, and even the side of his face, were decorated with colorful body art, much of it gang tatts. A stepladder was tipped over onto the alley floor a few feet from the dangling corpse.

'Partner!' Gil yelled.

When the older cop saw the dangling corpse, he said, 'Somebody from that apartment building must've put in the call.'

Never having seen a suicide victim before, Gil said, 'Whadda we do now?'

Dan Applewhite said, 'Mostly we worry about this dude's head coming off and rolling down the alley.'

When the coroner's crew arrived, a floodlight was set up. One of the body snatchers said he'd go up the ladder to remove the noose if his partner and a cop could lift the corpse to give the rope some slack. By then several residents of the apartment building had their windows open and were gawking down at the macabre spectacle.

Gil gaped in horror at the feces-caked legs of the

dead man, and Dan Applewhite said, 'My young pard is big and way stronger than me. He'll help you.'

'I can smell him from here!' Gil cried.

'We'll wrap a sheet around him when we lift,' the body snatcher said. 'We never untie the knots. The coroner wants his knots intact. Hold your breath. It'll be all right.'

'Gross!' Gil Ponce murmured, gloving up.

By the time the stepladder was in place, and the lights and voices in the alley had caused several more illegal immigrants to pop their heads out of windows, D2 Charlie Gilford had arrived, pissed off for having to leave his TV just because some old cruiser did an air dance. One of the talent show contestants, a fat girl, had begun blubbering, and the killer panelists were pouring it on just as the phone rang.

Dan Applewhite said to the detective, 'Just an over-the-hill homie. Which means a middle-aged guy that never filed a tax return.'

Charlie gazed at the dangling man's full-torso and full-sleeve colorful gang tatts, then at young Gil Ponce walking disconsolately toward the stepladder as though to his own hanging. Finally, the detective sucked his teeth and smirked. Dan Applewhite noticed and said, 'I know what you're thinking, Charlie, but those people up there can hear you. It's obvious, so don't say it!'

But the night-watch detective was nothing if not obvious. Squinting at pale and queasy Gil Ponce, Compassionate Charlie Gilford yelled, 'Hey, kid, find me a fucking stick! *This* is what I call a *piñata*!'

FIVE

Flotsam and jetsam caught an early-evening call that they felt should have been referred to the CRO the next day. A Guatemalan woman who lived in Little Armenia complained that she couldn't drive out of her alley early in the mornings because of all the cars parked at an auto body repair business owned by a man who she thought was Armenian. She needed to get downtown to her sweatshop job in the garment district by 7:30 A.M., but the south end of the alley was often blocked. The north end had apartment buildings on both sides filled with Latino gang members, and everyone was afraid to drive or even walk in that direction.

'This is a quality-of-life issue,' Flotsam said to the mother of five, whose English was better than most.

'I do not understand,' she said.

'We got officers who deal with this kind of thing,' Flotsam said. 'They work in the Crow office.'

'Like the bird?'

'Well, yeah, same name,' Jetsam said. 'See, they warn people and then write citations if they do stuff like blocking alleys in the neighborhood.'

'I can sympathize,' Flotsam said. 'I mean, you can't

even use the alley because of thugs. Your kids have to bob and weave their way to school just to get through yellow tape.'

She understood the allusion to yellow tape. She'd seen plenty of it strung across crime scenes since migrating to Los Angeles.

'How do I call to this crow?' she asked.

'I'll tell one to call you tomorrow when you get home from work,' Flotsam said. 'You can tell them about the problem.'

When they cleared from that call, Jetsam decided to drive to the alley and have a look. The body shop was closed and there was only one security light on in the front of the building. Those at the rear were burned out or had been broken by vandals.

Jetsam pulled the car up near a chain-link fence where cars were stored, awaiting repair. He got out and shined his light around, lighting up empty oil drums, wooden crates, a Dumpster, and hopelessly damaged car tires and wheel rims.

'These fucking mini-lights!' he said. 'If I ever get chalked because I couldn't get enough light, it's gonna be the police commission and the chief who really killed me. Remember that, bro, and seek revenge.' Jetsam shined his light up at the window eight feet above the alley floor and began looking for something to stand on.

'What're you looking for anyways?' Flotsam asked, not bothering to get out of their black-and-white.

'That woman said there were lots of cars blocking the alley and I noticed that the shop didn't seem big enough to do that kind of business.'

'So?'

'So I was wondering about the rest of the businesses in this little strip. Like, the place next door has no sign on it. I was thinking the body shop might use that part of the place to work on the cars. If they use stuff like welding torches and flammable cylinders in a space that's only separated by a plasterboard wall from some dwelling units, there might be a fire ordinance that could be cited to close them down. See?'

'Lemme lock in on this shit,' Flotsam said, genuinely perplexed by his partner's behavior until the answer came to him. After a moment he said, 'I get it!'

'You get what?' Jetsam said, as he stood on a wooden box and then on top of an empty oil drum to shine his light into the window of the building next to the shop.

'This is all about Ronnie Sinclair!' Flotsam said. 'She's working Hollywood South now. You wanna run over there tomorrow and get some face time with the Crow sergeant and show how you're all obsessed about quality-of-life crap. So maybe he'll consider you next time there's an opening. And then, if dreams really do come true, you might even get to be Ronnie's partner. And she eventually might not find you as repulsive as she does now. Like, I'm on it, dude!'

Jetsam would have been really steamed by Flotsam's accurate assessment of his motives, but he was too busy being surprised by the business at hand. He said, 'Bro, climb on up here and look what's inside.'

'Don't keep me in suspense,' Flotsam said, not budging. 'Enlighten me.'

'This whole place is a wide-open storage and repair

area. There must be a couple thousand square feet of floor space in there.'

'So?'

'So I'm looking at six SUVs. New and almost new. A Beemer, a Benz, a Lexus, and, let's see, I can't tell what the others are. It's too dark.'

'Dude, this is a body shop. Did you expect these Armenians to be storing olives and goat cheese in there, or what?'

'I'm just sayin',' Jetsam mumbled, still peering in the window. Suddenly, he turned and said, 'Bro, they ain't Armos.'

'Okay, so what are they?'

'I can see a newspaper on a workbench right down below this window. I think it's in Arabic. I think they're Arabs.'

'Now I know why you don't have the word *detective* on your badge, dude. News flash: We got thousands and thousands of camel fuckers in L.A. So what?'

'I know what they're up to, bro.'

'Lemme guess. They're al Qaeda operatives?'

'They're repainting and selling hot SUVs. I'm calling the auto-theft detail tomorrow morning soon as I get up.'

'Why don't you go all radically *CSI* on me and start looking for stuff with DNA on it? I don't mind sitting here while you sleuth around. Maybe you'll find O.J.'s knife or Robert Blake's gun.'

'Do you think they really *could* be al Qaeda?' Jetsam said.

While Jetsam was annoying his partner with his sleuthing, Ali Aziz was counting the crowd at the

Leopard Lounge and ranting at his black bartenders, his white cocktail waitresses, and even his Mexican dishwashers. Ali wasn't worried about his rant upsetting his customers. All of them were men whose rapt attention was focused on a pair of topless dancers in G-strings, writhing around metal poles while music blared from a sound system that had cost Ali $75,000, even though he'd gotten a special discount from a customer who'd needed cash prior to beginning a prison sentence for fencing stolen property.

Ali Aziz had employed all manner of bartenders, both male and female: whites, Asians, Mexicans, now two black men whom he was going to fire next week, and even a man from the Middle East. They were all thieves, Ali Aziz believed. Ali's bartenders and his cocktail waitresses wore starched white shirts, black bow ties, and black trousers, but Ali always said that if bartenders served drinks completely naked with a manager watching them, they would find a way to steal from him.

Of course, Ali also thought that the U.S. government stole from him, as well as the state of California, as well as the city of Los Angeles. He fought back by keeping two sets of books for both nightclubs he owned, one with the real income, the other for IRS auditors. Whenever possible in years past, Ali had bought liquor from the addict burglar he knew as Whitey Dawson, whom he had met shortly after coming to America thirty years earlier, when Ali was twenty-two years old. He'd gotten word that Dawson had overdosed on heroin and died, and Ali was prepared to deal with Dawson's protégé, Leonard Stilwell. But soon even Leonard had stopped coming.

Of course, a prosperous businessman like Ali Aziz did not trust the late Whitey Dawson or Leonard Stilwell any more than he trusted his bartenders, and far less than he trusted his estranged wife, Margot, the thought of whom filled him with rage. Ali had always made sure that any liquor that came from thieves like Whitey Dawson was picked up by a friend or an acquaintance of one of Ali's Mexican busboys. Or by someone else not directly connected to him or to his businesses.

'You, Paco!' Ali yelled at a Mexican who was busy cleaning the table at the largest banquette.

The Mexican, whose name was Pedro, not Paco, had been employed by Ali for six months and said, 'I come, boss.'

'Where is my goddamn key? My key ain't on my desk!'

'I don' . . . I don' . . .' Pedro couldn't remember the English word for *comprendo,* his brow knitting into furrows. He kept his eyes lowered, fixed on Ali's diamond pinkie ring and on his huge gold watch as Ali shook a finger in the Mexican's face.

'Do not be so stupid!' Ali said. 'Key. *Llave.*' Then Ali muttered, 'Goddamn Mexican. I speak in Spanish. I speak in English. Goddamn stupid Mexican.'

At last Pedro understood. 'Boss!' he said. 'Joo not geev to me. Joo geev to Alfonso.'

Ali stared at Pedro for a moment, then said, 'Go back to work.'

Ali stormed back into the kitchen to scream at the sweating dishwasher, whose arms were submerged in soapy water, his head enveloped in a mist of steam.

After retrieving the key to the storage room from the apologetic Mexican, and after threatening to fire him and withhold wages for incompetence, Ali returned to the bar to check the crowd again.

He grudgingly had to admire the job that Margot had done with her interior decor. The room was first-class, and well designed to accommodate as many customers as the fire inspector allowed. Ali had balked at the price she'd paid for the wallpaper, with its wine-colored swirls bleeding into earth tones. And the wine-colored carpet she'd wanted would have cost more than the silver Rolls-Royce he'd test-driven last week, so he'd overruled her and bought chocolate-brown carpet at a discount price. Now that his business had improved and customers seemed happy with the refurbishing, he was glad he had listened to Margot. And he had to admit that the bitch had many talents. But he still wished that she were dead.

Leonard Stilwell had gotten fed up and quit his short-lived job at the car wash, and he hadn't been able to set up a sting of any kind since Whitey Dawson had died. Security had tightened everywhere and Leonard Stilwell needed rock cocaine. He was lapsing into severe depression in the rat hole of a two-room apartment he rented by the week in East Hollywood. It was what the manager called a 'studio apartment.' There was a room with a hide-a-bed that closed up against the wall so he could enter the kitchenette without walking across the bed. And the kitchenette was so small, an anorexic tweaker couldn't squeeze through it without turning sideways. To make matters worse, a biker and his biker bitch were living in the apartment next door, and they'd be outside working on their chopper at all hours, revving the engine so Leonard couldn't sleep. The dude didn't wear any biker colors or have shit logos attached to his leather jacket, but he was big, hairy, and ugly, and Leonard was scared to say anything to him. At times like this Leonard almost wished he were back in jail.

In fact, he was so desperate he decided to go out that evening and try to game some chump at the ATM in the shopping mall. There was a market there that he'd burglarized on two occasions back when Whitey Dawson was alive and not so heroin crazed. Whitey could disarm most of the alarms they'd encounter, and he was a master with lock picks. Leonard was no good at any of it but had always been available to Whitey. Now Leonard had fallen on very hard times and been forced to become resourceful.

He'd tried an ATM trap four times and each attempt had failed, but he'd learned a few things through failure. This time Leonard made sure he had strips of black film that would be undetectable when pressed against the black slot reader at an ATM. He folded over the ends of the film and attached glue strips on the folded portions. What he'd failed to do last time, he corrected by cutting slits on the film so the card didn't get kicked back out the slot by the mechanism.

It was getting close to the hour when most of the stores were closing in Hollywood, so he didn't waste time. He dressed in a clean Aloha shirt, reasonably clean jeans, and sneakers, in case he had to beat feet in a hurry. He drove his old Honda to the mall parking lot, leaving the car near enough to the ATM for a fast exit but not so close that a witness would see him jumping into it. He strolled to the ATM and pretended to be inserting a card to make a transaction. Instead he inserted the trap into the slot and pressed hard on the glue strips on the upper and lower lip of the card reader. Then he retreated and waited.

An elderly woman approached the ATM holding a child by the hand, probably the woman's grandson, by the looks of them. They appeared to be Latinos, and Leonard cursed his luck. If they were illegal aliens who didn't speak enough English to give up the PIN, it wasn't going to work. But on second thought, they were too well dressed to be illegals, and it gave him hope.

The woman inserted her card, but nothing happened. She punched in her PIN and waited. Still nothing happened. She looked at the boy, who Leonard guessed was about ten years old. Then Leonard strolled closer and heard them speaking a foreign language that wasn't Spanish.

Leonard pulled out an old ATM card he carried for this game, made sure that they saw it, and said, 'Excuse me, is there something wrong with the machine?'

The boy said, 'The card is stuck inside. It won't come out.'

'Lemme try it,' Leonard said. 'I've had this happen to me.'

The woman looked at Leonard and he gave her his biggest freckle-faced, blue-eyed, reassuring smile. She said something to the boy in that strange language and the boy answered her.

Up close, while he was trying to sell Leonard Stilwell to them, she didn't look so old, maybe the same age as his mother, who would be fifty-eight if she were alive. And up close this woman looked smart. And wary.

'Where're you from?' Leonard asked the boy.

'My grandmother is Persian,' the boy said. 'I am American.'

He should've known. They were all over Iran-geles. And he'd never met a poor one, so he was feeling pretty stoked when he said, 'See, I know what to do to get your card back. You punch in your PIN number at the same time that I press "cancel" and "enter." Then the card should just pop out.'

The boy spoke again to the woman, and she reluctantly moved aside for Leonard, who stepped up and put his fingers on the 'cancel' and 'enter' keys. She looked at him and he smiled again, trying not to swallow his spit. When he did that, his oversized Adam's apple bobbed, a sure sign of nerves.

'We have to time this right,' he said to the boy. 'Tell her she has to put in her PIN number now.'

Instead, it was the boy who moved next to Leonard. He said, 'I can do it. I'm ready.'

'Go,' Leonard said, and he watched the boy punch the five digits as Leonard pressed the 'cancel' and 'enter' keys.

And then Leonard stepped back, scratched his head theatrically, making dandruff flakes appear on his bird's nest of rusty red hair, and said, 'I'm sorry, it's always worked before. Can't help you, I guess.'

Leonard shrugged at the woman and, lifting his hands palms up, turned and walked toward the parked cars, where he crouched behind the first row and watched them. The woman and boy conversed for a moment and then went inside the store while Leonard sprinted to the ATM machine, carefully lifted the folded tips of the film, gently pulled, and captured the ATM card. Then he punched in the PIN, took a chance on asking for $300, the maximum daily withdrawal allowed by the bank whose name was on the card, and jackpot!

Fifteen minutes later, Leonard Stilwell was parking in the pay lot closest to Grauman's Chinese Theatre on Hollywood Boulevard, not even pissed off by the exorbitant parking fee because he had three bills in his kick. He was looking for Bugs Bunny, not the tall Bugs Bunny who often showed up on Friday night, but the short Bugs Bunny who always kept a stash of rocks inside his bunny head as he hopped around in his rabbit suit with a big foam-rubber carrot in his paw, saying, 'What's up, Doc?' to every tourist with a camera who got within ten yards of him.

The Street Characters were always out in numbers on soft summer nights like this one. He saw Superman, Batman, Porky Pig, and Spider-Man, one of several, in his predatory pose with one knee raised, looking more like a bird than a spider. Summer nights like this, when the smog conditions created a low sky, cutting heaven down to size, made people feel that paradise could be found right here on Hollywood Boulevard. They made this a magical place for anyone with hopes and dreams.

Leonard Stilwell, who knew something about Hollywood magic, watched an intent tourist with a purse dangling from a strap over her shoulder snap a photo of her husband, who was posing with Cat-woman. This, while a lean and nimble teenage boy expertly opened her purse and removed her wallet, disappearing into the crowd before she'd even asked Catwoman to pose for one more.

When it was time to pay the Amazon for the photo, the woman said, 'Oh, Mel! Melvin! My wallet's gone!'

Leonard hoped he'd never have to resort to the risky trade of purse and pocket picking, and as he sidled through the throng he heard Catwoman say, 'I hope you don't think I dress up and pose for free, Melvin. Nobody got *your* wallet, did they?'

When Leonard saw the Hulk, he was hopeful. He knew that the Hulk was a pal of Bugs Bunny because he once saw them leave together in the same car. But the Hulk was very busy at the moment with no less than six Asian tourists lining up to take photos with him. Ditto for Mr. Incredible, Elmo, and even Count Dracula, whose blood-dripping leer was too scary for photos with little kids.

Then Leonard spotted him. Bugs Bunny was doing a double shoot with the Wolf Man, both of them sandwiching an obese, fifty-something woman wearing a sequined 'I Love Hollywood' baseball cap, her chubby hands caressing the heads of both Street Characters.

When Bugs had collected his tip from the woman, Leonard approached him and whispered in a two-foot ear, 'I need some rock.'

'How much you got?' Bugs said.

'I can spend two bills. You good with that?'

'Good as gold, dude. I got some rock, and some

ice-that's-nice if you wanna do crystal. Wait one minute and follow me into the Kodak Center. I gotta take care of Pluto, then you.'

When Leonard looked back on that moment later in the evening, he thought it must have been his sixth sense as a burglar that saved him. All those years watching, waiting, studying people. Asking himself things like, Is that greaser looking at me the way one of the 18th Street crew would look at me? Or the way an undercover cop would look at me? Or, why is that nigger hooker working this corner tonight, when I never saw her or any hooker here before? Did that fucking little junkie from Pablo's Tacos tell the cops that I'd be taking off his boss's store tonight with the alarm code he gave me? Is that sneaky whore really a cop, or what?

Leonard did not like the look of the fat tourist in a new white tee with the Hollywood sign emblazoned across the front and back. Leonard didn't like his L.A. Dodgers baseball cap either. It was too well worn to belong to an out-of-towner. The bottom-heavy guy looked like he was trying too hard to appear touristy, and he wasn't quite fat enough for Leonard to say he couldn't be a cop.

Leonard stayed far back and was one hundred feet away when he spotted Bugs Bunny and Mickey Mouse's dog Pluto, their huge heads under their arms, standing outside a restroom. He saw the buy go down. And he saw the fat guy take off his Dodgers cap. And Leonard knew that was a signal, for sure.

The fat guy ran straight at them, and three other undercover cops came at them from other directions.

Bugs Bunny tried to dump the meth from his head by tipping it upside down. Pluto took the rock cocaine he'd bought and threw it backward across the floor.

The fat guy pulled a pistol from under his tee and yelled, 'Police! Drop your heads and raise your paws!'

So far, Ronnie Sinclair and Bix Ramstead had experienced an uneventful ten hours. In furtherance of their quality-of-life mission, they'd been involved in crackdowns on some of the nightclubs on Sunset and Hollywood Boulevards that were generating numerous complaints from other businesses and residents in the area. Nightclub customers parked wherever they found curb space, ignoring the color of curbs or whether portions of their cars might extend into the driveways of residential property. The nightclub patrons, especially those who frequented the topless clubs where booze was sold, also urinated and vomited on sidewalks and in planted areas and threw trash anywhere that was handy.

Those who preferred all-nude dancers would emerge with more sobriety, since ordinances prohibited booze to be served in those clubs, but the more enterprising customers found ways to flavor their soft drinks and setups with secreted containers of liquor. Some of the customers went so far as to make frequent trips to the restroom, where they'd withdraw plastic bottles of spirits from under their clothing and fill their mouths before returning to their tables, then spit it into their half-empty soft drinks. Bolder ones just poured it under the table into the setups. Still others just forgot about booze and ingested or snorted other drugs, which did the trick well enough.

The vice unit would work these clubs and cite or arrest for all sorts of violations, from prostitution to alcoholic beverage violations, but Ronnie and Bix were attending to the needs of the neighbors. In the short time she'd been a Crow, Ronnie was already getting to know the roster of chronic complainers by name. One of these was Mrs. Vronsky, who owned a twenty-nine-unit apartment building near the Leopard Lounge, one of the clubs that used the word *class* in all of its commercials.

'Officer Ramstead, thank you for being so prompt,' the old woman said in slightly accented English when they found her standing in front of her building. She was in her mideighties, short, still full figured, her white hair coiffed, and she wore slacks with a matching jacket that Ronnie thought would exceed her own budget.

'Of course, Mrs. Vronsky,' Bix said. 'I'd like you to meet one of our new community relations officers. This is Officer Sinclair.'

'Very nice to meet you, dear,' Mrs. Vronsky said, then turned to Bix. 'I have asked that man Mr. Aziz a thousand times to tell his employees not to park in our spaces here, but when they see a parking space open, they grab it. And then my tenants come home at midnight after getting off the swing shift, and what happens?'

'You have to call Hollywood Station to have them cited or towed,' Bix said sympathetically. 'I do understand, Mrs. Vronsky.'

'I've been patient, Officer Ramstead,' she said, her pale eyes watery. 'But the man ignores my calls.'

'We'll just have to keep citing and towing, won't we?'

Bix said, patting the old woman gently on the shoulder. 'But for now we'll go have a talk with him.'

'Thank you, Officer Ramstead,' she said. 'The next time I see you I shall have some of my homemade piroshki. Just the way you like it.'

'Oh, thank you, Mrs. Vronsky,' Bix said. 'Officer Sinclair is in for a treat.'

When they were walking toward the front door of the Leopard Lounge, Ronnie said, 'The look that old lady was giving you said, If only I were forty years younger. As it is, she'd gum you to death given half a chance.'

Bix smiled and said, 'It's just as easy to be patient with them. Last year she donated a thousand dollars to the L.A. Police Memorial fund along with a thank-you to "that nice Officer Ramstead at Hollywood Station." The boss gave me an attaboy for that. Wait'll you meet Mrs. Ortega. She's Puerto Rican and always makes me sit down and eat some baked fish and rice. And she never fails to suck the eyeballs out of the fish head.'

'Yikes!' Ronnie said, then followed Bix through the darkened doorway into the nightclub, finding the Leopard Lounge to be more posh than she'd imagined.

A burly Latino bouncer nodded at the uniformed cops and stepped aside when they entered. There were three bartenders pouring drinks with both hands, and a busboy was running trays of dirty glasses through swinging doors into the kitchen. The place was dark, but light enough that all customers and their tableside activities could be monitored by undercover cops as well as by the bouncer. The banquettes looked comfortable and the tabletops were clean, thanks to Latino busboys in white shirts and bow ties, working hard.

Ronnie was surprised by how pretty the cocktail waitresses were, and the two girls dancing onstage were knockouts. One of them looked to be part Asian and part white, her glossy hair hanging down nearly to her G-string as she gyrated under strobe lights.

A busty cocktail waitress walked toward the cops, smiled, and said, 'Table for two, Officers?'

'I gotta warn you, I don't like tropical toys in my mai tais,' Bix said, smiling back at her. 'Is the boss around?'

'He's in his office. Just a minute, I'll tell him you're here.'

She was gone for a moment, returned, and said, 'You can go in.'

Ronnie noticed the cocktail waitress giving Bix the big eye when they squeezed past her in the narrow corridor leading to the office, but he didn't seem to notice. Ronnie had decided by now that Bix was the elusive Monogamous Male Cop, a creature she thought was extinct, if it had ever existed in the first place.

Ali Aziz was sitting at his desk, which was covered with file folders, bills, and photos of prospective dancers, most of them topless. He was yelling in Arabic at someone on the phone. When he looked up at them, he forced a polite smile and motioned them to the two client chairs.

Ronnie thought the office was very nice, not at all what she'd expected. The wall coverings were subtle, mostly pale colors that complemented the earth tones in the carpeting, and drapes that concealed the single small window facing the alley. The only bling was on the person of Ali Aziz himself, who wore a creamy silk blazer with a monogrammed pocket, a black shirt and matching black trousers, a gold Rolex, and pinkie rings on both hands. He was middle-aged, balding, swarthy, and wasn't likely to get invited to the Jonathan Club downtown, she thought. But he'd fit in okay on the Nightclub Committee of the Community Police Advisory Board.

When Ali Aziz hung up the phone, he stood and reached across the desk to shake hands with both cops. He was several inches shorter than Bix and looked up with all of the cordiality he could muster, saying, 'Welcome, Officers. I hope there is nothing wrong? We are friends of Hollywood Station. I am knowing your captain well, and each year I give from my heart to the Children's Holiday Party and the Tip-A Cop fund-raiser.'

'It's the same complaint, Mr. Aziz,' Bix said.

'Parking?' With his accent he pronounced it *barking*.

'Yes, parking.'

'Fucking Mexicans!' Ali Aziz said, then looked at Ronnie and said, 'Sorry. I am sorry, Officer. I have so much anger with my Mexicans. I shall fire them. They do that illegal parking. I am sorry for my rude mouth.'

Ronnie shrugged and Bix said, 'We wouldn't like to get anybody fired. We just want your employees to stay out of the parking places belonging to the apartment building across the street. Even though the spots look empty, people who work late hours come home to find your employees' cars in their spaces.'

'Yes, yes,' Ali said. 'The old Russian lady, she is right. She calls me all the time. I have police coming here all the time. I do not mind. I wish for my customers to see the police here. They know this is a respectable club. But I am sorry for you to waste your time. I shall fix this problem. I am going to send flowers to the old Russian lady. Do you need money for anything? I shall give you some cash for the – how you call it? – Pals Program.' He turned the *p* into a *b* again.

'No cash,' Bix said, standing up. 'If you like, you can make a donation by check to the Police Activity League.'

'I shall do that tomorrow, God willing,' Ali said, standing to shake hands.

Ronnie was looking at the framed photos on a shelf over a big-screen TV. Three were studio shots of a beautiful boy, one taken when he was about two and another when he looked to be about five years old, wearing a suit, white shirt, and necktie in both photos. The third studio photo was of the boy posing next to his mother, he wearing a blazer and tie, she a basic black, V-neck dress with only a string of pearls hanging at her throat. She was a striking beauty, with hair the color of, what? Golden chestnut, maybe, full and heavy hair that any woman would die for.

Ronnie carefully touched the frame and said, 'Your family is very beautiful.'

'My little son,' Ali said, smiling genuinely for the first time. 'My heart. My life. My little Nicky.'

'Your wife should be in movies,' Ronnie said. 'Don't you think, Bix?'

'Uh-huh,' Bix said, hardly glancing at the photo.

Ali's smile turned sour then and he said, 'We are in a divorce battle.'

'Oh, sorry,' Ronnie said.

'No problem,' Ali said. 'I shall obtain my son from her. I have the best divorce lawyer in all Los Angeles.'

They said their good-byes, and when they left the nightclub, Bix said, 'So what's your opinion of Ali Aziz?'

'I wouldn't wanna work for him,' she said.

'Butter wouldn't melt in his mouth when he's talking to cops,' Bix said.

'Please,' Ronnie said, 'make that nonfat yogurt.'

As they were getting in their car to go end-of-watch, she said, 'He won't be a problem for long. That dude's so golded up, he'll probably drown in his pool someday if he goes in the deep end.'

And that's how their uneventful watch would have ended if they had not driven to the station by way of Sunset Boulevard. Traffic was only moderate that evening, but Sunset was blocked at Vine Street by a confusing flare pattern that a motorist had placed. They saw a black-andwhite that had been speeding north on Vine Street come screeching to a stop at the intersection. Bix turned on the light bar and drove west in the eastbound lane, turning south on Vine, and there it was: a major traffic collision.

'The TC must've just happened,' Ronnie said, as two cops from Watch 3 were running from their shop to a flattened old Chevy Caprice that had rolled more than once after having been slammed broadside by a two-ton flatbed truck that had blown the traffic light while racing southbound, driven by a teenage driver with a cell phone glued to his ear. The kid was bleeding from facial lacerations and was leaning against a door that was folded like a wallet from the force of the collision.

Bix leaped out and ran to the old car, Ronnie following. And one of the young Watch 3 cops yelled to them, 'Two RA's on the way! There's a woman and kid in there! They're bleeding bad and we can't get them out!'

The other cop, a bigger man, was kicking at the jammed rear door of the Caprice where they saw a child's head inside, gashed open from the crown to the forehead, blood running across her face from deep channels that had been opened to the bone.

'God!' Ronnie said. 'God almighty!'

And she began kicking the door also, after the big cop stopped and drew his baton. He tried using it as a pry, trying to muscle open the door while yelling to his partner, 'Get me a tire wrench! Anything to pry with!'

Bix could see through the shattered glass that the Asian woman behind the wheel was dead. Her chest had been crushed by the steering column and she stared lifelessly at the black sky through what was left of the roof.

Ambulance sirens were getting closer and Bix heard several voices shouting, and then he saw something move. He shined his light inside and realized that another child had been in the backseat of the car.

'There's another kid in there!' he yelled, just as the

big cop succeeded in prying the rear door open, and Ronnie saw clearly that the little girl's shattered skull was attached to her neck only by a few shredded knots of red, slimy tissue.

'God almighty!' she repeated and ran around the car to Bix and the other child he had found, hoping that this one was alive.

Bix, his mini-flashlight on the asphalt, was down on his knees, crawling under the car, trying to lift the portion of wreckage that had the child pinned. Ronnie could hear him grunting and saw him lifting with his back, and when she shined her light under the car, she lit the face of a four-year-old girl who turned out to be the second daughter of young Cambodian immigrants who had been in Hollywood for nearly five years.

The child's body was twisted and bloody, but her face and head were unmarked. She had a delicate, very pale beauty, and Ronnie crawled under the wreckage to help Bix try to lift the twisted metal.

It was then that the thing happened, the thing that Ronnie knew she'd remember for the rest of her career. Perhaps for the rest of her days. The little girl opened her eyes and looked directly into the straining face of Bix Ramstead, who had at last raised the chunk of wreckage high enough for Ronnie to pull her free.

Just before Ronnie grabbed her, the child said to Bix, 'Are you my angel?'

Controlling his labored breathing, Bix managed to say, 'Yes, darling, I am your angel.'

When they got back to Hollywood Station, Bix changed out of his uniform much faster than Ronnie did. When she left the women's locker room she saw him sprinting across the parking lot to his minivan, and she was pretty sure she knew where he was going.

After Ronnie arrived at work the next morning, she learned that the child had survived the ambulance ride to Hollywood Presbyterian Medical Center but died in the ER moments before her angel came running to her side.

SIX

ONCE A MONTH every patrol division of the LAPD was required to hold a CPAB meeting, pronounced *see-pab*, for Community Police Advisory Board. Hollywood Division held its CPAB meeting on the last Tuesday, the idea being to bring together community leaders, neighborhood-watch captains, the City Attorney's Office, the Department of Transportation, the L.A. Fire Department, and others, all to discuss crime and quality-of-life issues in the respective police divisions. The meeting was run by the division captain along with the CPAB president, whoever that might be.

The problems began almost immediately for the Hollywood Division CRO because, according to unofficial reports to the office of the chief of police, Hollywood was not like anywhere else. In fact, the unofficial report referred to Hollywood as 'America's kook capital.' Because it was a community meeting, residents of Hollywood could not be segregated or excluded due to irrational behavior, unless the behavior turned dangerous. Many of the same people showed up regularly at the meetings for free coffee and donuts. And, more often than not, havoc ensued.

Special arrangements had to be made to

accommodate the Hollywood Division CPAB meetings, and it was decided that a second meeting would be held the day after the official CPAB meeting. The names and addresses of the more peculiar and troublesome residents were culled from sign-in sheets at the CPAB meetings, and letters were sent telling them that their meetings would now be held on the last Wednesday of the month. The Wednesday gathering was officially renamed the 'Hollywood Community Meeting.' But the cops unofficially referred to it as the 'Cuckoo's Nest.'

Crows would say to one another, 'Are you going to CPAB or Cuckoo's Nest?'

The Cuckoo's Nest meeting was not run by the captain or any member of the command staff. Sometimes even the CRO sergeant wasn't in charge, preferring to leave it to one of the senior lead officers. The Crow would try to arrange for interesting guest speakers, such as a narcotics detective or a gang officer or a vice cop. In order to entice speakers, the Crow told them that this was a very low-key community meeting that the speakers would find enjoyable. Once the speakers discovered the truth, they never came back.

Ronnie Sinclair was tasked to assist at her first Cuckoo's Nest meeting the day after Jetsam became convinced that he might have stumbled onto an al Qaeda cell operating in Hollywood. Jetsam had phoned the auto theft team the moment he woke up that morning, but they were in court or otherwise occupied and away from the station. When one of them finally returned his call, the detective, whom Jetsam didn't know personally, was less than enthusiastic.

After hearing Jetsam's terrorist theory based upon

spotting one Arabic newspaper at a body shop that worked on expensive SUVs, the detective said to him, 'Do you know Arabic from Farsi?'

'Well, no,' Jetsam had to admit.

'The newspaper could have been left there by an Iranian,' the detective suggested.

'All the more reason to check it out,' Jetsam said. 'Remember the case last year where LAPD and the FBI popped those Chechens who had a racket where they got people to report expensive cars stolen and collect insurance payoffs? And then the cars were smuggled in big shipping containers to their country to help Muslim terrorists? Remember that one? Well, these SUVs were too newish and expensive to be worked on in a repair joint in East Hollywood.'

The detective was silent for a moment and then said, 'Are you saying you think these people are Chechen terrorists?'

'No, but maybe they're copycats pulling the same scam, and they're gonna smuggle hot SUVs to places like . . .'

'Baghdad?'

'Or like . . .'

'Tehran?'

'Aw, shit,' Jetsam said.

'You have my blessing if you wanna check it out yourself,' the detective said. 'But you catch 'em, you clean 'em. Right now I'm due in court, so I gotta run.'

After hanging up, Jetsam said to the phone, 'And we thank you for your call. Fuck you very much.'

Detective indifference and condescension is what brought Jetsam and his reluctant partner to the

Cuckoo's Nest meeting on Wednesday night. Of course it was a bonus for Ronnie Sinclair to observe a meeting conducted by an experienced Crow. The sergeant told Ronnie that Tony Silva would be a good one to emulate because he was patient and had a calming effect on most of the regulars if things turned violent.

'Violent?' Ronnie said in astonishment, but her sergeant only shrugged and walked away. She thought he must be kidding.

Twenty minutes before the Cuckoo's Nest was to start, Ronnie was surprised to see Jetsam enter the meeting room and wave her outside.

'What's up?' she said, walking with him to the black-and-white, where Flotsam sat behind the wheel.

Flotsam looked out at her and said, 'Don't blame me for this, Ronnie. Watch five only has three cars in the field tonight and he's got me beached. If Treakle finds out, he'll have us castrated.'

'I got something for a Crow to check out, Ronnie,' Jetsam said, giving her a piece of notebook paper with the address of the auto body shop and the address and phone number of the Guatemalan woman who phoned about their cars blocking the alley.

'What's all this?' she said.

'It's a quality-of-life deal,' Jetsam said. 'And it's an opportunity for you to go to this body shop and maybe, just maybe, end up with something pretty big.'

'It's Osama bin Laden,' Flotsam said. 'My pard thinks he's there, pounding out dents on Beemers and Benzes.'

'Dude, can you stop hacking on me for two minutes?' Jetsam said to his partner. 'You're spiking me like you spiked those barneys at Malibu this morning.'

Ronnie, who knew that Flotsam and Jetsam surfed almost every day before going on duty, said, 'Spiking? Barneys?'

Flotsam said, 'He thinks I shouldn't do surfboard self-defense on four squids that flipped us off and stole my juicies when I was rippin'. They thought it was cooleo till one of them caught my log upside his head when I snaked him on the next wave.'

'What?' Ronnie said.

'All I said was,' Jetsam said to Flotsam, 'you should cap the little surf Nazi if you wanna turn him into part of the food chain. Not torpedo him till he's almost dead in the foamy.'

'There's just too damn many languages spoken in this town,' Ronnie said rhetorically. 'Did you bring me out here for today's surfing highlights, or what? I got a meeting inside.'

'Take a few minutes tonight or tomorrow night,' Jetsam said quickly. 'Phone the woman about the Arabs at the repair shop. They got the joint vacuum-packed with some slammin' SUVs. I think they gotta be hot. You could warn them about blocking the alley and maybe take down some license and VIN numbers.'

'I'm not a detective,' Ronnie said. 'Call the auto theft detail.'

'Been there,' Jetsam said. 'They're about as lazy as Compassionate Charlie Gilford. A blocked alley affects everybody in the apartment house. I need a quality-of-life cop to get this thing kick-started.'

'That's not my area,' Ronnie said.

'You're the only Crow I know real well,' Jetsam said, 'except for Hollywood Nate. This is a job for a real cop. They couldn't have morphed you into a teddy bear already. If you want, we could meet you tomorrow at the body shop as backup, say around sixteen hundred hours? Right before they close.'

'*You* can meet her,' Flotsam said to his partner. 'I go on duty at seventeen-fifteen.'

'Dude . . .' Jetsam said in exasperation to his partner.

'This one ain't on my desktop,' Flotsam explained to Ronnie. 'Him and me, we're close, but we ain't Velcro close. I ain't down for this one.'

'Okay, okay!' Ronnie said, relenting. 'I'll give her a call later tonight and maybe I can stop by the body shop tomorrow afternoon. If I can, I'll give you a call on your cell. Will you be hanging ten at Malibu or remaining on dry land?'

'I'll be home,' Jetsam said. 'And ready to jam.'

After Ronnie went back inside, Flotsam said, 'You know you wouldn't be doing any of this if Ronnie was a yuckbabe instead of totally mint. Get over yourself, dude. She ain't never gonna be your fuck puppet.'

'This might be too much for you to download, bro,' Jetsam said, 'but this ain't about hose cookies. This is about what the Oracle always said to us: Doing good police work is the most fun we'll ever have in our entire lives. I know there's something going down in that repair shop. And whadda you got to do tomorrow except crawl along the sand and sniff around some salty sister whose whole life is smoking blunts and chugging coolers?'

Flotsam thought it over and said, 'Okay, dude, you're totally frenzied. I guess we better stop there on the way to work. Just to get it outta your system.'

'You're down?' Jetsam said.

'I'm down,' Flotsam said, with no more enthusiasm than Jetsam had heard from the auto theft detective or from Ronnie Sinclair.

After they were back cruising their beat, Jetsam said dreamily, 'Dude, ain't there something about Ronnie that's like . . . like being all flattened in dead water, and, like, here comes a beautiful peel breaking so clean from the top? And next thing, you're flying down the lane smelling that Sex Wax, and you get the blood surge? Know what I'm saying, bro?'

'You could LoJack that chick and still not park her in your crib,' Flotsam said. 'Look for a date on MySpace. She's too tall for you.'

'We're about the same height.'

'She puts on sky-high stilettos, then what? You'll look like Sonny and Cher.'

'But she's, like, smokin' hot,' Jetsam said. 'I bet that girl and me could put some antic in romantic! I'll bet she could make me harder than Gramma's biscuits!'

'You two would look like Tom Cruise and every babe he marries,' Flotsam said drily.

Officer Tony Silva got the meeting off to a good start with his soothing and reassuring manner. He'd instructed Ronnie to maintain a 'calm and professional smile,' no matter what happened. But he was getting close to the hazardous part of the meeting, when questions from the floor were permitted.

One of the eldest of the regulars, who couldn't get to the bathroom fast enough at the prior meeting, was responsible for a rules change. Tony Silva's Crow assistant, Officer Rita Kravitz, whose trendy eyeglasses said 'I am smarter than you,' was asked by Tony Silva to help with the cleanup last time, but she said to him, 'Instead of you sitting up there popping bubble wrap while you look calm and professional, go find yourself a goddamn mop!'

Cuckoo's Nest Rule 1 was enacted: 'No punch is to be served at Wednesday meetings.'

Ronnie was warned about 'Deputy Dom,' always the first to arrive and the last to leave. He was in his sixties, with a fringe of gray hair, and always wore an odorous, food-stained security guard uniform.

'Dom was absent for the first time last week,' Tony Silva told Ronnie. 'He was in jail, but the City Attorney's Office decided not to prosecute. He tried to pepper spray an entire Laotian family: father, mother, four kids, and a grandma. He said none of them were carrying passports, and that made them security risks.'

Ronnie learned that the cross-eyed guy in a bowling shirt with 'Regent Electrical Supply' across the back and 'Henry' over the front pocket was the one they'd dubbed 'Henry Tourette.' He was an unintentional disrupter, because he'd yell out 'Fucking-A-Bertha!' to every single statement offered by anyone. It was worrisome in that it provoked angry retorts from other borderline personalities.

Unfortunately, there wasn't much that the Crows could do about any of it, not in the land of diversity, where all behavior that was not overtly criminal must be understood and respected. Where people were *never* to be considered 'sick,' but only 'different.'

The sole 'weapon' that the Crows found somewhat

effective was the Community Service Completion Certificate. The CRO sergeant first encountered it when a young man who had attended meetings for three months without ever uttering a peep approached the sergeant and presented him with a folded document, saying it was given to him by a motorcycle officer.

'The officer wrote me a jaywalking ticket on Hollywood Boulevard,' the young man explained. 'My mother paid the ticket, and then the officer stopped me again a week later in the same place.'

'For jaywalking?' the sergeant asked.

'Yes, but this time I told him about the voices.'

'What voices?'

'The ones that tell me when to cross the street.'

'What did the motor officer say about that?'

'He said, "Why don't the voices ever tell you to cross on a *green* light?"'

'That sounds like Officer F.X. Mulroney,' the sergeant said. 'Did he write you another ticket?'

'No, he gave me this certificate and told me that I would have to attend every Wednesday night Hollywood Community Meeting for ninety days, and to stay away from Hollywood Boulevard. And if I did it, you'd sign my certificate.'

Thus, a tradition was started. The CRO sergeant signed the 'certificate' and announced to the entire assembly that the young man had completed three months' community service for jaywalking, and the other members at the meeting gave him a standing ovation.

Things started well at Ronnie's first meeting. Everyone seemed calm, even bored. They ate copious amounts of donuts, and Ronnie later wondered if elevated blood sugar had something to do with what happened later. Things started going sideways when one of the home owners, a meticulously groomed gentleman with a dyed transplant, stood and said, 'I'd like something done about the gay men who park in front of my house after the bars close and commit sex acts.'

One of the trannies, the best-dressed person at the meeting, said, 'If they're on the street, it's public property. Are you jealous?'

'Yeah,' said a woman wearing a lip ring, an eyebrow spike, and a tongue stud. The face jewelry seemed peculiar in that she was seventy-five years old if she was a day. 'Just stay in your house, and that way you won't know there's people blowing each other in this world.'

'Fucking-A-Bertha!' Henry yelled.

That set off the one they called 'Rodney the Racist,' a fiftyish Nazi wannabe, whose shaved skull was decorated with a backward swastika that he'd created with a mirror and Magic Marker.

Rodney raised his hand, and when Tony Silva acknowledged him, he stood and said, 'It's all these goddamn illegal aliens causing the problems.'

A burly senior citizen who resided in Little Armenia and was said to have made a few bucks before alcoholism rotted his brain stood and said, 'Immigrants make America great!'

The play Nazi said, 'What're you, an illegal alien?'

'I come to this country legal, you son of bastard!' the Armenian yelled.

'Yeah, through a drainpipe at the Tia-juana border!' a homeless transient yelled back.

'Order, please!' Tony Silva said from the front of the room. 'Please, folks! Let's stay on point and take turns!'

'He is Nazi and he eat shit!' the Armenian yelled.

'Spoken like a goddamn illegal Mexican!' the play Nazi shot back. 'Get a green card!'

'I am not Mexican!' the Armenian hollered, pointing to Officer Tony Silva. 'He is Mexican! I dare you call Officer Silva filthy names, you pig-shit Nazi.'

Widening his smile to no avail, Tony Silva said, 'Actually, my family is from Puerto Rico.'

A stick-thin woman looking slightly Goth with a hedge-clipper do turned and said to Ronnie, 'My little love dumpling claims my hemorrhoids look like Puerto Rico. Or is it Cuba?'

Tony Silva tried levity then. Sweat beads popping, he stood and said, 'To quote the ex-convict philosopher and celebrity thug Rodney King, can't we all get along? Can't we just get—'

He didn't get a chance to finish. The Armenian geezer made as though to attack the play Nazi but was easily restrained by Bix Ramstead, who'd been sitting quietly in the back row. That officially ended the Wednesday night meeting, and the distracted cops never saw the homeless transients stealing all of the remaining donuts, stuffing them under their grimy layers of clothing.

After locking up, Ronnie and Officer Tony Silva were standing in the shadows of the parking lot when she said to him, 'Tony, those people weren't just sitting there spouting designer slogans and trendy complaints. That was truly a cuckoo's nest. Some of those people are seriously crazy!'

'Crazier than Kelly's cat,' Tony Silva responded with his calm professional smile frozen in place.

'Fucking-A-Bertha!' a voice yelled from the darkness.

Meanwhile, some unusual police action was about to take place on Hollywood Boulevard, and Leonard Stilwell was present to witness it. He had placed himself directly in front of the Chinese Theatre because there were more tourists than usual meandering around the theater forecourt on this warm evening, looking at the movie star handprints in cement. If desperation was forcing him to try his hand as a purse pick, this seemed like the place to do it.

Of course, Leonard was streetwise enough to have spotted a few hooks waiting by the entrance to the subway station, young black guys ready to hook up customers to partners holding crack or crystal. The hooks liked the subway for quick retreat back to South L.A., where they resided. When the foot-beat cops or the bike patrol appeared, the hooks would vanish.

Leonard was hoping to see that skinny kid who had lifted the wallet from the tourist's purse while she was snapping pictures. The kid had moves, and if Leonard spotted him, he was going to offer him $20 just to give Leonard some tips. Leonard smoked half a dozen cigarettes while he watched and waited, feeling his palms dampen whenever he spotted a likely purse dangling from the arm or shoulder of a preoccupied tourist. He figured they were all wise to the jostling gag and would reach for their purses if someone bumped into them. That was the thing about the kid. He didn't touch her. He just drifted in like a ghost and was gone, leaving the purse hanging open and the wallet missing.

What Leonard failed to see was the start of an incident that did not make the *L.A. Times* but did rate a column in one of the underground sheets beneath a provocative headline and a story yammering about 'warrior cops.' The warrior cop in question was Officer Gert Von Braun, but it all got started by a sharp-eyed rookie.

Probationer Gil Ponce was teamed with Cat Song in 6-X-32 because Dan Applewhite was on days off. Gil was ecstatic to get away from his moody field training officer, and being teamed with someone as cool as Cat Song was definitely a bonus.

When Gil had occasion to work with a P3 or even a P2 whom he didn't know personally, he'd always address them as 'sir' or 'ma'am.' He still had a few weeks to go on his probation and he wasn't going to risk any negative comments from anyone.

When he got to their shop after roll call, she said, 'I'm driving, you're booking, okay?'

'Yes, ma'am,' he said to Cat.

'How old're you?' she asked after they were in their car.

'Twenty-three,' he said. 'Almost.'

'I'm thirty-three,' she said. 'Almost. But if you call me "ma'am," I'll get feeling so matronly I'll have to kill you and blame it on hormonal hysteria. My name's Cat.'

'Okay, Cat,' Gil said.

When she wrote his name in the log, she said, 'If we need it, can you translate Spanish, Gil?'

'No, sorry. My name's Hispanic but . . .'

'No need to apologize,' Cat said, raising a slender hand with manicured nails the same color as her lipstick. 'Somebody's always calling on me to translate Korean and all I can say is *kimchi* because I grew up eating the stuff.'

Later in the evening Gil Ponce was starting to mentally play How much would I give to trade Dan Applewhite for Cat Song? when they got the call to meet the foot-beat team at Hollywood and Highland.

It wasn't much. The foot beat had a plain drunk in tow and they needed a team to transport him to jail. He was a transient who'd been begging for change in the Kodak Center and apparently had been very successful.

'He's annihilated,' the older cop said to Gil, who wasn't sure if he should glove up or not. He knew that some of the older cops scoffed when the young ones drew on the latex gloves, but there had been roll call training about the prevalence of staph, along with some grisly photos of cops who'd picked up horrible lesions on their hands and arms and even their legs.

There was plenty of light from street lamps and headlights, and plenty of neon there on Hollywood Boulevard, but Gil shined his flashlight beam on the guy. He saw that the transient had a long string of snot dangling from one nostril and his cotton trousers were urine soaked. So Gil put on the gloves, glad to see that Cat did the same. Just before he took control of the reeling drunk, the guy started moaning, leaned forward, and vomited.

All four cops leaped back a few paces and Gil said, 'He's chunking all over his shoes! Oh, gross!'

It was this part of police work – the smell of the hanging body leaking feces or a drunk reeking from urine and vomit – that Gil Ponce feared he might never learn to accommodate. The blood and hideous trauma of every kind he could handle, but not the odors. And just as he was about to lead the drunk at arm's length to their shop, he was saved. He looked at the mob of tourists half a block away on the Walk of Fame and spotted a young guy with shoulder-length dark hair, a red tee, baggy jeans, and flip-flops, walking fast, a brown leather purse tucked under his arm.

'Hey!' Gil said. 'Look! A purse snatcher!'

Gil instantly started running south, and when the guy, who'd been glancing behind himself, turned and saw a strapping young cop sprinting his way, he wheeled and ran across Hollywood Boulevard, nearly getting creamed by an MTA bus. Four Street Characters in full costume began shouting encouragement when Gil had to stop for the fast-moving, westbound traffic.

An older woman, obviously the victim, was standing next to the Characters, screaming, 'My purse. He's got my purse!'

'Move your ass!' Conan the Barbarian shouted at Gil. 'He's running in sandals with his butt crack showing, for chrissake!'

'I'm paying your taxes!' Superman shouted. 'Get it in gear!'

'Zigzag through the traffic, you big chickenshit!' the Lone Ranger shouted, minus Tonto, who was in jail.

Even Zorro chimed in, and with his bogus Spanish accent said, '¡Ándale, hombre! Don't be such a wienie!'

And Gil Ponce, perhaps subconsciously spurred by the taunting of the superheroes, did just that.

Cat Song saw him nearly get hit by a Ford Taurus whose driver was busy checking out the freak show in front of the Chinese Theatre before jamming on his brakes to keep from killing the young cop.

Cat jumped in their shop and slowed traffic with her light bar and siren, turning the corner and driving west in the eastbound number one lane, stopping car traffic in front of the Kodak Center. She was broadcasting a description of the suspect and location of the foot pursuit, when a van full of tourists caused her to brake and blast them into awareness with her siren. The tourist van skidded sideways and screeched to a stop, gridlocking traffic in both directions.

Gil Ponce was amazed by the purse snatcher's foot speed. Of course, the guy wasn't wearing all of the gear on his belt that Gil was, but the thief was running in flip-flops. And Gil, who was in the best shape of his life, couldn't gain on the guy, who ran a broken field pattern through and around the hordes of pedestrians on the boulevard. Gil could see the long hair floating and the head bobbing. Otherwise, he wouldn't have known where in the hell the guy was.

Then he saw more heads bobbing their way through the crowd a block away, and he knew that some cops were running his way. Short-haired bobbing heads were chasing a long-haired bobbing head like a zany board game on Hollywood Boulevard, with Gil Ponce leaping high to see over the crowds, hoping the eastbound bobbing heads would meet the westbound bobbing head and gobble him up like Pac-Man. But suddenly, the whippet in flip-flops was gone.

The decision that the thief made to zip around the corner, running south on Orange Drive, turned out to be unwise. Because after following the foot pursuit on the radio, several cops were fanning out and trying to guess where the thief would run, and one had figured correctly that it would be through the parking garage.

Some of the foot pursuit information was broadcast by Cat Song, her shop still trapped in traffic while she boiled in frustration, cursing everything, including tourism in general. Yet the more her siren howled and her light bar winked, the more confused the out-of-town motorists became, and the gridlock grew more impenetrable. The other foot pursuit information came from five cops who'd parked west of the Chinese Theatre and were broadcasting on their rovers while running through the crowds.

The one copper who had everything doped out perfectly was Gert Von Braun. There were lights all over the parking structure, but there were dark places where a wide person dressed in a navy-blue uniform could hide. She was behind a concrete wall when he ran to the structure, puffing and panting, looking behind himself, the purse in his hand now.

He never slowed and never saw Officer Von Braun holding her PR24 baton in a rising-sun samurai pose before she stepped out from the shadows and whirled in a 360-degree whip with amazing agility for a woman in a size 44 Sam Browne. She was holding her baton in a Barry Bonds two-handed baseball grip when she swung for the bleacher seats. The baton struck the purse snatcher across the chest, and he might as well have slammed into the side of a bus. His right flip-flop continued hurtling forward, along with his left eye. It popped from its socket and rolled, clicking across the pavement, scooting off the curb, and coming to rest against the tire of an illegally parked car.

The first to arrive at the scene of arrest was Gil Ponce. The purse snatcher was proned out, hands cuffed behind his back, making creaking raspy sounds as he sucked at the air but couldn't get enough of it. His empty eye socket glistened in the neon glow from the boulevard.

Gert Von Braun handed the purse to Gil Ponce, who was still wearing the latex gloves he'd donned when asked to take charge of the putrid drunk. Gil looped the purse strap over his arm and was putting his baton back in the ring when the surfer cops pulled to the curb and parked.

The surfers alighted from their shop, and Flotsam looked at Gil, saying, 'You need somebody to accessorize you, dude. That purse does not match your shoes and gloves.'

Gil quickly peeled off the gloves and stuffed them in his pocket, and Jetsam removed the cap and straw from a cup of Gatorade he'd been drinking and said, 'Here, bro. Rehydrate before you pass out.'

Gil took a gulp of Gatorade and handed it back to Jetsam while Flotsam and Gert Von Braun, each holding an arm, lifted the purse snatcher to his feet.

'My eye!' he said, wheezing. 'I lost my goddamn eye!'

Flotsam shined his flashlight beam on the thief's face and said, 'You did lose it, dude. There's just a hole in your face now. Stuff it with toilet paper before you get to the slam or those jailhouse meat packers will add a whole new meaning to eye-fucking.'

'Do you know what that eye cost!' the thief yelled, his baggy jeans and boxers now down so low his penis was exposed.

Taking out her handcuff key, Gert Von Braun uncuffed his hands, saying, 'You missed a belt loop. In fact, you missed the whole belt. Do me a favor, put that thing away while we look for your eye.'

Shining his flashlight beam around the pavement, Gil Ponce said, 'There it is. Under the tire of that car. Gnarly!'

'Pick it up, will ya?' the purse snatcher said to Jetsam, who was sitting on the fender of his shop, looking down at the glass eyeball, sipping his Gatorade.

'I ain't picking up nobody's eyeball,' Jetsam said. 'You can pick up your own fucking eyeball, bro.'

'Get gloved up again, boy,' Flotsam said to Gil Ponce. 'And pick it up. Every man's got a right to his own eyeball.'

'Why did I transfer to this lunatic division?' Gert Von Braun asked rhetorically and strode across the sidewalk. 'There's not a real man on the midwatch.'

And she squatted, shined her light under the car, picked up the glass eyeball, ungloved, and then strode over to Jetsam and dunked the dirty eyeball into the surfer's drink. And swished it around.

'My Gatorade!' Jetsam cried in disbelief to all present. 'She dunked an eyeball in my Gatorade!'

'Girlie men,' Gert Von Braun muttered, and she handed the eyeball to the purse snatcher, saying, 'Stick this in your head, dude.'

There were two civilians watching the action from a hundred feet away. One was Leonard Stilwell, who then had decided that purse picking wasn't for him. Along with him was a young guy who looked like a transient but was a stringer who wrote pieces for the underground rags. The stringer was thinking he might submit this piece to the editors at the *L.A. Times,* who were always harping about LAPD's 'warrior cop' ethos. He'd already decided on his headline: 'The Eyes Have It with Warrior Cops.'

Gert Von Braun said to Gil Ponce, 'I'll see you at the station.'

'I think maybe there is one real man on the midwatch,' Flotsam said, watching Gert get in her shop. 'At least we didn't get spit at.'

Finally having negotiated her way through the traffic on Hollywood Boulevard, Cat Song double-parked across from the parking structure and trotted over to the group of cops, where she saw the purse snatcher wipe something on the front of his T-shirt and then use both hands to do something to his face.

But her mind was on her young boot, who had nearly gotten himself killed, and she was very mad when she pulled Gil Ponce aside and said quietly, 'You almost got pancaked by that head-up-ass tourist in the Ford. You were very lucky. Dumb and lucky.'

'I misjudged his speed,' Gil Ponce said.

'Listen, man of steel,' she said, 'you can play Russian roulette, date Phil Spector, or otherwise self-destruct on your own time, but not on mine. There's no place for a kamikaze kid in my shop.'

'I'm sorry, Cat,' Gil said. 'But we got him. We got the guy!'

Jetsam walked over to Cat Song and pointed at Gert Von Braun driving away. 'She dunked an eyeball in my Gatorade!' he said. 'And swished it around!'

'What?' said Cat Song.

SEVEN

THE NEXT DAY was one where all the watches had to listen to roll call training prepared by the LAPD's Behavioral Science Services about recognizing suicidal behaviors. The California Highway Patrol, which was a much smaller law enforcement agency than the LAPD, had been experiencing a frightening suicide cluster. Eight of their officers of both genders had committed suicide in the prior year alone, the rate being five times higher than the national average for law enforcement. Suicide was a subject that cops did not wish to talk about. It was disturbing to think about and unnatural that far more cops murder themselves than are murdered by criminals. And that if they stay on the Job long enough, they will have worked with or around some cop who does it.

They preferred to treat it much like others in high-risk jobs treat death, the way fighter pilots treat the deaths of colleagues by blaming nearly all air crashes on pilot errors that they themselves would not have made.

Cops would say, 'He probably got into massive debt and couldn't find a way out.'

Or, 'She probably was into drugs or booze and it all got to be too much.'

Or, 'He probably had some bipolar shit in his DNA and just went mental. So why didn't he just hang out at UCLA and shoot law students before they metastasize?'

The first question that a cop asked the sergeant who read the material at day-watch roll call was 'Why the CHP? They got it made. Like working for the auto club. Triple A with guns. How hard is that? Why should they be capping themselves?'

And another cop said, 'What if they had to live under a federal consent decree like we do? Along with a police commission full of cop-hating political hacks? They'd be setting themselves on fire like Buddhist monks.'

The training bulletin was meaningless to the young coppers at the various roll calls. Why were they being briefed about it? Whatever drove those poor bastards to bite it had nothing to do with *their* young lives.

The senior sergeant, who recognized the defense mechanisms and knew that the BSS shrink assigned to Hollywood Station was the loneliest underworked guy in the division, said, 'Yeah, I guess reading this material is a waste of time. It could never happen to us tough guys, could it?'

That morning, before Ronnie and Bix Ramstead could tend to their many calls for quality-of-life service, they were to assist two other Crows with Homeless Outreach, that is, cleaning out the transient encampment in the Hollywood Hills. The other Crows on that assignment were Hollywood Nate Weiss and Rita Kravitz, neither of whom wanted to be there.

Their task was to roust the transients and write

citations for trespassing in a mountain fire district. They called it 'hitting the billy goat trail,' and for this one, even Nate wore boots and BDUs, the black battle-dress uniform favored by SWAT officers. The encampment was behind the Hollywood Bowl, in the hills and canyons where one could see the lighted cross on the promontory overlooking the John Anson Ford Theater's parking lot. That parking lot was where older Hollywood cops used to go after night watch for a brew or two, sometimes with a few badge bunnies joining in the fun. That was before the former chief of police, whom they called Lord Voldemort, put a stop to it and to most other activities that provided any enjoyment whatsoever.

Rita Kravitz started complaining the moment they parked their Ford Explorer and started up the steep hillside. She slipped twice and had to grab at some brush and tumbleweed, getting thorns in her hand and breaking an acrylic nail.

'Goddamnit!' she muttered after the second fall. 'Now a scorpion will probably sting me.'

'Or you might step on a rattlesnake,' Nate said, climbing behind her. 'They say the babies are the deadliest.'

'Shut up,' Rita said.

Then Bix Ramstead slipped and skidded down the slope a few feet until he grabbed a handful of brush and pulled himself upright.

'I'm too old for this,' he said.

Ronnie, who wasn't having an easy time either, said, 'Everybody's too old for this. How the hell do the homeless geezers do it?'

'They must have a helicopter stashed somewhere,' Hollywood Nate said, wiping sweat from his brow. 'This is steeper than a dinner tab at the Ivy.' Then he added, 'Where I happen to be going next week with a director pal of mine.' Nate was disappointed that everybody was too tired and grumpy to give a shit.

When they finally got to the encampment, there were only three little tents in place, made from blue tarps that had probably been stolen from a construction site. A homeless transient was cooking a hot dog over a small fire pit dug into the dry earth.

'Morning, Officers,' he said when he saw them.

He looked seventy, but he could have been fifty. His clothing was typical: a sweatshirt over a T-shirt over another T-shirt, even on this hot, smoggy day. And a pair of baggy dungarees, none of it having been dipped in soapy water for several weeks. Or months.

'I recognize you,' Bix Ramstead said. 'I thought we told you to leave last time I was here.'

'I did leave,' he said.

'But you're still here,' Bix said.

'That was then. This is now.'

'You weren't supposed to come back.'

'Oh,' the guy said. 'I didn't know you meant forever.'

'Why don't you go to the homeless shelter?' Bix said.

'Too many rules,' the transient said. 'A man's gotta be free. It's what America's all about.'

'I'm getting all choked up,' Rita Kravitz said. Then she looked in the second makeshift tent, where a fat woman was snoring, surrounded by empty cans of Mexican beer. Rita kicked the bottom of her filthy bare feet until she sat up and said, 'What the fuck?'

Hollywood Nate went to the third tent and heard more snoring. Powerful chainsaw snores, along with wheezes and whistles and snuffling.

'Hey, dude!' Nate said. 'Rise and shine!'

The snoring continued, rhythm unbroken. Nate grabbed the tent and started shaking it.

'Earthquake!' he yelled. 'Run for your life!'

Still there was no change in the pattern of snores or the whistling snuffles.

Nate grabbed the tent in both hands and shook it violently, yelling, 'Get your ass up!'

And it worked. A deep voice from within the tent bellowed, 'I'll kill you, you motherfucker! I'm armed! If I come out, you're a dead man, you son of a bitch! Hear me? Dead!'

Nate leaped back and drew his Glock, tripping on a loose chunk of sandstone and falling flat on his ass, tumbling backward several feet down the hillside.

Ronnie drew her Beretta and so did Rita Kravitz. Bix Ramstead pulled his nine and his baton, just in case deadly force was not in the cards. And they all started yelling.

'Crawl out!' Rita Kravitz ordered. 'Hands first!'

'Let's see your hands!' Ronnie ordered. 'Your hands!'

'Now!' Bix Ramstead ordered. 'Crawl out now!'

As Hollywood Nate scrambled to his feet and advanced on the tent, looking for cover if the guy should come out shooting, the tent flap was thrown open and four guns were deployed diagonally, leveled at the tent.

A wizened transient with a wild white beard halfway down his puny bare chest popped his head out, holding his 'weapon,' a piece of broom handle, and saw the four cops pointing pistols at him.

He offered an apologetic, toothless smile and said, 'I'm just not a morning person.'

Things were getting desperate for Leonard Stilwell. Nothing was working out in a world where trust was eroding. The old burglary targets had gotten harder what with more sophisticated alarms and window bars. His short flirtation with purse picking had terrified him after seeing what happened to the long-haired guy in flip-flops. He'd tried the ATM scam for three nights straight and never again was able to score the way he had with the Iranian woman. One of the chumps figured it out right away and threatened to call the cops.

He had no rock left, no crystal meth, not even a blunt to mellow him out before he hit the streets, contemplating a degrading life as a common shoplifter. Then he thought of old customers to whom he had sold stolen cases of liquor. He thought of Ali Aziz.

It was late afternoon by the time he arrived at the Leopard Lounge on Sunset Boulevard. The nightclub would not be open yet, but he knew workers would be there cleaning and setting up. This was the hour when he used to drive up to the back door with Whitey Dawson and get his prearranged cash payment from Ali. Leonard banged on the front door and was admitted by a Mexican busboy who recognized him. Ali was in work clothes behind the bar, checking the stock.

'Ali!' Leonard said, slapping palms with the nightclub owner.

'Leonard!' Ali said with a grin, displaying the gold

eyetooth that Leonard figured was a status symbol in shitty sand countries.

'Can we go in your office and talk?' Leonard asked. 'Just for five minutes?'

'For my old friend Leonard, yes,' Ali said.

And Leonard was glad he'd worn his only clean T-shirt and freshly laundered jeans. His sneakers were worn out, but he felt that he didn't look as poor and desperate as he really was.

When they got inside the office, Ali said, 'You got some liquor for me, Leonard?'

'Well, no, not yet. But I'm working on it.'

Ali turned sullen. He didn't ask Leonard to sit. If this thief wasn't selling liquor, what could he possibly want?

'So?' Ali said, sitting on the corner of his desk.

'I got this deal in the works, Ali,' Leonard began, 'but I need an advance. Not much, but enough to pay a guy to give me an alarm code.'

'Advance?' Ali said, and he started fidgeting with one of his gold pinkie rings, the one with a big white stone that Leonard doubted was real.

'Maybe . . . five hundred?'

'You wish to borrow five hundred dollars?' Ali said, incredulous.

'As an advance against my fee when I deliver the stock.'

'You are going crazy,' Ali said, standing up. 'Crazy, Leonard.'

'Wait, Ali!' Leonard said. 'Two hundred. I think I could shake the alarm code loose for two hundred.'

'You waste my time,' Ali said, checking the face on his huge gold watch.

'Ali,' Leonard said, 'we done lots of business in the past. I can still help you out. I got several plans in the works.'

Ali Aziz glanced at the photos on the shelf over the TV. Then at Leonard, then back at the pictures. He went around his desk and sat in his executive chair and motioned Leonard to the client chair.

Leonard's legs were shaky and his hands were sweating now. He needed some rock bad. Perspiration was running down his freckled cheeks from his rusty hairline, and sweat beaded under his sockets, beneath the vacant blue-eyed stare. But he was full of hope and he waited.

Nearly a minute passed before Ali spoke. When he did, he said, 'Leonard, you are a good thief, no?'

'I'm the best,' Leonard Stilwell said, trying to look confident. 'You know that. We never had no trouble when Whitey and me sold you liquor. No trouble at all.'

'No trouble,' Ali said. 'That is so. But now Whitey is dead.'

'And if I just had the alarm code that this guy said he'd . . .'

Ali shook his head, waving his hand palm down, and Leonard shut up.

'You are giving me a big idea,' Ali said. 'About the alarm code. You enter and steal from business buildings many times,' Ali said. 'You also can enter and steal from a house, no?'

'Yeah, sure, but why would I want to? There's nothing in most houses. Even the big houses up where you live. People don't keep cash laying around no more.

Everything's done with credit cards. And a lot of that fancy jewelry you see at red carpet events? It's fake.'

'How you know where I live?'

'You told me one time,' Leonard said. 'Up in the hills. Mount Olympus, right?'

Ali nodded. 'Okay, but I do not live there no more. My bitch wife is living there with my son. We are in a very big divorce fight. The house is sold and we must wait for escrow to close up.'

'Sorry to hear that,' Leonard said, unable to concentrate fully. Thinking how fast he was going to drive his Honda to Pablo's Tacos or the cyber café and score something to smoke, wondering how much he could get out of this Ay-rab.

'I am thinking that I need for you to enter my house on a Thursday. At four o'clock in the day. There is something I must have for my divorce fight.'

'What something?'

'Bank papers. Very important.'

'Can't you just ask for them? Or have your lawyer do it?'

'Impossible,' Ali said. 'My bitch wife is not going to give them. She wishes to use the documents against me.'

'Are they in a safe? I never done a safe.'

'No, just in a desk drawer.'

Now Leonard was perspiring even more. This didn't sound right. He didn't like the way Ali was explaining it. There was too much hesitation, like he was making it up as he went along. If he'd only smoked one little blunt to mellow him out, he could think better.

Finally he said, 'Another reason I never did much

housebreaking was 'cause there's always a chance somebody will walk in on you. I'm not into violence, Ali.'

'No violence,' Ali said. 'That is why Thursday is the correct day. My wife does the exercise that afternoon. The maid finishes housecleaning at four o'clock. She sets the alarm, she locks doors, she goes. Her grandson collects her in front. Then you enter my house and get the bank papers for me.'

'I don't know, Ali,' Leonard said. 'It ain't that easy. How about the alarm? You got the code?'

'I am sure that my bitch wife changes all locks so my key is no good. And she also changes the regular alarm code. But I do not think she can change the code for the maid. Lola is a most stupid Mexican who cannot see good up close. Stupid old woman cannot find most of dirt in the house neither. I want to fire her, but my wife says that Lola is very good with my Nicky. Okay, Lola many times forgets her correct code and many times she sets off alarms. My wife is not changing the code for Lola, no way. That code I give to you.'

'Lemme lock on this,' Leonard said. 'I break in through one of the access doors that's alarmed, right? A door that's used for entering and leaving, so there's no panic at the alarm company? Not as long as I enter the maid's code within a minute or so, right?'

'Absolutely correct,' Ali said with a reassuring smile.

'You could do the same,' Leonard said warily.

After a short hesitation, Ali said, 'No, I cannot. Number one reason: I cannot permit for someone to see me doing such a thing. My lawyer would explode like . . . like . . .'

'An IED in Baghdad.'

'Precisely. Number two reason: I do not know how to enter a door that has the lock in place without making big damage.'

'Why is that important? When she finds the papers're missing, she'll know somebody broke in and stole them.'

'No, no,' Ali said, and after a thoughtful pause he continued. 'She must not learn that the papers are of so much value and she must not know they are missing. You see, there are many other documents there.'

Now Leonard was certain that something was wrong and that Ali was winging it. But at least it didn't involve violence, so Leonard said, 'Windows are out of the question. And I'm sure you got a motion detector. Is there an attached garage?'

'Yes, the garage attaches to the house.'

'Do you think she changed the code on the garage door opener?'

Ali thought for a moment and said, 'I do not think so. The gardener has a door opener and so does Lola.'

'Do you have one? I mean besides the one that's probably built into your car.'

'Yes, I have the old one.'

'I'm sure the front door has a dead bolt and probably the other doors, but how about the door leading to the garage? A dead bolt? The kind you have to turn?'

'Dead bolt?' Ali pondered. 'Yes.'

'And another lock, right? One on the doorknob or handle that locks by itself when the door closes unless you turn a little thumb-turn on the inside?'

'Yes, that is correct. On the doorknob. It is a very old lock.'

'And is the alarm pad right inside that door?'

'Yes.'

'Okay,' Leonard said. 'Here's the deal. Most people don't bother to throw the dead bolt on the access door from the garage to the house. They feel comfortable that two doors are between them and the street. And besides, they're always bringing something in or out of the car to the house. Do you think your maid might lock the dead bolt on that door when she sets the alarm and leaves?'

'Absolutely no,' Ali said. 'When I was living there, I always drive into the garage and use my key for only the doorknob lock. But when my wife is home, no knob lock. No nothing.'

Leonard thought, if he was going to lie, he should lie large. He had to have this job. He said, 'I can pick any ordinary lock, so your wife won't know it's happened. I'll need your garage door opener and an exact idea of what papers I'm looking for and where to find them. And I'll need your maid's alarm code.'

'And you are very certain nobody will know you enter into the house?'

'Not unless your wife is paranoid and calls the alarm company to see if her maid came back for some reason. But would she?'

'No, my bitch wife will not do that,' Ali said.

'If your garage opener don't work or if the dead bolt is thrown on that access door, I'm outta there,' Leonard said.

'Is okay with me,' Ali said.

'So where do I find the bank papers, and what do they look like?'

'Look for the brown folder. Big one. With the year two thousand and four on the outside. You shall find it when you open the bottom drawer in the white desk. It is in the office room next to the kitchen. Other brown envelopes are there too, but do not touch. Leave other papers. You understand?'

'I guess so,' Leonard said. 'So how much do I get for this job?'

'I give you the two hundred dollars you say you want.'

'Fuck that!' Leonard said. 'That was an advance. This is housebreaking and it's dangerous and takes special talent.'

'Okay, okay,' Ali said. 'I give you four hundred dollars after you give me the bank documents.'

It was the biggest gamble that he'd taken in a long time, but he decided to go for it. Leonard said to Ali Aziz, 'Two hundred now. One thousand more when I give you the papers.'

'You crazy, Leonard,' Ali said. 'No way.'

Leonard was fully prepared to back down, but he gambled again. Standing up, he said, 'I'm outta here. Good luck, Ali.'

'Okay, okay,' Ali Aziz said. 'I agree.'

Now Leonard quickly swiped at his face to stem the rivulets of perspiration and said, 'But what if the papers ain't there? I still risk state prison. I still want the thousand.'

'But how shall I know if you go in there and try?'

'Tell me something that's in the house that your wife won't miss. Some little thing.'

'Napkin,' Ali said. 'She have very special cocktail

napkins. Look inside baskets on the countertop in the kitchen. Has her initial printed in gold on every napkin. Bring one to me if you don't find no bank papers. I see that napkin, I pay you.'

'You'll give me the thousand anyways? No argument?'

'Yes, I shall not argue.'

Leonard put out his hand. Ali looked as though he didn't want to touch it but did. 'We got the deal,' Ali said.

'Call me on my cell when you're ready. I'll stop by here same time as today. Have the garage door opener and the alarm code for me. Now I'll need the two hundred.'

Ali reluctantly pulled out his wallet and peeled off four $50 bills and handed them to Leonard Stilwell.

'One thing more,' Ali said. 'When you finish with the job, you meet me down where you see the Mount Olympus sign. I shall be there in my car. Black Jaguar.'

'That's weird,' Leonard said. 'Why don't I bring them here?'

Ali hesitated yet again. 'Maybe I look at the papers and don't find the certain document I need. Maybe I ask you to go back, look somewhere else.'

'No fucking way!' Leonard said. 'I go in one time and that's it. What're you trying to pull?'

'Okay,' Ali said quickly. 'If the correct document is not there, is okay.'

'Are we finished here?'

'You leave that door with no lock on the knob. Very important. No lock.'

Now Leonard was totally confused. This thing was

going sideways before it started. 'Unlocked? But you said you didn't want your wife to know anybody had busted in her house. If she gets outta her car and finds the knob lock ain't set, what's she gonna think?'

'She shall think the stupid old Mexican maid forget to lock the doorknob again. No problem.'

'This ain't right, Ali,' Leonard said, brow wrinkling. 'There's something wrong here.'

'I wish for her to fire the stupid Mexican maid,' Ali explained. 'My bitch wife says Lola is good for my son. I do not think so. My wife finds the door unlocked again, maybe she decides to fire Lola. That shall be good for my Nicky.'

'Look, why don't you and me just do the job together?' Leonard said. 'All I gotta really do is pick that lock and let you in. That way, you could look around anywheres you want. You could check her underwear drawer and sniff her panties if you want. And I could leave you in there and go about my business. Don't that make a lotta sense?'

'No, Leonard. I shall never go inside the house, no way. Not till my divorce is finish. I must not take a foolish risk. Someone see me go into the house, what do you think happens to my divorce fight? Do the job like I tell you and I pay, no problem. Okay?'

'Okay, but you still wanna meet me there in your neighborhood rather than right here?'

'By Mount Olympus sign, Leonard.'

Leonard felt the four President Grants in his pocket and thought, if he could smoke a little rock, this whole thing might clear up in his mind. Maybe then he could figure out what this goat fucker was really up to.

'I'll come here when you call me,' Leonard said to Ali Aziz, using the desk notepad to write down the number of his throwaway cell phone. 'By the way, what's the address?'

When Ali recited his Mt. Olympus street and house number, Leonard wrote it down on a second notebook sheet.

'No, Leonard,' Ali said, watching him. 'You write down the wrong number. Last two are not correct numbers.'

Leonard showed Ali his knowing smile and said, 'That's a little trick I learned from Whitey Dawson. 'I always subtract two from the last pair of numbers in the address of a job I'm gonna be working. That way, I don't have to memorize nothing. Guys forget stuff when they gotta memorize things. If the cops stop me and find the address, it ain't gonna mean shit to them.'

'Very clever, Leonard,' Ali said. 'I think you are a clever man.'

'You gotta do your homework,' Leonard Stilwell said, thinking about the rock he'd be smoking that night. Figuring he had lots of time to see his Fijian neighbor and learn how the hell to pick a lock.

EIGHT

L ATE THAT DAY, after the Homeless Outreach had been concluded and the hills behind the Hollywood Bowl were encampment free for the time being, Ronnie kept her appointment with the surfer cops. She arrived with Hollywood Nate at 4 P.M. and parked in front of an auto body repair business in East Hollywood that was ostensibly diminishing the quality of life for a few hundred Hispanic people at the other end of their shared alley. Bix Ramstead was at the station catching up on paperwork and 'constant caller' phone messages that he'd been postponing. It was estimated that about 30 percent of all CRO complaints were from the same callers.

The surfer cops were already there, standing by Flotsam's pickup truck in their normal street attire of T-shirts and jeans.

'Thanks for coming,' Flotsam said, glancing uneasily at Nate, whose expression said to him, Are you an innocent bystander, or what?

'So why don't you come in with us and make sure I do it right?' Ronnie said to the surfers.

Jetsam followed Ronnie inside, and Flotsam trailed, whispering to Nate, 'The game's afoot, dude. He think he's Holmes, but I ain't no Dr. Watson.'

The proprietor of Stan's Body Shop was not an Arab, not an Iranian, nor an immigrant from any foreign country. He was a fifty-year-old white Anglo native of Los Angeles named Stan Hooper, and he was very surprised to see two cops in uniform and two other guys who looked like cops enter his place of business.

Ronnie said, 'Good afternoon, sir. We're from Hollywood Division Community Relations Office. Here's my card.'

While Stan Hooper looked at the card, she said, 'We have a complaint from residents at the other end of the alley that cars from your shop are often blocking the alley early in the morning, and apartment residents can't get their cars out when they need to go to work. In fact, I noticed three cars parked there now with barely enough room for a VW Bug to squeeze by.'

Stan Hooper wiped the grease from his hands and said, 'We'll move them right away, Officer. I'm sorry. This place is too small for us but it's all we can afford right now. I'm looking for more space. I try to keep the alley clear, but sometimes customers park there before I can tell them not to.'

'Business must be good,' Ronnie said, looking toward the open door leading into the main room, where body work was in progress on a white Lexus SUV that was taped and primered.

'Too good, but I shouldn't complain,' he said, looking at the surfers, wondering why it took four cops to deliver the warning. 'I don't want no tickets. I won't let it happen again.'

Jetsam said, 'Nice rides you got in there.' And he

strolled into the large open area, where the work was being done.

'He's one of our officers,' Ronnie said to Stan Hooper. 'He likes cars.'

Stan Hooper followed Jetsam into the work bay and said, 'Two of those are for sale. My customer said I could sell them if someone wants to buy. I wouldn't take no commission if an officer from Hollywood Station wanted one of them. The Mercedes is really nice and the price is pretty good.'

The surfer cop began writing down license numbers and VIN numbers, and Stan Hooper said, 'Something wrong, Officer?'

Jetsam said, 'We got a few reports about hot SUVs being repainted and having license plates switched. It's just routine.'

'I never been in trouble in my life!' Stan Hooper said. 'You can check. I got a reputation with insurance companies for doing honest work at an honest price, and we specialize in SUVs. We can even straighten bent frames if they're not too bad. Insurance companies refer SUV owners to us all the time.'

At this point the other three cops knew that Jetsam was just trying to save face when he said, 'I wasn't thinking of you. I was thinking of the owners of the SUVs. Do you know them personally?'

'I know two of them from way back. I've worked on their cars for ten, fifteen years. The other two I don't know. One's an old guy, lives in Los Feliz district. The other's a woman. Drop-dead gorgeous. Lives in Hollywood Hills somewheres. One of my guys drove her home.'

'Are any of your workers from the Middle East? Arabs maybe?'

'Arabs? No. Three're Mexican, two're Salvadoran. One's an Okie. That's about it.'

Jetsam looked sheepishly at the other cops, and Stan Hooper said, 'The woman customer has a name that sounds like maybe an Arab name, but she's American. Her SUV was full of old magazines and newspapers written in a Middle East language. They were laying around the shop last time I looked. I wish she'd come and pay me and pick up her car, but she hopes I can sell it for her.'

Stan Hooper handed the repair estimates to Ronnie, who glanced at them perfunctorily just to help Jetsam gracefully exit, and she saw the name Margot Aziz.

'Aziz,' she said. 'Would this customer be related to Ali Aziz who owns a nightclub on Sunset?'

'You got me,' Stan Hooper said, shrugging.

Hollywood Nate suddenly got very interested. He looked over Ronnie's shoulder and saw the familiar address on the work order, and he memorized the phone number.

'How much does the lady want for the SUV?' Nate asked casually.

'It's three years old but has very low mileage. It had some body damage but nothing major. Somebody smacked into her in the parking lot at Farmers Market, she said. She'll take twenty-eight.'

'Twenty-eight thousand,' Nate said. 'That's a little high, isn't it?'

'Maybe she'll come down,' Stan Hooper said.

'Keep the alley clear, please,' Ronnie said, turning toward the door.

When the four cops were back outside, Ronnie said, 'A Mercedes SUV? And you recently bought a Mustang, I believe. Are you on the take, Nate?'

'Nice ride. I always admired these Mercedes SUVs.'

'See you guys,' Ronnie said. 'I'll leave you to run license and VIN numbers if you wanna stay on this case.'

When the surfer cops got back in Flotsam's pickup to drive to Hollywood Station, Flotsam said, 'Dude, I know Ronnie rocks your libido, but this kinda move ain't gonna help you become a Crow.'

Jetsam said, 'At least I got it right about the Arabic newspaper.'

When they arrived back at Hollywood South, Ronnie found Bix sitting at a desk with his BlackBerry in front of him, still making tedious phone calls. And Nate seemed in a hurry to make a few calls of his own, but not in the office, where the others were working. Nate walked outside and dialed the number on his cell, surprised at how cotton mouthed he was when she answered.

'Hello . . . Margot?' Nate said.

'Yes. Who is this?'

'It's Nate Weiss. The police officer you met?'

'Oh, yes,' she said. 'How'd you get my number?'

'You won't believe what a coincidence this is,' Nate said. 'But today I had occasion to be at Stan's Body Shop and I saw your SUV there and learned it's for sale.'

'Yes, it is,' she said.

'I'd like to talk to you about it,' Nate said. 'I might be interested.'

'I'm asking twenty-eight thousand.'

'Would you be willing to negotiate?'

After a few seconds she said, 'I might.'

'Could I come by and talk to you about it?'

'When?'

'Oh, after I get off work this evening?'

'What time would that be?'

'I could get to your house as early as eight o'clock.'

'My au pair is not available tonight,' Margot said. 'I'm afraid I'll be occupied with my five-year-old son. It'd be better if you come tomorrow night.'

'Tomorrow night at eight?'

'That'll be fine,' Margot Aziz said. 'One question, Officer Weiss.'

'Call me Nate. What's the question?'

'That's my dinner hour and I'm not a bad cook. How about sharing some homemade pasta and mango chicken salad with me?'

When Hollywood Nate Weiss closed his cell phone, he actually felt giddy.

After Margot Aziz hung up her house phone, she used her pay-as-you-go cell phone and rang another go cell that she'd bought for a beautiful Amerasian topless dancer.

'It's me,' Margot said when Jasmine answered. 'I can't wait any longer for the number one draft pick. Remember the other one I mentioned to you? He's coming here tomorrow night. I'll see how it goes. He might work out.'

'I'm getting sick and tired of this,' the dancer said. 'If something don't happen soon, I'm pulling outta the whole thing. It's too nerve-racking.'

'Be patient, honey,' Margot said. 'We've worked hard getting into the man's head. We've got him primed. It'll just be a little while longer.'

Since there wasn't a full moon, the watch commander hoped for a quiet night. A full moon over Hollywood meant that anything could happen and usually did. Most of the things were not the sort that the police discussed with the business community at meetings of the Community Police Advisory Board.

Dan Applewhite was using up some of his accumulated overtime days, so young Gil Ponce had been assigned to ride with Gert Von Braun. They hadn't been out on the streets more than thirty minutes after sunset when 6-X-66 got a call in Southeast Hollywood regarding a silent burglar alarm at a furniture store. When they arrived and did a routine check of windows at the store, Gert's new eight-inch flashlight began blinking. She tapped it a few times and the light went out.

'Goddamn this piece of shit!' she said. And she tapped it again and switched it off and on a few times.

And then Gil Ponce got a first-hand look at Gert's EST, the explosive temper syndrome that other cops talked about privately.

'Motherfucking political hacks!' she snarled. And hurled the flashlight against the block wall at the rear of the furniture store, debris flying.

Gil just watched but said nothing, and she turned to him, saying, 'We're gonna stop at a drugstore and buy a goddamn flashlight that works!'

It sounded to Gil Ponce like a challenge, so he swallowed and said, 'Yes, ma'am. Okay.'

'Don't call me ma'am, goddamnit!' she said, getting into their shop, squeezing her bulk between the steering wheel and backrest.

'No . . . Gert,' Gil said, slipping into the passenger seat as quickly and quietly as possible, keeping his eyes on the streets.

An hour later, Compassionate Charlie Gilford was once again called away from one of his favorite reality shows to meet 6-X-66 at the scene of a possible homicide, where the body was missing and a baby was dead. It was the kind of location that the committees that were dedicated to the beautification and renewal of Hollywood liked to think was so far off the boulevards that one needn't consider it a Hollywood neighborhood at all. But it was.

It happened at a Brentwood slumlord's three-story Hollywood apartment building. There was an outside stairwell under the roof at the rear of the property, which was used by various homeless transients as temporary housing. They slept, drank, urinated, and even defecated there, belying the adage about not shitting where one sleeps. All outdoor metal piping had been stripped and stolen long ago, and before brass hinges were replaced with steel, at least one transient was stabbed while kicking down the door of an empty apartment just to get the shiny treasure. Hispanic children did not dare walk barefoot for fear of discarded syringes.

One of the Honduran residents of the building, who had passed the stairwell from the parking lot on his way to the transient-free staircase at the front, spotted what appeared to be bloodstains on the concrete walkway where the trash bins were located. He poked his head inside the stairwell area, holding his breath against the stench, and saw more blood. He followed the trail to the corner under the stairwell and there saw thick viscous chunks of blood, and something that looked like raw oysters, but he just didn't want to know. There was dried spatter on one wall and a Rorschach pattern on the concrete floor beside a blanket stiff from blood drenching, as well as articles of discarded clothing. The Honduran thought the scene was so horrible that rats would flee from it. But he was wrong. There were rats.

And under a cardboard box in the other corner he found a dead baby. Not a fetus, but a full-term baby with the cord still attached. It was a boy but he could not tell any more about it. He knew that he should not disturb this scene and ran to his apartment to call the police. When he told his wife about what he had found, she returned with him to the stairwell to await the police officers' arrival.

Despite her husband's protests, she went back to their apartment and fetched a bath towel, refusing to let the body lie on the dirty concrete floor. She picked up the dead baby, who was not stiff, rigor mortis having come and gone, and placed the body on the third step, folding the towel over the tiny body.

'*Pobrecito,*' she said, and offered a prayer for the baby and for the mother if she was still alive, but the Honduran woman did not think that the mother could have lived. All that blood!

When 6-X-66 arrived at the scene, Gert Von Braun said to Gil Ponce, 'You better do the talking here. They probably don't speak English any better than George W. Bush.'

Here we go again, Gil Ponce thought, and he said, 'I'm sorry, Gert. I don't speak Spanish.'

She gave him a doubtful look and muttered the familiar refrain: 'Fucking Hollywood. Nothing's ever the way you expect.'

The Honduran man directed his remarks to young Gil Ponce. 'Very bad thing happen,' he said in passable English. 'Blood ees all over. We see thees dead baby.'

He led them to the stairwell and pulled back the towel. Gert shined the beam from her new flashlight onto the body and said, 'Looks like it's been here awhile. Wonder where Momma went.'

The Honduran said to Gil, 'Much blood over there.' And he pointed to the blood-caked blanket.

When Gert shined her light on the wall, she said, 'That looks like spatter. This might be more than a homeless woman giving birth. We better treat this as a homicide scene. Call the night-watch detective. Tell him we got something that looks like pizza topping without the crust.'

'We stay here?' the Honduran said to Gil Ponce.

Gert Von Braun said, 'I'm ten years older than him. Talk to me, why don't you?'

'Sorry?' the man said, not understanding.

Gert said, 'Never mind. Talk to him.' She was used to it with people from male-dominated cultures.

'Go to your apartment,' Gil said. 'But a detective will come and speak to you soon. Okay?'

'Okay,' the man said.

Compassionate Charlie got there well before the coroner's crew. He spoke with Gert and Gil, looked at the spatter and the vast blood loss someone had suffered, and got the Homicide D3 at home, telling her what they'd found. The D3 said she'd phone the detectives who were on call and get back to him.

And that was when the fattest transient any of the cops had ever seen staggered onto the scene. He was a homeless alcoholic who'd been arrested many times on the boulevards where he panhandled tourists. He was a middle-aged white man, perhaps a few years older than Detective Charlie Gilford, but very much larger. He wore a battered fedora, a patched, dandruff-dusted sport coat, and a greasy necktie over a filthy flannel shirt, perhaps his attempt to retain a drop of dignity.

When he lurched unsteadily toward the stairwell, the neck of a wine bottle protruding from his coat pocket, he didn't even see the cops until Gert Von Braun lit him with the beam from her new flashlight.

Charlie Gilford said, 'Jesus! This double-wide juicer must weigh three bills easy.'

'Uh-oh,' the fat man said when he saw them. 'Evening, Officers.'

Gil Ponce gloved up and patted him down, removing the wine bottle as the man looked at it wistfully, his breath like sewer gas, facial veins like a nest of pink worms. The fact that his face had color and had not turned lemonade yellow was a testament to his still-functioning liver.

'What's your name?' Charlie Gilford asked him.

'Livingston G. Kenmore,' the man said, lurching sideways until Gil Ponce steadied him.

'Whadda you know about this?' Charlie Gilford asked.

'About what?'

'The blood. The dead baby.'

'Oh, that.'

The cops looked at one another and back at the drunk. Finally, Charlie Gilford said, 'Yeah, that. What happened here?'

'About the blood or the baby?'

'Let's start with the baby,' Gert said.

'It belongs to Ruthie. It's dead.'

'We know it's dead. Who's Ruthie?'

'She was sleeping here,' he said. 'She was big as a house, but she still was doing guys for ten bucks. Ruthie didn't get too many takers at the end. Her belly was out to here.' He patted his own enormous belly then.

'Where's Ruthie now?' Charlie asked.

'She went to the homeless shelter two days ago,' the fat man said. 'You can find her there now. She wasn't feeling too good after she had the baby. Poor thing. It was dead before it came out. She bled a lot.'

'Did you help her have the baby?' Gert asked.

'Her friend Sadie did,' he said. 'She went to the shelter with Ruthie. You can go there and ask them about it. I tried to stay outta their affairs. They're businesswomen, if you get my meaning.'

'Are you telling us that all this blood came from Ruthie?' Charlie Gilford said.

'No, some of it came from Ruthie,' the man said, looking at Charlie like he was stupid or something.

'Did some of it come from Sadie?' Charlie asked.

'No,' the fat man said. 'Some of it came from me.'

'From you?' Gert said. 'Where from you?'

'From my schwanze,' he said. 'See, I been having lots of trouble peeing, so I went to the clinic a few weeks ago and had some surgery. A doctor put a catheter clear up my willie with one of those balloons inside my bladder to hold everything in place. But the other night after I drank a couple forties and a quart of port, I got mad at it and ripped it out. Blood squirted everywhere.'

Both Charlie Gilford and Gil Ponce involuntarily uttered painful groans from stabs of sympathy pain. Gil doubled over a bit and Charlie grabbed his own crotch while Gert sneered at the two of them. Gil already knew she thought they were all just a bunch of pussies, so he stood up straight, took a deep breath, and told himself to maintain.

Gert said to the drunk, 'You mean your thingie bled that much?'

'You can't imagine,' the big man said. 'I almost called nine-one-one. Wanna see it?'

Both Charlie Gilford and Gil Ponce said, 'No!' But Gert Von Braun said, 'Yeah, whip it out.'

He did. And while Charlie Gilford and Gil Ponce got busy looking in other directions, Gert shined her beam on the fat man's penis and said, 'Whoa, that's gnarly! You gotta have a doctor stitch it up. That thing looks like the pork sausage my mom used to make.'

The detective said to Gert and Gil, 'How about you two driving Mr. Kenmore here to the shelter and grabbing Ruthie and Sadie. In case they used different names, he can point them out. Treat this like a possible homicide. They coulda killed the baby.'

'Oh, no!' the fat man said. 'She was going to adopt it out. She thought she could get maybe two thousand bucks for it if it was white. And sure enough it was. She cried when she saw it was dead. She wouldn't hurt the baby. It was stillborn. I'm a witness. I put it in the corner and covered it with a box. We wouldn't throw it in a Dumpster or anything like that. They were gonna come back and take care of the body like responsible citizens.'

'We gotta corroborate everything you told us and we'll need you to help us do it,' Charlie Gilford said.

That was Gert's cue, and she headed out to the front street to get their car and drive it around to the parking lot so they didn't have to walk so far with the fat drunk.

'Just find the two women,' Charlie Gilford said to Gil Ponce. 'Bring them to the station and we'll let the Homicide team decide how they wanna handle all this.'

Gil said, 'If the women don't wanna come, do we place them under arrest?'

'Absolutely,' Charlie Gilford said. 'We got a dead baby. This is a crime scene until somebody tells us different.'

'Nobody committed a crime,' the fat man said, reeling again and grabbing the corner of the concrete wall. 'Ruthie woulda been a fine mother.'

Charlie Gilford said, 'Yeah, well, that's heartwarming, but I doubt that our Crows will wanna share this tearjerker the next time they meet the folks from the Restore Hollywood project.'

And while Charlie Gilford was dialing the Homicide

D3 again to tell her about the new developments, and Gil Ponce was watching the detective, eager to ask more questions about his further duties, nobody was watching Livingston G. Kenmore. He just couldn't stay upright any longer. He staggered a few steps over to the darkened stairwell and saw a pad of some kind on the third step and sat down on it.

'Holy shit!' Gil Ponce yelled. 'Get up! Get up! Get the fuck up!'

It all happened just as the D3 on the other end of the line said to Charlie, 'Is there any obvious trauma to the dead baby?'

'Oh, yeah,' said Compassionate Charlie Gilford after turning toward the commotion. 'There is now.'

NINE

THE CROWS HAD a recurring problem and it had to do with the Nightclub Committee's complaints about hot dog vendors. The prior evening, the vice unit, working in concert with the Crows and night-watch patrol, initiated Operation Hot Dog.

The night-watch and mid-watch patrol officers had been too busy and too short staffed to deal with the vendors, and things had gotten out of hand. On Hollywood and Sunset Boulevards, where so many nightclubs were springing up – clubs whose purported ownership changed nearly as often as the tablecloths – Latino hot dog vendors were setting up carts to catch nightclub customers coming and going during the wee hours. On the night of Operation Hot Dog, there had been more than fifty vendors cited for illegal sidewalk sales, and their carts had been impounded. Now the station parking lot was jammed with carts and rotting hot dogs, and everyone was wondering if the 'wienie sweep' had been a bit overzealous.

Ronnie got relieved of any responsibilities for Operation Hot Dog when she and Bix Ramstead were asked to meet 6-A-97 in Southeast Hollywood. The Crow who usually took care of calls in that neighborhood was on a short leave due to a death in his wife's family. There were not many black residents living in Hollywood Division, and the absent Crow, a black officer, had established a rapport with some of them.

Six-A-97 had responded to a complaint regarding shopping carts, five of them, that were lying around a wood-frame cottage rented to a Somalian couple. When Ronnie and Bix arrived, the older of the two waiting cops nodded to Bix Ramstead.

'We're not trying to kiss this one off,' he said, 'but you Crows deal with chronic-noise complaints and quality-of-life shit, right?'

'And "quality of life" covers a lot of territory,' Bix said wearily. 'What's the deal?'

The cop said, 'The woman who called us says the people who live in that little house are from Somalia and the husband doesn't like black people, so she can't talk to them.'

'Somalians *are* black people,' Bix said.

'Yeah, but he doesn't like American black people. So she wants us to talk to the guy and tell him that in this country, you can't just walk off the market parking lot with shopping carts. In fact, she says the Somalian even jacked a cart from her teenage son when he tried to take it back to the market. She says the guy just doesn't get it about shopping carts.'

'So did you try talking to the guy?' Ronnie asked.

'He won't answer,' the cop said, 'but the woman swears he's in there. Can you take over? We got some real crime to crush.'

There it was, Ronnie thought. They were real cops, the Crows were something other.

'Okay,' Bix said. 'What's her name?'

'Mrs. Farnsworth.' The cop was obviously happy to dump this one on the Crows, since patrol officers believed that Crows never did a day's work anyway.

Mrs. Farnsworth was a stout woman with straightened gray hair combed in a Condi Rice flip. Her bungalow, across the street from the Somalians', had a geranium garden in front and was freshly painted. She invited the cops in and asked if they'd like a cold drink, but they declined.

'I'd like to handle this my own self,' she told them, 'but that Somali man is mean. He has a big scar down the side of his face and he never smiles. His wife is very sweet. I talk to her when she passes on the way to the market. She's about twenty years younger than him, maybe more. And she left him once. I didn't see her for maybe three weeks and I don't know where she went. Then a week ago she came back.'

'We'll have the shopping carts picked up,' Bix said. 'Any idea why he keeps taking different ones?'

'I think he's plain crazy,' she said. 'I tried to ask him to turn down his music one night and he screamed at me. Called me a nigger. I said, "Whadda you think *you* are?" He didn't answer.'

'Anything else you can tell us about him? Something that makes you think he's crazy?'

'I talked to his wife a couple times when he had a big party with some Somali friends on New Year's. She said they just chew something called *kaat* and eat their spicy food and gamble all the time. Every one of them has their birthday on New Year's, that's why their party lasted for three days.'

'Why New Year's?' Ronnie asked.

'They're so damn backwards, they don't know when they were born. They just pick any year they want for the immigration papers, and make the birthday fall on New Year's so it's easy to remember. That's what she told me. They're that ignorant. And he has the gall to call *me* a nigger.'

'What's his name?' Ronnie asked.

'Omar,' Mrs. Farnsworth said. 'I found out they're all named Omar, or Muhammad. I don't know his last name.'

'Are you sure he's home now?' Bix asked.

'He sure is,' she said. 'And she is too. That damn music was blaring an hour ago and then it went off and he ain't left the house. I been watching it. He just don't wanna talk to the police, is all.'

'We'll knock and see if he'll open the door,' Bix said. 'And we'll call the store and get the carts picked up.'

'I can tell you this,' Mrs. Farnsworth said. 'His wife is scared of him. You can see that. I'm surprised she come back to him, but maybe she just didn't have no money and nowhere else to go.'

They crossed the street and Ronnie knocked at the door of the cottage while Bix stood to the side, trying to peek into the window through a rip in what looked to be muslin curtains. No answer.

She knocked louder and said, 'Police officers. Open the door, please.'

They could clearly hear some movement inside and then an accented voice said, 'What do you want?'

'We just need to speak to you for a minute,' Ronnie said.

The door opened, and a tall, very dark man with the chiseled facial structure often seen in the Horn of Africa stood in the doorway. He wore only black trousers and tennis shoes, and he was unmistakable by virtue of the pale scar running from his hairline down the right side of his jaw to his throat. His irises were gunmetal blue.

Ronnie said, 'We've received complaints about loud music and about the shopping carts in your yard. Do you know it's against the law to take shopping carts home from the market? That's theft.'

'I will take them back,' he said with a rumbling voice from deep inside him.

'What's your name?' Ronnie asked.

'Omar,' he said.

'And your last name?'

'Omar Hasan Benawi,' he said.

'Why do you take so many carts, Mr. Benawi?' Bix asked.

The man stared at both cops for a moment and said, 'If they steal one cart I have more.'

'If who steals one cart?' Bix asked.

'Them,' he said.

'Who?' Ronnie asked. 'Neighbors?'

'Them,' he said without elaborating but looking off vaguely in the distance with those gunmetal eyes.

'Is your wife home?' Bix asked.

'Yes,' he said.

Ronnie said, 'Let us see her. Now, please.'

The Somalian turned and mumbled something, and a bony young woman wearing a maroon head scarf, pink cotton dress, and sandals came to the door. She wasn't as dark as her husband, but like him, she had sharply defined features, and large, velvety eyes.

'Do you speak English?' Ronnie asked.

She nodded, glancing up at her scowling husband.

'Did you hear what we said to your husband?'

'Yes,' she said. 'I hear.'

'Do you understand that you cannot play loud music at night and that you cannot take shopping carts home from the market?'

'Yes,' she said, looking at her husband again.

'Are you all right?' Bix Ramstead asked.

'Yes,' she said.

'I'd like to talk to you about the shopping carts. Can you step outside, please?' Ronnie said.

The young woman looked at her husband, who hesitated and then nodded. His wife walked onto the porch and followed Ronnie to the front yard, where Ronnie put an overturned cart upright.

Then in a quiet voice, while Bix kept the husband busy by getting names, phone number, and other information, Ronnie said, 'Is there something wrong with your husband?' Ronnie pointed to her head and said, 'Here?'

The young woman glanced back at the house and said, 'No.'

'What is your name?' Ronnie asked.

'Safia,' the young woman said.

'Don't be afraid to tell me the truth, Safia,' Ronnie said. 'Has he hurt you in any way? If he has, we can take you to a shelter where you'll be safe.'

'No, I am fine,' Safia said.

'And your husband,' Ronnie said. 'Is he fine? Up here?' And she pointed to her head again.

'He is fine,' Safia said, eyes downcast.

'Does he have a job?' Ronnie asked.

'No, not now,' Safia said. 'He look for job. I look for job also. I clean houses.'

'How old are you?' Ronnie asked.

'Twenty-one,' she said. 'I think.'

'Do you really want to stay with your husband?' Ronnie asked. 'Is he kind to you?'

'I stay,' the young woman said, looking at Ronnie now. 'My father give me to Omar. I stay.'

Bix left the Somalian on the porch and approached Ronnie and Safia then, saying quietly, 'You do not have to stay with him.'

Speaking slowly and articulating carefully, Ronnie said, 'This is America and you are a free woman. Would you like to get your clothes and leave with us? There are people who can help you.'

'No, no!' the young woman said emphatically. 'I stay.'

Ronnie pressed a business card into the young woman's hand and said, 'Call if you need help. Okay?'

The young woman hid the card in her sleeve and nodded.

Bix Ramstead went back to see Mrs. Farnsworth and gave her one of his business cards, writing his personal cell-phone number on the back of it. 'If you suspect anything really bad is going on over there, I want you to call me. I can be reached at this number anytime.'

And that's how it was left. Bix and Ronnie stopped by the market two blocks away and notified the kid who picked up shopping carts abandoned in the neighborhood that there was a jackpot in Omar's yard.

They went about their business, hoping it was the last they'd hear of Omar Hasan Benawi.

Half an hour later, while driving to Hollywood South, Bix Ramstead said, 'I have a very bad feeling about that Somali couple.'

'So do I,' Ronnie said.

Los Angeles experienced a rare summertime thunderstorm at twilight. The rain came down hard for twenty minutes and then it stopped, and a gigantic rainbow appeared over the Hollywood Hills. It was a magic moment, residents said. And the rain led to an incredible moment that would be remembered in LAPD folklore for years to come. It occurred minutes after the midwatch hit the streets, and the surfer cops were there to see it.

The Gang Impact Team, called GIT, had made arrangements with the watch commander to use two of the midwatch cars and two from the night watch on a surprise sweep of the 18th Street gang. GIT had the highest felony filing rate at Hollywood Detectives and loved to jam the street gangsters, but morale had been suffering ever since the U.S. district judge overseeing the federal consent decree wanted all six hundred LAPD officers assigned to gang and narcotics units to disclose their personal financial records as part of the anti-corruption crusade. However, since that information could be subpoenaed, a cop's bank account information, Social Security number, and much else could end up in the hands of lawyers for street gangsters. Cops were threatening to quit their present assignments rather than let that happen, and their union, the L.A. Police Protective League, was waging a battle on their behalf. It was another of many oppressive, paper-intensive skirmishes during the dreary years of the federal consent decree.

The information that GIT had was that the 18th Street crew were going to cruise south in their lowriders into Southeast L.A. to help other Hispanic gang members mete out street justice to some black gangsters who were suspected of shooting a Latino. More than half of the Los Angeles homicides in the prior calendar year were gang related. The informant indicated that the 18th Street homeboys would be waiting by a chain-link fence next to an apartment house in Southeast Hollywood, where most of them lived. When the cops arrived, eleven of the cruisers were perched on the top of the fence or leaning on the portion that was pulled from the posts and rolled in a tangle of steel wire. At a prearranged signal on the police tactical frequency, the patrol units swooped in, led by two teams of Hollywood gang cops.

None of the homies had seemed particularly disturbed and nobody ran. Several who were smoking cigarettes continued smoking. Nobody tried to toss any crystal or crack. They kept chatting among themselves as though the cops were putting on a good show for their benefit. The crew were not proned out on the ground due to the deep rain puddles that had formed under and around the fence, so the usual commands were modified:

'Turn and face the fence!'

'Interlock your fingers behind your head!'

'Do not move or talk!'

Then the cops began patting down each homie and pulling them aside to write FI cards. The gang cops took various members of the crew to their cars for more private conversations, but all in all it was a disappointment. The consensus was that the information had somehow leaked and the crew were expecting to be jacked up. The gang cops were mad and embarrassed.

During the first twenty minutes of the episode, when a few of the crew were copping attitudes, a cruiser dressed homie-hip in a baggy tee and khakis – with the usual face tatts consisting of spiderwebs and teardrops – turned to his crew and grinned, proudly displaying two gold caps. Like several of the others, he wore a red-and-white bandana around his shaved head.

He said, 'Yo, this ain't right,' to one of the Hispanic gang cops who'd arrested him in the past.

'What ain't right, *ese?*' the gang cop said.

'We're just hangin', man. Ain't no law being broke around here.'

'Homes, I would never accuse you of law breaking,' the gang cop said.

The cruisers were all grinning at one another, and the gang cops became more certain that somehow they had anticipated this sweep.

Flotsam wasn't the least bit surprised and said to Jetsam, 'Dude, have you ever heard of a cop keeping a secret?'

'Might as well give it to *Access Hollywood*,' Jetsam agreed. 'You want it out there? Telephone, telegram, tell-a-cop.'

The surfer cops were waiting for the gang unit to give them the okay to clear, when a motor cop pulled up. He wasn't just any motor cop. He was Officer Francis Xavier Mulroney, a hulking, craggy, old-school veteran who still wore reflector aviator sunglasses and black leather gloves. He had thirty-seven years on the LAPD, thirty of it riding a motorcycle. He was usually assigned to the Hollywood beat, where his nickname 'F.X.' seemed wildly appropriate. He stepped off his bike and walked through the standing puddles, boots splashing any cops who didn't get out of his way.

With his helmet and those boots and his paunch and those glasses, he looked to Jetsam like the guy that played General Patton in that old World War II movie. In fact, he even sounded like the guy, kind of gravelly.

'What's this cluster fuck all about?' he said to the nearest of the two Hispanic gang cops.

The gang cop shrugged and said, 'Nothin' much, looks like.'

Then the motor cop said, 'Why ain't these *vatos* facedown in the fucking water instead of standing around giggling like girls? What, you don't prone out these hanky heads when it's rained?'

The gang cop smiled agreeably and said, 'Roger that message, F.X. I wish we could still do things like back in the day.'

Referring to the May 1 immigration rally in MacArthur Park, which got negative national attention when the LAPD used force on demonstrators and reporters, F.X. Mulroney sneered and said, 'This is May

Day all over again. Like, oh, dear me, let's not rough people up. Shit! Sister Mary Ignatius tuned us up worse than that when I was in the third fucking grade!'

'Roger that,' the gang cop said patiently.

The motor cop said, 'When I came on the Job, we were taught, "When in doubt, choke 'em out." This is why when I retire next year, I'm driving my bike onto the freight elevator at Parker Center and I'm running it right up to the sixth floor and leaving it in front of the door to the chief's office. With a sign addressed to all LAPD brass, the police commission, and the mayor. A sign that says, "Put this crotch rocket between your legs. You got nothing else there." That's what I'm gonna do.'

Clearly, nobody doubted him. Then one of the cops from the night watch turned toward his car to stow his beanbag shotgun.

The old motor cop snorted and said, 'Beanbags. When I came on the Job, beanbags were used by little kids to throw at cutout clowns. That's what they've turned LAPD into, a bunch of clowns!'

'Roger that too,' the gang cop said with a sigh. 'We hear you, F.X. Loud and clear.'

Now the other cops were even more eager to get away from there, what with F.X. Mulroney on the scene. But the homeboys perched on the fence or leaning against it were giving the old motor cop the stink eye. A few of them actually laughed at him. And then a big mistake was made.

The homie with the gold teeth said in a stage whisper to one of his crew, loud enough for F.X. to hear, 'He's so old they should have training wheels on his baby hog.'

All of the 18th Street cruisers chortled at that one.

The motor cop took three big strides in those black, shiny boots toward the night-watch cop standing by the open trunk of his shop, where he was putting away his beanbag gun.

'Lemme borrow this for a minute,' F.X. said, and he pulled the cop's Taser from his Sam Browne.

'Hey!' the cop said. 'Whadda you think you're doing?'

'We only got those bulky old piece-of-shit Tasers in our saddle-bags. This is the new one, ain't it?'

'What're you doing?' the cop repeated.

The old motor cop showed the young night-watch cop what he was doing.

'Homes,' the motor cop said to the banger with the gold teeth, and to all the other food-stamp homeboys in their $200 Adidas, 'don't ever keep an electric appliance around your bathtub. And don't *ever* stand in a rain puddle and lean on a chain-link fence. A bolt from heaven could strike.'

And he fired a dart that was attached to the gun by a twenty-one-foot copper wire, right into the tangle of fencing.

When the prongs bit and hooked onto the wet steel, fifty thousand volts made a crackling sound and arced a blue dagger like in Frankenstein's lab. And the cops watched in astonishment as the homies started doing the Taser dance.

Two dropped off the fence and three fence leaners fell ass-first in the rain puddles. The rest leaped clear after experiencing shocks, mostly imagined, and everyone began screaming and cursing.

'He fucking electrocuted me!'

'I'm suing!'

'All you cops are witnesses!'

'I got a burn on my ass!'

And F.X. Mulroney joined in the chorus, crying out, 'But I was only doing a spark check! Shit happens!'

'*Pinchi* cop!' Gold Tooth yelled. 'He shocked us! You saw it!'

'My lawyer!' a homie yelled. 'I'm calling my lawyer!'

Flotsam and Jetsam stared as Officer Francis X. Mulroney spread his arms wide, looked up at the darkening sky, and cried, 'God knows I'm innocent! Even Bill Clinton had a premature discharge!'

'I'm fucking suing!' Gold Tooth yelled.

F.X. Mulroney bowed his head then and murmured, 'Oh, the horror. The horror!' Flotsam whispered to Jetsam, 'F.X. always goes over the top. He's, like, way dramatic.' Jetsam whispered back, 'In Hollywood everybody's an actor.'

All the drama caused Flotsam and Jetsam to walk quietly to their shop, start the engine, and drive away before anyone noticed they were gone.

Most of the other bluesuits were doing the same, and the gang cop pulled Gold Tooth aside and said, 'Homes, I think you better forget all about this . . . accident.'

'Accident, my ass!' the homie said.

The gang cop said, 'Can you imagine what'll happen if this story gets out? That crazy old motor cop can retire anytime. You can't hurt him. But everybody'll be laughing like hyenas. At you, dude. At your whole posse. MS Thirteen will laugh. White Fence will laugh. *El Eme* will laugh. All the Crips and Bloods from

Southeast L.A. that done your people wrong, they'll laugh the loudest. You'll hear fucking laughter in your sleep!'

Gold Tooth thought it over and huddled with his crew for a minute or two. When he returned, he said, 'Okay, but we don't want nobody to know about this, right? All your cops gotta keep their mouths shut.'

'If there's one thing cops can do, it's keep a secret,' the gang cop said.

When they were two blocks from the scene, Flotsam said, 'Dude, do you realize we were a witness to Hollywood history being made? That old copper just brought down a whole crew with one fucking shot!'

'We didn't see nothing, bro,' Jetsam said. 'We were already gone when history was being made.' After a pause, he said, 'When he's ready to pull the pin, do you think that loony old motor cop will really, like, drive his bike up to the chief's office and leave it there with a sign on it?'

'What motor cop?' Flotsam replied.

TEN

IT WORRIED RONNIE SINCLAIR that her partner, Bix
Ramstead, was so troubled by the encounter with the
Somalians. They were at Starbucks on Sunset
Boulevard, both doing some paperwork before going
end-of-watch. Bix, never garrulous, had been unusually
quiet all day.

The third time he brought it up he said, 'Sometimes
I think being a copper turns you into an animal in more
ways than one. The hair on my neck hasn't settled down
since we first laid eyes on that scar-faced Somali. That
guy's fifty-one-fifty, for sure.'

'He's way out there, no doubt,' Ronnie said, 'but
what could we do about it? There was no evidence of
violent behavior. I gave her every chance to walk outta
there and she flat-out refused. What could we do?'

'Nothing, I suppose,' Bix said. 'But wasn't your blue
radar blinking? That dude's gonna hurt that girl.'

'He's probably hurt her already,' Ronnie said. 'Lots
and lots of times. He owns her, according to their
customs. You know we couldn't pick her up and bundle
her out on the basis of blue radar, Bix.'

'Of course,' he said, 'but it still bothers me.'

'The way I look at stuff like that is, it's not my

tragedy. I have to see it, but I don't have to take it home with me. I let it go.'

'My wife's told me that for years,' Bix said. 'That's one of the reasons I got into CRO. Her telling me I was bringing too much shit home with me for too many years.'

'She was right,' Ronnie said, thinking that every once in a while she'd run into a cop like Bix Ramstead, someone who didn't have the right temperament for the Job. Somebody who couldn't let it go.

He suddenly looked a bit embarrassed, as cops do when they indulge in uncoplike self-revelatory talk. He turned the conversation to her. 'You ever gonna get married again, you think?'

'I'm not in the market,' Ronnie said. 'I've proven to be a bad shopper. Besides, I'm concentrating on passing the sergeant's exam. But if I ever get married again, it will *not* be to another cop.'

Bix smiled and said, 'Smart girl.'

And Ronnie thought, If you weren't already bought and paid for, buddy, I might make an exception. She was surprised by how much she liked Bix. Those sensitive, dusky gray eyes of his could make a girl's knees tremble.

She said, 'Will you be staying on the Job until the bitter end?'

'Until I'm fifty-five, at least,' he said. 'I've got a couple of teenagers who'll have to get through college, and my daughter is talking about becoming a physician. I won't be retiring any time soon, that's for sure.'

Ronnie almost suggested that he might consider an inside job somewhere, one that would keep him from the likes of Omar Hasan Benawi and his pitiful wife, but she thought she shouldn't be offering career advice to a veteran like Bix. Besides, the Community Relations Office was the next best thing to an inside job. How much real police work would they ever have to do as Crows?

She said, 'A couple of us are heading up to Sunset after work for a few tacos and a tequila or two. Wanna come?'

Bix hesitated, but he obviously trusted Ronnie and could confide in her in ways he might not to a male officer. He said, 'I'd better not join you. I have a bit of a problem.'

'Problem?'

'I haven't had a drink for almost a month, and I'm reluctant to go places where everyone else is powering them down.'

'Sorry, I didn't know,' Ronnie said.

'It's nothing major,' Bix said. 'I've been dealing with it for years. On the wagon, off the wagon. I deal with it.'

'I hear you,' Ronnie said. 'My first ex was an alcoholic in denial. Still is.'

'I'm not an alcoholic,' Bix said quickly. 'I just don't handle booze very well. When I drink, my personality changes. My wife, Darcey, put me on notice last month when I came home hammered, and I'm grateful she did. I feel a lot better now. Getting too old for that nonsense.'

Ronnie didn't know what else to say, and Bix obviously thought he'd said too much. They finished their cappuccinos and their reports silently.

*　　*　　*

Hollywood Nate Weiss could not wait to log out at 7:30 P.M. He'd changed from his uniform into a pricey white linen shirt, and black jeans from Nordstrom's. He'd thought about really dressing up but figured it might make him look like some schmuck who'd never had a private supper at the home of some flaming hot, bucks-up chick in the Hollywood Hills. Which was the case exactly.

While driving to Mt. Olympus he thought of half a dozen opening remarks he could say to her, but rehearsing aloud made them sound dumber than they did in his mind. He almost parked on the street in front but decided that as a guest he was entitled to pull into the bricked motor court. The lot was quite expansive for a view site in the hills, where land was scarce, and the motor court was large enough for an easy U-turn. The house itself was deceivingly large, with a Spanish-tile roof, white plaster walls, exposed beams, and lots of arches, a style that realtors liked to call 'early California.' A cinch to sell, especially to non-Californians who found it romantic.

Nate was very happy to see that there were no other cars in the motor court. He'd been worried that the babysitter might have decided to stay with the kid at Margot's house. Or that maybe Margot had invited somebody else to her pasta supper. He attempted to stay calm, trying on the affable but poised mini-smile he'd used successfully in his last piece-of-shit movie, and rang the bell.

Margot showed him that dazzling smile when she opened the door. She too was wearing jeans, low-cut designer jeans, and a yellow tee that stopped six inches before the jeans began. His eyes went from her eyes directly to that tan, muscular belly. She'd pulled back her heavy butterscotch hair and pinned it with a tortoiseshell comb.

Extending her warm, dry hand, she took his and said, 'Officer Weiss. You look so different in civilian clothes.'

'The uniform makes the man, huh?' He tried to keep the tremble out of his voice, needing one drink to mellow out.

Seeming to read his mind, she said, 'What can I get you to drink? And to answer your question, you don't need a uniform. In fact, you look much younger now.'

Nate tried on a broader smile and said, 'Wine?'

'Name your flavor.'

'Whatever you're having.'

'Pinot grigio it is,' she said. 'I'm not a wine snob. Just give me an honest California pinot and I'm happy as a lark in the park. Come in and pour while I finish the pasta.'

Nate entered and was drawn at once to the living room, with its view of Hollywood and beyond. Blankets of lights, some twinkling, some still, and the summer smog hanging low and dark against the golden glow of sunset actually calmed him. The view wasn't as good as some he'd seen from houses in the Hollywood Hills farther west, but this would do. He couldn't imagine how many millions a home with a view would cost around there.

As far as the furnishings, it looked a trifle overdone, like many of the westside living rooms he'd seen in *Los Angeles* magazine and the *L.A. Times*. An unpleasant image of the Arab ex sitting on one of those plush sofas smoking a hookah flashed and faded.

Nothing could spoil it for him. It all smelled like big bucks to Hollywood Nate Weiss.

'You know,' he said, 'from here even the smog looks beautiful.'

Margot chuckled and he thought it sounded charming and warm. Everything about her was warm.

She said, 'Come on, boy, let's away with us to the kitchen, where you can pour us some grape. I need to let my hair down whenever my five-year-old stays over with our au pair.'

Nate followed her into a very large gourmet kitchen with two stainless-steel side-by-side refrigerator-freezer combinations and a commercial gas range and oven, also done in stainless steel. There were three steel sinks, and he wondered which she'd choose when she drained a pan of pasta. Too many choices!

He picked up the corkscrew and the bottle of pinot grigio and tried to peel off the neck seal and extract the cork like he'd seen sommeliers do it on those occasions when he could afford to take a date to an expensive restaurant. He had some trouble with the cork, but she didn't seem to notice.

'Have you been a police officer long, Nate?' she asked.

'Yeah, almost fifteen years,' he said.

'Really?' Margot said. 'You don't look old enough.'

'I'm thirty-six,' he said. Then he added, 'You don't look old enough to have a five-year-old child.'

'I could have one a lot older, but I'm *not* telling you my age,' she said.

'I already know,' Nate said. 'Your driver's license, remember?'

'Drat!' she said. 'I forgot.'

Nate poured wine into the glasses and put one on the drain board by Margot.

'Does your son stay with your nanny often?' Nate asked.

'Only on very special occasions,' Margot said, and there was that coy smile again.

He took a big swallow then but told himself to slow it down, way down. He began thinking of acting tricks, such as pretending that this was a movie starring Nate Weiss. Trying to get himself into character but uncertain whom the character should resemble. Hollywood Nate Weiss simply had no frame of reference for a date like this one.

'So are you really interested in the Mercedes?' Margot said.

'Of course,' Nate said nervously. 'Why else would I have called?'

She stopped slicing the mango. Repressing a grin, she glanced at him before saying deadpan, 'I can't imagine.'

Nate felt his face burning. He *was* like a kid around this woman! 'Am I lame or what?' he finally said. 'Sure, I love the Mercedes, but I just bought a new car last year. You should kick me right outta here.'

Margot brought the wine bottle to the bar counter, topped off his glass, and said with sudden seriousness, 'I was glad you called, Nate.'

'Really?'

'Really,' she said. 'To tell you the truth, I've been frightened about something and I was thinking about talking to the police.'

'Frightened of what?'

'Let's have supper and then we'll talk,' Margot said.

Gert Von Braun was teamed with Dan Applewhite for the first time after he returned from his days off. The other cops figured that putting Doomsday Dan with someone as explosive as Gert would produce a match made in hell. The surfer cops had bets on how long Gert could listen to Dan talking about the worldwide Muslim calamity on the horizon, or the imminent collapse of the world financial markets, before she threw a choke hold on him. What they didn't know was how much Dan and Gert's mutual loathing of Sergeant Treakle would produce a bond that nobody could have predicted.

It began when Sergeant Treakle informed Gert that the accidental discharge of the shotgun was going to result in an official reprimand for certain, the first in her eleven-year career. She was ready for it, of course, but not in the way the information was delivered.

Sergeant Treakle, who rarely bothered to learn any cop's first name, called her into the sergeants' room and said, 'Von Braun, you will be getting an official reprimand for your carelessness with the shotgun.'

'I figured,' Gert said and prepared to leave.

'Furthermore,' he said, and she paused at the doorway, 'it will result in a serious penalty if such a thing should ever happen again.'

Gert's rosy complexion went white around her mouth and she said, 'You think it's ever gonna happen again, Sergeant?'

'I'm just giving you a word to the wise,' the young

sergeant said, looking away nervously. Gert's collar size was larger than his, and it was rumored that she had embarrassed a male cop at Central Division when he'd boozily arm wrestled her at the Christmas party.

She forced herself to stay calm and said, 'Thanks for the words of wisdom.' And again she tried to leave.

But Sergeant Treakle said, 'Part of the problem could be your physical condition.'

That stopped her cold. In fact, she took a step toward his desk and said, 'What about my physical condition?'

'Your weight,' he said. 'It must be hard to move around quickly enough when something unexpected happens. Like your cell phone falling and you trying to grab it, and accidentally hitting the shotgun trigger. Police officers must be ready to think and act quickly. Like athletes, as it were.'

Gert dead-stared Sergeant Treakle for a moment and then said very softly, 'I've passed every physical since I came on the Job. And I was first in the agility test for women in the academy. And I've competed twice in the Police Olympics. Now I have a question for you. Have you ever heard of EEO laws?'

'Equal Employment Opportunity?'

'That's right, Sergeant,' she said. 'It's all about discrimination in the workplace. And I'm giving you a gift right now by forgetting about this conversation. Because you're *offending* me in a very personal way.'

Sergeant Treakle blanched and said, 'We'll talk later. I've got some calls to make.'

By the time Gert Von Braun joined Dan Applewhite in the parking lot, the grim set of her jaw told him that it wasn't the time to tell her that staph infections had stricken several officers in neighboring divisions and an outbreak was imminent.

She drove in silence for five minutes, and when she spoke, she said, 'Have you had any personal dealings with Treakle?'

'Once,' Dan Applewhite said. 'He told me I had a sour expression when talking to citizens and that my attitude needed improving. He said he was sure I could improve my outlook on life by attending Bible study with him. He's a born-again and got baptized in a pond somewhere, with people singing on the bank.'

'He told you that?'

Dan Applewhite nodded. 'I told him I'm a Unitarian. I could tell he didn't know what that was.'

'Neither do I,' Gert said, then added, 'we had a sergeant like him at Central Station. Things started happening to that guy.'

'What kind of things?'

'Mostly to his car. If he forgot to lock it, he'd find a string tied from his light-bar switch to the door. Or he'd find the plastic cord-cuffs hanging from his axle making noise while he was driving. Or he'd find talcum powder in his air vent. It'd make his uniform look like he was caught in a blizzard.'

'That's kid stuff,' Dan Applewhite said.

'Once when a truck got jacked that was hauling huge bags of popcorn and candy to a chamber of commerce holiday party, we recovered it and somebody filled the sergeant's private car with popcorn. I mean from the floor to the roofline. You looked inside his windshield and all you could see was popcorn.'

'That's kid stuff,' Dan Applewhite repeated.

Gert said, 'Then one night somebody paid a skid row derelict ten bucks to do some asphalt skiing. The cop who did it borrowed an old piece of plywood roofing from one of the makeshift lean-tos where the transients sleep and tied a piece of rope to it and attached the rope to the sergeant's car while he was inside a diner. And the derelict was promised another ten if he'd hang on for a whole block. He did, but it was pretty gnarly. Sparks were flying and the derelict started yelling and it pretty much all went sideways. People on the street were shocked, and the captain's phone rang off the hook the next day. IA investigated the night watch for a month but never caught the culprit. All the derelict would say was, the guy who hired him was a cop and all cops look alike when they're in uniform. The sergeant got ten days off for not looking after his car.'

'Well, that's not childish,' Dan Applewhite said. 'It's much more mature when you can get an asshole like that a ten-day suspension.'

It was less than a half hour later that Sergeant Treakle himself rolled on a call assigned to 6-X-66. Dan Applewhite groaned when he turned and saw the young supervisor pull up in front of an apartment building in Thai Town that was occupied mostly by Asian immigrants.

'Chickenlips is here to check on us,' he warned Gert, who was knocking at the door.

The caller was a Thai woman who looked too old to have a twelve-year-old daughter but did. The girl was crying when the cops arrived, and the mother was furious. The girl's auntie, who was a decade younger than the mother, had been trying to calm things. The auntie spoke passable English and translated for the mother.

The trouble had started earlier in the day when the local clinic informed the mother that her twelve-year-old daughter's bouts of vomiting were the result of an early pregnancy. The mother wanted the culprit found and arrested.

Of course, the cops separated the kid from her mom, Gert walking the child into a tidy bedroom, talking to her gently, saying, 'Wipe your eyes, honey. And don't be afraid.'

The child, who was all cheekbones and kewpie lips, had lived in L.A. since she was eight, and her English was good. She stopped sobbing long enough to say to Gert, 'Will I be taken to juvenile hall?'

'You won't be taken anywhere, sweetie,' Gert said. 'All of this can be handled. But we must find out who put the baby in you.'

The child dropped her eyes and asked, 'Am I in trouble?' Then she began sobbing again.

'Now, now,' Gert said. 'There's no need to do that. You're not in trouble with us. We're your friends.' Then sensing someone behind her, she turned and saw Sergeant Treakle standing there watching.

Gert tried but failed to suppress the sigh that popped out of her, then said to the sergeant, 'I wonder if you'd mind letting us females talk about this in private.'

Sergeant Treakle arched an eyebrow, grunted, and returned to the kitchen, where Dan Applewhite was getting a list of potential suspects for the follow-up by detectives. The child had no siblings, but there were uncles, cousins, and neighbors who were possibles.

Sergeant Treakle looked at his watch a couple of times, and when Gert left the girl in the bedroom and came back to the kitchen, he said, 'Who's the daddy?'

'I don't know,' Gert said. 'The sex crimes team will have to talk to her.'

'All that time and you don't know?' Sergeant Treakle said.

Her voice flat as a razor, Gert said, 'The child says she doesn't know how it happened.'

Sergeant Treakle guffawed loudly and said, 'She doesn't *know*?'

Knowing his religious views, Gert Von Braun said, 'Tell me, Sergeant Treakle, what if the young girl's name was Mary? And the baby inside her was gonna be named Jesus, would you still scoff? After all, Mary didn't know how the hell it happened either. *Did* she now?'

The sergeant's jaws opened and shut twice, but nothing came out. He started to say something to Dan Applewhite, but nothing happened there either. He left the apartment and hurried to his car to make a negative entry in his log.

When they got back to their shop and started driving, Dan Applewhite took a good look at Gert Von Braun. He was a lot older and knew he wasn't much to look at. And he couldn't seem to keep a wife for very long, no matter how much money he spent on her. But he was starting to develop feelings he hadn't had for a while. Despite her bulk and scary reputation, Gert Von Braun was starting to grow very attractive.

'What say we stop at Starbucks, Gert?' he said impulsively, then added something that usually interested other female partners. 'I'd love to buy us a latte and biscotti.'

Gert shrugged and said, 'I'm not much for sissy coffee, but I wouldn't mind an In-N-Out burger.'

And *zing* went the strings of his heart! He grinned big and said, 'Okay! One In-N-Out burger coming up!'

'With grilled onions and double the fries,' Gert added.

He was back at an ATM that night, a different one this time, on Hollywood Boulevard. Leonard Stilwell had worked diligently to set the film trap with the glue strips in place. He couldn't sit around his room waiting for the job with Ali. The advance that Ali had given him was gone, smoked up in his pipe and lost on those goddamn Dodgers after he was stupid enough to make a bet with a sports book who'd beaten him 90 percent of the time.

Despite his prior misgivings and fear of all the cops he'd seen around the Kodak Center, the area offered an irresistible attraction in the persons of all those doofus tourists. So after casing carefully, he'd decided that a certain one of the ATMs wasn't quite as dangerous as the others because it was in a dark corner and provided an easier escape route to the residential street several blocks away where he'd parked his old Honda. Now he was watching that ATM. Several Asians with cameras dangling from their necks almost bit. They'd be no good to him unless they spoke enough English to accept his 'help.'

The ATM customer who finally stopped was the one he wanted. The guy was at least seventy years old and so was his wife. He was carrying a bag from one of the boulevard souvenir shops and she was carrying another one. They wore walking shorts and tennis shoes and their baseball caps had pins all over them from Universal Studios' tour, Disneyland, and Knott's Berry Farm. Her brand new T-shirt said 'Movies For Me' across the back. Just looking at them made him imagine the heavenly smoke filling his lungs.

The guy put his card into the slot but nothing happened. He punched in his PIN and looked at his wife. Then he looked around, presumably for help, just as a younger man with hair the color of an overripe pumpkin, a wash of freckles, and a howdy-folks smile walked to the machine, holding his own ATM card in his hand.

'Are you finished with your transaction, sir?' Leonard said.

'There's something wrong with the machine,' the tourist said. 'My card won't come out and the dang thing doesn't work.'

'Golly,' Leonard said, as syrupy as he could manage. 'I've run into this before. Do you mind if I try something?'

'Help yourself, young man,' the tourist said. 'I sure don't wanna be calling my bank and canceling my card. Not when we just got to Hollywood.'

'Don't blame you,' Leonard said. 'Let's see.'

He stepped forward, put his fingers on the 'enter' and 'cancel' keys, and said, 'Way it was explained to me is, you punch in your PIN number at the same time you hold down "cancel" and "enter," and it should kick out the card. Wanna try it?'

'Sure,' the tourist said. 'Let's see, I hold down which two keys?'

'Here, lemme help,' Leonard said. 'I'll hold the two keys down and you just go ahead and punch in your PIN number.'

'I'll hold down the keys,' a deep voice behind Leonard said.

He turned and saw a guy his age. A tall, buffed-out guy looking him right in the eye. Leonard's Adam's apple bobbed.

'This is my son,' the tourist said. 'There's something wrong with the machine, Wendell. This fellow's helping us.'

'That's nice of him,' Wendell said but never took his stare from Leonard's watery blue eyes, not for an instant.

Leonard said, 'Go ahead and punch in your PIN number.' But he didn't dare look at the keyboard. In fact, he made it a point to look away.

'Nothing,' the tourist said. 'Not a goldang thing happened.'

'Well, guess you'll have to cancel it,' Leonard said. 'It was worth a try. Sorry I couldn't help you.'

As he was sidling away, he heard the woman say, 'See, Wendell, there's lots of real nice, polite people in Hollywood.'

Leonard felt like weeping by the time he'd walked several blocks to his car. He needed crack so bad he couldn't think of anything else. He wasn't even hungry, although he hadn't eaten a real meal for two days. And to make matters worse, there was a police car parked behind his car with its headlights on, and two cops were giving him a goddamn ticket!

'Is this your car?' Flotsam asked when Leonard approached, keys in hand.

'Yeah, what's wrong?' Leonard said.

'What's wrong?' Jetsam said. 'Take a look where you're parked.'

Leonard walked around to the front of the car and saw that he was halfway across a narrow concrete driveway belonging to an old two-story stucco house that was crammed between two newer apartment buildings. He hadn't noticed the driveway when he'd parked, not after he'd circled the streets for twenty minutes, looking for a parking place where he wouldn't get a goddamn ticket like this.

'Gimme a break!' Leonard said. 'I'm between jobs. And even if I wasn't tapped, I couldn't give my ride to those goofy wetbacks at the pay lot. They'll back your car right up onto the fanny pack of the first tourist dumb enough to take a shortcut through the parking lot, and then what?'

'Too late,' Flotsam said. 'It's already written. Lucky you came back, though. The guy in that house wanted your car towed.'

'No mercy,' Leonard said. 'There ain't a drop of mercy and compassion in this whole fucking town.'

Jetsam had his flashlight beam close enough to Leonard's face to see the twitching and sweat. He raised the light to check Leonard's pupils and said, 'Got some ID?'

'What for?' Leonard said. 'I haven't done nothing.'

'You drive this car,' Jetsam said. 'You have a driver's license, right?'

Leonard reached in his pocket for his wallet. 'Not

a drop of mercy or compassion for a fellow human being,' Leonard said, taking the parking citation from Flotsam and handing Jetsam his driver's license.

Jetsam took the license and walked back to their shop and sat down inside it.

'Aw, shit,' Leonard said. 'What's he doing, calling in on me?'

'Just routine,' Flotsam said, giving Leonard a quick pat-down.

'That's what they always say,' Leonard whined. 'Do you guys ever give a person a break? I mean ever?'

'Whadda you been arrested for?' Flotsam asked.

'You're gonna find out in a few minutes,' Leonard said. 'Couple of small-time thefts is all. I learned my lesson. I'm just a working stiff now. Between jobs.'

When Jetsam came back, he said to his partner, 'Mr. Stilwell here has two priors for burglary and one for petty theft.'

'The burglaries were reduced to petty theft,' Leonard said. 'I pled guilty and I only got county jail time. The petty theft was for shoplifting when I had to steal some groceries for an elderly neighbor who was sick. Jesus! Can't a guy get a second chance?'

By then, both cops figured him for a crackhead or maybe a tweaker, and Flotsam said, 'Mr. Stilwell, you wouldn't object if we took a look in your car, would you? Just routine, of course.'

'Go ahead,' Leonard said. 'If I said no, you'd find an excuse to do it anyways.'

'Are you saying no?' Jetsam said.

'I'm saying just do what the fuck you gotta do so I can go home. I give up. There ain't a drop of mercy and compassion and charity left in this whole fucking city. Here.'

He pulled the keys from his pocket and tossed them to Jetsam, who opened the door and did a quick search for drugs in the glove box, under the seats and floor mats, and in other obvious places. All he saw was a note behind the visor with an address on it. He recognized the street as one on Mt. Olympus near the house where a multiple murder involving Russian gangsters had occurred. He jotted the address down in his notebook.

When he was finished, he nodded to Flotsam and said, 'Okay, Mr. Stilwell, thanks for the cooperation.'

By then Leonard was shaking his head in disgust, and when he got into his car, he was mumbling aloud about the merciless, pitiless, fucking city he lived in.

'Let's drive up to Mount Olympus for a minute,' Jetsam said when they were back in their shop.

'What for?'

'That guy had an address behind his visor. What would a loser like that be doing up on Mount Olympus? Except casing a house, maybe.'

'There you go again,' Flotsam said. 'Dude, you are determined to go all detective and sleuthy on my time. Maybe the guy's looking to become a gardener or something. Did you think of that?'

'He's the wrong color. Come on, bro, it'll just take a few minutes.'

Flotsam headed for the Hollywood Hills without another word and, finding the winding street, followed it up to the top.

Jetsam checked addresses and said, 'This number don't exist.'

'Okay,' Flotsam said. 'You satisfied now?'

He turned around just as Jetsam spotted a familiar car in a driveway a few houses away from where the street address should have been.

'That's Hollywood Nate's ride!' he said.

'That Mustang?'

'Yeah.'

'Dude, there's lots of Mustangs in this town.'

Jetsam grabbed the spotlight and shined it on the car. 'How many with a license plate that says SAG4NW?'

'What?'

'Screen Actors Guild for Nate Weiss. How many?'

'So?'

'Maybe we should stop and see if the resident knows a Leonard Stilwell.'

'Look, dude,' Flotsam said. 'We already dragged Hollywood Nate into one of your wild goose chases. We ain't gonna interrupt whatever he's doing in there with another of your clues. And knowing him, whatever he's doing in there involves pussy, that much is totally for sure. So he is not gonna be happy to see us, no matter what.'

'Bro, this could be something he should know about.'

'It's the wrong goddamn address!' Flotsam said. 'You can tell Nate all about it tomorrow. That thief we just shook ain't gonna be killing no residents on this street tonight. You good with that?'

'I guess I gotta be,' Jetsam said.

'Tomorrow you can call Sleuths R Us if you get more brainstorms.'

'Bro, do you think you could stop ripping on me

about that?' Jetsam said. 'So I made a mistake about the SUVs. Can't you just step off?'

Flotsam said, 'I'm off it. Somebody's gotta prove there's a drop of mercy and compassion in this whole fucking city. Are we gravy, dude?'

'Gravy, bro,' Jetsam said. 'Long as you don't mention it again.'

'I'm off it forever,' Flotsam said. 'And that's the truth, sleuth.'

ELEVEN

Of COURSE, Hollywood Nate didn't know anything at all about the surfers' debate taking place out on the street in front of the Aziz home. He was sitting at the dining room table, sipping wine and looking into the amber eyes of Margot Aziz, who kept topping off his wineglass and trying to persuade him that she made the best martinis in Hollywood.

Finally he said, 'I'm just not much of a martini guy. The wine is great and the pasta and salad were sensational.'

'Just a simple four-cheese noodle,' she said. 'Your mom called it macaroni and cheese.'

'I should help you with the dishes,' he said. 'I'm good at it. My ex-wife was dishwashing obsessive and turned me into a kitchen slave.'

'No dishes for us, boyo,' she said. 'My housekeeper will be here in the morning, and she gets mad when there's not something extra for her to do.' Then she said, 'Did you have kids with your ex?'

'That was the one good thing about my marriage. No kids.'

'Can be good or bad,' she said. 'Nicky is the only

good thing about my marriage, which will soon be officially over, praise the Lord.'

Nate looked around and said, 'Will you get to keep this house?'

'We're selling it,' she said. 'Which is sad. This is the only home Nicky's ever known. Did your wife get to keep your house?'

'It was an apartment,' Nate said. 'More or less a pots 'n' pans divorce. She came out of it way better than I did. Married a doctor and now lives the way a Jewish princess was meant to live. Her father hated it when she married a cop. She shoulda listened to him. I shoulda listened to him.'

Margot said, 'My Nicky is five years old and deserves to keep the lifestyle he's always had.'

'Sure,' Nate said. 'Of course.'

'I worry a lot about him, and that's part of what I need to talk to you about.'

'Okay,' Nate said. 'I'm listening.'

'I've become afraid of his father.' Then she stopped, took another sip of wine, and said, 'Sure you won't have a martini? I've just gotta have one when I talk about my husband, Ali Aziz.'

'No, really,' Nate said. 'You go ahead.'

Margot Aziz got up and walked out of the dining room and into a butler's pantry, then to the kitchen, where Nate could hear her scooping from an ice maker. He got up and joined her, watching her make the cocktail.

'I'm not a big-city girl,' she said. 'I'm from Barstow, California. Where desert teens spend Saturday night dining at the historic Del Taco fast-food joint and getting deflowered at the prehistoric El Rancho Motel. I dreamed of being an entertainer. Danced and sang at all the school assemblies and plays. I was Margaret Osborne then, voted the most talented girl in the senior class.'

She was quiet for a moment, and when they reentered the dining room, she said, 'A James Bond vodka martini. Shaken, not stirred. Can't I tempt you?'

'No, really, Margot, I'm feeling just perfect.' He wondered if 'tempt' was meant as a double entendre, hoping it was.

She tasted the martini, nodded in satisfaction, and said, 'The problem was, when I came to Hollywood and started looking for an agent and attending cattle calls and auditions, I discovered that every girl here was the most talented girl in her school. Changing my name from Margaret to Margot didn't glam it up much.' She gave a self-deprecating shrug.

'I suspected you were a dancer,' Nate said. 'Those legs.'

'Since turning thirty I've gotta work harder to keep things in place.' She sipped again, put the martini down, and said, 'I wasn't born to all this. My dad worked for the post office, and it almost broke my parents to put my older sister through college. Lucky for them, I didn't want that. I wanted to dance, and I decided I was going to give it all I had. And that I did for nearly four years. I did waitressing to buy food and keep my car running. And then I did other things.'

Nate thought he'd heard this story before. Or seen it in just about every movie ever made about showbiz wannabes. He waited while she lowered her amber eyes as if ashamed, and he finally said, 'Other things?'

'I became a topless dancer at some of the clubs on the boulevards. It was good money compared to what I'd been surviving on. Sometimes I made five hundred dollars a night on tips alone.'

She looked at him as though awaiting a response, so he said, 'A girl's gotta make a living somehow. This is a tough town.'

'Exactly,' she said. 'But I never danced at the totally nude clubs. Those no-liquor joints that do totally nude attract servicemen and other rowdy young guys. I'd never take all my clothes off.'

'I understand,' Nate said, but he was wondering how big a difference a G-string made. He remembered a screen-writing class he'd taken at UCLA. Reductive. This freaking story was reductive.

'And then I got a job at the Leopard Lounge,' Margot said, 'and I met Ali Aziz.'

'Your husband,' Nate said.

She nodded and said, 'He owned two clubs. I danced at the Leopard Lounge for more than two years and made quite a lot of money, by my standards. I moved into a very nice condo, and Ali kept taking me on dinner dates and buying me expensive presents and behaving like a real gentleman. And he kept begging me to move into this house with him, but I refused. And finally he convinced me that he would be a kind and loving husband. Fool that I am, I accepted his proposal and married him, but only when he agreed to a proper marriage with no prenuptial. By the way, have you ever heard of my husband?'

'The name's familiar,' Nate said. 'We have a Nightclub Committee that's run by our Community Relations Office. I think maybe I've seen the name.'

'He makes sure he donates to all of the Hollywood police charities. You may have run into him at police events. He's chummy with lots of the officers at Hollywood Station.'

'Yeah, I do think I've heard of Ali Aziz,' Nate said, wondering how chummy Ali would be with the Jewish cops at Hollywood Station.

'My parents were not thrilled when I told them about Ali, but I took him home to Barstow just before the wedding and they were very impressed by his good manners. He even assured my mother that if we had children, they would be raised Christian.' This time when she paused, she took another sip from the martini and yet again topped off Nate's wineglass.

'Back then it was peachy, huh?' Nate said, thinking, she was the most exciting woman he'd ever shared a meal with in his entire life, but this sappy story was killing his wood!

'For sure,' Margot said. 'The honeymoon was in Tuscany and he bought me a little Porsche for a wedding present, and of course I never had to set foot in the Leopard Lounge again, except to help him with the books. The last real work I ever did in that place was when I talked him into a major refurbishing and he let me do the design.'

Nate sneaked a look at his watch. It was 10:30 and they weren't even close to getting naked. And all the goddamn wine was making him gassy. Pretty soon he'd be farting!

He said, 'So after a few years of marriage, what? He was no longer a gentleman?'

'He's a fucking pig!' Margot said it so viciously it startled him.

'What happened?'

'Women. Cocaine. Even gambling. And the scary thing, he kept talking about leaving Hollywood. Leaving America. Going back to the Middle East with Nicky and me.'

'Nice,' Nate said. 'I can just see you in a burka, or one of those other beekeeper outfits.'

'He said I'd like Saudi Arabia. Claimed he had connections there, even though he's not a Saudi. I said I'd die first, and that he wasn't taking my son anywhere.'

'And that started the fireworks?'

'Definitely,' she said. 'And it resulted in my filing for divorce and starting a really big-time dispute over the division of property. But that's another story.'

Nate finally decided that even if all this was gospel, it was hard to feel sympathy for rich people. He offered an official police response, saying, 'Has he hurt you or threatened you in any way?'

'That's why I wanted to talk to you tonight,' she said. 'He *has* threatened me, but in very subtle ways.'

'Like how?'

'Like when he comes to pick up Nicky for his visit. He'll say things like, "Enjoy this while you can." Or, "A boy needs his father, not a mother like you." Then he makes signs.'

'What signs?'

'He points a finger at me like a gun. Once he mouthed the word *bang*. Things like that.'

'That's not much in the way of a threat. And it'd be his word against yours.'

'That's what the other officer said.'

'What other officer?'

'I've talked to another of your officers about it. An officer I met last year with my husband at one of the Tip-A-Cop fund-raisers. I can't remember his name. I told him what was going on, but he said that I should talk it over with my divorce lawyer. He said that so far, my husband hadn't done anything criminal that I could prove.'

'Took the words right outta my mouth,' Nate said.

'But last week when Ali brought Nicky home, he said something that made my blood run cold.'

Nate remembered his screen-writing professor saying that no screenplay should ever contain those last three words. 'Yeah?' he said, trying to muster enthusiasm.

'He said if I didn't agree to sign certain business documents, something very bad would happen.'

'What documents?'

'Documents pertaining to the businesses, the stock portfolio, and properties we own.'

In a minor way Nate had an understanding of divorce law, and at last something piqued his interest. He said, 'You mean you're an owner right along with him of everything?'

'Yes, of course,' she said.

And now Hollywood Nate started getting a woody once again. This Barstow babe must be a world-class piece of ass to have rigged a deal like this with a dude from the Middle East! Nate said, 'He wants you to sign off on certain things?'

'On certain things I can't even talk about. Signatures I agreed to give so that he could avoid certain tax liability, as well as others of his dealings I can't discuss.'

'Back to the very bad thing that would happen,' Nate said. 'Did he describe what might happen?'

'He's too smart for that,' Margot said. 'But he drew his finger across his throat.'

Here we go again, Nate thought. Finger across the throat. Every time she said something he was ready to buy into, she came up with lines that could have come from the piece-of-shit movies he'd appeared in.

Nate said, 'Did you tell your lawyer about it?'

'Of course,' she said. 'But he told me Ali would deny it, and just to change my locks and alarm code. Which I had already done.'

'Anything else by way of a threat?'

'Yes. One night last week I saw him standing on the street when I came home from dinner with a girlfriend. He was half a block down behind a parked car. He ducked when I drove past, but I'm sure it was him. When I got in my driveway, I saw taillights driving down the hill.'

'Did you call the police?'

'Yes. I called Hollywood Station and talked to an officer at the front desk. I told him I wanted a car to patrol my street, and if they found my husband, to stop and investigate. The officer said he would tell the area car to be on the lookout for Ali prowling around. I insisted that he make a record of my call. My lawyer advised me to be sure that there is official verification of every incident.'

'So you've told the cop you met at the fund-raiser, and you called Hollywood Station, and now you're telling me. Any other police officers know about this?'

'Yes, last Saturday night I was sure I heard footsteps beneath the bedroom balcony at about eleven P.M., and I called Hollywood Station again. And two officers arrived, along with a sergeant. They didn't find anything.'

'Do you remember the sergeant's name?'

'Let's see . . . no, but he was young and officious. He issued a lot of orders to the officers.'

'Did he have lips?'

'What?'

'Was his name Treakle?'

'That's it. Sergeant Treakle.'

Well, Nate thought, she's done everything but put it on MySpace and send up smoke signals. Help! Ali Aziz is threatening me, but I can't prove it.

'Does your husband still see your son?' he asked.

'Oh, yes. I had to agree to reasonable visitation rights. Ali has a luxury condo in Beverly Hills and a full-time housekeeper and au pair. There was nothing I could do about it.'

Nate felt his woody withering again, especially when she said, 'Won't you let me make you a vodka martini? It's a wonderful mood enhancer.'

And yet hers wasn't half finished. This chick was way more interested in pouring booze into him than into herself. What about *her* mood? It occurred to Hollywood Nate Weiss that wealthy people could be very perplexing.

He once again declined a martini and said, 'If you're

really scared of him, have you considered moving away?'

'I have,' she said, 'and I will. But in the meantime I went to a gun store in the Valley where they have a pistol range and I took a shooting lesson. The gun store owner said I'm a fast learner. I'm thinking of buying a pistol. Do you like the Glock or the Beretta?'

'Whoa!' Nate said. 'Are you *that* scared?'

'I am,' she said. 'I'd have bought a gun already, but with Nicky getting into every nook and cranny in this house, I've been afraid to do it. The alternative is more expensive but might be wiser.'

'And what's that?' Nate said.

'I've been thinking about hiring someone from a security firm to stay here in the house until it closes escrow. Oh, did I tell you that I sold it already?'

'No, you didn't,' he said.

'Well, I did. With the agreement of my husband and his attorney. And with proceeds to be shared. I'll just need someone here for forty more days, maybe less if the buyer can close early. We have bedrooms and bathrooms we've never used. But then I thought, Who knows what kind of person might be employed by those security firms? And I got to thinking, there might be a police officer from Hollywood Station who'd be interested in a very nice room-and-board arrangement for a month or so. I think I could feel safe with a real police officer being here. Is that feasible, do you think?'

Now Nate was so baffled by this woman that he decided to test her. He said, 'I might be interested.'

'I was hoping to hear that, Nate,' Margot said with

a little sigh. 'I'm truly scared for my safety and for my son's.'

'Where're you moving to?' he asked.

'Haven't decided yet,' she said. 'That's another thing our lawyers are fighting about. He doesn't want me to take Nicky out of Los Angeles, but we're trying to show the court that Ali's business environment does not make this the ideal place to raise Nicky. Ali knows I love San Francisco and New York. But until that's settled, I'll rent a condo for Nicky and me right here in L.A.'

'Good luck with your battle,' Nate said.

She took another tiny sip from the martini glass, her voice sultry now, and said, 'What do you drink besides wine? Let's take a pair of fresh cocktails out onto the balcony and talk about this further.'

And then it kicked in: the cop's survival instinct, honed by all the years of playing Guess What I'm Really Thinking with countless miscreants on the streets. She had drunk far less wine than he had, and she'd hardly tasted her martini. And those eyes – the color of good whiskey, Jack, maybe, or Johnnie Black – were mesmerizing, but Nate's response to more drinking was dictated by blue radar, not raging hormones.

He said, 'Okay, I'd love to talk about it further. But I'm just not that much of a cocktail drinker. I'll hang on to my wineglass. You go ahead and have another James Bond special.'

He saw the immediate disappointment on her face. And then he heard a cell phone chime from the butler's pantry. Margot excused herself, went to the pantry, and picked up her go cell from the countertop.

'Yes,' she said and listened. Then she closed the pantry door and whispered, 'No, honey, he won't do.' She listened for a moment and said, 'He's not a drinking man.' She listened some more and said, 'Please, baby, don't say that. I'm going back to number one. I'm going after him very hard. Please. Give me a week.'

While Margot Aziz was in the butler's pantry, Hollywood Nate Weiss made a very tough decision. He was going out on that balcony for more talk, but he was going to make a serious move on her to see where all this was going. And if she resisted and tried one more time to pour booze down his throat, he was outta there. This is Hollywood, he thought, and there are extremely unusual people around these parts – gorgeous, scary people who could turn smoking male wood into a steaming pile of sawdust.

Nate didn't get a chance to execute his strategy. When Margot came out of the butler's pantry and back into the dining room, she said, 'Nate, I'm terribly sorry. That was my au pair. Nicky's got a fever and she's worried. I've gotta drive over there right now and pick him up.'

'Sure,' Nate said, not as disappointed as he might have predicted. 'Anything I can do?'

'No, I'll call you tomorrow. I have your number.'

When Hollywood Nate was walking out the door, it occurred to him that he should get her cell number too. He started to ask for it but thought he'd better leave. She had a sick kid to deal with. And anyway, he wanted to see if this stunning, rich, very strange woman *would* call him tomorrow. The amazing thing was, he'd been so bowled over that he hadn't done what he always did when he met a likely babe. He hadn't even told her about his SAG card and that he'd appeared in two TV movies.

As he was driving home that night, he remembered what his first field-training officer had said to him when he was a boot, fresh out of the academy: 'Son, that badge can get you pussy, but pussy can get your badge.'

Jasmine was scowling when she stormed out of the dancers' bathroom into the dressing room, wearing only her yellow G-string and red stiletto heels. She put her throwaway go cell in her locker, where she kept her street clothes.

One of the stage-sharing dancers that evening, a broad-shouldered redhead called Tex, was sitting in a recliner, looking at photos in a fan magazine. Tex was top heavy from saline overload and was wearing a G-string, a cowboy hat, a short sequined cowgirl vest, and white cowboy boots.

Tex said, 'What's wrong, Jasmine? Boyfriend trouble?'

'Yeah, boyfriend trouble,' Jasmine said, her face darkened by rage and frustration.

'If we could invent a vibrator with a twenty-word set of responses, we'd never need them,' Tex said. 'What is he, a gambler, an addict, or a boozer?'

'This guy's definitely not a boozer,' Jasmine said. 'Which is too fucking bad.'

Tex was about to ask what Jasmine meant by that, when Ali Aziz popped his head in the door without knocking, and said, 'Jasmine, I got to see you.'

'My next set's coming up, Ali,' Jasmine said.

Ali was dressed for the evening in a blue double-breasted, raw-silk blazer, a blue silk tie, and a white shirt with monogrammed cuffs. He said, 'Tex can take your set. Come.'

Tex rolled her eyes and said, 'This job sucks in more ways than one.'

When Jasmine entered the office, Ali closed and locked the door, sat in his desk chair, and poured himself a glass of Jack Daniel's. Jasmine stood and waited. Lately, he'd call her in there just to rant, especially if he'd been drinking, so maybe if she was very lucky, it wasn't for a hummer after all.

'Fucking bitch!' he said. 'Cunt bitch!'

It could only be one person he was talking about. 'Margot?' she said.

'Fucking bitch!' he said. 'She don't do nothing my lawyer says. Nothing I say. She always tries to keep my Nicky away from me. She only gives him to me when the judge makes her. She requires me to spend lawyer money for everything. Every week more lawyer money. Fucking bitch!'

Ali took a big gulp of Jack and said, 'You have been knowing her for three years. You helped her to decorate this place. You are her friend. I need for you to be my friend. I need for you to help me more.'

'Help you even more?' Jasmine said.

'Watch out for my Nicky. The house will be in the close of escrow soon and she will move to a condo. That is what she says to my lawyer. But now I want you to watch.'

'Ali,' Jasmine said, 'I already am sort of watching out for Nicky, just like you said for me to do. Sort of.

But I only get to see Margot, what? Once a week? She lives on Mount Olympus. I live in Thai Town. Jesus, Ali, gimme a break.'

'She says to me that she is going to take Nicky away from California when the house is finish with the escrow and the divorce is over. She says to me that her lawyer is going to make this happen. She says to me that she has a boyfriend and this is none of my business. She says to me all of this on the phone yesterday. I am going insane, Jasmine! My Nicky! He is my life!'

'Okay, Ali, I'll tell you something I didn't wanna mention. The last time I phoned her, I was sure she was all weirded out on something. Probably coke. And Nicky was there, because she yelled at him real mean.'

Suddenly, Ali Aziz started sobbing boozily and pulled a red handkerchief from the pocket of his blazer.

Jasmine watched and waited, and before he stopped she said, 'I guess I could pay her a personal visit twice a week. Maybe take her some of the Chinese cookies she loves. I might be able to find out if the boyfriend's staying at the house. And maybe I could ask her straight out if she's doing coke again.'

Ali stopped weeping then and said, 'I ask her, I beg her, I say, "Please, Margot, whatever happens, do not go back into the life of cocaine. You must take care of our Nicky." When I first met her, she was spending all her money on cocaine. A beautiful, young dancer who was doing so much cocaine. Soon I was more than her boss. I was her friend and she quit the cocaine. Then pretty soon I was her husband.'

'Yeah, you told me,' Jasmine said, thinking how she hated taking the last set. But now she'd have to take it for Tex while she listened to this shit for the hundredth time.

'Jasmine, I want for you to see Margot and to tell me what is what. I shall pay for it. Do not worry, I shall pay you for the time you use. I must know what is in her head. Is she truly wishing to take my Nicky away to a different state? Maybe to do cocaine again with this new man? Without my Nicky I shall die, Jasmine!'

'I'll do what I can, Ali,' Jasmine said. Then she added, 'Tell me, Ali, what happens to your situation if Margot dies?'

'Margot die? God willing!' Ali said. 'I shall have my son then. But do not think that I can make such a thing happen. I am a businessman. I am a loving father. I am no killer.'

'Of course you're not,' Jasmine said. 'But I'm curious about your deal with her. About how you got all your holdings so tangled up with her.'

'Fucking lawyer! Fucking accountant!' Ali said. 'I got rid of them, but too late. They said to me I can escape from taxes if she is on the deeds and licenses for certain things. Stupid bastards! Now I must suffer for it.'

'What if you die?' Jasmine said. 'Who gets your piece of the money and property?'

'You talk too much of death, Jasmine,' Ali said suspiciously.

'You want me to spy for you? Okay, but I gotta know what's going on. I don't wanna be part of any violent plots.'

'No! No violence!' Ali said quickly. 'I am not a violent man!'

'So tell me, when you die, who gets all your wealth?'

'Nicky, of course. My lawyer is, how you say, executor. But all goes to Nicky. I weep to think of my Nicky with no daddy and only his bitch cunt mother to take care of him.'

'It's hard for me to figure how a smart businessman like you married without a prenup in the first place,' she said.

Ali said, 'You did not know her when she was a young girl. The most beautiful dancer in all Los Angeles. A young girl with eyes that make you go dizzy. So smart she could make me act stupid. She always refuse to give me the blow job. She refuse to even give me kisses more than a few times. She made me to believe she is a virgin. She made me so stupid I run out and buy her a very big diamond ring. She still will not give me sex even one time. I say we sign a business contract and we get married. She say to me no marriage with a business contract. I was the most stupid man in Los Angeles because she made my brain sick. I make her my wife. No contract, no nothing. Two years after that, I listen to my stupid lawyer and stupid accountant, who get her name mixed up in everything. I save some tax money, but look where I arrive to today!'

Jasmine grinned then and said, 'How were the blow jobs after all that?'

'Okay,' he said. 'But not like the ones you give to me.'

'If you were to die, it'd be real nice to be Nicky's mother,' Jasmine said. 'There'd be ways his mother could cut into Nicky's fortune.'

'Why do you talk like that, Jasmine?' Ali said. 'Stop! You make me feel sick.'

'I'm only saying what you must be thinking,' Jasmine said. 'If I'm going into the spy business in the middle of a very bitter divorce involving ... how many millions?'

'Please, Jasmine, stop now!' Ali said.

'I'm just saying. I just have to be careful what I'm getting into, is all. She might have very bad friends who could see the tremendous advantage to her if you would pass away suddenly. And as your agent I might find myself in serious trouble. Whadda you know about this new boyfriend, for example?'

Ali was holding his head in his hands now, getting a headache. 'Nothing. I know nothing.'

'How do you know he's not some coke dealer from her younger days? How do you know what the two of them are scheming about? He might be a very dangerous man.'

'I beg you to stop,' Ali said.

'I just hope it all works out for you, Ali,' Jasmine said. 'For your son's sake.'

Ali said, 'When Nicky is older, I think he shall see his mother is a cunt bitch. And he shall want to come and live with Daddy. That is what my new lawyer says. He tells me I must have very much patience.'

'Okay, I'll do more undercover work for you, Ali, but I'll need serious compensation for it.'

'Yes, yes,' Ali said. 'If she is doing cocaine with this man, you must tell me very fast. Then I can tell my lawyer and we maybe can go to the judge to get back my son. This country have very insane laws.'

'You mean I might have to give a deposition or something?' Jasmine said. 'I wouldn't like that.'

'I shall pay you, Jasmine,' Ali said. 'You shall not be sorry.'

'To betray my friend?' Jasmine said. 'And to maybe run the risk of her new pal finding out about it? That's gotta be worth a lot.'

'I shall pay you plenty,' Ali said. 'Nicky is my life.'

'Okay, I'll see what I can do,' Jasmine said.

'Thank you, Jasmine, thank you,' Ali Aziz said. 'Now, please come here and make me feel like a man once more.'

'Not again,' Jasmine muttered but nevertheless got down on her knees in front of Ali's chair while he unzipped his fly, wishing he'd taken Viagra.

TWELVE

THE FOLLOWING MONDAY AFTERNOON, an extraordinary photo was taken by Officer Tony Silva in Laurel Canyon. A drunken porn producer in a Ferrari, coming from an all-day shoot at his studio on Ventura Boulevard in the San Fernando Valley, swerved head-on into a pair of eucalyptus trees, doing damage to the front end of his car but not activating the air bag.

The Crow had just dealt with another in the endless complaints about peeping paparazzi from one of the second-rate actors who lived in a rented house in the hills, when he came upon the accident, which a nearby resident had called in. However, Tony Silva was the second cop to arrive, the first being Officer F.X. Mulroney.

The LAPD motorcycle was parked twenty feet behind the Ferrari, whose engine was still running, and the driver, who would later blow an astonishing .37 on the Breathalyzer, was casting panicky looks over his left shoulder. The porn producer was concentrating on what he thought was the road in front of him but was really open space between the two trees, where his car was wedged and immobile.

With his decades of experience in such matters, F.X. Mulroney immediately understood that as far as this motorist was concerned, he was still negotiating the curves on the canyon road, no doubt with double vision. And by the time Tony Silva got out of the CRO's Ford Explorer, F.X. Mulroney had already been at it for a while and was short of breath from his 'pursuit' of the Ferrari.

Tony Silva later said that with a video camera he could have had himself a huge hit on the Internet, but all he had was his cell-phone camera. The grainy still photos he shot were of F.X. Mulroney, in full motor cop regalia, running in place beside the Ferrari, his black boots pumping up and down while he shouted, 'Pull over! Pull that fucking car over!' to the porn producer, who was gunning the engine and looking back, desperate to speed away from the relentless motor cop who, as in a dream – or in his case, a nightmare – seemed to be pursuing him on foot!

'I don't wanna have to shoot ya!' F.X. Mulroney yelled. 'Pull to the curb and turn off your engine!' Then, as always, F.X. Mulroney went totally over the top and yelled, 'Watch out for the woman and baby! Pull right! Pull right!'

For a moment the high-performance engine revved to full rpm, the wheels turning sharply, and this allowed the car to climb a foot or so up the trunk of the larger of the eucalyptus trees, tires smoking, engine roaring. But then it settled back down, coughing, sputtering, and dying when the engine finally blew.

F.X. Mulroney noticed Officer Tony Silva for the first time then, but he couldn't speak. He had to bend forward with his hands on his knees to catch his breath after such a long 'chase.' Then F.X. stood tall, removed his mirrored aviator sunglasses, and said to the camera, 'Am I glad this asshole finally pulled over. I was just about outta gas.'

The porn producer looked up at the old motor cop standing beside his car. And with eyes at half-mast, he opened the door and said, 'My compliments, Officer. I thought I lost you a couple times, but you caught me fair and square.'

Ronnie felt that Bix Ramstead had seemed different for most of the day. He was uneasy, agitated, nervous. They'd spent several hours knocking on doors, dealing with the myriad calls from the constant complainers who were so well known at the Community Relations Office. It was tedious work, and on past occasions Bix had seemed temperamentally perfect for the assignment. But not today. He wasn't as patient as usual. His practiced responses didn't seem as sincere. He looked at his watch when people were pouring out their troubles, most of which the cops could do nothing about. The fact was, the callers were lonely and wanted attention from officialdom, but all they had were the Crows from Hollywood South.

On the last call they did together, Ronnie and Bix were standing in the kitchen of an eighty-year-old white-stucco bungalow, listening to the complaint of an elderly Salvadoran immigrant whose children hadn't been to visit her in three months. Her English was good enough that they came to understand that her life was being made miserable by her next-door neighbor's frequent yard sales, which attracted a bad element who threw trash on her property and urinated in her driveway in broad daylight.

When she stopped long enough to answer the phone in her bedroom, Bix went to the sink and helped himself to a glass of water. In the corner of the kitchen he spotted a mouse in a glue trap. The mouse, firmly stuck by its belly, feet, and legs, looked up with eyes both frightened and sad, as though the creature knew it was hopeless.

Ronnie heard Bix Ramstead say to the mouse, 'Sorry, buddy, I'd help you if I could, but I can't even help myself.'

When the Salvadoran woman returned to the kitchen, she picked up the trap and drowned the rodent in a bucket of water on the back porch. Then she continued reciting her many complaints about her neighbors.

After completing that visit, Bix said, 'Let's go back to the office and get another car. I think we should split up and deal with as many calls as we can for the rest of the day. We've gotta get our backlog caught up.'

Ronnie agreed but couldn't help wondering what Bix had meant when he'd spoken those words to a doomed mouse.

In recent years, Alvarado Street in Rampart Division had come to resemble a commercial thoroughfare in Tijuana. Most of the shops and businesses displayed goods that spilled out onto the pavement, and those sidewalks were mobbed by Spanish-speaking pedestrians at all hours of the day and most of the evening. The sights and sounds and smells were all from beyond the imaginary line that marks the southern boundary of the United States of America.

There was a particular *farmacia* in that neighborhood that had been frequented by Ali Aziz since 9/11, when he had had to give up his trips to Tijuana. Prior to that catastrophe, he'd found it well worth a drive across the international border for all the prescription diet drugs, tranquilizers, and stimulants required by his dancers. But after 9/11, he got sick of being directed to the secondary inspection area every time he was coming back and subjected to interrogations and searches the moment he answered the question 'Where were you born?'

On the last occasion, the prescription drugs he'd bought in Tijuana were confiscated by a U.S. Customs officer who rightly doubted the legitimacy of Ali's prescriptions issued on the spot by Tijuana doctors who worked with the *farmacias*. After that, Ali talked with his Mexican employees and was directed to the Alvarado Street pharmacy owned and operated by Jaime Salgando, who would sell anything without a prescription to Ali Aziz for three times what a legitimate pharmacy would charge. Prescriptions required expensive office visits to physicians by his entire stable of dancers, and Ali did not want to pay for those, especially when they wouldn't prescribe large enough quantities of the drugs that the dancers needed.

So far, Ali had never been turned down by Jaime Salgando, but today would be a test of the pharmacist's loyalty, and of his greed. Ali had with him a single capsule, something he had stolen from the medicine cabinet in his former Mt. Olympus home. That theft had occurred on the day that he had removed all of his clothes and personal property under the humiliating scrutiny of a security guard hired by Margot to see that he took only what they had agreed upon through their respective lawyers.

When the guard was not watching, Ali had impulsively removed a single magenta-and-turquoise 50-milligram capsule from Margot's vial of sleeping aids. This was shortly after he'd read a news account in an Arabic-language newspaper about a rich Egyptian who had been arrested for trying to poison his elder brother by doctoring his sleeping medication. The prescription drug was the only one that Margot had ever used for occasional insomnia, and it was prescribed by her doctor in West Los Angeles. Ali had never known her to take more than a single capsule once or twice a week, usually on nights when she claimed to be under stress. The vial held thirty capsules, and she would replace it about every four months.

He had been very frightened the day he'd opened that medicine cabinet and shaken out one capsule and slipped it into his pocket. But having that capsule all these months had somehow bolstered his confidence and quelled his frustration and outrage with the American system of justice and with American women who knew how to manipulate the system. Having that capsule made him feel less impotent while he was being ground down by that baffling legal machinery. The capsule told him that he had the power to end it should things ever become intolerable. If she ever made him fear for the safety of his son.

There were a dozen Latino people in the small

pharmacy when Ali entered. A young woman working at the forward cash register said something to him in Spanish and smiled. Ali did not understand but smiled and pointed to the lone pharmacist at the rear of the store. Ali was glad to see that there were only two customers waiting for prescriptions. He took a seat in a chair surrounded by shelves full of vitamin bottles and herbal cures and waited. When the second woman had paid for her prescription, he stepped to the counter and smiled at Jaime Salgando, a balding, sixty-year-old Mexican with drooping eyelids, a thin pebble gray mustache, and an air of total confidence.

With barely a trace of a Spanish accent, the pharmacist grinned and said, 'Ali! Where have you been hiding?'

'Hello, brother Jaime,' Ali said with an insincere grin of his own.

They shook hands and Jaime said, 'What's the problem? You need more Viagra to keep up with all your gorgeous employees who fight to take you to bed?'

'God willing,' Ali said, maintaining the grin.

'I think I have everything you might need,' Jaime Salgando said. 'How can I help you, my friend?'

Ali gave him a list of the usual meds: diet pills for Tex and antianxiety for Jasmine. And because Margot always had her prescriptions filled at a pharmacy near her doctor's office, her needs were unknown to the pharmacist, so Ali asked for a specific 50-milligram sleep aid, supposedly for Goldie.

When Ali handed the list to Jaime Salgando, the pharmacist said, 'Goldie has switched to a different medication?'

Ali shrugged and said, 'I pay no attention. You got that one?'

'Yes,' said the pharmacist. 'And how are you keeping, Ali? Your health is good?'

'Very good,' Ali said.

As the pharmacist worked, Ali said, 'How is business, brother?'

'Not as good as yours, Ali,' Jaime said. 'And my employees do not look like your employees.'

Twice Jaime had enjoyed dates with Tex, compliments of Ali Aziz for pharmaceutical services rendered. Ali said, 'Tex is missing you. When shall you come back to see her, Jaime?'

The pharmacist sighed and said, 'Next time I must double up on Viagra. One tablet is not enough when I am with that girl.'

Ali forced a laugh that was more nervous than he wished it to be and said, 'You tell me when, brother. She is there for you.'

'At my age that is very nice to know,' Jaime said.

When Jaime Salgando was finished with Ali's entire order, Ali paid him and said, 'Jaime, I got a terrible problem and I need more help.'

'That is what I am here for,' Jaime said.

'I need a capsule of poison. Fifty milligrams.'

'What for?' the astonished pharmacist said.

'I got to kill a dog. I must put poison in the meat.'

'What dog?'

'My Russian neighbor on Mount Olympus is very rich. He is a very bad gangster. He got this big dog. Fifty kilos. The dog is a killer. Last week the killer dog almost got my Nicky. My son! The housekeeper carried Nicky inside the house just in time. I went to this Russian. He tells me go to hell.'

'Did you call Animal Control? Or the police?'

'No, I am afraid of this Russian. He is a very dangerous man. All my neighbors are afraid of the Russian and his dog. All neighbors talk. We say we shall poison this Russian dog. Next time the dog gets out, we give it poison. The Russian must never know who done it.'

'I don't know, Ali,' Jaime said. 'This is not a good idea.'

'You read about the Russians in Los Angeles who kidnap and murder the people for money? He is a connection to them. He is a dangerous man. His house is for sale now. He shall be moving away, God willing. We are all scared of him, but right now we are more scared of his dog. Please help us.'

'This is a crime.'

'Everything is a crime in this goddamn country,' said Ali.

'Yes, but this is different. My drugs are to help, not to kill.'

'One of my neighbor gave the idea. We put the poison capsule into the meatball. I do not care what kind of poison.'

'Why did you say fifty milligrams?'

'My neighbor thinks we need fifty milligrams of stuff they put into pest poison to kill this big dog. And fast, so the dog don't suffer. We have no wish to be cruel people.'

'I think your neighbor might be talking about strychnine,' said the pharmacist. 'When I was a boy working on a ranch in Mexico, we used to bait coyotes and kill them, but with less strychnine than fifty milligrams. Far less.'

'The Russian dog is big like two, maybe three coyotes,' Ali said.

'I don't know about this,' Jaime Salgando said.

Ali was ready for him. He put five $100 bills on the counter and said, 'Please, brother, for me. I'll make the date for you with Tex and Goldie. Both at the same time. You shall never forget the date. You need lots of Viagra for this one!'

Ali felt his chin tremble, but he fought to keep the sly smile in place as Jaime Salgando mulled it over.

Then the pharmacist said, 'I'll have to get what you need from a supplier I know. I'll drop it at your club on Thursday evening at six o'clock.'

'That is good, brother,' Ali said. 'But please make sure, one capsule that we can stick inside the little meatball. I see this Russian many times feed him little Russian meatballs from his hand.'

'I'll tell my friend what is needed for the bait,' the pharmacist said.

'When you want the three-way date, brother?'

'On Saturday evening,' the pharmacist said. Then he added, 'Nobody must ever know about any of this, Ali.'

'No,' Ali said. 'Nobody must ever know, or this Russian shall kill me! And thank you, brother, thank you. You have save the life of my son!'

'I'll see you on Thursday with your order,' Jaime said. 'At the Leopard Lounge.'

Affecting a lighthearted farewell, Ali said, 'Yes, my

brother! And Tex shall wear her cowboy hat and cowboy boot for you on Saturday night, I promise!'

When Ali got to his car, he tore open the paper bag and was relieved to see that Goldie's sleep aids were identical to the turquoise-and-magenta capsule in his pocket. It had cost him $200 just to be sure that the manufacturer of Margot's sleep aids had not changed the colors or size of the capsule in recent months. He might have to put a few extra capsules of the sleep aid in her vial so that things didn't happen too soon. He wanted her to die when he was ready, and not before.

On his drive from Alvarado Street back to Hollywood, Ali began to fret about Jaime Salgando. But the closer he got to Hollywood, the more his fears seemed irrational. If three months from now Margot were to die, why wouldn't it be considered a suicide over her affair with that new boyfriend, whoever he was? Or, if murder was suspected, why wouldn't the new boyfriend be the object of the inquiry? Who knows what intrigues the boyfriend may have been plotting with Margot. The police might surmise that she had threatened to leave the boyfriend and he was punishing her. Her pig boyfriend would be the target of the police investigation, not Ali Aziz.

Even the most fearful scenario did not hold up when he looked at it with courage and reason: that Jaime Salgando might have a terrible attack of Christian conscience and inform the police that on one hot summer day he had supplied Ali Aziz with 50 milligrams of poison, ostensibly to kill a dog. But that was the silliest fear of all. If Jaime did such a thing, what would happen to his license, his business, his life? Jaime was a man who had taken money from Ali for years, unlawfully dispensing drugs for dancers at the Leopard Lounge. Jaime, the loving father and grandfather who had bedded a number of those dancers to whom he was unlawfully providing drugs. And how could Jaime ever prove that he gave Ali Aziz a 50-milligram capsule of poison? No, Jaime Salgando had committed too many crimes behind the counter at his *farmacia*. Jaime was the least of the worries of Ali Aziz.

His main concern would be to gain legal custody of Nicky when Margot was found dead. Ali knew that her family, those insignificant people in Barstow, California, would fight for custody in order to have control over their grandson, the heir to Margot's fortune. Or rather, Margot's half of Ali's fortune, the wealth that the bitch had stolen from him through all her trickery. And truth be told, he would let them have everything she had stolen from him – all of it – if only they would not initiate any custody fight for Nicky. All that Ali Aziz wanted was his son.

When Ali got to the Leopard Lounge that afternoon, he went to his office, locking the door behind him. He sat at his desk, turned on the desk lamp, dried his hands, and drank a shot of Jack to steady them. Ali found it absolutely astonishing how, despite his fear, the thought of soon possessing that deadly capsule made him feel extremely powerful. He would have the power of life and death. With the unexpected gifts of drugs that he would be giving to his dancers, he felt entitled to special blow jobs with no complaints. Ali decided to call one of the girls into his office. And he wouldn't be needing Viagra. Not today.

Ronnie and Bix Ramstead's ten-hour duty tour – excluding the half hour for a meal break referred to as code 7 – was to end at eight that evening. But when Ronnie signed out, Bix still hadn't returned. She'd called him on his cell twice but couldn't reach him. She was so worried that she was about to mention it to the sergeant prior to his leaving for a meeting with the Graffiti Committee. Then her cell rang.

'It's me,' Bix said when she answered.

'I was getting concerned,' she said.

'Sorry,' he said. 'I got tied up.'

Ronnie thought she detected a slight slurring of speech but hoped she was wrong. She said, 'You coming in now?'

Bix said, 'Check me out, will you? I'll be back later to turn the car in.'

Now she was sure of it. She said, 'Why don't I come where you are? We could get a bite to eat.'

'No, I'm gonna grab a burger with a cop I know from my North Hollywood days. Just check me out. I'll be back soon.'

And that's how it was left. If it had been anyone other than Bix Ramstead, Ronnie Sinclair, being so new to the Community Relations Office, would not have complied. She thought about talking to one of the other Crows about it, but she did not. Ronnie liked Bix as much as any cop she'd ever known at Hollywood Station. She was feeling very nervous and worried when she checked out both Bix and herself that evening.

Ronnie knew she'd have a restless night, worrying about the possibility of Bix Ramstead and his LAPD car getting involved in a DUI collision.

There was trouble in Southeast Hollywood that evening involving more than fifty Filipino and Mexican men. They had gathered in a warehouse that closed its doors for the day at 6 P.M. but whose back door had been left unlocked by an employee who'd made secretive arrangements with all the other sporting men who worked in the warehouse. One of the storage bays had been roped off, and tattooed workers in company shirts or wife beaters were drinking beer and tequila as they gathered around a fighting pit made of plywood that had been temporarily nailed in place to provide an arena for the grisly spectacle about to take place.

Several trucks arrived and very soon steel cages were being carried into the warehouse and stacked against the wall. Each of twelve cages contained a fighting cock, and every bird was squawking in terror from the commotion. Mexican music was blaring from an old boom box, and voices of drinking men shouted bets to one another in Spanish, Tagalog, and Spanglish prior to prepping the birds for the bloody fights to the death, scheduled to begin at 8:30 P.M.

It might have gone off as planned except for one young Mexican forklift operator named Raul, who had made the mistake of telling his wife, Carolina, a Mexican American girl born and raised in East L.A., that he would be busy that evening and would be coming home late.

'Busy doing what?' she said.

'I cannot tell you,' he said.

'Whadda you mean you can't tell me?' she said.

'I swore a secret,' he said.

'You better unswear it, dude,' she said. 'I wanna know where you're going.'

It was always like this. The forklift operator had wished a thousand times that he'd married a real Mexican girl. These brown coconuts, milky white on the inside, were nothing but nagging *gringas* with Hispanic names.

'I have made a promise to my friends,' he said.

'I think maybe you're gonna be visiting your old squeeze,' she said. 'That bitch Rosa with the big *chi-chis*. Well, you can forget about coming home afterwards.'

He sat down on the kitchen chair and hung his head and surrendered as he always did and told her the truth. 'We are having a bird fight at the warehouse.'

'A bird fight?' Carolina said. 'You mean you're making roosters kill each other? Like that kinda bird fight?'

'Yes,' he said. 'I am only going to bet twenty dollars. No more.'

'You ain't betting shit,' she said. 'Because you ain't going to no bird fight. It's against the law in this state, in case you didn't know.'

'All my friends will be there, Carolina!' he pleaded.

'You go out this door and I'll call the cops about the bird fight,' she said. 'It's cruel and disgusting!'

Her husband went into the bedroom and slammed the door. Ten minutes later, while he was in there pouting, his wife picked up the phone and quietly dialed 9-1-1.

*   *   *

One hour before the 8:30 P.M. cockfight was about to commence, a hastily gathered raiding party had been put together by the assistant watch commander at Hollywood Station. Three patrol units from Watch 3, and two from Watch 5, were assigned to the raid, accompanied by the two teams of vice cops who were available on short notice. A pair of Animal Control employees were to be dispatched to meet the LAPD officers thirty minutes after the raid began, in order to impound the fighting cocks. Everyone was expecting to be writing a lot of citations and maybe booking the event organizers. The animal cruelty code section carried a $20,000 fine and/or one year in county jail.

The Watch 5 midwatch officers tasked were Cat Song and Gil Ponce, along with Dan Applewhite and Gert Von Braun. Most of the cops thought it might be an interesting assignment. There hadn't been many cockfighting raids conducted in the heart of the city, and none of the cops had ever seen a fighting bird.

On their way to the staging area parking lot, from where they would converge on the warehouse, Gert Von Braun made a startling confession to Dan Applewhite.

'As far as big birds're concerned, I look at them like they're nothing but snakes with wings. Thinking of those roosters is creeping me out.'

Doomsday Dan was stunned. He didn't think Gert Von Braun was afraid of anything. At that moment, she stopped being this intimidating mass of angry female cop and seemed like nothing more than a sweet and vulnerable girl!

He was absolutely tender when he said, 'Don't worry, Gert. If anything should go wrong with the killer birds, I'll be there for you. One summer when I was a kid in Chino, I worked on a chicken farm, culling eggs. I'm a rooster wrangler, is what I am. You just get my back and deal with the drunk Mexicans and Filipinos, I'll do the rest.'

'Oh, yeah,' she scoffed, 'I can just see you there with your pepper spray, telling an insane rooster with knife blades on its feet, "Okay, birdbrain, *bring* it!" Sure, you will. My hero.'

When they arrived at the staging area, the cops turned off their headlights and got out to talk to one another. It was then that they learned of an awful turn of events: The vice sergeant who was supposed to lead the raid was unavailable and had been replaced by a patrol sergeant from the midwatch.

'Chickenlips Treakle!' Cat Song moaned when she got the word.

'Appropriate choice, considering the nature of the event,' young Gil Ponce noted.

'He'll find a way to fuck it up totally,' Gert Von Braun said. 'If a rooster fight can get any more fucked up than they are to begin with.'

'I hear *that*,' Doomsday Dan concurred. 'Treakle in command makes me wanna have a sudden back attack.'

And to make matters worse, Sergeant Treakle, shining his new mini-flashlight beam on the raiding party until he spotted his Watch 5 officers, approached Dan Applewhite and said, 'I'll be riding in with you and Von Braun.'

'Sergeant, don't you wanna drive your own car in

case we need extra shops to transport prisoners?' Gert said.

'No, Von Braun,' he said curtly. 'I want you to drop me fifty yards from the warehouse for a very quick reconnoiter before I give the go command on my rover.'

Sergeant Treakle was especially nervous. He kept obsessively rubbing lip balm across his mouth, but he turned his back when he did it. Like he was sniffing coke.

Dan Applewhite whispered to Gert, 'Why's he need ChapStick? He's got no lips!'

A bearded Latino vice cop, wearing an Ace Hardware work shirt and kneeless jeans, spoke up then, saying, 'Wouldn't it be better if I do the reconnoiter, Sergeant? Your uniform is a tad conspicuous.'

'Thanks for the input,' Sergeant Treakle said icily. 'I'll manage.'

'Okay,' the vice cop said, 'but I hope this caper don't get "fowled" up.' He looked around at the other silent cops and said, '"Fowled" up? F-o-w-l?'

The others groaned or guffawed, and Sergeant Treakle made a mental note to find out the name of this smart-ass vice cop. He looked at his watch and said, 'Applewhite and Von Braun, let's roll!'

'Let's roll?' the vice cop said after Sergeant Treakle was gone. 'Christ almighty. That fucking attack gerbil thinks he's on United flight ninety-three!'

Another midwatch unit, one that had not been assigned to the raid, happened by at that moment after hearing the radio communication setting up the rendezvous. Jetsam was driving, and Flotsam, who had had a very strenuous morning at Malibu, was riding shotgun and nursing an injured shoulder. He was relating the entire tale to his partner.

'Dude, I was ripping on that juicy when I got shut down,' Flotsam informed him.

'A total wipeout inside the barrel?' Jetsam said.

'I got pitchpoled, dude. The nose went vertical and I went horizontal, and the board snapped the leash and catapulted straight up in the air. And I'm talking my U-boat. See, I'd pulled the old longboard from my quiver this morning, and there I was, waiting for nine feet of glass to come down on me like a mortar round!'

'Shit, why is there radical surf every time I gotta go to the dentist or something?' Jetsam said.

'The worst part of it is, I swallowed maybe half a gallon of foamy and I'm all coughing and gagging, and what happens? This totally awesome dudette in a white thong bikini comes up and she says, "Are you okay?" I look at her and I see the most excellent Betty I've ever seen at Malibu. Remember the salty sister we seen at that midnight rager last month? The one that was jumping over the fire pit topless with a tequila bottle in each hand? That one?'

'Are you telling me this one was as cooleo as *that* one?'

'Mint, dude. Totally prime.'

'Did you get her number?'

'Dude, I could hardly breathe. I'm all gasping. I'm all choking. Then I'm, like, feeling the IHOP waffles come chugging up my throat.'

'Oh, no!' Jetsam said. 'You barked the dog?'

'I lunched it,' Flotsam said, nodding. 'Barfola.'

'Don't tell me more!' Jetsam cried but wanted to hear it all.

Flotsam said, 'Dude, I blew chunks all over her. She screamed and jumped in the surf to wash off the spooge and I never saw her again. I was soooo bleak.'

'Bro,' Jetsam said softly. 'That is, like, one of the saddest stories I ever heard.'

Cat Song and Gil Ponce were the last team to leave the staging area parking lot, when 6-X-46 drove up, flashing headlights at them.

Jetsam pulled close to the other car, facing the opposite direction, and said, 'The game's afoot, huh?'

'Yeah, and we gotta go now,' Cat said. 'Treakle's in charge.'

'Aw, shit,' Jetsam said. 'Sorry for you.'

Flotsam looked at the cageless old black-and-white parked in the lot and said, 'Which supervisor belongs to that piece of shit?'

'Chickenlips,' Cat said. 'He's on a sneak-and-peek mission, checking out the target. We can't talk. Gotta go.'

'Catch you later,' Jetsam said while Cat drove away, following the caravan of police units ready to swoop into the warehouse parking lot.

Flotsam massaged his aching shoulder while Jetsam switched from the Hollywood base frequency to the tactical frequency just in time to hear Sergeant Treakle's high-pitched radio voice.

'All units converge on target!' Sergeant Treakle said, spraying saliva on his rover. 'Converge, converge, converge!'

'He gets pretty excited about a bunch of chickens, don't he?' Jetsam said.

'I bet that dude's got women's tits,' Flotsam said. 'Let's go get a burrito.'

While the surfer cops were sitting in their car on Sunset Boulevard enjoying some Tex-Mex, one of the cars that was checked out to the Community Relations Office drove up the hill to Mt. Olympus and into the driveway of Margot Aziz. The driver got out of the car but didn't close the door. He tried to will himself to get back into the car but could not. Then he closed the car door quietly, walked to the front door of the house, and rang the bell. He heard footsteps on the inside marble foyer and knew she was looking through the brass-enclosed peephole.

When the door opened, she threw her arms around his neck and kissed him repeatedly on the mouth, cheeks, and neck as he tried to push her away. Her eyes were bright and wet in the moonlight streaming down, drops clinging to her eyelashes. He felt wetness on her cheekbones, and could taste it when she kissed him, and he wondered why her tears were not salty.

'I was afraid you wouldn't show up,' she said. 'I was afraid you'd never come again. I left four messages on your cell today.'

'You've gotta stop doing that, Margot,' said Bix Ramstead. 'My partner might pick up my calls sometime.'

'But I haven't seen you in twenty-nine days and twenty-nine nights!' She pulled him forward into the foyer and closed the door. She wanted to smell his breath for alcohol, but he kept pulling back when she tried to kiss him again.

'I can't stay, Margot,' he said. 'I've got a police car here. I've gotta get it back to the station.'

'Do it and hurry back,' she said. 'I'll make some supper for you.'

'I can't,' he said. 'I just stopped by to tell you that you gotta stop calling me. You're gonna get me in trouble.'

'Trouble, Bix?' she said. 'Trouble? I'm the one in trouble. I'm crazy in love with you. I can't sleep, I can't think. We have something, Bix, and you can't throw it away. I'm almost free of Ali now. Then I'm all yours. Me and everything I have!'

'I can't. I've been going crazy too. Thinking of you. Thinking of my family. I'm no good for you. We're no good for each other.'

'You're the best man I've ever known,' she said, and then she put her face against his badge and held him hard with both arms.

'I gotta go,' he said again, but he wasn't pulling away from her now.

'I've tried to be patient,' she said. 'The only thing that's held me together is knowing that your family went to your in-laws' for a visit. You see, I've marked my calendar, Bix. You're all I think about. I'm selfish. I want you here with me every night while they're gone. I want the chance to convince you how right we are for each other.'

'I can't think straight tonight,' he said. 'I'll call you tomorrow. I've gotta get the car back to the station.'

She released him and he looked at her. Then he

kissed her, and for certain she smelled the booze on his breath.

'Tomorrow, darling,' Margot said, smiling hopefully. 'I'll be waiting for your call.'

When Bix Ramstead backed out of the driveway and turned back down the hill, he didn't see the Mustang parked a block farther up. Hollywood Nate had waited since Friday for her call that never came. He too had had a few drinks that evening after getting off duty. And impetuously, he had driven up to Mt. Olympus, intending to knock on her door. Intending to find out just what the hell was going on in that woman's head. But as Nate had approached her driveway, he'd seen a police vehicle. He'd driven past the driveway, turned around, parked, and waited.

Nate didn't have to tail him very long to be sure that the driver was Bix Ramstead. He was tempted to follow Bix to the station for a friendly face-off, to compare notes on Margot Aziz. But he decided that he'd better wait until he was completely sober before trying something like that.

After finishing their burritos, Jetsam and Flotsam drove back in the direction of the cockfight raid instead of toward their beat.

'Where you going, dude?' Flotsam said.

'To take a look at the big chicken caper.'

'Why?'

'You ever seen a fighting rooster?'

'No, and I got no desire.'

'Might be educational.'

By the time they pulled into the warehouse parking

lot, everything was under control. All of the Mexican and Filipino spectators were inside being questioned and having Ficards filled out on them. Everyone was being checked for wants and warrants, and a few were being cited. There was nobody outside the building except Gil Ponce, standing by a stack of metal cages containing the fighting cocks, which were still squawking furiously and pecking at the steel confining them.

Jetsam drove up to the young cop and said, 'What's going down in there, dude?'

'Nothing now,' Gil said. 'Just FI-ing everybody and running them for warrants. Gonna book a few. You shoulda been here when we first arrived. One of the organizers of this thing tried to get away, but Gert threw a body block that knocked him flat.'

'Yeah, she would,' Flotsam said.

Then a lithe figure came through the darkness, carrying a steel crate. When she got close, they saw it was Cat Song.

'That rat dog bastard,' she said to the surfer cops. 'Treakle's making us carry the birds out here instead of waiting for Animal Control to do it. He wants to lock up the warehouse and go brag to the watch commander about his great chicken raid and leave us to babysit the birds until Animal Control arrives. I've got feathers and chicken shit on my uniform!'

She stacked the cage on top of two others and the fighting cocks made a louder racket at the new arrival.

'How many birds you got?' Jetsam asked.

'I don't know,' she said. 'Ten, twelve. Haven't counted them.' Then she turned to Gil Ponce and said,

'Come on, sonny, I'm not carrying these things all by myself.'

When they walked back inside the warehouse, Jetsam glanced at Flotsam, who looked like he was about to start whining about his shoulder again.

Jetsam turned out the headlights, jumped out of the black-andwhite, and opened the back door on Flotsam's side.

'What're you doing, dude?' Flotsam asked.

He watched in amazement when Jetsam grabbed the top crate and swung it into the backseat of their shop, saying, 'You had a bad day at Malibu, bro. I'm trying to cheer you up.'

'Just whadda you got on your desktop?' Flotsam said anxiously.

'Now, bro, don't suck the cool outta this situation,' Jetsam said, closing the door and getting behind the wheel.

'What situation?' Flotsam wanted to know, and soon found out.

Jetsam drove, lights out, and wheeled into the parking lot, where a lone black-and-white was parked in the darkness. And he said, 'You still carry that Slim Jim in your war bag?'

'Dude, this is totally uncool,' Flotsam said.

Jetsam got out of the car and said, 'Bro, this is fate at work. Look at that old cageless black-and-white sitting there waiting for us. Don't bitch out on me. This is our destiny!'

'Stay real, dude!' Flotsam said, but nevertheless he was fascinated watching Jetsam get gloved up and slide the Slim Jim inside the car window until he unlocked the door.

'Go to sleep, chicken,' Jetsam said to the caged bird when he transferred the cage through the rear door of Sergeant Treakle's car. But when he opened the rooster's cage, he got his finger pecked.

'Ow!' he said. 'This ungrateful chicken bit me. And I was starting to like him 'cause he looks so much like Keith Richards.'

'This ain't cool, is all I got to say,' Flotsam said. But actually he thought it *was* pretty cool. If they didn't get caught.

When Jetsam closed and locked Sergeant Treakle's shop and they drove away looking for a likely Dumpster in which to toss the empty cage, Flotsam said, 'Do you think the boot might panic and dime us when that heel-clicking, no-lips little Nazi starts trying to figure out who boosted the chicken?'

'I ain't sure if Ponce's still a probie,' Jetsam said. 'He might own his pink slip by now. Anyways, Cat Song would shove one of those Korean metal chopsticks in his eyeball if he tries to put us behind the grassy knoll. We're gravy, bro.'

Sergeant Treakle was pleased as punch with the raid when all was said and done. Citations were written to three men who had been drinking in the parking lot when the cops swooped in. Five were arrested for public drunkenness or for outstanding traffic warrants. None were cited for being spectators at the cockfight because it hadn't started yet. The two organizers were arrested and booked at Hollywood Station on the animal cruelty charge.

After Animal Control arrived and took custody of

the birds, Sergeant Treakle made sure that the warehouse was secured and the burglar alarm set. He was meticulous and proud of the job they'd done. And because he was riding with Gert Von Braun and Dan Applewhite, they had to wait until the bitter end. They were hungry and cranky, and both had soiled uniforms from helping to haul the fighting cocks out of the warehouse.

When everyone was gone or driving away except the two midwatch units, Sergeant Treakle said, 'Now, Von Braun, I have a treat for you and Applewhite.'

'What's that?' Gert said doubtfully.

'I'm inviting you to take code seven with me. I'm treating. You name the eating spot.'

With the odor of the frantic birds and the chicken shit still in her nostrils, Gert Von Braun said sourly, 'Oh, goody. Let's go to KFC, Sergeant Treakle. I want wings and a drumstick.'

Gil Ponce suppressed his giggle when he saw that their supervisor was glowering.

'On second thought, you and Applewhite can clear,' Sergeant Treakle said with a frosty glance at Gert. Turning to Cat he said, 'Song, you and Ponce can drive me to my car.'

Gert mouthed the words *Sorry, Cat* when she and Dan Applewhite walked to their car.

'Thanks, partner,' Dan said to Gert. 'Treakle gives me heartburn so bad I feel like I need a bottle of antacid in my holster with an IV drip attached.'

Sergeant Treakle got into the backseat of Cat and Gil's shop and they drove quickly to the parking lot staging area without conversation. Upon getting out of their black-and-white, he said, 'Stay here till I get it started. The electrical system in that old car is dicey.'

Cat sighed and put the car in park and shook her head at Gil, and they waited. As it turned out, she was eternally glad they did or they might have missed it.

The exhausted bird was down on the floor in the back, apparently asleep, when Sergeant Treakle unlocked the driver's door and got in, thinking the odor of those horrid birds just wouldn't go away. The bird apparently stayed asleep when Sergeant Treakle pulled the door closed. The bird didn't budge when Sergeant Treakle started the engine. But when Sergeant Treakle tooted his horn to signal to 6-X-32 that they could go ahead and clear, the fighting cock exploded in a whirring tornado of claws, horrifying screeches, and flapping wings!

Gil Ponce heard strange sounds, and he picked up the spotlight and shined it on Sergeant Treakle's car. Then he said, 'Cat! Sergeant Treakle's being attacked!'

'What?' Cat Song said, slamming on the brakes.

Then they both gaped, frozen for an instant, as the enraged rooster raked the back of Sergeant Treakle with sharp claws and pecked at his skull, all the time beating powerful wings and screaming like a cat.

But as loud as the fighting cock shrieked, he wasn't shrieking half as loudly as Sergeant Jason Treakle, who fell gurgling from the car onto his face. Cat Song ran to the car and poked her baton at the furious bird, driving it back until she could close the door again.

'Oh, my God!' Gil Ponce said. 'Sergeant Treakle, are you injured?'

But Sergeant Treakle couldn't talk. He was making fearful strangling sounds and trying desperately just to breathe.

'Call for an RA!' Cat said to Gil Ponce. 'And get that Animal Control truck back here! And then bring me a bag! He's hyperventilating!'

'A bag?' Gil Ponce said. 'Where'll I get a bag?'

'Forget the bag! Just make the calls!'

'Okay!' Gil said, running to their car.

When he came back, Gil found Cat propping their supervisor upright, easing him gingerly against the door of his shop. He yelped when his wounded back touched metal, and Cat told him to ignore the pain and try to breathe normally.

'Is Sergeant Treakle gonna be okay?' Gil Ponce asked.

'I think so,' Cat Song said. 'But he had quite a shock, and he got beat up pretty bad. And he's just *covered* with chicken shit.'

By the time the paramedics arrived and treated the wounds on Sergeant Treakle's head, neck, and back, the team from Animal Control had showed up as well. Cat opened the car door for them, then jumped back. But they captured the now docile bird without incident and caged it in the back of their van. The lieutenant was on a day off and the acting watch commander was called to the scene. He happened to be the oldest patrol sergeant at Hollywood Station and was well aware of young Sergeant Treakle's methods and reputation.

Cat was standing near enough to overhear the senior sergeant say to Sergeant Treakle, 'Maybe we should keep this outrageous prank quiet. It's just the kind of story that little *L.A. Times* prick who covers the LAPD would love to get on a local headline. The Department would look silly, and so would you.'

'*Me* look silly?' Sergeant Treakle said. 'I didn't do anything to deserve this! I'd like Internal Affairs to interrogate every officer who was out here and put them all on the polygraph!'

That touched a nerve with the elder supervisor, who had been around long enough to know how unreliable the polygraph is, especially with the overdeveloped superegos of those who make up the police service. He knew that a sociopath's poly chart is essentially flat lines, but a cop's looks like a witch's hat if you so much as ask him if he's jerked off anytime in the last decade.

'I know you don't deserve this,' the old sergeant said soothingly. 'Nobody deserves this. But everyone who reads the *Times* would laugh at us. Laugh at *you*. If we launch an investigation, it would leak in a heartbeat. Right now, nobody knows about this except Song and Ponce and the paramedics. I'll talk to all of them.' When he said it, he turned toward Cat, who pretended to be writing in the log.

'They shouldn't get away with this!' said Sergeant Treakle.

'But we can't go off half-cocked,' replied the old sergeant.

' Half-*cocked*,' said Gil Ponce, giggling, until Sergeant Treakle scowled at him.

'But I know in my gut who did it!' Sergeant Treakle said.

'Who's that?'

'That smart-ass vice cop. The Hispanic guy with the beard. I just know it was him.'

'Look, Treakle,' the old sergeant said. 'Do you want your family and friends to read a headline that says—'

'Okay, I get it!' Sergeant Treakle said, finding the headline possibilities unbearable to contemplate. 'But I know it was that vice cop.'

'Maybe you should ask the captain for a transfer to some other division,' the old sergeant said. 'Get a fresh start somewhere else. Does that sound okay?'

'I can't wait,' Sergeant Treakle agreed. Then, for the first time, he was heard to utter an obscenity. He sat and pondered for a moment and said, 'Fucking Hollywood!'

Sergeant Treakle refused to be transported for further medical treatment at Cedars-Sinai when Cat Song said they might need to wear biohazard outfits to clean him up. And he drove the cageless shop back to the station on his own – feathers, chicken shit, and all.

The senior sergeant then spoke with Cat and young Gil Ponce about the need to keep the incident quiet for the good of Hollywood Station. And they indicated that they understood the gravity of a situation where a prank caused injury and terror to the junior supervisor – who would likely be transferring out of the division ASAP. They assured the senior sergeant that they wouldn't breathe a word of it.

Before an hour had passed, Cat Song had phoned Ronnie Sinclair at home, text-messaged Gert Von Braun, and managed to reach Hollywood Nate on his cell phone, knowing how much he loathed Sergeant Treakle. Everyone thanked her effusively for sharing and promised they wouldn't breathe a word of it.

Gil Ponce, being one of the officers who had declined an invitation to participate in Bible study with Sergeant Treakle, whispered all the details to Doomsday Dan in the locker room at end-of-watch – with a theological question attached. The young cop wondered if it was possible that in the first instant of being suddenly enveloped in great dark wings and hearing unearthly screeching in his ears, Sergeant Treakle may have smelled sulfur and believed that he'd been seized by the Antichrist himself!

'It's heartwarming to think so,' the older cop replied. Then he added, 'The Oracle always said that doing good police work was the most fun we'd ever have. Well, there's a pair of anonymous coppers out there who did some *great* police work tonight. I hope they remembered the Oracle.'

THIRTEEN

Two of the crows at Hollywood South had worrisome thoughts the next day about Bix Ramstead, but neither was aware of the other's concern. Ronnie wanted to know if Bix had fallen off the wagon and been drinking on duty the night before, and Nate wanted to know what the hell Bix Ramstead was doing up on Mt. Olympus at the home of Margot Aziz. But neither had the nerve to ask him.

That morning, Ronnie and Bix were tasked to do follow-ups to neighbors of various tanning salons, an aromatherapy salon, an acupuncturist, and a chiropractor. All complaints had come from neighborhood residents and businesspeople, and most concerned illegal parking and night-time noise. There was an accusation of prostitution directed at tanning salons because of an excessive number of men entering and leaving all day and late in the evenings. One of the tanning salons and the aromatherapy salon had been busted in the past by vice cops posing as customers, but both businesses were said to be under new management.

As Ronnie and Bix were getting ready to hit the streets, their sergeant was involved in a peculiar debate with Officer Rita Kravitz about running an errand to the Church of Scientology Celebrity Centre to pick up a generous donation check it had offered for the Special Olympics fund-raiser. Rita gave the sergeant a couple of lame excuses as to why she was too busy to handle the job and suggested he send one of the guys.

'But you might run into John Travolta or Tom Cruise up there,' the sergeant said. 'Wouldn't that make your day?'

Officer Rita Kravitz pushed her newest and trendiest-ever eyeglasses up onto her nose and with a curl to her lip said, 'I might also get taken prisoner by those robots and brainwashed till I turn into a smiley-faced, twinkly-eyed cult cookie. And if you think that can't happen, ask Katie Holmes.'

The other Crow with Bix on his mind was having a late-morning Danish and cappuccino at his favorite open-air table in Farmers Market, listening to a former director and three former screenwriters at the usual table railing about the ageism that had killed their careers and promoted mediocrity in Hollywood.

'The last meeting I took was with a head of development who was twenty-eight years old,' a former screenwriter said.

'All they wanna do is preserve their jobs,' another one said.

'They'd rather have a flop they can blame on somebody else than take a risk on their own that might produce a hit,' a third one said.

The first one said, 'Every time my stuff gets rejected, they say it's not enough "outside the box," whatever

that means. Or not enough "inside their wheelhouse,"
whatever that means.'

The former director said, 'Bottom line, they're
terrified of people our age because they think we might
know something about making movies that they don't
know. And they're right!'

There was a chorus of amens to that one.

Nate wasn't enjoying the show business grousing.
All he could think of was how Margot Aziz had looked
when he'd first seen her here, and how she had not
called him, as promised. He figured that Bix Ramstead
might have had a lot to do with that. Nate tried
rehearsing half a dozen approaches he could try with
Bix to find out the truth. First, though, he'd have to
get Bix alone, away from Ronnie Sinclair.

Nate finished his cappuccino and started on his
rounds. He had three calls to make on apartment
dwellers about chronic-noise complaints. He was
already starting to think that this quality-of-life shit
was way more tedious and boring than he ever thought
it could be. But at least he had last night's adventure
of Sergeant Treakle and the rooster to sustain him.
He would've loved to share the story with somebody,
but so far today, he couldn't find anyone at Hollywood
Station who didn't know all about it.

Nine hours into their ten-and-a-half-hour shift, Ronnie
and Bix were tired. All they'd accomplished so far was
to issue warnings to salon proprietors about the need
to screen their workers to make sure that temporary
employees were not turning tricks when the boss wasn't
around. Of course, they knew that most of the temps

were hired precisely because they were more than eager to offer special services to safe and willing customers.

Their last tanning salon was on Sunset Boulevard near Western Avenue and was called Miraculous Tan. This one was larger than the others and seemed to be catering to an all-male clientele. The employees were saline Suzies in short shorts, Miraculous Tan T-shirts, and tennis shoes. When the bluesuits walked into the reception area, two male customers waiting on the sofa dropped their magazines and quickly departed.

The receptionist said, 'Please wait, Officers. I'll get the manager.'

'Maybe we better take a closer look at this one,' Ronnie said. 'Seeing us made those dudes run faster than my Sav-on panty hose.'

Bix nodded. He had spoken very little all day and his eyes weren't as bright and clear as they usually were. Ronnie had tentatively tried directing conversation toward the previous night, when Bix had asked her to log him out, but each time she did, he'd change the subject.

The manager was as tall as Bix. Her hair was ash blonde and hung over her breasts in two pigtails. She was bulging with saline implants and had heavily rouged apple cheeks, resembling the stereotypical milkmaids from porn flicks they showed at the adult stores on Hollywood Boulevard. She was dressed in a white vinyl skirt, pink long-sleeved cotton blouse, and white wedges.

'I'm Madeline. How can I help you?' she said with a toothy smile that was impossibly white next to her crimson lip gloss.

Ronnie was too tired and it was too hot a day for subtlety. She said, 'We're getting numerous complaints from your neighbors that they're suspecting illegal activity is going on here during day and evening hours. Also, we're hearing that your customers are causing noise disturbances at night, and parking illegally.'

'Oh, that,' Madeline said. 'We've changed management. That was before I came here two months ago. One of the girls was doing her own thing and nobody here knew about it. The vice officers arrested her. Your Detective Support Division knows all about it.'

'We've gotten complaints more recently than two months ago,' Bix said.

'I'll bet they're from the older Asian people who have the tailor shop two doors down, right?'

'We can't discuss who the complainants are,' Ronnie said.

'No, of course not,' Madeline said, 'but they're always complaining about something. You can ask any of the businesspeople around here.'

'When we walked in here, two of your customers almost ran over us to get out the door,' Ronnie said.

'Maybe they had some problems of their own with the law,' Madeline said.

'Mind if we have a look around at your business?' Ronnie said. 'I may want to try your services sometime. Especially one of those spritzer tans.'

Madeline didn't look happy about it but said, 'Of course. Follow me.'

The cops followed Madeline into a long hallway with five doors on each side, all of them closed. She led them to an intersecting hallway and turned right, toward a large, tiled room that looked like it was meant for showers.

'This is for sunless tanning,' Madeline said. 'As a matter of fact, one of our employees is getting ready to go in now. She has a heavy date tonight and wants to look her best.' She turned to Bix and said, 'If you would turn your back, Officer, I'm sure Zelda wouldn't mind demonstrating how it works.'

Bix walked a few paces farther down the hall and faced the wall.

'Zelda, honey, you can come out,' Madeline said, knocking on one of the closed doors.

The shapely, young platinum blonde was wrapped in a towel. A plastic shower cap completely covered her hair, and booties covered only the tips of her toes and the bottoms of her feet. Her eyes opened wide when she saw Ronnie standing there with the boss. She hurried to the sunless tanning room, whipped off the towel, revealing her own implants, and hung it on a hook by the doorway.

'Zelda has cream on her palms, fingernails, and toenails,' Madeline explained to Ronnie. 'We don't want the tanning liquid to get in the nail beds or on her palms or the bottom of her feet. That would look totally unnatural.'

Zelda faced a bank of spigots on the middle of the wall and pushed a button. The tanning liquid sprayed out, covering her in a mist. She pressed the button again, turned around, and tanned the other side. When she was finished, she was dripping with goop the color of buckskin, and she began patting herself dry.

'We could offer you a police discount, Officer,' Madeline said to Ronnie, 'if you'd like to make an appointment sometime.'

Bix joined them when Zelda was back in her changing room, and they continued their tour of the establishment, looking into one of the little rooms with tanning beds inside.

'Looks claustrophobic,' Bix said. 'Like getting in a coffin and pulling down the lid.'

'Not at all,' Madeline said. 'We give you tiny dark goggles to cover your eyes, and you're only in there for about eight minutes at any level of tanning power you choose. It's a lot more pleasant than baking in the hot summer sun.'

Ronnie said, 'Maybe I'd like this kind of power tan better than the spritzer variety. More bang for the buck.'

While she and Madeline were talking about tans, Bix continued down the hall, subtly trying doorknobs, but they were locked. Behind the third door he heard a woman moaning. It was loud and unmistakable.

Madeline noticed him listening and quickly came forward, saying, 'We can't disturb our clients, Officer. Please follow me and I'll show you—'

'There's somebody moaning in there,' Bix said. 'A woman.'

'Maybe she fell asleep and is dreaming,' Madeline said. 'Really, I must—'

'Isn't that dangerous?' Ronnie said, exchanging glances with Bix. 'Somebody falling asleep under those tanning lamps?'

'They shut off automatically,' Madeline said, and

now she had Ronnie's arm, trying to guide her back down the hallway.

Then they heard a man in that room cry out, 'Do it to me, baby!'

'Got a key?' Bix said.

'I'll . . . I'll look for one,' Madeline said, hurrying back toward the reception area.

Ronnie winked at Bix and knocked lightly on the door, saying, 'Hey! The vice cops're here! Split up and get in separate rooms. Hurry!'

Within seconds the door opened and a plump naked man ran out, holding all of his clothes in his arms. He saw the uniformed cops, said, 'Oh, Jesus!' and dropped the clothes, his erect penis pointing directly at Ronnie.

Inside the room, an eighteen-year-old honey-haired employee with eyebrow, nose, and lip rings, wearing a Miraculous Tan T-shirt and nothing else, was trying to get her shorts pulled up over her hips.

She said, 'I was just trying to tell him his tanning time was up. Honest!'

While Bix got on his radio and asked for a unit to assist, Ronnie pointed to the man's penis and said, 'I hope you had plenty of tanning lotion on that thing, sir.'

Seeing that the cops weren't about to buy her story, the girl said, 'When I went in to wake him up, he was laying there pounding the clown! I didn't have nothing to do with it! Honest!'

'Why, you lying little bitch,' the man said, his tumescence deflating.

It was turning out to be a different sort of day for the Crow team, who didn't often get to make a felony arrest. After questioning the customer and the young employee, both of whom clearly implicated the salon manager in soliciting acts of prostitution and signed a report to that effect, Ronnie and Bix arranged for Madeline to be transported to Hollywood Station, interviewed by the vice sergeant, and booked for pandering.

A transporting unit arrived, and it happened to be the surfer cops who'd just cleared from roll call. Jetsam jumped on this one when he realized from the broadcast which Crow needed an assisting unit.

While Jetsam was chatting up Ronnie, Flotsam looked at Madeline's driver's license and said, 'Holy crap. Madeline's a man! Name of Martin Lester Dilford.'

The manager was standing silent, having admitted nothing, and Jetsam took out his handcuffs, saying, 'Well, I guess I'll do the pat-down here, since she's a guy.'

'No, you won't,' Madeline said. 'I'm not a man anymore. And I won't be put into a cell with men. And you won't put your hands on me.'

'You're a tranny?' Flotsam said.

'Transsexual, if you please,' Madeline said. 'I haven't had time to change my name legally yet.'

'Pre-op or post-op?' Ronnie asked.

'Post-op,' Madeline said. 'As of three months ago, and I'll strip and prove it if you like.'

'Then I guess I'll be doing the pat-down here,' Ronnie said. 'Just relax, Madeline.'

The desperate situation of Leonard Stilwell had gotten considerably worse. He was failing at every attempt to make a buck, and Ali Aziz had not phoned him yet about doing the job on Mt. Olympus. He had even driven up Laurel Canyon one afternoon and taken the right turn into the Mt. Olympus development, not doubting that there were more Italian cypress planted there per acre than anywhere else in the world. Leonard drove the streets and thought it looked pretty formidable. There were security company signs everywhere, and he saw a few homes where uniformed security people were standing in the driveway. He was not encouraged.

Leonard had been reduced to shoplifting from discount stores, but even boosting small merchandise wasn't so easy anymore. It was at the cyber café where Leonard got drawn into a humiliating plot to commit the most pathetic crime he could imagine.

There were more than a hundred computers for rent in the cyber café, and lots of jackals and bottom feeders whom Leonard knew, tweakers mostly, used the computers to sell stolen items and make deals for crystal meth and other drugs. Leonard had a cheap little CD player with headphones that he'd boosted and nearly got caught with when he'd bypassed the checkout counter. None of the other scavengers in the parking lot of the cyber café would trade him so much as a single rock for the CD player. One of the base heads actually sneered at him. He was about to give up when a tweaker he'd seen before but didn't know by name gave him a nod.

The tweaker was a white guy several years younger than Leonard but in far worse condition. He was jug-eared, with small, close-set eyes and pus-filled speed bumps all over his sunken cheeks. He had only a few teeth left in his grille and he grinned at Leonard. They recognized each other's desperation and that was enough. Names were not needed.

'I need a driver,' the tweaker said to Leonard. 'I seen you getting out of that Honda. You open for a job?'

'Let's break it down, dude,' Leonard said.

The tweaker followed Leonard to his car, which was parked in front of a donut shop in the same little strip mall. After they got in Leonard's car, the tweaker lifted his T-shirt and showed a small-caliber revolver stuck in his waistband.

'Freeze-frame!' Leonard said. 'I ain't into guns.'

'This ain't real,' the tweaker said. And he put the gun to his head and pulled the trigger. It clicked. He grinned and said, 'It's a starter pistol. Unloaded.'

'I think you better get outta my car,' Leonard said.

'Don't flare on me, dawg!' the tweaker said. 'You don't gotta do nothing but drop me off on a street. That's it. Drive me around till I see what I'm looking for and drop me off. You don't even gotta pick me back up at the scene of the crime.'

'At the scene of the . . .' Leonard rolled his eyes and said, 'Why don't you just call a taxi?'

'We might have to drive around awhile till we spot him. And if something ain't right, we may have to follow him for a little ways. I can't have a cab driver witness.'

'A witness to what? You're gonna chalk a guy with a fucking starter pistol?'

'I ain't gonna dump the chump. I'm gonna jack his truck. And afterwards, I'm gonna meet you in the truck and give you two Ben Franklins. You won't even be there when I jack it.'

'Lemme track. You saying I'm gonna get fucking chump change for a hijacking?'

'Man, I ain't jacking a Brinks truck.'

'What're you jacking?'

'An ice-cream truck.'

'There ain't a fucking sane human being left in all of Hollywood,' Leonard said to the steering wheel as he gripped it tight.

The tweaker said, 'See, this greaser that drives the truck, he brings his cash payment every other week to some other greaser that lent him the money to buy the truck.'

'How much cash is he carrying?'

'That's my business.'

'Get outta my car.'

'I'll give you three Franklins.'

'Out.'

'Three-fifty, and that's it.'

'Three-fifty,' Leonard said. 'I risk, what? Maybe five years in the joint for chump change?'

'Later, man,' the tweaker said, opening the door.

'I'm good with it,' Leonard said quickly. 'These are hard times.'

'Okay,' the tweaker said with a gap-toothed grin. 'There ain't no risk to you at all. I cased this good. You just drop me near where the guy's selling ice cream. The cash is in the metal box he keeps behind the seat of the truck. I scare the fuck outta him and jump in his truck and drive it maybe six blocks away to some safe place where you're waiting for me. I jump in your car, and you drive me back here to the cyber café.'

'Dude, I want my three-fifty no matter what you end up getting from him.'

'I'm cool with that,' the tweaker said.

'So when do we do it?'

'In one hour,' the tweaker said. 'In the meantime, could you buy me a Baby Ruth bar? I got the craves so bad I could eat a fishbone sandwich if they'd dip it in chocolate.'

Leonard stared for a moment at the 'Help Wanted' sign in the window of the coffee shop. He wanted to tell this lowlife slacker to get a fucking job. He wanted to, but he couldn't. Three-fifty would buy enough rock to tide him over until the fucking Ay-rab called him for the housebreaking job.

He looked at the tweaker and pulled a dollar bill from his pocket. 'Go in there and buy yourself a chocolate donut. Tell them to dip it in powdered sugar. It'll get you by for a couple hours.'

The hijacking was to occur on a residential street in East Hollywood, one of the few neighborhoods where a vendor could make a few dollars. Rogelio Montez was the driver of the little white truck, which played nursery tunes from a large outdoor speaker attached to the roof as he cruised the streets. He was an immigrant from the Yucatán, and this was the best job he'd ever had in his life.

Rita Kravitz, the Crow who oversaw quality-of-life complaints in that neighborhood, had contacted

6-X-66 at midwatch roll call to help her out with this ice-cream vendor. Rita Kravitz briefed the patrol officers about a chronic complainer who lived on the street, a woman who had nine school-age grand-children and saw pedophiles everywhere.

'The alleged suspect drives one of those Good Humor sort of trucks,' Rita Kravitz had told them, 'and he comes by pretty late on summer evenings. Maybe seven o'clock. Just write a shake on the guy and make sure he's not driving the truck with Mister Wiggly exposed. The old lady's already accused her mailman, the meter reader, and one of the presidential contenders of being a willie wagger. Although she's probably right about the presidential contender.'

Gert Von Braun said, 'Okay, but you should call *Dateline* for this kinda deal. They're the ones with all the hidden cameras and lotsa time to set up on these guys.'

Gert Von Braun and Dan Applewhite had gotten teamed again because Doomsday Dan requested it, now that Gil Ponce was just about off probation. Gert told the senior sergeant that she didn't mind at all working with Doomsday Dan, and the astonished sergeant later told his fellow supervisors that there truly is someone for everyone in this world.

When 6-X-66 cleared, they went straight to the neighborhood, found the vendor, and flagged him down, using the excuse that he had only one functioning brake light. Instead of writing him a ticket, they wrote an FI card from the information on his driver's license.

He spoke very little English and seemed contrite about the brake light, and grateful not to be getting a citation. He looked so threadbare and poor that Dan Applewhite insisted on paying for the ice-cream bars that the guy wanted to give to them. Then the cops remained parked at the curb while he drove off, his truck playing merry tunes enticing Latino children from their homes with coins and dollar bills in their fists, all jabbering happily in Spanglish.

Gert and Dan sat, contentedly licking their ice cream and chatting. They were growing ever more comfortable with each other, and the real bonding of police partners had begun. And of course, they'd never heard of Leonard Stilwell and knew nothing of how his life was intersecting the lives of Crow officers. It was quite pleasant to eat ice cream on that hot and dry summer evening when twilight rays of the setting sun cast a magical aura over the land of make-believe, with not a smudge of dark cloud above Sunset Boulevard.

Leonard Stilwell knew he was making a very bad mistake as he drove the tweaker toward the residential streets in East Hollywood, where the ice-cream driver was supposed to be working. First of all, the tweaker kept playing with the starter pistol, twirling it, putting it under his T-shirt inside the waistband of his jeans, and then doing quick draws.

When they were passing L. Ron Hubbard Way, a short street off Sunset Boulevard that fed into the Dianetics Building, Leonard said, 'I know you need to smoke some ice real bad, but could you, like, try to chill? You're making me nervous.'

The tweaker put the gun inside his jeans again and said, 'Get over yourself, dawg, and stay in the game.

For my pickup, you look for me one block south of Santa Monica, two blocks east of the Hollywood cemetery. Whatever that fucking street is.'

'Kee-rist, dude,' Leonard said, 'that's the third time you told me. Your short-term memory's gone!'

'Okay, okay, I'm just sayin'. Don't I gotta, like, keep you dialed in and make sure you got your mind in the day?'

'*My* mind?' Leonard said. 'You're worrying about *my* mind?'

They were a block away from the ice-cream truck when the tweaker spotted it. 'There it is, man!' he said. 'Burn a right!'

'I see it,' Leonard said, driving slowly, keeping an eye on the tweaker, who looked like he'd jump out and start running, given half a chance.

When he was six houses away from the truck, Leonard pulled around the corner and stopped.

The tweaker said, 'Remember, you gotta meet me at—'

Unable to bear another repeated direction, Leonard interrupted, saying, 'Dude, keep this in your fucked-up memory bank. If the cops get onto you, you're gonna have to outrun them in a vehicle that moves at about the speed of prostate cancer. But if you live through it and you bring me less than three-fifty, I'm gonna knock that last corn nut you call a tooth right outta your grille!'

'Chill, Phil!' the tweaker said. 'You're gonna get what's coming to you. Now bang a U-ee and split.'

With that, Leonard drove off, making a U-turn and watching the tweaker in his side-view mirror. The tweaker immediately began slouching toward the ice-cream truck. The last Leonard saw was the scarecrow jogging, then sprinting, in full attack mode.

Gert and Doomsday Dan were just finishing their ice-cream bars and Dan said, 'Okay, we observed the vendor's normal activity and there's nothing abnormal about it. Let's log this and get on with the rest of our lives.'

'Yeah, he's clean,' Gert said, 'but when you think about it, this would be a good job for a pedophile. Selling Eskimo Pies, Push-Ups, and Big Sticks all day long. Like, Hello, little girl, would you like to lick a big stick? Know what I mean?'

'You got a point,' Dan said as Gert started the car.

'Man, there's a guy that needs ice cream bad,' Gert said.

The tweaker was in an all-out sprint when they saw him in the next block. He ran straight at the vendor, who was giving two ice-cream bars to a girl about ten years old who held a younger girl by the hand. The truck's engine was running and 'It's a Small World' was playing noisily.

The tweaker hit the driver hard with his shoulder, sending him sprawling. The children screamed, dropped their ice cream, and started to run. The tweaker pulled his starter pistol, pointed it at the face of the supine Mexican, and said, 'Stay down or die!'

Then the tweaker leaped into the truck and drove away.

'Goddamn!' Gert Von Braun said, squealing out from the curb, turning on her light bar as Dan Applewhite got on the radio and said, ' Six-X-Sixty-six is in pursuit of a two-eleven vehicle!'

The location and description of the pursued vehicle got garbled by the howling of the siren, and after clearing the frequency for the pursuit car, the radio PSR said, 'Six-X-Sixty-six, repeat the location! And did you say an ice-cream truck?'

That was enough to alert a television news crew who monitored police calls. Within minutes, there was a crew speeding toward East Hollywood. Nobody wanted to miss *this* pursuit. An ice-cream truck?

Leonard Stilwell had been sitting with his engine turned off and was worried that it might not start. That would be just his luck. After a few minutes he started it. But then he got worried about overheating the old Honda and switched off the ignition again.

When the police unit was two blocks away but speeding toward him, he heard the siren. It was coming from the direction of the Hollywood cemetery. He figured it might be an ambulance. Yeah, he thought, probably an ambulance. But thirty seconds later, he said, 'Fuck this!' started the car, and pulled away from the curb. No matter who that siren belonged to, Leonard Stilwell had just resigned from the hijacking business.

The tweaker was gunning the engine of the ice-cream truck for all it was worth, but it wasn't worth much. The truck was sputtering and the transmission was slipping as the truck headed north on Van Ness Avenue. Driving south on Van Ness in his direction was the tweaker's wheelman, fleeing in his Honda.

The tweaker almost swerved into him head-on and yelled out the window, 'You bastard! You chickenshit asshole! Don't leave me!'

The pursued and pursuers, with 6-X-66 still the primary, blew right past Leonard in the opposite direction, and he wheeled west on Melrose, heading anywhere but to the cyber café, where there would no doubt be cops looking for him as soon as the tweaker got busted and spilled his guts. But the tweaker didn't know his name and certainly hadn't written down his license number, and anyway, the loser was so brain fried he probably wouldn't even remember what kind of car Leonard owned. As soon as Leonard got safely back to his apartment, he intended to call Ali Aziz. He needed that job. He needed money *now*.

The pursuit was coming to an end after the ice-cream truck rumbled north on the east side of Paramount Studios, then passed the Hollywood cemetery and turned west on Santa Monica Boulevard. There it caused a traffic collision when a Toyota SUV, trying to avoid broadsiding the ice-cream truck, swerved into the rear of an MTA bus. The tweaker nearly caused a second collision when he pulled a hard left onto Gower Street, nearly rolling the ice-cream truck, and slammed to a stop on the west side of the Hollywood cemetery, abandoning the truck.

Gert Von Braun had almost gotten in a TC of her own at Santa Monica and Gower, where she was stopped cold by a pair of elderly motorists who couldn't tell where in the hell the siren was coming from in the fading twilight and just stopped, completely blocking the intersection. When Gert, red faced and fuming, got around them and squealed south onto Gower Street, the cops spotted the abandoned truck.

A man walking a dog waved at them and yelled, 'The guy climbed the fence and ran into the cemetery!'

The mausoleums and tombs on the cemetery grounds contained the mortal remains of Rudolph Valentino, Douglas Fairbanks, Cecil B. DeMille, and many other Hollywood immortals. A pair of security guards opened a gate for Gert Von Braun and Dan Applewhite, and now there were three other Hollywood night-watch and midwatch cars wheeling into the cemetery.

The tweaker had been running frantically through the park, and for no reason anyone could later determine, he ran to the obelisk rising into the blue-black sky with the Hollywood sign visible in the background, to the north on Mt. Lee. He waited while cops and security guards searched the cemetery grounds on foot with flashlights, and with spotlights from the police vehicles. It was there at the obelisk that the tweaker made his last mistake of the day, after being spotted by Gil Ponce, who was teamed with Cat Song.

The tweaker later told a paramedic on their way to the ER that he'd been hanging on to the starter pistol only because he wanted the police to have it if he wasn't able to get away. This, in order to prove that he hadn't used a real gun in the hijacking. The tweaker said that when he saw about two tons of blue running his way, and when a young cop spotted him and began shouting commands, he got worried about the starter pistol in his waistband, scared that the rookie would see it and panic. He said he tried to draw it out with only three fingers, like in the cowboy movies, and drop it on the ground.

But the LAPD hadn't taught Gil Ponce with cowboy-movie training films, and it was too dark to see a three-fingered draw. When the tweaker pulled the gun from his waistband, he saw orange balls of flame and was jolted back against the obelisk, struck in the upper body by two of three rounds fired by Gil Ponce.

Cat was running fast, her nine in both extended hands, when Gil fired the rounds. After the tweaker was on the ground and other cops were running to the obelisk and Cat had gotten on her rover and requested a rescue ambulance, Gil Ponce said, 'He pulled a gun, Cat! I had to shoot him!'

'I know you did,' she said, putting her arm around the young man. 'I would've done the same thing. You did good.'

By the time the tweaker arrived at the ER, he was deemed to be in a serious but not critical condition. However, after a seemingly successful surgery, he died three hours later of a pulmonary embolism. Surgeons reported that one of the rounds had dotted the *i* on the tattoo across his bony chest, which said 'Mom tried.'

Despite the tweaker's statement, which the paramedic repeated in a TV interview, it was widely believed that the trapped and surrounded robber had intended to die. In fact, the TV reporter who covered the incident from the start of the pursuit came on the eleven o'clock news and described the events in the Hollywood cemetery. After reciting a long list of film stars who were interred there, he told his audience that police had withheld the name of the deceased until next of kin could be located.

Then, in response to a question from the anchor desk, he said, 'It is the opinion of this reporter that, despite what was said to the paramedic in the rescue ambulance, what we have here is another tragic case of suicide-by-cop. To believe that the cornered robbery suspect was trying to comply with police commands when he pulled what appeared to be a deadly weapon from his waistband flies in the face of credibility. If he'd wished to surrender, he would never have done something so stupid.'

Leonard Stilwell, who was lying in bed when he saw that newscast, knew from long experience that in Hollywood, things are seldom as they seem. And he muttered to the TV screen, 'Dude, that idiot's entire brain would fit in a coke spoon.'

FOURTEEN

Early the next morning Hollywood Nate got a phone call at home from his CRO sergeant at Hollywood South. The surfer cops had been trying to reach Nate and had left a cell number with the sergeant. When Nate called the number, Jetsam answered, and Nate could hear the sound of crashing surf in the background.

'Why am I being summoned by the headache team?' Nate wanted to know.

'Bro, Malibu is radical today!' Jetsam said. 'You should be here. My partner is out there with two little newbies in thongs the size of tire patches.'

'I see,' Nate said. 'You had to give a surf report to somebody and I won the prize?'

'No, bro,' Jetsam said. 'I gotta talk to you about something.'

'Talk,' Nate said.

Jetsam said, 'I wish I could do it in person at the station, but our hours and yours don't match too good.'

The rest of it faded, and when the signal returned, Nate said, 'I can't hear you.'

'Shit!' Jetsam said. 'Meet us at Hamburger Hamlet at noon straight up.'

Then it was Nate who said 'Shit!' The signal was gone and Nate figured it was probably because the goofy surfer had failed to charge his cell.

Nate was supposed to meet Rita Kravitz to talk with three members of the Homeless Committee, but he felt obliged to postpone that and meet with Flotsam and Jetsam, who would be at Hamburger Hamlet, expecting him. Hollywood Nate could only hope that Jetsam wasn't in his sleuthing mode again. The last episode had gotten him supper with Margot Aziz, but that was all it had gotten him. She still had not called.

Late that morning Leonard Stilwell dragged himself out of bed without having slept more than two hours altogether. He'd awakened several times with nightmares and had lain awake for hours before falling into a brief but fitful sleep. For most of the night, he'd contemplated how he had barely survived catastrophe the previous evening as a result of being driven to desperate measures. He was lucky to be alive and free but had no prospects whatsoever, except for the job with Ali Aziz. His weekly rent was due in two days and he hardly had enough money to put gas in his car and enough food in his belly to keep from feeling weak and nauseous. He ate the last of the breakfast cereal right out of the box, since he had no milk, drank a cup of coffee, didn't bother shaving, and got in his car, determined to drive straight to the Leopard Lounge and demand another advance from Ali Aziz.

Leonard had to bang on the kitchen door before one of the Mexican workers looked out and opened it.

'Where's Ali?' Leonard asked.

'He ees een the office,' the young guy said, obviously uncertain if he should have opened the door for Leonard.

Leonard walked past him, entered the main room, where another Mexican was vacuuming and cleaning tables, and continued down the long hallway to Ali's office. He didn't bother to knock.

'Leonard!' Ali said, irritated by the abrupt entrance.

'I gotta talk to you, Ali,' Leonard said.

'I tell you I shall call.'

'Yeah, well, I can't wait no more,' Leonard said.

Ali Aziz glared at him. Leonard's freckled face looked blotchy. His blue eyes seemed even more empty and stupid-looking than usual. His rusty red hair was a tangled mess and he hadn't shaved in days. Ali thought he must be a fool to be involved with this thief. If only he himself knew how to open a locked door. He was starting to wonder how long it would take him to learn such a skill and if a locksmith could be hired to teach him.

Then Ali said, 'I shall need you soon.'

'Well, soon ain't soon enough,' Leonard said. 'I'm busted, man. I need money now. I'll wait, but only if I get another advance.'

'No, Leonard,' Ali said. 'I give you one advance. We make the deal.'

'Four hundred more,' Leonard said. 'I gotta pay my rent and I gotta actually take some nourishment once in a while. You ever think of that?'

'We shall do the deal next week,' Ali said. 'I promise you.'

'You said a Thursday. Tomorrow is Thursday.'

'This week, no,' Ali said. 'Next week for sure.'

'I'm outta here,' Leonard said, turning toward the door.

'Okay!' Ali said. 'Leonard, please. Go out to the kitchen and tell Paco to get you food. Eat. I see you in twenty minutes, okay?'

Leonard reluctantly obeyed, wondering what kind of food they'd serve in a joint where all the customers really wanted was to look at bare ass and jerk off.

When Leonard was gone, Ali pulled his worry beads from the desk drawer and fingered them while he dialed the number of the *farmacia* on Alvarado Street.

'*Bueno.*' Jaime Salgando answered it himself.

Affecting a jaunty tone he did not feel, Ali said, 'What is happening, Jaime? You do not hire a girl to answer the phone no more. Business is very bad?'

Recognizing the voice and accent at once, Jaime Salgando said, 'Ali, old friend! And how are you today?'

'Fine, brother, I am fine,' Ali said. 'But I must have a very big favor. I must ask my friend to please come for the date tonight and bring what I ordered from you. The girls are very much ready for you. This night is very much better for them.'

'I can't, Ali,' Jaime said. 'My granddaughter is in a school play this evening and I have to be there to see her.'

'Jaime,' Ali said, 'this is most important. I must have it. Another child on my street almost got attacked yesterday. From this killer dog.'

'I'm sorry, Ali,' Jaime said. 'I can't disappoint my granddaughter.'

'Can I come to the store and pick up my order today? I do that, okay?'

'But I haven't seen my friend yet,' the pharmacist said. 'I don't have what you ordered.'

Ali thought of how desperate Leonard looked, and now it was his turn for desperation. He worked those worry beads for all they were worth until he came up with a plausible story. Ali said, 'Jaime, my brother, I am so sorry. There is another reason that Saturday date is no good.'

'What is that?'

'Tex, she is getting married on Saturday. Big wedding. We all shall go to it. She says to me she cannot have fun with old friend Jaime no more after that. Even Goldie shall go to this wedding. I have new girls to work that night. I never meet these girls before. I hire the girls from the agency. I cannot ask new girls to have a special party with my friend Jaime. I am sorry.'

The pharmacist was silent for a moment and then said, 'Strange. I never think of these girls as doing normal things like getting married.'

'But Tex says if her friend Jaime can come tonight, she can give him a very great time. Like, how you say, it is her getting married party?'

'Bachelor party,' Jaime said. 'Or bachelorette, in this case.'

'Exactly!' Ali said. 'And Goldie says, "Oh yes, that is going to be very much fun."'

Again the pharmacist hesitated before speaking. 'All right. I'll make a call and deliver your order to you at seven o'clock. I'd like to watch the show for a while. Then I'd like to have my private party and be home by midnight.'

'All shall be as you wish, brother!' Ali said. 'The dinner reservation shall be ready and so shall Tex and Goldie!'

'I didn't like that motel last time,' Jaime said. 'It wasn't very clean. I want to go to that nice one by the Leopard Lounge.'

'Anything, brother,' Ali said.

After he hung up, Ali scrolled to Tex's cell. When she answered, he said, 'Tex. You shall not do the special party on Saturday. You must do the party tonight. Get Goldie. Come tonight, eight o'clock.'

He had to hold the phone away when she yelled, 'Goddamnit, Ali, I told you I needed tonight off! I got a date I been looking forward to! I ain't doing the old Mexican tonight and that's final!'

Ali felt his blood rising. The planning, the expense, the anxiety, the fear, it was all getting to be too much. He was doing all of this for his son. To save his beloved son from his son's bitch mother. His motives were pure and he was being obstructed by everyone!

Ali heard himself yell into the phone, 'I shall pay you big bonus! I shall pay Goldie big bonus! But you shall come tonight! You are listening to me?'

'Keep the bonus, Ali!' Tex yelled back at him. 'You can fuck the old Mexican yourself, for all I care!'

Ali began choking with rage now. His eyes were bulging and he'd broken the strand that held the worry beads. He screamed into the phone: 'You do like I say or I fire you! You got to fuck the old Mexican! I am the boss! The boss don't got to fuck no old Mexican!'

He was panting, and he swallowed his spit and felt

light-headed and unsteady. He thought he might vomit. The worry beads were scattered all over his desk.

Then Tex's voice said calmly in his ear, 'It better be a big fucking bonus, Ali. And I mean it literally.'

Four of the eleven senior lead officers at the Community Relations Office were on vacation. Ronnie and Bix were filling in for the Police Explorer Program, which involved kids of both genders ages fourteen to twenty. Many of the former Explorers went on to join the LAPD when they were twenty-one years old. Ronnie liked working with the kids, who were open and eager and idealistic. She hoped they could hang on to some of that if they did become regular police officers. Of course, there was no way she could warn them about the premature cynicism that she and her colleagues had to battle throughout their careers. For these kids, cynicism was not on their desktop.

Bix Ramstead was starting to worry her more each day. Through casual conversation she learned that his wife and two children had left for their vacation, along with his wife's parents, to her parents' lakefront home in Oregon. From what he said and didn't say, Ronnie gathered that Bix's father-in-law, a retired judge and a demanding perfectionist, might not have been a best friend to his son-in-law. In any case, Bix seemed relieved not to be spending two weeks with the judge.

Since his family had gone, Ronnie thought she could see a difference in his eyes, his voice, even the steadiness of his hands. She was positive that he was drinking, and not just a little bit. Ronnie didn't think that Bix should be alone in his house for two weeks.

That day, while the two cops were taking code 7 at a good little restaurant in Thai Town, sharing a spicy, hot shrimp salad, she said, 'Must get lonely for you with the family gone.'

'I've got our dog, Annie, to keep me company,' he said. 'How about you? You're always alone.'

'I'm used to it,' she said. 'But you're used to a wife and a couple of adolescents charging around. How're you coping with silence?'

'I get to watch whatever TV program I like,' Bix said. 'With a big, slobbery dog sleeping in my lap. And I don't have to make the bed.'

'You know you're always welcome to join us for our burrito rendezvous on Sunset Boulevard. Sometimes Cat shows up, or Hollywood Nate. Rita Kravitz is usually there, and Tony Silva. The boss comes by once in a while. In fact, we might be going there tonight.'

'No, thanks,' he said. 'I think I'll try for eight hours' sleep, if Annie will let me. She sleeps crossways and takes up most of the bed. She kicks like a mule in her sleep and passes enough gas to launch the Goodyear blimp.'

Ronnie hesitated, then said, 'Are you still concerned about the, you know, booze thing when you go out with a bunch of coppers?'

'It enters my mind,' Bix said, 'but that's not the reason.'

'How long's it been since you had a drink?'

'I don't count the days like an alcoholic does,' he said. 'But it's been well over a month.'

'Do you miss it?'

He shrugged and said, 'I can take it or leave it.'

Ronnie Sinclair knew that Bix Ramstead was lying.

'No shoes, no service,' the imperious hostess at Hamburger Hamlet – one of the legion of otherwise unemployable liberal arts majors who staffed nearly every nonethnic restaurant and bar in Hollywood – said to the surfer cops when they walked through the front door.

'Bro, I didn't notice you were shoeless,' Jetsam said to his partner when they returned to Flotsam's GMC pickup to get his sneakers. 'You gotta show some class.'

'Why do you take me to fancy establishments where you gotta wear shoes?' Flotsam said. 'I'm so used to running around the beach all day, I don't know if I got flip-flops on or not. You think I spend a lotta time looking at my own feet?'

'Since we're not packing, I hope nobody tries to steal our boards,' Jetsam said, their guns being under the seat of the locked truck. 'Anyways, the wusses that run the consent decree would go all PMS-ey if we capped a surfboard thief.'

'Only if they're oppressed minorities,' Flotsam said. 'If they're white, you can shoot them down like rabid pit bulls and back over them in your truck five or six times.'

'Check the city demographics, bro,' Jetsam said. 'We're the oppressed minority.'

When they re-entered Hamburger Hamlet, they got disapproving looks from the hostess, this pair of surfers in baggy T-shirts and board shorts, with salt still clinging to their sunburned faces, and sand falling from their hair. They couldn't have looked more like surfers if they'd been wearing half-peeled wet suits, but at least she could now count four sneakers on their sockless feet, so they got seated in a booth to await the arrival of Hollywood Nate Weiss.

They only had to wait ten minutes, and both were hydrating with their second iced tea when Nate entered and sat down.

'To what do I owe the pleasure of doing lunch with you two sand crabs?' Nate said.

'Wanna cold drink?' Jetsam said when the waitress came over to their table. She was an Asian with very nice legs.

'I'll have what they're drinking,' Nate said.

'Iced tea coming up,' she said. 'Lemme know when you want something else.'

Nate checked her out as she was walking away and said, 'I might just do that.' Then he said to Jetsam, 'So you wanted face time. What's up?'

Flotsam assumed his 'I got nothing to do with this' pose, and Jetsam said, 'Last Friday night we wrote a parking ticket to a guy named Leonard Stilwell. The name mean anything to you?'

Nate looked puzzled and said, 'Nope.'

'Wormy-looking white dude. Maybe a tweaker, maybe a crackhead. Fortyish. Medium height. Red hair, freckles, black Honda with primer spots?'

Nate shook his head and said, '*Nada*. Am I supposed to know him?'

Jetsam said, 'I dunno, but he had an address in his car, and just for the hell of it we checked it out, because this dude shouldn't be having an address up on Mount

Olympus. Not unless he's going there to clean out their garage or something. He's got a couple priors for burglary.'

'Still not tracking,' Nate said.

'So we don't find the address,' Jetsam said. 'The number's off a little bit. But right near there where the address should be, we see a car.'

'*His* car?' Nate said.

'Not *his* car,' Jetsam said.

That brought things to a sudden stop. Nate frowned slightly and said, 'You saw my car?'

'SAG4NW,' Jetsam said. 'So we thought you should know about this burglar Stilwell, is all.'

Flotsam corrected his partner, saying, '*He* thought you should know. Me, I'm neutral in this matter.'

Hollywood Nate didn't speak for a moment and then said, 'It was the wrong address, you said.'

'Yeah, but there was no street address to exactly match the one on the piece of paper. If I remember right, the address you were visiting ended in four eight? His address ended in two six. But then the street turns and the numbers are totally different. The house you were in is closest to the number he wrote down.'

Flotsam was sick of this. He said to Nate, 'Dude, my pard thinks whoever lives in that house might be a future crime victim or maybe a present criminal if they're connected to this dirtbag Leonard Stilwell. That's, like, the shorthand version of this here drama.'

'What's, like, the longhand version?' Nate said.

'The longhand version is that my pard is all goony over Sinclair Squared, and he would love to become a Crow and work with her, even though she don't know a surfboard from an ironing board. But come to think of it, whenever somebody asks her to iron something, she divorces him. And since she don't marry nobody unless his name is Sinclair, I wish he'd either change his name to Sinclair or stop all this Sherlock shit, because it's wearing me down!'

Jetsam just looked at his partner, astonished. He'd never seen Flotsam so exercised.

'What's his crush on Ronnie got to do with the burglar?' Nate asked Flotsam, as though Jetsam weren't there.

'He heard that Ronnie and Bix Ramstead were working that part of the Hollywood Hills, kissing ass with all those rich whiners up there, and he's, like, trying to bring the spotlight on this and score points with Ronnie and maybe the Crow sergeant.'

Jetsam still stared at his partner in astonishment and finally said, 'Bro, why didn't you switch to my frequency? I didn't know you were all vaporized about this!'

'I been trying to for days,' Flotsam said. 'You ain't been the same ever since you fired off flares over the SUVs in the body shop. You're, like, totally spring-loaded. You just don't listen to body language no more!'

'I didn't know you were all bent, bro!'

'Work out your domestic partnership later,' Nate said. 'I can tell you that the person who lives in that house is not some kind of crook. As to being a target of this guy Stilwell, I just don't know.'

'Is she your squeeze?' Flotsam said with a leer.

'Hey, I don't ask you about your Bettys,' Nate said.

'Dude, you are hormonally spirited!' Flotsam said admiringly.

Rebounding from Flotsam's tirade, Jetsam said to Nate, 'It wouldn't hurt to ask your squeeze – I mean, the person who lives there – if she knows a Leonard Stilwell. If she don't, it might be something to talk over with the burglary dicks. Trust me, bro, that pus bucket Stilwell is a waste of good air, and he's up to no good.'

'I'll give her a call,' Nate said, 'and see what she knows.'

'Is she a hottie or just rich?' Flotsam said to Nate with that same annoying leer.

'She's just somebody with a car for sale,' Nate said. 'I was talking to her about her SUV.'

It had slipped from Nate's mouth before he could stop it, and Jetsam jumped on it. 'Hey, bro! That's the SUV from the body shop, ain't it? The one you talked to the guy about?'

Nate saw both surfers looking at him expectantly now. He decided to tell the truth. He said, 'Yeah, that's the one. And yeah, she's a burner babe, but nothing happened.'

'This is destiny at work, bro!' Jetsam said with a flourish. 'There's only a few degrees of separation here. We're all part of some inscrutable plan!'

Nate was speechless until Flotsam said, 'He gets like this after we been surfing. He sits out there on the water and gets, like, these visions. They make him go all surfboard simple for the rest of the day. He'll be okay later.'

'At least you should bounce for the iced tea,' Nate said, finishing his drink.

'Yeah, dude, it's on us,' Flotsam said. 'But if you

want my opinion, you oughtta shine them Hills honeys. All that sculpted flesh and five-karat diamonds look good, but there's, like, better ways to escape your humdrum existence. Grab yourself a log and come to Malibu. We'll be your gurus.'

Jetsam agreed, saying, 'Bro, it's way wack to go all frothy over Mount Olympus bitches, who think their shit should be gilded and hung on gold chains.'

Flotsam concurred, saying, 'Yeah, they think their turds should be bronzed and kept in trophy cases, dude.'

'Come to Malibu, bro,' Jetsam said. 'Maybe you'll have a vision too and find your true self.'

Nate stood up then, nodded, and said, 'Am I ever glad I came here today. All this time I've been buying lottery tickets and stalking talent agents, and the answer was right before my eyes. I just couldn't see it till you sea slugs dialed me in. It all comes down to a surfboard. The stuff that dreams are made of!'

There was no better time of day in Hollywood than twilight, as far as Ronnie Sinclair was concerned. The way the setting sun blasted through the low-hanging summer smog actually burnished the pollution into garish wine-colored clouds. After which, a scarlet glare was cast over the boulevards announcing to all: This place is unlike any other. Here even the toxic gases are beautiful!

After lunch, followed by a perfunctory visual check to see if there were signs of the homeless encampment springing up again, Ronnie drove them back toward Hollywood Boulevard. Bix Ramstead answered his cell phone and the look on his face startled her.

Bix reddened and whispered into the phone, 'I'm working. I can't talk. I'll call you later.' He snapped the phone shut and said, 'My brother Pete. He's a pain. Always borrowing money, never paying it back.'

'Yeah, my sister used to be like that till her husband made it big,' Ronnie said, looking at Bix, who was smiling but not with those heavily lashed gray eyes she loved. And she knew he was lying again. That was not brother Pete on the cell call.

'Maybe I oughtta join you guys the next time you go up to Sunset Boulevard for a Mexican dinner,' Bix said abruptly. 'With my family gone, I guess I should get out and mix a bit. Gets lonely talking to a dog, even one as smart as Annie.'

'I'll bet she's smarter than most of the people we call on every day,' Ronnie said. 'I found out that our posse won't be doing our Mexican thing tonight after all, but if you're not busy, I'd be glad to meet you there.'

She had never detected a sexual vibe coming her way from Bix Ramstead and she didn't detect it now when he said, 'I might do that. When, right after we go end-of-watch?'

'Okay by me,' she said. 'And I'll pop for it, since I'm a semiprosperous single copper with nobody to spend my money on but me and two goldfish.'

Then another phone call came in, this one on Ronnie's cell. She picked it up and said, 'Officer Sinclair.'

'It's Nate,' Hollywood Nate said to her. 'Can I talk to Bix?'

'Sure,' she said, handing Bix her phone and saying, 'It's Nate.'

'To what do we owe the pleasure?' Bix said to him.

Then the smile was gone. His face darkened yet again. His lips turned down and he said, 'Yeah, I know the resident at that address.' After a moment he said, 'I, uh, I'll see you back at Hollywood South and we can talk about it. In an hour, okay?'

When he hung up this time, he felt he definitely owed his partner an explanation, so he said to Ronnie, 'Just some Hollywood Nate deal. A person on Mount Olympus that I dealt with on a prior call might be a burglary target. Some guy with four-five-nine priors had the resident's address in his car, or a similar address to that one. It's just bullshit, I'm sure. It's nothing.'

The brooding look on his face said that it was not nothing to Bix Ramstead. And Ronnie Sinclair knew that he was lying to her yet again.

Ali Aziz couldn't eat a bite all day. He mulled over his plan a dozen times and he couldn't stop sweating. He even used the shower in the dancers' bathroom and steamed himself clean, letting the hot water pelt his balding dome until it turned pink. He went to the closet in his office and changed into a clean silk shirt. He shaved his face, doused himself with cologne, and flopped onto the leather sofa in his office and tried to nap, but he could not.

He didn't want food or whiskey or women. He only wanted this torment to be over. He wanted Margot to be gone forever. He wanted to have his son, Nicky, and to take him away from this terrible city, from this terrible, godless country someday. Here, there was no respect, no love, no truth. Everything here was a lie.

*   *   *

Jaime Salgando showed up half an hour early at the Leopard Lounge. When he entered Ali's office, he said, 'Traffic was light for once.'

Ali looked approvingly at Jaime's double-breasted pinstriped suit, wondering if it was a Hugo Boss. And at his starched white shirt with shooting cuffs and gold links and at his sky-blue necktie with a perfect knot, and he said, 'This is how gentlemen dress. In my country, in your country, men have respect. In this country, no respect.'

Jaime said, 'Thank you,' and sat in the client chair nervously, wanting to get the business finished.

'The girls shall arrive at eight o'clock, like you say,' Ali said.

'Yes, yes,' Jaime said, 'that gives us a chance to do our business. I have an acquaintance at a compounding pharmacy who helps me with these unusual orders.'

'What is the meaning of "compounding"?'

'They mix a lot of drugs and medications for special prescription orders. This employee is from the village in Mexico where I used to spend my summers. He was able to help me, but it cost me six hundred dollars.'

Ali looked at him, trying to keep his smile in place. He knew that Jaime was lying to him, but he was powerless. Everyone lied to him. By forcing Jaime to come tonight instead of Saturday, he was going to pay a price. Ali took the roll of hundreds from his gold money clip and counted out six bills, placing them on the desk.

'Of course, my brother,' Ali said. 'We got to pay for good service always. That is the American way.'

Jaime Salgando picked up the bills and put them in his pocket and withdrew a small pill envelope with his pharmacy's name on it. He opened it and dropped two green capsules on the desktop, then put the envelope back in his pocket.

Ali nearly panicked. 'Two?' he said. 'I need *two* capsules to kill the dog?'

'No, you only need one of these to easily kill a fifty-kilo dog. The other is just in case the dog does not take the bait or if something goes wrong. Then you can try again some other time.'

Ali's relief was palpable. 'You are a smart man, brother,' he said. 'Very smart. Yes, is good to have the, how you say, backdown?'

'Backup.'

'Yes, we got the backup now. Very good. Very good.'

'I'd like a drink while I wait for the girls.'

'Yes, yes,' Ali said. 'Anything. You want champagne? I got good champagne for special customers.'

'I want a bottle of good champagne brought to the motel,' Jaime said, very businesslike and matter-of-fact. 'Make it two bottles. And an ice bucket. And three glasses, of course. But for now I'd like a double shot of tequila. The Patrón Silver that you serve to your special clients.'

'You got it, brother,' Ali said, but now his forced smile had turned grim and produced white lines around his mouth. Ali was starting to loathe Jaime Salgando nearly as much as he loathed the other thieves with whom he was forced to do business. Almost as much as he loathed Leonard Stilwell.

By the time the pharmacist had finished his tequila

shooter, there was a knock at the door and Tex entered with Goldie.

'Jaime, you rascal!' Tex drawled. 'I'm so glad you could make it tonight!'

'Me too!' Goldie said. 'This is just too cool for school!'

Both women giggled when the courtly pharmacist rose and kissed their hands. They were both dressed in black Chanel knockoffs with spaghetti straps, as though for one of their nights on the Sunset Strip. Goldie wore three-inch open-toed heels, but because the pharmacist had special needs, Tex did not wear hers. She wore lizard-skin cowboy boots that she used in her act, and a new snow-white cowboy hat with a rhinestone *T* across the crown.

When Jaime Salgando and the dancers were gone, Ali locked the door and took the green capsules out of his desk drawer and looked at them. For what this evening was costing him, he wished he could have put one of them in the pharmacist's tequila.

Ali reached into the back of the drawer and brought out the magenta-and-turquoise capsule he had stolen from Margot's medicine cabinet, along with the coke spoon and razor blade that he used when he had to give the girls a toot in exchange for services. He put the items on a clean sheet of bond paper along with the two green capsules and a funnel he'd fashioned from a sheet of heavier bond. He carefully pulled open the sleep aid and dumped the contents into the trash basket. Then he wiped his hands and held them palms down in front of him to make sure they were not trembling.

He very carefully pulled open the green capsule and

poured the contents into the homemade funnel. It looked something like a mixture of cocaine and sugar might look. Then he picked up the empty magenta-and-turquoise capsule with tweezers and funneled the lethal dose into it. The green capsule contained a bit more than 50 milligrams, so there were some granules left over and it concerned him. But the pharmacist had seemed very confident that this would kill a 50-kilo animal, so there must be more than enough to do the job.

He was going to dump the remaining granules from the green capsule into his trash basket, but instead he took the residue into his bathroom and flushed it away. He washed his hands thoroughly and for no logical reason burned the paper he had used. He put the lethal capsule, which now looked like just another of Margot's sleep aids, into an envelope along with the other deadly green sister and stored them far back in his middle drawer alongside the full vial of capsules.

His only concern now was that Margot might only have a few capsules left in her sleep aid vial. And that would mean he'd be afraid to add too many more, for fear of making it obvious. If that was the case, she'd die in the next few weeks rather than in the next few months, after she had gone to wherever it was that she was taking his son. Ali feared that outcome. He wanted her to be found dead in that other place, so that there would be little reason for investigators to look for answers back in Hollywood.

Then he felt his heart go hollow as he thought of where she might go to live when the house closed escrow, those places she had talked about. San

Francisco? New York? If the judge permitted this, he might not be able to see his precious boy from the time she moved away until she died. The thought of not seeing Nicky for two months or more made Ali Aziz put his face down on his folded arms and weep.

FIFTEEN

M AN, YOU AIN'T RIGHT for this work,' his neighbor known as Junior said to Leonard Stilwell that evening while Ali Aziz wept and the Mexican pharmacist partied.

Leonard and Junior had been practicing for twenty minutes with a TR4 tension bar and a double-diamond pick that Leonard was planning to borrow from Junior for the job tomorrow. Junior's apartment, three doors down the hall from Leonard's, was about what Leonard had always found in a parolee's crib: Cuervo bottles, porn mags, a half-eaten chocolate cake, candy wrappers everywhere. The room was so small, the giant Fijian would have had to stand in the kitchenette to make the bed, which he never did. He had huge hands and lots of jailhouse tatts that were nearly invisible on his dark skin.

After getting Junior away from the cartoon channel, Leonard was kneeling on the floor with the door open, trying to unlock the double-sided dead bolt with a thumb-turn on the inside. He was interrupted when a fat cockroach crawled up his neck, causing him to yelp and do a roach dance, slapping at his neck and shaking like a wet dog.

'They do not hurt you, bro,' Junior said. 'Back home we eat them bugs if they too dumb to get off our food.'

'I'm scared of roaches,' Leonard said. 'I grew up in Yuma with six brothers and sisters and a drunk old man that never worked. Cockroaches crawled all over us when we were sleeping, and so did the rats.'

'Bro, back home we eat them rats too. No problem.'

'Okay, lemme try again,' Leonard said.

The tension bar looked to Leonard like a very slender Allen wrench, and the pick, which Junior called a rake, was like a four-inch needle with what looked like a couple of camel humps on the end of it. The fact of the matter was, Leonard had never picked a lock in his entire life and had never bothered to learn from Whitey Dawson, not even once on the dozen jobs they'd done together.

'Man, you was not born for this work,' Junior said. 'You sure you wanna take the job? You gonna fuck up and get busted.'

'I seen it done lots of times when I had a partner,' Leonard said. 'It looked easy when he did it.'

'Why don't you cut that partner in on this job, bro? I don't think you gonna be teachable.'

'He's dead.'

'Too bad, man. Wish I could help you but I promise my mommy I ain't gonna do no crime no more.'

'Show me again,' Leonard said. 'One more time.'

The big Fijian held the tension bar in his massive hand, inserted it, and said, 'See, bro, the tension bar turn the cylinder.' He slid the pick inside with the other hand and said, 'The rake, it lift up the pin.' Then he turned the knob easily and handed the little tools to Leonard, saying, 'My granddaddy could do this, and he lost one hand to a mako shark.'

'Lemme try once more,' Leonard said, and he concentrated on copying the big Fijian's finger moves.

He inserted the tension bar and said, 'With this I turn the cylinder.' Then he inserted the pick and said, 'With this I lift the pin.' And he felt it.

'Yes!' he said when he turned the knob.

He did it once more, and again it worked.

'You there, bro!' the Fijian said.

'I'll bring them back to you tomorrow night,' Leonard said, putting the instruments in his pocket.

'You get caught, man, you don't know me. You never heard of nobody from Fiji. Not even Vijay Singh.'

'I'm good with that,' Leonard said. 'And when I bring the tools back, you'll get the President Grant, like I promised.'

'If you ain't in jail,' the Fijian said.

'Later, man,' Leonard said, walking out.

'Hey, bro,' the Fijian said, 'I just remember. Could you gimme a ride to the clinic? I caught the clap from some whore, and the doc say come back for a checkup.'

'Yeah, I'll drop you,' Leonard said. 'Where you being treated?'

The Fijian aimed a fat index finger at his genitals and said, 'Down there.'

When Ronnie and Bix returned to Hollywood South to turn in their car and check out, Hollywood Nate was waiting with his feet up on a desk, reading *Daily Variety*. Bix didn't look happy to see him.

'Go on ahead,' Bix said to Ronnie. 'I gotta talk to

Nate for a minute. I'll meet you at the restaurant, okay?'

'Okay,' she said, glancing at Nate, but he just gave her a little wave, betraying nothing.

Ronnie entered the women's locker room to change out of her uniform, more uncertain than ever about her partner. There was something going on other than secret drinking. But what would it have to do with Hollywood Nate Weiss, who was sitting there like a sphinx? If she only knew Bix a little better, she'd just grab him and blurt out some questions she wanted answered. But for now she didn't feel she had the right to intrude.

Bix and Nate walked outside and stood on the step in front of Hollywood South. Traffic was light on Fountain Avenue for such a balmy summer evening. At times like these, old residents of the neighborhood could almost smell the flower gardens and citrus trees that everyone used to cultivate back in the day. But now, in the most traffic-choked city in North America, there was only the smell of engine exhaust.

'Now, what's this about?' Bix said, sitting on the step.

Nate also sat and said, 'Like I told you on the phone, the surfers jacked up some dude with four-five-nine priors who had an address in his car. It was a bad address but the closest number to it belongs to someone named Margot Aziz.'

Bix Ramstead gave Nate a blank look and said, 'What's that got to do with me?'

'Flotsam and Jetsam were wondering if this guy might be employed by the homeowner. His name's Leonard Stilwell. A white dude about forty, medium height and weight, red hair and freckles. He drives a shitty old black Honda with primer spots on it. If he's not working for the homeowner, he might be targeting the house for a four-five-nine. That's what our sleuthing surfers think.'

'Again, what's that got to do with me?' Bix said.

Nate had given Bix enough bait, but he hadn't come close to taking it. So Nate decided to tell a half-truth.

'They drove up Mount Olympus a little later and saw one of our cars up there.'

Of course Bix thought that 'our cars' referred to police vehicles, and he said, 'What night was that?'

'I don't know,' Nate said, telling another half-truth. 'But they checked and found out who was driving the car that night.'

Bix Ramstead looked like he was pondering it and then he said, 'Well, if it was the night before last, it was me.'

And that was all he said. He looked at Nate as though it was his turn to talk.

Nate said, 'I'm not asking you about your business, Bix. It's just that they thought this dude Stilwell is bad news and they just wondered—'

Interrupting, Bix said, 'I know the woman who lives there. Last year we met at a Tip-A-Cop fund-raiser, and she calls me with problems occasionally.'

Nate would always look back on this moment and regret that he'd not been brave enough and honest enough to show and tell, to compare notes on Margot Aziz. But all he said was 'I don't suppose the problem had to do with somebody who fit the description of this guy Stilwell?'

'No,' Bix said, looking less tense, more forthcoming.

'Actually, she's worried about her husband, Ali Aziz. Do you know the Leopard Lounge?'

'Topless joint on Sunset?'

'That's it.'

'Yeah, I know where it is.'

'Ali Aziz is the owner. Anyway, they're in the middle of a raging divorce and custody battle, and she's afraid he's gonna do her harm.'

'Is he one of those nightclub-owning gangsters, like the Russians?'

'No,' Bix said. 'He's just some semi-sleazy operator from the Middle East who found his American dream selling T and A.'

Now Nate was the one feeling less tense. It was all in sync with what Margot Aziz had said to him. Of course, the big question tormenting Nate was whether Bix was more than just a professional acquaintance of Margot's. Again he tried to summon the nerve to ask Bix, and to reveal to him that she had almost offered to let Nate move into her house, and that she'd spent an evening trying to pour booze down his throat.

But all he could bring himself to say was 'So do you think somebody should ask if she knows Stilwell?'

'I don't see why we should add to her worries. She's paranoid enough about her husband. After all, you said it was a different house number.'

'Yeah, but the number he had doesn't exist, and the Aziz address is the only one close to it.'

'If it's bothering you, I guess I could call her tomorrow and ask if she knows the guy. Maybe he's giving her a price on window washing or something.

She happened to mention the house is in escrow and she'll be moving.'

'It's not bothering me. It's bothering those log-head surfers.'

'I can call her,' Bix said. 'Maybe tomorrow.'

Nate tried to make it sound casual when he said, 'Is she an older woman?'

'Why do you ask that?' Bix said.

'Well, if she's an older woman, I wouldn't wanna scare her.'

'An older woman in a custody battle?'

'Oh, that's right, I forgot,' Nate said. 'She can't be that old.'

Bix said, 'I'll give her a call tomorrow, just to be on the safe side.'

And that was all the nibbling around the edges that Hollywood Nate was prepared to do. He was convinced that Bix Ramstead was more than an acquaintance of Margot Aziz's. Because anybody on the planet, when asked if Margot was an older woman, would have said that far from being an older woman, she was a Hills honey who could stop traffic at noon on Rodeo Drive or anywhere else, no matter how much competition was out there. But Bix hadn't done that.

'Well, I gotta change and meet Ronnie for some *carne asada*,' Bix said. 'Wanna join us?'

'Naw, I think I'll go in the workout room and hit the treadmill,' Nate said. 'I got my physical coming up in two weeks.'

'Catch you tomorrow,' Bix said.

And suddenly Nate Weiss didn't feel so bad about not telling the whole truth to Bix Ramstead, because he was absolutely certain that Bix had been lying to him.

Midwatch unit 6-X-66 was having an uneventful tour of duty so far. Gert Von Braun had written a ticket to a guy in a Humvee who'd been gawking at a dragon hustling tricks on Santa Monica Boulevard. He blew through the stoplight at Western Avenue, almost broadsiding a car full of Asian kids. Then they'd refereed a family dispute involving a soldier just back from Iraq whose wife had moved in with her boss's son and wouldn't let the soldier have personal property that he said belonged to his mother.

Then, two hours into their watch, they'd received a message on their MDC computer that sent them to the bungalow of a ninety-year-old lifelong resident of East Hollywood who claimed that a possible home invader was watching her house. When Gert and Dan Applewhite arrived, they found the old woman sitting in a rocker on her front porch, stroking a Persian cat. A light burned inside and a cable news channel was on.

You could count the old woman's bones through flesh the color of antique ivory, but she seemed very alert and described the suspicious man to Gert and Dan as having black hair and 'large, liquid brown eyes.'

When Gert asked if she had any idea who the man was, the old woman said, yes, his name might be Tyrone Power.

Gert, who was nearly twenty years younger than Doomsday Dan, said, 'Is this Tyrone Power a black man or white?'

'He's white,' Dan said to Gert.

Gert looked at Dan and said, 'How do you know?'

Instead of answering Gert, Dan said to the old woman, 'Was he wearing a black mask, by any chance? And did he carry a sword?'

'No,' the old woman said. 'Not this time.'

'On other occasions?' Dan asked.

'Oh, yes, sometimes,' she said.

'Did he ever carve a Z on any objects around here?'

'He might have,' she said. 'He's very handsome.'

'I know exactly where this man is,' Dan said.

'You do?' the old woman said.

'Yes, and I'll see to it that he doesn't come around bothering you again. You don't have to worry about it. Do you live with someone?'

'Yes, I live with my daughter. She's at work.'

'Well, you can sleep tight. We'll take care of that fellow.'

'You won't hurt him, will you?' she said. 'He's very handsome.'

'I promise we will not hurt him,' Dan Applewhite said.

When they were walking to their shop, Gert said, 'So, okay. Who's this Tyrone Power?'

'You're too young to know, but he was a big movie star.'

'And you say you know exactly where to find him?'

'Yes, in a mausoleum at the Hollywood cemetery,' Dan Applewhite said.

Gert cleared by pressing a button on the MDC keyboard and they resumed patrol, Dan driving and Gert keeping score. She logged the call and then looked over at Dan.

'You know what I heard about you?' she said.

'What's that?'

'I hear you're a serial groom, that you've been married four times.'

'That's a lie,' he said. 'Three times.'

'You don't like to stay married very long, huh?'

'I've been married a long time,' he said, 'but to three different women.'

'Got kids?'

'Only one,' Dan said.

'How old?'

'Twenty-six. He's a computer geek, and a whiner like his mother. How about you?'

'Never been married,' she said. 'This job isn't conducive.'

'You've got lotsa time,' he said. 'You're young.'

'Look at me. I don't have anybody breaking down my door,' she said.

He turned and did take a good look at her and he said, 'Whadda you mean?'

'I'm wide,' she said with defiance in her eyes. 'Ask Treakle.'

'You care what Chickenlips thinks?' Dan said. 'I think you look healthy. I'm sick of anorexic women. My last two wives figured out a way to throw up more food than they ever swallowed.'

'My dad's a skinny German,' she said, 'but my mom's Dutch, with big shoulders and wide hips. From picking too many tulips, I guess. I favor her side of the family.'

'I like the way you look,' Dan said.

Gert smiled slightly and said, 'Tyrone Power, huh? I'm gonna have to educate myself. He played Zorro?'

'Long before Antonio Banderas,' Dan said. 'You like old movies?'

'I haven't seen too many, but yeah, I do.'

'I know an art house cinema where they even show silents. You should go with me sometime. I mean, not like a date or anything. I know my sell-by date is way past.'

'You're not that old,' she said.

'You don't think so?' said Doomsday Dan.

The incipient flirtation was interrupted by another computer message, directing them to an address familiar to Ronnie Sinclair and Bix Ramstead.

When 6-X-66 arrived at that address and knocked, a portly black woman came to the door. She pointed across the street at a wood-frame cottage where two shopping carts were overturned in the tiny front yard.

'I'm Mrs. Farnsworth,' she said. 'I've called you all about the people over there. About the shopping carts in the yard and about the noise.'

'Is that what this is about?' Gert said. 'Noise?'

'No, this is about the quiet,' she said. 'It's too quiet over there. At this time of evening they usually got this weird Somali music blaring. But not tonight.'

'Maybe they're not home,' Dan said.

'They're home,' Mrs. Farnsworth said. 'I seen them through their windows an hour ago, but now the blinds are down.'

'Maybe they went to bed,' Gert said.

'Honey, they don't go to bed till two, three A.M.,' Mrs. Farnsworth said. 'At least *he* don't. He yells at her all the time. And I know he beats her, but she won't say nothing whenever I get a chance to ask her about it.'

'It's pretty hard for us to go knock on people's doors and ask them why they're being so quiet,' Dan said.

'There's a young man,' Mrs. Farnsworth said, 'a young white man. He used to drive her home once in a while. She cleans his house, is what she told me. He lives with his handicapped parents and he has a good job and he's good to her, she said. One day I seen him drop her off, and her husband came outta the house with only his underwear on and he grabbed her arm and started jabbering in their language and dragged her into the house and slammed the door. After that she took the bus home from her housecleaning jobs. He's a very mean man and she's a very sweet and frightened girl.'

Gert looked at Dan and he said, 'We can knock and try to think of some reason for doing it. Just to make sure everything's okay.'

'The shopping carts,' Mrs. Farnsworth said. 'He's been warned about that before.' Then she went to a bookshelf and removed a porcelain vase with some cards inside. She handed one to Gert, saying, 'The officer wrote his personal phone number on the back of the card and said I could call him anytime.'

Gert read it and said, 'Officer Bix Ramstead.' Then she said to the woman, 'We'll knock and see what's what.'

'Please,' Mrs. Farnsworth said. 'I'm really worried about that girl. And so was that Officer Ramstead. You could see it in his face.'

Gert Von Braun and Dan Applewhite crossed the

residential street, needing their flashlights to keep from stepping into the potholes that the city of Los Angeles hadn't the financial resources to repair.

They listened and heard nothing inside. Dan knocked. No answer.

Gert walked a few steps to the window and listened. Dan knocked again. No answer.

Dan said, 'There's nothing more we can do here.'

Gert put her palm up to hush him and pressed her ear to the door. 'I think I hear something,' she said.

'What's it sound like?'

'It's very faint. Like a man chanting or something. In their language, not ours.'

Dan drew his baton and banged it on the door, good and loud. Gert kept listening after he stopped.

'Anything change in the sound?' he said.

She shook her head and tried the knob. It was locked.

'Maybe we should call a supervisor,' Gert said. 'To give us an okay to enter.'

'And take the chance of drawing Chickenlips Treakle?'

'Forget the supervisor,' Gert said.

Both cops walked back to the street. Gert said, 'Put your light on this.'

Dan held the business card and lit it for her with his flashlight beam. She took out her cell and dialed the handwritten number on the back of the card.

The Crows were in their street clothes: Ronnie in a striped, tapered shirt, and jeans from Banana, and Bix in a yellow polo shirt and chinos from the Gap. Ronnie thought he was even better-looking out of uniform.

LAPD blue seemed somehow unbecoming to him. Ronnie had ordered the chile *relleno* plate and a margarita. Bix had ordered two *carne asada* tacos and a cold *horchata,* made of rice water and cinnamon. Ronnie had hesitated before ordering an alcoholic drink in front of Bix but then figured it would make him even more uncomfortable to know she was avoiding booze for his sake.

They were halfway through dinner when his cell chimed. Ronnie wondered if it might be the mysterious caller who'd made him so uncomfortable. The one he'd lied about, saying it was his brother Pete.

He looked at the number and didn't recognize it. 'Hello,' he said.

'This is 6-X-66, Von Braun here,' Gert said. 'Is this Officer Bix Ramstead?'

'Yeah,' he said. 'What's going on?'

'I got your number from a Mrs. Farnsworth,' Gert said. 'It's about some Somalians that live across the street from her. She tells me you know something about them.'

'What happened?' Bix said.

'It's weird,' Gert said. 'Apparently they're in there, but they won't answer the door. The house is way too quiet to suit Mrs. Farnsworth, and I can hear the guy inside chanting some voodoo or something.'

'Are you going in?'

'We don't know whether to back off or bang on the door some more or what.'

'Did you call a sergeant?'

'No, we're afraid we'd get Treakle. He'd turn it into a fire drill.'

'I'll be right there,' Bix said.

When he closed his cell, he pulled some bills from his wallet and put them on the table. 'That was a midwatch officer. It's the Somalians. Something's wrong and they won't open the door.'

'Where're you going?'

'He might open the door for me. I established some rapport with him.'

'Bix, you're off duty,' Ronnie said. 'Let a supervisor deal with it. You shouldn't get involved.'

'Finish your dinner, Ronnie,' Bix said. 'I'll call you when I check it out.'

'This is not your responsibility,' Ronnie said.

'I feel I should've done more,' he said, turning toward the door. 'I had a gut feeling.'

'We did what we could at the time,' Ronnie called after him. 'If something bad happened there, it's not your tragedy, Bix!'

She didn't know if he heard that last part or not. Bix Ramstead was running out the door to the parking lot.

Mrs. Farnsworth was standing on the street by the black-and-white. She'd given Gert and Dan each a cup of coffee, which they were finishing when Bix Ramstead drove up and parked his personal car, a family-friendly Dodge minivan.

The cops gave their empty cups to Mrs. Farnsworth, who said, 'Evening, Officer Ramstead.'

'Hello, Mrs. Farnsworth,' Bix said. 'I'm glad you kept my card.'

'It's real quiet in there,' she said to Bix. 'And it's

never quiet in there. And he got real mad at her last week when a young white man she works for gave her a ride home. If he'd hit her, I woulda called you. But he just grabbed her arm and got in her face and yelled angry Somali talk. And she took the bus home the next day without the young white man. It shouldn't be so quiet in there like it is tonight, Officer Ramstead. I'm scared for that girl.'

A moment later, all three cops were back on the front porch of the wood-frame cottage. They stood silently and listened. There was only the hum of traffic on the nearby four-lane avenue and the sound of a dog barking close by and the whirring of cicadas in the yard next door and faint salsa music from somewhere down the block. Then they heard the sound of a deep male voice, chanting prayers.

Bix knocked at the door and said, 'Mr. Benawi, it's Officer Ramstead. I spoke to you last week about the shopping carts, remember?'

They listened again. The chanting stopped.

Bix said, 'Mr. Benawi, please open the door. I need to talk to you. It's okay about the shopping carts. I just need to know that everything else is all right. Open the door, Mr. Benawi.'

The chanting started again and Gert Von Braun felt a shiver, but it was a warm, dry summer evening with a Santa Ana blowing hot wind from the desert to the sea. Dan Applewhite felt the hair on his neck tingle and he knew it wasn't caused by the Santa Ana.

Bix Ramstead said, 'We're not leaving until you open the door, Mr. Benawi. Don't make us do a forced entry.'

The chanting stopped again. They heard padded

footsteps. Then Omar Hasan Benawi's rumbling voice on the other side of the door said, 'There is nothing for you here. Please leave my home.'

'We will, Mr. Benawi,' Bix said. 'But first I need to talk to you face-to-face. And I need to see your wife. Then we'll all go away.'

'She will not talk to you,' the voice said. 'This is my home. Please go away now. There is nothing for you here.'

They heard the padded footsteps retreat away from the door, and the chanting began once more.

'Well, shit!' Dan said.

'Now what?' Gert said.

'This is what the federal consent decree has done to the LAPD,' Bix said to Doomsday Dan. 'What would you have done back when we were real cops?'

Dan looked at Bix Ramstead and said, 'We're white, he's black. We better not do something hasty. I can't afford a suspension right now.'

'Answer my question,' Bix said to Dan. 'What would you have done six years ago, before a federal judge and a bunch of politicians and bureaucrats emasculated us?'

Dan Applewhite glanced at Gert Von Braun and said, 'I'da kicked the fucking door clear off the hinges and gone in there to see if that woman is okay.'

'Exactly,' Bix Ramstead said.

And he took three steps back, then ran forward and kicked just to the right of the doorknob, and the door crashed open and slammed against the plasterboard wall.

Bix Ramstead's momentum carried him into the darkened living room. Gert Von Braun and Dan

Applewhite drew their nines and followed him, casting narrow beams of light around the shabby room. Dan took the lead, trying to illuminate the ominous hallway leading to other rooms at the rear of the cottage.

The chanting had stopped. Now there was no sound at all, except for the traffic on the busy avenue half a block away. The first room was stacked with cardboard cartons, aluminum cans, and refundable bottles. Their flashlight beams played over the boxes, and then the cops advanced one behind the other to the last room, where a dim light was burning. Dan Applewhite pressed his back to the wall, his Beretta semiautomatic in his right hand now, and he crouched and peered around the corner.

'Son of a bitch!' he yelled, and he leaped upright, dropping his little flashlight and holding the Beretta in both hands. 'Down! Get down on your belly!'

Gert, holding her light in one hand and her Glock in the other, sprang forward, crouching below Dan's extended arms, and yelled, 'Down, goddamn you!'

Bix Ramstead edged into the crowded space and looked in the room.

The Somalian was on his knees then, wearing only the black trousers he wore when last Bix saw him. He was also wearing half-glasses, his eyes looking like tarnished dimes, and he clutched a Koran in his right hand when he slid down into the prone position.

Bix Ramstead mumbled, 'In the name of God!'

Lying prone, Omar Hasan Benawi said, 'Yes, in the name of the one true God. She did the shameful thing with a white man. Now I give her to the white man.'

There was dried white paint spatter on one wall, and puddles of paint on the threadbare carpet had dried and were hardening. Dried paint smeared the other walls and had dried in streaks on the window blinds. The Somalian's hands were white with dried paint and there were smears on his bare torso and on the tops of his bare feet, and the front of his trousers was caked with white paint. A cheap table lamp lay broken on the floor, and an empty five-gallon can of paint was lying on the floor beside the bed alongside an eight-inch paintbrush. There was dried white paint all over the coppery bedspread.

And on the bedspread was Safia, the wife of Omar Hasan Benawi. She had been strangled with the cord he'd jerked from the table lamp, and the ligature lay coiled like a serpent on the pillow beside her head. Naked, she looked tinier, more frail and fragile and vulnerable, than Bix Ramstead had remembered her. And more childlike. She was lying supine on the bed with her head on a pillow, and her arms were crossed over her small breasts, as her husband had posed them. And she was white.

He had painted every inch of her white. From the bottoms of her delicate feet to the crown of her small round head, she had been painted dead white. Even her opened lifeless eyes had not been spared. Dried paint clogged the cavernous orbs that Bix Ramstead remembered so well.

When Dan was handcuffing the Somalian's hands behind his back, the prisoner said, 'Now she is yours to bury with other white dogs in your infidel places of the dead.'

'Shut the fuck up!' Gert Von Braun said. 'And listen while I advise you of your rights.'

There were dozens of employees of the Los Angeles Police Department at that crime scene before the sun rose. One of the first was the night-watch detective Compassionate Charlie Gilford, who was about to go end-of-watch when he got the call from Bix Ramstead. He just had to see this one, so he jumped into a detective unit and drove to Southeast Hollywood as fast as he could.

After he took in the grotesque scene in the little bedroom, he walked out on the front step and directed his nuggets of wisdom at a pair of night-watch coppers who'd been called to assist with scene preservation.

'Fucking Hollywood,' the disappointed detective said. 'You can blame this kinda shit on the movies. I'll bet this fifty-one-fifty was sitting there watching TV and got the idea from *Goldfinger,* where they did the same thing to James Bond's snitch. Different color paint is all. This don't show any imagination. This Somali wing nut's nothing more than a second-rate copycat.'

Ronnie Sinclair received a call from Bix Ramstead just before she went to bed. He told her what they'd found in the cottage and that he'd be at Hollywood Station until the early-morning hours, doing reports and being interviewed by Homicide detectives. Bix told Ronnie that there was no telling what time he'd get home and would need to take tomorrow off. He said he'd left a long message on their sergeant's voicemail explaining what had happened.

Before the conversation ended, Ronnie Sinclair said to Bix Ramstead, 'It was not our fault. It is not our tragedy.'

He didn't respond to that.

SIXTEEN

Tᴴɪs ᴡᴀs the thousand-dollar day! Leonard Stilwell awoke before dawn and did something he almost never did. He went for a stroll along the Walk of Fame before the tourists arrived, breathing deeply, even shadowboxing for a few minutes, jabbing and hooking until the midget at the newsstand on Hollywood Boulevard said, 'I wouldn't take that pussy jab into a ring, buddy. Even Paris Hilton would kick your ass.'

'How would you like me to try it on you, you fucking termite,' Leonard said.

But when the belligerent midget scuttled forward, saying, 'Bring it, you turd licker!' Leonard got away fast, before the little maggot started gnawing on his leg.

Leonard wanted to go to the Starbucks on Sunset but didn't have enough money. Instead he drove to Pablo's Tacos, where all the tweakers hung out, and he bought a cup of Pablo's crappy coffee and a sweet, greasy Mexican pastry. Then he went home to rest and wait. But first he stopped and stole an *L.A. Times* from the driveway of a house two blocks from his apartment.

*   *   *

The only reason Ali Aziz slept so soundly was that he'd swallowed two of the magenta-and-turquoise sleep aids with a double shot of Jack Daniel's. He did have a slight headache when he awoke, and he recalled that Margot would never take one after she'd been drinking alcoholic beverages. He had a hot shower and then a cold one. Then he sat in his robe with a cup of tea and looked out from the balcony of his condo, where the view encompassed some of the commercial real estate of Beverly Hills.

It couldn't compare with the view from Mt. Olympus, from the house that he loved and that had been stolen from him by his bitch wife. Someday, God willing, when he had his son all to himself, they would live in a place where the boy could have land under his feet, perhaps a dog to run with, or even a horse to ride. There were places like that in some parts of the San Fernando Valley and in Ventura County, but they were disappearing fast with the influx of people clogging the freeways. Still, he would live in a place like that for his son's sake, and he'd make the long daily drive to his Hollywood businesses without complaint. He would do that for his son. He would do anything for his son.

At 2 P.M., Leonard Stilwell arrived at the Leopard Lounge. He found Ali Aziz in his office and he sat in the client chair in front of Ali's desk. Without comment, Ali removed a garage door opener from his desk drawer and slid it across to him.

'How much do I get if this don't work and we have to shitcan the whole plan?'

'It shall work,' Ali said solemnly.

'How can you be sure?'

'One day last week when I know my wife was not home, I drove by and pressed on the button. The door opens and closes.'

'Okay, gimme the alarm code,' Leonard said, and Ali pushed a piece of paper across the desk.

Ali said, 'Alarm pad is right inside on the wall. I want these things back to me when we meet later. And my big envelope, for sure.'

'Yeah, yeah,' Leonard said. 'You get all the incriminating evidence and I get my thousand bucks, all at the same time.'

'You shall have it,' Ali said.

'I better have it,' Leonard said. 'Or else.'

'What is your meaning?' Ali said. '"Or else"?'

'Nothing,' Leonard said. 'We got to trust each other, is all. Don't we, Ali? And we gotta keep real quiet afterwards.'

Ali did not like the words that had just come from the mouth of the thief, but he thought he should say nothing about it. Not now.

'Ten minute after four o'clock, you do it,' Ali said. 'You park fifty meters past the house, up on top of the hill. No houses there yet. Nobody shall pay attention.'

'And I meet you by the Mount Olympus sign down below after I do it.'

'That is exactly correct,' Ali said.

'I'll see you then,' Leonard said.

After Leonard had gone, Ali sat motionless and thought about those words: *Or else*. He wondered if he had underestimated the thief. What if Leonard threatened to tell Margot that he had been paid to enter her house and steal an envelope? It would mean nothing to Margot. There was no document of any value whatsoever in that house, and Margot knew it, only legitimate file folders with bills and check stubs that they were told to keep for several years in case of a tax audit.

But that would get Margot thinking about why Ali would pay a thief to enter her house. And she would call her lawyer. Ali didn't want Margot to think too much. He hated her, but he admired her mind. Margot was a very clever woman. Look how she had stolen half his fortune. If Leonard ever talked to Margot, it would put Ali in great jeopardy.

He opened his middle desk drawer and withdrew the envelope with the backup green capsule in it. He placed a clean sheet of paper on the desk. He removed the coke spoon and razor blade from the drawer, along with the vial of magenta-and-turquoise sleep aids, and emptied a sleep aid into his trash basket. Then he made another little funnel.

When he had completed his work, there were now two special magenta-and-turquoise capsules in the little envelope. Two deadly sisters side by side. He would carry one of them with him this afternoon and he would leave the other behind. In case there ever was an *or else* coming from the thief Leonard Stilwell.

At 3:30 P.M., moments after Ronnie Sinclair had tried unsuccessfully for the third time that scorching summer afternoon to reach Bix Ramstead on his cell, Leonard Stilwell had just left a drugstore where he'd bought latex gloves. He was driving up to Mt. Olympus a bit ahead of schedule. As his Honda was chugging up the hill, he saw a Latino teenager and an older woman passenger driving down in a smoke-belching Plymouth. He wondered if that was the maid with her grandson. He drove past the house and continued up to a turn in the street where there were no houses because of the steep terrain.

Leonard parked the Honda, got out, and locked it. He remembered Whitey Dawson telling about a time when he and some crack-head pulled a burglary at a supermarket and succeeded in attacking an ATM without setting off any alarms whatsoever. But the crackhead screwed up during their exit and set off the silent alarm, and when they got outside they discovered that their car had been stolen. They both got caught flat-footed when cops responded to the alarm. He'd learned a lot from Whitey Dawson, but not how to pick a lock.

Just after 4 P.M., Leonard chose a purposefully brisk stride to walk down the steep street to the Aziz home. Whitey Dawson had never believed in slinking around and arousing suspicion. Upon approaching the house, Leonard hit the button on the remote control in his pocket and held it down. When he was in front of the driveway the door opened. He ducked under the rising door and used the remote to stop and close it before it had finished the sequence. When he was safely inside the garage, he donned his latex gloves, took the tools from his pocket, and approached the door.

'Fucking Ay-rab!' he said when he saw that it was

not an old knob setup. It was a bronze-handled, single-sided dead bolt, no doubt with a thumb-turn on the inside.

He told himself to stay calm. That shouldn't matter at all. Old knob, new handle, what the fuck was the difference? He found the light switch and turned on the garage light. It was fluorescent and provided more than enough illumination. He knelt in front of the handle and inserted the tension bar, then the pick, and he repeated Junior's words.

'Tension bar turns cylinder. Rake lifts pin.'

For a few seconds he thought it felt like the setup on Junior's door. But then he lost it. He removed the tools, took out a penlight, and squinted at the key slot. It looked pretty much like the one at Junior's crib. So why did it feel different?

He tried it again. This time he used all the terminology, mumbling it like a mantra: 'Insert TR-four tension bar to turn the cylinder. Then insert double-diamond pick to lift the pin.' He moved his bony fingers delicately, gracefully, just as Junior had moved his brown sausage fingers. Nothing happened.

He choked back a sob of frustration. Ten Ben Franklins just to turn a fucking cylinder and lift a fucking pin! A Fijian gorilla with the brain of a cockatoo could do it with his eyes shut. And that gave him an idea.

Leonard shut his eyes and inserted the tension bar and the pick. Blind people develop a special touch, he told himself. He felt for the cylinder and the pin, but he only felt metal scraping metal.

He opened his eyes, and this time a wet balloon of

a sob escaped his lips. 'Jesus!' he said. 'Why can't I get just one fucking break?'

Then he had a head-slapping moment. The gloves! The fucking latex gloves had diminished the feel. The touch.

He peeled off the gloves. He wiggled his fingers. Even though it was a blister outside and ovenlike in the garage, he blew on his fingers and flexed them like safecrackers do in the movies. He held the tension bar and the pick as lightly as he could. Like two delicate bugs he didn't want to harm.

He inserted the tension bar. He inserted the rake. He felt for the cylinder and he felt for the pin. He also felt the sweat pouring down his face. He was tasting it. It was flowing under the neck of his T-shirt. Flop sweat, a Hollywood malady.

He couldn't feel shit! He threw the tension bar and pick onto the concrete floor. If they were bugs, the little fuckers would be dead.

Leonard Stilwell groaned when he stood up. It was over. He was going to blame it on the new door hardware. Maybe that fucking sand nigger would give him something for his attempt. Maybe a President Grant. If not, maybe an Andrew Jackson. But in his heart Leonard knew better. That towel head would want Leonard to return the two-bill advance that he'd already smoked up.

He bent over to pick up the tension bar and pick. His back had stiffened, and feeling unsteady, he grabbed at the door handle for support. And the handle dropped. And the door opened. The maid Lola had failed to set the thumb-turn on the inside handle!

'Holy shit!' he said, stumbling inside, fumbling for the notebook paper in his pocket as the alarm's warning chirp sounded. He couldn't find it! The security breach would show on the computer in the office of the security provider in a few more seconds if he didn't . . .

He found it in his pants pocket! He looked at it and punched in the maid's code and the warning tone stopped. Then he stepped back out to the garage and retrieved the tension bar and pick. He put on the latex gloves and, for good measure, used the tail of his T-shirt to wipe the door handle that he'd grabbed on to. Nobody was going to *CSI his* ass.

When he got inside, he walked to his right, entered the kitchen and then the dining room, where he could see the view of Hollywood. He'd never been in a home like this. As scared as he was, he had to admire it for a moment. It was hard to take it all in. The extravagance! Now he wished he'd demanded more for this job. Ali was always poor-mouthing about how his wife had made him almost broke. Look at this! What was an extra thousand to that fucking goat eater? To a man who had lived in a house like this?

Leonard Stilwell believed that was a weakness that had held him back all his life. He was too generous and too trusting in his fellow man, and what had it gotten him? He tore himself away from the sights and got down to business. He found the little office near the kitchen, where Margot Aziz paid her bills. He opened the drawer that Ali had described to him and found the large envelopes, labeled by year. He looked through them until he found the folder for 2004. He tucked it under his arm and returned to the door, setting the thumb-turn that the maid had forgotten to set.

He was into the garage and the spring-loaded hinge on the door was in the process of closing the door behind him when he remembered. Ali said more than once for him to leave the door unlocked. Leonard stopped the door just in time. He unlocked the thumb-turn so that the maid, Lola, would catch hell for not setting it, just as Ali had ordered him to do. Of course Ali would never find out from Leonard that Lola had failed to set it in the first place.

But when he was walking away from the house, Leonard regretted that he hadn't set the thumb-turn. Fucking rich assholes never give working people a break. He didn't want to be responsible for the dumb old Mexican woman getting her ass chewed out. But he figured the divorce was so bitter that Ali's ex would never fire the maid, if only to spite Ali.

On the other hand, the Mexican maid probably had family who would take care of her, and Social Security, and maybe welfare checks, and everything else the U.S. government gives to the millions of wet-backs in this country. The same federal government that turned him down the last time he applied for SSI assistance based on his poor health and addiction to rock cocaine. Some county social worker would always point to some shitty job like dishwasher and expect him to take it. In 2007 Los Angeles, it didn't pay to be a white man.

After being seated safely behind the wheel of his Honda, Leonard opened the big folder to see if he could spot what it was that made this worth so much to Ali Aziz. But all he found were receipts, check stubs, and banking lists of cleared checks. Just ordinary household crap that anyone might keep around for a few years.

As he was driving down the hill to meet Ali Aziz, a lot was going on inside the head of Leonard Stilwell. He kept looking at the file folder. How could it be so important? And then there had been Ali's insistence on the door being left unlocked to get the ex-wife more pissed off at the Mexican maid. But if the house was in escrow and the ex-wife was moving, the maid would be history anyway. It didn't hang together and never had from the first moment Ali had tried to spin it.

When he got down to the Mt. Olympus sign, he saw Ali's Jaguar farther down the road, facing up the hill. He parked on the opposite side of the road, got out with the file folder, and crossed to Ali's car.

He handed the folder through the open window, and Ali said, 'Good, Leonard. You done a very good job. Give me the garage opener and the piece of paper with the alarm code, please.'

'It wasn't easy,' Leonard said, handing both items to Ali. 'She has new door hardware. If I wasn't an expert, I never coulda picked the lock.'

Ali gave Leonard a roll of hundred-dollar bills, saying, 'It is all there, Leonard. Thank you for helping me.'

'It was a different lock setup. Not like you said it was,' Leonard repeated.

'You leave it unlocked?' Ali said, suddenly concerned.

'Yeah, sure,' Leonard said.

'Okay, Leonard,' Ali said, starting his engine. 'Come by the Leopard Lounge sometime. I shall buy you a drink.'

Leonard looked at Ali and said, 'Because I had such a lotta extra work to do on the new hardware, it took more time and put me in more danger. I think I deserve a bonus.'

Ali pushed the gearshift back into park and said, 'We have a deal.'

'Yeah, but you didn't get it right and it made the job very tough and risky. I think I should get another one of them Franklins.'

Ali dropped the shift into drive and said, 'Good-bye, Leonard.'

Then he made a U-turn and drove back down toward the boulevards, as though to return to his business.

Leonard had a hunch then and decided to play it. He took his time getting into his Honda, waiting until Ali's Jaguar had vanished in the Hollywood traffic. Then he started his car, made a U-turn, and drove back up Mt. Olympus, passing the Aziz house, turning onto the street farther up the hill, and parking behind a gardener's truck. Leonard got out and walked back to the corner and watched the house of Margot Aziz fifty yards down the road.

He only waited five minutes until Ali's Jaguar appeared, driving past his former home and parking in nearly the exact spot where Leonard had parked prior to his burglary. Ali got out of his car and walked to the garage and opened it. And Leonard could see the large file folder in Ali's hand. He was returning it, just as Leonard thought he would. This wasn't about a fucking folder full of canceled checks and household shit.

*   *   *

Ali saw for himself that Margot had changed the lock on the garage access door as she had done on the others. He hadn't counted on that, but he doubted that it had presented any difficulty for Leonard Stilwell. Ali was furious that the thief had tried to get another hundred dollars out of him. Ali put on a pair of latex gloves he'd gotten from his nightclub dishwasher, examined the handle, and opened the door.

He used the maid's code to silence the alarm chirp and closed the door behind him, checking his watch. Another thing about Margot was that she was a creature of habit. She went to Pilates every Thursday and stayed until 5:30, no matter what. Then she would pick up Nicky at the home of the nanny and take him somewhere and feed him junk food that he liked, food she would never eat. Ali hated her for that as well. When he got custody of his son after her death, he would see to the boy's healthy diet. Lots of yogurt and lamb and rice and vegetables.

He quieted his fears by remembering the stories in the news a few months earlier about two Los Angeles women who were on vacation in Russia and were poisoned by thallium, the toxic metal that was first suspected in the murder of former spy Alexander Litvinenko until polonium-210 turned out to be the killer. Also, he remembered that Los Angeles County health officials had found that a popular brand of Armenian mineral water contained large amounts of arsenic. And then there was the local and national recall of premium pet foods found to be laced with rat poison that was killing cats and dogs. Poison was everywhere. If it happened after she was gone from Los Angeles, there was no way that anyone could suspect Ali Aziz, no matter how much he gained from her death. Nicky would get her estate and he would get Nicky. In essence, he would have everything back as it should be.

After replacing the large folder in the small office, Ali climbed the stairs to the master bedroom and felt pangs of nostalgia. He had loved this house. He had loved being married to Margot in the early days, and having the most beautiful baby he had ever seen, and making more money in his two nightclubs – especially the Leopard Lounge – than he had ever dreamed possible. He had loved Margot then. Or, more accurately, had been bewitched by her. She was the most perfect woman who had ever stepped on his stage. All natural, no silicone or saline, not even now, as far as he knew. Before she became a discontented, scheming bitch, the sex she had given him was like nothing before or since. During those early years with Margot and his infant son, Ali had been a completely contented man. A devoted husband, a loving father, a considerate boss who seldom required blow jobs from employees.

Ali felt the nostalgia more painfully when he entered the master bedroom. There used to be a photo of him on the wall by the dresser, but it was gone. The enormous walk-in closet was even more full of her clothes than it had been when he lived there. The bills that came to his lawyer's office were an outrage and had taken up so much argument before the judge that Ali had decided it was cheaper to pay them than to pay the hours that his lawyer billed to him.

He looked in his former walk-in closet, prepared to see the clothes of the lover Jasmine had told him about,

but it was now more than half full of her overflow.
He guessed she owned fifty pairs of shoes, maybe more.
And those were just the dressy ones. The others – flats,
sandals, athletic shoes – numbered in the dozens as well.
There was no sign of men's clothing.

He entered the bathroom and was happy to see that
there was no trace of any man living in the house. After
talking to Jasmine, he'd been afraid that the boyfriend
whom Margot had flaunted in her telephone calls might
have completely taken over this bedroom suite. He
couldn't get his mind around an image of this man in
this bedroom, naked with Margot. And where was
Nicky during those times?

Ali couldn't put it off any longer. He had to do the
terrible job he came here to do. He removed the little
envelope from his pocket and then opened the medicine
cabinet. But Margot's sleep aids were gone. Panic
struck! They should be there. They were always there,
high on the top shelf, where Nicky couldn't get to them.
He began opening drawers. He opened the medicine
cabinet on his side of the bathroom. He opened lower
cabinets, even though he knew she wouldn't keep
prescription drugs there.

Ali ran back into the master bedroom and started
opening drawers in the two massive walnut dressers.
Then he went to the upright chests of drawers and
opened them. It was hot in the house with the air
conditioner timed to come on thirty minutes before
she returned home. He was perspiring heavily. He could
smell himself. He told himself to be calm, to only look
in high places that Nicky couldn't possibly reach.

Ali entered his former closet, the one that now held

her overflow. On the top shelf he saw a jewelry box, the one where she kept her costume jewelry. He took it down. The vial of magenta-and-turquoise capsules was there! He was so shaken he had to sit.

Ali went to her vanity dresser and sat down on the padded chair she used when brushing her hair before retiring. He emptied the vial onto the dresser top and took the deadly capsule from the envelope. He put it into the empty vial and then scooped the other capsules on top of it. He opened the new vial that he'd gotten from Jaime Salgando and added six capsules from it to her vial, because hers was half empty. She wouldn't notice the few extra capsules, but they would provide the extra time for her to be living elsewhere when it happened.

He put her vial back in the jewelry box and placed it on the top shelf where he'd found it. He looked around the master bedroom for the last time. He knew he would never see it again, and it brought tears to his eyes. It would all have been perfect if she had not turned out to be such a coldhearted, conniving American bitch who stole his money and broke his heart.

When he got to the garage access door he reset the thumb-turn as he believed it was before Leonard had picked the lock for him. He removed his gloves, opened the garage door, and closed it quickly after stepping outside. Then he walked up the hill, very pleased that there was no traffic passing and there were no gardeners on the nearby properties. When he got in his car, he made a careful U-turn and proceeded back down to the boulevards.

*   *   *

The gardener had moved the truck behind which Leonard Stilwell had parked, and a woman in the next house watched him when he walked to his car.

Leonard smiled at her and said, 'Do you know which house Madonna lives in? I seem to have the wrong address.'

The woman looked at him suspiciously and said, 'No, I don't. I don't think there's anyone by that name on this block.'

'Oh, well, I'll try farther down,' Leonard said with a wave.

While driving down the hill, he couldn't get it out of his mind. Ali hadn't hired him to take something out of that house. He'd been hired so that Ali could get into that house. And it had nothing to do with the big folder that Ali had carried back inside. He'd been in there for thirteen minutes. What was he looking for? He couldn't have been stealing something that she'd miss or he'd have wanted Leonard to make it look like a burglary. Yet that's what Ali did *not* want.

Leonard pulled to the curb at the first sewer opening he saw, hopped out of his car, and tossed the latex gloves down the hole. Now let's see them try to *CSI* my ass again, he thought.

When he got back in the car, he took the tension bar and lock pick from his pocket and put them in the glove box. He was two blocks from the cyber café, where he figured to score plenty of rock with some of the Franklins he had, when it hit him: the answer to the Ali Aziz puzzle. Suddenly, he was on it. There was only one thing it could be. That fucking devious Ay-rab had planted a listening device in his ex-wife's house!

If Leonard were to drive up there later tonight, he was sure he'd find somebody parked on that street who shouldn't be there, somebody hired by Ali to monitor what was happening in the little lady's bedroom. Leonard figured that this was the kind of shit that crazed rich people did during their divorces. People who didn't really appreciate what was worthwhile in life.

So it had all been a lie, Leonard thought. Ali Aziz had hired him under completely false pretenses and had lied to him about nearly everything. Well, he had known something was wrong from the get-go and should have guessed sooner that Ali was a complete phony and liar. That's the way it was nowadays. There wasn't an honest person left in the whole fucking town.

SEVENTEEN

TERRIBLE EVENTS were to take place on Hollywood Boulevard early that evening, events that left tourists screaming and children in tears. And Leonard Stilwell, flush with greenbacks and desperate for rock, walked right into it.

Things hadn't been peaceful along the Walk of Fame in front of Grauman's Chinese Theatre for some time. There was always a Street Character getting busted for something or other by the Street Character Task Force. Arrests had involved the red Muppet Elmo and Chewbacca and Mr. Incredible, to name a few. And the Crows had meetings where they tried to gather the hundred freelancing Street Characters – many of whom duplicated the same cartoon icons, and many of whom were drug addicts – to warn them that laws against aggressive panhandling would be enforced to the letter.

And it wasn't that the Street Characters were only fighting the law, they were fighting one another too. For example, when a tourist was snapping photos of a Superman, a SpongeBob SquarePants might hop into the shot and try to hustle half the tip. This caused clashes among the Characters, some of them physical, as well as the forming of cliques. On a given day, one or two of the Spider-Man Characters might align with a Willy Wonka, who might be feuding with a Catwoman or a Shrek. And that might torque off Donald Duck, or the Wolf Man, or one of the many Darth Vaders. It could get ugly when teams like a Lone Ranger and Tonto or a Batman and Robin got hacked off at each other, especially since their tips from tourists depended in no small measure on the partnership itself. What was a Robin without a Batman?

But that was what happened on that Thursday evening, a few hours after Ali Aziz had been so busy perpetrating the future murder of his ex-wife. And shortly after Leonard Stilwell, with a thousand bucks in his kick, could not score at the cyber café or at Pablo's Tacos because of a mini task-force of narcs who were jacking up every tweaker or street dealer anywhere near those two establishments.

It could have been that everyone, including Street Characters, was particularly gloomy from the announcement that there would no longer be a Hollywood Christmas Parade, an event inaugurated by the Hollywood chamber of commerce in 1928. The popular parade had featured Grand Marshal superstars such as Bob Hope, Gene Autry, James Stewart, Natalie Wood, Arnold Schwarzenegger, and Charlton Heston. But as Hollywood had lost much of its glamour in recent years, so did the parade. Recent Grand Marshals included Tom Arnold, Dennis Hopper, and Peter Fonda. And it had finally gotten so bad that they even had to settle for a local politician, Los Angeles mayor Antonio Villaraigosa. That was probably the parade's death knell.

So, on Hollywood Boulevard, on a scorching summer evening when the bone-dry air hit you in the face like a blast from a hair dryer, and the temperature inside Street Characters' costumes was unbearable, the stage was set for riot. And to make things worse, a labor dispute was going on, and a local union had a group of members with signs and pickets demonstrating in front of the Kodak Center because of nonunion workers being employed there. A woman officer in plainclothes from LAPD's Labor Relations Section was monitoring, but that was the only police presence.

Just after sunset, when Hollywood takes on its rosy glow, and the hundreds of tourists in front of Grauman's Chinese Theatre feel the buzz that says, anything can happen here, something did. Some said that Robin started it, others blamed it on Batman. Either Robin called Batman 'a big fat chiseling faggot' or Batman called Robin 'a whiny little sissy punk.' Nobody was ever sure where the truth lay, but there was no doubt that Robin threw the first punch at his partner. It was a hook to Batman's ample gut and Batman's plastic breastplate didn't protect him much.

He went, 'Oooooof!' And sat down on Steve McQueen's footprints, preserved in the cement of the forecourt.

Then a Spider-Man, one of the larger ones who had been aligned with that particular Batman during a recent Street Character feud, put a hand on Robin's face and shoved him down onto the concrete imprint of Groucho Marx's cigar.

Then Superman and his pal Wonder Woman – who was actually a wiry transvestite with leg stubble – called

Spider-Man a 'pukey insect' and proceeded to beat the living shit out of him while tourists screamed and children quaked in fear.

Leonard Stilwell had parked his Honda in the parking lot closest to the Kodak Center. He didn't give a damn about the excessive parking charges, not with all those Franklins in his pocket. He figured to catch up with Junior tomorrow and give the Fijian back his tools, along with a President Grant.

He was surprised to discover that no matter how much money he had, sometimes there were things that money couldn't buy. And so far that afternoon and evening, he could not buy rock cocaine anywhere. He hoped that one of the hooks from South L.A. who hung around the subway station might have a few rocks on him. If not, he could risk trying one of the Street Characters in front of the Chinese Theatre, but only as a last resort. He still remembered clearly what had happened at the Kodak Center to big Pluto when he had the dope in his head.

The woman officer from Labor Relations Section had run to the melee, holding up her badge and yelling, 'Police officer!' but Superman and Wonder Woman wouldn't back off and Spider-Man was moaning in pain. And the trouble was far from over.

Batman, having recovered from the blow to the belly, suddenly needed a bowel movement badly. He saw that the labor union pickets had a large trailer parked at the curb, along with an Andy Gump porta-potty attached to it.

Holding his wounded gut, he ran crablike to the

Andy Gump, opened the door and stepped inside, and relieved himself with an eruption that could clearly be heard by the outraged pickets guarding the trailer.

When Batman emerged from the Andy Gump, one of the pickets, a diminutive fifty-two-year-old black man, who happened to be the local union representative, said, 'Hey, dude, nobody said you could take a dump in our Gump.'

'Batman craps wherever he wants,' said Batman.

The little union steward said, 'Batman is jist some jiveass flyin' rat in a funky ten-dollar cape, far as I'm concerned.'

'You're lucky I didn't shit in your hat, you ugly little nigger,' said Batman.

The union rep, who had been a pretty good Golden Gloves bantamweight thirty years earlier, said, 'Ain't no fuckin' bat gonna front me, not even Count Dracula!'

On the eleven o'clock news that night, the reporter who witnessed the mini-riot showed his audience a Batman cartoon panel and said that what happened next was just like in the comic books: 'POW! WHAM! BAM!'

'However,' he added, 'it was the caped crusader who got clocked and kissed the concrete.'

Thus, Batman became the second superhero that day to be taken to the ER for multiple contusions and abrasions.

By then, the Labor Relations cop had put out a help call, and the midwatch units just clearing from roll call, with plenty of daylight left, were on their way. Gert Von Braun and Dan Applewhite arrived first and pulled

Superman and Wonder Woman away from Spider-Man, Gert grabbing Wonder Woman by the shoulder-length auburn tresses – which suddenly came off in Gert's hand.

'Mommy!' a young girl shrieked. 'Wonder Woman is bald like Daddy!'

Two other night-watch units arrived, and soon there were hundreds of tourists snapping photos like mad and a TV news van caused a traffic jam on Hollywood Boulevard. Leonard Stilwell decided that this was no place for him. He started jogging around the tourists on the Walk of Fame, heading toward the parking lot, but ran smack into 6-X-46 of the midwatch.

'Whoa, dude!' Flotsam said. 'It's him!'

Jetsam grabbed Leonard's arm as he was hotfooting it past the cops and spun him around. 'I been thinking about you, bro,' he said.

Leonard recognized them at once, those heartless, sunburned cops with the bleached-out spiky hairdos. 'I got nothing to do with that ruckus back there,' Leonard said.

'Let's see that piece of paper in your car,' Flotsam said. 'The one with the address written on it.'

'What piece of paper?' Leonard said.

'Don't fuck with us,' Jetsam said.

'I'm not!' Leonard whined. 'I don't know what you're talking about, man!'

'The paper with the address up on Mount Olympus,' Flotsam said. 'Do you remember now? And you better give the right answer.'

'Oh, that paper,' Leonard said.

'Yeah, let's go to your car so I can see it again,' Jetsam said.

'I ain't got it no more,' Leonard said.

'Why did you have it in the first place?' Jetsam said.

'Have what?' Leonard said.

'Screw you, bro,' Jetsam said, reaching for his handcuffs.

'Wait a minute!' Leonard said. 'Gimme a chance to think!'

'Think fast, dude,' Flotsam said. 'My partner's outta patience.'

'I wrote down an address that I got outta the newspaper,' Leonard said. 'It was about a job. Somebody needed a housepainter.'

'You're a housepainter?' Flotsam said.

'Yeah, but I'm outta work at the moment.'

'I been thinking about painting my bedroom,' Flotsam said.

'Should I use a semigloss enamel on the bedroom walls or a latex?'

Leonard was getting dry-mouthed now. The only latex he knew about involved the gloves he used on his jobs. He said, 'Depends on what you like.'

Jetsam said, 'Do most people use oil-base enamel or water-base latex on their bedroom walls?'

Leonard said, 'Enamel?'

'Let's go visit your car, dude,' Flotsam said. 'Maybe that piece of paper's still there.'

When they got to the parking lot, Leonard led them to his car, parked in the far corner. 'You ain't got no right to search my car and you know it,' he said.

'Who says we're searching your car?' Jetsam said. 'We just wanna see that piece of paper again.'

'Then you'll stop hassling me?' Leonard said. Jetsam

looked at Flotsam and said, 'He says we're hassling him.'

'I'm shocked. Shocked!' Flotsam said.

Leonard opened the car door and got in, reaching for the glove compartment.

'Wait a minute, dude,' Flotsam said.

'I'm gonna see if I put it in the glove box,' Leonard said.

'Wait till my partner gets around and can see in there,' Flotsam said. 'That's how cops get hurt.'

'Me hurt you? Your feelings or what?' Leonard said disgustedly as Jetsam opened the passenger door, his hand on the butt of his nine.

'Now go ahead and open it,' Jetsam said.

Twilight was casting long shadows by then, and Jetsam used his flashlight to illuminate the glove compartment.

Leonard remembered where the note was then and reached up under the visor, saying, 'Here it is.' But Leonard didn't remember that he'd tossed the tension bar and pick in the glove box.

'What's this?' Jetsam said, his flashlight beam on the locksmith tools.

'What's what?' Leonard said. And then he remembered what!

'Those strange little objects in the glove compartment,' Jetsam said. 'Do you, like, use them to pry off the lids from paint cans?'

Leonard looked in the glove box and said, 'They been in the car since I bought it. I don't know what they are. Are they illegal? Like kiddie porn or something?'

'Get outta the car,' Jetsam said. 'And gimme your keys. I don't think you'll mind if I look for more strange objects, will you?'

'What's the use?' Leonard said. 'You'll do it anyways.'

When Leonard Stilwell was standing outside the car, and Jetsam was looking under the front seats and in the trunk, Flotsam patted down Leonard Stilwell, felt the bills in his pocket, and said, 'What's this?'

'Just my money,' Leonard said.

'How much money?' Flotsam said.

'Do I gotta answer that?' Leonard said.

'If you know how much you got, then we'll figure it's your money,' Flotsam said. 'If you don't know how much you got, we'll figure you just picked a pocket or a purse in front of the Kodak Center. And we'll go look for a victim. Might take a long time.'

'A thousand bucks,' Leonard said. 'Ten Ben Franklins.'

The surfer cops looked at each other again and Jetsam said, 'You got a thousand bucks in your kick? Where'd you get it?'

'Playing poker,' Leonard said.

'And you got locksmith tools,' Jetsam said, 'but they just happened to be in your car when you bought it?'

'Yeah, that's right.'

'And you can't pick a lock?'

'Man, I can hardly pick my nose!' Leonard said. 'You guys're harassing me! This is police harassment!'

'Tell you what, dude,' Flotsam said. 'If you can spell *harassment,* we'll let you go. If you can't, we'll take you to Hollywood Station to talk to a detective. How's that?'

Leonard said, ' H-e-r . . .'

Fifteen minutes later, Leonard Stilwell was sitting with Flotsam in an interview room at Hollywood Station, and Jetsam was in the detective squad room, explaining what they'd found to Compassionate Charlie Gilford, who was irritated to be pulled away from his tape of *Dancing with the Stars,* where Heather Mills McCartney hit the floor but disappointed Charlie when her prosthetic leg stayed attached.

'What we got here is some lock picks and a thousand bucks and a guy with a four-five-nine record,' Charlie said, never eager to do any work whatsoever. 'That's pretty thin for a felony booking. How about that wrong address note? Can't we pull a victim outta that somehow?'

'The burglary dicks might be able to do it tomorrow,' Jetsam said. 'That's the reason we lock him up tonight, right? To give them forty-eight hours. Come on, this guy's dirty. I just know it!'

'Lemme get a coffee and think about it,' Charlie said.

Since the federal consent decree had gone into effect six years earlier, the nighttime detective could no longer approve a felony booking. Now the detective could only 'advise' a booking, and then it went to the patrol watch commander for a booking 'referral.' It seemed that the federal government and its legion of overpaid civilian auditors and overseers didn't like declaratory phrasing and active verbs that sounded too aggressive. Their preferences created a lot more paperwork, as did everything about the consent decree. But in the end, it all amounted to the same thing. A felony suspect went to the slam for forty-eight hours while the detectives tried to make a case that they could take to the district attorney's office.

Jetsam was disgusted. While Charlie was gone, the surfer cop took out his notebook and, sitting at one of the desks, dialed the cell number of Hollywood Nate Weiss just before Nate went end-of-watch.

Jetsam explained what had gone down and said, 'Did you ever get a chance to ask that friend of yours on Mount Olympus about this guy Stilwell?'

'No, I didn't,' Nate admitted. 'But I talked to someone who knows her a lot better than I do and he said he'd ask her about it.'

'Did that someone ask her?'

'I don't know,' Nate said uncomfortably.

'Look, bro, you gotta help us,' Jetsam said. 'I was hinked-out by this dude the first time I saw him. He's a burglar. I just know he pulled a job where he stole a thousand bucks, but we got no report on it yet. I think it happened up there on Mount Olympus at the house where you were, or close by there.'

The line was silent for a moment and Nate said, 'I'll make a call right now and get back to you.'

'Thanks, bro,' Jetsam said. 'That house up there? It gives off bad juju.'

Nate rang the home of Margot Aziz, who had just pulled into her garage with her son, Nicky, who was asleep in his car seat. She got Nicky out of the car and was carrying him to the door on the first ring. She tried the handle but the door was locked.

'Damn!' she said. The door was never locked. Lola had forgotten so many times that Margot had stopped reminding her. This had to be the one time Lola had locked it, now, when Margot was hoping for a call from Bix Ramstead, whom she'd been trying to reach all day.

Margot managed to dig her keys from her purse while still carrying her sleeping five-year-old and got the door open just as the phone stopped ringing. She punched in her alarm code to shut off the electronic tone and ran to the kitchen phone, picking it up after the voice message had concluded.

She played it back, but it was the wrong cop. She heard a voice saying, 'Margot, this is Nate Weiss. Please call me ASAP. This is about a police matter that might concern you.'

A police matter? She picked up his card from the desk in the little office by the kitchen but put it down again. A pussy matter, more like it. After their evening together she had never called him as promised, and now he'd obviously decided to press her. He'd probably tell her that he wanted the job of moving in as her house protector during the remainder of the escrow period.

You had your chance, bucko, she thought. It was too bad he wasn't a boozer like Bix Ramstead. She liked Nate's looks and his sexy manner.

Hollywood Nate made a decision. He was going to do the show-and-tell with Bix Ramstead. He was positive that Bix must have something going with Margot Aziz, and he knew Bix was married with two kids. Well, that was too bad. Nate didn't like embarrassing the guy, but this Stilwell thing had gone on long enough. He was going to tell Bix everything about his evening with

Margot, and then either he or Bix was going to find out if anything peculiar had happened around her house lately. Anything that might explain why a lowlife burglar with an address written down that was close to hers had lock picks and a thousand dollars in his pocket. Nate knew from experience that Margot was a smart woman. If the Stilwell business made any sense at all, she might be able to figure it out for them.

Of course, Nate was aware of the Somali murder the prior evening and that Bix had had a long night and was not on duty today. He dialed Bix's home and cell numbers but was taken to voice mail at both of them.

'Bix, it's Nate Weiss,' he said on each voice mail. 'I've gotta talk to you about Margot Aziz ASAP. It might be very important. Call me.'

He looked in the office and discovered that Ronnie had just signed out. He went to the women's locker room, stuck his head in the door, and yelled for her.

He was relieved when she said, 'Yeah, I'm here.'

A few minutes later Ronnie emerged in her street clothes, and Nate said, 'Do you know how I can reach Bix?'

She shook her head and said, 'I've tried four times today with no luck. I think that weird murder last night had an effect on him. I'm kinda worried, to tell the truth.'

'Doesn't his wife know where he is?' Nate said.

'The wife and kids are outta state, visiting her parents. They won't be back till after the weekend.'

'So I won't be able to talk to him till tomorrow?'

'Maybe, maybe not,' she said. 'He called the sergeant today and took tomorrow off as well. He's got a lotta comp time on the books and said he needed a couple days to do family business.'

'You think he went outta town?'

'I don't know, Nate,' Ronnie said. 'Bix is a mysterious guy. And so are you these days.'

'What's that supposed to mean?'

'You and Bix. What's the secret you're sharing? Or is it a guy thing?'

Nate paused for a few seconds and said, 'There's this woman who lives up on Mount Olympus. She may have been burglarized today. It's a long shot, but Flotsam and Jetsam got themselves a suspect, and you know how obsessive they are. They want somebody to talk to her right now, but she's not home. I just called.'

'What's Bix got to do with it?'

'We both know her and I think Bix probably has her cell number. It's a long story.'

'So it *is* a guy thing,' Ronnie said, deeply disillusioned. Bix Ramstead, the last of the monogamous cops. An alcoholic in denial. And a womanizer to boot?

'Good luck,' Ronnie said. 'I gotta go home.'

Nate found Flotsam and Jetsam in the detective squad room and said to them, 'Okay, you guys know that I'm familiar with the woman who lives at the Mount Olympus address, but I'm not as familiar as you guys think I am. I tried to reach her and I left a message. Why don't you just book the asshole and let the dicks sort it all out tomorrow when the lady's at home?'

'Our sentiments exactly, bro,' Jetsam said, 'but Charlie Gilford's acting all PMS-ey tonight and don't wanna give us a booking approval without an eyeball witness, a videotape, and a confession signed in blood.'

Just then Compassionate Charlie came out of the interview room where he'd been talking to Leonard Stilwell. He had a 5.10 report in his hands, which made the surfer cops hopeful. He wouldn't be doing paperwork if he was going to kick the crackhead out the door.

'Okay, I'll five-ten him and advise a booking for four-five-nine,' Charlie said. 'Book the lock picks and the thousand bucks, and we'll let the burglary team deal with it tomorrow.'

'All right!' Jetsam said.

'He said he won the thousand betting on the Giants against our Dodgers with a stranger he met at a pool hall,' Compassionate Charlie said with disgust. 'Any resident of this town who'd even think up such a disloyal fucking story deserves to go to jail.'

Margot Aziz tried reaching Bix Ramstead yet again. She was acutely aware that his wife and family would be returning home in a few days. That's all the time she had. All the time she would ever have with *that* man, she was sure of it. If it didn't work with Bix, she'd have to come up with an entirely new plan. But would Jasmine hold still for it? Her greed was being overwhelmed by fear and she was already talking about aborting the scheme, even after Margot had put so much time and effort into Bix Ramstead in recent months. Never once in all that time would Bix agree to spend the entire night in her bed. Never once did she have the opportunity to put the plan in motion. It was giving her a headache thinking about it. The stress was getting unbearable.

People thought she could survive forever on a $7 million net worth. Her lawyer estimated that $7 million, more or less, would be her share after all the real property and other assets, including a growing stock portfolio, were divided. But this was before the lawyer's exorbitant fees would be deducted at the end of the ordeal.

The attorney had told her that with proper investments, she and Nicky could live 'comfortably.' And she'd laughed in his face.

Margot had reminded him that hundreds of homes in the Hollywood Hills were presently for sale for more money than the 'comfortable' amount, a few of them for twice that. How could Nicky be raised in his present living standard if she had to spend at least four or five million on a decent house? And did the lawyer know what house maintenance costs were around here? And did the bachelor lawyer have *any* idea what a trustworthy au pair charged? And how about the fees at a good school? Nicky would be in kindergarten come September, and the annual fees would cost more than the Barstow home her parents bought when they'd gotten married. Margot told him that she understood very well what a day-to-day money struggle was all about, but she was determined that Nicky never would.

About Nicky. That's where she and her lawyer had their biggest disagreements. He told her that when he was through with Ali Aziz, the nightclub proprietor would be afraid to ever be a day late with child support payments. She'd told him that was a joke, that she knew

Ali Aziz as well as she knew herself. And there was no doubt whatsoever that he would secretly divest himself of his entire net worth and make clandestine plans to convert all his holdings to cash. And then take his son away from her, away from America, forever.

The lawyer had insisted that Ali Aziz, a naturalized citizen, would never do any such thing. Living in a Middle East country again after having lived a lavish Hollywood lifestyle was beyond the attorney's imagining.

Margot had reminded the lawyer that Osama bin Laden had also been rich and had given it up to live in a cave. And she doubted that Osama would have to spend big bucks on cocaine in order to get his blow jobs. And then she'd asked the lawyer to verify a supposition. She'd asked it casually enough: If Ali passed away at any time during or after the divorce settlement, would his fortune go to Nicky with her as executor?

The lawyer had answered that, as far as he knew, Ali's new will named his attorney as executor, but that, yes, his fortune would go to Nicky. And then she thought about Ali's attorney. He seemed like a reasonable man, as lawyers go. He'd blush when she'd stare at him for too long. She could work with him on behalf of her son. There would be approximately $14 million for her and Nicky. They could get by on that. She was still young, still had her looks. There'd be lots of wealthy men out there after she extracted Jasmine from her life.

And even if she never found the right man, Nicky would come into his inheritance in thirteen years.

Margot could not guess what his $7 million, properly invested by Ali's lawyer/executor, would look like by that time. Nicky would take care of his mother then. She'd be forty-three years old and her ass would be falling like a bag of wet laundry, and she'd need someone to take care of her.

Margot looked in Nicky's room and saw that he was sound asleep. She went to her bedroom and undressed, then had a hot shower, and, turning on the bedroom TV, channel surfed. She gave up and switched to one of the easy-listening cable channels, then set the burglar alarm, deciding to turn in early.

Margot went to the closet and brought down the jewelry box where she'd been keeping her sleep aids after catching Nicky one afternoon up on her bathroom sink rummaging through her medicine cabinet looking for cough drops. She got a glass of water from the bathroom and sat in front of her vanity mirror, brushing her hair for a few minutes. Then she removed the top from the vial.

Margot thought of Ali then, of how he didn't like her taking the sleeping capsules for fear that any drugs would cause her to revert to the cocaine use that she'd conquered years before. She turned the vial on its side in order to shake a capsule into her hand. And at that very moment, when she was thinking of Ali, Rod Stewart began singing 'We'll Be Together Again.' And she felt a shiver jetting through her neck and shoulders.

Margot thought, No, we will *never* be together again. Not in this world, not in the next, if there is one. The very thought of Ali Aziz and what she must do made her hands tremble. She dropped the vial on the dresser top and all of the magenta-and-turquoise capsules spilled out.

Margot scooped the capsules back into the vial. One was left on the dresser top and she put it in her mouth and swallowed it. Then she swallowed another, despite her doctor's admonition that one was enough. Tonight she needed to sleep uninterrupted.

Before retiring for the night, she called Bix Ramstead's private cell number one more time and left a message saying, 'Bix, I *beg* you to call me!'

EIGHTEEN

VIOLENT NIGHTMARES tormented Leonard Stilwell all through the night. He'd been in a cell with three other guys, including a tatted Latino strong-arm robber who'd somehow learned that a prisoner late in arriving – a thirty-two-year-old insurance agent – had been booked for sexually abusing his girlfriend's eight-year-old daughter.

The Latino had been minding his own business until then and hadn't said anything to anyone the whole time that Leonard had been in the cell with him. But when he received the word about the child molestation, he got up and without warning began beating the insurance agent's head against the wall of the tank, causing a laceration on his skull that spattered blood onto Leonard's T-shirt.

When the jailers heard the screams, both men were pulled from the tank. And as the attacker was being led away, Leonard heard him yelling to the jailers, 'Me, I'm a robber! That's what I do! Him, he's garbage!'

Later, Leonard was on his bunk, sleeping fitfully, waking often with night sweats. During one of those waking periods, he decided that he was getting too old for this life. He was through doing petty stings and scrounging for rent money. When he got out, he was going to get a stake and begin life anew, and he thought he knew how to do it.

After they were awakened for what Leonard called fried roadkill and fake eggs, he uttered a spontaneous comment to his remaining cellmate, an old con artist with refined features and a mane of white hair who had bilked three elderly women out of their life savings.

'Man, I've had enough,' Leonard said to him. 'Way more than enough. This ain't what I planned for my life. This ain't what I had in mind.'

The old con man replied, 'Destiny is pitiless, son. Nobody ever started out in life wanting to be a proctologist either, but shit happens.'

The residential burglary team who got the arrest report on Leonard Stilwell had a heavy load that week and were able to devote very few hours to a follow-up. One of them got Leonard out of his cell and interviewed him with much the same result that Charlie Gilford had gotten. The detective's partner, D2 Lydia Fernandez, drove to the address of Margot Aziz and knocked on the door at 10 A.M.

Lola was vacuuming the living room and Nicky was watching *Sesame Street* in the family room, with the volume turned up loud so he could hear it over the vacuum noise. Margot, still in her nightgown and robe after a drug-aided nine-hour sleep, answered the door. A woman not much older than Margot, looking businesslike in a matching summer jacket and skirt, showed Margot her badge and presented a business card, saying, 'Good morning, ma'am. I'm Detective Fernandez and I'd like to ask you a few questions.'

Margot stepped out on the porch and said, 'I'd invite you in but we'd have to communicate in writing. I have a five-year-old in there.'

The detective smiled and said, 'I'll just need a moment. Do you know a man named Leonard Stilwell?'

'I don't think so,' Margot said. 'Why?'

'This man?' the detective said, showing Leonard's mug shot.

Margot took the photo and said, 'I've never seen this man, as far as I know. Can you tell me what it's about?'

'Possibly nothing,' Detective Fernandez said. 'He had an address in his car that's close to yours but not right on. He has a burglary record and he had some tools that could be used to enter a locked door. I'm going to check with every resident on this block.'

'A burglar?' Margot said. 'How scary.'

'Was your house or property disturbed in any way yesterday?'

'Not at all,' Margot said. 'My housekeeper was here most of the day, and a few hours after she left, I came home with my son. The doors were locked and the alarm was set when I entered. Should we be worried about this man?'

'There's no need for alarm,' the detective said. 'Just be aware that there're always opportunists like him looking for an easy target.'

'Thanks for telling me,' Margot said.

When the detective was turning to leave, Margot said, 'Could I trouble you for just a minute about another matter?'

'Okay,' the detective said and stopped.

Margot said, 'I'm not worried about burglars, but

I'm involved in a very nasty divorce and my husband's made some veiled threats. I'd like the patrol car in this area to drive by from time to time. Would you please remind Sergeant Treakle at Hollywood Station? He was here one night.'

'I'd suggest you give him a call,' the detective said. 'Any note I leave for him might get misplaced in the piles of paperwork at our station.'

'I'll do that,' Margot said.

She stood on her porch and watched the detective entering the driveway next door. Now Margot had another name to add to the list of police officers she'd apprised of worrisome threats from Ali Aziz.

When Margot reentered the house, she motioned for Lola to turn off the vacuum and said to her, 'We have to be more careful about security, Lola. That was a police officer. There might be burglars in the neighborhood.'

The Mexican woman said, 'I be careful, missus. I always lock doors and set the alarm.'

'Yes, Lola, and you'll have to start remembering to always set the lock on the door to the garage. We can't be too careful these days.'

'Yes, missus,' Lola said. 'I am sorry. I forget that one.'

'You didn't forget yesterday,' Margot said. 'So just do it like that every time.'

Lola looked perplexed because she couldn't remember setting that thumb-latch yesterday, but since she was getting praised for it, she figured she must have done it for once.

'Yes, missus,' Lola said with a fourteen-karat smile.

*　　*　　*

Ronnie Sinclair made two calls that day to the homes of chronic complainers about trash removal, one of the objects being a twelve-foot sofa with the springs hanging out of it. How it got into the front yard of a vacant house was anyone's guess, and the complainant said it wasn't there yesterday. It was during moments like this that Ronnie thought about becoming a real cop again.

But then she looked on the bright side. She was in street clothes today instead of her uniform because of a dinner meeting she had to attend. And she had no radio calls to answer and got her SLO pay bonus. Moreover, she had time to study for the sergeant's exam. Still, there was a wistful feeling every time she saw a black-and-white roaring to a call with lights flashing and siren wailing.

Ronnie was sure by now that Bix had fallen off the wagon and hit the deck hard. With his wife and kids out of town and with days off, she figured he was binge drinking. After learning that Leonard Stilwell was in jail, she didn't really have an excuse to bother Bix with more phone calls. It was still hard to accept that he might be just another Hollywood Nate, tapping some rich bimbo up on Mt. Olympus. She'd expected much more from Bix Ramstead.

Then she started to wonder why she was so troubled by it. She wondered if there was resentment here because Bix had never so much as uttered a sexual innuendo or shot a suggestive glance in her direction. Was it that her pride was hurt? That Bix might prefer one of those Laurel Canyon stone-washed Crate & Barrel addicts who outgrew their tramp stamps by the age of forty and lived with tattoo remorse or laser scars?

Or maybe that he'd prefer one of those Hollywood Hills trophy bunnies in all that distressed second-skin denim, married to middle-aged guys who still dressed like middle school but never in uncool pastels, the lot of them mentally exhausted from trying to think up screwier names for their babies than the movie stars routinely came up with? Is it that I'm a jealous bitch with wounded pride? Ronnie Sinclair asked herself.

The detectives had found nothing on Mt. Olympus or on any report that would marry Leonard Stilwell to a burglary or theft of $1000. The day-watch patrol officers had come in with several arrests that would require extensive investigation, so at 3 P.M. the overworked detectives permitted Leonard to be released from custody, and he was given back his money and his tools. The desk officer at Hollywood Station looked at Leonard like he was nuts when he asked if the officer could break a $100 bill for the pay phone because he'd left his cell in his car.

The desk officer called Leonard a cab, which was driven by a Pakistani, who transported Leonard to the parking lot on Hollywood Boulevard by Grauman's Chinese Theatre. After a raging argument with the parking attendant, they settled on a parking fee of $85 for leaving his Honda parked for twenty-six hours, and Leonard gave the leftover $15 to the cabbie. He was now down to nine Ben Franklins.

Trying to keep all his anger and frustration under control, he dialed Ali's office number and got voice mail. He said, 'Ali, it's Leonard. I need to see you at six o'clock. Be there, man.'

Then Leonard drove to IHOP and loaded up on pancakes, ham, fried eggs, and hash browns, wolfing it all down so fast the waitress was gawking at him. After that, he drove to his apartment building, wrapped a $50 bill around the tension bar and lock pick, and slid it under Junior's door. Then he went to his room, collapsed on the bed, and fell asleep.

When Ali got to his office, he picked up the voice mail and listened to it three times. There was nothing good going to come of this. He could hear a shaky defiance in Leonard's voice. The 'Be there' was particularly worrisome. It had to be about money.

It made Ali open the middle drawer of his desk. It was just a precaution. He would wait until he saw Leonard before he took any action. Leonard was stupid and he was not. He could outwit the thief and probably reason with him, but just in case, he had to have another option.

Ali had intended to give the vial of sleep aids to the first of his girls who gave him a good blow job, but now he had better use for them. Ali took two magenta-and-turquoise capsules from the vial and emptied their contents into the trash basket. In a few minutes he intended to refill them with powdered sugar from the kitchen. He placed the deadly capsule into the vial near the top. Like in Russian roulette, one could shake a capsule out of the vial and perhaps survive. Or perhaps not. Before Leonard Stilwell arrived, Ali decided he would place the vial on the desktop in plain sight.

*   *   *

Bix Ramstead had a violent headache, as well he should, given the quantity of booze he'd consumed in the last thirty-six hours. He'd woken up in his clothes, sharing the sofa in his living room with Annie, the Lab/shepherd mix he'd rescued so long ago. Annie, staring directly into his face, whimpered and wagged her tail when his eyes opened.

'Hi, Annie,' he said and winced.

He pulled himself upright and stretched his back muscles side to side, then limped into the kitchen and rinsed out Annie's dish.

'Want some breakfast, girlfriend?' he said, and Annie sat watching him with the special devotion that rescued dogs were said to possess.

He tossed three aspirin in his mouth and washed them down while mixing Annie's kibble with boiled chicken and a hard-boiled egg. He panicked for a second when he couldn't remember if he'd fed her last night, but then he saw the empty can of dog food on the sink and knew that he had.

After Annie was happily eating, he made sure the doggy door was open, giving her access to the backyard, and he refilled her bowl on the back porch with fresh water. Then he made some coffee and poured himself a bowl of cereal and a glass of orange juice. He got the orange juice down but couldn't manage the cereal.

Bix gathered the two empty bottles of vodka and the dozen beer cans and put them in a trash bag. They'd be collected before he picked up his wife and kids from the airport. He was afraid there would be no way he could hide the drinking from Darcey. She knew him too well and he'd promised her too much. He recalled the last vow he'd made to her: 'Even though I do not believe I'm an alcoholic, if I ever get drunk again, I'll go to AA for help, I swear.'

And she had said, 'As much as I love you, I'll take the kids and leave if you don't.'

He brought the coffee cup to his mouth, and a sob escaped him. He put down the spoon and fought for control.

The cell phone sounded and he didn't know where it was. For a moment he forgot that he'd asked for and received a compensatory day off today. He followed the sound and found the cell on the sofa, where it had fallen from his pocket. His hangover prevented him from reading the screen without his glasses.

He managed a painful hello.

'Bix!' Margot said. 'Thank God!'

'Margot, why're you calling me?' he said.

'I've got to see you!' she said. 'It's urgent!'

'I thought we'd settled this,' he said.

'You've got to come. I don't know where else to turn.'

'Is it about us?'

'No, I swear. It's about Ali. I think he's insane.'

Now the pain was hammering over his right eye. 'You've got a lawyer. You've got the law on your side.'

'They can't help me if I'm dead. I think I need to buy a gun.'

'Jesus, Margot!' Bix said. 'Your fears're exaggerated.'

'Detective Fernandez from Hollywood Station came by today. There was a suspicious character arrested who had an address in his car that they think might have something to do with me.'

Through the fog Bix remembered. 'Oh, yeah,' he

said, 'I was supposed to mention that guy to you. His name is Stillwater or something.'

'Leonard Stilwell,' she said.

'Yeah, that's it,' he said. 'It didn't sound like much. Frankly, I forgot about it.'

'I can tell you about that too if you'll just stop by.'

'Margot . . .'

'Come and talk to me. That's all, just talk. If you think I'm being hysterical, I swear I'll never call you again.'

'I'm sick today, Margot,' he said. 'I'll drop by in the afternoon, but only for a few minutes.'

'Wonderful!' she said. 'Can I help you? What's wrong?'

'I slipped,' he said. 'I got blitzed last night. I'm sick today.'

'Poor Bix!' she said. 'I've got a secret potion for hangovers that I learned when I was a dancer. There were lots of hangovers in the Leopard Lounge, that's for sure.'

'How about five o'clock?' he said.

'Can you make it later?' she said. 'Lola's here today until five. How about six-thirty?'

'Okay,' he said. 'Now I gotta go lie down.'

'Take some vitamin B and C,' she said. 'Lots of it. Drink plenty of juice and water, and put a cold towel over your forehead and eyes. Try to catch a nap.'

'I'll see you at six-thirty,' he said.

Bix thought it over. He felt safe with her in the daytime. The sun was still high enough at 6:30 on these long summer days. It was after sundown that the enchantment always started, the times when he could not resist her.

He'd once admitted that to Margot, and she'd said cheerily, 'Why, Bix, didn't I ever tell you? I'm a vampire!'

Margot Aziz found her go phone and called Jasmine moments after she hung up from her call to Bix. It was difficult not to betray the excitement she felt.

When Jasmine answered, Margot said, 'It's me. Where are you?'

'Where am I?' Jasmine said, annoyance in her voice. 'I'm home trying to get a little rest after your husband made me dance four sets last night because that cunt Goldie took the night off, claiming she had an ankle sprain.'

'Get on your throwaway. I'll call you right back.'

In a moment Margot rang the number of the pay-as-you-go phone she'd bought for Jasmine, who answered with a bored, 'Yeah, so what's up?'

Margot said, 'It's gonna happen!'

'I've heard that before,' Jasmine said.

'Tonight!' Margot said.

That got her attention. She said, 'Don't tell me that if it isn't true, Margot. I can't deal with it no more.'

'Tonight, baby!' Margot said. 'Take the night off.'

'Ali will kill me!' Jasmine said, and Margot almost laughed.

Jasmine realized what she'd just said and muttered, 'Damn! That's sick.'

'It's your turn to sprain an ankle,' Margot said. 'I'll have my friend under control before midnight, for sure. You be ready to do what you gotta do then.'

'Midnight?' Jasmine said.

'Right around midnight,' Margot said.

'I was starting to think it was like a game,' Jasmine said. 'Not real, you know?'

'It's real, baby,' Margot said. 'We'll have it all.'

'Will you call me when it's time?'

'You be sitting in your car a block from the club no later than eleven-thirty. Sometime after that you'll get the call, and then you gotta be good, honey. Real good.'

'I will be,' she said.

'Make that mascara run,' Margot said.

'I can do it,' Jasmine said. 'I just hope you can.'

'I love you,' Margot said, ending the call.

Margot poured a cup of coffee and called the nanny in order to have Nicky picked up for an overnighter. The nanny was used to it and got well paid for overnighters. There was nothing for Margot to do now but to prepare herself mentally.

She decided that after a few months she'd kiss off Jasmine with a nice 'severance package.' Margot figured that $100,000 would be enough for her. Of course, Jasmine would rage and threaten to expose Margot, but what could she really do? Admit to being a co-conspirator and accomplice? And what could she prove if she did make such an outrageous claim? No, Jasmine would take the money and fall in love with someone else. Just like the song, she fell in love too easily, but only if the lover was very rich. That reminded Margot to retrieve Jasmine's go phone in the next few days and dispose of it. Just in case.

Sheer emotional exhaustion kept Leonard asleep for an hour. When he got up, he showered and even shaved.

He put on a clean T-shirt and faded Levi's jeans that weren't too grungy and his best pair of sneaks. He smoked a cigarette and amped up on coffee and began a rehearsal. He had to strike the right 'tude going in, was how he figured it. He had to be ready to be just too cool when the fucking Ay-rab started waving the verbal dagger in his face.

The Leopard Lounge had enough dancers in the stable to keep the club crowded in late afternoon, and happy hour prices were not necessary. Leonard counted more than forty cars in the parking lot at 6:10 P.M., and it made him feel more justified than ever in making demands for a decent fee for services rendered.

He once again entered the office of Ali Aziz without knocking, and found Ali seated at his desk with a bottle of Jack and two glasses. Near the bottle were some letters and a blank envelope, along with a vial of magenta-and-turquoise capsules.

Ali, who had also been mentally rehearsing, had the toothiest smile that Leonard had ever seen on him.

'Leonard, my friend!' Ali said extravagantly. 'I am very glad to see you. I have got back the important document, thanks to my friend Leonard. Everything is correct again!'

Leonard sat in the client chair and said, 'Yeah, well, I'm happy you're happy, because I think we got more business to discuss.'

'I wish to order some food for my friend. I feel like a new man. A nice steak, perhaps? T-bone? Rib eye?'

Leonard gave a head shake, not knowing what to make of the new Ali, and he said, 'Naw, I ate at IHOP.'

'A drink?' Ali said, pouring two hefty shots of Jack Daniel's.

'Okay,' Leonard said, picking up the nearest glass.

'You look like you are tired,' Ali said. 'You are getting enough sleep, no?'

'I get enough,' Leonard said.

'I am getting good sleep,' Ali said. 'I take sleep medicine that one of my dancers gave to me.'

'That's good,' Leonard said, thinking he might try switching from smoking rock to booze if he could afford good stuff like this.

Ali said, 'I am going home in one hour because I was awake at five o'clock this morning to do inventory. My bitch wife no longer does inventory for me, so I must do all things.'

'Yeah, life is tough,' Leonard said. 'You shoulda been with me last night. Even your sleeping pills wouldn't a helped.'

'Where you were last night?'

'In jail.'

'Oh, God!' Ali said. 'What did you do wrong?'

'Nothing,' Leonard said. 'Except that I did that job for you. And the cops found my tools and rousted me, and I spent the night in jail, even though they couldn't prove nothing and had to kick me out this afternoon.'

'Oh, God!' Ali said again. 'You didn't say nothing about—'

'Of course not,' Leonard said. 'But I still got popped behind that business I did for you.'

'I am so sorry, my friend,' Ali said, pouring another double shot for Leonard. 'That is why you look so sleepy.'

With two capsules full of powdered sugar concealed in his left hand, Ali reached for the vial of capsules on the desk. Ali unscrewed the top and appeared to shake out two capsules onto the desktop, dropping the two that he'd palmed. Then he screwed the top back on and put the vial near the bottle of Jack.

Ali made it very apparent that he was putting the capsules into his mouth and swallowing them down with a shot of the Scotch, saying, 'This is very good sleep medicine. I shall be feeling very peaceful soon. And then, maybe one hour from now, I shall go to bed and sleep for ten, twelve hours. You only want eight hours, you swallow down one capsule. Wonderful sleeping.'

'Yeah, that's nice, but maybe we oughtta talk,' Leonard said.

Still brimming with bonhomie, Ali said, 'You try.' Then he unscrewed the top again.

'I ain't ready to go to sleep,' Leonard said.

'No,' Ali said, 'not for now. You try later. You shall thank me. If you like them, I get you all you want.'

Leonard had never been one to turn down drugs of any kind, and he gave a nod while Ali dumped the capsules onto the desktop and put the empty vial in the drawer. Then he pushed a plain envelope across to Leonard with his fingernail and, with a mirthless smile, said, 'One hour before you wish to sleep, swallow down two.'

Leonard scooped the capsules into the envelope, folded it, and put it in his pocket. Then he said, 'I been thinking that my pay for what I done for you is pathetic. You just said how much I helped you. But what happened to me? I went to the slam and spent the fucking night with maniacs and child molesters and gangbangers.'

Ali stopped smiling then. His brow wrinkled and he said, 'I feel great sorrow for you, my friend.'

Leonard said, 'Yeah, well, I ain't looking for pity. I just want proper compensation.'

Ali knew he had guessed correctly. It was blackmail. He'd probably demand another two hundred. Maybe even five. And he'd be back in a few weeks. And a few weeks after that. Ali was glad he had decided to give Leonard the other deadly sister. It would be the only way to stop these petty demands that would eventually get expensive, and even dangerous.

Trying to maintain an attitude of sympathy mixed with puzzlement, Ali said, 'How can I help you, Leonard?'

'I think ten thousand bucks will help a lot,' Leonard said.

Ali could not remember a time when he needed to control so much outrage. He sipped some Jack and, with a quiver in his voice, said, 'You wish for me to pay you ten thousand? Am I hearing the correct words?'

'It's only a loan,' Leonard said. 'I got an idea for a small business. I need a stake.'

'A loan,' Ali said without intonation.

'Yeah,' Leonard said. 'I'll pay you back in maybe a year, eighteen months tops, with twenty percent interest. That's fair, ain't it?'

'But Leonard, ten thousand is very big money,' Ali said.

'Not to you,' Leonard said. 'I seen your ex-house.

I seen this club packed to the walls, with money laying all over the bar and the tables and even on the stage. How much did you make on a case of that hot liquor I used to supply you? Come on, Ali, ten grand ain't much for you to lend to a friend.'

'I shall have to think,' Ali said. 'You come back in three, four days. We are going to talk some more.'

Suddenly Leonard said, 'What would your ex–old lady say if she knew you paid me to steal a folder from her desk?'

Ali knew that his voice might betray the rage welling up from his belly, so he took another sip of Jack Daniel's and said, 'My bitch wife? She would say no, Ali has no care about documents in this house. She would not be believing such a thing, Leonard.'

Emboldened by Ali's deferential manner and by the liquor warming him, Leonard went for it. With sweat dampening his T-shirt, he said, 'What would she say if I told her you planted a bug in her house?'

Ali was genuinely perplexed and said, 'A bug?'

'A listening device,' Leonard said. 'I bet she'd hire a security company to sweep the joint and they'd find it. Where'd you put it? In the bedroom?'

Hanging on to a semblance of a smile, Ali said, 'You talk very much shit, Leonard.'

'I hung around and saw you go in that garage, Ali,' Leonard said. 'And you were carrying that folder you never wanted in the first place. And you were in there for thirteen minutes. What would the little woman say about them little nuggets of information?'

Ali Aziz blinked first, unsmiling, his teeth clenched. Then, voice trembling, he said, 'I do not put no bugs in the house. I just read the document and put the folder back in the house. That is all.'

'I guess you could try to sell that to the little woman,' Leonard said. 'But she ain't gonna buy it. And after they do the electronics sweep and find the bug, you are gonna be in a world of hurt when her lawyer tells the judge. Actually, what you done was a serious crime, Ali. You committed a felony, entering that house and planting a bug.'

For a frightening moment, Ali Aziz thought about the pistol in his desk drawer. He quickly came to his senses, knowing he could never get away with that. Not here, not now. Instead, with a voice hoarse and raspy, he said, 'I understand. I shall give you the business loan, Leonard. But I do not have so much money here. Come back next week.'

'I want it now, Ali,' Leonard said. 'We can start with what you got on you. I seen you peel off five grand right outta your pocket one time after Whitey and me got you a load of booze.'

Without a word, Ali Aziz reached a trembling hand into his trousers pocket, pulled out his roll of $100 bills, and tossed it on the desktop, gold money clip and all.

Leonard finished his drink, poured another, and removed the money clip and pushed it back to Ali. He counted while Ali sat trying with all of his self-control not to leap across the desk and get the thief's skinny neck in his fingers and squeeze.

After he finished counting, Leonard said, 'You let me down. You only got twenty-one hundred here. Go to your safe and get the rest. Whadda you got, a floor safe?'

Ali Aziz could barely get out the words, but he managed to say, 'Please go to the bar, Leonard. Have one more drink. Come back and I shall have the money.'

'Sure,' Leonard said. 'But you don't gotta worry about me seeing your safe. I never steal from a friend.'

Leonard Stilwell's legs were rubbery when he walked down the passageway to the main room, and he knew it wasn't the booze. He had just pulled off the biggest score of his life! It was scary but he'd stung that fucking Ay-rab with ease, and there was no reason he couldn't do it again before Ali's ex-wife moved out of the house.

What was it Ali had said? Escrow was closing pretty soon? After that, and after the divorce shit was all worked out, a shakedown wouldn't work anymore. In fact, Ali could retrieve the listening device himself by then, or he might even have somebody else break into the house and get it out of there in order to get Leonard off his back. But Leonard thought he ought to be able to burn Ali Aziz one more time, maybe in a few days, before Ali had a chance to react to what had just happened to him. Leonard figured that in business, timing was everything.

He was so utterly stoked, with more money in his pocket than he'd ever had in his life, that he sat by the stage and stuffed a $20 bill into the G-string of the dancer, a big, busty babe in a cowboy hat who'd licked her lips and winked at him. Then, when he finished his drink, after tipping the cocktail waitress $10, he walked back down the passageway. But suddenly he stopped and felt a wave of fear sweep over him. It was safe enough here with all the people around, but he thought of how Ali's face had gone deathly pale. That swarthy camel fucker had turned whiter than Leonard for a minute there. Whiter than a corpse.

Leonard grabbed the first busboy to walk past him, handed the Mexican a $10 bill, and said, 'Come with me to the boss's office.'

He knocked this time, then pushed the door open gingerly, holding the Mexican by the arm and saying, 'Ali, I brought the help with me.'

Ali was sitting at the desk, staring at the doorway, his hands folded under his chin. The look on his face was as grim as Leonard had seen on the strong-arm robber last night after he got the word that their new cellie was a short-eyes kiddie raper.

Ali said, 'Please come in.'

'I'll leave the door open,' Leonard said. Then to the Mexican, 'What's your name, son?'

'Marcos,' the kid said.

'Okay, Marcos, hang there for a minute,' Leonard said, leaving the door open so that Ali knew there was a witness, in case violence was on his mind. Then Leonard hurried across the room to Ali's desk and picked up the stack of currency awaiting him.

'Good-bye, Leonard,' Ali said. 'I do not want no more loans between us.'

'Don't be a drama queen,' Leonard said. 'This is what they call squid pro quo. That's lawyer talk and it means we're straight with each other.'

When he left the office, he handed the busboy another $10 and said, 'Thanks for being my bodyguard, son.'

Ali Aziz entered his little half bathroom, closed the

door, locked it, turned on both water taps to muffle the
sound, and, gripping the sink, screamed until drool
ran down his chin.

NINETEEN

BIX RAMSTEAD WAS FEELING much more alive after having had a nap and a shower and shave. He dressed in a pale blue Oxford shirt and clean chinos and swallowed some aspirin to diminish the raging headache. He felt resolute enough to resist Margot Aziz now, while the sun was still high enough over the Hollywood Hills and his resolve had not been shattered by six or eight ounces of booze. That's all it took when he was around her, that alluring young woman so different from his wife.

Bix didn't believe that Margot was truly in love with him, as she claimed. Her miserable marriage made her think so. But to have a woman like Margot Aziz professing her love for him, so passionate for him, had been overwhelming. Margot wasn't shy like his wife, Darcey. She was assertive and sophisticated and always knew just what to say. She was mischievous and funny and made him feel more worldly, more important, than he was or ever could be. And Margot made him feel *young* like her.

When Bix was able to step back and analyze it soberly, none of it made sense. They had been intimate for only five months. They'd had sexual encounters only half a dozen times in those five months, always in hotels, where she'd rented a room and waited for him until he got off duty. And always she had provided drinks to allay his fears and guilt. He'd been besotted by this perplexing young woman who claimed she'd never betrayed her husband before meeting Bix, and who made him believe it.

Bix parked his minivan in her driveway and Margot answered the door very quickly. She was dressed the way she often was when they had evening clandestine meetings. She wore creamy tailored pants that hugged her body, a simple black shell, a delicate gold necklace, no earrings, no bling. Her ears were perfect and she seldom adorned them. Her shoulders were wide and square, her tan was year-round.

Bix was glad she was not wearing low-cut jeans and a rising jersey that exposed her muscular belly, as she sometimes dressed for a daytime rendezvous. That's when she looked most sensual.

'Hello, darling,' she said.

'I can only stay long enough to hear the story and offer some advice,' he said.

'Of course,' Margot said. 'Come in.'

When they were inside the marble foyer, Margot said, 'Let's sit on the terrace and admire the smog, shall we? The toxins are so lovely this time of day.'

He followed her through the living room to the sliding doors and walked outside. There was a pitcher of iced tea already there and some smoked wahoo tuna, cream cheese, chopped onions, capers, and a crunchy French baguette, already sliced.

'We'll smell awful after eating this stuff, but what the hell,' Margot said.

Bix sat, feeling dry-mouthed, and sipped some tea. Then he said, 'Tell me about it, Margot. What's going on?'

'His threats are more overt now,' she said.

'Overt how?'

'He talks blatantly to Nicky in my presence when he's picking up our son for his overnighter. He makes sure I hear him telling Nicky how beautiful Saudi Arabia is. Or he tells Nicky that he'll love seeing the Giza pyramids in Egypt. Stuff like that.'

'He's just trying to goad you,' Bix said. 'That guy's locked into America. In fact, he's locked into his businesses here in Hollywood. He's going nowhere.'

Margot loaded up a slice of baguette with wahoo and cream cheese and onion, topped it with a few capers, and handed it to Bix. He thought she had the most beautiful hands he'd ever seen, and, as always, her nails matched the lip gloss she was wearing.

'I always talk to Nicky when he comes back from outings with his father,' Margot continued, 'but lately he's clamming up. I know that Ali has ordered him not to tell me what his father's planning.'

'He's five years old, Margot,' Bix said. 'Ali's not gonna be making travel plans with a kid that young. It's just talk, trying to get Nicky in touch with his father's culture. That's all it is.'

'The last time Ali came for him, my son was a different child when he came back.'

'Different how?'

Margot sipped her iced tea and said, 'I took Nicky

to bed with me that night and I hugged and kissed him and asked him what he and his daddy talked about. And he said, "Are you going to come and live with us, Mommy?" And I asked him where, and he said, "When I meet my gramma and grampa." And I said, "You've met your gramma and grampa lots of times. Remember when they came here, and when we drove to Barstow?" And he said, "My other gramma and grampa. Who live far away across the ocean."'

'That doesn't imply he's gonna run off with Nicky,' Bix said.

'I've got information from a good source that he's put the Leopard Lounge up for sale with a broker. It's all on the Q.T. And he's dissolving every asset he owns that's not part of the divorce action. He's very sneaky. Ali's got secret assets we haven't been able to find.'

'That still doesn't mean he's ready to leave the country. Does Nicky have a passport?'

'Do you know how easy it is to leave this country for the Middle East with a child if you have plenty of money? You just hop in your car and drive your child three hours south and cross the border into Tijuana. After that, it's a piece of cake to arrange for passports and flights to anywhere you want.'

'Your imagination is getting the better of you,' Bix said.

'There's more,' Margot said. Then she stopped and said, 'Would you mind if I had a drink? It'll make it easier to talk about.'

He didn't look pleased but said, 'Go ahead.'

She returned with a triple shot of premium vodka, on the rocks in a tumbler, just the way he liked it. With a slice of lime hanging on the lip of the glass instead of a lemon twist inside it, also the way he liked it.

She squeezed the lime into it, took a sip, and said, 'Oh, that's better. That's much better.'

Bix looked at his watch and said, 'Get on with it, Margot. I wanna get home before dark.'

'Why? Your family isn't home.'

'I've gotta feed Annie,' he said.

'She can't eat after dark?'

'I can't be here after dark,' he said.

'Why?'

'You're a vampire, remember?' he said, smiling just a bit.

Margot chuckled then, a sound he loved to hear, and she said, 'Oh, darling, I've missed you so much.'

'You were going to tell me more,' Bix said, avoiding her amber eyes. 'Something you needed my advice about, remember?'

'He said he's going to kill me,' Margot said suddenly and took another sip of vodka.

'Who'd he say this to?'

'I'm not sure,' Margot said, 'but I think it was one of his dancers. I got an anonymous call. My new number's unlisted, but of course he has it. She could have found it in his desk directory.'

'Why would he be crazy enough to tell a dancer he was going to kill you?'

'He uses cocaine heavily in his office. He shares it with his dancers for sexual favors. When he's high on coke, he talks way too much. He reveals things he shouldn't. He mixes his drugs and doesn't even remember what happened later. That's what I think happened.'

'What did the anonymous caller say?'

'She said, "Be careful. He's going to kill you and take your son." Then she hung up.'

'You didn't recognize the voice?'

'No, but I'm sure it was one of the dancers.'

'You're speculating.'

'Based on experience.'

'Did you tell your lawyer.'

'No.'

'Why not?'

'He'd say what you're saying. It's speculation. Someone's trying to scare me. I'm being an alarmist. Et cetera.' Then she stopped and her chin quivered, and she put her hand to her eyes, saying, 'Excuse me, Bix, I'll be right back.'

Margot Aziz left him there alone with the sweating tumbler full of his favorite ice-cold vodka. His face felt fiery hot and he wanted to pick up the glass tumbler and hold it against his cheek to quell the heat. He wanted to hold the glass against his lips.

She was gone for a few minutes, and when she returned, her eyes were a bit moist, as though she'd been crying, and she held a tissue in her hand to prove it. She noticed that the vodka level in the tumbler had dropped. Only a little. But it had dropped.

She said, 'Excuse me again, I want to freshen this.'

Bix Ramstead felt his heart pounding. This woman. The sight of her. The touch of her skin. Her scent. He had the taste of vodka on his tongue, as he always had when he was with her. This was all so familiar and so frightening.

When she returned, she set the tumbler on the

outdoor table with the fresh vodka in it and a fresh slice of lime hanging on the lip of the glass. She looked at him in earnest and said, 'Bix, you always carry your gun off duty, don't you?'

'When I come to Hollywood, yeah,' he said. 'When I'm at home in Studio City, I'm not packing. Not when I go to the market or to the movies with my kids.'

She said, 'Are you packing now?'

'It's in the car,' he said. 'Why?'

'I'm gonna buy a gun as soon as possible. I can't stand this fear I'm living under. I want you to tell me what to buy.'

'If it makes you feel any better,' he said, 'then buy one. Just get a wheel gun. A thirty-eight revolver. They're simple. They don't misfire. They're easy to use. Anyway, you're never gonna fire it.'

'Any particular make?' she said.

He looked at his watch then and said, 'I better be going. I might run into traffic, driving over Laurel Canyon. I don't think I should get on the freeway tonight.'

'One drink,' she said. 'For the road. For old times' sake. In a little while the traffic will be light and you can whiz home and feed Annie.'

He hesitated just long enough for her to know she could pull it off. She slid the tumbler full of vodka in front of him and said, 'I'll fix myself another.'

Then she got up and went to the kitchen. She took her time, and when she returned, she saw that the vodka level had dropped again, but this time more than a little. And she had poured a triple shot into that one.

'Darling,' she said, sitting with her fresh drink.

'Thank you for coming. There was no one I could turn to. Nobody I could trust but you.'

His hand trembled when he picked up the tumbler and drank again. 'I've gotta get away from here before sundown,' he said.

Margot chuckled again and, yes, he absolutely loved the sound of it. Just as a massive swarm of insects rose like ashes in the sky, tainting his lovely view of multicolored shards of smog over Hollywood.

The crack pipe was red-hot when Leonard Stilwell put it down on the sink counter that evening. He'd finally been able to score some rock at Pablo's Tacos, and he'd driven straight back to his apartment with the rock and with four chicken tacos loaded with guacamole. He'd stayed well away from Hollywood and Highland for fear of running into that pair of cops who looked to him like surf rats.

The crackhead dealer who'd sold him the rock said that he had six grams for sale, and Leonard said, 'Wrap it up. I'll take it all.'

'Cool!' the dealer said. 'Plastic or paper?'

Leonard had been smoking ever since, trying to watch TV but unable to concentrate. When he was feeling both mellow and elated, that combination he loved to feel, he decided to take the advice given to him by Ali Aziz and turn in early for a good night's sleep. The envelope with the capsules was on the cheap little nightstand beside his bed and he shook out three capsules. But then he thought he'd better not push it and dropped one back inside the envelope. He popped two in his mouth and washed them down with a beer.

Then he stripped down, got under the covers, and prepared himself for sweet dreams. Nobody who saw the pile of Ben Franklins he'd stashed inside a pot in the kitchen could say that Leonard Stilwell was anything but a Hollywood success story.

The sun had flamed out unnoticed in wispy clouds of rosy smoke without Bix Ramstead giving a single thought to vampires. Two hours after he'd taken that first sip from Margot's drink, his speech was somewhat slurred, his eyes were 80 proof glossy, and night was on them, light sparkling all over Hollywood.

A large raven flew up from the canyon into the blue-black sky with wildly beating wings, screeching at a mockingbird that was diving at the ebony flyer. Bix Ramstead watched that raven escaping from the feathered tormenter, seeing it fly away from the Hollywood Hills to the safety of its nesting place.

Margot saw him watching it and said, 'It's getting too cool and dark for ravens and crows. Let's go inside.'

When they were seated side by side on one of the enormous pistachio green sofas, he tried to focus on the glass sculpture hanging from the travertine wall and convince himself that he was not drunk. Mellow music from several speakers surrounded them, and the lamps in the living room and foyer were on dimmers and had been turned low.

'Hope you don't mind that it's all Rod Stewart tonight,' she said. 'I'm still an old-fashioned girl from Barstow.'

'In the oldie song "Route Sixty-six," Barstow is mentioned,' Bix said, having trouble pronouncing consonants. 'You ever heard it?'

'Really?' Margot said. 'Don't think I know that one.'

'You're too young,' Bix said. 'Ask your mom and dad.'

'I think I will, next time I see them,' she said. 'By the way, they're as worried about Ali stealing Nicky from me as I am. He's their only grandchild and they adore him. They hate his father, of course, and they hated it when I was a dancer at the Leopard Lounge. They never understood that I did what I had to do to get by. Hollywood is a pitiless place.'

'What's your dad do?' Bix said, trying not to gulp this drink. Sip, he told himself.

'He's retired from the post office,' Margot said.

'A civil servant,' Bix said. 'Like me.'

'Bix,' Margot said, looking more serious, 'would you do me a huge favor and bring your gun in here?'

'What? You wanna shoot crows on the hillside? I'm a Crow, remember?' Those consonants again, they were getting tangled on his tongue and in his throat.

But it sounded exceptionally funny to him and he laughed before taking another big hit from the tumbler. He was trying to remember if this was his fourth or fifth drink. He was sure he could handle six, but Margot poured so heavy he was going to stop after five. Was this number five?

Margot said, 'I believe I told you that I took a shooting lesson at a gun store in the Valley. And I'm sure you're right about a revolver being what I should buy, but the nine-millimeter pistol I fired in that lesson seemed comfortable to me. If that's a word that applies to a gun. Would you mind getting yours so I can ask you a few questions? Or I can get it if you give me your car keys.'

'I'll get it,' Bix said with a sigh. 'I gotta pee anyway.'

It took him two attempts to get up from the sofa, and he weaved when he crossed the living room to the powder room off the foyer. After he'd flushed the toilet, he looked at himself in the mirror, trying to focus on his pupils. Was he drunk? He thought he'd better not have another vodka. Maybe some fizzy water. After that, he was going home.

The second he opened the door to his minivan to retrieve his holstered nine from under the seat, Bix Ramstead felt it: a hint of danger. His neck hair bristled when he touched the gun, and he shivered. Cop instincts that he'd developed over nearly two decades were telling him to get into that van and drive down that hill and never drive back up again. But he decided he was being ridiculous. He was having a pleasant time and would be flying off to his nest very soon. After one more drink.

While he was gone, Margot removed from the drawer in the butler's pantry two magenta-and-turquoise capsules that she'd taken from her jewelry box earlier in the day. She pulled one apart and poured it into the drink, stirring it before dropping in the ice. She didn't like the way it failed to completely dissolve, and she didn't really think it would be needed tonight, but there was no sense taking a chance that he'd somehow summon enough sobriety to drive away from there. The granules were clinging to the ice, and she thought he'd get very little of it into his system, so she took the second capsule and added it, then flushed the empty capsules away. She prepared herself another tumbler of plain tonic, ice, and lime.

When Bix got back inside the house, a fresh drink

was waiting for him on the massive glass-and-steel coffee table. He sat down heavily again and withdrew the Beretta from its holster. After taking a sip from the fresh drink, he said, 'Is this the kind of gun you fired?'

'Yes,' she said. 'I just liked the feel of that kind of pistol, but I'm unsure how the safety works. I wouldn't want anything that would be too easy for Nicky to figure out if, God forbid, he ever found it.'

'It's your job to see that he never does,' Bix said emphatically. 'That's why buying a gun is a bad idea.'

'What is that on the frame?' she said. 'Is that the safety?'

'No,' Bix said with the careful articulation of the inebriate. 'It's a decocker. With this gun you don't have to sweep a safety up from the safe position before firing. We can just draw, aim, and squeeze the trigger. The first round is double action and takes more trigger pull. Then the rest are single action while the gun ejects the empty shell casings. Afterwards, we sweep the decocker down to safely drop the hammer, then back up to the fire position, and we're ready again.'

'What's the bottom line?' she said. 'You only have to pull the trigger, right?'

'Squeeze with the pad of your index finger,' he said. 'Don't pull, yank, or jerk.'

'Got it,' she said. 'I think I'll buy one of those.'

Bix got the hiccups then and Margot got up, saying, 'I'll get you some bitters and lime. Works every time.'

Bix holstered the gun and took a long gulp of vodka, but it didn't stop the hiccups. She returned with a saucer. On it was a wedge of lime soaked in bitters.

'Bite on this and suck hard,' she said with a grin.

He did as he was told and shuddered, saying, 'That tastes awful!'

'Wash it down,' she said, and he did, with more vodka.

'Is that better?' she said.

He sat quietly for a moment and said, 'My hiccups are history.'

'See?' she said. 'Would I ever steer you wrong?'

Another Hollywood Crow had too much to drink that evening. Hollywood Nate was enjoying his day off and had gone alone to an early first-run movie in Westwood, later stopping at Bossa Nova on Sunset Boulevard, a restaurant that stayed open until very late and was frequented by cops. He saw a black-and-white in the parking lot, but he didn't know the two cops inside. After he ate, he drove to Micelli's on Las Palmas, thinking he might see a few cops, but there wasn't anyone he recognized in there either. He stayed and had a glass of house red. Then another.

Nate was mellow when he got into his Mustang. And because he was, he again did something that he would never admit having done. Something he would never forget and always wonder about, the thought of which would later fill him with profound regret. He drove up the hill to Mt. Olympus.

He'd never gotten her out of his mind, even though the initial lust he felt for her had subsided. It was the mystery of her. Who was she? What was she about? He didn't know what he'd do if he saw her red Beemer pulling in or out of her driveway. He didn't think he had the gall to walk up and ring her bell at this time of night. To say what? Yes, Margot, I'll take the job as your live-in security guard. And why haven't you called me?

He was a grown man, thirty-six years old, and this was childish and silly, and yet he kept driving up into the Hollywood Hills. Up to Mt. Olympus for no reason that made any sense whatsoever. When he got there, he saw a blue Dodge minivan and he recognized it. Bix Ramstead often parked that minivan near Nate's Mustang in the south lot, and once he'd told Bix the minivan looked like a vice squad hand-me-down and asked if Bix had to steam clean the cargo area and rake out the condoms after the hookers had been transported to jail.

Seeing that minivan made him face another possibility that he did not like to consider. Was he simply jealous that Margot Aziz could prefer Bix Ramstead to Hollywood Nate Weiss? Nate passed the address, turned around farther up the hill, and stared at the house of Margot Aziz as he drove slowly down past it again. He thought that Jetsam had been dead right. That house had an aura.

TWENTY

I'M DRUNK!' BIX Ramstead finally admitted.

'You're just a bit tipsy,' Margot said, removing the throw pillow between them on the sofa while Rod Stewart sang 'You Go to My Head.'

'Gotta go, Margot,' he said.

Still not touching him, she said, 'How about a good-night kiss for the road?'

Quickly, she slid over next to him, and he felt her breath on his neck. She kissed him with lots of tongue, and then she kissed his face and neck and ran her hands all over him while he groaned softly.

'Let's go lie down for a while, sweetheart,' she said. 'Until you're feeling more alert.'

'I can't—,' he said, but she cut him off with more kisses.

'You're sweet, Bix,' she whispered. 'You're the sweetest man I've ever known.'

'I can't, Margot,' he said without conviction.

'You've never even seen my bedroom,' she said. 'Let me show it to you.'

He would've been surprised by her strength if he'd been sober enough to appreciate it. She half lifted him to his feet, put his arm around her neck, and led him to the carpeted staircase.

'I gotta go feed Annie!' he said, but she had an arm around his waist, and, holding up much of his weight, she started up the stairs.

'Shhhh, baby!' she said. 'Wait till you see my bedroom. You can feed her later.'

Margot was panting by the time she got him upstairs and into the bedroom. She walked him to the bed, and he stood swaying when she pulled back the spread and top sheet. Then she let him fall back onto the bed. This was not how she had imagined it would happen. She thought she'd have to get him pretty drunk, but not utterly blitzed like this. After sex, sleep would naturally follow. That was how it was supposed to happen, but she'd been too fearful that he'd have an attack of conscience. She'd poured too heavily. The only bonus was that she wouldn't have to ball him after all.

He was up on one elbow, unable to focus, seeing two Margots, when she quickly peeled off her top and stepped out of her pants.

'See!' she said cheerily, just in case he had any noncompliance left in him. 'No underwear!'

He was nearly unresponsive, eyes closed, breathing through his mouth.

Naked, she worked methodically, pulling off his shoes and socks, undoing his belt, unzipping his chinos, pulling them down and off. Then she peeled off his briefs and he seemed barely awake when she unbuttoned his Oxford shirt and got him out of it.

When he opened his eyes, looking past her at the open doorway, she nearly panicked. He couldn't get up now! He couldn't leave now! She climbed on him, sliding along his body, moaning, uttering endearments, running her hands over him, leaning down to kiss him when he tried to raise up.

'Baby, baby,' she murmured. 'I want you!'

All he said to her was '*Some* angel I am.'

'Yes, yes,' she said. 'You *are* my angel. You *are!*'

It was more of a sex simulation than the real thing, and it required much more effort for her. She was panting from exhaustion by the time he fell into a deep slumber. She gathered his clothes, folded them, and put them in her closet. When she came back to the bed, she strained and pushed and lifted until he was under the covers, his head on the pillow, snoring softly.

She put on a robe and ran downstairs. She retrieved his holstered gun from the coffee table but left the empty vodka bottle and the two glasses on the table, pouring some vodka into her tumbler of tonic to prove that they'd both been drinking heavily.

Then she crossed the foyer to the front door and unlocked the thumb-latch, making sure that the door opened easily. She ran back up to the bedroom and put Bix's holstered gun on the nightstand at his side of the bed, along with his car keys and wallet. Then she turned out all of the lights except a lamp on the second floor at the top of the staircase. She wanted Ali backlit when he entered her bedroom.

Gil Ponce had gotten back to regular duty in record time after the shooting of the ice-cream hijacker was found to be in policy and the BSS shrink had peeked inside his head. Gil's quick return was probably due to the TV media's being so quick (and incorrect) in calling the incident a suicide-by-cop, thus giving the LAPD bureaucrats plenty of cover.

Six hours into their watch, Cat Song and Gil Ponce took code 7 in a restaurant that Cat frequented in Thai Town. That meant phoning ahead for their dinners so that the food could be served the moment they sat down, giving them the whole thirty minutes to get through the courses.

Cat told Gil that the main course was named for her, and he smiled when they brought out a whole baked catfish. Cat talked to Gil about the satay and the curry, and, using a fork, she flaked off the tender flesh from the fish and spooned it onto his plate. They drank Thai iced coffee, and when the bill came, Cat insisted on paying it, leaving a good tip for the owner.

When they got back out to their black-and-white, Gil driving and Cat riding shotgun, he said, 'Why're you being so nice to me? It's not my birthday.'

'I'm always nice to everybody,' she said. 'And you're so close to finishing your probation, I thought we should celebrate. You won't be a probie that we can kick around anymore.'

'You've been especially nice,' Gil said, driving west on Sunset Boulevard at 11 P.M.

'I hadn't noticed,' Cat said, clearing from code 7 and, seeing their MDC blinking, hitting the message-received and display button.

She opened and acknowledged the message, then hit the en route key, and Gil looked at the message on the dashboard screen, saying, 'Illegal parking. That's near that nightclub, what's it called? The Leopard Lounge?'

'It's a titty bar masquerading as a fancy nightclub,' Cat said. 'Somebody's always complaining about the parking around there.'

When they were still a few minutes away, Gil said, 'There wouldn't be another reason why you've been treating me like you're my—'

'If you say mommy, I'll give you a shot of whup-ass spray,' Cat said, touching the canister on her Sam Browne.

'Big sister, I was gonna say.' Then Gil added, 'Is it about the shooting?'

'You tell me, Gil,' Cat said. 'I haven't seen you crack a smile since that night in the Hollywood cemetery.'

'Well, it was scary with those FID investigators jacking me up. They aren't gentle. The shrink was okay, but I just told him what I thought he wanted to hear.'

'Who cares about any of them?' Cat said. 'I told you a minute after you shot that guy that you did good. That I woulda done the same.'

'I know, but, well . . .'

'Well what? You shoulda had ESP and known the tweaker was packing a starter pistol? Is that what?'

'I don't know. I just feel . . . different now.'

'Sure, you do,' Cat said. 'You're supposed to. You took a life – through no fault of your own. He made the choice, not you. I was there, boy. I heard you yelling at him to put his hands on his head and get down and prone out. I heard it!'

Gil Ponce said, 'I don't like the other guys slapping me on the back and calling me a gunfighter. I don't like that.'

'Screw them too!' Cat said. 'Macho dipshits. None

of them ever fired their weapons outside the pistol range. Those that have wouldn't go around patting your ass over it.'

'Well, I wouldn't want anyone else to know that you and me talked about this,' Gil said.

'That's just your Hispanic machismo,' Cat said.

'I'm not really Hispanic,' he said.

'Let's not go over that again,' she said. 'Now, listen to me, partner, I don't know how to dial you in except to keep saying you did exactly what any copper woulda done and shoulda done at that moment in that place. And I'd hate to think that my safety could be jeopardized from now on because you're gun-shy.'

He said, 'Cat, I don't want you—'

'Lemme tell you a true story,' she said, interrupting him. 'Five years ago, I had a partner for two months. A nice guy. We were working Watch three. He married a woman with four kids who was a peace activist, and pretty soon he decided to resign from the Department. Said he wanted to go into a line of work where he'd never have to use violence on anybody. And on the last day we worked together, he made a little confession to me. Because of his wife's haranguing, he hadn't loaded a round in his nine since before we started working together. It's the closest I ever came to pulling my baton and beating another cop right into the ground.'

'Why're you telling me this, Cat?' Gil asked.

'Did you clean your nine after the other night?'

'Yeah.'

'Did you reload it?'

'Of course.'

'Then I feel safe. Because this is all about me, not

about you. I've got a two-year-old at home who needs his momma. I've got a good copper here with a loaded nine who's got my back. So I feel safe. End of story. Any questions?'

After a moment of contemplation, Gil Ponce said, 'Thanks, Cat.'

'For what?' she said.

Gil Ponce paused, then said, 'For the Thai dinner, of course. It was great.'

'Don't mention it,' Cat Song said.

There wasn't any parking for blocks around the Leopard Lounge at

11:15 on a soft summer night like this one, when a Hollywood moon brought hordes of people out for revelry on the boulevards. Gil parked their black-and-white in a red zone on Sunset Boulevard and they walked south to the source of the call, a large apartment building with parking spaces in front.

The person reporting was a well-coiffed, well-dressed elderly woman who answered the door at the manager's office and said with a Russian accent, 'I'm Mrs. Vronsky. I'm the one who called.'

'Yes, ma'am,' Gil said.

'At this time of night I should be in bed, asleep,' she said, 'but if I go to sleep, I'll get woke up when my tenants come home and can't park. A man just pulled into space number two, and when I yelled at him, he said something ugly to me. Then after I called for you, he drove away.'

'Then there's nobody for us to cite at the moment,' Cat said. 'Call us if it happens again.'

'Do you know Officer Ramstead?' Mrs. Vronsky said. 'He's a friend of mine.'

'Community Relations Office?' Cat said.

'Yes, that's right,' Mrs. Vronsky said. 'He often comes by in the daytime and helps me with the parking problems. It's all because of the nightclub, you know.'

'Yes,' Cat said, 'we sympathize.'

'Officer Ramstead is a very kind man and he likes my homemade piroshki,' the old woman said. 'If I had some, I'd invite you in and pour you some tea, and you could taste it.'

'Some other time,' Cat said, giving Gil a look that said, Lonely old lady.

'Oh, look!' Mrs. Vronsky said. 'Another one.'

Sure enough, a four-year-old white Corvette that had been cruising slowly along the street, looking for parking, had wheeled into one of the vacant spaces in front of the apartment building. The driver of the car turned out the headlights but did not get out.

'We'll check this one,' Cat said, and both cops walked out to the front of the building.

'Come back when I have some piroshki!' Mrs. Vronsky called after them.

Gil Ponce was surprised to find a young woman sitting in the car when he walked up on the driver's side. A beautiful young woman who looked to be of mixed race, with dark Asian eyes. She jumped when he tapped on her window with his flashlight.

She lowered the window and said, 'Yes, Officer?' Then a beam shone along her dashboard and she saw Cat at the passenger window.

'Do you live here, ma'am?' Gil said.

'No, I don't,' she said. 'Is there a problem?'

'You're parking on private property in a resident's parking space,' Gil said, thinking that this girl was smokin' hot!

She blinked, smiled, and said, 'But Officer, I'm not parking. I just stopped here because there's no place on the street. I'm waiting for a car to leave a parking space at the Leopard Lounge. I work there.'

'May I see your driver's license and registration?'

Jasmine looked in her purse, retrieved her wallet, opened it, and said, 'Oh, crap! Today I bought some underwear at Victoria's Secret and paid by credit card. The girl asked for my driver's license too. I must've left my license and my Visa!'

'How about your registration?'

She handed it to Gil Ponce, who shined his light on it and said, 'Jasmine McVicker.'

'Yes,' she said, drumming nervously on the steering wheel, looking at her watch. It was 11:25 P.M.

'Do you have anything else that proves you're Jasmine McVicker?' Gil asked.

She said, 'I only have the one credit card. Look, Officer, you can walk across the street to the Leopard Lounge and anybody'll tell you I work there.'

Gil looked at Cat over the roof of the 'vette, and Cat gave a shrug that said, Your call.

The fact was, young Gil Ponce wanted to go inside the Leopard Lounge and see what an upscale titty bar looked like. He said, 'Let's find a place to park your car and see if you're who you say you are. If you are, I'll give you a warning for driving without a license but no ticket. Fair enough?'

Just then, Jasmine's cell phone rang and she grabbed it from her purse. Margot's voice came on in a whisper, saying, 'Showtime.'

Quickly Jasmine said, 'I'll be delayed. A very nice police officer has detained me for not having my driver's license.'

'Goddamnit!' Margot whispered. 'Get rid of him!'

'I'll be as quick as I can,' Jasmine said, clicking off. To Gil she said, 'Where do I park?'

'Right up at the corner, in the red zone,' Gil said. 'My partner can watch your car so you don't get a ticket while you and me run inside for a minute.'

'But then I'll have to come back out and move my car to some legal place before I can go back in again! I have to see one of the other dancers about something important and I'm late!'

'Better than getting a traffic citation, isn't it?' Gil said. Then he added, 'Are you really a dancer?'

Jasmine was desperate. If there hadn't been a woman cop with him, she'd have given him her address and offered him a late date. Anything to give her fifteen minutes of goddamn parking so she could do what she had to do!

'Okay, okay!' she said. 'But let's just leave my car here for two minutes and run across the street. Please, Officer, it'll save time!'

Gil shrugged at Cat, who gave a nod, having figured this one out. Cat had pumped up her young boot's sagging morale to the point where he wanted to stroll into the topless bar with this hottie and check out the other flesh onstage. And who knows? Maybe get Jasmine's phone number. They lose their innocence fast, these male rookies, Cat Song thought.

While Jasmine was locking her car, purse in hand, and Gil Ponce was making a mental list of cliché questions – such as how did such a beautiful girl end up dancing at the Leopard Lounge – Cat Song walked to their shop, opened the door, and listened for radio calls.

After they got inside the nightclub, it didn't take thirty seconds for Jasmine to wave one of the harried, perspiring bartenders to the end of the bar to identify her for Gil Ponce, who couldn't have cared less. He could barely hear the bartender over the erotic, pounding beat from Ali's $75,000 sound system, and he just nodded at everything the man shouted over the nightclub din. Actually, Gil Ponce was preoccupied, gaping at two dancers onstage, pole writhing under strobes, one of whom was Ali's stunning new star, Loxie Fox, her G-string studded with tightly folded $5 and $10 bills.

Cat Song snapped him out of it when she suddenly appeared behind him, saying in his ear, 'Excuse me, Officer Casanova. I'm so glad you got your mojo back, but I thought you might like to know, there's a hell of a pursuit coming our way from Rampart Division. Would you care to jump on it, or would you rather just sit this one out for a rainbow drink with an umbrella in it?'

Officer Gil Ponce raced out of the Leopard Lounge without asking for Jasmine McVicker's phone number. Without even saying good-bye to her.

Jasmine hurried to the dancers' bathroom and locked the door behind her. She opened her purse and grabbed the eyedrops she'd bought in a shop on La Brea. It supplied cosmetics to makeup artists working in film and television, drops that helped actors to cry their eyes out on cue. She poured them into both eyes, heeding Margot's admonition to 'make that mascara run.' When she was finished, her vision was so blurred she could hardly see her face in the mirror, but she knew she looked like hell. She was ready. Showtime.

Ali's office door was locked, and Jasmine figured he was counting the cash. On big nights like this one, he made numerous trips to the bar to retrieve large currency notes, replacing $100 bills with $50s, $20s, $10s, and lots of $5s, which was the smallest tip that customers offered in this upscale nightclub.

Jasmine knew that Ali arranged for private security pickups at the end of the night when the money pile in his safe grew too large. She'd seen that often enough. She also knew that the money he took in at the Leopard Lounge was greater than the IRS, or Margot, or God almighty, would ever know about. And that if Margot thought she was getting half of Ali's assets, she was kidding herself. Jasmine had informed Margot that she believed there was a safety deposit box, but she didn't know where. Margot told her to work on it.

Jasmine banged on the door frantically and yelled, 'Ali!'

'Who is there?' he called out.

'Jasmine! Open up!'

She knew he was looking through the peephole at her and then he opened the door, startled by her appearance.

'What has been happening to you?' Ali said, closing

the door and locking it. 'I thought you were having an ankle sprain?' He was looking weekend sharp, in one of his monogrammed white dress shirts and a charcoal gray Valentino suit, with black loafers.

Through a fluffy blur she could see that on the desktop there were stacks of currency. She ran to the client's chair and sat while Ali stood between her and the desk, instinctively guarding his money.

'I just left Margot!' she said, wiping the mascara from her face, looking up at him with eyes overflowing.

'What is happening?' he said.

'You told me to spy on her!' Jasmine said, trying to sob.

'Yes, yes!' he said. 'What is happening?'

'She's hoovering cocaine, Ali! She had lines laid out on her dressing table. There musta been three, four thousand bucks' worth of blow! I did one line, sort of, just so I could find out what's happening in that house.'

'What? Tell me!' he said.

'They wanted me to do a three-way,' Jasmine said. 'Her and him, but I told them no way. I told him I don't do kink. He was even more trashed than she was. I was scared of that guy!'

'Nicky!' he said frantically. 'Where is Nicky?'

'He was there,' she said.

'WHAT?'

It was so loud, she jerked back in the client chair, her head thumping against the tufted leather back.

'I tried to take her aside and talk sense to her. Him, he was just roaming in and out of the house in his Speedo. He'd jump in the pool and then he'd come inside and do a line. Then he'd jump in the pool and swim some more. He kept wanting her to swim, but I kept telling her it was too risky in her condition. I kept telling her to stay in her bedroom and go to sleep.'

Ali seemed to forget the money then. He walked around the desk and sat in his swivel chair. He pushed the stacks of currency aside and put his elbows on the desk and his face in his hands. In less than a minute his face was more tearstained than hers.

She worried then that he might be too devastated to act. She was trying to provoke unbridled rage, not debilitating grief. She said, 'Nicky wasn't right there when they were doing the lines. He was in his own bedroom.'

Ali wiped his eyes with the palms of his hands and said, 'Nicky has plenty energy. Nobody is going to keep Nicky in his bedroom.'

Deciding to use Nicky as the final card she'd play, Jasmine said, 'The guy's name is Lucas. He's a big, young guy, Margot's age. She met him at a nightclub on the Strip. I think the guy wants to take over Margot and her house, and he supplies her with coke.'

'Why is my son in the house tonight?' Ali said. 'Please tell me, Jasmine.'

'As much as I could find out, this is the way it's been ever since this guy entered the picture. He says she shouldn't waste her money on the nanny. He says the kid should stay at home like other kids.'

'Stay home?' Ali said, and she'd never heard him sound so bleak. 'Stay home to see his mommy like this? Sex, cocaine, and what more things?'

'I don't know if I should tell you more, Ali,' she said.

'Tell me, Jasmine,' he said. 'I beg you to tell me all. I must know.'

'Margot told me they been doing three-ways with other girls on a regular basis, with lots of coke to amp them up. And sometimes they do a lot more than that. Lucas brings girls and guys from the Strip and they all do cocaine, and then they all get weirded out and do one another. Anything they can think of.'

'And my Nicky,' Ali said. 'Where is my Nicky when these things happen?'

'From what I can tell, he's always in the house these days. I guess he's in his room when the really heavy stuff is going on. I don't think Margot would let him be in the bedroom when they start kinking it up. Unless he just walked in on it. I really can't say for sure, Ali. I'm sorry. I tried to find out as much as I could.'

'How many people are in the house tonight, Jasmine? Only Margot and this man?'

'Yeah, that's all there was when I left,' she said. 'But Lucas was talking about calling some friend on the Strip. He's a fucking animal and he's ripped.'

'You are a good friend to me,' Ali said. 'I thank you.'

'Are you gonna call your lawyer?' Jasmine said. 'I don't wanna get dragged before a judge. I'm telling you what's happening, but I'm not doing a deposition for some lawyer. I'm scared of that man Lucas. And I still gotta work in this town.'

'What good is a lawyer?' Ali said. 'Margot shall say you lie if we talk to my lawyer. She shall look and talk like the perfect mother when she sits down with the lawyer or the judge. Everybody looks at her and smiles. Beautiful mother.'

'I can't see what good it would do to call the cops either,' Jasmine said. 'They couldn't go in there and check on the kid unless they had a warrant or some kind of firsthand information. And I'm not talking to cops, Ali. You can fire me, but I'm not talking to cops or to lawyers. I did what you asked me to do and now I'm out of it. I want no more to do with your ex-wife and her twisted friend. I'm real scared.'

'Yes,' Ali said. 'I shall pay you the bonus. You are a good girl.'

She was losing him again. She had seen the rage rise and fall and rise again. Now it was ebbing. She'd given him too much to process. He was beaten down by it. He looked like he might start weeping and not stop. She was watching it slipping away. All the money she and Margot would share. It was time to play her last card: the ace of spades.

She said, 'There's something else, Ali. . . . No, never mind.'

Wearily he said, 'What? Tell me all, Jasmine. Please.'

'I don't know if I should. I don't have proof of anything, and there's nothing you can do about it anyways.'

He raised his eyes from his desk and looked up at her, his dark-rimmed eyes boring into hers. 'Tell me,' he said.

'Well, there was one point when I heard Nicky hollering for his mom. It's when Lucas was outside in the pool and I was in the bedroom with Margot, telling her she had to get herself together, that her son was calling for her.'

'Yes, yes?' he said, his voice pleading to hear, and not wanting to hear.

'She was too into the blow. I couldn't get through to her. Then I heard Lucas come from the pool. I heard him coming up the stairs. I heard him walk down the hall to Nicky's room. I peeked out and saw him, wearing only the Speedo, open Nicky's door and go in and close it behind him.'

'Oh, God!' Ali said. And then he began murmuring in Arabic. Jasmine guessed it was a Muslim prayer. After a few seconds he stopped.

'I'm not saying anything terrible happened in there, Ali,' Jasmine said. 'But he was in there for quite a while. Maybe ten minutes. Maybe longer. When he came out, Nicky wasn't yelling anymore.'

'Then you did *what?*' Ali demanded.

And there was no doubt about it. This was pure rage. He was scaring her. She said, 'Ali, I did what I could! When that man went into Margot's bathroom, I ran down the hall to Nicky's room and I opened the door and looked in.'

'He is okay?' Ali said. 'Please, Jasmine. My Nicky is okay?'

'The room was dark and he was under the covers, crying. I said his name but he wouldn't come out from under the covers. He knows me, but he wouldn't come out. Then I had to leave him because Lucas was out of the bathroom, asking Margot where I went. I ran back into the bedroom and said good night to both of them and came here as fast as I could.'

Ali's fists were clenched so tightly the knuckles were white as bone. He began to rise from his chair, and if he had been looking directly at her, she would have run for the door in fright. He said, 'Thank you, Jasmine.'

'Are you going there, Ali?' she said. 'Oh, I'm afraid. It could be dangerous for you!'

'And for Nicky,' he said quietly.

Jasmine stood and said, 'Are you taking your bouncer with you? You could, but it might trigger a confront-ation.'

'Thank you,' Ali said, walking stiff-legged toward the door. 'I must go there in peace. Alone. I shall only demand to see my son. If they do violence on me, I shall have a reason to call the police.'

'Wait!' she shouted, and it caused him to stop. 'You can't go there like that. Take your gun with you.'

Ali said, 'I do not threaten nobody. I shall take my son away. Nobody is going to stop me.'

'But, Ali!' Jasmine said frantically. 'You can't do it unarmed! That man is big and creepy and young. He won't let you take Nicky. He'll hurt you bad. Maybe Nicky too. Maybe you won't even be able to call the police. Then what? Take the gun as protection for *both* of you. Just in case of emergency!'

Ali stood motionless, then returned to his desk and unlocked a lower drawer and, removing a .32 caliber, semiautomatic pistol, put it inside the waistband of his trousers. And then Ali Aziz did the most amazing thing that Jasmine had ever seen him do. He walked out the door, leaving her in the office with the desktop stacked with money. She went to the door and spoke to him as he was walking down the passageway.

She said, 'I had a feeling it would come to this if I told you everything, Ali. So when I went out Margot's front door, I took off the knob lock. And they were both too ripped to have set the burglar alarm. You can just walk in, Ali. But for God's sake, be careful!'

He never turned around but said, 'Thank you, Jasmine. You are a good girl.'

When she was sure Ali was gone, Jasmine ran back inside his office and scooped all of the money from the desktop into her purse.

TWENTY-ONE

IT HAD BEEN an uneventful night for 6-X-66, but that was okay with them. Lately, they'd had enough of what Hollywood cops called Star Wars Nights to last awhile. The pursuit of an ice-cream truck ending up as a shooting in the Hollywood cemetery, along with the Somalian woman who'd been painted white, had practically given them carpal tunnel by the time they got through writing all of the reports.

They'd just handled a call that had taken them out of their area and into the Hollywood Hills. It hadn't amounted to much, only a jittery resident worrying about a parked car on Laurel Canyon Boulevard that turned out to belong to a neighbor's nephew visiting from Montana. Gert Von Braun and Doomsday Dan Applewhite were on their way down the canyon, Gert driving, when they saw a Jaguar make a hard right turn onto the lovely tree-lined road leading up to Mt. Olympus.

'That guy almost rolled it,' Dan said.

'Let's check him out,' said Gert.

She whipped a left and floored it, turning on her light bar. In a moment, the black-and-white had closed on the Jaguar, which pulled over in front of a palatial home halfway up the hill.

Ali Aziz was in the crisis of his life. If the police got him out of his car and spotted the pistol inside his belt, he'd no doubt be arrested for carrying the concealed weapon, even though he had legally purchased the gun several years ago at a gun shop. If he put the loaded pistol on the seat, he'd still have a lot of explaining to do and perhaps be taken to Hollywood Station for further investigation. If he tried to hide it under the seat and they noticed it, he'd be arrested for certain.

In that fateful moment, he even considered telling them the terrible things that Jasmine had said and asking them to accompany him to his home. But he knew that would end with Margot reassuring the cops that everything was fine and that they were in a bitter divorce and custody fight. And the cops would tell him to go home and speak with his lawyer and to the appropriate detectives in the morning. He had learned from experience how the laws of this country worked against people who were trying to do what is right. And in the meantime his son would be left in his bed, weeping in terror, and perhaps from unspeakable harm done to him.

Ali didn't have time and couldn't risk it. He decided in that brief moment to get his emotions under control and to run the bluff of his lifetime. Ali Aziz willed a small smile onto his face when the burly woman cop came up on his side of the car while her male partner stood at the passenger side, shining his light in the window.

'In a hurry, are we, sir?' Gert said.

'I am so sorry, Officer,' Ali said. 'I am Ali Aziz,

proprietor of the Leopard Lounge on Sunset Boulevard. I am in big hurry to the house of my ex-wife to collect my son.'

He gingerly reached into his coat pocket for his wallet while both cops shined their flashlight beams on his left hand. He prayed to God that they would not spot the gun when he removed his license for Gert. He also removed business cards bearing the name of the Hollywood Station captain as well as one from the division captain.

'I am always first to give plenty of my time to the Community Police Advisory Board,' he said. 'I give always donations to the holiday party for children. Everyone knows Ali.'

'Just curious,' Gert said. 'Why're you picking up your son at this time of night? Won't he be asleep?'

'Yes, you are correct,' Ali said. 'I work late at the nightclub and this is how I must do. Nicky is going to sleep in my car when I drive with him to my condo.'

Gert Von Braun didn't like his plastered-on smile and she didn't like the beads of sweat forming at his hairline. Her blue antenna was sending signals, but the address on his license was up the hill near the top of Mt. Olympus, and everything he said made sense. She looked over the roof of the Jaguar to Dan Applewhite, who shrugged.

'Drive more carefully when you have your son in the car, Mr. Aziz,' she said, handing Ali back his license.

'Yes, yes, Officer,' Ali said. 'I shall drive with great care.'

When the cops returned to their black-and-white, Ali drove slowly up the hill to the house on Mt. Olympus.

*   *   *

Margot had received the two-ring warning call from Jasmine twenty five minutes earlier. It meant that Ali was on his way. The go phone was on vibrate and she didn't need to answer it. She had been seated naked on the chair in the darkened master bedroom, on the opposite side of the king-size bed in which Bix Ramstead slept. She got up, went to his side of the bed, and removed his pistol from the holster on the nightstand. She walked back around the bed and out to the terrace through the sliding door that she'd kept open. After she got to the railing, she looked out into the canyon and hurled the throwaway phone into the brush below.

She walked softly to her walk-in closet for a robe and laid it across the chair. But she would not put it on. Bix had last seen her naked, not that he'd remember. Then she sat back down on the chair and waited for the sound of a car in front.

Ali Aziz parked in the driveway rather than on the street in case he had to get away fast with his son in one hand and a gun in the other. He closed the door of the Jaguar quietly and walked to Margot's door, grateful that the security lights in the garden had not been turned on but there was moonlight. He looked up at the bright, glowing moon.

The door was unlocked and Ali blessed Jasmine for it. He entered, leaving the door open for his fast exit. He'd decided to go straight to Nicky's room, take him out of bed, and run with him down the stairs and out. Tomorrow, he and his lawyer, with Jasmine's help – and she would help when he offered her $25,000 – would go to the police, as well as to the judge who'd presided over their divorce proceedings. And if there was any justice at all, he would never have to return Nicky to her again. He prayed that the drug-dealing monster had not harmed his son.

There was a light on. The lamp at the top of the staircase on a marble table under the huge mirror that had cost him a fortune. He ascended, turned left, and crept along the hallway to Nicky's room, finding the door wide open. He stepped inside, but the bed was made and Nicky was gone! What had they done with him? He returned along the hall to the master bedroom. Could Nicky be in bed with them? The double doors were wide open. He adjusted the gun inside his belt so that it was more accessible. A few more quiet steps and he'd be through the double doorway into the master bedroom.

He stood in the doorway. He could hear faint snoring, but it was very dark. He took another step forward. There was only one person lying there, sleeping on what he knew to be her side of the bed. Was it Margot? Was she alone in the bedroom? Where was the man? Where was Nicky? He was confused. He took another step inside. And another, his pupils adjusting to the darkness. And then he heard the loudest shout he had ever heard from the lips of Margot Aziz.

'ALI, DON'T SHOOT! PLEASE DON'T SHOOT! DON'T SHOOT!'

'What?' he said. 'What? Margot?'

And Ali Aziz saw three fireballs and perhaps heard three explosions, but perhaps not. He was slammed down onto his back by the fireballs. It was a tight pattern fired from a distance of four feet after Margot stepped from behind the closet door and stood between Ali and the bed, crouching slightly and firing two-handed, just as the instructor had shown her at the pistol range. Ali's chest heaved and began leaking blood, then bubbled from an arterial spurt. His heart stopped almost instantly, pierced by one of the 9-millimeter rounds.

The explosions that smashed Ali Aziz to the floor also brought Bix Ramstead onto the floor, feet first. He leaped from bed and stumbled to his knees, not knowing where he was.

'Bix! Bix!' Margot screamed. 'The lights! Turn on the lights!'

But Bix didn't know where the lights were. Bix was trying to decide where *he* was, and he wasn't even sure who was yelling his name. He saw a lamp and reached for it but knocked it from the nightstand.

Margot Aziz did not want light. She had dropped Bix's pistol onto the floor and, with tissue in her left hand, was feeling around Ali's waist and in his pockets. But there was no gun! Where was the fucking gun? Working frantically in the darkness, she managed to get her hand under him but it wasn't there either! Then she accidentally touched his crotch and felt hard metal inside. The gun had slipped down inside his briefs when he'd fallen.

Bix Ramstead figured out that he was in the bedroom of Margot Aziz, and he yelled, 'Margot! Where are you! Where's the light switch!'

She saw him lurching naked toward the open doorway, toward the lamp outside, just as she got her hand down inside Ali's crotch and worked the gun up and out, using the sheets of tissue between her fingers and the steel. She picked up the pistol and placed it beside Ali's outstretched right hand.

Margot wadded the tissue in her left hand and, putting her right hand on Ali's bloody chest, smeared some blood on her own chest and cheek for dramatic effect, screaming, 'Ali! Ali! Bix, I think he's dead!'

Bix Ramstead found the wall switch by the door, turned on the bedroom lights, and said, 'Get away from him! Don't touch him!'

Margot stood up, put her bloody hand to her face, and screamed, 'He's dead! Ali's dead! Oh, dear God!'

Bix Ramstead swayed and scrutinized the scene in horror, saying, 'Where's my clothes? Where's my goddamn clothes?'

'Ali!' Margot screamed, running into the bathroom, kneeling at the toilet, and making gagging sounds, while Bix found his clothes in the closet and picked up the telephone that had fallen onto the floor beside the bed.

When Margot heard him making the call, she stopped gagging and put the tissues in the toilet and flushed them away. When she came out, Bix was talking to the watch commander at Hollywood Station.

Margot washed Ali's blood from her hands but not from her face or chest. She went to the closet and put on suitable pajamas, a full-length satin robe, and bedroom slippers. Then she walked toward Nicky's room to sit and prepare herself for the questioning.

The last words she would ever speak to Bix Ramstead were uttered when he was downstairs in the foyer, waiting in the doorway for the arrival of police. She was upstairs, standing at the railing outside Nicky's room, and she looked down at him.

'You were right, Bix,' she said. 'We were very bad for each other. But I want you to know that I'd rather he'd killed me tonight than see you brought into this horrible nightmare. I'm very, very sorry.'

The call was given to 6-A-15 of Watch 3, the morning watch, but when midwatch unit 6-X-66 heard the location, Gert Von Braun said to Dan Applewhite, 'Hey, that's the address that was on that guy's driver's license!'

When midwatch unit 6-X-46 heard it, Jetsam said to Flotsam, 'Bro, that's the house on Mount Olympus!'

Soon there were four black-and-whites parked on the street in front, one of them belonging to the watch commander. And Bix Ramstead was standing on the porch in front of the house, telling them not to come inside but to keep the street clear for the coroner's van, criminalists from Scientific Investigation Division, and the two Hollywood homicide teams that were coming from home. Only a successful telephonic argument by the area captain, who said that this incident should be contained as much as possible, kept Robbery-Homicide detectives downtown from being called out, as they often are in high-profile cases. With an LAPD cop involved, this was very high profile.

The surfer cops stood in the driveway, and Jetsam looked up at the moon illuminating the tile roof on the two-story house. For a few seconds, cobwebs of cloud floated across that dazzling white ball high in the velvety black sky over Hollywood.

And Jetsam said to his partner, 'The Oracle would have told us to beware tonight. There's a Hollywood moon up there. And bro, this fucking house is *full* of bad juju.'

TWENTY-TWO

FLOTSAM SAID TO JETSAM, 'One of the corpse cops just arrived.'

Hollywood homicide D2, Albino Villaseñor, was the first detective to arrive from home. He parked on the street and emerged from the car with a plastic briefcase and a flashlight, wearing the same brown Men's Wearhouse suit that he'd worn every time Flotsam had seen him.

His bald head glinted under the luminescence provided by the Hollywood moon, and his white mustache looked wild and feline from his having slept facedown in bed. He nodded to the surfer cops and plodded toward the arched doorway in no particular hurry to see another of the multitude of dead bodies he'd seen during his long career.

He turned toward the street when a white van with a TV news logo on the door climbed the steep street and parked as near as it could get to the driveway. And close behind it was a news van from another Los Angeles TV station. The toney Mt. Olympus address on the police band was drawing them from their beds.

After the detective was inside the foyer, Flotsam said to Jetsam, 'Dude, do you think a homicide dick gets a secret high when someone else gets laid low? Wouldn't that, like, give you the guilts?'

'It'd creep me out, bro,' Jetsam said. 'And it looks like there's gonna be an opening in the Crow office, for sure.'

By this time, the forensics van had arrived and criminalists wearing latex gloves and booties were in the bedroom, treating the situation like a full-scale murder investigation, even though Bino Villaseñor had been informed by the patrol watch commander that the only crime committed had been perpetrated by the decedent. But with an LAPD cop even peripherally involved, great investigative care was to be taken, per orders from the West Bureau deputy chief. Just in case things turned out to be more dicey than they seemed.

'Here come the body snatchers,' Flotsam said when the coroner's van was waved into the driveway by one of the morning watch officers who'd received the original call.

When Bino Villaseñor got inside, he found Dan Applewhite in the kitchen with Bix Ramstead, who sat staring at his coffee cup, eyes red and ravaged.

The detective, who did not know the Crow personally, nodded at him. Bino Villaseñor, speaking in the lilting cadence of the East Los Angeles barrio where he'd grown up, said to Bix, 'Soon as somebody else from our homicide team arrives, I'd like them to take you to the station. I'll get down there as soon as I can.'

Bix Ramstead nodded and continued to stare. The detective had seen it before: the unnerving, hopeless look into the abyss.

The detective said to another of the morning-watch cops standing in the foyer by the staircase, 'Where's the lady of the house?'

'Up in one of the bedrooms to your left,' the cop said. 'She's with a woman officer from the midwatch.'

Bino Villaseñor climbed the stairs to the upper floor, looked in the master bedroom where lights had been set up, and did not enter while the criminalists were at work, but he could see that blood had drenched the carpet under Ali's body. The detective turned left and walked to Nicky's bedroom, where he found Margot Aziz, still in pajamas and robe, dried blood on her cheek and chest, sitting on the bed, apparently weeping into a handful of tissues. He didn't know the burly female officer with her, but he indicated with a motion of his head that she could leave. Gert Von Braun walked out of the bedroom and down the stairs.

'I'm Detective Villaseñor, Mrs. Aziz,' he said to Margot. 'We might need you to come to the station for a more formal statement, but I have a few preliminary questions I'd like to ask.'

'Of course,' Margot said. 'I'll tell you whatever I can.'

Bino looked around the huge bedroom, at the mountain of toys and gadgets and picture books and the biggest TV set he'd ever seen in a child's bedroom, and he said, 'Where is your son?'

'He's spending the night with my au pair,' she said. 'That's why I ... well, that's why Bix and I ... you know.'

'How long have you and Officer Ramstead been

intimate?' the detective asked, sitting on a chair in front of a PlayStation and opening his notebook folder.

'For about five months.' She almost said 'on and off' but realized how inappropriate that would sound and said, 'More or less.'

'Do you often sleep together here?'

'This is the first time we've ever slept together anywhere. On the other occasions we went to hotels for brief interludes.'

'Tell me what happened after you and Officer Ramstead went to sleep.'

'I heard a noise.'

'What kind of noise?'

'Ali's car. The window was open and I heard it, but of course I didn't know it was him. It could have been someone visiting next door. There's a Russian man living there who gets visitors at all hours.'

'What'd you do then?'

'I've been frightened for some time about my husband. He's irrational . . . *was* irrational. He hated me and wanted to take my son from me any way he could. I've told my lawyer, William T. Goodman, numerous times about threats my husband made. I can give you my lawyer's phone number.'

'Later,' the detective said. 'Did you tell anyone else about the threats? Did you report the threats to the police?'

'I tried to,' she said. 'I told it to Officer Nate Weiss of the Community Relations Office, and Sergeant Treakle, and Detective Fernandez, and of course Bix Ramstead.'

That surprised Bino Villaseñor, who said, 'Did any

of the officers talk to you about making a police report against your husband for making terroristic threats?'

'Nobody seemed to think the threats were explicit enough to qualify as a crime. Everyone seemed convinced that a successful businessman like Ali Aziz wouldn't do anything irrational. But I knew he was an insanely jealous and dangerous man, especially where our son was concerned. I knew he'd eventually try to steal Nicky from me. What I didn't know was that he was insane enough to come here to murder me.'

'How'd he get in? Did he still have a key?'

'Not that I know of,' she said. 'I changed the locks when he turned vicious during our divorce and custody battles.'

'How about the alarm? Didn't you change the code when he moved out?'

'Yes,' she said, 'but . . . sorry, it's hard to talk about.'

'Take your time,' the detective said.

'I'm ashamed. So ashamed. But the truth is, Bix and I were drinking quite a lot. He drank a lot more than I did, and I had to practically carry him up the stairs. And, well, we made love. We were both exhausted. I simply could not get up again to set the alarm. I dozed off. I don't know, maybe I felt secure with a police officer . . . with Bix in bed with me. I'd forgotten that the front door was unlocked.'

'Why was it unlocked? Doesn't it have a self-locking latch on it?'

'Yes, but Bix unlatched it when he went out to his car to get something.'

'To get what?'

'His gun.'

'He went outside to get his gun? Why?'

'I wanted to buy a gun as protection, and I needed to know how things like the safety button work. I asked Bix to show me. You see, I was convinced that Ali might snap one of these days. And apparently he did.'

She could see that the detective was very interested now. He'd stopped making notes. He looked her in the eye and said, 'Let's go back to where you heard the car in the driveway. What did you do?'

'I tried to wake Bix. I poked him. I called his name. He wouldn't budge. He was out cold, snoring. He was *very* drunk when we went to bed.'

'Then?'

'Then I crept to the landing and looked down and I was almost sure I heard the front door creaking on its hinges. And I ran back in the bedroom and shook Bix and said his name, but it was no use. Bix's gun and keys and wallet were on the nightstand. I took his gun out of the holster. You have no idea how terrified I was.'

'And then?' the detective said, and his dark eyes under wiry white eyebrows were penetrating.

'Then I didn't know what to do!'

'Did you try to phone nine-one-one?'

'There wasn't time! I could hear his footsteps on the stairs! He was coming fast! I was panicked!'

'Then?'

'I ducked behind the closet door! He came in the room! He had the gun in his hand! He was walking toward the bed with the gun pointed! I thought he was going to shoot Bix! I leaped out and I got between him and Bix and I yelled! I yelled, "Ali, don't shoot!

Please don't shoot! Don't shoot!" But he turned and pointed the gun at me and I fired!'

She buried her face in tissues then, said, 'Excuse me,' and got up and ran into Nicky's bathroom, where he heard her turn on the water in the sink.

When she returned, the dried blood was no longer on her cheek and chest, and she said, 'I'm sorry. I was feeling nauseous. And I didn't know there was blood on me till I looked in the mirror just now. I guess I knelt beside him. I don't even remember that. You'll have to ask Bix what happened then. I don't think I fainted, but I just have no memory of what happened after I fired.'

'How many times did you fire?' the detective asked.

'I don't know.'

'Had you ever fired a handgun before?'

'Yes, in the Valley at a gun shop. I went there thinking about buying a gun because of Ali. I took a shooting lesson and decided I'd ask Bix about which gun I should buy. I can give you the name of the gun shop. I have it downstairs in my phone file.'

'Is there anyone else you told about the threats your husband made against you?'

'I don't have any close girlfriends to confide in. My entire life involves taking care of my son. Let's see, other than the police officers I named . . .' Then she said, 'Yes, two more police officers.'

'Who're they?'

'The ones who came the night Sergeant Treakle was here. I thought I heard footsteps outside on the walkway between my property and my neighbor's. I felt sure it was Ali, but the officers looked around and couldn't find anything. You can get their names from Sergeant Treakle at Hollywood Station.'

The detective cocked an eyebrow, closed his notebook, and said, 'Speaking of Hollywood Station, I think it would be helpful if you would come down to the station now for a few more questions and a more formal statement.'

'Are you accusing me of something?' she said.

'No, it's just routine,' the detective said.

'I can't possibly go there,' Margot said. 'I've been through a great trauma. As soon as your people are out of my house, I've got to have my au pair bring Nicky home. There's a lot for me to do, as you can imagine. I'll be here at my house to help you any way I can, but I won't go to the police station unless my lawyer agrees to it and goes with me. And that would happen only after I get some sleep. I'm exhausted.'

'I see,' Bino Villaseñor said, studying her more closely than ever.

A sergeant from Watch 3 told 6-X-66 that one of his morning-watch units would take over, and the midwatch team could go end-of-watch. While 6-X-66 was heading back to Hollywood Station, Gert Von Braun said to Dan Applewhite, 'I wish we'd pulled that guy outta his Jaguar. Maybe we'd have found the gun.'

'We had no probable cause,' Dan said. 'His driver's license had the Mount Olympus address on it, and his registration too. It all checked out.'

'I almost always make a guy get out when it's late at night to see if he's DUI. Maybe I got intimidated because he was a big-bucks guy from the Hollywood Hills, with lots of LAPD business cards in his wallet.'

'Gert, he wasn't DUI. He was cold sober.'

'Maybe we shoulda written him a ticket.'

'That woulda delayed what happened by ten minutes, is all.'

'I don't feel good about the way we handled it.'

'Look, Gert,' Dan said, 'that guy was determined to kill his wife and he got what he deserved. Stop beating yourself up.'

'It's not him I'm thinking about. It's that Crow, Bix Ramstead. How well do you know him?'

'I've seen him around for years, but I never worked partners with him,' Dan Applewhite said.

'He's through, for sure,' Gert said.

'Bix Ramstead made his choices, just like Ali Aziz,' Dan said. 'What happened to both those guys has nothing to do with you and me.'

'I guess so,' Gert said. 'But I don't feel right about it.'

'We're off tomorrow,' Dan Applewhite reminded her. 'So how about doing a Hollywood thing? How about going with me to one of those old movies I told you about? Maybe one starring Tyrone Power. If you wouldn't mind going out with a geezer.'

'You're not so old,' she said.

It was still an hour from sunrise when Bino Villaseñor was seated across the table from Bix Ramstead in one of the interview rooms at the Hollywood detectives' squad room. They had talked for forty-five minutes uninterrupted, all of it recorded.

Bix Ramstead's eyes seemed sunken in their sockets. He still had the unsettling stare when he wasn't directly answering a question, what the detective called 'the stare of despair.' His mouth was dry and gluey, and when he spoke, the dryness made his lips pop.

Bino Villaseñor said, 'You must need a cold drink bad. And so do I.'

The detective left the interview room for several minutes, and Bix put his head down on his arms and closed his eyes, seeing strange images flashing in his mind. When the door opened again, Bix could hear voices outside talking quietly.

Bino Villaseñor put two cold sodas in front of Bix, who was dehydrated from so much alcohol. Bix popped one open and drank it down, then the other. The detective sipped at his and watched Bix Ramstead.

'Is that better?'

Bix nodded.

'We've pretty much covered it,' the detective said, 'unless you have any more to offer.'

Bix took a deep breath and said, 'No. To summarize: I was stinking blind drunk and I don't remember much of anything after going upstairs. I did hear her yelling "Don't shoot." I'm sure of that much. And I damn sure heard the shots. And I saw him dead on the floor, or seconds from death, with blood gushing from chest wounds, and a gun by his hand. Nothing could've saved him. I did not talk to Margot about anything after that and did not contaminate the scene in any way. I told her to sit in her son's room until police arrived. I went downstairs and waited. And I'd give my right arm or both of them if I could set the clock back to seven last night, when I decided I could handle one shot of vodka.'

'Okay, Bix,' Bino Villaseñor said. 'I believe you.'

Bix looked up then, the first time the detective could see some life in his eyes, and he said, 'Don't you believe *her?*'

'I guess I'll have to,' the detective said. 'The stories fit like a glove. A latex glove. But I'll always wonder about a few things. That woman told no less than half a dozen cops from Hollywood Station and Hollywood South that her husband was threatening her. She may as well have made a video for YouTube entitled *My Husband Wants Me Dead.* She even took a shooting lesson and wanted to buy a gun. And finally, she managed to get the greatest corroboration in the world. A veteran married police officer, with nothing to gain and everything to lose, was right there as a witness to the event.'

Bix looked at the detective and said gravely, 'Do you actually think we conspired to murder her husband?'

'No, I don't think *you* conspired with anybody,' the detective said. 'You wouldn't be dumb enough to put yourself right in the bedroom during a capital murder. There'd be lots better ways for you to get it done. But buddy, you *were* dumb enough to destroy your career. Yet I got this very uneasy feeling about a woman who manages to get her boyfriend in bed for the first time on the very night that her husband decides to murder her in her sleep.'

'I'm not her boyfriend,' Bix said.

'What are you, then?'

'I don't know what I am anymore,' Bix Ramstead said. 'Are we through here?'

'We're through, except that Internal Affairs is outside, waiting to get at you next.'

Bix gave the detective a bitter smile then and said, 'Why would I bother to talk to IA? As you've pointed out, my career is over. My pension is lost. My children will be seeing this filthy story on the news. Their classmates will ask them humiliating questions. And my wife, she . . .'

He stopped there and Bino Villaseñor said, 'You're not gonna talk to them?'

Bix took his badge and ID card from his badge holder, put them on the table, and said, 'You talk to them.'

Bino looked in those despairing eyes and instantly thought of the Behavioral Science Services shrink. 'Okay, Bix, screw IA. But there's a couple of news teams outside, waiting to jump all over you. How about letting me call the BSS guy for you? You need to talk to somebody right now, buddy.'

Bix said, 'No, I have to go home now and feed Annie.'

Before the detective could say anything further, Bix Ramstead stood and walked out the door of the interview room, out of the detectives' squad room, and out the front door of the station, toward his minivan in the north lot, where the surfer cops had driven it.

He hadn't gotten to the parking lot when one of the on-scene reporters, a tall guy with a full head of flaxen hair, wearing light foundation that had smudged the collar of his starched white shirt, leaped from a van, holding a mike. He ran after Bix Ramstead with a camera operator trailing behind.

Bix looked around for a moment until he spotted where the surfer cops had parked his van and was halfway to it when the reporter caught up with him, saying, 'Officer Ramstead! Officer Ramstead! Can you tell us how long you and Margot Aziz have been lovers?'

Bix ignored him and kept walking.

The reporter matched him stride for stride and said, 'Do you and Mrs. Aziz have future plans?'

Bix ignored him and kept walking.

The reporter said, 'Have you phoned your wife about this yet? Have you spoken to your children?'

Bix ignored him and kept walking.

As they reached Bix's minivan, the reporter asked the ultimate cliché question that Bix Ramstead had personally heard a hundred media hacks ask victims at terrible events.

The reporter said, 'How do you feel right now?'

And that got Bix Ramstead's attention. He turned and said, 'How do *you* feel right now?' And he swung a roundhouse right that caught the reporter on the side of the jaw, knocking him back against the camera operator and sending them both sprawling onto the asphalt of the parking lot.

As Bix was driving away, the reporter picked himself up and yelled, 'Man, you are *really* in trouble now!'

It was late morning by the time Bix got home. The killing of Ali Aziz had happened too late to make the morning newspaper, but he was certain it would've been on the morning TV news. He had feared that his brother might be waiting for him.

When he unlocked the door, Annie ran from the bedroom and leaped on him with energy he hadn't thought she had at her age. She was bursting with joyful whimpers, licking him and bouncing like a puppy. He knelt down and held her in his arms and said, 'Oh, Annie, I didn't feed you last night. I'm sorry. I'm so sorry!'

Then Bix sat down on the floor, his face in Annie's fur, his arms around her neck, and wept.

When he was able to get up, Bix ignored the flashing on his answering machine. Instead, he went to the kitchen and prepared a huge breakfast for Annie, giving her two hard-boiled eggs, several ounces of boiled chicken breast, and her kibble. He mixed some nonfat cottage cheese in the bowl and put it down on the kitchen floor.

While Annie's face was buried in the food, he walked out the back door and filled her water bowl to the brim. But while he was doing it, he heard the flap in the doggy door open, and Annie poked her head out to make sure he wasn't leaving her again.

'Oh, Annie,' he said. 'I'm here.'

Then Bix went back inside, and Annie returned happily to her breakfast while he entered his son's bedroom. Bix looked at a baseball trophy and at photos of Patrick playing ball with Annie when she was a pup, and one of Patrick graduating from middle school. Then he entered his daughter's room and picked up a photo of Janie and his wife, Darcey, sitting side by side on the piano bench. He couldn't remember what they were playing when he'd taken the photo and he was surprised to see that Janie had inherited her mother's lips. How had he never noticed that before?

He entered their bedroom then, his and Darcey's. She'd never liked the photo of her when she was pregnant with Janie, but he loved that photo for the serenity in her face. He was very glad that his daughter's features favored Darcey and not himself.

Bix opened the closet door and reached on the high shelf, back behind a pair of hiking boots he wore whenever they went camping. He opened a zipper case and removed his off-duty gun, a two-inch stainless-steel revolver. When he got to the kitchen, he saw that Annie had cleaned the bowl, so he opened the refrigerator and put all of the remaining chicken into the bowl along with more kibble and cottage cheese.

He went to the wall phone and called the LAPD emergency number, got a PSR on the line, and gave his name and address. He asked that a patrol unit be sent code 2. Then he opened the front door quietly, not wanting Annie to see him leaving again. He walked to the front yard and took the revolver from his pocket.

When Annie heard the gunshot she stopped eating. She ran to the living room and looked out the window. Then she bolted through the doggy door into the backyard and ran along the side of the house to the chain-link fence that prevented her from going into the front yard. She stood up on the fence with her front paws until she could clearly see him lying on the grass.

Then Annie started howling. She was still howling when the first black-and-white arrived.

TWENTY-THREE

H E'D FALLEN ASLEEP watching TV and awoke feeling
like Rosie O'Donnell was sitting on his head. He
had a humongous headache when he got up that
morning. He was looking for something to blame it
on besides the two pipeloads of rock he'd smoked,
and all those 40s he'd guzzled. Then he remembered
those little capsules that Ali Aziz had given him. He
vaguely recalled popping two of them before he passed
out.

Leonard Stilwell turned on the TV, since he couldn't
stand silence, and began drinking ice water. After that
he drank a glass of orange juice before going back for
more water. He'd never been so thirsty in his life and
his head was killing him. It had to have been the
sleeping meds. Leonard opened the drawer of the
lopsided chest of drawers that contained two pots, a
frying pan, two dinner dishes, a bowl, a few knives,
forks, spoons, socks, some underwear, and two clean
T-shirts. On top of the T-shirts he found the envelope
with the magenta-and-turquoise capsules.

He should've known better than to use anything that
fucking Ay-rab had given him. He took the envelope
into his tiny bathroom and dumped the remaining

capsules into the toilet. It took two tries to get them all flushed away.

When he came back into the kitchen, one of the local morning news anchors, a hottie whose heavily penciled eyebrows were used as emphasis, was talking about a killing. Leonard felt like adjusting the TV vertical to keep those bouncing fucking eyebrows in one place. When he turned up the volume to hear if for once she had something sensible to say, he heard 'Ali Aziz.' Then she went on to the next story.

'Holy shit!' Leonard said, switching to every other local channel. But the news was either over or somebody was talking about some horrible fucking recipe you couldn't get Junior the Fijian giant to choose in place of a bowl of cockroaches.

He quickly got dressed, took four aspirins, and ran downstairs to his car, driving a couple of blocks to a residential street where he could steal an *L.A. Times*. Then he drove back to his apartment and looked all through the newspaper, but he saw nothing about Ali Aziz. He turned on a local channel again and saw an LAPD spokesperson just winding up his brief statement on the suicide of some LAPD cop and the fatal shooting of nightclub owner Ali Aziz by his former wife, who'd been mixed up romantically with the dead cop.

The first thing that Leonard Stilwell thought was, There goes my chance at another Ali Aziz shakedown! The second thing he thought was, How can I make a buck from this by telling the rich widow that Ali bugged her house? The answer was obvious: He couldn't. Not without revealing his own part in it. And he'd seen enough of Hollywood jail.

Leonard Stilwell told himself to look on the bright side. He had ten grand plus. He had the stake he needed to get out of crime and go into the business he'd been contemplating. Still, it was a goddamn shame that the hotheaded Ay-rab had to get himself smoked like that just because some cop was porking his old lady. It was the only time in his life that Leonard Stilwell had found himself right in the middle of a big-time soap opera, and he couldn't figure out how to squeeze a fucking dime out of it!

Late that morning, Detective Bino Villaseñor had nearly completed his reports and was eager to go home, when he got the word that Officer Bix Ramstead had shot himself. Everything changed in an instant. Both the area captain and station captain were in meetings with the West Bureau commander. And the detective knew without a doubt that this thing was going to be discussed with the chief of police himself before Bino Villaseñor ever slept in his own bed.

The detective called the law offices of William T. Goodman, Esq., and was politely told that Mr. Goodman's client Margot Aziz would be making no further comment to anyone unless compelled to do so by court order. Mr. Goodman said that he would accept any subpoena pertaining to this terrible tragedy on behalf of his client at any time in the future.

At 2 P.M. that day, after spokespersons for the chief of police had been badgered and hounded by reporters, Detective Villaseñor found himself in a conference room on the sixth floor at Parker Center with police brass and representatives from the district attorney's office.

Bino Villaseñor had been preparing himself for this meeting all day and had expected dozens, if not hundreds, of detailed questions. But by the time he arrived, all of them had already read his reports and seemed satisfied. The questions were few.

A deputy district attorney said, 'Detective Villaseñor, is there any doubt in your mind that Officer Bix Ramstead was *not* part of a plot to murder Mr. Ali Aziz?'

'No doubt whatsoever,' the detective said. 'In my opinion, he killed himself out of shame and remorse. The officer had lost everything and couldn't face the disgrace he'd caused to himself and especially to his family.'

The deputy district attorney said, 'Is there any doubt in your mind that Mrs. Margot Aziz did not plot to murder Mr. Ali Aziz?'

Bino Villaseñor looked around then at all that brass, everyone expectant. And he said, 'If this was a setup and Officer Ramstead was a fall guy needed for corroboration, only Margot Aziz knows how she pulled it off. Getting Bix Ramstead in that bedroom for the first time might not have been so tough, but getting Ali Aziz in there with his own registered gun in his hand and murder on his mind, well, I just can't imagine how she coulda timed it so well. I'm real sorry that Officer Ramstead is dead, but her story and Bix Ramstead's story are the same story. And every employee of the Leopard Lounge who was there last night has been contacted today. Including a dancer named Jasmine McVicker who popped in the door for a few minutes to have her identity verified for a midwatch unit. And nobody saw Ali Aziz leave the club last night, not even the bouncer, who'd left for fifteen minutes to stop a brawl in the parking lot.'

The deputy district attorney said, 'Did you speak to Mrs. Aziz's attorney about a family trust or wills involved in this case? As a motive for murder?'

'That was one of my first questions to him,' Bino Villaseñor said. 'Margot's executor is her father in Barstow, and everything she has goes to her son, Nicky Aziz.'

The district attorney said, 'And how about the estate of Ali Aziz?'

'His lawyer informed us that he is the executor, and all of Ali Aziz's assets go to Nicky Aziz.'

The deputy district attorney said, 'As far as you are concerned, then, this is a case of self-defense and not a murder, am I correct?'

'Correct,' Bino Villaseñor said. 'At least for now.'

The deputy district attorney said, 'And her lawyer will not produce Margot Aziz for further questions unless by subpoena?'

'Correct,' the detective said. 'The last thing he said to me was that she's going on an extended vacation to get away from the press, possibly on a cruise. He said that her son has been taken to his grandparents' home in Barstow, and that Margot Aziz would not be returning to Hollywood until what he called the "ugly scandal" is no longer in the news. He said that she's distraught and mentally exhausted.'

The bureau commander said, 'You did a good job, Detective. And you look a bit exhausted too. Why don't you go home?'

'I got a few good rounds left in me, Chief,' said Bino Villaseñor, 'but on this one, I'm shadowboxing with ghosts.'

At the end of that long day, the sergeant in charge of the Community Relations Office told all Crows at a very solemn meeting that Bix Ramstead's family was planning to have a private funeral service as soon as the coroner released Bix's body to their mortuary. Then their sergeant told a few anecdotes from happier times he'd had with Bix, and he invited others to do the same.

Ronnie Sinclair had to dab at her eyes several times while others were talking about Bix, and she declined when asked if she'd like to say anything about her partner. Ronnie wanted to tell them about the time Bix became an angel to a dying child, but she knew she'd never be able to get through it.

TWENTY-FOUR

Twenty-one days after the bodies of Bix Ramstead and Ali Aziz were put into the ground at different cemeteries, a cruise ship of Norwegian registry was docked at the port of Istanbul. The entry to Istanbul through the Bosporus, with Europe on one side and Asia on the other, had been thrilling, and Margot Aziz was looking forward to exploring the Turkish port city with other passengers she'd met.

Margot had had no trouble at all finding passengers, especially among the single men, who wanted to be her escort whenever they'd gone ashore at other ports. But none of them interested her very much, and she'd decided to visit the Topkapi Museum and the Grand Bazaar of Istanbul with Herb and Millie Sloane, a married couple from San Francisco.

At the end of their exhausting day, they decided to dine at a highly recommended restaurant rather than return to the ship at the dinner hour. They enjoyed a feast, sampled local wine, and had a very pleasant time. When they got back to the ship, Margot told the Sloanes that she was tired and didn't feel like going to the shipboard nightclub show that her friends planned to attend. The last thing she said to them was that she needed a good night's sleep.

The only thing that had spoiled things for Margot that day was the need to respond to a few annoying calls from Jasmine McVicker, whining about how she should have been invited along as a companion. Margot couldn't make her understand how suspicious it would have looked at this time and decided that the girl was an idiot. She'd have to pay her off and get Jasmine out of her life sooner rather than later. But for now Margot needed rest.

An hour later, Margot Aziz staggered from her stateroom and screamed for the steward. He was a German named Hans Bruegger, who said in his statement that Margot Aziz seemed to be experiencing muscle spasms. He said that her backbone arched and she went into convulsions. She was taken from the ship and rushed to the finest hospital in Istanbul but died of asphyxiation in less than an hour.

The Turkish authorities made immediate inquiries, and at the request of the U.S. State Department, Margot's body was released and flown to California for the postmortem and time-consuming toxicology tests. However, a Turkish pathologist publicly ventured an opinion, based on symptoms and a cursory examination, that he saw indications of something akin to the poison used to kill rats and other pests. The word *strychnine* appeared in news reports. The restaurant where Margot had dined was visited by Turkish health officials, but they could find nothing amiss. And the Sloanes gave statements saying that they'd experienced no ill effects from what they'd eaten and drunk at the restaurant. No rat poison was found anywhere. Nor was pesticide containing strychnine found anywhere on the ship.

When the body of Margaret 'Margot' Osborne Aziz arrived home, local reporters engaged in lots of speculation about whether her cruel death could be another case of an American being mysteriously poisoned abroad. It didn't take long for TV reporters to introduce a sinister suggestion that infuriated Turkey's tourist industry, namely that Americans were no longer safe from extremists in any Muslim country, democracy or not.

An angry spokesman for the Turkish Consulate General in Los Angeles said that in his opinion, Margot Aziz's death had nothing to do with Muslims and that suicide should at least be considered as a motive for her poisoning. He suggested that the recent tragic shooting of her husband may have been too much for her to bear. That statement outraged Margot Aziz's lawyer, who called it preposterous, and it brought another furious response from James and Teresa Osborne, Margot's parents in Barstow, California, who were in the process of becoming legal guardians of their wealthy grandson, Nicky Aziz.

There were two people in the city of Los Angeles who were nearly as upset as her parents over the death of Margot Aziz. One was a beautiful Amerasian dancer whose only payday for her nerve-racking work had been the $4,700 she'd stolen from the desktop in Ali Aziz's office on the night he was murdered. Jasmine McVicker spent three days in bed grieving after the report of Margot's death appeared on the TV news. She would forever wonder if somehow Margot could have been a murder victim herself. The thought of it terrified her.

The other Los Angeles resident who was profoundly distressed by Margot Aziz's death was a Mexican pharmacist on Alvarado Street. He had no idea if his former client Ali Aziz could have been a murder victim, but he feared that Margot Aziz probably was. And he thought he knew how it might have happened.

His wife noticed that the pharmacist seemed obsessed with news concerning the case, and she wondered why he had become so diligent about attending Mass, not just on Sunday but sometimes during the week as well. She often saw him on his knees in front of a statue of the Virgin of Guadalupe, his fist pressed to his heart, as though begging forgiveness.

And at Hollywood Station, Detective Bino Villaseñor said to the homicide D3, 'When spouses commit murder, the women use poison, the guys use guns. In this case, the woman used a gun and the guy—'

'Is dead,' the D3 said. 'Ghosts can't poison people, not even in Istanbul. Let it go, Bino. This case is closed.'

'I guess I'll have to,' said the old detective. 'But something's wrong here, and somebody knows it.'

That week, Leonard Stilwell decided that it was time to launch his legitimate business enterprise. He'd also decided that Junior the Fijian was to be his partner, but Junior didn't know it yet. Early in the afternoon, the time when Junior usually woke up, Leonard knocked on the door of his apartment to spring it on him.

'Junior,' Leonard said to the still sleepy giant when he got him out of bed. 'You and me, babe. We're going into business!'

Junior, who was sitting there barefoot in his baggy shorts and wife beater, said, 'Bidness, bro?'

'Yeah, it's time for both of us to start a new life. I'm taking a piece of what I got from that job I done with your lock picks, and I'm setting us both up in legit business.'

Junior grinned big, showing two gaps in his grille, and said, 'My daddy is gonna be proud! Whadda we do?'

'We're selling something, that's what. And people are gonna buy it.'

'Whadda we sell?'

'Happiness,' Leonard said.

'You mean like crack? Or crystal meth?'

'No, I said legit business. We're selling goodwill. We're gonna be Characters.'

'Everybody say you already a character, Leonard,' Junior said, grinning again.

'No, no, I mean Street Characters. Like up at Grauman's Chinese Theatre. That kind of Character.'

'I wanna be Spider-Man!' Junior said.

'Jesus Christ, Junior!' Leonard said. 'Where the fuck would you get a Spider-Man costume big enough? And would anybody buy into the idea of a spiderweb holding *your* big ass? The fucking thing would have to be made of steel cable.'

'Okay. Superman, then,' Junior said.

'Right, a Superman that looks like someone who eats missionaries? I don't think so,' Leonard said. 'What I got in mind is retro. Know what that means?'

'No,' Junior said.

'Back to basics,' Leonard said. 'See, all these Street Characters are trying to one-up each other. Trying to keep up with whoever's hot right now. That's why there's so many Batmans and Spider-Mans. We ain't gonna go that route.'

'Who we gonna be?'

'Mickey Mouse and Pluto, his dog,' Leonard said.

'I get to be Mickey Mouse!' Junior said.

'Oh, yeah, a 'roided-up megarodent,' Leonard said. 'No, dude, I'm the main man.'

'You mean the main mouse,' Junior said with a giggle.

'I'm Mickey,' Leonard said. 'You're Pluto the dog. Pay attention!'

Junior stopped picking goop from his toenail with a dinner fork and said, 'I hear you, bro.'

'Okay,' Leonard said. 'See, everybody loves Mickey Mouse, but nobody out there on Hollywood Boulevard has ever had a first-class Mickey costume like you see at Disneyland. Well, now I got enough bucks to buy me the best. And we're gonna get a real break on the Pluto costume because the Pluto that was out there had a first-class outfit. But he got busted by the narcs a while back for stashing dope in his head. I know who's taking care of his crib, and we'll buy the Pluto costume cheap. He's gonna be needing bucks for crystal the minute he gets outta jail, so he won't give a shit. Lucky he's a real big guy, so the costume should fit you, no problem.'

'What's Pluto do?' Junior wanted to know.

'He barks. He's a fucking dog!'

'How do I make it sound?'

'You just say what a dog says. What's a dog say in Fiji? "Woof!" Right?'

'No,' Junior said. 'I seen "woof" in American cartoons, but in Fijian cartoons, dogs don't say "woof."'

'Well, you're an American dog, so you say "woof," okay?'

'Okay, bro,' Junior said. 'Woof.'

'Now, here's the deal,' Leonard said. 'We always go straight to the little kids. The little kids don't really give a shit about Darth Vader and Frankenstein and all those other scary Characters. And the cute Characters, like SpongeBob and Barney? They're boring. But the little kids love Mickey Mouse. Their parents love Mickey Mouse. Their grandparents love Mickey Mouse. You and me, we'll steal the business from all those other jerkoffs by going back to cartoon roots.'

'Whadda you do when I say "woof"?' Junior asked.

'Let's rehearse it,' Leonard said. Then, in as squeaky a falsetto as he could manage, Leonard said to an imaginary tot, 'Hello! My name is Mickey Mouse! What's yours?'

'Junior,' said Junior.

Leonard said, 'No, I ain't asking *your* name, for chrissake!'

'Okay, okay, I get it. Do it again,' Junior said.

'Wait for your cue,' Leonard said. Then, again in a squeaky falsetto to an imaginary tot, Leonard said, 'Hello! My name is Mickey Mouse! What's yours?'

'Pluto!' said Junior.

'Oh, fuck,' said Leonard Stilwell. 'This is gonna take some work.'

Hollywood Nate Weiss had occasion to make a call in Laurel Canyon that afternoon. A resident had been complaining to the Community Relations Office about a neighbor's yard sales. They'd been happening at least once a week, and it was, according to the complainant, 'unbecoming' to other property owners in Laurel Canyon. After Nate spoke to the neighbor, who agreed to curtail the activity, Nate was driving back when something made him take a left turn up to Mt. Olympus.

He drove to the former home of Ali and Margot Aziz and parked in front. He thought about Margot and about Bix Ramstead. If only he'd obeyed the impulse and gone up to the door and rung the bell on that last night, when he'd seen Bix's minivan in the driveway. He didn't like thinking about Bix. Nate believed the way Bix died had unnerved all of them. But they'd never admit it. It couldn't happen to them. They were tough guys.

Then the front door opened and two young children ran out, a boy and a girl, followed by their pregnant mother. They were heading for the mailbox when they noticed the black-and-white, and the woman said, 'Is there anything wrong, Officer?'

Nate smiled and said, 'Not anymore. You've got a beautiful house.'

'We're very excited about it,' she said. 'And we know about its history.'

'You'll write your own history,' Nate said, and they all waved as he drove back down from Mt. Olympus.

When he got to the stop sign at Laurel Canyon, a Porsche 911 flew past him southbound, cutting off a car that had been trying to make a safe left turn. Nate pulled in behind the Porsche, turned on the light bar, and tooted his horn.

She had all the markings of a Hills bunny, with highlighted hair curled and tousled like Sarah Jessica Parker's. She had violet eyes and a sprinkle of freckles across her nose and cheekbones under one of those salon tans like Margot's. Her saline-enhanced bustline reached out and touched the steering wheel.

'Your license, please,' Nate said.

'Was I going too fast?' she said with a blazing orthodontic smile. Her license showed her to be thirty-two years old, and she wasn't wearing a wedding ring.

'Yes, and that was a very unsafe pass,' Nate said. 'We've had several bad traffic collisions on this road.'

'I recently got this car,' she said, 'and I'm not used to it. I hope you don't have to write me a ticket!'

He noticed her fingers tugging subtly at her skirt until her athletic thighs were exposed. Then she said, 'We just moved in. Guess I need someone local to show me the lay of the land.'

'Just a moment,' Nate said and walked to his shop.

When he returned, the Hills bunny's skirt was almost up to her seat belt, and she said, 'I think that if an officer wanted to get to know a girl better, he wouldn't write her a ticket.'

Hollywood Nate said, 'I think you're right. Sign here, please.'

Keep reading for an extract from *Hollywood Moon*, the third instalment of Joseph Wambaugh's series about the cops of Hollywood Station. *Hollywood Moon* will be published by Quercus in May 2009.

'Hollywood Nate rents midgets,' the long-legged, sunbaked surfer cop who the others called 'Flotsam,' said to his partner, while 6-X-32 was passing Grauman's Chinese Theater, cruising east on Hollywood Boulevard at twilight.

The dying spangled sunlight ricocheted off the windows of the taller buildings, and his shorter surfer partner, also weathered and singed, who of course they called 'Jetsam,' glanced at the driver through the smoked lenses of his wraparound shades and said, 'What?'

Flotsam wore his two-inch hair gelled up in front like a baby cockatoo, and Jetsam's was semi-spiked, both coifs streaked with highlights not provided by sun, sea or nature. And with just enough gel to get it done and still not irritate the watch commander, a lieutenant in his early fifties, twenty years their senior, and very old school.

'In fact,' Flotsam continued, 'last Wednesday, Nate hired one to bowl with him for twenty bucks an hour. That's when five coppers from the mid-watch and Watch 2 got together at the bowling alley in the Kodak Center with a bunch from North Hollywood and

Wilshire. I heard that Nate, like, stole the spotlight with his midget.'

'Where did you hear about Hollywood Nate and midget love?' Jetsam wanted to know.

'I got it from Sheila,' Flotsam said, referring to Officer Sheila Montez, a midwatch P2 who both surfer cops lusted for. 'And I ain't saying he loves little people, but dude, he's so cinematically dialed-in he devised this way to capture the attention of all the bowling alley Sallys. His little fella gets all flirty and cute with the Sallys and it sets things up for Nate to move in and close the deal.'

Officer Nathan Weiss, a hawkishly handsome, thirty-six-year-old, physically fit gym rat, was called 'Hollywood Nate' because he possessed a SAG card and had actually appeared briefly in a few TV movies. And he always volunteered to work every Red Carpet event at the Kodak Theater, in his thus far futile quest for cinematic discovery and eventual stardom.

Jetsam envisioned those feverishly hot Sallys as he shot a casual glance toward the Walk of Fame where lots of curb creatures were already out. He saw a tweaker sidling closer toward the purse of an obese tourist who was busy yelling at her much smaller husband. The tweaker backed off and slithered into the crowd when Jetsam gave him the stink eye as the black-and-white passed. The Street Characters: Batman, Superman, (two Supermen, actually), Darth Vader, Spider-Man and Cat Woman, were all mingling with tourists in the forecourt of Grauman's Chinese Theater, posing for camera shots in an endless quest for tourist bucks.

'Maybe we oughtta hire a midget too,' Jetsam said.

'I used to bowl a lot when I was married to my second ex-wife who I miss like a prostate infection. It was a low rent bowling alley in Long Beach, and I was like, the only bowler in the whole place who wasn't sleazed out. Even my second ex – who loved bowling, Leonardo DiCaprio, and pharmaceuticals – was inked up, a butterfly on her belly and my name on her ass. Her girlfriend told me how that prescription-zombie screamed like a cat when they lasered my name off. I'da coughed up two weeks' pay for the video. Her exotic girlfriend, by the way, might be worth your attention, bro. She's an Indian.'

'Feather or dot?'

'Dot.'

'No way, dude,' Flotsam said. 'Every time my laptop goes sideways I get one of them on the line and always end up tossing my cell phone against the wall in frustration. I buy more cells than every cartel in Colombia. But I agree, we should definitely not overlook the target rich environment at the Kodak Center.'

Jetsam said, 'Being where it's located makes it like, the most lavish bowling alley this side of the palace of Dubai. Maybe we can't afford it?'

'Can't is a frame of mind that don't hold our photo,' Flotsam said. 'Hollywood Nate claims that on certain nights it's full of bowling alley Sallys hoping Matt Damon will come in to roll a line or two, or maybe Brad Pitt, when Angelina's in Africa looking for sainthood with people even skinnier than she is.'

Jetsam said, 'I hear what you're saying, bro. I mean, there's gotta be opportunities on those lanes for coppers as coolaphonic and hormonally imaginative as the four hundred pounds of male heat riding in this car.'

Flotsam thought about it some more and then said, 'There's a midget that works at the newsstand on Cahuenga. And there's that roller skating midget at Hollywood and Highland. The one that throws water balloons at tourists? He'd crawl in a clothes dryer for twenty bucks an hour.'

'A *plethora* of midgets ain't gonna get us our way,' Jetsam said, showing off the new vocabulary he was acquiring from his community college class. 'We gotta think original. Maybe we could, like, hire a clown to bowl with us. That would amaze those ten-pin tootsies.'

'I'm scared of clowns,' Flotsam blurted, and it was out of his mouth before he could take it back.

'You're what?' Jetsam said, and this time he turned fully toward his partner, as the late summer sun dropped into the Pacific and lights came on in Hollywood, the fluorescent glow making the boulevard scene look even weirder to the swarming tourists.

Flotsam and Jetsam had been mid-watch partners and fellow surfers for more than two years, but this was the first time Jetsam had learned this incredible secret: his tall rugged partner was afraid of clowns!

'Maybe I said it wrong, dude.' Flotsam quickly added. 'It's just that they, like, shiver me. The way a snake creeps you out, know what I mean?'

'Snakes don't creep me out, bro,' Jetsam said.

'Rats then. I seen you that time we got the dead body call where rats were all eating the guy's eyeballs. You were ready to blow chunks, dude.'

'It wasn't the rats themselves, bro,' Jetsam said. I

just wasn't ready for an all out rodent luau.'

'Anyways, I'm just saying, clowns like, make me like all . . . goose bumpy. I mean, maybe I saw too many movies about slasher clowns or something, I don't know.'

'This goes on my desk top,' Jetsam said with a grin. 'I'm holding onto this.'

Referring to their patrol car, which LAPD cops called a 'shop' because of the 'shop numbers' on the roof and doors, Flotsam said grimly, 'What happens in our shop stays in our shop, dude. So hit your delete button.'

'I feel ya, bro,' Jetsam said. 'And next time a boule-vard clown squirts a tourist with a water gun, just stay in the car and roll your window up and lock the doors. I'll man-up for both of us. And I'll taze the first ass-hole that calls my partner a sissified whimpering bitch.'

While 6-X-32 was cruising the boulevard, two home-less middle-aged panhandlers in east Hollywood, named Axel Minton and Bootsie Brown, were pushing a man in a wheelchair along the sidewalk to a graffiti-tagged neighborhood market frequented by local pensioners. It was a store where Axel and Bootsie often begged for change from the residents of the neighborhood, mostly Latino and Asian, who bought groceries there.

Axel was a spindly white man, with sprigs of gray hair, who would drink anything from a bottle if a label indicated alcohol content. Bootsie was a black man, blind in one eye, who slept in a storage shed behind the apartment building where eighty-eight-year-old pensioner Coleman O'Toole lived. They both wore layers, sooty and drab, molded to their forms like fungus, until you weren't sure where the fabrics left off and they began. And each was not many gallons away from wandering Hollywood Boulevard – like all those other self-lobotomized colorless specters in pull-tab necklaces and football helmets, or maybe wearing bikini bottoms on their heads – pushing trash-laden shopping carts, chanting gibberish or yodeling at terrified tourists. The Hollywood cops called it 'gone to Dizzyland.'

Each transient had wheeled Coleman O'Toole to the store many times for a modest fee. This time they were both pushing the wheelchair and bickering when they stopped in front and entered, leaving Coleman O'Toole parked in the shadows.

While Axel and Bootsie were inside loading up on shelf items, which included three quarts of 100 proof vodka and three quarts of gin, another octogenarian transient called Trombone Teddy shuffled by. He'd been a good bebop sideman back in the day, or as he put it, 'When I was a real person.' Teddy, who was well known to officers at Hollywood Station, looked curiously at the figure in the wheelchair. Then he used his last few coins to phone the police, and the call was given to 6-X-32 of the midwatch.

Axel and Bootsie's bottles of liquor and several bags of snacks were stacked on the counter. The part-time clerk, who called herself Lucy, was a white transsexual in a blinged out T-shirt, low rise jeans, nosebleed stilettos, and magenta hair extensions piled so high she wouldn't feel being conked by a bottle of Corona, which could easily happen in that store. She adjusted her silk scarf to better conceal the healing from recent surgery to remove her manly apple, and looked at the transients curiously.

Being acquainted with both of them as well as with

Coleman O'Toole, she said, 'Is Coley throwing a party, or what?'

'It's his birthday,' Bootsie said.

'No, it isn't,' the tranny said. 'His birthday was last month, same as mine. He bought me a card.'

'It ain't his birthday, dummy,' Axel said to Bootsie. 'It's the anniversary of his retirement from the railroad. He has a party every year to celebrate his current life of comfort and ease.'

Lucy looked at Coleman O'Toole's pension check and at the endorsement. The signature looked like the old man's scrawl. 'Why don't you wheel Coley inside?' the tranny said, squinting out the window at the wheelchair figure alone in the darkness.

'You wanna check his ID, see if he's old enough to buy booze?' Bootsie said with a wet, nearly toothless grin.

'Yeah, you wanna card old Coleman?' Axel said, snuffling and grinning wider than Bootsie. 'Actually, the old bugger's sick. Puked half way down the street. You don't want him in here unless you got a bucket and mop.'

'And all this booze is gonna cure him?' Lucy said, then shrugged and started ringing up the items, just as 6-X-32 pulled up in front of the store and was met by Trombone Teddy.

The cops hardly noticed the old guy in the wheelchair, and Flotsam said, 'Did you make the call, Teddy?'

'Yes, sir,' Teddy said. 'Is there a reward for capturing a couple of crooks for check fraud?'

'Whadda you mean?' Jetsam said.

'If you would put in a word to the store owner would he give me a few bucks for blowing the whistle on a pair of thugs?'

'We ain't qualified for high level business negotiations, Teddy,' Flotsam said. 'But I gotta think somebody'd buy you a forty or two.'

'Okay,' Teddy said. 'I'll take a chance that generosity still exists in this ungrateful goddamn world. Go inside and you'll find two thieves cashing a stolen check.'

'This better be righteous, Teddy,' Flotsam said, walking inside with Jetsam at his back.

The tranny, who was as tall as Flotsam in those heels, was surprised when the cop appeared and said, 'Can I see that check?'

Pushing the check across the counter, Lucy said, 'Something wrong, Officer?'

'That's what we wanna know,' Jetsam said.

Flotsam examined the check and said, 'Are either of you Coleman O'Toole?'

It was Lucy who said, 'No, they're not, Officer. Coley's the one out there in the wheelchair. These two sometimes wheel him down here to buy groceries.'

'Coley's the salt of the earth,' Axel said, looking uneasy. 'I'd fight a whole pack of pit bulls for old Coley. He's a fellow wine connoisseur.'

'Connoisseurs don't drink wine in a paper bag,' Jetsam noted.

'Coley's my man,' Bootsie said. 'When some no-account neighbor put lye in his gin bottle one time and he ended up wif a tube in his stomach, it was me that poured some good whiskey into the tube so he could get drunk.'

'That's a touching testament to friendship,' Flotsam said, putting the check on the counter.

He walked to the door, nodding to Jetsam who stayed

inside while the grocery transaction was being completed. Lucy was counting out the change when Flotsam came back inside.

Axel Minton looked at the cop's expression and said, 'Uh oh.'

The tranny's eyes were theatrically done, so as to be seen from balcony seats, and those amazing orbs moved from Flotsam to the transients and back again, before she said, 'Don't tell me that's not Coleman O'Toole out there in the wheelchair!'

'Oh, yeah,' said Flotsam. 'I'm sure it's him. He's strapped in and rigged up nice as you please.'

'What's the problem then?' Lucy asked.

'It's that he won't be needing all this booze,' Flotsam said. 'Him being deceased and all.'

'Uh oh,' said Bootsie who pointed at Axel. 'It was his idea after we found Coley layin' on the floor, colder than Aunt Ruby's poon.' Then he looked at the tranny and said, 'Sorry for my rude mouf, Miss Lucy.'

'You lying rat!' Axel said to Bootsie. Then to the cops, 'He was the one noticed Coley had already signed his check!'

'Tha's right, Officer,' Bootsie said, 'but it was this here pissant that pointed to Coley layin' there quiet as a bedbug on your pilla, and said ol' Coley woulda wanted us to cash it and have a Irish wake!'

'Okay, you two turn around and put your hands behind your back,' Flotsam said. And sotto to Jetsam, 'Better notify the night-watch detective about the corpse in the wheelchair and our two grave robbers. While we're waiting for the body snatchers I'll take care of Teddy.'

As Jetsam led the handcuffed miscreants out to their

car to await the arrival of the coroner's van, Flotsam bought a pint of Jack for Trombone Teddy to show that generosity still exists in this ungrateful goddamn world.

ACKNOWLEDGEMENTS

Once again, special thanks for the terrific anecdotes and wonderful cop talk goes to officers of the Los Angeles Police Department:

Mike Arminio, Richard Blue, Tom Brascia, Ken Brower, Joe Bunch, Vicki Bynum, Paula Davidson, Francesca Flores, Maggie Furmanski, Beatrice Girmala, Brett Goodkin, Maria Gray, Craig Herron, Art Holmes (ret.), Jeff Ingalls, Roger Jackson, Jim Jarvis, Alisha Jordan, Richard Kalk (ret.), Mike Kammert, Al Lopez, Kathy McAnany, Julie Nony, Ed Pandolfo, Danny Pesqueira, Ralph Sanchez, Armen Sevdalian, Jeritt Severns, Mike Shea, Bill Sollie, John Washington, Jerry Wert.

And to officers of the San Diego Police Department:

Don Borinski, Andra Brown, Joel Bryden, Rob Burlinson, Henry Castro, Kim Collier, Joe Cristinziani, Reggie Frank, Robin Hayes, Ken Impellizeri, Nick Kelbaugh, Charles Lara, Noel McElfresh, Wende Morris, Gib Ninness, Tony Puente (ret.), Joe Robertson, Dave Root, Adam Sharki, Jerry Stratton, John Tefft, Roxie Vigil, Judy Woods, Kelly Yatch, Randy Young.